HE SAID HE COULD CHANGE

By Chelsea Labzda

To my mom, who always believes in me and supports me.

This book is a work of fiction. Names, characters, businesses, organizations, places, and events other than those clearly in the public domain are either the product of the author's imagination or are used fictitiously. Any resemblance to actual persons, living or dead, is purely coincidental and not intended by the author.

Prologue

I need a change.

That is all I can think about while on my Saturday morning run. Granted, this is not the first time I have thought or felt this, but I know the feeling is getting stronger and harder to ignore. I don't run as far as I used to, but it has brought me a sense of peace, which has been hard for me to find lately. I used to run about five or six miles at a time, but now it is more like two. Either way, I'm glad I've gotten myself back into it. It almost feels like free therapy. Mother Nature seems to know what's best for me. The neighborhood is a bit hilly, which I find somewhat exhausting, but it is also comforting to see some of the older widows walking, usually with their dogs. I never talk to them, though. In fact, I don't talk to many people at all these days.

Today is somewhat of a warm day, and I notice I am sweating a bit more than usual, although it never gets too hot in the mountains. I live in Asheville, North Carolina. I have lived here for about six years with my husband, Rodney.

Rodney is fine.

Rodney is nice enough, has a promising career, and, on paper, I know people would think I was nuts to complain. Rodney and I have a fairly decent relationship. We have date nights and travel together. Well, I guess we don't travel much anymore. We are nice to each other overall. However, he used to be nicer.

Much nicer.

I like Rodney. I do.

In fact, I love him.

But… Rodney is what I need to change.

Chapter 1

Moving

My name is Amelia. I had moved to Asheville after living in New York City for several years—I just wanted a fresh start. While New York City always sounded glamorous to me, living there was a different story. Almost a nightmare looking back at it. I lived in a 400-square-foot studio apartment. It was impossible to entertain, but most people I knew would tend to meet at bars anyway, since we all had small apartments. I lived on the Upper West Side, which was more of a family area than other parts of the city.

I didn't date too much in the city, which probably sounds weird since there was such a large population that I could surely find someone to enjoy spending my time with. The first dates and the getting-to-know-each-other conversations soon felt forced and mundane. I never seemed to click with anyone, so I just went out with friends and lived in the moment.

I worked as an assistant in a fashion showroom – we set up appointments with buyers who would come in to see if they wanted to order any of our lines for the stores they worked for. I did like the job overall, but the pay was mediocre at best, and it seemed it would take a long time for me to move up in the company. Mainly because it was so small, and the only time a position became available was when someone left. Or died. That happened once. I felt it would be bad karma to try to get that woman's position, so I never applied.

New York wore on me much quicker than I had anticipated when I planned to move there during college. The days seemed to fall into a routine, and on weekends, I was too tired from the Monday-to-Friday grind to take advantage of living in the city. One day, I remember it like it was yesterday, I was taking a fresh springtime walk with one of my neighbors, Amanda. I don't think I had ever expressed to Amanda that the city was wearing on me, mainly because a part of me just assumed that it was part of being an adult. As Amanda and I finished our loop around the pond in Central Park, she asked me if I could do anything I wanted, what would it be? I blurted out almost faster than I even knew what I was saying – an interior designer! I was more surprised by this than she was since it hadn't crossed my mind before. Amanda very casually said, "Well, that makes complete sense for you! You're so artistic and have a natural way of working with people." We then switched topics, and Amanda started telling me about a new guy she would have drinks with later that afternoon.

As the weeks and months passed, I started to feel increasingly claustrophobic in the city. I began to consider moving, but I was unsure where to go. None of my friends seemed to understand how I felt, so I didn't have anyone to talk to about it. I tried researching articles online about "America's Best Cities to Live In", but every city I looked at seemed to have its pros and cons. I felt confused and eventually just continued with my life.

Many of my friends were starting new relationships, causing our friend group to drift apart. I didn't exactly have a strong desire to build new friendships, so I started doing more and more things by myself. The problem with living in a big city like New York City, though, is that even though you are surrounded by so many people, it can feel somewhat lonely. Loneliness isn't the worst feeling for me, but it does get a bit old.

Walking home from work one night, I decided to stop at a café for a vanilla latte. It was a Friday, so I didn't care if the caffeine would keep me up a bit later than normal. In fact, I'd prefer it. As I sat in the café by myself at a table for two, a text from Amanda popped up on my phone. "Happy Friday! Random, but my aunt mentioned her friend is looking for an interior design assistant and has not had any luck locally. I should mention my aunt lives in Asheville,

North Carolina. I've been there once and it is so beautiful! Let me know if you'd like to connect with her."

"YES," I replied.

I've read about Asheville. It was much smaller than New York City but had unique forests, and I could go hiking in the Blue Ridge Mountains. I know people in New York who have not been able to break into interior design, so another perk would be learning the industry while still being in a creative field. My mind was racing, and I blamed the latte. This was just a text from Amanda, and I had already started planning a huge move in my head. I took some deep breaths and brought myself back to earth when my phone buzzed again. "LOL – okay, I will give your number to my aunt to give to her friend. You just have to promise to come back and visit me if this happens!!"

"Deal! Thanks so much, Amanda – you're the best!"

After I finished my latte, I decided to go to a restaurant and order myself a glass of wine. I mean, why not? This one text could be life-changing, and I could start a brand-new chapter. I was still definitely getting ahead of myself, but I didn't care. I felt happy and excited, and needed to celebrate.

That weekend, I researched everything I could on Asheville and Interior Design. The housing prices there were drastically cheaper than rent in Manhattan. I couldn't help but think of all the leftover cash I would have for shopping! I quickly remembered I'd need a car, but that was fine. I had managed to set aside some money over the last few years, so it seemed to all work out relatively quickly in my head. I remember thinking I should have a going-away party, but then, equally as fast as that thought came into my head, I remembered I didn't have too many people I'd been good at keeping in touch with. So perhaps a lovely farewell dinner with Amanda. Speaking of Amanda – I had no clue when I would be hearing from her aunt's friend, but I was more than anxious. I just wanted this to work out somehow. I was ready to leave the city. I was prepared for a fresh start. Just then, my phone rang so loudly it made me jump. I looked at the area code, and it was one from Asheville.

When I answered, a woman introduced herself as a friend of Amanda's mom, Susan. Her name was Charlotte. Charlotte was very easy to talk to, mainly because she did most of the talking. She almost sounded to be in a bit of a frenzy. She told me she had interviewed several women in Asheville, but no one was the right fit for various reasons. Some women only wanted to work part-time, while others had little passion for design. I assured her I wanted (and needed) a full-time job, and while I just had fashion in clothing as a background, I was just as interested, if not more, in learning about interior design. She told me what she thought was a fair salary and said she would pay $5,000 to help with my moving expenses if I accepted the offer. Even though Charlotte seemed desperate to get some help in her office, she told me to think about it for at least a week before agreeing to such a significant change in my life.

I didn't need a week to think about it, but to avoid acting too desperate, I agreed to call her back the following weekend. Even though I only had one conversation with Charlotte, we just seemed to click. I couldn't wait to tell Amanda about the phone call. I couldn't wait to give notice at my job. I couldn't wait to start this next chapter of my life.

As the weekend went on, I wondered if I would miss much about my city life. Of course, there are some things I would miss, but I felt there would be so many more things I would not miss. Such as riding on jam-packed subways during rush hour. Or the fact that when not using the subway system, I had to rely mainly on my own feet for my transportation. Taking the subway during rush hour was never fun – everyone would be packed on the train like sardines. Not to mention how it gets bitterly cold in the winter, making it daunting to go up the street for groceries. Then it is totally the opposite in the summer – you start to sweat after a block.

At least in Asheville, I would have the luxury of a vehicle again. Even though I didn't know anyone who lived in Asheville, for some reason, it didn't faze me. That was probably because I moved to New York City without knowing a soul. I moved to New York City from Kansas, and most of my friends at the time thought it was crazy to leave. It was a small town where everyone knew each other. I couldn't help but feel that Asheville was a good compromise for me. I liked the fact that there were mountains, nature, and new areas to explore, which, let's be honest, Kansas didn't have much for me in terms of exploring. Asheville was full of new restaurants and trendy neighborhoods being built. I'm not sure why I felt all this positivity towards Asheville and this new job, but maybe I was meant to meet the man I am supposed to marry there. I mean… eventually, it had to happen.

When I woke up that Sunday morning, I decided it was best to write my resignation letter. Even though I had to wait a week before I gave Charlotte my decision, I knew what it was. Of course, I did not turn in my resignation letter that week, but knowing I would be soon was a good feeling.

The following week really seemed to drag on. One nice thing, though, was that I felt like whatever I was tired of in the city didn't seem so bad anymore. That was most likely because I knew my days were numbered when I was at my job. I didn't put too much effort into it; instead, I looked for furniture and apartments in Asheville. The fact that I could easily afford a one-bedroom again, or even more, made me feel like a millionaire. I even looked up social activities to try to meet people. Maybe I never put much effort into New York City because I sensed I wouldn't end up there.

On Thursday night that week, I stopped at a restaurant by myself to get some dinner; since I was alone, I just sat at the bar. Typically, when I'd go out alone, people next to me at the bar were rather strange, and I was lucky if they even talked to me. When they did strike up a conversation, they often just seemed weird and would make me lose my appetite.

Not that night, though.

Chapter 2

A man in a suit sat beside me and started a conversation. He was charming, good-looking, and engaging. That hadn't happened to me in all my years in New York City, so I had to laugh at the universe. It was almost like it was trying to entice me to stay by dangling this most likely emotionally unavailable man in front of me.

I figured I would chat with this man and see what he was all about. His name was Louis. Louis was 32 and in finance. I had dated men in finance before, but never had good luck – for various reasons. Louis and I enjoyed a nice glass of wine together and then another.

Shockingly, the conversation just flowed and was actually fun. Louis made me laugh quite a bit, which was interesting as I found most men rather unfunny. It was just so weird; I mean, what are the chances I am days away from officially accepting a job in another city, and I meet a man who didn't immediately repulse me?

I decided I needed to capitalize on my time and figure out as much as possible about Louis. When we were finishing up our drinks and food we had ordered, I asked if he would want to have another drink at my apartment, as it was only a couple of blocks away.

Louis looked at me, surprised, "Why, I'd be delighted!"

I have never done this, but he seemed harmless enough. And if he became a stalker, I was about to move anyway, so it didn't matter if he knew where I lived.

The short walk was a bit chilly, so I was thankful to get to my place, and by the time we walked up to the 4th floor, I was no longer cold. Louis was very polite upon seeing my apartment and even made a ridiculous comment about its spaciousness. I poured us a glass of red wine – he seemed to gulp it down, but I just chalked it up to nerves. We chatted a bit about the city and our jobs – I didn't exactly tell him I was planning to leave the city in a matter of weeks. Technically, I hadn't accepted the job yet, so if this was my knight in shining armor, I could still change my mind and stay in New York.

Well… Two hours later, I came to the full realization that Louis was indeed not my knight in shining armor. I was on my second glass of red wine – and he was on his seventh. I kept count – unsure if I was more in shock or in awe of how much this man could drink. Eventually, he started to slur his words. I made up a lie and told him I needed to get up early for a meeting - then he began to pout. I wasn't sure if I had ever seen a grown man pout – but Louis had this act down.

He begged to stay over….as he poured himself another glass of wine. I guess the more wine he drank, the less I had to pack up and move… that was the only silver lining I could find in this situation. I should have just left him at the bar where I found him. Lesson learned.

Either way, I still needed to get him out of my apartment.

"I really need you to head out – I've got to get to bed." He mumbled something in return. Great – there is no way this man can even be thrown into a taxi. I finally told him to sleep on the couch, but I could tell that idea didn't sit well with him as he crawled into my bed. He miraculously could form a sentence then, but the sentence was "more wine, please."

"Excuse me? Don't you think you have had enough?"

He repeated, "More wine, please." I thought that perhaps if I had poured more wine, he would fall asleep. So, I got up, opened a new bottle of red wine, and gave him a glass. As I was putting the bottle away, I went to tell him not to spill the wine, but when I looked up… the wine glass was already empty. I was speechless. How did he drink that so fast? My plan worked because he fell asleep within about five minutes after mumbling more nonsense.

By that point, it was just past midnight, so I made myself comfortable on the couch and then made a plan to wake up at 6 am and kick him to the curb.

I was surprised to find that I slept through the night. Apparently, drunk men are rather exhausting. I woke Louis up and told him I was late and that he needed to leave so I could get ready. Louis looked very confused and immediately asked when we could see each other again. I really don't know how I did not burst out with laughter, but somehow I managed to keep my composure.

"I'll text you," I said.

He was one of those men who insisted I send my number to his phone while I was right in front of him. DING!! His phone went off with a text from me. I didn't have the mental capacity to worry about dodging his texts in the near future. I just needed this man out of my apartment and my life.

"It was great to meet you!" I lied. I instantly regretted that comment, but to my defense, I had not exactly been in that position before.

I walked Louis downstairs and did not even wait to see if he had gotten a cab. As I walked back into my apartment, I counted the wine bottles he had consumed. Four.

Lovely.

Since I still had a little time before work, I started cleaning and trying to get rid of any evidence from the night before so I wouldn't have any reminders when I got home that evening.

Chapter 3

When taking the subway to work that morning, I decided to get off the train a couple of stops early and walk through Midtown. I couldn't help but notice that most people seemed so stressed and in a hurry. It made me anxious just watching all the rushing going on around me.

Asheville wouldn't be like this. It would be a town where people had time to stop and smile at you. Maybe even time to smell a rose or two.

My office was relatively quiet that day, and we had only a few appointments. This gave me more time to daydream about my conversation with Charlotte this weekend. I knew it would go well because I was genuinely excited about the opportunity, and she would be able to hear it in my voice. I grabbed a sandwich at the deli downstairs for lunch and ate it in a nearby small park. More people watching. I liked seeing all the dogs and their owners walking around the city. For city dogs, I remember them looking rather happy to be on their walks. I suppose many of them didn't grow up with fields around them to run and play in, so they probably didn't know what they were missing.

That was another thing – I felt most people who lived in the city for a long time were born there. It was what they were used to and their actual home. So many transplants I met seemed to get burnt out in a few years and move back to the area they were from or elsewhere with a slower pace. I was craving that slower pace. Sometimes, I felt I barely had time to think while living in the city.

My afternoon went by fast, especially when my boss, Debra, told me I could go home at 3 pm. For a second, I wondered if I should get a bite to eat somewhere, but after the previous night's fiasco, I decided it would be best to stay in and order a pizza.

I never wished away a weekend, but I was eager to return to work on Monday morning and give my notice.

Friday night was great. It was just me, a great New York pizza, and a Hallmark movie. The pizza was something I would miss when I moved. All the sirens I constantly heard when I opened my window would not be missed.

As I was drinking my coffee the following morning, my phone buzzed. It was a text from Charlotte that asked if now would be a good time to chat. It was only 10 am! She had to have been as excited as I was to have me take the position if she reached out so early in the day.

When Charlotte phoned me, she cut to the chase and said, "Hi Amelia! I'm so excited to talk to you again, and I hope you had a great week. Did you, by chance, have any time to think more about the offer? "YES," I blurted out, which cut her off mid-sentence. Charlotte laughed, "Well then! I am not sure who is more excited about this – me or you! Susan just raved about you, so I know it will be a great fit for the both of us – I hope you are ready to decorate some beautiful mountain houses in Asheville with me!" I remember briefly finding it odd that Susan had raved about me, considering I had never met her, but I guess Amanda spoke highly of me.

Charlotte and I then went over logistical information. I would give my two weeks' notice, and I would get to work on finding a place to live in Asheville and line up movers. While she was eager to have me start, she was also very flexible about my start date since I was moving from several states away. When we hung up, I let out a scream of excitement and joy – only to be immediately stopped by my neighbor pounding on our adjoining wall.

Maybe Asheville would have a lovely, small house I could rent, so I wouldn't need to deal with neighbors as much…

Following our phone call, I immediately got to work looking for houses to rent. I figured it didn't need to be perfect, as I could move again after I got to know the area better. One of the first ones I saw looked to be almost perfect for me. It was a quaint two-bedroom, two-bath home just on the edge of downtown. I knew that would be useful as I wouldn't have a vehicle when I move down.

When I called the realtor, she offered to do a virtual walk-through since I was not local. I loved the inside even more than I had expected to. The kitchen had black and white tile – something I had always wanted. The bathrooms were updated, and there were even walk-in closets. A walk-in closet was an absolute dream after living in New York. There was also a front porch with a couple of rocking chairs and some beautiful potted plants.

"When is it available?" I asked. The realtor, Samantha, replied. "Well, the owner wanted to have it deep cleaned this week, but then it is up for grabs."

"I'd love to put in an application to rent it," I said. Samantha emailed me the rental application after we hung up.

A few hours later, Samantha called me back and said that the property owner had accepted my application. Samantha and I worked out several dates for me to schedule the movers' arrival.

I could not believe how easily this was all happening. It felt like it was meant to be. Next step: I called around to get quotes and line up movers. That was a bit more expensive than I had anticipated, but Charlotte was going to advance me $5,000 for moving expenses, so it wasn't a problem.

That afternoon, I decided to take a run in Central Park. On my way home, I picked up some boxes to start packing. I had never been more excited to pack in my life. Since the spring weather was getting warmer, I figured I could start by packing my coats, boots, and sweaters. I put on some classical music, poured myself a glass of wine, heated a slice of leftover pizza, and started assembling boxes and filling them with the items. I finished packing a few boxes and then decided to sit by the window and feel the cool breeze come in. Of course, there were the background noises of sirens and cars honking…

Sunday morning, I woke up and finished my resignation letter. I made sure I was extra nice to try to leave that door open in case something fell through in Asheville—although I was pretty confident it wouldn't.

It was a beautiful day, so I decided to grab some lunch and go relax in the park and people-watch. Something told me I would not be doing quite as much people-watching in North Carolina.

Monday morning came quickly, and I busted through the doors to our office with such force that a couple of my colleagues looked up in confusion. I guess it was safe to assume I was ready to give my notice. My boss heard the commotion and called me into her office.

"Is everything all right, Amelia?" she asked.

I broke the news of my departure to Debra, and she couldn't have been more supportive. In fact, she had been to Asheville on a vacation once and said she would make me a list of some of her favorite restaurants.

"Amelia – I don't blame you for wanting out of this city – the only reason I'm still here is because my husband can't imagine doing anything besides working on Wall Street." Debra then seemed to have a change in her composure and looked me dead in the eye and said, "Now, what I don't want you to do is meet a man in Asheville who makes you forget who you are – you're one of the most talented people to have ever worked for me, and I know you are much more intelligent than this position allows you to demonstrate. Amelia – promise me you won't ever forget who you are."

I had never seen this side of Debra, and I almost didn't know how she wanted me to react.

"I…promise," I slowly said.

I couldn't help but feel that was almost a warning message of some sort from her. After I left her office, the workday was full of questions from coworkers about where I was headed after my two weeks were up. I was never too close with any of my coworkers, and it was a bit annoying that it took me to quit for some to show interest in my life.

Oh well. Too little, too late.

I answered most of their questions as vaguely as I could. For some reason, I'd always taken pride in keeping my personal life separate from many of the people in my day-to-day life. I wasn't sure if this was necessarily a good thing or even that healthy.

Maybe it would even come back to bite me someday…but hopefully not.

Chapter 4

The next couple of weeks were a blur. They went fast, which I was thankful for. I packed a lot and stopped at my favorite shops and restaurants for the last time. As far as missing any people I had met in New York, there weren't many. I valued my friendship with Amanda, but she had gotten busier and busier with her new boyfriend. And I actually couldn't blame her for that because he was a surprisingly nice guy.

I had lined up movers to drive my stuff down to Asheville the Saturday after my last day of work.

The movers were quick—I guess that happens when you have only enough items to live in a studio in New York City. I cleaned up a few final items in my apartment and took one last look around before leaving to catch my flight to Asheville. For some reason, it didn't feel hard for me to leave.

Maybe it had just run its course.

I grabbed my suitcase and headed for the door. The movers would arrive in Asheville the next day, so

I planned to stay at a hotel in downtown Asheville for the night.

I was beaming with joy during the entire cab ride to the airport. I was excited to move to New York for the first time, but it was safe to say I tried to stay longer in the city than I should have. It had truly lost its magic for me. All of the thoughts I had racing through my mind about how my new life would be in Asheville – the possibilities were endless. Not only was I excited about learning more about interior design, but I was also certain I would have better dating luck there. The men had to be more down-to-earth than those I had encountered in New York.

"Where ya headed, miss?" asked the cab driver.

"Asheville!"

"Where's that?" Maybe Asheville wasn't as famous as I had thought.

"Well, sir, it's in Western North Carolina – I'm actually moving down there."

The gentleman laughed. "Oh yes! It's out in the Smoky Mountains – I saw a TV show about that area once. Looked beautiful and quite the change from the Big Apple."

I replied, "And a change is exactly what I am looking for!"

The rest of the drive went smoothly. Of course, we hit the typical New York traffic, which added some time to the trip, but I had planned for that. When we pulled up, the driver helped me with my luggage and wished me all the best. I must say he was one of the nicer drivers I had, but it didn't surprise me, as everything with this move had just been unfolding so nicely.

It was somewhat surreal being at the airport – all of my things were packed and on their way to Asheville. I had tied up all my loose ends in the city between work and my apartment, and lined up the cutest house to rent. I was going to have a front porch! And a small backyard! I was even excited to see green grass in my daily life. I would only see grass in the city if I walked to Central Park, which was just on the weekends.

Once I checked my luggage and went through security, I had time to grab a glass of wine at an airport bar. The bartender was a friendly woman. She asked what I wanted to drink.

"A pinot grigio, please!"

"The six or the nine-ounce pour?" she asked.

"I guess I should be somewhat responsible, so I'll take the six-ounce." She winked at me and proceeded to pour me the nine-ounce. Bless her.

"Where are you flying to?"

"Asheville!" I replied, grinning ear to ear.

"For a trip?"

"No – I'm actually moving there." The woman looked confused.

"For a man?"

I let out a little laugh, "No – for a job, but I am hoping I can eventually find a man, too."

"Well, I'm glad you're moving on your own – I always get a bad feeling when women come to this bar and tell me they are doing anything for a man. I so often get a bad gut feeling...but maybe I'm just jaded."

"Do you get a bad feeling for me?" I asked,

"I do," she immediately replied. "Which...is odd considering you said you aren't going there for a man you already know. Oh, who knows, honey – I'm just a crazy woman. Don't listen to me."

Her tone was a bit unsettling, but I decided to brush it off and get back to being excited.

Chapter 5

Meeting Rodney

After landing in Asheville, I grabbed my luggage and headed outside to hail a taxi. It was still light out, and the days were getting longer as summer approached. The airport in Asheville was small and much more manageable than JFK. When I got into the cab, I gave the driver my hotel address. The hotel I found was in downtown Asheville, and I was beyond eager to put my stuff in my room, get out, and explore a bit. Not to mention, I was starving, so some dinner was in order.

The drive to the hotel was gorgeous. I had not seen so many trees in ages, and the air smelled so fresh and clean. Asheville didn't have a significant layer of smog like New York City did. The mountains were prettier than I imagined, and not to mention the traffic – I felt like there wasn't any! I was flooded with good feelings and excitement.

When we got to the hotel, I checked in. The gentleman at the front desk gave me a map of Asheville and pointed out several popular restaurants within walking distance. I went to my room to do more research on the restaurants. I could not help but notice the beautiful view of the mountains from my room.

I felt like I was in Heaven.

I jumped in the shower and put on a pair of jeans and a white blouse. I blow-dried my hair and applied some makeup, and I was off to my first official night in Asheville.

As I walked out of the hotel onto the street, I couldn't help but notice how few people there were compared to New York City. I had looked up a few different restaurants in the hotel room, and since they were all within a couple of blocks of each other, I decided to walk by each and decide from there. Except when I got to the first one, it was so cute and charming, I wanted to go in.

It was an Italian restaurant and had gotten great reviews. When I walked in, I told the hostess it would just be me dining in, and as I looked around, I noticed a small section of the bar facing the window. I asked if I could sit there, as I would be able to check out the people of the town as they walked by.

I ordered lasagna, Caesar salad, and a glass of pinot grigio. The food was better than I expected—or maybe I was just hungrier than usual. When the waitress came and cleared my plate, I asked if it would be okay if I ordered another glass of wine and just hung out for a little while.

She looked at me, a bit confused, and said, "Honey, of course! My name is Holly —just shout if you need anything." As I watched the people walk by, I couldn't help but notice that people seemed so down-to-earth. Or at least they appeared that way. People were dressed more casually than in the city, which I found also went along with the energy of Asheville.

"Excuse me, miss?" A voice came out of nowhere, startling me a little. I whipped my head around and saw a tall, handsome man. "I'm sorry! I didn't mean to surprise you—I just wanted to check if anyone was sitting in this seat next to you—all the others are full."

I quickly glanced around the restaurant, and he was right; the place did fill up.

"Oh yes, of course! Please do! I should be leaving soon anyway."

He sat down next to me. "Well, I hope I'm not running you off! I was just on my way home from doing some errands, so I wanted to grab a glass of wine and do some people-watching. This spot is great for that."

I laughed a little. "Yes! I was just doing that myself, although the people-watching here isn't quite what I am used to."

"Oh?" The man replied. "Well – where do you usually do it?"

"New York City," I replied.

"New York City!? Well, I have never been there, but I can only imagine that Asheville is a bit less interesting when it comes to our mutual hobby of people-watching. What brings you to Asheville, if you don't mind me asking?"

There was something I enjoyed about this man. He had a very calm demeanor, and while we were making conversation, he didn't seem too pushy. He just seemed like a... normal guy. I haven't met one of those in years.

"I actually just moved here! Today!"

"What?! Wow! Well, welcome to Asheville! I hope you love it here just as much as I do! Since you're going to be a local, I should introduce myself – I'm Rodney."

Rodney.

I don't think I have ever met a Rodney in my life.

"I'm Amelia – you are the first person I have officially met here, Rodney."

Rodney and I continued to talk, keeping the conversation light and making comments as people walked by in front of us. He had such good energy that I found myself really enjoying him. Before we knew it, the restaurant said it was the last call.

"Oh wow! What time is it even – it seems sort of early?" I asked.

"Oh, they close down pretty early here – it's only 9:30 pm."

"9:30 pm?! I guess I'm not in New York anymore. They don't close most places until at least midnight."

Rodney laughed and replied, "Well—I don't want to be too forward, but there is a bar just down the block, and they—if you can believe it—are actually open until 11 pm if you are up for another drink."

"Absolutely!" Wow. I almost shocked myself with how quickly I agreed—hopefully, I didn't come off as too desperate.

"Great! I can tell you the best local places to go in Asheville!"

Rodney asked the server for the bill, "Can you please put her on my tab?"

"What?! No – you do not need to do that – I ordered an entire meal, and you just got some drinks."

Rodney looked at me and said, "It was your first meal in your new city! I have to give you a warm welcome and make sure you don't want to run back to New York before sunrise." He grinned. I swear there was almost a twinkle of light in his smile.

"Well, thank you so much – this has been a delightful first meal! I will have to come back and try some of their other items."

As we both stood up, I noticed he was several inches taller than me and seemed to be in good shape. There was definitely an attraction on my end, but I did not know if that feeling was mutual.

While on our walk to the next stop, we talked more about the town, restaurants, and shops we were passing. We ended up at a bar called Mac's. It was technically a brewery, but thank goodness they offered wine since I am not a beer drinker.

"Do you want to sit at the bar or a table?" Rodney asked.

"The bar is fine with me."

We grabbed a couple of seats, and Rodney immediately started telling me about the most popular restaurants, the best places for fresh food, different farmers' markets, and even some areas to shop for clothing.

"Amelia – I just realized you said you moved here, but I don't think you told me why."

"Oh, my goodness!" We both laughed at how easily we kept getting sidetracked. "Well, I am starting a new job as an interior design assistant next week. Although I may start a little this week, my boss has been flexible and wants to make sure I get settled in my new place a bit."

"Interior design, huh? Well, that is definitely something I know nothing about. In fact, I could probably use some help in that department."

"And what is it that you do for work?"

"Oh, I'm a software engineer. Boring stuff, really, and us engineers have a reputation for being socially awkward."

I laughed, "You? Awkward? Oh my – I don't think you have been awkward at all! Although I did move from New York City - just last week - I saw a woman tap-dancing on the subway, so… Maybe I have a high threshold of awkwardness."

He laughed, and there was that charming smile again.

Rodney was a delight. I was a bit sad as the night was ending, since we managed to make it to our second-to-last call of the evening.

"Can I walk you back to your hotel? It is late, and while Asheville is a relatively safe area, I would feel better knowing you got back safely."

My mind didn't go to the safety factor but to the fact that I could spend some more time with Rodney, so of course, I agreed to let him walk me back to the hotel.

The hotel was less than a mile away, and we were back at the hotel in no time. While we were saying our goodbyes, I realized I was not sure if we would even see each other again, and that is when Rodney asked, "Can we exchange numbers? I mean… we don't have to, but I had a really nice evening with you, and I'd love to see you again."

I didn't even answer. I just started blurting out my number. You'd think I had never been asked for my number in my life the way I threw the information at him. At that point, I was getting a bit embarrassed by some of my behavior and was sure it would be a turn-off to him. I thanked him for the lovely evening and the warm welcome to Asheville, and then headed up to my room.

When I got to the room, I changed into my pajamas and settled into bed. As I looked out of the window, I could see the outline of the mountains in the sky. What a fantastic night I had just had. Great hotel, great meal, and even better company…of a man I just met. I don't recall ever being this excited after meeting someone. It was refreshing to meet in person rather than online, where you often build up expectations in your mind before you meet.

Chapter 6

Before I knew it, I was waking up to sunlight hitting the mountains outside of my room. I slept so well, and I am sure the fresh mountain air had something to do with it. Today was a big day as the movers were scheduled to arrive at my new house around noon. I decided to throw some clothes on and walk to a nearby café for breakfast. I must admit – I was hoping to run into Rodney, but at least we did exchange numbers, so I could hope to hear from him in the coming days. As I was having some breakfast, my phone buzzed. I couldn't help but wonder, maybe it was Rodney?! But it was the movers letting me know they were about an hour outside of town.

It buzzed again – RODNEY!

I was so excited to see his name on my phone in a text.

"Good morning, Amelia! I had a wonderful time last night. I hope you got some good rest. Since you are just getting your furniture today, you probably won't have anything to eat. If you'd like, we can grab dinner again. No pressure!"

I texted back, "That sounds great!" We then agreed to touch base later to see how the move was going, so we could decide on a good time to meet.

After finishing my breakfast in the café, I headed back to the hotel to grab my things. Once I packed up my suitcases, I grabbed a taxi to my new home! I was so excited to see it in person, finally, and it was only a couple of miles from the hotel.

When I was dropped off at the house, I just stood there and stared at it for a bit. It was so quaint and perfect. It had white siding, dark green shutters, and the nicest front porch with rocking chairs. My realtor, Samantha, pulled up just after I was dropped off and handed me the keys.

"So glad you made it here safely, Amelia!" Samantha said.

"Thank you! I had a really nice night last night downtown – it's such a cute town and I love seeing the mountains all around."

As we walked toward the house, Samantha took the keys out and handed them to me. "Welcome home! I'll do a quick walkthrough with you to see if you have any questions."

As I opened the front door, I was amazed by the space. Now – I am sure it was because I had been so used to living in a tiny studio apartment for several years prior – but it still seemed more spacious than the photos let on.

"My goodness! I will need to go furniture shopping as I don't have all that much arriving from my New York apartment."

"Didn't you mention you are going to be an interior design assistant?"

"Yes – that is right."

"Well, I am sure you will find just the perfect pieces in no time then!"

We heard a loud truck, and when we looked out front, we saw the movers just arriving.

"Well, honey, I'd better be on my way and let you settle in a bit. If you need anything, you call me, okay?"

"Will do! Thanks for all of your help," I said to Samantha.

I saw Samantha off, then went to greet the movers and started showing them where to place things.

The movers only took about an hour to set up my furniture. After they left, I plopped down on my couch and had a moment of peace and solitude. It was my first official house instead of an apartment. I would definitely need to get some more furniture and wall hangings to help make the place homier, but overall, it was the perfect place for me.

I texted Rodney to let him know the movers were done and that I was going to start hanging up some of my clothes so I could get ready to grab a bite to eat with him. I had a walk-in closet, so I can't even express the anticipation of putting my clothes away and having plenty of room to spare.

Rodney suggested a couple of restaurants, and once we decided which one to meet at, I started unpacking my clothes.

I wanted to look nice tonight, so I found a navy dress that was both casual and classy. I paired it with a pair of tan high heels. I put some extra time into my makeup and hair, and then ordered a taxi to meet Rodney downtown.

How lucky am I?! I couldn't help but think to myself. I was able to move to the perfect town, find the perfect home to live in, and seemingly meet the perfect man—well, I guess, compared to the men I had been meeting.

Rodney seemed different—it was hard to explain.

As I was dropped off at the restaurant, I saw Rodney sitting at a table next to the street window. He smiled at me, and my face lit up with happiness.

It was another Italian restaurant, but I had told him that it was one of my favorite cuisines. Throughout dinner, we talked a lot about our past and how we arrived at where we are now in life. Rodney didn't have any siblings, and his parents had both passed away several years ago.

"Well, I am so sorry to hear that. To say the least…" I said.

"Hey… I guess that's life sometimes. What about you? Any siblings, and where do your parents live?"

"Well… I don't think I have any siblings. I grew up in the foster care system and was adopted around age seven. My adoptive parents live in Kansas – but we aren't that close. I mean… We don't really talk, but I've never been able to connect with either of them fully. Not exactly my favorite story to tell by any means…"

Rodney had a confused look on his face – I could tell he didn't know what to say, as most people don't.

"Well, I suppose a limited family can keep things a bit simpler. Who needs that family drama anyway?" he said with a slight smile.

"Okay – now that we've got that out of the way, can we please talk about something more fun?" I asked. "Such as what wine should we order next?" We both laughed and got the mood back to the happy one it had been.

The night seemed to fly by once again, and I was thoroughly enjoying myself. "You know, Amelia, I think we should go out again."

"Well, I happen to agree with you there!"

"And let's say we even go out again after that – then maybe we would decide to try dating each other. And do you know what one of the best things about me is?"

"What's that?" I asked.

"I can change."

"What do you mean?"

"People always say men can't change – but I pride myself on being somewhat of a chameleon throughout life. And if you ever grow tired of something about me – I'll just change it!" He smiled as he was telling me this.

I was a bit confused. I thought about it for a second and figured someone in his past must not have liked something about him, and maybe he didn't want to run into that again. I am not sure, as this was just a guess, and I only had about five seconds to think about this since I was sitting right in front of him.

But…maybe he was joking, and I wasn't picking up on the humor.

"Well, I appreciate you saying that, but there isn't anything I want to change so far. So, we've got that going for us!" We both laughed.

We wrapped up dinner, and I went home to sleep in my house for the very first night. Even though I had hardly unpacked my things, I already felt at home. As I laid in bed, I couldn't help but daydream of all the lovely furnishings I could find for the house. According to Rodney, it sounded like Asheville had a lot of unique boutiques.

I replayed some of our evening and couldn't help but be thankful for having a fantastic second night out with him. I thought for sure I'd have to get on one of those treacherous dating apps to meet someone here - especially since I didn't even have friends who could introduce me to anyone.

Before I knew it, all my daydreaming had me drift off to a peaceful sleep.

Chapter 7

My first few years in Asheville were honestly amazing. My job was personally and financially rewarding and satisfying. Charlotte was a great boss, but we never grew too close outside of work. She was always traveling to design shows or designing people's homes in other states - sometimes even other countries! Charlotte was very good at what she did. Often, she would just email me a list of items to order and make sure the deliveries were smooth. So I never had anyone breathing down my neck, which I appreciated.

Rodney and I had begun dating. It was one of the easiest relationships I had ever had, although I hadn't had that many to compare it to. We had done some traveling together and, of course, loved our nights out to dinner. We would also go hiking, and loved to watch thriller movies together.

The only thing that was a bit difficult for me was forming friendships. I worked alone in an office, and Rodney said most of his friends had moved away after college. So, we were each other's main friends. There is nothing wrong with that, but sometimes I'd see a group of women out to dinner having wine and laughing, and I was always a bit envious of those situations. I once befriended a woman whose home Charlotte helped design—but then she got pregnant with twins, and we lost touch once they were born.

Tiffany. I liked Tiffany, but I guess our lives just went in very different directions.

One afternoon, I was sitting at my desk, somewhat zoning out since it was a Friday, and I was ready for the weekend. My cell phone rang so loudly, it made me jump.

I looked down and saw it was Rodney.

"Hello?" I answered.

"Hi! Did you have plans tonight?"

I laughed a bit because Rodney knew I hardly ever had plans. "Nope – I am wide open. Did you have something in mind?"

"Great! I booked a nice dinner at a new restaurant in town – I hope it will be a special night for us."

"Oh, that sounds fun to try something new – I ordered a new dress online this week that fits perfectly, so I will wear that."

"Sounds good – pick you up at 7 pm?"

"That works for me - see you then!" I said as I hung up. I finished up a couple of things around the office, locked up, and headed home.

I wondered what Rodney meant by making it special. It was just an ordinary weekend, so I didn't quite understand what he meant by that. I guess I'd be finding out in a couple of hours.

When I got home, I sat on the back porch with a glass of wine and stared at the sunset. I couldn't see the total sunset, but it was enough to make me appreciate it. After all, I never saw it while living in New York City. Speaking of New York, I didn't think about it much anymore. I was so used to my life in Asheville and had adapted well to it. I should have kept in better touch with some of my friends, and at the very least, Amanda – but Amanda had gotten married and had kids. It seemed like anyone I knew who had kids, well, very clearly, had different priorities. At least initially, but then, as time went on, I guess it felt harder to reach back out.

Before I knew it, I had finished my glass of pinot grigio. Looking at the time, I decided to pour myself another half-glass before I got ready. As much as I enjoyed my time with Rodney, I also enjoyed my time alone at my house, which had become my sanctuary. I had decorated it exactly as I wanted—in a traditional style, with many vintage pieces I had collected over the years at nearby antique shops.

Rodney's house was fine. I mean, it was typical bachelor style, I suppose, and he seemed to be a bit of a hoarder. I was a minimalist, and Rodney sure liked his "things." We hadn't discussed living together, which maybe should have been a bit odd to me that we never discussed moving forward, but I guess I wasn't in a big rush and was okay with how things were. I definitely liked and appreciated my alone time.

I finally decided to throw myself in the shower and get ready. Plus, I was already looking forward to drinking some more wine. It was Friday, after all!

It is always much easier to get ready when you know what to wear, especially when it is a new outfit. I found this gorgeous silk dress online, and it was on clearance, making it even more exciting.

Just as I finished applying my makeup, I heard the doorbell ring. I grabbed my clutch and met Rodney at the door, and then we headed to dinner.

The restaurant he took me to had recently opened and had such a romantic atmosphere. We often went to more casual places, so this was a nice change. Each table had flowers, candles and the lighting was dim overall, which in my opinion made everyone look better, so I appreciated it.

Rodney and I had been talking about our days since he picked me up—nothing out of the ordinary. We ordered an appetizer and our entrees. He seemed nervous for some reason, which I found peculiar, but I really didn't put too much thought into it. After the server cleared our plates, he asked the server for a glass of one of their finest wines. I looked at him, puzzled.

"Why are you ordering that for us?"

"Well, Amelia – I will tell you when we get our wine."

I was confused.

Finally, the wine was delivered to our table—a cabernet sauvignon. I am not a red wine fan, but this was delicious.

"Okay, Rodney – enough with you being weird – what's this all about?" I asked.

"Amelia – I want you to move in with me."

I almost dropped my expensive wine.

"Huh?!"

"We've dated for over a year and are often together anyway. I mean, you pay rent now. You could stop paying rent and save money if you just lived with me."

He had a point there.

"Well… umm… that could be an idea." For some reason, this was very overwhelming. I should be excited. Why wasn't I? I've been dating this man for over a year, as he just pointed out, and I love him. So, what was the problem with me? It was almost like I had this deep gut feeling that I suddenly didn't know him.

I had too much wine. That was it. I am just overthinking, and the alcohol isn't helping.

Rodney stared at me, looking a bit dismal over my reaction.

"You know what?! I think this sounds like a fantastic idea!"

"You do?!" Rodney exclaimed.

"Yes! But can we PLEASE redecorate some of your rooms?!" We laughed as Rodney happily agreed to let me take over the decorating.

The rest of the evening was rather fun as I told him some of my ideas for different rooms. He had a four-bedroom house, and a couple of the rooms were somewhat empty, which would make it easy to move some of my furniture in. I will admit—his home had huge walk-in closets. My rental house had big closets, but his were even more spacious. What woman doesn't like that?!

"When is your lease up?" Rodney asked.

"I have to double-check, but I'm pretty sure it was switched over to a month-to-month lease when I renewed after the first year."

"Well! This just gets easier and easier!"

There it was again. Suddenly, I had this gut feeling I shouldn't be doing this. Enough, Amelia – I told myself. Enjoy the evening and revisit this thought on another day – should it even come up again.

"Thank you for ordering that fine wine – I loved it!"

"We can have a lot more when we LIVE together!" Rodney exclaimed with a giant smile.

I smiled back. This is good. This is exciting...Isn't it?

After dinner, we went back to Rodney's house and picked out a movie to watch. It was an action movie, which I didn't care for but I lied and said I was fine with it. In reality, while we watched it, I kept replaying our conversation at dinner over and over in my mind. Why did he want me to move in? I mean, I guess it is a normal part of a forward-moving relationship.

Do I have low self-esteem? I feel like I should be happy, but for some reason, I just… wasn't.

Before I knew it, I had fallen asleep on the couch. It had been a very long week and even longer day.

Rodney woke me up after the movie so I could get up, wash my face, and crawl into bed. It was considerate that he never left me on the couch because once he did, and my neck hurt for a week.

See? He's nice. He's thoughtful.

I woke up in the morning to birds chirping outside the window. I must say, sometimes I get woken up by traffic at my house. Rodney's house is in a more proper neighborhood and is quieter all around. I was feeling much more comfortable about the idea of moving this morning. I am sure I just drank too much wine, and it made me paranoid. Why wouldn't I want to live in a bigger home that I could help decorate and have bigger closets to continue my shopping habits? I was being crazy last night - end of story.

Rodney made me breakfast – a cheese omelet and bacon. While it was good, and I didn't mind eating like this sometimes, I was a bit worried it would be hard to get him to eat more healthily, like I did when I moved in. Oh well. I can cross that bridge when I come to it. After breakfast, I left his house to head back to mine.

That afternoon, I just did some errands and some cleaning. Rodney and I were not meeting that Saturday evening because he had to focus on a work project, so I had a night to myself. I decided I had better really enjoy these last couple of months at home. So, I did my favorite thing – poured myself a glass of wine, cooked one of my favorite pasta dishes, and turned on some reality shows. Since I didn't have any drama of my own, it was a bit fun to watch someone else's.

Hopefully, I can still have some nights like this to myself at Rodney's. It will be an adjustment to living with someone else full-time, but change is good and promotes growth, right?

Right.

The next couple of months went by pretty fast. I spent my days going to work and researching different ways to decorate Rodney's house. He seemed really flexible with all my suggestions, which was nice. I had slowly started to bring some of my things over on the weekends, so the actual move wouldn't have to be all at once.

On the actual day I moved in, everything went seamlessly. Rodney had plenty of room for all of my stuff – granted, I didn't have a ton – but it was still nice that I didn't need to get rid of anything I didn't want to. I decided to part with some of my furnishings, and of course, it is always a good time to go through clothing and donate anything I hadn't been wearing.

On my first official night living with him, Rodney had picked up some Chinese food for us. We sat down to eat, and he looked at me and said, "Amelia, I can't tell you how happy I am that I not only met you but that you are also now living with me. Thank you for moving in, and I promise to make you so happy!"

"Well, you already make me happy!"

"Okay, good—and remember, if I start to not make you happy, I can change!" he said with a wide smile.

I had a flashback to our second night when he mentioned he could change. I don't know why, but that just struck me as so odd. And this current conversation was also a bit off. Do men go around offering to change? I am pretty sure most women *want* men to change, and they either can't or won't.

"Well, thank you for saying that, Rodney, but everything will be just fine with us! I can feel it."

And actually, everything was fine. We eased into living together and settled into new routines. I had my job, and in my free time, I went hiking and planned trips for us. Rodney and I both enjoyed traveling. We had traveled a lot around North Carolina - the beach was one of my favorite places. We had found some on the Outer Banks that were not as crowded, and it was one of my happy places.

Chapter 8

One weekend, about a year after I moved in, we traveled to a town in North Carolina called Corolla. The town's beach was part of a state park, which had wild horses in it. If you were lucky, you would sometimes see the horses come out of the dunes and onto the beach. I loved seeing this happen. I loved horses and the beach, so seeing both at once was such a wonderful experience.

We had been on the beach that day and went back to shower before going to dinner. As I was getting ready, I noticed Rodney looked extra dressed up.

"Wow! Look at you! What's the occasion?" I asked.

He was nervous. Rodney was never nervous. He shuffled his feet as he replied, "Well, the restaurant we are going to looked a bit nicer according to the reviews, so I just thought I'd put in some extra effort."

Since I hadn't gotten dressed yet, I changed my mind about what I would wear and picked a slightly nicer dress for the evening.

As we walked out of the condo we had rented for the weekend, I saw him grab a bottle of champagne.

"Why are you bringing champagne to the restaurant?"

"Well – you know what – I was told the sunset was going to be extra nice tonight, so I thought we should go down to the beach for a little pre-dinner champagne."

"Say no more – that sounds like a wonderful way to start the evening! Can we come back here first to rinse our feet off?"

Rodney laughed – he knew I hated sand even though I loved the beach.

"Oh, of course – I wouldn't have it any other way for you."

I took off my heels and put on flip-flops, and we headed to the beach. Our condo was on the beach, so it was just a short walk down the path. The evening air was cooling off slightly. We spread out a blanket, and I went to grab the champagne glasses from the bag he had put them in.

'Wait!" Rodney exclaimed.

I was annoyed. All I was trying to do was pour some champagne – what was there to wait for?!

Rodney looked nervous again. I was really starting to get confused by his behavior now.

"Wait for what, Rodney?"

"I…uhh… I… I just have to talk to you for a second."

"Okay, well, I'm right here in front of you – so what is it?"

"It's just that – Amelia – ever since the first night I met you, I knew you'd be someone special in my life."

OH, MY GOD. Is he proposing???

My brain started connecting all the dots like crazy.

"And I really can't imagine my life without you."

OH, GOD. He is.

"So, you know I had a whole speech prepared, but I'm just so nervous, I am just going to ask: Amelia, will you please marry me? Please?" Rodney pulled a ring out of his coat pocket. It was simple yet elegant, and I will say it was my taste.

Do men say please in proposals? Wait. I needed to focus on the moment. For some reason, I got a giant pit in my stomach. Was I actually surprised this was happening? I mean, I live with the guy, and we get along; it is the only logical next step. I needed to answer. When I tried, I felt this insane sense of dread. Rodney was staring at me and waiting for me to say something. Obviously. I yelled at myself in my head and pulled myself together.

"YES!"

"Really?!" Rodney exclaimed.

"Yes, yes!" I forced it out of my mouth.

"This is wonderful, Amelia! I'm going to be the most perfect husband for you!"

Just then – almost on cue – some horses ran down from the dunes and brought me a sense of calmness. I am pretty sure you are supposed to be happy when you're proposed to, but it was hard for me to put into words. I just had this feeling it wasn't right. But then again, I have had these random feelings at all the major turning points in our relationship, and everything has been completely fine. So, per usual, I figured I must be overthinking things again.

Maybe I have just read one too many romantic thrillers.

Rodney was great. I am now engaged. And I'm happy.

Right?!

I will say that Rodney seemed so happy I had said yes. So happy that, between him and me, we shared the whole bottle of champagne. I will admit it was a beautiful evening. Watching the wild horses to the north and the gorgeous sunset to the south was surreal. My anxious feelings had started to subside, and I could finally just enjoy the moment.

As the sun had just finished setting, we gathered our things, went to the condo to rinse off our feet, and headed out to dinner. The restaurant was less than half a mile away, so we decided just to walk. As we walked in the neighborhood, we held hands, and I felt good—happy—which is how you are supposed to feel.

We went to a restaurant overlooking the harbor. During dinner, Rodney seemed so happy. I mean, I was too – but he was just a lot happier than I had ever actually seen him.

"Amelia – when do you want to get married?"

Goodness. I barely had a ring on my finger, and we are jumping to wedding planning?!

"Umm."

"Okay, I know it is soon. I guess I have been thinking about this for a while, and you just started this evening."

"That is very true!" I laughed.

"I was thinking something small?" Rodney said.

I laughed. "Rodney, of course, it will be small! We don't really have any family and barely have any friends!"

Rodney laughed too. "Oh, okay, well, you have a point there! Okay – so we will elope!"

"Elope? Well, I suppose that makes sense. Plus, I have always heard wedding planning can be so stressful – not to mention expensive. I think it would be fun to go dress shopping, though! Oh, you know what, Rodney – maybe I could even fly to New York City for a weekend – I used to always walk by a beautiful wedding shop there, and I am sure I could find the perfect dress."

"Well, a perfect dress for my perfect bride-to-be – that sounds good to me!"

Chapter 9

New York. I hadn't been back since I left. Which, I guess, has been about three years now. I was just so done with it when I left; I had barely ever missed it. The thought of returning for just a weekend, though, excited me. I could go to my favorite bakeries and restaurants. It would be fun to take a jog through Central Park again. It is springtime too, so it won't be cold. I could even catch up with Amanda. She'll be so excited that I am engaged and getting married. I haven't spoken to her much over the years, so it would be great to catch up in person.

After our trip to the beach, we headed back to Asheville, and I got to planning—well, planning as much as someone could for an elopement. There still seemed to be an awful lot of decisions to make, though. The dress, hair, makeup, and flowers.

Over the coming weeks, I must admit I was a bit sidetracked at work with looking at bridal magazines.

There were just so many different types of dresses to choose from. I tried to narrow down a style – I was thinking I wanted lace. I went online and called a bridal store I used to walk by on the Upper West Side of Manhattan, near where I lived.

"How soon do you want to come in? We are usually booked months in advance, but we just had two different cancellations for this weekend. Is that too soon for you?" the sales clerk asked.

"I'll take them!" I blurted out. "I mean, I will take one of them!" The sales clerk and I both laughed. "Sorry! I am just so excited!"

"Well, that is understandable, my dear! Do you have a wedding date in mind?"

"No – we are just going to elope, but have not decided the timing yet."

"Very smart of you! You have no clue how many stressed-out brides I deal with every week! It takes the fun right out of it if you ask me. Okay – we have an 11 am or 3 pm this Saturday – which do you prefer?"

If I take a Saturday morning flight, I should be able to get there by 3 pm.

"3 pm sounds great!" I said.

"Okay – let me get your information, and you'll be all set."

That evening, I went home and told Rodney the bridal store had an opening, so I took it and will fly up just for the night. He had no interest in coming with me. Which was fine – I wouldn't be there for too long, and it would be nice to focus on my own schedule rather than play tour guide with him.

I had gotten a morning flight to New York and landed at JFK airport around 11 am. I grabbed a taxi and headed to a hotel I booked near Central Park. It was just enough time to drop off my bags and get some lunch before the 3 pm wedding dress appointment.

It was oddly nice to be back in the city—quite the opposite of the feeling I had when I left.

I stayed at a hotel on the southwest end of the park near Columbus Circle. I must say, when I walked into the lobby, it was fancy, unlike the hotels we had in Asheville. It felt so classy and upscale. I did splurge a bit since I was in town to pick out (hopefully) a wedding dress.

I had texted Amanda to see if she could meet up, but she was out of town with her family. There really wasn't anyone else I had kept in touch with, so it was all me this weekend. Granted, I was only in town for one night. It was such short notice, so I felt terrible asking for any time off from work.

A cute little Greek café was next to the hotel, so I popped in for lunch. I pulled out some of my bridal magazines to review once more. I wanted to show the shop's salespeople some of the styles I was leaning towards. So far, I have been thinking of something simple, all lace. Well, a simple silhouette. I was really excited to go dress shopping. Hopefully, they didn't mind that I was doing it alone, as I know most people have friends and families to go with them.

It was a bit odd that Rodney and I really didn't have a circle of friends or family. I will say – there was no outside drama. And between the two of us, there wasn't even much drama. We hardly ever fought, and if we did, it was about trivial items like where we should eat dinner. We never could complain about each other's in-laws because frankly, we didn't have any.

I finished my Greek salad and started to make my way to the bridal shop. It was just a twenty-minute walk, so I figured I'd get some steps in. The buildings on the Upper West Side were so fun to look at, and it was nice to see all the different types of people out and about. Tulips were planted in many of the street planters and were all popping up with fresh blooms—definitely a charming aspect of the city.

When I arrived at the shop, I took a moment to remember all the times I had walked by it and marveled at the dresses in the window. And here I am! I am actually able to go in and try on dresses.

I walked in and went to the check-in desk. "Hi! I am Amelia and have an appointment at 3 pm."

"Welcome! Let me see who you are assigned to work with. Oh, you are working with Laura. She's great—you'll love her. She is finishing up with another appointment. Can I offer you some champagne while you wait for just a little?"

This day keeps getting better and better.

"Yes! That sounds lovely! Thank you."

As I sat in the waiting room, I heard a buzz on my phone. I looked down to see a text from Rodney. "Amelia – I hope you find the perfect dress! Don't worry about how much it costs either! I already can't wait to see you tomorrow." I was lucky I met Rodney. He was very easy-going overall. Although the man clearly had no clue how expensive wedding dresses could be.

"Amelia?"

I looked up to see a woman smiling at me.

"Hi! I am Laura! I am so glad to meet you, and I hear you are visiting from out of town?"

"Yes – well, I used to live in the city, just down a few blocks actually, but now I live in Asheville, North Carolina."

"Well! Welcome back to the city, and we simply must find you a dress today, then. I have excellent luck with out-of-town guests. Do you have any types of dresses you are interested in?" Laura asked.

"I do! I brought some pictures to show you."

"Oh, fantastic – I always love a bride that comes prepared." She grabbed my magazines and started flipping through all the marked pages. "Well, you clearly have a style you are interested in. Classy, elegant, simple. Come on – let me show you to your fitting room and I can start bringing some dresses for you to try on."

We started walking back and passed what seemed to be their champagne bar in the shop. "Lucy, we need a refill in bridal suite four, please," Laura winked at me.

"Umm, can I come back every Saturday?!" We both laughed.

"Dress shopping can be stressful, and you know what, Amelia? I am glad you are here solo. You have no clue the number of opinions some of these brides get from having family involved, and they start to second-guess what they actually like."

I guess she was right. I mean, it wasn't like I had the option to have family, and my ability to make friends was… relatively nonexistent.

I sat down in the bridal suite. It was much bigger than a standard dressing room—basically the size of a small bedroom. It had multiple full-length mirrors and seating areas.

Laura went out to gather some dresses and before I knew it, she was pushing up a rolling rack full of them.

"Okay, Amelia. I picked out six dresses for you to try on. We will see what you like and dislike about each one, and I can update the selection from there."

This was great. I wonder if this is how rich people feel when they go shopping for everyday clothing. I could definitely get used to this.

I tried the first one. Eh. It was too plain, it had lace, but not the type I had imagined. The second one was better, but overall, it had a little too much detail. The third dress—as I pulled it off the rack, I heard Laura say, "You know this one stood out to me for some reason, so I am excited to see if you like it!"

As I slipped it on, she helped button up the back. It had long sleeves, which I did not imagine liking at all, but they were see-through lace. The body was a white fabric covered in lace as well. The dress was fitted and flowed out nicely from the hips. This dress seemed a bit too complicated for me. I envisioned something simpler.

"Go ahead now – go look in the mirror," Laura told me.

As I turned around to walk to the three-way mirror, I was in such awe. It was perfect.

"Well?" Laura inquired. "Do you like it?"

"Oh, Laura, I don't like it – I am in love with it! This is just breathtaking. I'm obsessed!"

"Do you want to try more dresses on to be sure?"

"Oh, I am sure! This is the dress for me, and I must admit you are fantastic at your job!"

Laura laughed. "Well, sometimes I just have a little extra luck on my side. Now, let's go get your measurements and order this dress for you."

After ordering the dress, I walked outside and wondered where I should go next. It was before sundown, so I thought it would be nice to take a stroll along the Hudson River. I heard my phone go off, so I looked to see a text from Rodney. I realized I had forgotten to respond to him earlier.

"Amelia – how is the dress shopping? I am hoping you didn't decide to run off with another man and forget all about me while you are up there."

I stopped in my tracks. What was he even talking about? Rodney had never displayed any jealousy, but I guess I have also never been out of town solo since knowing him—but still… good grief.

"Hi! I am sorry I forgot to respond. I got so sidetracked. I found a wonderful dress! I am on a walk now, will grab some dinner in a bit, then give you a call tonight from the hotel."

I didn't acknowledge his comment about another man. I realize I forgot to text him back, but it had only been a couple of hours. It was definitely odd to me, but maybe he was joking? It didn't feel like a joke, though, but then again, I guess it is hard to tell via text.

My walk was lovely. It felt so nice to be back in the city. I was really shocked about how different I felt now compared to when I left, but I guess time heals us and lets us forget some bad feelings.

While on my walk, I looked up some restaurants and decided to try a new seafood one that slightly overlooked Central Park. It was also next to my hotel, so that was convenient. As I finished my walk and headed back to my hotel, I popped into a couple of boutiques along the way. My goodness—I must say the fashion was much different than in Asheville. Asheville had many perks, but shopping wasn't one of them.

I stopped at the hotel to shower and change, and then walked to the restaurant. It was pretty busy, but I could be seated at a table for two overlooking the park. I started with half a dozen raw oysters and a glass of celebratory wine. My dress was so beautiful – I couldn't wait to get it delivered and try it on.

Just then, my phone went off, and it was another text from Rodney. "Amelia, when will you be at the hotel? Are you going to be out all night?"

All night? It was 7:00 pm. He clearly is not used to me going out of town.

"Hi dear – I will be back at the hotel in just over an hour or so and will give you a call! Miss you!" I texted back.

I do not know what has gotten into him, but I must admit it was a bit annoying. I mean, I am sitting alone in a restaurant trying to be happy about my day. He must just be anxious.

I had the best seared scallops for dinner and then headed back to the hotel. I was somewhat dreading calling Rodney. I was hoping he would be normal on the phone…

Chapter 10

After the phone call, I was relieved. He was back to normal. Maybe I should have been better at communicating more, but I was just gone for a night, so I didn't really think about it much. After we hung up, it was only about 9 pm, and I couldn't help but want to take advantage of being back in the city. I threw my coat on and went to walk around a bit.

The city at night made me feel so alive – well, it was the city that never sleeps, so that made sense. I walked several blocks, looking at the lit-up buildings, and was just mesmerized by it all. I passed a quaint little bar on a corner, so thought I would stop in. I felt a little guilty not telling Rodney I had left my room – but this way, he wouldn't be sending me any weird texts. Besides, I was going back to Asheville tomorrow and would see him then.

The bar had lots of books in it that you could take to read. I guess it was a coffee bar in the morning. It was decently crowded, but there were a few empty tables and also some openings at the bar, so I grabbed a seat. I ordered a cosmopolitan. Something different I figured. The crowd seemed very relaxed – not like the New York people I was used to from when I lived here. Maybe I was not going to the right spots? Well, it doesn't matter now.

Just then, a man walked up, "Do you mind if I sit here, miss?"

"Not at all!" I responded. The last time a man asked if he could sit next to me was in Asheville, and it was Rodney.

"I won't be here too long. I am meeting some friends just down the way, but I heard they are running late. They are a wild bunch, so I thought it would be smart for me to come in here since it is more low-key and I can decompress from my work week a bit."

"Oh," I really did not know what to say, and I hadn't talked to a random man in years at this point. Being engaged—was I even allowed to? I was always with Rodney in Asheville, so this never happened.

"Oh, I am sorry! You probably had a hard week yourself and are in no mood to talk to a random stranger like me. I'd tell you I'd stop talking, but that is not really who I am. The only thing I can tell you is I only have about 30 minutes to disrupt your life."

We both laughed. "I apologize – you aren't disrupting me. It's just that – I don't live here anymore and perhaps I've forgotten some of my social skills."

"Well, where do you live?"

"Asheville."

"Oh! I have never been, but I've heard it's beautiful! What brings you back to the city?"

"Well, actually, I just got engaged and flew up to pick out a wedding dress today."

"You must love that dress because your face just lit up when you talked about it."

"Oh, I do! I really, really do!"

"Well, the next question is when is the big day?"

"Umm, I am not sure how big of a day it can be since we are just eloping."

"Oh. Easy. Smart. Simple. Too bad he met you first! My name is Hudson, by the way."

Hudson. That was a nice name.

"Amelia," I said as I shook his hand.

"So, Hudson – what's your story? Married? Kids?"

"Oh... no. Came close to getting married once, but it just didn't work out, I guess." His demeanor completely changed, and suddenly, he seemed so sad. Then he snapped out of it. "But hey! That's life, right – and why we are lucky to get new chances and new beginnings! And what better place to start over than in New York City!"

"Oh – did you just move here?" I asked.

"No, but I am just saying it is still a pretty easy place to start over." Hudson smiled.

There was something about the way he said that. It was hard to explain.

"So, you're getting married and had the nerve to not even meet me first."

"Ha! Well, trust me. I lived here and tried to date, and it was *a nightmare*!" Hudson and I said at the exact same time.

We talked for just a bit longer, and it was fun. He was very smart and funny, and I felt an odd sense of familiarity with him.

"I need to go meet my friends, Amelia, but I am happy I met you, and while I am not happy you're running off to marry someone else, I am happy you found your perfect dress!"

"Oh! Can I show you a picture?"

"Absolutely!"

"Sorry, but I'm a woman, and we love these things."

I pulled out my phone and showed him a picture of me in my dress.

Hudson's expression completely changed. It was almost as if he were in shock.

"Well?" I asked.

"Amelia… you are stunning. The dress is okay, too," he smiled. "You sure you know what you're getting yourself into? With this guy, I mean. Is he nice to you?"

It was so odd. Hudson barely knew me, and he knew absolutely nothing about Rodney. He seemed so genuinely concerned, though it was hard to dismiss it.

"Oh yeah, he's fine."

"Fine?! Just fine, Amelia? He'd better be the most amazing man ever to walk this earth if he's getting to marry you. I know I just met you – but I usually have a sixth sense about these things."

This was getting so strange.

"Okay, I really gotta go. Can I ask you, now you're a taken woman, so I can't ask for your number, but can I take a picture of your phone with you in that dress?"

I laughed at the craziness of this.

"Amelia, what if you're my soulmate – how am I ever gonna prove to people I met my soulmate at this crazy little bar surrounded by books?" We both laughed.

"Okay, fine." I pulled my phone out again, and he took a picture of me in my dress.

"Now listen – do you see that building out there – with the red lights up at the top?" Hudson had a very serious tone all of a sudden.

"Yes…"

"I work on the 23rd floor. You seem like a really great person. If you ever need anything, tell security you want to see Hudson on the 23rd floor. They will let you up."

"Umm…okay... uhh… thank you?" I was so confused. Maybe it was the cosmopolitan.

"Okay, Amelia – take care of yourself and enjoy the rest of your time in the city. Sorry for being so blunt… I am not usually like this, but sometimes we need to follow our gut."

And that was it. He left.

Just then, the bartender asked if I wanted another cosmopolitan.

"I sure do!"

Chapter 11

The next day, I woke up sad to leave the city. It had been a short trip but a wonderful one. I found the dress of my dreams and took some nice walks around the city.

Hudson.

I forgot about meeting him. He was so nice… and yet oddly so concerned about me. I had never had an encounter like that before. I guess it really didn't matter, though – I was about to head back to Asheville and will never see him again.

I got my things together and grabbed a cab to the airport. I had some time and was hungry, so I wanted to get a salad at a place to eat in the airport. It was so funny – I recognized the same woman bartender who talked to me the day I moved to Asheville. She had a very distinctive look, which is why it was easy to remember her…oh… and the fact that she had a bad feeling about me moving. Well, time to prove her wrong.

"Hi!" I exclaimed.

"Here, let me get you some menus – are you eating too, or just drinking?" she asked.

"I think I just want a salad or something – so a food menu would be great."

As she handed me the menu, she stared at me, "You seem familiar – I imagine you fly through here a lot?"

"No. Not really. In fact, I have not been here since I moved to Asheville, which was several years ago."

Suddenly, her face changed. "Yes! I remember you, honey. How are things there? Please tell me they are good…"

"They are! I just got engaged!"

I could barely finish the word, and her expression completely changed.

"Well – just remember if something goes wrong, you can always come back to the city."

"Oh…. Umm…" I was confused yet again.

"So, what do you want to eat?" she asked.

"Let me have a grilled chicken Caesar salad, please."

I was getting more excited about leaving New York and returning to Rodney. Between the random man last night and the lady at the airport today, I want to be around more positive people. I didn't understand how random strangers could be so concerned about me

– especially when nothing was wrong! At least Laura at the bridal store was wonderful.

When I arrived back in Asheville, Rodney picked me up, and we went out for a nice meal. I must say, even though I had only been away from him for two days, I was happy to be back. I was so used to being around him that a couple of days felt more like a couple of weeks without him.

While at dinner, I told him all about my trip—well…most of it. I did not mention that I left the hotel room after we talked. There is no need for him to worry about anything.

"You should really come to New York with me sometime!" I said.

"Ehh… my home is Asheville," Rodney somberly replied.

"I didn't say move there with me – I mean to go visit for a weekend. The city does have a lot to offer, you know."

"Umm, well, it just seems like a lot of people too – and so much crime. I'd rather never go there if I am being honest."

This attitude annoyed me. Am I really okay with marrying a man afraid of New York City? Maybe "afraid" isn't the right word, but he definitely wasn't open to it on my behalf. While frustrating, I guess he does go to many other places. Perhaps I will keep New York as my special place.

"Well, Amelia – now that you will officially get your dress – we need to figure out the next steps."

"I agree! Let the fun continue. Do we elope at a destination and combine it with a honeymoon experience?" I asked.

"That could be fun! What kind of destination? Should we do something easy like Las Vegas? I know you have always liked Vegas. But we don't need to have Elvis marry us – we could find a nice hotel to do it in. Or should we do something like Hawaii or Jamaica?"

"Hmm… Jamaica could be nice? Or Vegas. Or Hawaii!" We both laughed. "Well, at least we have some ideas to research and can decide in the coming weeks," I said.

That night, as we were getting into bed, Rodney seemed a bit off. I asked if he was okay, and his face changed. "Well… if I am being honest, I didn't like it when you were in New York. I had a bad feeling you were going to meet someone else, and I don't think I could handle it if you left me."

"Left you?! My goodness, Rodney – what are you even talking about? I was gone for one night. You know I'd never leave you."

"Promise?" Rodney asked.

"Of course!" I said.

Why did I have to promise? I felt a pit in my stomach, and a wave of uneasy emotions came over me to the point that I felt a little sick. I talked myself down.

I had a whirlwind of a couple of days, and I am sure we were both just overtired.

The next several weeks were so exciting. I spent so much time looking at bridal jewelry, flowers, and hairstyles. I also spent time researching places to elope. Las Vegas sounded fun, but I was on the fence about it. Hawaii looked great, but the plane trip was quite the ordeal. Jamaica was becoming increasingly convincing.

I found an all-inclusive resort that offered elopement packages and even had a photographer on-site, along with someone who could do my hair and makeup. The flights from Asheville were not too long, so it made sense. Once I had explained all my reasoning to Rodney, he was entirely on board.

I was due to get my dress in the coming days, so we started looking up plane tickets and the best time frames for us to elope.

"We may as well go this summer – say in June?" Rodney said.

"I agree! That is about five weeks from now, but why wait?" I must admit—all of the bridal and marriage stuff had gone to my head. I am sure there was a part of Rodney that just wanted it over with. "How long should we go for?"

"A week? Is that too long? Maybe five nights?" Rodney said.

"I think that sounds perfect! This is easy – we should be professional wedding planners!"

Rodney laughed. "You are so easygoing, and I am fortunate to marry you."

He was right about that for sure.

The following five weeks passed quickly, and I was excited to go to Jamaica. We would arrive on a Sunday. I had a spa day planned for us both on that Monday, and on Tuesday, we would have the elopement ceremony. On Wednesday, we would relax, and on Thursday, I had some excursions planned for us – or at least I was setting aside the day for something if we decided.

I started exercising more, eating healthier, and treating myself to facials and skin treatments to look my best in our photos. I admit my efforts paid off.

Work had been mundane, and I was ready for a new adventure in Jamaica. Rodney and I had been getting along splendidly, which we usually did, so that was no surprise.

Chapter 12

The day finally arrived, and we were going to Jamaica to elope. We were flying out of Asheville and had a layover in Atlanta. Rodney upgraded us to first class on the Atlanta flight, so when we boarded, they offered us some champagne, which we both accepted.

As we sat down in our spacious first-class seats, we toasted each other. It finally felt like the start of our vacation. I was feeling relaxed yet excited. The flight was a few hours, and when we arrived at Montego Bay Airport, we got off the plane and looked for a shuttle to take us to our resort. We quickly found the bus, and as we were the last to board, we took off after several minutes on the hour-long journey to the hotel.

Rodney grabbed my hand as I sat beside him, and we looked at each other excitedly. We were always good travel companions, and I looked forward to adding another trip to the books.

The road was awfully rough, with lots of curves—I was relieved to have finally arrived, as I had started to feel a little carsick. Once I got off the bus, I saw the resort. It was magnificent! It was four stories in the main building. As we walked into the reception hall, we were greeted by the hotel's staff, who were eager to help us get our room and take our luggage. The reception hall was two stories high and had beautiful marble floors. I noticed I could see the ocean at the other end of the hall and could not wait to check it out.

As we checked in, we were given a map of the resort—it was much bigger than I had even realized. We were then led to our room—I let Rodney pick it out, so I was not sure which one he had reserved.

I noticed that the door said "Suite" next to the room number. As we were led into the room, my jaw dropped. "This is stunning!" I exclaimed. The hotel butler smiled, then assured me I had not seen the best part and motioned for me to follow him out to the balcony. As we walked through the sliding doors, the balcony wrapped around part of the building, offering beautiful ocean views.

The butler then said he would leave us to get settled in and was off.

"Rodney!" I exclaimed! "You've outdone yourself! Look at the beautiful water and white sand beaches!"

"Well, you were the one who found the resort – I simply just asked for one of the top rooms," he said, grinning.

From our balcony, we could see a good portion of the resort's offerings. Once we had an idea of where everything was, we decided to explore the rest of the suite. There was an open living room just inside the balcony, and off to the side was the bedroom. The bedroom had a king-size bed with white linens, along with an extra sitting area facing the ocean.

The bathroom was astounding. It was all marble, with a large tub big enough for both of us and a huge walk-in closet.

Just then, I noticed Rodney was no longer behind me.

"Rodney?" I yelled.

"In here!"

I walked out of the bathroom, through the bedroom, and into the living room, where he was exploring the kitchen.

"Look at this, Amelia! This is some fancy bourbon – I wonder how much it is?"

"Free!" I said with excitement. "It's an all-inclusive, remember? It's all free, well, in terms of the food and drinks. Our spa day and any other excursions aren't."

"Wow! Well, what do you say I make us a couple of drinks, and we walk down to the beach and explore a bit?"

"Fine by me! Let me hang up some of our clothing and freshen up while you do that."

I was in heaven, and it hadn't even been an hour at the resort. I could not wait for what this week had in store for us.

As I hung up our clothing, I felt so relaxed and calm. It had been a busy couple of weeks lining up the final details for our elopement, but in the end, it all came together, and now I could truly start to enjoy myself.

"Okay, Amelia – I made you a lavender vodka spritz."

I laughed, "How on earth did you make that?"

"You need to come look in this kitchen – it's a bartender's dream!"

I left the room and went to meet Rodney in the kitchen. "Oh, wow! You weren't kidding! Well, let's head down to the beach, enjoy our drinks, and take in some of our surroundings."

Rodney grabbed the room key, then my hand, and we headed out.

The beach had such pretty sand—white and super soft. The sun was starting to set, and the water was clear.

Rodney was looking at a pamphlet we had gotten at check-in. "They have five restaurants – maybe we should try a seafood one tonight?"

"Fine by me!" I said as I took a sip of my refreshing vodka lavender spritz that Rodney had made. "Rodney, I need you to recreate this drink at home—it's incredible!"

"It was easy too! So, I can make that happen."

We sat down on some beach chairs and dug our feet into the sand. We both let out a deep sigh. It had been a busy but good day. I loved it here! We both did.

There was always something about being on the beach for me. I felt like I could clear my head and feel at peace. The ocean always had a way of instilling hope in me – no matter what I was going through.

After relaxing for a bit, we started to head towards the seafood restaurant Rodney had mentioned. It also overlooked the water and had an outdoor seating area. It was decently crowded, and the food smelled so good.

"Did we even eat lunch, Amelia?" Rodney asked.

"Oh my! I think we were so distracted we forgot to! No wonder that drink felt so strong." We both laughed.

"Okay - well, let's make sure to get an appetizer that we can start munching on soon. How about some fried calamari?" Rodney asked.

"Oh, that sounds excellent!"

We had a lovely dinner overall—the food was fantastic. Rodney and I talked about the day and how we were so happy we booked Jamaica because so far, everything felt perfect.

When we went to bed that evening, we left the sliding glass door in our bedroom open to hear the ocean waves crashing on the sand. Rodney was out like a light – and I stayed up a little longer, gazing out at the ocean from the bed.

When I woke up in the morning, happiness washed over me. I smelled coffee coming from the kitchen and was excited for our couples' massage in a few hours. We had the afternoon free to relax on the beach or do anything else we could think of.

I got up out of bed to see my soon-to-be husband making me a cup of coffee.

"There you are, my darling!" Rodney said as he handed me a cup of coffee. "How did you sleep?"

"Thank you! The coffee smells wonderful! And I slept so well – I loved hearing the ocean during the night."

"I agree. I figure we have two options from here on out."

"What's that?" I asked.

"We either never leave this resort – or come back very often."

"My vote is we just don't leave!" I said as we both laughed.

I went out to sit on the balcony and take in the morning view of the ocean. The weather was a perfect 78 degrees outside. I looked around the resort and saw some of the other couples. It was an adults-only resort which also had two adjoining resorts next door.

As I basked in the sun, I lost track of time and realized I needed to start getting ready to head down to the spa. I went inside to find Rodney reading a magazine.

"Honey, we need to get ready to head downstairs to the spa."

"Oh, okay – how long is the massage again?" Rodney asked.

"Sixty minutes—then we can use some of the facilities, like the sauna or steam room, if we want," I said.

When we walked into the spa, we were greeted by two lovely women who said they would be giving us the massages. They were both from Jamaica and had the accents to match, so it was fun chatting with them about our stay so far. We had told them we were going to elope the following day, so they both loved hearing that news.

They led us into a dimly lit room that smelled like a field of lavender. I was already relaxed, and the massage hadn't even started.

They asked each of us if we had any areas of tension that they wanted us to focus on. Since we were on vacation, we could not think of any specific area where we were having issues.

They dimmed the lights, put on some soothing music, and began the massages. The woman working on me seemed to know what she was doing, and I was feeling more peaceful by the second.

Then suddenly, as she was massaging my back, she stopped. "Ma'am," she whispered to me.

"Yes?"

"Are you okay? Am I hurting you at all?" She asked.

"No, not at all, it feels wonderful."

She seemed to hesitate, then started to work on my back again.

During the rest of the massage, she would randomly stop, and I would hear her sigh. I had no clue whether this was normal. Maybe her hands were tired and she had to take little breaks.

After the massage, the ladies left us in the room to get dressed.

"Oh shoot!" Rodney exclaimed.

"What's wrong?"

"I forgot my wallet in the hotel room – I will have to go get it to tip them."

"Oh – well, how about I walk back with you, and I can bring the money back to them," I said.

"Do you want to? I'm the one who forgot my wallet – I can do it."

"No, it is fine. Plus, this way, you can have time to make me another lavender vodka spritz!" We both laughed.

"Ohhhh, I see what you are doing now. Okay, well, I can try to think of a new drink to make for myself – should we go lie on the beach for a bit this afternoon?"

"Yes, please – I wouldn't mind getting a little more color before our big day tomorrow," I said.

We explained to the ladies that I would return after we went to the hotel room to grab some cash. The room wasn't far, so I was only gone about 15 minutes or so.

When I walked back into the spa, only the lady who had been massaging me was at the desk. She almost looked relieved to see me. Which, I thought, was weird.

"Here you go!" I happily held out the cash to give to her. I noticed her name tag said Wanda.

She grabbed my hand and held it. "Miss, are you okay?" she asked quietly.

"Umm – are you kidding me? You just gave me the best massage I've ever had!"

"No, no – that is not what I mean."

And cue my confusion.

"It is just that… It's that…" She mumbled.

"What?" I asked.

"You seemed *really* tense during the massage."

I laughed a little. "But I'm not! I'm on vacation! And I love this resort!"

"No…." She said again. "I have never massaged anyone so tense in my life. If you don't feel it, it must be your subconscious trying to tell you something. Are you sure you know this man you are marrying tomorrow?"

I laughed again. "Yes! I appreciate your concern, but I have known him for years now, and we live together."

She shook her head. "Honey – something deep down is telling me you don't."

"Don't what?"

"Don't know him," Wanda said. "Your body is trying to tell you something, but you are not listening, my dear."

"Well, thank you for telling me this, but I am usually pretty in tune with my emotions." I started to back away and told her to have a good day. I wasn't sure how else to get out of that conversation.

"Good luck to you, my dear!" Wanda yelled as I pushed the doors open to leave the spa.

Chapter 13

As I entered the hotel room, Rodney was just finishing up our cocktails. "Thanks for going back and doing that. Did everything go okay? You look perplexed."

"Oh… yeah, it was fine. One of the ladies was talking to me, and it was a bit weird…" I probably should not have even said that. What was I supposed to do, tell Rodney I couldn't marry him because some random woman who gave me a massage said not to? Obviously not. I snapped myself out of it. "But more importantly – look at these beautiful drinks!"

Rodney handed me my drink. "Thank you! What did you end up making for yourself?"

"I made a passion fruit martini." He handed me his drink to try it.

"Oh wow… this is excellent! At least we know now if you ever lose your job, you can easily become a bartender."

Rodney smiled as he started to grab our stuff to head down to the beach.

We found a couple of beach chairs and situated ourselves. There was a slight breeze, and it was 75 degrees. Perfect. I sprayed on some tanning oil, hoping to get a bit more color before tomorrow.

"I can't believe you will be my wife tomorrow!" Rodney said to me as he reached over and squeezed my hand.

I smiled back at him. "I know! I hope it goes well with the photographer. At least the weather should be perfect."

"Everything will be just fine! Don't worry – it will all come together perfectly," Rodney assured me.

We each lay in the sun for a bit, reading magazines and soaking up the sun. Eventually, we went swimming to cool off. The water was so clear! I loved being able to see to the bottom. Some smaller fish would swim around us, which was neat to see as well.

After lounging in the sun for the afternoon, Rodney pulled up a list of restaurants for us to review. "Umm, how about the French one?" I asked.

"That sounds good to me! What time do we need to be up in the morning?" he asked.

"Well – how about I just tell you when and where to show up while we are at dinner."

Rodney laughed and agreed.

"Speaking of dinner, how about I head up to the room before you, since I need to shower and it will take me a bit longer than you to get ready. You can stay and enjoy the beach a bit longer."

"That works for me!" Rodney replied. "I hope our marriage is as easy as this week is!"

"Ha! It will be," I said with a smile.

I headed up to the room to shower and get ready for dinner. I picked out a light blue strapless dress I had ordered for the trip. It was knee-length and flowed out from the waist. I matched it with some pearl earrings and a pearl necklace.

As I was just about ready, I stared out into the ocean from the balcony. It was just so peaceful looking over the ocean. It was like everything in my mind was able to become still.

Just then, I heard the door open and turned around to see Rodney walking in.

"Wow! You look stunning, Amelia."

"Just wait until tomorrow!" I replied with a smile.

Rodney quickly showered and got dressed for dinner, and we were off.

The French restaurant was at another resort, so we had a short walk there. It was a beautiful evening, though, and it was nice to see more of the resort along the way.

When we arrived at the restaurant, we were seated at a table overlooking the water.

"What should we get?" I asked Rodney.

"I think we should order the escargot as an appetizer to get the real French experience. Have you ever had that?"

"Umm… no, but let's give it a shot! Although I have a feeling, I won't like it much…" I replied.

When the waitress came, we ordered escargot, a bottle of French red wine, and our entrées. I had chosen a salmon entrée, and Rodney had chosen a roasted chicken entrée.

"Okay, Amelia, I still need you to tell me where to meet you tomorrow."

"Oh! That's right! I am having someone come to the room to do my hair and makeup at 10 am – she said it will take a few hours."

"Goodness!" Rodney exclaimed. "You don't even usually wear a lot of makeup. How on earth can someone spend three hours applying it to you?"

"Well, there is my hair too, don't forget," I said with a smirk.

"So, back to what I was saying, she will come to the room from about 10 am to 1 pm. Then I will need to get dressed. How about you come to the room, shower, and get ready, and I'll wait on the balcony? After you leave, I will put my dress on."

"Are you sure? You know I'm a fast showerer," Rodney said.

"Yes, honestly, it will be good for me to have some time to take some deep breaths anyway!"

"Okay – so I will come to the room around 1 pm, or whenever you text me. Then I will head down to where they will perform the ceremony and wait for you."

"That sounds perfect. We are supposed to be there at 2 pm, and we will have the photographer take some photos afterwards around the property and on the beach."

Just then, the escargot arrived.

"Umm... should I try one first?" I asked.

"Ha – sure! Go for it!" Rodney said.

I picked up a snail with my fork, stared at it a bit, and then threw it in my mouth. Chewy. It was very chewy. The flavor was okay since it had been drenched in garlic and butter, but…

"Oh no! Judging by your face, I'd say you are not going to be having a second one!" Rodney said.

I vigorously shook my head no. I wanted to spit it out, but forced myself to swallow it.

"Give me the wine!" I shouted as I laughed a bit. "I need to wash this down! Give me some bread too!"

Rodney laughed as he went in for a snail. "Well…it's not my favorite, I will admit, but at least we are both a bit more cultured now for having had escargot."

Over dinner, we enjoyed the fine wine and our entrees. We talked about how excited we were to be eloping. We both agreed we would have the easiest marriage and could look forward to many more trips in the future. I kept envisioning the next day and how my makeup and dress would look. A part of me couldn't believe I was finally getting married.

We wrapped up dinner and headed back to the hotel room. We had discussed sitting on the balcony for a little while, but then both agreed that we had a big day tomorrow and should get a good night's rest.

We got dressed for bed and got into the comfy king-size bed.

"I am so excited to see you tomorrow, Amelia! I can't wait to see your dress," Rodney said.

"It's going to be a wonderful day for both of us," I said as I smiled at Rodney.

We both drifted off to sleep.

Chapter 14

The next thing I knew, I woke up drenched in sweat and felt sheer dread running through my body. What was wrong with me? Did I get sick from the snails? I looked over at Rodney, who was still sound asleep. I decided to get out of bed so I wouldn't wake him.

I felt like I was having a panic attack, or maybe I was getting sick. I couldn't quite tell, especially since I had never really had a full-on panic attack.

Was it something I ate? It didn't seem so.

Was it just my nerves about getting married? As soon as I asked myself that, my body felt worse. I wiped my forehead. It didn't feel hot, but it was wet with sweat. My arms were even sweating.

I was so confused.

Not only was I feeling physically ill, but I was almost feeling mentally ill, too.

Should I wake up Rodney? No. I can't do that. Plus, he'd probably not even know what to do with me since I didn't even know what to do with myself.

I decided to sit in a chair and see if I could relax a bit.

Getting married is a big decision, and perhaps I had become so caught up in planning the details that I didn't take the time to reflect on what marriage meant to me and what it would feel like.

Would I make a good wife? Would Rodney be a good husband? Oh, of course he would! Why on earth am I asking myself this? He has never once given me cause for concern.

Well, there was that one time in New York when he seemed very concerned about me leaving him. But I am sure that he was just nervous about me traveling alone.

And…I am sure this is all just my nerves. But I must admit, it didn't feel like just nerves. It felt like something more. Something deeper.

I really didn't know what to do at that moment. It was the middle of the night. I mean, was I not going to go through with marrying Rodney? Of course, I am going to marry him. I was in that chair for almost two hours. Overthinking everything I could. I finally calmed myself down and began to feel sleepy, so I crawled back into bed, careful not to wake Rodney.

Just as I was falling back asleep, the alarm went off. I jolted up. Looked next to me and found that Rodney wasn't in bed. I had an odd sense of relief that he wasn't in the room with me. I let out a huge sigh.

"Is that you awake in there?" I heard Rodney's voice coming from the living area.

My heart started to beat so fast. I didn't know what was wrong with me. It had to just be circumstantial anxiety.

Rodney walked in with a mimosa in his hand. THANK GOD. I thought to myself. Maybe some champagne would make me chill out.

I forced a smile on my face as I reached out for the mimosa.

He laughed, "Whoa, it almost seems like you're more excited for that mimosa than to see me."

"Oh, I am sorry, my dear, I just didn't sleep much. I think it's just nerves and all," I told him.

"You aren't getting cold feet on me, are you now? I think that is my job as a man, and I am feeling perfectly fine and happy!" he said to me.

He went to the bathroom to shave, and I headed to the fridge and poured more champagne into my mimosa, which I had already half finished. This probably was not the healthiest way to handle things, but maybe I just needed something to take the edge off so I could get back to enjoying my day.

It was, in fact, my wedding day! I was determined to snap myself out of it and let myself enjoy it.

I looked down at my watch – it was 9:30 am.

"Rodney!" I yelled as I walked into the bathroom. "It's time! Time for you to get going! I need to start getting ready."

"Okay, okay – I think I will head down to the pool and maybe the beach to occupy myself while you are getting your hair and makeup done. I'm allowed to come back at 1ish, right?"

"Right, but I will text you to be sure," I said. Rodney grabbed his towel and headed out the door.

"Sounds good, darling. I cannot wait to see you later."

I suddenly felt more at ease. Clearly, the champagne was kicking in and doing its job. Or was I just feeling better because Rodney had left the room? No. It can't be that. I am simply being crazy right now.

The hair and makeup girl was supposed to arrive in about fifteen minutes. In the meantime, I sat down and tried to take some deep breaths.

I had only taken about five deep breaths when there was a knock at the door. As I got up to open it, the girl almost screamed. "Ahh!! The day is finally here for you! I'm Heather, and I am so excited to get started with you!"

Heather's excitement caught me so off guard that it actually helped calm my nerves.

She walked into the room and saw the champagne bottle. "Oh! I see you are already getting this party started!"

"Well… you know, those wedding day jitters, I suppose," I replied.

"Oh, sweetie, I see it all the time. It's perfectly normal!"

"It is?!" I asked with a sense of relief.

"Why yes! I mean – one man for the rest of your life – not to mention hoping you look the absolute best. It's a lot for anyone! I will say the fact that you're eloping must be a huge weight off your shoulders. I do many weddings with lots of family, and boy, it can get tense. I swear the bride is never even relaxed."

"Wow…thank you for saying those words to me. I have been wondering all sorts of crazy things, but you put my mind more at ease."

"Oh, Amelia – like I said, I have done this before. I could sense you were nervous right when you opened the door."

"You could?" I asked.

"Ha, well, yes! But we want you to be nervous now versus when you're walking down that aisle. Plus, you don't want that nervous energy hanging around you when you are doing your photos."

She was right about all of it. I sat down in the chair I had moved into the vanity area in the bathroom, and she opened what appeared to be a carry-on suitcase, but it was full of makeup.

"Is that ALL makeup in that suitcase?" I asked.

Heather laughed. "You are not the first person who is amazed by all the makeup I have, but I work with lots of different skin tones, so I need to be prepared for all of them."

"That's true," I replied.

She wiped my face with cleansing cloths, then started applying serums to my face and under my eyes. The serums were cool to the touch, helping me become more relaxed.

"Now I have the inspirational makeup and hair photos you sent me, so I am going to do my best to recreate the look," Heather said. "So, how are you enjoying your stay so far?"

"Oh, I simply love it here! Aside from my bout of nervousness last night, it has been total bliss. What brought you to work in the islands?" I asked Heather, as she was clearly from a southern state, judging by her accent.

"You know, it is the weirdest thing, but I used to always vacation here with my family from Alabama when I was growing up, and once I started doing hair and makeup, someone told me it is easy to get gigs with resorts, and they even provide room and board. I thought about it a bit, and now I do it each year. Usually just for a month or so at a time, so my clients back home don't get too upset with me living my island life," she smiled.

Heather had a calming way about her. I was very thankful I was spending this time talking and getting to know her, as it helped take my mind off things.

"I ask all of my clients, do you want to face the mirror as I work, or do you want to face the other direction and see it all done at once?"

"All done at once, please!" It sounded so exciting to go from waking up a stressed-out mess to bridal beauty. Heather was working on me over the next few hours. She seemed to be so detailed in everything she did. So precise.

We chatted along the way, but not about anything too serious, which I appreciated. She wasn't asking me much about Rodney—she was mainly giving me makeup application tips and telling me about her relationships. Heather was currently single.

"Honey, let me tell you my last relationship was just over a couple of years, and that man decided he wasn't going to put in the effort I deserved anymore," Heather said.

"Oh no, I'm sorry to hear that," I said.

Heather laughed. "Girl, it was a blessing! Now I am doing hair and makeup in the islands! I had told him of that idea, and he thought I was crazy for even suggesting it. And his loss because he could be out on the beach relaxing with Rodney right now, getting free drinks!"

"Men can be really dumb sometimes, but I am glad it is all working out for you! Are you dating now, or no?" I asked.

"Well, not really. Maybe I will again one day, but I don't want to go out of my way to meet someone. If it is meant to happen, it will. That's my philosophy."

I liked Heather. She seemed grounded and full of life. I also appreciated that she wasn't one of these people I barely know, trying to tell me to be careful about Rodney.

Heather added a little more hairspray to my hair and said, "Okay! We are done!! Are you ready to see your new look?"

"Absolutely!" I said as she started to spin the chair around to the mirror.

Wow! I looked so beautiful. I have never looked so good in my life. My makeup was better than I hoped, natural yet glamorous. My hair was in the most perfect bun I have ever seen. It was simple but sleek, and I loved it.

"What do you think?" Heather asked.

"I'm obsessed!" I said with a huge smile.

"Oh, good! I am so glad. You already have so much natural beauty. All I did was slightly enhance it with the makeup. And I told you a lot of the things I did, so hopefully you can recreate the look on your own if you want."

"Umm, I think I'd prefer to hire you full-time and have you do my makeup and hair every day instead," I said as we laughed.

Heather then started gathering up all the makeup and hair tools she had used on me. She was so nice, I was sad to see her go.

"You know I am on social media, if you want to follow me, if you have any makeup questions, or need anything in the future," Heather said to me.

"Oh, I am not on social media. I feel like I would waste too much time on it," I said.

"Well, you are definitely not wrong about that. I also have some business cards with my email on them." She pulled one out from her bag and handed me one.

As she went to the door, she saw a photo of Rodney and me on the counter that the resort had taken of us when we arrived.

She stopped, looked down at it, and slowly picked it up. "Is this Rodney?"

"Yes, it is."

"Oh." She stared at it a bit longer, then put it down. "Well, good luck to you," Heather said in an almost somber way. She gave me a heartfelt smile and was out the door.

Confused, I looked at the picture myself. Rodney's eye looked darker than usual, but it was probably just the lighting. However, I don't know why she acted a little weird about it. Oh well. I needed to go put on my dress.

Chapter 15

I glanced at my hair and makeup again in the mirror. Heather did a miraculous job on me. I went to pull the dress out of the closet. Even though it was full-length and had long lace sleeves, it wasn't a hot day, so I expected to feel very comfortable in it. I laid it out on the bed and unzipped the back. Fortunately, I could zip it up myself once it was on. As I walked to the full-length mirror to get the complete look of myself, I was in awe. I looked prettier than I have ever seen myself! Having my look come together so well finally excited me to get married, celebrate, and forget my nerves.

I went to grab my phone to text Rodney that he could come up. I went out onto the balcony to sit and reflect while he got ready. I closed the drapes so he would not be able to see me.

I heard the door open, and I yelled, "Hi!!! I am out here, so obviously don't come out. Just let me know when you are about to head down to the beach area."

"Okay, that sounds good! I'll hurry so you aren't stuck out there too long," Rodney said.

After only about twenty minutes, Rodney was ready to go. "Okay, I am going to head out – I will go downstairs now."

"That sounds good! I'll meet you with the minister at 2 pm on the dot!"

"I will be counting down the minutes to see you and your dress, Amelia!" I could hear Rodney say with a smile.

Then I heard the hotel door shut, and I went back inside. I had some white flats, but wasn't going to wear them until dinner since we were getting married on the beach.

Just then, a knock at the hotel door – I opened it to be greeted by a beautiful bouquet of white roses that one of the hotel wedding planners delivered to me.

"Oh my! I forgot I even requested these!" I said.

The woman laughed, "Oh, that is not the first time I have heard this. People get so caught up in the day that you'd be amazed at what they forget. That is where we come in to make sure it all comes together. Now, is there anything you need me to carry downstairs?"

"Hmm." I thought about it. "I don't think so?"

"Okay, well, how about you wear some shoes down, and I can hold on to those for you once you get onto the sand?"

"That is a fantastic idea!"

Just then, another knock at the door. I opened it and was greeted by the photographer.

"Amelia! You look beautiful! I hope you don't mind, but I thought we should get a few shots of just you before we go down. Oh, and I'm Brittney – the photographer, if you couldn't tell."

We spent the next fifteen minutes or so taking pictures. We took many out on the balcony with the ocean view and some in the hotel room's sitting area. Once we got some shots, I slipped on my shoes and grabbed my bouquet, and we started to head down towards the beach where we would be married.

I was so excited. I couldn't wait to see the look on Rodney's face when he saw me.

We came to an area where I was shielded from the beach and from Rodney. Janice helped fluff my dress, ensured my veil was lying correctly, and took my shoes for me. Brittney went ahead of me and took some photos of Rodney, then some of me as I started walking out.

"Well?" Janice looked at me. "Are you so happy!"

I automatically replied, "Oh yes! I have been looking forward to this day for so long!"

"You look so beautiful! He is a very lucky man!" Janice looked around the corner and saw Brittney motioning that they were ready for me. "Okay – go ahead! Go get married!" she said with a smile.

As I slowly turned the corner, I saw Rodney and the pastor. Rodney looked so handsome! Like the true gentleman that he is. He got the biggest grin I had ever seen on his face when he looked at me.

As I approached him, I saw he had shed a tear or two. The pastor told us to hold hands.

The pastor had us say our vows, and before I knew it, we both had said "I do," and that was it. We were married…

I felt like the luckiest woman in the world.

Chapter 16

Marriage (Past to Present)

"Rodney?" I asked as I walked into our house after coming home from work. To my relief, I didn't hear him say anything back. Then I saw a note on the counter that he had gone for a walk. Okay, good. I probably have about 30 minutes or so until he is home.

I went to the refrigerator, poured myself a glass of wine, and sat down on the couch. We had dinner reservations at 8 pm. It was only 5:30 pm, though, so I had some time to wind down from my workday.

It's been a couple of years since we got married. If I could go back in time, I honestly don't think I would do it again. It's been so stressful. I can't even say why. There is no pressing issue about our relationship. We both have jobs and our health. Yet we seem to fight so often. Rodney used to be so laid back, and now he has become so high-strung and anxiety-ridden, it is flat-out exhausting at times. I suggested therapy multiple times, but he never wanted to go. I eventually gave up on asking.

We used to travel a decent amount, but now Rodney never seems to want to go anywhere. Our life has quickly become like Groundhog Day, and sometimes I feel so bored and confined. Maybe more than sometimes. Often.

I heard a loud noise that made me jump and almost spill some of my wine.

"Hello!! Amelia!!?" Rodney yelled.

Our house wasn't even that big. I had no clue why he needed to yell.

"I'm in the living room," I replied.

"What are you doing?" he asked.

I looked at him. "Umm. Just relaxing for a few minutes before I shower and get ready."

"Okay. Well, how long will it take you to get ready?"

"Rodney, we've been together for years, you know exactly how long it takes me," I said, trying to hide the fact that I was already annoyed with him.

"Well, I thought we could grab a drink before dinner."

I sighed. "Okay, so you're saying I need to go get ready now. Fine."

"How much time do you need to relax anyway?" he asked me, also annoyed.

"Don't worry about it, I will go get in the shower and try to hurry."

Deep breaths. Deep breaths. That is what I had to tell myself often these days.

Rodney used to be so easygoing and understanding of my needs, but these days, it's like he thinks I should be a clone of him.

Is this what happens in marriages? I certainly don't think all of them can end up this way. I still don't have any friends in this town, so I can't compare our relationship to others.

As I was in the shower, I decided to try to reset my mind. It was Friday after all, so I wanted to look forward to the night. I had no plans on Saturday, so I could sleep in. Rodney and I both liked to sleep in on the weekends. And since we did not have any kids or pets, it was very easy to do so.

Once out of the shower, I planned my outfit: a simple black top with a cream knee-length skirt.

"Are you ready? I want to go!" Rodney yelled. That man really had no patience.

"I'll be ready in ten!" I yelled back.

Once in the car, I asked, "So where did you want to go before dinner?"

"A new brewery opened."

"Oh great, just what this town needs, another brewery," I said.

"Well, we can just try it out. At least it is something new to try."

"That's true," I replied. "I feel like we get stuck going to the same places all the time."

"But we know they are good. Besides, I hate being let down when we venture out of our normal places," he said.

"Well, I just hope they have wine."

"They do, I called and asked," he said.

"Oh! Well, thank you for doing that."

Sometimes, Rodney was fine. Overall, though, it is hard to explain.

He's changed.

It seems like he is hardly ever in a good mood, and it gets very hard to navigate. I feel we are always one wrong word away from a fight.

We never used to fight. I hate fighting. I've now grown accustomed to it.

When we pulled into the brewery, Rodney immediately started to point out what was wrong with the parking lot. "You know, they could have gotten a lot more spaces in here if they had the entrance on the opposite side."

"Well, maybe the owner didn't want that," I said, then immediately wondered why I was even commenting on a parking lot layout.

"It would be much better for their business. People just don't think anymore," Rodney angrily said.

Oh, the complaints from this man. I hear them almost every day. I swear the wind could blow from the wrong direction, and he could easily lose his mind over it. It makes it hard to be around him day in and day out. I guess I signed up for this… but actually, I didn't. I'd have never gone on a second date with him if he had complained this much. Complaints about nothing if you ask me.

"Well, let's go in, and hopefully, you will at least like their beer selection," I said, once again trying to steer the mood in the right direction.

When we walked in and looked at the menu, I knew what his reaction would be.

"How can they charge these prices?! They won't make it more than a few months running a business like this."

"Well... maybe one day you can open a brewery and make all the decisions, and it will be the most profitable and smoothly running brewery in the nation."

He looked at me, unamused.

"Okay, fine, maybe just in Asheville," I smiled.

Sometimes it would be nice if I weren't the only one trying to be positive in this relationship.

After the brewery, we went to the Italian restaurant where I had initially met Rodney when I first moved to Asheville. I couldn't help but remember how excited I was to start fresh in a new city. I felt so full of life back then—at least compared to now. Ugh. I almost did not like going to this restaurant because I would often compare how I was feeling now to back then and couldn't help but become a little depressed.

Even though we frequented the spot, since it was in the restaurant industry, there seemed to be a lot of turnover, so we never got to know any of the staff for long.

"What are you having?" Rodney asked.

"Oh, I don't know, I'm thinking the spaghetti with meatballs."

"But you had that last time? You really need to try new things," he said.

Here we go again. Rodney had become so critical of me that sometimes I would try to call him out, and other times, it was just easier to go with it to keep the peace.

"That's true," I replied, "Okay, how about the vegetable lasagna?"

"If you are suddenly becoming a vegetarian, I guess."

Clearly, I wasn't going to suddenly become a vegetarian just after I said I wanted the meatballs. What is wrong with this man?

"What are you getting?" I asked.

"I think the meat lover's pizza."

"But didn't you have that last time?" I questioned when I knew it wasn't worth it.

"Yes, but it is what they are known for. So, of course, I want it again."

Does this man hear himself? He is off his rocker.

"Well, yes, it is good – you are right. And this way, I can have a piece too!"

"What? You are a vegetarian now, though."

And I'm done. It's best to try to totally change the subject or drink more wine and have a conversation in my head. I keep trying to find ways to communicate more positively with Rodney, but it doesn't seem to work.

Luckily, he pulled out his phone and started reading some articles. I wasn't sure what he was reading, and I also didn't have it in me to pretend to care. I was just happy we could stop conversing for a bit. As I took another sip of my pinot grigio, I started planning my weekend in my mind. I had been wanting to get back into running, so I was thinking about starting my day off with a short run. Then, I will probably just go to the grocery store and do a few minor errands.

Before I knew it, our food arrived. I was served my vegetable lasagna, and then they put down Rodney's massive pizza. It looked delicious, but I knew it was not worth my energy to even ask for a slice. The last thing I needed was unwarranted vegetarian comments again.

We ate our meal mostly in silence. Towards the end, Rodney asked what I wanted to do when we got home.

"I guess we can watch a movie," I told him.

"Sure, there is a new action movie out that I've been wanting to see," Rodney said.

An action movie. He knows I hate action movies, and I find myself so bored that I try to just fall asleep.

"Rodney, you know I hate action movies, can you watch it on your own sometime?" I pleaded.

"Well, you got to pick the last movie we watched."
"Yes, but the difference is I always try to pick movies we'd both enjoy. The last thing I would do is make you sit through a two-hour romantic comedy."

He laughed. "Like I would ever do that anyway!"

"My point exactly... well, whatever. We can watch what you want."

"Well, now you sound mad, and I don't want to deal with you being grumpy all night," he said.

"Rodney, it's fine. Let's get the check and go."

No one said a word on the car ride home. This has become increasingly frequent. I get reluctant to bring up how unhappy I've become, though. Once when I did, it almost wasn't worth it. Rodney essentially had a meltdown and kept telling me he would change and would never do anything to risk losing me. He changed, alright... for a few days' tops. It wasn't much of a change. He just acted a bit more humbly and was nicer. Sort of the way he was when I first met him. humbly

But then he quickly fell back into his strange moods and critical ways.

When we got back home, we started the action movie. I made us some popcorn and gave the movie a shot, but twenty minutes in, I knew it wasn't for me. I pulled out my phone and started looking up new coffee cafes in town. I was thinking it would be nice to go to a café tomorrow, read a magazine, and just relax a bit.

Luckily, Rodney didn't seem mad that I wasn't paying attention to the movie. I never know what will set him off. Which, quite frankly, is exhausting.

Chapter 17

The next morning, I woke up excited to have the day to myself and try a new coffee café. First, I went for a run, then quickly showered and headed towards the new café. It was on the edge of downtown and looked adorable from the outside.

When I walked in, it was just as adorable on the inside. There were only a few other people in there, so plenty of open seating. I ordered a mocha latte and found a cute little table by a bunch of magazines. I grabbed a few off the top and started flipping through them. One article I opened was about marriage and why people sometimes leave them.

I read it.

The article wasn't exactly helpful. It was all about marriages that ended because of infidelity or physical abuse. Thankfully, we didn't have that in our relationship. So, I couldn't help but wonder, do people get divorced because their partner has become moody? It seemed like a drastic thing to me to end our marriage over some bad moods. Sigh. I just kept going in circles in my mind.

I didn't want a divorce, but at the same time, do I want to live like this forever? Rodney is just not the same anymore. When I try to bring it up, it only causes fights. He won't go to a therapist; he won't even read a self-help book. So, how much longer do I stay?

The only plan of action I seemed to have was to focus more on myself, mainly by getting more exercise, cooking new meals, and going to these nice little café outings on occasion.

The other articles I was reading were about how hard it is to find decent men these days. Several women of various ages said it was easier to be single than to deal with the dating world. They said they focused on their friendships and still traveled and tried new things, just didn't solely focus on finding a relationship to make themselves feel complete.

That life sounded pretty good to me, I must admit. Then again, I did have that life in New York City. Ugh. The circles continue.

I found another magazine with horoscopes. I read mine, and while I find them all a bit cliché, I did like something I read. It said, "Your soul will know the right time to make a move."

That was nice, straightforward advice. It was simple yet seemed so wise.

I finished looking at some fashion magazines and decided to head home.

When I pulled in, I saw Rodney trimming some of the bushes in front of our house.

"Hi, dear!" I said as I walked up. "How has your day been? It's beautiful weather out today, isn't it?"

Rodney seemed annoyed.

"Well, it would be nice if I didn't have to do all this yardwork alone," he muttered.

"I didn't know you were doing it. I will go in and change and come out to help you."

"Ha – of course, right when I am finishing up, you offer to help. Did you at least go to the store last night to pick up chicken for me to grill?"

"Oh…well, no, I didn't, but I didn't know you wanted me to. Did you text that to me? I must have missed it," I said as I checked my phone.

"No, I told you at dinner last night that I planned on grilling. You never listen to me," Rodney said.

"Oh…sorry, I must have missed that. I can run to the store now and grab some, though."

I didn't even bother going into the house. I just turned right around and drove to the local grocery store. I do not recall us talking about having chicken for dinner. Also, is it that big of a deal if I actually missed what he said? I felt his reaction was a bit uncalled for. Or very uncalled for. I also did not know he was doing yard work.

This is when I get frustrated. I try to mind my own business, but it backfires. I obviously would have helped him with the yard work and stopped to get chicken. I can never tell what he will get mad at me about. It is just getting so old.

Again, I find myself asking, "How long do I put up with this? " I do not foresee it changing. Maybe I will say something at dinner tonight… which reminded me to grab an extra bottle of wine. I may need it to deal with any tantrums he decides to throw.

After leaving the store, I tried to coach myself to get the courage to say something at dinner. Or maybe I should mention it after dinner so I don't ruin my meal. It was always hard to figure out a good time to bring up something to Rodney, as it seemed there was never a good time.

After I got home and gave Rodney all the groceries I had bought for dinner, we both started to prepare the meal. I turned on some music, so there was less of a need to talk. I decided to wait until we were almost done eating before bringing anything up. Otherwise, he'd probably fly off the handle, and I would leave the table without eating. I was hungry tonight and didn't want to risk that outcome.

Rodney didn't seem to notice we weren't talking. I swear he could exist in this relationship just fine if I were a warm body and he never had to speak to me. It was too bad for him that I did not feel the same way.

We ate dinner mostly in silence. This was such a waste of my Saturday night, and I was beginning to think this was a waste of a relationship.

"So, Rodney…"

"What, Amelia? I can already tell you're in a bad mood, and I am trying not to ruin my Saturday night," he said.

Lovely.

"Well… I just can't help but notice we don't seem to be on the same page too often anymore."

"So? We are married. I don't know what you expect."

"I expect us to still enjoy each other, have fun, and be friends like we used to be. And it was not even that long ago that we were like that!"

"Amelia, I don't know what you want from this conversation. Nothing's going to change. I'm happy. You need to learn to be happy."

I sat there in disbelief. Am I supposed to be happy with my husband constantly being miserable and rude to me? What planet was this man on?

"Well, if that's the case, I don't want to be in this marriage anymore," I said.

Chapter 18

I wasn't planning on saying that.

Once I said it, it actually didn't feel that bad. I felt a weight lifted off of me.

Rodney stopped eating and looked at me. "What happened till death do us part?" he asked.

"Umm, well… I do believe in that, but I also believe in my happiness. And being treated right," I replied.

"Well… what if I change?" he asked.

"Rodney! You literally just told me nothing is going to change! Plus, we've been through this before. It is flat-out exhausting, and I am sick of it."

Feelings of relief flooded over me.

Maybe this is actually the right decision for me.

Rodney was quiet. He just sat there and stared at his plate.

"Amelia, you aren't allowed to leave me," he said.

"Actually, I am. I'm not saying that is what I want, but I know I want to be happy, and I have become increasingly miserable over the years. I try to tell you, I try to have a good attitude and stay positive, but nothing I do seems to make a difference."

I do not know where I found the courage to say this, but the more I said, the better I felt.

I will say, the more I talked, the stranger Rodney became.

"I will change! I will work on myself, I promise, Amelia! I love you! You can't leave me, you just can't! I can't live without you."

"Rodney, I want to believe you, but the truth is…I don't. Listen, how about I take some time for myself to really clear my head, and maybe that will help you to do the same."

"What do you mean?" he asked.

"Maybe I need to go on a trip for a week or two and clear my head."

"Two weeks!?" he exclaimed.

"Well, as I said, I don't want us to get a divorce, and I do not want to make an overnight decision. This is something I do take seriously."

"Well, where would you go?" Rodney asked.

"Maybe the beach? I feel like that could be a good place for me to relax and take some time for myself. And you can do the same here. Maybe you won't even miss me, who knows?" I said.

Rodney got quiet again.

"So, when do you think you will go?" he asked.

"Well, let me talk to Charlotte at work tomorrow. Or I will give her a call since she is working out of town per usual. Maybe I will go next weekend."

It felt bizarre to say this to Rodney, but maybe I just needed a good vacation by myself. Perhaps it would make him appreciate me more.

"I do not think you should go. This is a really bad idea, and I won't lose you." There was something odd about the way he was speaking to me. A part of me felt a little…scared. Maybe scared wasn't the right word, but I was definitely uneasy.

"Well, honestly, Rodney, it seems like this is the first time you are even hearing me. Do you realize how often you just dismiss me? It makes me upset, and it is a very lonely feeling."

Rodney didn't respond right away. He sat there for a moment, swirling his red wine around in his glass. He then finished it in one giant gulp and suddenly smashed the glass down onto the edge of the table, instantly shattering it all over the floor and table. I froze with both shock and fear.

"You are NOT leaving me!" he yelled.

I didn't move. I didn't know what to say and was terrified to say anything. Rodney has never acted like this. Ever.

He then got up, grabbed his car keys, and I heard him slam the front door and drive away.

I had more emotions running through me than I knew what to do with. I felt very scared, and my only thought was that I somehow needed to calm the situation down. I also needed to get myself out of it. That had become very apparent.

I got up and grabbed a broom to start cleaning up all the glass. I really do not understand why Rodney felt it was okay to break a glass; he is lucky neither of us got cut. I wanted to cry, but also wanted to keep my focus. Once I cleaned up the glass, I put away the food and washed the dishes.

I did not know where Rodney had gone, but I assumed it was probably to a bar or something.

I wish I had a friend to text or call. It's pathetic how I am not close to anyone in this town.

I looked at the dining room after I had put everything away. It looked like nothing had happened. Did it happen? Yes, I know it did, but because I had never seen Rodney have an outburst like that, a part of me wished it was just my imagination.

I had no clue what to do next. I guess I will get ready for bed and maybe read a book to try to decompress, if that is even possible.

I decided I wanted to sleep in the guest room—the guest room for guests we never have. I won't get a wink of sleep if I am next to Rodney tonight.

When I crawled into bed, I started looking up hotels and houses to rent on the Outer Banks. I found a cute little cottage on the beach that was within walking distance of shops and restaurants. Perfect. This is just what I need, and at the moment, I have no desire to ever return from the coast once I get there. I should be able to arrange to go next weekend for a week or two with work. I will ask Charlotte first thing on Monday morning if I can take some time off and work remotely, if she'd like me to. Hopefully, I can think clearly when I'm there and away from this mess of a situation.

Just then, I heard the door open and footsteps come down the hall. I could tell Rodney had stopped right outside my door, but then he walked away without knocking on it or opening it. Good. I have no desire to hear one more word from him tonight.

Eventually, I fell asleep. When I woke up, I smelled bacon. Rodney must be cooking breakfast. I had no idea how he'd act when I left the room I had slept in, but I may as well find out.

When I walked into the kitchen, Rodney looked at me. He didn't seem to have much expression, but finally, he broke the silence.

"Listen, Amelia, things got out of hand last night, and I am sorry. I should never have broken that wine glass. It was unacceptable behavior. The bottom line is, I will do anything it takes not to lose you. I promise you, I can change."

Ugh. Well, I guess he was right to apologize, but I worry if he did that once, would he do it again? Should

I forgive him so easily? I just wanted to be at the beach. Alone.

"Thank you for your apology, but I will need some time to think about this," I said.

"Okay. In the meantime, do you want some eggs and bacon?" he asked.

"Sure. Then I'm going for a run. We have some fruit, and I will cut it up for us." I headed to the refrigerator and pulled out some watermelon and grapes.

I felt somewhat numb to everything.

We ate breakfast and said little other than that the weather was nice

After we cleaned up, I put on my running sneakers. On my run, I was sure I'd go to the beach by myself for a week, maybe two. I would play it by ear. My plan was to stay on the quiet side this week and not bring up leaving or ask Rodney for much.

I suddenly had this overwhelming feeling that I was done with Asheville. And more importantly, Rodney. I don't want to get ahead of myself, though. I am understandably still upset from last night, so I need to give myself time to cool down and collect my thoughts.

The first thing I did when I got to work on Monday morning was send Charlotte an email asking if I could take some time off or work remotely if needed. She responded right away.

Hi Amelia,

Of course! Maybe just check in once or twice a day for any urgent emails, but I don't have many projects in Asheville at the moment anyway. I will be in sunny California this week, but don't hesitate to reach out. Go ahead and give yourself two weeks if you want. You hardly ever take time off.

-Char

She is so nice. I hardly see her, but she is very accommodating whenever I need anything.

It wasn't too terrible with Rodney that week, but there was definitely an elephant in the room at all times. And I kept my distance as much as I could. He would ask me just about every day, "What's wrong?" I knew if I was honest, it would turn into another fight, so I would say "nothing" and go about my day.

I started going for morning runs before work. This way, I avoided him more in the mornings, and it was really only in the evenings that we had to coexist.

Towards the middle of the week, he approached me. "Amelia, remember I can change."

"I know, Rodney," I responded. Uninterested.

"So why don't you give me a chance to do that before you run off to the beach for a week?"

"The thing is, when people truly want to change, they just do. They don't say over and over for years, they can change and never actually change. Does that make sense to you?" I asked.

"Yes. It does. I'm going out to dinner. Do you want me to bring you something back?"

"No, I will just make myself a salad or something. Thank you, though. I hope you have a nice dinner," I said, ecstatic that he would be out of the house for the evening.

He left pretty quickly, and I grabbed a frozen meal from the freezer and turned on a reality show for me to watch in peace. Rodney hated the shows I enjoyed, to the point that it was easier for me to watch them when he was out of the house.

As I enjoyed the house to myself, I couldn't help but think that if we were to divorce, it could always be like this: peace, harmony, white wine, and reality TV. My dream. These days anyway…

Rodney continued to go out for dinner by himself each night for the remainder of the week. He never told me which restaurants he went to, but I also didn't care enough to ask. All I knew was that it was great to have the additional space from him. We didn't fight because we barely saw each other.

I was counting down the days until I could go to the beach and truly decompress.

When Friday evening came, Rodney left to go out to dinner, and I eagerly started to pack my bags. Since it was warm out, I mainly packed summer clothes, swimsuits, and books. I was looking forward to getting lost in a few novels.

Before I knew it, it was 9 pm. I decided to get ready for bed, turn on some mindless TV, and hopefully fall asleep to it. Just as I was drifting off, I heard the front door open and then slam shut so loudly it seemed like the walls shook.

I froze in fear that Rodney was going to come into my room. He didn't, though; instead, it sounded like he went into the kitchen and he turned on the stereo very loudly. Great. I assumed he was drunk and angry about my leaving in the morning. I felt I had two choices. One was not to ask him to turn the music down and risk losing a lot of sleep. Two was to ask him to turn down the music politely, but that would likely lead to a fight.

At first, I went with option one. I tried to sleep for an hour or so, and of course, I couldn't. I looked at the clock; it was 11 pm. I decided to get up and go see what Rodney was doing, and to my surprise, he was asleep on the couch. Fantastic! I turned off the stereo and went back into my room, excited to finally get some sleep. Rodney had really changed lately, but for the worse, it seemed. Fine by me. It was just making my decision to go to the beach even easier.

I finally fell asleep close to midnight and woke up around 9 am. Not quite as early as I'd hoped to get up, but that was fine. It was about an eight-hour drive to the beach, so I had a long drive ahead of me and wanted to get on the road soon. And more importantly, away from Rodney. Who knows if he was even up yet.

I finished packing as much as I could in my room and then headed out to the kitchen. I smelled coffee, so I knew Rodney must have gotten up.

"Morning!" he said instantly as I went into the kitchen.

"Good morning, how was it sleeping on the couch last night?" I asked. Really not caring at all about his sleep quality since he hindered mine, to say the least.

"It was okay. I got up and went to bed around 3 am. Are you still going to the beach?"

"Yes."

"Oh. Well, I really don't want you to go," he said.

"Rodney, I know you don't, and it's not like I am exactly in love with the reason I'm going, but something needs to change," I said, clearly frustrated.

I decided I'd skip coffee and pick one up on the way out of town. I went back to my room and grabbed my suitcases. I had a carry-on and a regular-sized suitcase.

Rodney did not help me put them in the car, but I knew he was upset, so I really couldn't blame him.

Just as I went to get into the car, he grabbed my arm very hard and forcefully.

Startled, I looked up at him.

"I promise you, Amelia, I will change while you are gone. I can and I will."

Chapter 19

Twenty minutes later, I was leaving a coffee shop with a French Vanilla latte and pulling onto the interstate that would lead me to the beach. I had such a freeing feeling that I presumed would only get even stronger, the further away I got from Rodney.

The weather was beautiful, which was helpful for an easy drive to the coast. I was due to arrive just around dinner time, so I planned to check into the cottage, unpack a little, take a short walk on the beach, and then treat myself to dinner.

As I was driving, I was surprised at how fast the drive was going. It was fun to play the music I wanted without having to listen to Rodney's boring podcasts or his choice of music. I had to stop once for gas and some snacks, but then got back on the road.

Before I knew it, my GPS told me to pull off at the exit, and I would have about an hour on some back roads.

When I pulled up to the cottage, there was a keypad on the door to let myself in. As I looked around, I couldn't help but feel it was simply perfect! The space was modern with a feminine touch, and when I opened the windows, I could smell the salt air and even see part of the ocean from the living room and front porch. This was going to be a wonderful two weeks!

I went back to my car and lugged my suitcases in. Since the sun was close to setting, I decided to take a walk on the beach in the morning and get dressed for dinner. There was a seafood restaurant less than half a mile away that I could walk to. It was actually the restaurant that Rodney and I went to after he proposed on the beach, but they had good food, and I was starving. I'd have more time to research other places in the coming days.

I put on a black summer dress and headed to the restaurant. When I walked in, I was greeted by the hostess.

"Good evening! How many?" she asked.

"Umm... just me." I felt really weird saying that.

"Okay, do you want a table by the window or one outside?"

"Actually, can I just sit at the bar?" I asked.

"Of course! Follow me!"

As I followed her to the bar, I found an empty seat between two women and sat down.

A woman bartender immediately came up to me, "Hi there! What can I get you to drink?" she asked.

"Hi! I'd love a pinot grigio, please!" I said with a smile. After that eight-hour drive, I was ready to have some wine and relax for the evening.

"Are you on vacation?" the woman to my right asked.

"Well…yes. I guess you could call it that."

She looked at me a bit confused, so I decided to offer some more information.

"To be honest, I am here alone, trying to clear my head about my marriage."

"Oh. Well, nothing like some good salt air to clear your mind! I got divorced three years ago and never looked back," she said.

"I am sorry to hear that!"

She laughed. "Honey, I just told you I never looked back! We were married for seven years, and let's say it wasn't exactly fun towards the end of it. I finally got the courage to leave and bought myself a small condo just down the road. We lived in Atlanta together, so I don't even need to worry about running into him. It's heaven for me!"

I had never talked to such a happy divorced person. She really seemed to have made the right choice for herself.

"Do you have any regrets at all?" I asked.

"I'll have another cabernet!" she said to the bartender, then looked at me, "My only regret is I didn't leave sooner. I knew in my gut he didn't treat me right. Now with that in mind, I have not found my prince charming just yet, but I sleep soundly every night, and no one is complaining to me about God knows what every day. And I live at the beach! Henry never wanted to leave Atlanta."

"I'm Amelia, thank you so much for sharing your story with me."

"Nice to meet you, Amelia. I'm Suzy. How long are you in town for?"

"I think about two weeks. I was going to stay one, but it' s so nice here, I'm sure I will do two."

"Oh, definitely worth staying two weeks, because if you plan to go home and tell your husband you want a divorce, it will be a whole can of worms you probably never expected. Men can't seem to take rejection well… and they always make a hard time worse," Suzy said.

Just then, the woman to my left hung up on a call she was on and jumped right into the conversation. "Not to eavesdrop, but she's right. When I told my first husband that I wanted to leave, he went crazy. He managed to drag our divorce out for over nine months. So many attorney fees, but I am sure that was part of his plan."

"But you know what, ladies?" She eagerly asked both of us. "Worth every penny! And I met my second husband a year later and couldn't be happier."

"My goodness, I really appreciate you both telling me these stories. They are very motivating," I told them.

The three of us started chatting and shared random stories about our dating experiences. We laughed so hard. I don't even remember the time I laughed that hard. Needless to say, Rodney had become such a miserable person that it was hard to ever have any fun with or around him.

"Okay, girls, I need to get going," Suzy said. "Amelia, I'm sure we will run into each other over the coming weeks."

The other woman and I also decided to leave. She and her husband were leaving early in the morning, and I wanted to go to the cottage and sit out on the porch for a bit.

The walk home was short, and the air felt refreshingly cool. I grabbed a sweatshirt, poured myself a little more wine, and went out to the porch. There was a couch, a couple of chairs, and a rocking chair. I plopped down in the rocking chair and took a deep breath of the ocean air.

It was amazing how much lighter my energy felt ever since I left Asheville this morning. I could only imagine how much better I would be feeling in the coming days.

As I relaxed on the porch, I couldn't help but feel the universe was guiding me by having me meet the two women earlier, both of whom had been divorced and came out on the other side much happier. Maybe if I see Suzy again, I can open up to her a bit more about Rodney.

I started to get a bit sleepy, so I went inside, pulled out my pajamas, and got ready for bed. The bed was so soft, and the room had a window facing the ocean, so I made sure to crack the window open just enough so I could fall asleep to the crashing ocean waves.

I slept straight through the night, and when I woke up, before I even opened my eyes, I remembered I was at the beach – and alone! I stretched out over the whole bed and opened my eyes to look out the window. It was a gorgeous, sunny day with blue skies.

I eagerly got up and went to make myself a cup of coffee. I couldn't wait to take a walk on the beach and do some seashell hunting.

Just then, I heard a buzz from my cell phone. I looked down and saw a text from Rodney.

Crap. I thought to myself. I never texted him when I got here. He is going to be so upset with me.

"Morning, darling! Did you make it to the beach okay?"

Darling? He never called me that. I was also shocked that I forgot even to text him when I arrived. I was so happy to be here…away from him… that it completely slipped my mind.

It also occurred to me that maybe we shouldn't even talk during this two-week stay, but honestly, if I were to divorce him, we'd hardly ever speak again, so I figured an extra couple of weeks wouldn't hurt. I was going to make sure not to text him every day. And I was going to keep the overall communication to a minimum.

I texted him back apologizing for not letting him know I got there, and also let him know I was getting ready to take a walk on the beach.

He replied, "Sounds good, my dear. I'm getting ready to run some errands. Enjoy your day!"

It was a bit odd to me that he was being rather friendly, considering the reason why I was at the beach, but… better than him being a jerk.

I finished my coffee, put on my flip-flops, and headed to the beach. There was a boardwalk near the cottage that led directly to the beach, making it very easy to reach.

The weather was impeccable. There was a light breeze, and it was probably around seventy degrees. The sand was firm near the water, which made it easier to walk. I decided to head south towards a pier. I came upon a group of men with fishing rods lined up. I asked one, "Are you catching anything?"

"No ma'am! But any day is a good day on the beach, so I'm still a happy camper!" he said with a huge smile.

"Well, good luck to you, sir! Enjoy the beautiful morning!"

"Oh, I am! The forecast calls for similar weather all week, so if you're here, maybe one morning I can report back on a fish I caught," he said with a smile.

People genuinely seemed happier at the beach. And I admit I was already becoming one of them. I walked south toward a pier, occasionally walking with the ocean at my feet and taking some breaks to look for shells. I felt so relaxed and couldn't even remember the last time I felt so at ease.

After the beach, I headed to the store to buy some food and drinks to have on hand during my stay. It was a small local grocery store, but it had everything I needed. On the way back, I passed a little restaurant on the water advertising oysters for their happy hour, which started at 3 pm. I looked at the time, and it was just after 2:30 pm. Perfect! I thought to myself. I will go and unpack all of these groceries, then take myself out for some oysters.

It was alarmingly refreshing to be on my own schedule and not have to check in with Rodney at all, which reminded me that I need to take some time to sit down and really think about what I want to do with our marriage…

After unpacking the groceries and quickly changing, I jumped back in the car and headed towards the oyster spot. I wanted to try another restaurant for dinner, so I was going to make sure I didn't overeat.

As I walked up, the host greeted me. "Hiya! Do you want to sit inside or outside?"

"Outside, please, and it will be just me," I said.

I followed the host through the restaurant and outside. They were on the opposite side of the ocean, so they had tables on a lovely dock by the intercoastal.

"Is this okay, miss?" she asked.

"Oh, it is great! It is such a beautiful day out, isn't it?!"

"It is, and you're in luck if you like oysters. Some say we have the best in the state," she said with an enthusiastic smile.

I glanced at the menu and was in heaven. There's so much seafood to choose from, but I decided to stick with the oysters for now. When the waitress came over, I ordered a dozen oysters, three different varieties, and a glass of sauvignon blanc.

There were a few older couples at nearby tables, but overall, it wasn't crowded.

I remembered what I had told myself earlier…I need to think about my marriage. Do I want to stay in it? No. I immediately thought to myself.

Just then, the waitress delivered my wine. I took a sip, then asked myself again if I should stay in my marriage.

NO.

This time, it almost seemed like a subconscious no.

Let's say I do decide to leave Rodney, then what? Where would I move to? Could I afford it? I had so many questions running through my mind, it was overwhelming. In a way, I wanted to stop thinking about it and enjoy my time at the beach.

I do think I need to leave Rodney, but how I will go about even telling him and deciding what to do afterwards just all seemed so much.

"Here ya go, miss!" I jumped. A waiter placed my oysters down. I was so deep in thought that he had completely startled me.

"Oops, sorry, I didn't mean to sneak up on you like that."

"Oh no, no, you are fine, I was just lost in my own thoughts. These oysters look delicious!" I said.

"Oh, they are. People come from miles away to have them. I hope you enjoy them and stay out of those thoughts. You're at the beach!" he said as he laughed.

It was nice to have permission to stop thinking so much, even if it was from a total stranger.

After I finished the oysters and my wine, I headed back to the cottage to shower and take a nap since I was feeling a bit tired.

After my nap, I decided to sit out on the porch and read some magazines. I had interior design magazines that I was skimming through. I had learned so much from Charlotte – maybe I could become a designer on my own? If I leave Rodney…

When I leave Rodney.

The salt air was so refreshing. Would I move to the beach? Ugh, I probably couldn't afford that. Well, there was no "probably" about it. It was too expensive.

Would I move back to New York City? Maybe. I couldn't believe I was considering that a possibility. New York isn't cheap either, but there are jobs available.

I started to feel overwhelmed again.

Maybe I will run into Suzy tonight. She seemed to have a good head on her shoulders and clearly had a lot of courage to leave her husband and move out to the beach on her own. I wondered what she did for a living and how she supported herself. Rodney was the breadwinner in our household, and I was quite worried about the finances if I were to leave him.

Ugh, this was all too much to think about. Then again, I suppose I do need to think about it and come up with a plan. I wish Rodney could have just stayed normal and nice. He was so great when we first met, and in the first years we dated.

So nice.

So supportive.

So wonderful.

And now here I am on a solo trip at the beach, trying to clear my head and figure out what I need to do to get myself out of this marriage. Or do I just stay?

No.

I can't.

I won't.

Chapter 20

I got up from the porch, jumped in the shower, and got ready for dinner. I wore a light blue sundress. I decided to put in a little more effort than usual and looked at myself in the mirror. I couldn't help but smile at myself. I thought that I looked beautiful. Then I immediately tried to remember the last time Rodney had even complimented me. It's been years of him being critical and pointing out endless flaws. I am sure this has affected my self-esteem, and I haven't even realized it. It's been years since I even thought I looked as pretty as I did tonight, and I am sure that is a result of being away from Rodney, even if it was only for a couple of days.

I grabbed some tan high heels, threw on some jewelry, and was off to dinner. Although it wasn't far, I decided to take a taxi there since I was wearing heels.

The restaurant was new, having opened just months prior. It had great reviews online, so I was excited to try it.

As I walked in, I saw multiple fish tanks with the most beautiful fish. There were also beautiful chandeliers hanging throughout the restaurant. It was more upscale than I had realized, so I was glad I dressed up.

As I walked to the hostess stand, I asked if I could sit at the bar. The hostess led me to the bar, and I immediately saw Suzy! I felt some relief even just seeing her.

"Miss – can I sit over there by that woman?" I asked.

"Of course you can!" she said with a smile.

Just then, Suzy looked up and saw me.

"Amelia!" she exclaimed. "I thought I'd see you again, but not this soon. What a pleasant surprise. Did you have a nice day?"

"Oh, I really did, Suzy. It was so nice just to be…"

"Alone?" she asked.

"Yes," I sighed.

"Oh, honey, get yourself a glass of wine, and we can have our very own therapy session. I feel like I have definitely been in your shoes before."

There was something about Suzy that just calmed me. I had only met her once, but I felt I could open up to her, and not only would she not judge me, but she would help me figure out a plan.

"I just got here, I ordered some calamari; you're welcome to have some if you want," Suzy offered.

"Oh yes, I love calamari. This restaurant is beautiful. I'm happy I can try it out tonight."

"How was your day?" I asked.

"Oh, all my days are good. No one gives me an attitude, tells me what to do, or tells me who I can and can't talk to. It is very hard for me to even find something to complain about these days."

"Do you work?" I asked.

"Nope," Suzy said.

"Oh, well, what do you do for money?"

"I had quite a large inheritance. But Amelia, I didn't even know I was going to have an inheritance. It was the craziest thing. You see, I put off my divorce for years because I didn't know how I was going to support myself. Finally, I became so miserable that I just told myself I would figure it out. I was in the process of looking to rent a place, and then I got a call from an attorney, and he informed me that one of my aunts, whom I barely knew, had left me… well, let's just say it was enough money to buy my dream home at the beach.

"Wow," I didn't even know what else to say.

"That is not going to happen to me, though. I barely have any family."

"That's not my point, Amelia!" Suzy exclaimed. "My point is that life always catches us when we fall. Or should I say jump! Once you make that decision to start the next chapter of your life, doors will begin opening like you wouldn't believe."

I wasn't sure about this advice. Sure, it sounded good in theory, but I feel like I am too much of a realist to 'trust in the process' as they say.

"Haven't you been told to trust the process?" Suzy asked.

I couldn't help but laugh. "Funny you should ask, because I don't think I do trust the process. Is my husband being so terrible part of the trusted process?"

"Well, it won't be once you decide to start living for yourself again and not accept his behavior. If you don't mind me asking, what is the problem with him anyway?"

"Rodney," I said.

"Rodney? I've never met a Rodney," she said.

"I don't recommend it," we both laughed.

"Oh, Suzy, it's so weird. When we met, we were so in love. I met him the first night I moved to Asheville, and we just hit it off. He was fun, polite, kind... I could go on about how amazing he was for years. It was the weirdest thing, though. Once we got married, he…changed."

"Did he become lazy? Stop putting in effort?" she asked.

"Yes, that was a part of it. It's almost like he has become an entirely different version of himself, though. It's tough to explain. He is just simply not the man I met. And I know people do change a bit over time in relationships, but I feel it's just too much. He has gotten so critical of me, too. Almost mean."

"Well, that's no fun!"

"It really isn't. And since it was somewhat gradual, I feel like I have slowly become accustomed to it, to the point where I often forget what it should be like. How it was…"

"Do you think he'd go to therapy?" Suzy asked.

"No. I have asked so often that I eventually just gave up on asking."

"What does your gut tell you? Do you want to leave him?"

"YES."

Just then, my phone buzzed.

Since it was sitting on the bar, we both looked down automatically.

It was from Rodney.

I opened the text and read it out loud, "Hi darling, I hope your trip is going well. Make sure to spend some extra money on treating yourself, and I can't wait to see you when you get back."

"Is he always that nice?" Suzy asked.

"No. He was nice via text the other day, too. It is a bit bizarre to me."

We sat in silence for several seconds before Suzy said, "He knows you are going to leave. These men can sense that we're done with them from miles away."

"You think?"

"Oh, I know. Right before I gained the courage to leave my marriage, he started being so nice to me that it almost made me second-guess what I was doing.

Then, when I stood my ground, that is when he made it a living nightmare with all the attorney's fees."

"Rodney doesn't like to spend money. Well, he used to not mind, but over the years, he has become more frugal, so I don't see him wanting to spend a lot of time with an attorney. Besides, if I tell him I want a divorce, what can he actually do to stop me?"

"Legally, not much, but you'd be surprised what some of these men are capable of. Did you ever have any doubt about him at all, Amelia?" Suzy asked.

"Well… yes. And you know what's weird, I often encountered strangers who even questioned my relationship with him."

"What do you mean?"

"It's hard to explain, but over the years, even if I wasn't with Rodney, people would ask in a roundabout way if I knew what I was doing by marrying him."

"That's really weird. Strangers?"

"Yes, total strangers. From random bartenders to a lady who gave us massages in Jamaica. At times, it felt like a warning, but also, they were complete strangers who did not know Rodney or me, so I just dismissed it."

"Maybe all of those people were intuitive, though?"

"Maybe," I replied. "But also, what was I supposed to do, call off my wedding because someone I had never met before told me to?"

"I get what you're saying. I'd probably have done the same thing as you. The thing is, you also had a gut feeling at times, right?"

"Yes…I did," I said.

"That is the part you can't ignore. Your gut. Who knows, maybe this is all one giant lesson for you to learn to trust your gut."

"Maybe. At least I have the time here to try to come up with a plan. I think I may move back to New York City. I never thought I'd want to go back there, but living in the mountains for so long has made me crave the city life again."

"That makes sense because it was where you lived before you met your husband. So, it may even be a subconscious pull to get you back," Suzy said.

I suddenly got such a bad feeling.

Suzy must have seen it in my face because she grabbed my arm. "What's wrong?"

"I don't know, for some reason, I just imagined myself telling Rodney I want to leave him, and this overwhelming feeling came over me. A terrible one."

"I think that is normal, Amelia. It's a big change, but as cliché as it sounds, take one day at a time. People get divorced every day in this country, and you'll be able to handle whatever comes your way. You need to believe that."

While Suzy was saying positive and kind things to me, I guess I didn't believe her. This was a feeling I had never experienced before. It was on an entirely different level.

"Okay, let's talk about something more fun. This is all getting depressing," I said.

We finished the evening just talking about various things, including places we've traveled to and places we both still want to go to. Our favorite places to shop. Our favorite wines to drink. I started to feel better and more myself again.

After dinner, I went back to the cottage and decided to sit out on the porch and listen to the waves crashing onto the shore. As I was sitting there relaxing, my phone buzzed. It was Rodney. I had forgotten to even respond to him at dinner.

My heart sank. This won't be good.

I looked down at the text, which said, "Goodnight, darling! You must be enjoying yourself, and that is what life is all about. Talk soon! Xoxo"

"What?" I said out loud.

I was so confused. These texts didn't even sound like Rodney.

Do I respond? I guess I will.

"Sorry – I was out and missed your earlier text. Hope you're well, have a good night."

That message was nicer than I'd have preferred, but I do admit he has been throwing me for a loop with his nice text messages.

I decided to turn my phone off completely after that. I did not want to risk having to hear from Rodney the rest of the night. I came on this trip to clear my head, but it has been a bit harder than I thought it would be. Between how I would tell Rodney I wanted to leave him, deciding where I would move and work, and being overwhelmed by the dark feelings that surfaced about the entire situation.

It was just much more than I had anticipated needing to navigate.

I will say Suzy was a nice silver lining. It was comforting to have someone to bounce my ideas off of and also to talk about fun things and laugh a bit. I think not having any friends in Asheville had been wearing on me. That would be a goal of mine if (when) I move back to New York City. Friends. Lots of them. I could join various clubs and make much more of an effort than I did there or in Asheville.

I decided to call it a night and got dressed for bed. I read a little in one of my magazines, then drifted off to sleep.

All of a sudden, I woke up to a crashing noise coming from the living room. It was so loud! I froze in fear as I grabbed the edge of my bed.

Rodney.

Rodney must have driven to the beach and found me. He must have tracked me here.

Bang!

I heard the noise again. I was terrified. I wanted to scream and cry and stay silent all at the same time.

As I lay still in bed, waiting for the noise again or for Rodney to come into my bedroom, I noticed the wind outside. It was storming. Badly.

Maybe it wasn't Rodney? Just then, I heard the loud noise again, and this time it did not scare me nearly as much. The fact that I heard it three times, and each time it sounded the same, led me to believe it was something blowing against the house.

Suddenly, I felt much less scared, got out of bed, and opened the bedroom door. Right away, it dawned on me that there was a screened front door and I had forgotten to latch it, so the storm must have been blowing it open and shut.

I couldn't help but laugh at myself a little for getting so frightened.

I opened the front door, latched the screen door shut, and crawled back into bed. As I was falling back to sleep, a sudden thought came to me. Why was I so scared of the thought of Rodney coming to find me? Sure, it would make sense to be confused, but not frightened to death. Ugh.

Luckily, the range of emotions eventually exhausted me, and I fell back to sleep. I woke up in the morning to the birds chirping and the waves crashing. I smiled. Then I remembered the night before.

Rodney sending nice, calm texts, and then me being completely terrified he may have shown up at my cottage. It wasn't making sense. Something was definitely off, but at the same time, what was it?

Perhaps just my subconscious sensing the big change of me moving out and starting all over again. That would make sense.

I got out of bed, made some coffee, and headed down to the beach. I could feel myself calming down and reminded myself that I was fully capable of whatever life throws at me. Of course, that is easy to say when you are casually strolling along on the beach in perfect weather, while also being on vacation from work.

Work.

Ugh. I doubt I'd be able to work remotely for Charlotte from New York, as I know she likes a presence in the Asheville office. I really would have to start all over on the job front.

I can do it.

I can start applying for jobs online that are based in New York City. Maybe get something lined up before I move. That would be perfect.

Housing.

Crap.

How do I afford that? Rent is sky high in Manhattan. Rodney and I joined accounts after we got married. I do have my own credit card, though, so maybe I can rely on that if I need to. Well, I am clearly overthinking. Rodney couldn't keep all of our assets from me, especially since I had my own income.

I find that at the beach, I go from being completely happy and at peace to then freaking out about everything possible.

The next several days at the beach went by quickly. It felt a bit like Groundhog Day while I was there. I would have delicious seafood meals and wine, followed by panic attacks, and then calmness. As the days went by, though, I felt comfortable knowing I had reviewed as many scenarios as I could about how things would go with Rodney, and what would happen if I found a place to live, a job, etc.

I'd sit many nights on the cottage porch, with a glass of wine, listening to the crashing waves while simultaneously going over every possible outcome with Rodney and our upcoming divorce.

Chapter 21

Divorce

As much as I never thought I would want one, I am now fully confident that I not only want a divorce from Rodney, but I need one. I have to think he may feel a sense of relief when I break the news to him. The man has not been putting in effort for years. He doesn't seem to care if he impresses me or not.

A part of me felt that we just grew apart over time, and there's nothing wrong with that. Ultimately, there was no wrongdoing. No cheating, no abuse. No crazy family drama. (You need to have a family to have the family drama…) So, in reality, it should be smooth sailing to move forward with this divorce. I couldn't see how we would fight about money when we can see on paper what each of us makes.

We could live amicably for a couple of months, or however long it took to finalize the divorce, and then I could head back to New York. Who knows? Maybe we will even grow to be friends over time and some distance, and he will visit me in the city. That was somewhat of a nice vision. I always wanted him to come to New York, but that never appealed to him in the slightest.

In theory, this divorce should be a piece of cake. As Suzy reminded me, though, there is a chance that Rodney won't want the divorce and will make my life a living hell.

In all honesty, I have no clue how he could do that. If he makes me miserable, I will leave, deal with the divorce from Manhattan, and fly back if necessary.

Before I knew it, it was my last day at the beach. I did my usual routine of taking a walk or two on the beach, lying out to get some sun, and finding fun restaurants to eat at. Even though each day felt a bit the same, they were, for the most part, wonderful.

I decided to return to the restaurant I had visited on the first night, hoping to run into Suzy again and also try their crab cakes. Even though I had run into Suzy a few times, we never did exchange numbers. I suppose it would have been weird to even ask for hers since I would be leaving the beach… most likely for good if my plan to return to New York City works out.

I did my hair and makeup, picked out what was probably the only dress I had yet to wear, and headed over to the restaurant. I walked in and promptly let the hostess know I preferred the bar area. To my dismay,

Suzy wasn't there. I grabbed a seat and ordered an espresso martini.

When the bartender delivered it, it looked like a work of art. Just as he set it on the bar in front of me, I heard a woman say, "Make that two espresso martinis!" I looked up, and it was Suzy!

"Oh, Suzy! I am so glad to see you!" I exclaimed.

"Well, it's your last night! If you weren't at this bar, I figured I'd go check the one across the street too," she said as we both laughed.

"So, are you all prepared to start your new life, Amelia?" she asked.

"I think so. Wait, I know so!" Suzy had been coaching me to speak more confidently about what I wanted from my relationship and life in general.

"That's my girl! It will be great, maybe hard at first, but eventually you will see that light at the end of the tunnel. And once you get to that divorcee light, you'll love it there."

"I hope so," I said. "It has been so great to be at the beach and visit with you. I really appreciate all of the listening you've done."

"Oh, please, you are very enjoyable to talk to. It's a damn shame your own husband can't see that, but then again, men often have a knack for learning about life the hard way."

"So, you aren't friends with your ex? You never talk to him?"

Suzy looked at me. Then looked at her martini and took another sip.

"Amelia, no. The way that man treated me in the end, no. A friend wouldn't have done that in a million years."

"Oh," I said, a bit disheartened on behalf of Suzy. "I'm hoping that Rodney and I can remain friends."

"Amelia, I am telling you right now, hope for the best, plan for the worst. I don't think you understand what an emotionally upset man is willing to do to someone."

"Oh, Rodney is harmless overall," I said, as I then instantly remembered him breaking the wine glass on the dinner table.

"Men can change on a dime, and it usually is not for the best," Suzy said.

Ugh. This feeling of dread washed over me once again.

"With that being said, I need to head out. I told some neighbors I'd come back early and spend some time catching up with them since they just got into town."

"Oh, well, I am sad to see you go, but that should be a fun evening."

"Amelia, it has been so great to meet you and spend some fun evenings with you. It's all going to work out for you. If it doesn't initially, just hang in there. In the end, everything works as it should."

We hugged each other goodbye, and she was off.

"Sir! Can I put an order of crabcakes in?" I asked the bartender.

I am going to miss the beach and the freedom I have had here. Although I guess it was a good indicator of what I truly want for my life. And that is to be away from Rodney. Friendship sounds nice, but then again, that may only be in a perfect world. Suzy was probably right that Rodney may not be on board with this divorce.

The crabcakes were delicious, but after I finished them, I had this feeling of dread come over me again. After tonight, I had to drive back home to Asheville and put my plan into action. I paid my bill and headed back to the cottage.

Once I got back, I decided it would be good to pack up a little so I could get an early start in the morning to drive back. I didn't want to go back. A part of me just wished I could drive from the beach straight up to New York City and start my new life. Could I? Would that be completely wrong to do? Crazily enough, the thought of never seeing Rodney again and just telling him over the phone that I wanted a divorce didn't seem nearly as nerve-racking as going back and telling him in person.

Ugh. I had to go back. It isn't like Rodney was that terrible of a husband to warrant me never seeing him again. But the thought of just going to New York, for some reason, was very calming, versus what I was actually going to do.

That night, I hardly slept. I had slept so well when I first arrived at the beach. But knowing my peaceful time was coming to an end was very upsetting. By the time my alarm went off, I was still exhausted but also knew I had to get up and face the day.

I packed up my car and headed out. The eight-hour drive felt like twenty hours. I had so many emotions running through my head. I hated it.

Then I had a thought: what if I didn't tell Rodney tonight that I wanted a divorce? For some reason, I had been thinking I needed to walk right in and say 'hi, how are you? I want a divorce.'

I could wait at least a day. Besides, it's not like there won't be a discussion after I tell him, and after this long drive, I may not have the mental capacity to do that. My new plan was to go home, have some dinner, and catch up with Rodney a bit. I needed to get a good night's rest, especially since I had hardly slept the night before.

I eventually saw a sign on the highway that said Asheville was 60 miles away. I had a terrible feeling about arriving home, but by now I was getting used to those feelings. It was becoming easier and easier to ignore them. I am sure that wasn't healthy, but what was I even supposed to do about them?

Each passing mile felt longer and longer to me. Once my exit came up, I noticed I started to break out in a little bit of a sweat. I hardly ever sweat, so that was weird. It must have been a side effect from the anxiety I was having.

I had only been gone for two weeks but the town felt different to me. I must have been so focused on detaching from my life as I currently knew it while at the coast.

Finally, the street to our neighborhood came up.

I wanted to cry. It took every ounce of me not to turn around and never look back.

Then I snapped out of it and shoved those feelings down again. I was probably just over-tired from lack of sleep and the long drive.

'Get a grip, Amelia,' I said to myself.

Chapter 22

As I turned onto our street, I noticed a blue truck in front of our house. The neighbors must have someone visiting.

I pulled up to our house and saw our mailbox had changed. Why did Rodney feel the need to replace our mailbox? I'll have to ask him over dinner.

I pulled into the driveway and saw new flowers and bushes.

'What was wrong with the ones before?' I asked myself. Sure, they looked nice, but I wouldn't necessarily say any better, just different. I used to have red and purple flowers planted along our walkway, but now they are all white. It wasn't like Rodney to not consult me on flowers in the yard, as he knew I cared more than he did about them.

Maybe he was just bored while I was gone and channeled his energy into some new landscaping…and a new mailbox. Seemed like a big waste of money since everything was fine before.

As I put the car in park, I felt my stomach grumble. Oh, my goodness, I hadn't eaten on my entire drive! I was so mentally distracted with my drive home. I needed to get inside and eat something before my blood sugar dropped too much.

I got out of the car and decided to leave everything in it besides my keys and my phone. I can go get a snack and then unload the car.

As I walked past the white flowers, I couldn't help but feel a little annoyed. What was wrong with my flowers before?! I had been fertilizing and watering them, and they were at the peak of the season with their blooms.

I walked up the steps of the house, reached for the doorknob, and went to open the door. I suddenly noticed there was a different doorknob.

That's when I noticed the doors had small windows up top. Rodney got a new door, too?

Just then, the door flung open to the point I jumped a little since I wasn't expecting it.

"Darling!! I've missed you so!"

I couldn't help but stare at Rodney for a few seconds. He was dressed in a nice button-down shirt and khaki pants. He never dressed this way, so preppy. He was usually more rugged, and especially when he wasn't at work, he was not the type to dress nicely.

"Well? Haven't you missed me, too?" he asked as he laughed a bit.

"Oh, of course, I'm sorry, I just haven't eaten all day and am afraid my blood sugar is low," I said as I walked into the entryway.

I looked around a little. I didn't recognize anything. Literally - anything.

"What's wrong, dear? Tell me what's wrong," Rodney pleaded.

"Everything," I managed to say.

Just then, everything in my eyesight went dark, and I completely passed out.

When I came to, I woke up in a bedroom I had never seen. I mean, the layout was what I was used to, but all the furniture and décor were different.

Rodney walked by and saw me awake. He came in and pointed out the glass of orange juice on the bedstand. "Drink this, it will help with your blood sugar."

I grabbed the glass and gulped it down.

"You hit your head when you fainted. We need to call a doctor to have you checked out."

"No, no, I am fine," I insisted.

Why on earth was I even saying that? I glanced around the room again. The room was painted a light gray. It used to be white. There was a new bedspread. New rugs. A new dresser. New…everything.

What was happening???

"Sweetie, you should get some rest then. I want to call a doctor, but if you prefer, I will wait. I will leave you for a bit. I have plenty of food in the kitchen as I have been preparing a nice meal for us. Come out when you are ready, or call me if you need me." Rodney then gave me a soft kiss on my forehead.

He never did that. Not once in all our years together did he ever kiss my forehead.

I had so many different emotions running through me that I couldn't even tell how I was feeling.

I got up and walked around the room. I looked down at our wedding picture that had been in a frame on our dresser.

It was different. The dress I was wearing in the picture was a strapless one. I wore a long-sleeved wedding dress when we got married. Then I saw another framed photo of us, but… it wasn't me. Well, it was, but I didn't recognize the outfit I was wearing in the picture.

I walked towards our bathroom, which was connected to the bedroom.

There were different towels and different wallpaper. My shampoos and conditioners were not the ones I had been using. I picked one up… it was half empty. So, it wasn't brand new. I started to feel dizzy, so I sat down on the toilet seat.

What happened? Why is everything so different? Why do I remember everything so differently?

I almost felt so overwhelmed that I started to shut down emotionally. Probably some defense tactic. Who even knows at this point?

I smelled food coming from the kitchen. It reminded me I still had not eaten anything.

I got up and slowly walked down the hall towards the kitchen. There were pictures hung in the hall that I had never seen. We never used to have anything hung in the hallway.

The smell of the food was becoming stronger and stronger to the point that I felt my stomach growling.

When I entered the kitchen, my heart sank even further.

All the cabinets were a different color. They used to be wooden, and now they were white. They looked like brand-new cabinets, too. I then looked up and saw that the dining room table was set.

My mind instantly flashed back to when Rodney got so upset with me that he broke a wine glass on the table. He broke it on the edge of a square table; this one was now circular.

Feeling lightheaded, I grabbed a stool at the breakfast bar – of course, those were different too.

"Amelia, are you okay?" Rodney asked, seeming genuinely concerned. "You look like you've seen a ghost."

I do not think I was ever so speechless in my entire life. What do I even say without sounding completely crazy? I went to the beach for two weeks and came home, and everything was different. I'd be shipped off to the insane asylum stat.

Think Amelia, think. Do I play the part? Until I figure out just what the hell is going on.

"Amelia?" Rodney said.

"Oh…nothing, I just… I just need to eat something, I think."

"Well, of course you do! I'm roasting a chicken and some vegetables."

Chicken and vegetables? Rodney has been a red meat-and-potatoes kind of guy for years. If any vegetables were ever cooked, I was the one who cooked them.

I was racking my brain to figure out what had happened this evening. I had just spent two wonderful weeks at the beach when I decided I wanted a divorce. I drove home to tell Rodney, but I was nervous and forgot to eat. I remember leaving all my stuff in the car and coming in to get something to eat. I noticed all of the new flowers outside of the house, and when I walked in, the entire entryway was decorated differently.

And then…Then I passed out.

My phone. My purse. They must still be in the car.

"I need to go get my purse. I just remembered I left it in the car," I said.

"What are you talking about? You told me your purse was stolen at the beach. And your phone was in it. I knew you shouldn't have gone there alone. I was afraid of something like that happening to you without me to watch out for you."

"Huh?" I said, confused again.

"You really must have hit your head harder than I thought," Rodney said.

"My purse wasn't stolen. What are you talking about?"

"The last time I heard from you was a couple of days ago. You called from someone else's phone and assured me you'd be home today."

Rodney was acting so normal. So calm.

He went to get some plates from the cupboards. They were plates I had never seen before, but I must admit, they had a beautiful design.

"Here, make yourself useful and put these on the table, will you?" he asked.

"These plates are beautiful," I said.

Rodney laughed. "Oh, of course they are, you picked them out! You always have the best taste."

Yes, I did have good taste.

No, I did not pick these plates out.

I have never felt so out of place in my life. I had so much to say, but at the same time, nothing at all.

After I finished setting the new dining room table, I sat down at it. Just then, Rodney plopped down a glass of wine.

"Here you are, dear, your favorite."

I looked up at him. "Pinot grigio?"

"Yes! Okay, so maybe your memory isn't totally gone after that fall," he said in a joking way.

He went back to the kitchen, and I turned around in my chair to face him.

"So, I really don't have my phone?"

"I'm afraid not, and apparently the Good Samaritan who stole your purse at the bar hasn't tried to contact me to get it back to you."

I just had my phone. I know I did.

"Don't worry, darling, we will get you a new phone. Hey, maybe with a new number you won't get as many spam calls - a silver lining, I'd say! I'm just so thankful you are back, Amelia."

"Me too?" I managed to say.

Rodney put the food on the table.

"This looks amazing. When did you start wanting to eat healthy?" I asked.

Rodney just looked up at me. "I don't know, I suppose when I was born. What kind of a question is that anyway? We both always eat healthy."

I do. He doesn't.

"Cheers!" He lifted his wine glass to mine. "To you making it safely home, I can't wait to have you in my arms tonight."

I almost threw up. I barely know what is going on around me; the last thing I can possibly think about is sleeping in his arms.

The dinner looked so wonderful, I thought to myself. I took a bite of the chicken, and I couldn't help but exclaim, "This is great, Rodney! Where did you learn how to cook?"

Rodney looked at me weirdly. "I've always been a good cook…"

No. He hardly ever cooked, especially recently. I felt like I needed to watch what I said because whenever I said anything, he made me feel like I was completely crazy.

Am I?

Chapter 23

No! I'm not. This situation sure is crazy…and I can't explain it…but I am not crazy.

"So, what were you up to while I was gone?" I asked. I figured I needed to try to act somewhat normal and hopefully could piece things together more.

"Oh, you know, worked a lot. I made sure to water all the flowers you planted out front, too. I don't know why you had to go and plant all new plants, but I suppose if that's what makes you happy…" Rodney trailed off.

Was this all a game to him? Am I supposed to completely freak out in front of him and call him out? But then again, what was I calling him out for? Changing literally everything in the house while I was gone? That sounded crazy.

The man could barely pick up a pair of his own socks, let alone redecorate anything. Each time I asked him for advice on something, he never cared and always left everything up to me. Which just made me assume he had no taste.

"Well, I just thought the yard could use a little refresher, that's all. Thank you for watering them."

"Finally, you say thank you! I was waiting for that." Rodney smiled and reached his hand across the table to grab mine. "I think it's in your best interest to never leave me like that again…wouldn't you agree?"

What? This was all so bizarre that I could hardly keep up.

"Well, it was nice to have some time to myself."

Rodney squeezed my hand so tightly that it almost hurt me. It frightened me, then he let go and went back to eating his meal.

"It's good to be back, though," I managed to say.

Rodney smiled. "That's what I like to hear."

As we finished eating, Rodney got up to clear the dishes. I started to help.

"Amelia, go relax on the couch. I will clean up. You've had a stressful day. I will clean and then meet you on the couch, and we can find a movie to watch. Why don't you pick out something you'd like to watch?"

Rodney never let me pick out movies. I couldn't help but be just a little excited.

"Well, if you insist. That is very nice of you, and thank you again for dinner."

I walked into the living room, fully expecting to see all new furniture, and I was right.

We used to have leather couches, and now they were beautiful, light gray ones. The area rug was stunning!

Wait – did Rodney have an affair? And had the woman completely redecorated the house while I was gone? No. That made no sense at all. Plus, he never once expressed interest in other women. No woman would make the house look better just so I could stay with him.

I sat down and looked around the room I had never seen before. I felt a bit better after finally eating a meal, but mentally, I couldn't explain how big a mess I felt. I was so overwhelmed. And tired. As strange as it was, a part of me was looking forward to crawling into bed and going to sleep. Maybe this was all a bad dream, and I'd wake back up at the beach.

Just thinking of bed made me tired, and I decided to lie down on the couch while waiting for Rodney. Before I knew it, I had fallen asleep.

Rodney came into the room and tried to wake me. I was so exhausted I could barely open my eyes. Usually, when I fell asleep on the couch, he'd leave me there, but this time, before I knew it, he was picking me up! Between the wine and the exhaustion, though, I almost felt as if I'd been drugged, so I just acted like I was still asleep.

He brought me into our room and gently put me into bed. Covered me up, turned out the lights, and left the room. I wanted to take the time to try to get my thoughts straight, but I couldn't. It would have to wait until the morning. Before I fell asleep, I prayed I'd be waking up back at the beach…

When I sensed the morning light coming in through the window, I stretched a little and smiled. I was at the beach! I could get up and take a walk just like I had been doing, and forget what a terrible dream I had just had.

I opened my eyes.

I wasn't at the beach. It wasn't a bad dream. I was in my home, where I didn't recognize a single thing.

I couldn't help but wonder if something really did happen to me when I fell.

I turned over, and Rodney was sleeping next to me.

"Rodney!" I said, a bit louder than usual for the morning.

Rodney rolled over towards me, opened his eyes, and smiled at me. "Good morning, darling!"

"Rodney, tell me why I don't remember anything. What happened? I don't understand."

"I told you, you must have hit your head harder than we both thought. I will call the doctor today. In the meantime, just try to relax a little."

Relax? Was this man out of his mind?! Or was I the one who was out of my mind…

He grabbed me and pulled me into his arms. He used to do that. When we first met. He hasn't done that in years at this point, though. A part of me felt a sense of protection being so close to him, which, after this recent turn of events, I was oddly thankful for.

After a little bit, we got up, and I went to my closet. I realized I hadn't looked at it last night since Rodney had just given me one of his t-shirts to wear. I opened it, fully expecting to see all new clothing, but it was all the same! I had a rush of relief come over me. It was so nice to finally see some familiar items in this house! I browsed through the clothing, wanting to hug all of the items close to me. I was so happy. I got dressed and headed to the kitchen.

Rodney was making us breakfast. "I am making us some sliced fruit and a vegetable omelet. Is that okay with you?" he asked.

"Yes, that sounds so delicious," I said.

"You know, I never understand those people who will eat fast food for breakfast, I mean, what a bad way to start your day!"

Rodney used to eat fast food all the time. He WAS one of those people. I guess he isn't anymore, though.

"Ugh," I groaned as I sat down.

"What's wrong?" Rodney looked alarmed.

I hadn't even meant to let out that groan; it was just all feeling overwhelming again and making my head hurt.

"Oh, nothing, I'm sorry. Still waking up, I guess."

I had no clue how to act. Part of me felt like I should play the part, and part of me wondered, did I really just forget everything in our house? But why wouldn't I have forgotten my clothing? And I didn't forget Rodney.

At the moment, I wish I had.

When he came to sit down to eat, I couldn't help but ask, "So I really don't even have a phone?"

"I told you. Your purse was stolen. We will get you a new phone this week. Don't worry. Why, who do you need to call so badly?"

I thought about that. I guess he was right. I mean, I don't have any friends…or at least none that I remember.

"Don't I have any friends who'd want to hear I was back in town?" I pleaded.

He put down his fork and sighed. "Amelia, I wish that were the case, but you and I both have had such a hard time making friends here…so no. Unless you need to call your boss? I assume you have to go back to work tomorrow?"

Charlotte! Yes! I had my job. Charlotte will know what to do. Oh, but she is in Japan now at an interior decorator seminar. Well, I will see when she is coming back when I go in tomorrow. Thank goodness I have her to talk to about all of this.

"Yes, you are right, I do go back tomorrow. It has been nice having a break, but it'll be good to get back into my routine a bit."

I had a flashback to all those dreaded feelings I had had while at the beach… was that all foreshadowing? Ironically, I missed those feelings. They weren't good, but they sure as hell were better than how I am feeling now. As crazy as it sounds, I probably should have driven to New York. At least I had my purse then…I do not think someone stole it.

I think Rodney is lying to me. But why? Well, I had been saying we should maybe separate.

Another flashback. He often told me that he could change and that he'd do anything to keep me.

But why? Why go this far out of his way to have me stay? That didn't make sense to me, but if I'm being honest, not much is making sense this weekend.

"What do you want to do after breakfast?" Rodney asked me.

To run away.

That was what I wanted to do.

"I don't know. Maybe I'll go for a walk."

"That sounds great! I'll go with you!"

Rodney never walked with me, no matter how often I asked him to.

"You will?"

"Why yes, it is a lovely morning outside, and we always go on walks together."

No, we don't. Ugh.

"Sounds great. I will go get my shoes and change," I said.

As we headed out the door, I saw white flowers that Rodney said I had planted. I completely regretted not turning right around when I saw the yard so different, but I didn't know that was the least of the changes I'd be encountering.

"Whose truck is that parked in the road?" I asked.

"Uhh, mine? Whose would it be?" he looked at me, confused.

"Rodney, you have an SUV, not a truck. You always said you were never a truck guy."

"Amelia, I don't know what you want me to say right now. Let's forget about my truck and enjoy our walk," he said, sounding a bit annoyed with me.

We got to the end of the driveway, and I asked, "Which way should we go?"

"Amelia, you know we always go to the left."

"We do?" I questioned.

It was weird. I felt like there were some things he said that I knew weren't right, but then some I seemed to actually not know.

"Left it is!" I said.

Rodney was walking at a good pace, I noticed, and after a few houses, he gently grabbed my hand to hold.

"I really did miss you when you were at the beach." He looked at me rather genuinely, I must admit.

"I missed you, too."

"What did you spend all your time thinking about down there?" he asked me.

"I don't remember," I said, adding a blank stare to go along with it.

I did remember. I know I did. It was easier at the moment to go along with the theme of the weekend. I did not see it in my best interest to blurt out that I wanted a divorce.

"I'm so sorry. I can only imagine how frustrating this must all be for you to not remember so much. I am just so glad you remember me."

I remember you smashing your wine glass on the kitchen table and coming home drunk, blasting music…

"Me too, Rodney," I said with a sweet smile.

A car was approaching us with an older lady. She slowed down and rolled down the window.

"What a lovely morning out for a walk, isn't it! Amelia, I'm glad to see you've returned from the beach."

I had never seen this woman before.

"You and me both, Beth! I missed her so much. I don't want to let her out of my sight anytime soon," Rodney said, laughing, as he put his arm around me.

"I have to go get dinner on. You two enjoy your day!" she said as she sped off.

"Who was that?" I immediately turned to Rodney.

"Oh dear. You don't remember Beth? She is one of our sweetest neighbors."

"We don't know any of our neighbors," I said back, a bit frustrated, which Rodney could sense.

"Hey, hey, calm down. You've been through a lot. I am sure your memory will come back soon. I will call the doctor first thing in the morning and get an appointment for you."

Do people actually even lose their memories? I feel like that is something you only see in a movie. I suppose I had to wait until I could see a doctor. Without a phone… or my purse…I was pretty much reliant on Rodney for, well, everything.

Which is not in my character. I have always taken pride in being self-reliant and not needing anyone else. I couldn't help but wonder if I had taken that to the extreme. It is a bit absurd that no one else would be worried about me or try to get in touch with me, but Rodney's explanation did make sense. I don't remember us having any friends.

I really liked Suzy at the beach, but didn't bother getting her number since we both assumed I'd be moving back to the city. New York City. The thought of the city brought me some relief. That had to mean something.

Who knows? Maybe I would still end up there, and this was just a bitch of a glitch in my plan. It made me feel better for thinking like that.

Chapter 24

Positive.

I remember Suzy saying I needed to keep positive. Lord knows I am going to need a lot of positivity to get through this situation.

We finished up our walk, and Rodney said he was going to go to the store.

"Can I come?" I asked.

"Well, of course you can come, but why don't you stay here and rest up some more?"

I didn't have the energy to convince Rodney I wanted to go, and then I thought maybe some time to myself would be good for me.

"Do you want me to pick up anything? Why don't you write down on this piece of paper what you want me to pick up for you?" Rodney gave me a notepad and a pen.

I wanted some apples, bananas, and olives. I had been enjoying olives on my salads at the beach, so I figured I could start having that at home, too.

I gave the note to Rodney. He shoved it in his pocket but didn't even look at the list.

"Okay, I shouldn't be long. Call me if you need anything…oh. Um. Well, forget I said that. I'll be home soon."

I wasn't too sure of what to do with myself. Walking around the house and seeing so many different things made me sick to my stomach. I then realized I had not been in the backyard. I figured I'd go relax on the porch and once again try to make sense of things. As I walked out to the patio, it was just how I remembered it… minus, of course, the furniture. It was gorgeous. All of the furniture seemed in such pristine condition. The couch was orange-and-white striped. It reminded me of a seaside resort.

All of a sudden, I heard some water as I stepped further outside. What is that? I quickly scanned the area, and my eyes fell upon the cutest little water fountain. I had always told Rodney I wanted one, but he kept making excuses and said they would be too much upkeep.

He was firm in that decision, I remembered, and wouldn't budge.

I sat down. Again, it just doesn't make sense. Half of the stuff in this house is so much better than when I left, and it's all things he wouldn't have cared about or outright told me not to buy.

He wouldn't do all of this to keep me. He wouldn't. No one would. I mean, there was new carpeting and new wallpaper! And now a new fountain amongst the landscaping and just about everything else in the house. All of that takes time to pick out and install. I know this from working with Charlotte. Most of her projects go on for months.

I was only gone for two weeks.

Right? Yes, of course, it was only two weeks. I couldn't leave work for longer than that anyway.

I was able to relax a little while sitting on the porch. I closed my eyes and felt the sun on my skin, and as I heard the water trickle from the fountain, I imagined myself at a hotel in Italy.

Except I imagined myself with another man.

I suddenly opened my eyes. Who else would be with me? It was weird. I felt like I almost had a premonition. I was in such a relaxed state, and it was like my mind was so open to everything. Maybe I should take up meditating. I should do everything I can to focus more and keep my mind calm.

Just then, I heard the front door open. I got up from the patio and went inside to meet Rodney.

"I'm so glad you're back. I'm craving an apple," I said.

"I didn't get any apples," Rodney said as he was unpacking some of the groceries.

"Why not?" I asked.

He looked up at me. "I didn't know you'd be craving an apple, I guess."

"But I wrote them on my list."

"What list?" he said as he pulled out some bananas.

"The list you asked me to give you! I wrote apples, bananas, and olives."

"Well, I guess I was sort of successful at reading your mind because I did get bananas."

"Rodney, why would you ask me what I wanted, give me a piece of paper to write it on, and then not get the other two items?"

Rodney turned around as he went to put some milk in the fridge. "Because there was no list, Amelia. I didn't ask you to give me a list, and as a result, you didn't give me one."

I stood there, dumbfounded. How can I prove that I gave him a list if he claims I didn't?

"But!" Rodney exclaimed. "I did get you your favorite wine."

"Oh, I do love that kind!" I said.

"Of course, you remember the wine," he laughed. "How about we pour a glass and go sit on the patio?"

"Sure." I already missed my imaginary Italian vacation…

As we went back to the patio, I brought up the fountain. "I love that fountain. When did you get it?"

"Oh, I suppose we got it about a year ago. The second I suggested we get it; you were on board."

That is not what happened. It was my idea, and he always said no. I started to wonder if he would eventually slip up if I just kept asking about things.

I took a seat on the couch.

"Why are you sitting so far away? Come over here." Rodney pulled me towards his side of the couch and put his arm around me. I relaxed into his chest. It was a familiar feeling that I welcomed. I started to think maybe it was good sometimes to give in and feel peace whenever I could.

My mind did not let me feel peace for very long, though. At the beach, I had this nagging feeling that something was wrong, and now I still have that. The only thing now is I can look around and clearly see what was wrong.

Everything.

I felt like I was at Rodney's mercy. Since I didn't have my purse, wallet, or even cell phone, what could I do? In a way, I was lucky he didn't kick me out into the streets. It would be nice to get a hotel room to clear my head, but I don't have my credit cards. Then again, the whole point of my going to the beach was so I could clear my head, and now I am more confused than ever.

It was a defeating feeling.

"What's for dinner?" I asked. "Or should we go out?"

"I'm not so sure you should be going out just yet. I think we need to get you to the doctor before we do too much."

I couldn't help but feel like I was being held hostage a bit. At least I would be able to go to work tomorrow.

"As for dinner, I'm trying a new tofu recipe."

Rodney has never tried tofu, at least not to my knowledge. Whenever I'd make it, he'd use it as an excuse to go out by himself and grab a burger.

"You are?" I questioned.

"Yes, you were the one who taught me it can take on many different flavors. It is such a versatile food item. I'm sad you are not remembering so many things about us."

I couldn't help but laugh a bit, "You think you're sad?! Put yourself in my shoes. I have no cell phone or credit cards, and apparently no friends or family who even care enough to check in on me. And on top of all of that, I do not remember this house or apparently much about our relationship."

Rodney hugged me tight, "Well, at least I remember you, and I am always here to take care of you. I won't let anything happen to you."

I couldn't help but think, what would even happen to me? I thought that was a weird thing to say.

Reluctantly, I hugged him back. I tried to pull away, but he held on for a little longer.

He released me from his hug but grabbed onto my arms. "Okay, let's go inside, and I will start prepping some food. We can turn on some classical music, and

I will pour you some more wine in the meantime. How does that sound?"

It honestly sounded great. But there is just something off about this entire situation.

"It sounds great!" I said.

As we made our way back inside, Rodney did just that. Put on some classical music, poured me another glass of chilled white wine, and started pulling out cutting boards, knives, and vegetables.

We never used to listen to classical music. I do have to admit it was pleasant and somewhat soothing. Or was that the wine? Maybe both.

"So, are you looking forward to going back to work tomorrow?" Rodney asked.

"Umm, I guess… it is sort of hard to look forward to anything right now."

"I bet it is. Well, maybe getting back into a routine will help you. And I will be calling the doctor first thing in the morning.

"Okay… What recipe are you using? It smells wonderful!" I said.

"It's a honey teriyaki recipe I found. I am making the sauce, sautéing the vegetables in it, and then adding in the tofu."

As I watched Rodney cook, I found it a bit weird. I recalled him being like this in the beginning of our relationship, but not lately. As I continued to rack my brain for what had possibly happened to my memory, nothing made sense. Maybe I could find some clues when I go to work tomorrow. Perhaps I can get Charlotte on the phone and talk to her.

After we had dinner, we settled in and watched some TV. We talked, but not a ton, which was nice since it gave us more of a quiet evening.

"Rodney, I need to go to bed. I'm sorry, I am just so worn out," I said to him.

He turned off the TV.

"You don't have to go to bed. I'm the one who is tired."

"It's fine, dear. There is nothing wrong with me getting into bed now, too. I have been reading a book that I can read for a bit until I am more tired."

Reading? Rodney doesn't read.

"What are you reading?" I asked.

"Just a book on relationships. I know ours is great, but figured, why not see if I can learn more about ways to keep you around. Besides, you know what they say, 'happy wife, happy life!'"

Umm. Okay? It's like I left town, and Rodney started to become my dream husband. What wife doesn't want their husband to read more about relationships, especially voluntarily!

"Well, it takes two, so let me know if you pick up any tips or tricks you can fill me in on," I said with a smile.

"Oh, stop, you're the perfect one. Always have been, always will be."

Well… can't say he was wrong about that. That is also what had been frustrating me; I have felt for years that I was still putting in consistent effort in our relationship, and Rodney was not. I understand it is normal for people to get comfortable with each other, but it was like he became another person.

A lazy slob. If I'm being honest, a rude one too. That is what led me to the beach to think of a plan and decide on my next steps in life. Now that he seemed to be back to who he was, and who I wanted him to be… do I just stay?

Chapter 25

No.

I immediately got that gut feeling.

Of course, I had gone on for years not listening to my gut, and now I felt I finally wanted to, but can't. At least, not until I get my ID and phone back.

After I got ready for bed, I went into the room and saw Rodney in bed reading. Just like he said he would do.

As I crawled into bed, Rodney turned out the lights and wrapped his arms around me. I almost hated that I felt a sense of security in his arms. I was so exhausted, I think I fell asleep within minutes and slept straight until 7 am when my alarm went off.

When I woke up, I noticed that Rodney wasn't in bed. I smelled coffee. I guess he was already up? He usually sleeps till the very last minute he possibly can.

I got out of bed, grabbed my robe and walked into the kitchen.

"Good morning!" Rodney happily said.

"Umm. Morning."

"I have coffee ready for you, and I sliced up some fruit. Would you like a piece of toast too?"

"Oh uhh. Sure. I mean, yes, thank you. You didn't have to do all of this, you know."

"Sure, I do! Why wouldn't I want to make sure my wife's day starts right?"

"I guess that book is paying off…" I said with a grin.

Rodney smiled back, poured himself a cup of coffee, and sat down next to me.

"I hope your first day back to work goes well. How about we go out to eat tonight? You are probably ready to get out and about a bit again," he said.

"Yeah, that would be nice. I hope work goes well, too. Charlotte is in Japan, but I may try calling her and see if there's anything major I missed. You are driving me to work, right? Since I don't have my license."

"Yes, of course. Do you want me to pick you up for lunch?" he asked.

"No, that's okay. Maybe I will just bring something so I can focus on catching up on my emails and all."

"It's not healthy to sit in the office all day, but I understand you want to catch up. You should ask Charlotte if you can go part-time."

"Why?" I asked.

"Well, I make enough money at my job. We don't even need your income. At the same time, I understand it's important for you to have some structure."

"But Rodney, you know I love working."

"I know, I know. But darling, I want you to be able to enjoy life more. You could have extra time to go shopping and perhaps find ways to meet some friends."

I feel like he should be more concerned about my ability to remember things before I make more changes in my life. Besides, if I worked part-time, I wouldn't have the money to support myself if we got divorced.

When we get divorced… I heard myself immediately think.

"Rodney, that is nice of you to say, but how about we make sure I can get through this day first before I think about making any changes in my life," I said with a smile.

"Deal!" he responded.

As we got into his truck, I was about to ask when he got this thing and what happened to his SUV, but I knew he would tell me something that didn't make sense.

I had a thought, though, in his car, I'd always keep a small bottle of hand sanitizer in the passenger door. I looked in all of the compartments in the door, but there was nothing. In fact, absolutely nothing. No tissues, hair ties, or old receipts. It was so clean that it seemed like a brand-new truck.

It would be extreme to buy a new vehicle while I was away for only two weeks, but then again, the entire house is different…so maybe it is right in line with the theme of being extreme.

Luckily, my office was only a couple of miles away. I remembered exactly how to get there.

As we pulled in, I couldn't get out of the car fast enough.

"Amelia, wait! You need to kiss me goodbye."

Ugh. I didn't want to. I forced myself to turn around and hug him and give him a quick kiss goodbye.

"I'll pick you up at 5 pm, okay?"

"Make it 6 pm, I am sure I have a lot to catch up on," I said.

"Okay, good luck today. See you tonight!"

Finally, he was pulling out of the parking lot. I walked up to the office and punched in the door code. It opened. I remembered the office key code…

Once I walked in, everything was exactly how I left it! I could have cried, I was so happy. The feeling of seeing all the same furniture and even the same stacks of mail as I left them was so comforting.

As I sat down in my office chair, I had never thought that simply sitting at a familiar desk could bring me so much joy.

I opened up my computer and started going through some emails. I sent one to Charlotte, letting her know I was back and wanted to connect with her on the phone. It was about a twelve-hour time difference, so it was the evening as I was writing it. I kept it short and to the point. About five minutes after I sent it, she replied. I eagerly opened it.

Amelia!

Welcome back! I hope you are well rested.

I have been swamped here, so how about I give you a call towards the end of the week?

-Char

End of the week?! Ugh. I didn't want to wait that long, but I also didn't want to be a pest since she had just given me two weeks off.

I decided I just needed to buckle down and focus on work and getting caught up.

One email I received was from someone requesting fabric samples. I loved going to the fabric store, so I figured I could go that afternoon.

Wait.

I don't have a car. I couldn't take a taxi because I didn't have any money, and it was too far to walk. I will need to ask Rodney to borrow one of his credit cards so I can go tomorrow.

The day flew by, and it was the most normal I had felt since I was at the beach. Before I knew it, it was almost 6 pm. As I finished up for the day, I saw Rodney pulling into the parking lot.

I locked the door behind me and started to walk towards his truck.

His new truck, which he claimed wasn't new.

Rodney got out of the truck, came up, and gave me a giant hug.

"Oh, I missed you, darling. I hope your day wasn't too strenuous," he said.

Before I left for the beach, he would barely say hi to me when I would return home from work. This was definitely out of character.

"Oh, it was fine, I guess. Where are we going to dinner? I'm starving," I asked.

"Did you need to go home, or should we go straight to dinner?" Rodney asked me.

"I'm ready to have a glass of wine after my first day back!" I exclaimed.

Rodney laughed. "Okay, I know just the spot to take you."

We got into the truck and headed toward downtown. He pulled up in front of a little Italian restaurant. It was where I met him.

"This is where we first met?" I said.

"Yes! Oh good, I was hoping you would remember this spot since it is such a special place to us, plus I thought maybe it would help with some of the other memory…issues," he said hesitantly.

"Speaking of, did you call the doctor?"

"Crap. No, I am so sorry, Amelia. It was such a hectic day at work that it completely slipped my mind. I will call tomorrow," he said.

I didn't believe him. Your wife comes back from a beach trip and claims not to remember a single thing in the house? How could anyone have that slip their mind? I felt mad and frustrated, but also knew I could not do anything at the moment. As much as I hated it, I reminded myself I had to play Rodney's game until I could figure out what exactly was going on.

After returning to work and recalling all the details about my job and the office, I began to wonder what had happened to the house. It does not make sense that I would remember everything else in my life…

"Well, that is okay. Just call tomorrow, will you?" I asked with a fake smile.

"Of course! And again, I am sorry I didn't earlier," he said, seemingly sincere.

As we walked in, Rodney requested that we sit at the bar facing the window. It was where we first sat. It was such a fun and unexpected evening when I met him on my first night in Asheville. A part of me wondered where this relationship went so wrong.

We sat down and looked at the menu.

"What looks good to you?" I asked.

"How about you pick a couple of items, and we can share them. So, pick your top two favorite entrees!" he said with a smile.

This was weird because over the last several years, Rodney had basically criticized everything I wanted to order and also hated sharing his food with me. To the point I stopped even asking to have a bite of his.

"Well… okay. How about we share a garden salad and get the chicken parmesan?" I timidly asked.

"That sounds perfect! Do you want to get an order of calamari as well?" he asked.

"Oh yes, that sounds good!" Gosh, why hasn't it always been this easy with him? It was when we met, but he just ended up changing over time… it was almost like he switched back to his former self. The problem was that I knew he had another side to him, which was not the type of person I wanted to be with, let alone live with and be married to.

We chatted a bit about our days, nothing major, but it was relatively light and easy. Recently, our dinners had become so miserable for me because it seemed like Rodney was arguing with me over almost everything I said.

I couldn't help but think about what a doctor was going to say to me about everything I had been dealing with. I would probably sound like a crazy person to him. But then again, maybe I wouldn't?

Our food came, and it was such an enjoyable meal. The conversation stayed polite and friendly. Rodney was even making me laugh more than usual, too. I almost felt as if I was in an alternate reality.

As we finished up and drove home, once I saw those new bushes out front, I couldn't help but get a sinking feeling in my stomach. Being at work where everything was as I left it and going to a restaurant that was also familiar to me made me feel much more "normal." Knowing I had to walk back into this house, where absolutely nothing was familiar, was mentally draining and upsetting, to say the least.

"Home sweet home," Rodney said

I couldn't help but laugh a little. Luckily, Rodney didn't notice, but how on earth could he even say something like that to me when he knows I have complained about not recognizing anything?

Then again, how could I recognize something that I had never seen before…

We went inside, I showered, and then we settled in to watch some TV.

As we were getting ready for bed, right before I fell asleep, I said, "You're calling the doctor tomorrow, right?"

Rodney didn't respond. I immediately heard him snoring.

Chapter 26

When I woke up, Rodney was already out of bed. I put my robe on, and as I walked down the hall, I started to smell coffee.

"Good morning, my darling!" Rodney said as he approached me for a hug.

What's with all the hugging? He only did that for a very short time when we first started dating.

As he hugged me, he said, "Today is going to be a great day, I can just feel it!"

"What? Why?" I asked.

"Hey, I am just trying to be positive. It's good to set your intention for the day right when you get up."

Who was this man? I mean, I do like that he's been so polite and positive towards me, but it just doesn't add up. I instantly got the vision of him breaking the wine glass on the kitchen table.

That memory hasn't gone away.

Perhaps it is staying for a reason. As much as Rodney tells me I do not remember things, I do. I swear I remember everything.

Well… just about everything.

After breakfast, he drove me to work and hugged me again.

"I will make us something healthy for dinner tonight, and you are sure you don't need me to pick you up for lunch?" he asked.

"No, I'll be fine. I made a quick sandwich when you were in the shower this morning. I'll see you after work – 5 pm should be fine for tonight." I was eager to have him leave. My day yesterday was relatively peaceful, as I didn't have to be around him. There was not one person I encountered to tell me I didn't remember something.

At that moment, I couldn't help but think about how we can plan out our lives as much as we want…but things can very quickly go awry.

I needed to figure out how to get it back on track.

Something was not right about this situation, and I could feel it.

As much as I tried to focus on work that day, I couldn't help but also focus on what had happened during the last few weeks. I was at a complete loss for what I should do, aside from staying entirely dependent on Rodney. In a way, until I had my ID back, what could I do?

The police.

Could I go to the police? I guess I could explain my situation and see. I immediately googled the nearest police station, but it was a 15-minute drive.

Oh, screw it, I will call from the office.

I looked up the non-emergency number. Even though I felt like it was an emergency, I knew the police wouldn't see it that way.

"Asheville police," a man said when he answered the phone.

"Hello, uhh, umm," I started to get tongue-tied.

"Ma'am? You okay?" the man asked.

"Umm. Well, yes and no. You see, I really think I need to talk to an officer and explain what I'm going through."

"Are you in immediate danger?"

"No."

"Are you in a safe space?"

"Yes, yes, I am. It's a bit of a weird story, I'm afraid. And a long one."

"Okay, well, can you come into the station? I can let you talk to an officer."

"No, I am afraid not. You see, I was told my purse was stolen, so now I do not have my ID and can't drive."

"You were told your purse was stolen? By who?" he asked.

"My husband told me."

"Did you all report it missing?"

"No. Well, he told me I did."

"But you don't know if you did?" The man was growing increasingly more confused.

"Like I said, it's a long story, but I really need to talk to an officer."

"Okay, but you do know people drive without having an ID all the time if it gets stolen. You won't go to jail for something like that."

That had never even occurred to me. Rodney had made me feel like I just couldn't drive at all.

"Oh…I guess I didn't even think of that. Thank you for telling me."

"So, ma'am, do you need me to send an officer to you, or now that you know you can drive, do you want to come to the station?"

"Well, I guess I will just come tomorrow. Would that work?" I asked. I guess one more day wouldn't matter. Maybe it would give me some time to gather my thoughts more.

"Umm, yes, that will be fine. I appreciate your help. I will come tomorrow," I said.

"Sounds good, ma'am. Have a good rest of your day."

I had never considered going to the police, but maybe they could offer some help. I finally felt a little bit of hope. Between talking to the police tomorrow and Charlotte at the end of the week, something has to start making sense.

The day flew by, and before I knew it, it was 5 pm. I packed up my things and saw Rodney pulling in the parking lot.

My heart sank when I saw him. Something just was not right.

My heart sank even more when I saw him step out of his truck to greet me with his usual hug.

"Darling!" he said as he wrapped his arms around me. "How was day two? Are you feeling okay?"

"Oh, it was a good day. Nothing too crazy."

As we drove home, I mentally prepared myself to act happy and not let Rodney know how much I was questioning things. He'd have to slip up eventually if he did something wrong.

We pulled in, I went inside and changed into some more comfortable clothing, and met Rodney in the kitchen.

"What's for dinner?" I asked.

He laughed. "Someone must be hungry! I'm making us honey garlic shrimp, with rice and steamed broccoli."

"Wow, that does sound good!"

Rodney and I chatted a bit about our day. He was funny, polite, and engaging. Even though I didn't know what was going on in my situation, it was almost easy to forget that something was still wrong with it when he was so nice to me.

And fun.

And handsome.

I couldn't help but notice Rodney looked like he was shedding a few pounds and was looking more physically fit than he had in a long time. I am sure that eating healthier was paying off for him, and I have to admit, I was becoming much more physically attracted to him because of it. It always amazed me how quickly most men could lose weight by making even simple changes to their routines.

I was also drawn to what seemed like his entire new healthy routine—and positive attitude. He seemed so light and happy. It is hard not to be drawn to happy people, as I believe good energy is contagious.

I snapped myself out of it.

Something is still very clearly wrong, and I was determined to get to the bottom of it.

"Rodney, I'm going to drive to work tomorrow," I said boldly.

He stopped cooking and looked up. "But you don't have your ID."

"Yes, but that is fine. I realized people lose their IDs all the time and still drive until their new one comes. I will need to go to the DMV to request a new one. Perhaps I can do that tomorrow."

Rodney did not seem to like my suggestion. He was quiet for several seconds, then managed to flash a smile and say, "That sounds like a great idea, darling."

Well. That was easy enough.

"This actually would work out because I have to be in my office by 8 am for a meeting. I was going to try to change it, but I will leave it now," he said.

"Perfect! Okay, how much longer until we eat? I can't handle how good it smells for much longer. I need to taste it!" We both laughed.

"Here, I'll give you a small shrimp to try." Rodney scooped one up on a spoon and gave it to me.

"Oh my gosh, Rodney! You could quit your day job and become a chef at this point!"

Rodney blushed a little. "Well, thank you, darling, but the only one around here who needs to be thinking about quitting their job is you," he said with a smile.

I didn't have the energy to have that discussion again, so I started to set the table instead. As I was doing that, Rodney turned on some classical music in the background and poured each of us a glass of wine.

As we were sitting down, Rodney grabbed my hand across the table. "You know what one of my favorite days with you has been?"

"No, when?"

"Well, besides the day I met you, the day I married you."

The day we were married—my wedding dress. My mind flashed back to the picture of our wedding day, but my dress was different in the picture. Rodney noticed the concerned look on my face. I snapped myself out of it.

"Yes, that was such a wonderful day."

"What do you think about going back to the same resort for a little vacation at some point?"

"That could be nice." Would it, though? I'm really confused about how I feel and what I should feel.

"Rodney, this dinner is amazing."

"I'm so glad you like it! I'll clean up, and you can go relax on the couch."

"No, I will help you!"

"Darling, I insist. Go relax," he said.

"Well…if you insist, then I guess I have no choice."

"Can I have another glass of wine, though?" I asked as Rodney was heading towards the fridge."

He laughed. "That is just what I was going to get, a little more wine for us each. It is like you can read my mind, Amelia."

I definitely could not read his mind, but I did appreciate him being so nice to me.

The next morning, I woke up, excited to drive myself to work and… to the police station. I got out of bed, and of course smelled coffee brewing. As I walked into the kitchen, I saw freshly made scrambled eggs and sliced fruit.

"Good morning, darling, how did you sleep?" Rodney asked.

"Like a rock. I didn't even wake up once," I replied.

"That's good. So, are you sure you're feeling comfortable enough to drive?"

"Yes, definitely, besides it's not far," I said.

"Well..." Rodney was looking down and shuffling his feet. For a second, I was worried he'd talk me out of it or make up some excuse. "Just please be careful?"

Phew.

"Yes, of course I will! I can even call you from the office to let you know I made it. I'd text you, but I still don't have a phone..."

"Oh gosh, yes, I am sorry. I will go buy you one today."

Okay, well... it seemed like things are falling back into place a bit for me. Now I can drive, and will have my phone back.

"I need to call the doctor as well."

"Okay, I am off. I will call you when I'm at the office," I said.

It was weird being back in my car. As soon as I got in, the memories of my beach drive came flooding back to me. I was so determined to come home and tell Rodney we were done. I decided to shift my focus and remain in the present again. I am going to drive to the office, call Rodney, then drive to the police station.

"Hi, Rodney! It's me, I'm at work," I said.

"That was fast! All went okay?"

"Yes, it is so close, so it was fine. I'd better go. I have a lot of stuff to get to."

"Okay, my dear, let me know if you need anything, and I will see you tonight," he said.

As soon as I hung up, I grabbed my keys and headed to the police station. On the drive there, I had a lot of strange feelings. Was I really going to report my husband? Apparently, I was. Besides, I know Rodney is behind all of this. I don't understand why…But I know he is.

I pulled into the parking lot and had a bad feeling, but I am sure it was just nerves.

When I walked in, an officer was sitting behind a glass section.

"Hello ma'am, what can I help you with?" he asked.

"I uhh… umm... uhh…"

"Ma'am? Are you okay?"

"Yes, yes, I am sorry, I am just nervous. I need to talk to someone."

"About what?"

"Well, you see, it's kind of complicated. Someone stole my purse." It was the only thing that seemed to make sense when talking to the officer.

"Oh, okay, so you came here to file a police report. Walk through that door to your left, and it will let you back here."

I walked through the door and was no longer separated by the glass, and could see multiple desks and offices. The officer picked up the phone, asked another officer to come to the front desk, and hung up.

"Officer Smith will be right out to talk to you. I'm sorry about your purse. That is always such a hassle to deal with."

"Yes, it is. Thank you for your help."

Just then, the other officer came up to me, "Hi, I'm Officer Smith. Follow me."

I followed him down a hall and then into his office.

"So, your purse was stolen? When and where did this happen?"

"Officer, that's the thing. I was told it was stolen."

"You were told it was?" He looked at me, confused.

"Well, yes. You see, there is a bit of a story behind this stolen purse."

"I'm all ears," he said as he leaned back in his chair.

"You see, I live here in Asheville and went to the beach to clear my head about my relationship. I was there for a couple of weeks and had decided I wanted to come back and tell my husband I wanted a divorce."

"I'm sure he was thrilled to hear that," Officer Smith said.

"Well…that's the thing. I actually never told him that."

"Ma'am, I'm sorry, but I thought you came here to report a stolen purse?'

"Yes, so when I came back, I know this is going to sound very bizarre, but everything inside and outside of our house was different."

"Different? How so?"

"Everything. The landscaping, the furniture, the wallpaper, even framed pictures were different. Dishes, you name it, it was not at all as I left it. And when I walked into the house, I was so overwhelmed I passed out."

"You passed out because you were overwhelmed?"

"Well, I had forgotten to eat that day, or most of it, because of my nervousness."

"Well, what happened when you came back around?"

"I had asked my husband for my purse, not immediately but soon after, and he said it was stolen at the beach. He told me I reported it stolen."

"Did you?"

"That's just it, I don't remember it being stolen at all!"

"So… let me get this straight. You haven't been happy with your husband, which he probably knew to some extent, I am guessing. You go to the beach to work up the courage to ask for a divorce, but while you were away, he was busy updating the house. Probably to make you happier and to keep you with him. Some of us men don't realize we need to put effort in until it is just about too late. Your husband sounds like one of the smarter ones and tried fixing it just in the nick of time."

Wait, what? He isn't listening to me. Or am I not explaining it correctly?

"So, honestly, ma'am, if you don't even remember where your purse was stolen, I am not sure if there is a point in filing a claim. We can, just in case someone finds it and turns it in, but that almost never happens after this amount of time. In the meantime, I think you ought to appreciate all the effort your husband is putting into your home and relationship. Most guys would never do that."

Oh my God. I was the confused one now.

"But don't you think my story is odd? Things aren't adding up."

I could tell he was losing his patience with me a little.

"Ma'am, no offense, but perhaps you should be asking a therapist this. Us police officers really aren't in the business of arresting men for interior decorating."

"Well, that's just it, I work for an interior designer, and there is no way he could have pulled that all off, especially without my help."

"So, are you in the field itself?"

"Yes, sir."

"Well, that just makes this situation even clearer – he was trying to impress you in an area you are familiar with."

I give up. There was no way I was getting through to this officer.

"I suppose you're right. Well, I'd best get back to work and on with my day. Thank you for your time," I said, as I felt utterly defeated.

"You too, ma'am, and remember… maybe find a good therapist."

"Sure thing," I said and managed to crack half a smile.

Chapter 27

I could not get out of that police station fast enough. As soon as I got into my car, I broke down crying. I have no one to believe me! If the police won't, who will?

Charlotte.

I forgot she was going to call me this week. Oh, she has to be able to help. She will!

I dried my tears and sped back to the office.

As I dashed in the front door and opened up my email, I saw one from Charlotte.

THANK GOD.

> *Amelia – I am done with my meetings for the day – if you aren't too busy, call my cell so we can catch up!*
> *-Char*

I picked up the phone faster than ever before. This was it; this was going to be the call that saved me. Charlotte will believe me.

"Amelia! How are you? How was your vacation?" Charlotte asked.

Where do I even begin?

"Umm. It was good," I managed to say.

"Oh great! You went to the beach, right? Did you go with that boyfriend of yours? What's his name again? Oh, Rodney!"

Boyfriend?

"Well, he's my husband, but no, I went alone."

"Amelia!!! You got married! Oh my gosh, you didn't tell me! Did you elope?!" Charlotte was sounding so excited. How did she not remember I was married?

I was starting to have a hard time finding the right words.

"We got married a few years ago. But it hasn't been good lately, so I went to the beach to clear my head."

Charlotte was silent for a bit.

"Charlotte? Are you still there?" I asked.

"Yes, but, Amelia, what do you mean you got married years ago? Do you live with him?"

"Of course I do! I moved in with him before we were married."

"Why didn't you tell me you moved in and got married? I am so confused by this." Charlotte's tone went from excitement to concern.

"Charlotte, I'm so sorry, I thought I did. I had no reason not to, unless I was just so caught up in my head during the wedding planning. I really can't give you a proper explanation, and I am sorry for that. But listen, I went to the beach to clear my head and decided I wanted to leave Rodney and get a divorce. When I arrived home, though, the house was totally different!"

"Different? What do you mean?" she asked.

"Oh, everything, Charlotte, from the dishes to cabinet colors to the landscaping. It was like I came back to an entirely new house. I think Rodney is trying to convince me not to leave him, and also not let me because I think he took my purse, so I have no credit cards or ID at the moment. It's a living nightmare, and I don't know what to do. I even just went to the police, and they said it sounded like he was trying to make me happy."

"So… let me get this straight. You moved in with your boyfriend, got engaged, got married, and never told me. Now you are saying that your husband has drastically changed your house after you were away at the beach for a couple of weeks. Which you and I both know from a decorator's viewpoint, that is near impossible for even the best of us to accomplish, let alone a male."

I didn't know what to say. I sounded completely crazy to Charlotte, and I have to be honest, I can't even blame her. I had to try to do some damage control to save my job since it is literally all I have right now.

"I'm sorry. I realize none of this even sounds like it makes sense," I said, on the verge of tears.

"Amelia, I don't even know what to say. Let's just focus on work for now, and if you need to discuss this further when I am back…maybe we can. I'm staying here another week, then flying straight to Los Angeles to meet with some potential new clients. If you need anything, just email or call me per usual."

"Okay, sounds good. Thank you, Charlotte." And with that, we hung up.

I didn't get much work done for the rest of the day. I felt numb and confused inside.

Just then, the phone rang.

"Charlotte's Interiors, this is Amelia."

"Amelia."

It was Rodney.

"Amelia, are you there?" he asked.

"Oh, yes, yes, I'm here."

"I was able to get a doctor to make a house call. Would 4 pm today work?"

Well, by the way this day had been going, I wasn't sure if I should let myself have any hope about meeting with a doctor or not, but I supposed it couldn't hurt.

"Yes, that will be fine. I will leave work a little early and be back by 4."

I had no clue what I was going to say to the doctor.

Around 3:30 pm, I got in the car and headed home. I felt so hopeless after today. I needed to make a plan of action, but didn't know which way to turn.

As I pulled onto our street, I saw a car at the house. I checked the time, and it was only 3:40 pm. Rodney said the doctor was coming at 4 pm, unless he is just very early.

I walked into the house and saw Rodney and the doctor sitting in the living room.

"Amelia, this is Dr. Johnson," Rodney said.

"Pleased to meet you, Amelia." He extended his hand to shake mine.

"Yes, I am sorry I didn't think you were coming until 4."

The doctor looked at Rodney. Then back at me. "Let's all just sit down for a little."

We all sat down in the living room.

"Rodney has told me about what has happened to you over the last week or so."

He has?

"It sounds like you have been through a lot, and I'm sorry to hear this."

"Doctor Johnson thinks he knows what is going on with you, Amelia," Rodney said.

"You do?" I asked.

"This may be a bit challenging to hear, but from what it sounds like, when you hit your head, you must have given yourself selective amnesia. Or perhaps you hit your head while on your beach trip. Rodney mentioned you do not remember anything in the house, but do remember many other things. Is that accurate?"

I just stared at him.

He went on, "One might describe it as retrograde amnesia – this is the inability to recall memories from before the injury."

Amnesia? This could not be true.

I had thought my day was bad before, but this really takes the cake, to put it lightly. I felt like getting anyone on my side at this point was a losing battle. I needed to stay strong for myself, though, because I know something is very wrong with this situation.

"What can she do? Does she need to go on medication?" Rodney asked the doctor.

"Unfortunately, there are no medications currently available, but the good news is your memory will most likely come back over time."

"How much time?" I asked. While I did not believe this, I decided I needed to commit to playing the part.

The doctor looked down and shook his head. "Well, it really depends. It could last years, but I am hopeful that won't be your case."

"Is there anything I can do to help her in the meantime?" Rodney asked.

I wanted to yell at him to shut up. I am convinced he is the reason I'm in this situation anyway.

"Nothing in particular, but I feel that you should try to repeat stories and fun memories that you two had. The closer to the beach trip, the better, it may help. It may not, but we never know."

Well, I know he will be lying with those stories because we have not shared any positive memories in months.

"Well, folks, I'd better be going and leave you to enjoy your evening. Amelia, try to take it easy on yourself. These things can take time - no need for any additional stress on your mind at this time."

We both walked the doctor out.

Rodney then turned and hugged me. After my frustrating day, I let myself cry.

"Oh, I'm sorry, darling, this is so bad, but at least we have some answers now and can start to move forward. I am so glad we talked to the doctor because it just seems like everything makes sense now."

I sobbed into Rodney's chest, not for a sense of comfort, but out of a sense of extreme frustration. I had to play the part. I had to let him think I believe him and this doctor.

I needed to get out of this situation, but it was pretty clear it would not happen overnight.

Once I calmed down, Rodney took a step back and grabbed my hands. "I promise I will see you through this. You're my wife, it's my duty."

Ugh. The word wife made me cringe. The last thing I wanted to be was his wife.

"Thank you, my love, I don't know what I'd do without you," I lied.

"Let's go get some dinner. I have a chicken casserole and some steamed broccoli."

We walked towards the kitchen, and he pulled out a chair for me at the dining room table.

As I sat down, I simply could not believe what had happened throughout this entire day.

Rodney went to the kitchen and pulled a bottle of wine from the fridge. At this point, he may as well skip the glass and just put the entire bottle in front of me. He must have read my mind to an extent, because he filled the wine glass to the brim.

"Wow! That's a lot!" I said.

"Well, we were both just informed you are suffering from amnesia. I think we both deserve to have a full glass tonight. Besides, we can reminisce about old memories like the doctor told us to."

No thanks to that....

"It smells so good!" I said, which wasn't a lie.

"Oh, I'm glad! It's a new recipe and supposed to be lower in sodium," Rodney said as he brought the casserole dish to the table. "Let me quickly grab the broccoli."

As I took my first bite of the casserole, I could not believe how savory it was.

"Rodney, I will say, I definitely do not remember you being such a great cook." I did not remember it, but I swear he never was... or it had just been so long since he actually cooked for me.

"Just think of all the amazing meals I've made for you that you don't even remember!" he said with a little laugh.

I stared at him in disgust for a moment until I forced myself to laugh, too. Even if I did have amnesia, which I don't, would it be appropriate to make a joke so soon? Doubtful.

I decided I did not have the mental capacity for the rest of that evening to try to come up with a plan. I was mentally drained from the day, so I thought it was best to play along and let Rodney steer the conversation for the rest of the evening. I was very clearly a bit more reserved, but he either didn't notice or didn't care.

When I got into bed that night, I hoped I'd wake up with an idea about what to do. I woke up several times during the night and turned to face Rodney. He was sleeping so peacefully, like he didn't have a care in the world. That seemed to be the case with him, as long as I was a part of his world.

I didn't want to be a part of his world.

Eventually, I wore myself out trying to think of ways to explain what was happening in my life and fell back to sleep.

When I woke up in the morning, Rodney was out of bed, and per usual, I smelled coffee brewing.

It was Thursday. I was looking forward to going to work, as for the most part, I felt relatively sane there. I would not be feeling like that when Charlotte returns, though.

I got up, went into the kitchen, and was greeted by a hug and a kiss from Rodney.

"I made you oatmeal with fruit this morning, darling."

"Thank you, I appreciate it," I said with a smile.

We didn't exchange too many words that morning, which I was thankful for. As much as I was able to pretend things were okay, I knew in my heart they weren't. I just wanted to get to work and try to come up with a plan.

"Do you want me to drive you to work?" he asked.

"What? No, why? I can."

"Okay, I just know you had a lot of news delivered to you yesterday," he said as he grabbed my hand across the table."

"I'm fine, I promise, besides, he said my memory will most likely come back, so I think it is best if I try to act as normal as possible."

"That's true. Okay, well, call me from the office if you need me."

"Rodney, we need to get me a cell phone, remember?"

"Oh yes, you know I went to the store yesterday, but the line was so long I didn't have time. I will try again today."

"Thank you," I said as I cleaned up the kitchen and got ready to drive to work.

When I arrived at work, I made myself some coffee and just sat down at my desk and stared off into the distance. I really was not sure what to think. I did not know which way to turn. If I had money, I could just leave. But then again, I really need to get my ID replaced.

I logged on to my computer and looked up the requirements for getting a new driver's license. I was able to renew online using my Social Security number, but I needed a form of payment. The in-person option offered two ways to prove my identification. I could use my Social Security card and my passport. I decided I would gather those items while at home, assuming they were still in my closet where I left them, and go tomorrow to get a new license.

Something told me I needed to do this behind Rodney's back. The less he knew about my life at the moment, the better. Besides, if he didn't know I had a new ID.... he couldn't accuse me of having it stolen like he did before.

I decided I would spend my days creating a solid plan to escape. I wanted to go back to New York City. I wanted to be in a city so big that Rodney would have no chance of finding me.

Of course, I was on top of my work, but it was a bit slower while Charlotte was traveling anyway. Sometimes I wondered why she had an office at all, but I suppose it was a good place for her to keep track of all her jobs and files. She used to have more local business when I moved down, but has become much more popular globally by word of mouth.

As the day went on, I was eager to get home and make sure I could find my documentation in my closet. I prayed that Rodney hadn't moved it.

I finished up some emails, and before I knew it, it was 5 pm. I locked up and sped home.

Chapter 28

Thankfully, Rodney's truck was not there. He must still be at work. I went into the house, threw my work bags down, and went into the guest room. I have some extra stuff stored there, as Rodney had already mostly filled the main closet.

I flung open the door and looked on the top shelf. I breathed a sigh of relief when I found the box I had that was hidden behind some old shoeboxes.

I reached for it.

When I opened it, I breathed an even bigger sigh of relief when I saw my passport and Social Security card.

Thank God.

I grabbed the items to put into my work bag, and then I noticed something else.

A manila envelope.

What is in that? I wondered. I pulled it out of the box, and it was rather thick.

Oh, my God.

My mind raced back to when I filled this envelope. I opened it.

Cash.

Tons of cash.

I had completely forgotten that when we got married, Rodney was pressuring me into combining our bank accounts. Unfortunately for him and fortunately for me, I had just watched a crazy movie about a woman trying to escape a relationship, but she didn't have any of her own money since he locked her out of their accounts. I had literally watched it a few days before we met at the bank, and had gone there before to withdraw $20,000 cash. Rodney never asked how much I had in savings, so when we combined, there were no questions asked.

I fell down to the ground and cried a little. I would have cried more, but I knew Rodney would be home at any second.

Between that movie and all those strangers warning me about Rodney, I finally listened. Then I forgot I had actually taken some action, because overall things have been fine.

Until they weren't.

But… I finally felt some hope.

I was planning to visit the office tomorrow to research jobs and apartments in New York. And get myself out of this mess.

I put the box back and went to find my work bag, where I put both the money and the documents. I was not sure if that was the best idea with the money, but I needed to keep it in the office.

Just then, I had an idea. I needed to go back to the office right now, while Rodney was still not here. If he sees me leave, I will just say I forgot my bag at work.

I grabbed my keys and went out the door. I almost forgot to lock it. I was in such a rush. After running back to lock it, I made a dash to my car. Threw the bag in the trunk and sped off. Thank goodness there was no sign of Rodney. I knew once I was out of the neighborhood, I would be fine.

I arrived at the office, retrieved my bag from the trunk, and went back inside. I had some drawers in my desk that I could lock, and until now, I never really had much that needed locking. I put the cash and documents into the drawer and sat down to breathe another sigh of relief.

I didn’t stay long after that because I didn't want to answer any questions from Rodney.

I drove home and saw that Rodney was home.

As I pulled into the driveway and turned off the car, I smiled. I couldn’t believe I had put that money aside, and I also couldn’t believe I had forgotten about it. But boy was I thankful.

As I walked along the path with the new bushes, I found myself caring a lot less. Soon, I wouldn’t be seeing these bushes at all.

I walked into the house and, of course, it smelled wonderful from whatever Rodney was making.

"Hi darling! I'm in the kitchen!" He yelled.

I put my stuff down and walked into the kitchen to see a glass of white wine waiting for me.

It is too bad he is such a liar, because he can definitely pull off being a good husband.

"Oh, thank you! You really do know the way to my heart," I said with a smile.

It was much easier to act happy, knowing I now had a plan in the works to leave.

"It is such a lovely evening. Do you want to go sit outside by the fountain?" Rodney asked.

"Sounds delightful!" I responded.

"Well, you sure seem to be in a good mood. Did Charlotte come back?"

Oh gosh, I wanted to say no, she didn't, and I am glad because she thinks I am nuts too.

"No, but we talked yesterday, and it sounds like she will be back next week. What are you making for dinner?"

"I'm making garlic butter flank steak with rosemary potatoes and green beans," he said.

"That sounds so good! You know, your home cooking is becoming the highlight of my day," I said as I leaned into him for a hug.

I was so proud of my acting skills. I felt like I was finally getting a grip on my situation, how to deal with it, and most importantly… how to get out of it.

I made some light conversation until dinner was ready. And then we made more light conversation during dinner, which I was only engaged with on the surface.

I was trying to stay in the moment, but it was also a bit hard because, in my mind, I was planning every detail I could about leaving town.

Clothes. I had a lot of clothes and realized I should take a few items in my work bag each day and store them at my office until I was ready to leave town. Rodney would never notice them missing. Then I realized I could come home on my lunch breaks and take more. I planned on finding an apartment that would most likely have nothing in it, so I needed to be as strategic as possible in the coming days.

The next morning, I put my plan into action. I wore a sweater with a couple of t-shirts underneath, and brought a cardigan, and was able to get a few other garments into my bag without Rodney knowing.

I was hoping Rodney would leave for work before me, but he didn't. I will come home during the day and get more.

Once at the office, I stashed the clothes in a bag in our closet. Then I headed to the DMV. It was about 10 minutes from the office, so not far.

I walked in to find there was hardly anyone in line, which I appreciated since it was packed the last time I moved to town.

When I was called to the desk, I let the woman know I needed a replacement license and gave her my documents.

"Did you lose yours?" she asked.

"Umm, yes. At the beach."

"Oh, that's too bad! I hope the trip was good though!"

I smiled, "It was great. I mean, one can never have a bad time at the beach anyway."

"That's true." She returned my documents. "Okay, stand back just a couple of feet, and I will take your picture."

Once she took the picture, she let me know she would go pick it up from the printer.

Oh wow, you look so happy in this picture!" she said.

"I am," I smiled.

I drove back to the office and started looking up both jobs and apartments. Apartments worried me because I know they can be expensive in New York, especially in the good areas.

As I was going through listings, I grew even more worried. Many studios were at least $3,000 a month. Which would probably last me about three to four months with other expenses. Then I saw an ad pop up for affordable housing for women.

I clicked on it, not expecting much. The more I read about this building for women, the more excited I grew. It was for women in school or transition, provided two meals a day, included a bed, desk, and a dresser, and even had 24/7 security. I scrolled through the site looking for pricing.

$1200 for a single room. Oh my gosh, that will let me have plenty of time to find a job! I was so excited. I immediately picked up the phone to call and ask about the availability.

"Thank you for calling The Residences of New York. How may I help you?" a woman asked.

"Hi! I am looking to move to New York, and wondering if you have any availability? I'm moving there to find a job," I said, trying not to sound too desperate.

As I walked back towards the house, I reminded myself to take some deep breaths. I needed to stay focused...and fake in front of Rodney.

As I walked in, I went to the kitchen and he was already whipping up dinner.

"Hi darling! Were you out on a walk?" he asked as he came to hug me.

"Yes, it is such a nice evening out. It felt good to stretch my legs after sitting in the office all day," I said.

"Oh, I bet – too bad I wasn't home to go with you."

I was so glad he wasn't home to go with me. "Oh, we have plenty more nights to be able to, so don't worry about that," I lied.

It felt oddly good to lie to Rodney.

After all the things he has lied to me about…it was a small piece of mental revenge.

"What's for dinner tonight?" I asked.

"Chicken piccata with a Caesar salad," he replied.

"Sounds amazing per usual," I said with a smile.

I started to set the table and was preparing more lies in my mind to tell Rodney about my day in the office.

"I had such a busy day, my dear, how was yours?" I asked.

As he brought the food over to the table, I went to grab a bottle of wine for us.

"You know, it was a bit stressful, but I am just glad it's over and I can have dinner with my lovely wife."

Funny, we could not feel any different at the moment.

"I am sorry to hear that, mine was…a bit stressful too. Well, maybe stressful is not the right word. It was definitely busy… and productive." I guess that wasn't exactly a lie.

Rodney was supposed to have gotten me a cell phone that day, but I assumed he didn't. I also realized, if he did, he would be able to track me when I leave town and also probably know my every move leading up to that, so I thought it was best not bring it up. I would have to go to a store and buy a prepaid phone. When I get to New York, I can get a phone with a New York number.

It just occurred to me that my resume that I had been sending out had my old cell phone on it. Maybe I shouldn't worry about the jobs as much until I get to New York and get a little settled.

"Darling? Are you okay?" Rodney asked.

I realized I got lost in thoughts about my planning.

"Oh, oh yes! I am so sorry. I was just thinking about a work thing today with a client."

I reached out for his hand across the table. "You're much more important than my client, though, Rodney, please forgive me," I said with a smile.

"Of course, darling," he said as he squeezed my hand.

When he did that, I had a flashback of the night I got back from the beach, and he squeezed my hand so hard it hurt me.

I could not wait to leave. I could not wait to get back to the office tomorrow to finish up my planning.

After dinner, we cleaned up and went to watch a show that Rodney picked out. It was so boring that I let myself fall asleep on the couch. The extra perk to that was that I didn't need to sleep next to Rodney.

Even though there was only going to be a twin bed in New York for me, it would be all mine. I would not need to share it with a man who has been literally driving me crazy.

When I woke up the next morning, I had briefly forgotten I had fallen asleep on the couch. I was surprised to see I had slept straight through the night, but I needed the sleep. Rodney was not up yet, so I got up, made coffee, and sliced up some fruit for us. I could not wait to get back to the office to continue planning.

When Rodney awoke, I was already finishing up my breakfast.

"You're up early. Is everything okay?" Rodney asked.

"Oh yes, I just have a lot of work to get to for Charlotte, so I wanted to get an early start to the day," I said.

"That makes sense. I hate it when you have to work so hard. You really need to think about my offer to quit and enjoy your life."

I went to kiss Rodney goodbye. "I'll think about it, dear."

"Promise?" he asked.

"Promise."

Once I was at the office, I checked my email.

I had two replies to my job applications! Ironically enough, they both asked if I could call them towards the end of next week for an initial phone screening. This worked out perfectly, especially since I will be getting a new number and did not want to have to explain that right away.

I needed to think about my actual move.

How was I actually getting to New York?

I did want to bring some things, so buying a plane ticket would be too complicated. I can't take my car since Rodney could report it stolen, or me missing. I am sure he would come up with something. Plus, I don't need a car in Manhattan.

I'd have to rent a car and drop it off in the city. I could park it just down the street from Rodney's the night before. In the early morning, I could get to it, drive to the office, load up all my clothes and the things I've been slowly bringing into the office, and drive to New York.

I looked up how far the drive was from Asheville to Manhattan—ten and a half hours. I could easily do that in a day, especially if I leave at 3 or 4 in the morning. I would be able to drive to the apartment building, unload my stuff, and drop off the rental car the same evening. Parking was nearly impossible in the city anyway.

Just then, the phone rang in the office, and I nearly jumped.

"Hello?"

"Hi, is this Amelia?"

"Yes, it is. How can I help you?"

"Oh, I am so glad I got a hold of you, dear. This is Joy. I'm calling from The Residences of New York."

"Oh yes, hi, how are you?" I asked.

"Oh, I am good, dear, thank you for asking. Unfortunately, the other two rooms that had been available have been reserved, so I wanted to see if you are still interested in our last available room?"

"YES!" I halfway yelled.

The lady laughed, "Well, I am glad I called you then!"

I laughed too. "I'm so sorry, you actually just caught me in the process of planning my actual move, and I was just getting so excited to move back to the city."

"Oh, I did not realize you had lived here before. Well, the city will be more than glad to have you back!"

I had the biggest smile after she said that.

"How do I reserve the room? And how much will it cost?" I asked.

"Well, since the rent is $1200 a month, we do require a $300 down payment and the rest when you arrive. When did you want to come up again?" she asked.

"I am thinking next week, sometime between Tuesday and Thursday, so perhaps you can start charging me from Tuesday?"

"Oh, dear no, I will reserve it for you starting now anyway. So even if you want to come sooner, the place is yours. We don't start to charge until you actually move in. I can send you a form to wire the $300, if you have access to a bank?"

"Yes, I have a bank account, that will be fine," I said, still smiling.

She let out a breath. "Oh, good, I get so nervous asking people that because you have no idea the number of women who come here trying to escape their husbands or boyfriends, and they often don't have access to any funds. Those are always such sad situations, but we find ways to work with them. You wouldn't believe how grateful they are."

Wow. I really am ending up in the right place.

"Oh, I am sure. It is so nice of you all to do that," I said.

"Okay, well, I will email you the form. And remember…if you need to get out sooner, your room will be ready. We have someone at the front desk 24-7, so you don't even need to call ahead. We're here for you," Joy said.

I had tears come to my eyes. It felt like Joy knew I was in trouble. I don't know how she knew, but she did.

"Thank you so much! I can't even tell you how happy I am that this is all working out, Joy."

"Me too. You will love it here. We are a block away from the river and just a few blocks from Central Park. Call us in the meantime if anything happens. I have your email address….do you have a phone number?"

"Uhh…uhh… Not exactly. I will, though, next week. I want to get a local number," I said, worried about her reaction to me not having a phone number.

"I completely understand, dear, not to worry. Stay safe, and we will see you next week. I am looking forward to meeting you!"

"Thanks, Joy. Me too. I hope you have a great rest of your day."

Once I hung up, I could not help but cry tears of happiness and relief. I knew I still had to get some things in order and deal with Rodney for several more days, but I could manage.

Chapter 29

Charlotte. I need to tell her I am leaving. Something tells me that after our last call, she will have her own form of relief.

I emailed her.

Dear Charlotte,

I hope your trip continues to go well. After some thinking, I need to take some time off and regroup for a bit. With that being said, I am sending you my resignation. If it is okay, I am thinking of making it my last week early next week. Perhaps Tuesday or Wednesday.

I so appreciate everything you have done for me and taught me. You have changed the course of my career path, for which I will always be thankful.

I will leave a list of all our ongoing projects and their current status. Please let me know if there is anything else you need from me in the meantime.

All the best,

Amelia

After sending the email, another sigh of relief washed over me. With each step I made towards my new life, the better I felt.

I needed to find a rental car. Although I suppose they would be asking me the exact day I would pick it up and drop it off. Would Monday be too soon?

Maybe I should say Tuesday… it will give me a chance to bring more of my stuff to the office on Monday. However, I would need to pick it up on Monday evening and park it down the street. Okay, I will make it for Monday evening, but if I need to change it, I probably could.

I logged into a website and reserved a small car. I mainly needed to bring clothes and a few belongings, so that would be fine and better for gas, too.

Once lunchtime came, I decided I would drive home and try to gather more items while Rodney was at work. As I pulled onto the street, I saw that Rodney was not home.

Perfect.

I went to the kitchen and grabbed a couple of trash bags. I figured if Rodney did catch me, I would say I am donating them. Since it was going to be get colder in New York, I made sure to grab a lot of my jeans and coats, especially since they were expensive. I also grabbed sweaters and shoes, and some of my purses. Fortunately, I had so many clothes and accessories that you could hardly tell I took any.

I stuffed everything into the bags, checked out the window to make sure Rodney was not out front, then made a dash to my car. I popped the trunk and threw the bags inside. I was not sure if I should press my luck and fill one more bag, but I did. As I went back to my closet, I wondered what I should grab next. Date clothes! Eventually, I will want to go out on dates or out with new friends in the evening.

I grabbed nice blouses, dresses, skirts, and heels. I also grabbed some of my jewelry from a box I had in my dresser.

All of a sudden, I heard a car door slam.

I froze for a second, then ran to check the window. Thank goodness it was a delivery for the neighbors.

I ran out the front door, locked it behind me, then threw the bag into the trunk and headed to the office.

I was able to grab so many clothes that I don't even know if I need to bother with any more, but maybe I will take one last look this weekend for any pieces I really wanted to take with me.

When I arrived at the office, I quickly hauled my bags inside and put them in a closet. When I drive back to the office on Monday or Tuesday morning, I will have all my stuff consolidated in the closet and make sure to grab my remaining cash from the desk.

I sat down at the desk and let myself relax for a bit, and envisioned my new future. I honestly just needed to make it through this weekend and fake it with Rodney. I needed to try to act as "normal" as possible.

The thought of being with Rodney all weekend made me think I would prefer to leave town Monday morning. I would need to play that by ear since it would mean picking up the car on Sunday and parking it down the street. Maybe if I could get away from him for a little while in the afternoon, that would work out.

Ugh, this would all be so much easier if I had at least one friend! I was going to go out of my way to make many friends in the city.

I have learned multiple things from this nightmare, and one of them is the value of having friendships. While it was hard for me to make friends, I should have tried harder instead of basically giving up. I do not think I would be in this position at all if people had known more about my life. Even neighbors, we should have had them over for dinner and gotten to know them better.

I always prided myself on being so private, and I learned the hard way that I really needed to let people into my life. I will when I am in New York! In fact, I was looking forward to meeting other women in the building.

Another thing that occurred to me in that moment was that I did have multiple…warnings.

Warnings about Rodney.

So many.

All of a sudden, they came flooding back to my mind. The woman I met at the airport bar before I had even moved to Asheville -- someone who didn't know Rodney at that time – told me she had a bad feeling for me. Even the nice girl who did my wedding hair and makeup didn't even have to meet Rodney to know something was off. She took one look at a photo of him, and her entire demeanor changed. The massage therapist in Jamaica practically begged me not to marry him. She must have really trusted her gut… and I should have listened. Or perhaps even trusted mine more.

Thank goodness I pulled cash out of the bank at the last minute. That was the one thing I did that was making it possible to get out of this situation.

The rest of the afternoon, I was finishing up my list of projects for Charlotte. I wanted to leave her as many details as possible since I was not even giving a full two weeks' notice. Speaking of Charlotte, I wondered if she had emailed me back yet.

I opened my email and saw one from her.

> *Oh, Amelia, I hope this is not because I was a bit harsh on the phone the other day. By all means, you need to do what is right for you. Perhaps I should have spent*

more time in the office, rather than traveling around the globe so much. I got to thinking, and I really never gave you the proper time to let me into the personal side of your life. For that, I do apologize.

Feel free to lock up the doors at any time next week – and also feel free to reach out should you need anything. If you need a reference, you can certainly count on me to give you an outstanding one. I do appreciate all of your help over the years.

And please, stay in touch.

Thank you for all you have done!

-Char

Wow. That was a very nice email. I was so relieved, I really did not want to burn that bridge…just the one with Rodney.

I wanted to blow that bridge up and make sure it could never be repaired.

I looked at the clock and saw it was almost 4 pm. I did not want 5 pm to come. I did not want to see Rodney and be with him over the weekend. Plus, who knew what stunt he would try to pull next on me? This whole thing about him not wanting me to work was nuts to me, and maybe I even needed to play along if he brings it up again.

It is almost as if he wants to have complete control of me and my life. I don't understand why you would want to do that to anyone, especially someone you supposedly love.

I took a deep breath.

I am almost out of this mess. I have to stay positive and focused.

I finished some office tasks and started packing up for the day. Before I left, I checked the office to make sure that if I could leave Monday morning, everything was in place and I could grab it all as soon as possible.

I suddenly felt like changing my rental so I could pick it up Sunday night. I wanted to leave Rodney and this life behind.

Finally, I trusted my gut feeling instead of pushing it down like I had done for so long. I logged back onto the computer and updated the reservation. I figured I could take my car to the rental lot or somewhere nearby, drive the rental to our neighborhood, and park it down the street. I would need to arrange a cab service to pick me up at the rental and take me back to my car.

I printed out several cab companies and their phone numbers to take with me over the weekend. Since I still did not have a cell, I would have to figure out a time and place I could get to a phone and call them, but that should be easy enough.

Once I get the rental car situated and my car back at Rodney's house, I will need to figure out a quiet way to sneak out of the house and pray he does not wake up.

Red wine.

Red wine always makes Rodney sleep harder than usual.

I could ask him to make steak for dinner, and while he is out getting the steaks, I could get the rental. Then make sure to keep refilling his wine glass. I will fill mine too, but also make sure to pour most of it out when he is not looking to keep my wits about me.

I looked around the office and took it all in. It had been such a safe space for me for years, and especially in this last week. If all goes according to plan, I won't have any time to spend in here on Monday. I will have to be in and out at lightning speed.

I couldn't help but smile in that moment and find gratitude for everything I had gotten from this office and job. Charlotte had been very gracious in giving me bonuses…if it weren't for that, I would not have been able to take that extra money from the bank.

Now, to go home and endure one final weekend with Rodney.

I can do it.

Stay positive.

As I drove home, I noticed it was already 5:30 pm. I am sure Rodney would be asking me why I was late. I turned onto our street and saw his truck. Per usual, my heart sank, but I pulled myself back up quickly.

As I walked by the new landscaping, I cared the least I ever did.

As I walked into the entryway with nothing familiar to me, I also cared the least I had.

"Amelia? Is that you, my dear? I'm out back!" Rodney yelled.

I put my stuff down and walked towards the back porch. I saw he was sitting on the patio with a couple of cocktails.

"Hi! Sorry, I'm late; it's been a busy day at work. Are those margaritas?" I asked.

"Yes, I figured we could have a fun little cocktail to celebrate your week coming to an end. You've been through so much."

A lot more than my week will be coming to an end in a couple of days; little did he know.

"Oh, that is a fun little surprise, thank you!" I said as I grabbed the glass from him.

"I was thinking we could go out to a new French restaurant that just opened downtown. Would you be up for that?" he asked.

"Yes, that sounds delightful," I lied. The only thing that sounded delightful was driving myself out of this town and far away from this man.

After we talked about our days for a little over cocktails, we each got ready, and Rodney drove us to dinner in downtown Asheville.

"Oh, this looks very nice," I said as we pulled into the parking lot.

He reached across the console and grabbed my hand. "Only the nicest for you, my darling."

Ugh, I was so sick of him calling me darling. He started that while I was at the beach. He never called me that before, but I suppose it was part of his plan to reinvent himself while attempting to make me feel crazy. I must admit, his plan did work…until it didn't.

We went inside and were seated at a table for two. The place was nice, and I was hungry, so hopefully I could at least have a nice meal out of this situation.

"Wow, these prices are outrageous!" Rodney exclaimed as he looked at the menu.

I couldn't help but jerk my head up and look at him.

He slipped. That was the old Rodney talking. He used to always complain about prices when we'd go out, which, quite frankly, was a huge turn-off.

"Oh, what does it matter, though? We are celebrating tonight!" He seemed to have caught himself and attempted to correct his act.

I reviewed the menu and decided to pick out the most expensive item. The least this man could do was buy me a nice meal.

"I think I' m in the mood for a steak," I said.

"A steak?" Rodney asked.

"Yes, I read a review that their New York strip was amazing. And let's start with a dozen oysters!" I said with a smile.

I could tell he did not want to spend that much money. I was always so modest when ordering food with Rodney.

"Well, whatever you like, darling. I'm going to order the seared salmon."

"That sounds amazing – let's split a bottle of pinot noir, shall we?" I said, just as our server approached us.

I quickly scanned the menu and ordered one of the more expensive bottles.

"Excellent choice, madam," the server said.

Of course it was, I thought. It was almost $100. Rodney has taken most of my money, so the least he could do was buy me a nice dinner, even if he didn't realize it would be one of the very last.

"Can we also do a dozen oysters?" I asked.

"Oh yes, would you like to add caviar to them?"

I looked right at the server, "Oh, yes, we are celebrating, so let's add the caviar, thank you for suggesting that," I said with a smile.

The server's tone became a bit more upbeat. "Oh, what are we celebrating tonight? Is it a birthday or an anniversary?"

I looked toward Rodney, and then the server followed my lead and also looked at him.

"Uhh… well… uhh," Rodney stuttered. "It is sort of a long story."

The server seemed disappointed. "Okay, well, let me get that wine right out for you. I'll be right back."

"You are quite hungry tonight, it seems….and thirsty," Rodney said.

"I am!" I smiled back.

As much as I was dreading seeing Rodney after work, it actually wasn't that bad overall. I attributed this to the fact that I knew it was my last weekend. It was almost like I was able to relax…a little. I would not be fully relaxed until I was on the highway heading north.

The server returned and poured our wine.

"Wow, this is delicious, Amelia, great choice! You always make such great decisions," Rodney said.

If only he meant that. Some of the things Rodney says and does now are so lovely. I knew they weren't coming from a true place, but if they were, I would not be leaving.

If I think about it, he has turned himself into a much better version of himself.

Minus the fact that I still didn't have a cell phone. I almost had to laugh a little inside at how much effort he put into the house, yet he couldn't quite finish the plan of making me feel I actually suffered from amnesia.

The rest of our time at the restaurant went well and flew by. The wine helped me relax a bit, and the steak I ordered turned out so well. It was almost a shame that this was both my first and last time at this restaurant.

"Do you want to go grab a drink after this?" he asked.

"I guess. Where?"

"I don't know, I feel like we have not been downtown much lately, so we could just walk around and see if something sparks our interest."

"Sounds like a plan to me!" I said.

Rodney asked for the bill, and when he opened it, I could see him squirm at the total. He quickly gave the server his credit card, and we gathered our things to head out.

"Thank you so much for dinner, Rodney. I know that was expensive."

He put his arm around my shoulder as we walked out of the restaurant, "Anything to make you happy, my dear."

I put my arm around his waist and pretended to like walking so close to him.

As we walked down the road, I couldn't help but think that this week I'd be walking down the streets of Manhattan once again.

Alone.

I started to find it interesting when I reflected on my life. When I wasn't in a relationship, I really wanted to be in one. And now, I am making a literal escape plan to get out of my relationship.

Although I had to imagine this was far from a normal relationship. I worry it will be hard for me to trust a man…ever again. But maybe that wasn't the lesson in this mess. Maybe the lesson was that I needed to trust myself more.

As we approached what appeared to be a bit of a dive bar, Rodney stopped and looked in.

"Should we try this place? It's no French restaurant, but it looks interesting overall," he said.

"Oh, you know, as long as they serve wine, I am fine!"

We walked in and grabbed a couple of seats at the bar. We ordered our drinks and listened to the band. The band made it a bit tough to talk because they were loud, but I was fine with that.

After about thirty minutes, I saw Rodney yawn. "Do you want to go home?" I asked. "I'm getting tired too."

"Yes, it has been a long week for both of us," he said.

Oh, please. This man has no clue what a long week actually is.

Once we got home, we both went to bed. It was a little easier for me to sleep next to him, knowing I only had to do it for three more nights.

Chapter 30

When I woke up in the morning, Rodney wasn't in bed. I decided to stretch out and just relax for a little while, and enjoyed the empty bed.

After just a few minutes of my bliss, Rodney came into the room with a steaming cup of coffee.

"Good morning, darling. I brought you some coffee. I am going to run a few errands in a bit. Did you want to come?" he asked.

"Thank you for the coffee. No, I think I will have a slow morning and maybe go for a walk in a little bit."

"Okay, well, I will be gone for a few hours, I suppose."

Thank goodness! I have hardly been in this house alone at all, and not more than thirty minutes or so if that. My body was always extra tense around Rodney, so I was glad to get some time to myself.

I got up and went to finish my coffee on the patio by the fountain. I did love how he redid our patio. I am still so confused about how he picked out such nice things for the house, but at the same time, it didn't matter.

The only thing that mattered was getting out.

I spent part of my day going through some additional things in the house that had been mine. Suddenly, though, those "things" became just that. Things. It was rather ironic that returning to a house full of brand-new items and décor made me lose the value I once placed on material items.

I guess our priorities can quickly change when other things are at stake. In this case, it was my mental health. Of course, I know I would have to worry much less about that once I am back in the city.

Rodney had called the house and asked what I wanted for dinner.

"Up to you, my dear, I know whatever you make will be wonderful as always."

He laughed. "You're too sweet. Do you need anything at the store? Anything in particular you want for your work lunches this week?"

I smiled. There won't be any work lunches this week.

"Just some stuff for salads, I suppose."

"You got it, I will be home in a bit," he said.

My mind wandered off to my new city life. Christmas is coming up in a few months, and it would be great to see the tree in Rockefeller Center, as well as all the other fun holiday décor throughout the city.

I had a good feeling about this holiday season.

I wonder why? Obviously, I would be away from Rodney, but this feeling was deeper than that. Well, I guess time will tell.

Soon enough, Rodney came home.

"Well, what did you decide on for dinner?" I asked.

"Crab cakes with arugula salad."

"Sounds perfect."

"You know, would you want to grill steak tomorrow?" I asked.

"Sure, you know I love grilling, so I can make that happen for you."

"Let me start making the salad for us now," I said as I started unpacking the groceries he just bought.

The last time I had crab cakes was at the beach, which wasn't that long ago… who could have seen this crazy turn of events in my life, though? The women I had met at the beach both told me I'd be happier once I left Rodney. They also said he wouldn't make it easy for me.

How right they were.

One more day.

I can do this.

"Okay, I'm done with the salad. I'm gonna go sit on the couch and read a magazine, unless you need my help with anything?" I asked.

"Nope! I got it all under control," Rodney said as he leaned in for a kiss.

I found a travel magazine on the coffee table that I had never seen, but I also knew there was no point in asking where it came from. It had a section on traveling in Europe. I had never been to Europe, so I quickly lost myself in the articles.

Before I knew it, dinner was ready.

I went to the table, which Rodney had taken the initiative to set.

"Thank you for setting the table. I'd have helped."

"Oh, no worries, you looked very interested in your magazine. What were you reading?"

"Actually, an article about traveling through Europe."

"We should plan a trip there!" Rodney said.

"Oh yes, what a nice idea and a fun thing to plan," I said. Lying. Again. "Now let me try these crab cakes."

I took a bite. Wow. They melted in my mouth.

"Rodney! You've done it again! How are you such an amazing cook!"

He laughed. "I'm glad you like them. I don't know if it's that I am that great of a cook, or that I just find good recipes."

"Well, that is very humble of you, but I definitely think you have a huge part in these creations."

We ate rather quickly and discussed picking out a movie to watch after dinner.

After we cleaned up, we both went into the living room and sat on the couch.

"What should we watch?" he asked.

"Oh, I'm up for anything. How about you pick?"

"If you insist, darling." He reached for the remote and started scrolling through options.

He selected a documentary about the ocean. Honestly, I couldn't care less what he selected tonight. I was too focused on making sure the day went okay tomorrow.

And more importantly...the night.

I started to think about how I would get out of the house. I was counting on Rodney being a sound sleeper, but I still needed to take precautions to get out of the house quietly. Our back sliding glass door was probably quieter than the front door, which tended to squeak when opened and shut.

Shoes. What shoes would I wear? Sneakers made the most sense so that I could run to the car. I don't think I will even worry about changing my clothing. I will sleep in a casual pajama set and throw on a sweatshirt.

If I could make it to the rental… I have a feeling I would be fine. If Rodney woke up, he would first see my car in the driveway and look around the house. He would never suspect anything about my plan.

With that said, I need to leave him a note saying that I am leaving. The last thing I need is for him to tell the police I left and should not be on my own. Granted, I suppose he could throw the note out and make up some story. But I honestly would rather him be angry than worry.

Before I knew it, I heard Rodney snoring. I looked over and saw him slumped over on the couch.

Good. I won't have to sleep with him tonight - or at least most of the night.

I turned off the TV and got into bed.

All of the mental planning wore me out, and before I knew it, I had fallen asleep.

The next thing I knew, I was slowly waking up to the smell of coffee and the sun shining in through the window. I looked to Rodney's side of the bed. It seemed he never even got in it. Probably explains why I was able to sleep so well.

I got up and went to the kitchen.

"Good morning, darling!" Rodney said, just as chipper as ever.

"Hi – I am sorry, did you stay on the couch all night? I tried to wake you, but you were out like a light," I lied.

He laughed, "Yes, I woke up at 7 am and decided to get up and start breakfast. I seemed to have slept pretty well, minus my neck hurting just a bit."

"Okay, well, at our ages, that's not too bad!" I said.

I went to get myself a cup of coffee.

"No, darling, I can do that for you. Just have a seat at the breakfast bar."

As nice as it was that Rodney was always trying to do stuff for me, it sometimes made me feel helpless.

Plus, it never seemed to be coming from a place of authenticity.

Today was here.

Finally.

It was the last day I would ever have to see Rodney.

Hopefully.

As long as everything went smoothly this evening.

“I’m making something special for breakfast.”

Of course he is.

“Lobster eggs Benedict with Southern-style grits,” he said.

Well, I had to admit that did sound good.

“That sounds delicious! Do you need my help with anything?”

“All set – I have them in the oven, staying warm, so they are ready now,” he said as he went to grab some plates out of the cupboard.

We set up to eat at the breakfast bar, which I always preferred, so I didn’t need to be right across from him.

“Oh wow, you did it again! These are the best!” I admit I never had to lie about how good his cooking was.

Rodney took a bite, “Wow, you are right! I will for sure be saving this recipe.”

“What’s on your agenda today? I need to go to the home improvement store this afternoon. Would you like to come?” he asked.

Perfect.

"Actually, I think I am going to hang out here and catch up on some reading. Maybe even look into some European vacations as we discussed."

"I think that is a fine idea!" He smiled.

"Actually, not sure if you had anything in mind for dinner, but I am craving steak," I said.

"Steak? You just had it on Friday."

"Oh, I know, but yours is so good. Please?"

He laughed, "Well, sure then! I could go for some steak myself."

Thank goodness. Red wine and steak for dinner, and I could get the rental car this afternoon just as I planned.

We finished breakfast and cleaned up.

I grabbed some magazines and went out to the patio to read them, or pretend to.

After some time had passed, Rodney popped his head out.

"Okay, darling, I'm off to go do some errands. You sure you don't want to join me?" he asked.

"Yes, I'm sure. Let's be honest, I'd probably just slow you down anyway."

We both laughed.

I waited about 10 minutes after he left, then grabbed my wallet and car keys and drove to pick up the rental car. It was only about 15 minutes away.

I was nervous, but overall excited to put the next portion of my plan into action.

When I pulled into the lot, I tried to park where my car would not be in the way, since I would have to leave it there for a little while.

I walked into the office. "Hi! I'm here to pick up a rental for Amelia."

A young man looked down at his computer. "It says you aren't supposed to pick it up until 4 pm."

It was 2 pm. My heart sank a little.

"Oh, don't worry, ma'am! I was just kidding with you. We have a car ready. I'm sorry you looked awfully upset when I said that."

"Oh, oh, my goodness! Thank you, and I'm sorry.

I'm just eager to… take my trip."

He looked back at his computer.

"Wow! It says you're dropping this car off in Manhattan!"

"That's right, I am," I said with a huge grin.

"I've never been there, hopefully one day!" the young man said.

"Oh, I am sure you will get there, and you should! So much to do and see."

"Here are the keys for you. I will walk you out and show you the car."

I followed him out the front door and into the lot. We walked up to a small white car.

"Does this one work for you?" he asked.

"Oh, absolutely, plus I'm not picky. I'm hoping to make it in a day anyway."

"I had no idea it was that close! Maybe I should add this to my bucket list, to drive to New York City." His face lit up with excitement.

"Oh, I think you should! Or at least visit. It is the city that never sleeps after all, and do you like pizza?" I asked him.

"Who doesn't like pizza?!" he asked as he smiled.

"Well, New York simply has the best."

"You sold me! I'll definitely make sure to get up there someday. Call the office if you need anything along your drive or if anything goes wrong with the car, but I personally checked this one out myself, so you should be good to go."

"Do you mind if I drive the rental car home, and then come back here to pick up mine in a little?"

"Not at all!" he said, still smiling. It was refreshing to be around someone who seemed genuinely refreshing and was not faking it.

Or lying to me.

"Great, thanks so much! And see you in the city!"

"It's a deal, ma'am!"

I got in and quickly pulled out my list of taxicabs. I called the first one on the list.

"Taxi of Asheville, how may we help you?"

"Hi, umm, I was wondering if someone could pick me up shortly at 483 Creekside Drive?"

"Sure, I can have someone there in about 10 minutes. Is that too soon?"

"No, that is perfect! Thank you so much!"

This was going smoothly so far.

I started the rental car and headed home. Or, down the street…

As I pulled into the neighborhood, I parked the car outside of a home that was for sale and currently vacant. Just as I put the car in park, I saw the cab driving down the street.

I jumped out of the car and walked into the street.

"Are you Amelia?" the older gentleman asked.

"Yes! I am!"

"Well then, hop on in!" He smiled.

I quickly got into the car. "Sir, I do have to check, will you take cash?"

"Cash is king where I come from, so absolutely!" He laughed.

Everyone outside of Rodney seemed so jovial.

"Oh, fantastic. I'm not going far—just about ten minutes, towards the airport."

"Where are you flying to, miss?" he asked.

"Oh, well, you see, I rented a car. And I need to go get my car… It's a long story."

"Ah, shoot, you know every old man like me loves a good long story, but we only have about a ten-minute ride."

There was something about the way he said it. It was almost like he actually would have listened to me.

Even though…

The police didn't.

The doctor didn't.

Charlotte didn't.

Well, I guess Charlotte did try to backtrack a bit.

This gave me hope that maybe someone in New York would listen to me. And not only listen, but validate that I wasn't crazy.

We pulled into the lot. "There is my car over there," I said as I pointed towards it.

"Well, I hope you have a safe journey wherever that may be!" he said cheerfully to me.

I quickly hopped out of his car and into mine. I was a bit nervous driving back home, but I was sure Rodney would still be gone.

Just as I suspected when I pulled onto our street, his truck was nowhere in sight.

I let out a sigh of relief.

The first part of my plan worked. Now I will most likely be counting down the minutes until I can get out of the house tonight.

I decided to actually do what I said I would do earlier and sit and read some magazines. After all, I am sure Rodney would be asking me what European destinations I was reading about.

I looked around the patio and inside the house. Taking it all in. Which was an odd feeling. Usually, when one moves, one looks around and sees all of the memories one has made in a home.

But this wasn't my home anymore.

Chapter 31

It was so wildly different that it was almost hard to remember what it had been like before.

Just then, I heard the door slam. Rodney was back.

I went inside to greet him, "Hi! How were your errands?"

"All went as planned, so that was good, and I picked up some steak and potatoes for dinner. I feel like we have plenty of salad stuff."

"You're right. We do. In fact, I'm going to start making the salad."

"Perfect, and I will start washing the potatoes and marinating the steak. How about we have some red wine with the steak?" he asked.

Well, this couldn't get any easier.

"Love that idea!" I smiled.

Rodney went to get a bottle of red, opened it, and poured it into the two glasses I had grabbed from the cupboard.

"Cheers!" he said.

"Cheers!" I said as we clinked our glasses. We both took a sip, though mine was very small.

"I'm going to go out and check on the grill," he said.

When he went out, I poured my wine down the drain and started chopping vegetables for the salad. After several minutes, he came back in and noticed my empty glass. He didn't say anything; he just poured me more and topped his glass off.

Rodney prepared the potatoes to roast in the oven. "Let's sit outside? Everything in here is under control," he said.

"Sure, it is a beautiful evening, so we may as well enjoy it."

We grabbed our glasses and went out and chatted casually about our days. Nothing too intense, which I was thankful for. When Rodney went to check on the steak, I poured a little of my wine into a plant.

He came back and sat down. "This wine is excellent!" he stated.

"Oh, you're telling me! I can't seem to put mine down!" We laughed as I pretended to take another sip, and he took a large sip himself.

"We have about five minutes left on the steak."

"Okay," I said as I jumped to my feet. "I will head in and pull out the potatoes and set the table."

Once inside, I set the table and opened another bottle of red wine. We weren't done with the first bottle, but I wanted to make sure Rodney had easy access to more. I poured my remaining wine down the sink.

As Rodney came inside with the steak and we sat down at the table, I felt the joy of knowing this would be my last dinner with Rodney.

"The potatoes and steak are both wonderful, Rodney!"

"You know what's wonderful? That red wine. Pour me some more, will you?"

"I'd love to," I said as I grabbed the bottle. I poured myself more for show. "I can't believe how much I've had; it just goes down so smoothly. Why don't we turn on some music?"

"Great idea! I'm in the mood for some classic rock."

"You got it!" I said as I went over to the sound system.

When I came back, I could tell the wine was definitely hitting Rodney.

We finished eating, and Rodney had also finished his wine. I went to pour him more, but he stopped me.

"I should slow it down on the wine," he objected.

"Oh, live a little, Rodney! Let's relax and have some fun," I said flirtatiously.

Then proceeded to pour another glass.

I cleaned up dinner as he was going on and on about some work issue he was having. Frankly, he didn't seem to even be making sense, so it was safe to say he was rather drunk.

"Amelia, I'm so tired. Can we go to bed early?"

"Sure, of course. I'm done cleaning up, so we can get ready now."

He went straight to bed. He didn't even change.

I put on some casual pajamas as I had planned on. I placed a sweatshirt and some slip-on sneakers near the back door.

As I went to crawl into bed next to Rodney, I couldn't help but reflect on the fact that we did have a lovely evening. Was I second-guessing myself? I couldn't be. I mean, I guess I could wait another day or so, as I didn't have a time limit.

I suddenly didn't know what I wanted to do.

I felt paralyzed.

Just then, I heard Rodney drunkenly mumble…

"I told you I could change."

My eyes opened so wide, and my heart started to pound so hard that I was worried he would hear it!

I knew it.

I knew he was lying to me, and I knew he would eventually slip up. Only I never guessed he would be unconscious when doing so.

He was snoring so loudly. I had initially planned to wait till later in the night, but now seemed as good a time as ever to escape.

I rolled over and looked at him one last time. Shocked that this is what our once-happy and thriving relationship had turned into.

I got up and, as quietly and as quickly as I could, walked out of the bedroom and towards the back door. All along, my heart was beating out of my chest.

I grabbed my purse and pulled out the short note I had written to Rodney to place on the counter.

Dear Rodney,

> *I left. It shouldn't have had to end this way…but perhaps it's just karma catching up with you.*

-Amelia

I slipped into my sneakers, put on my sweatshirt, and slid open the back door.

Once outside, I made sure to stay steady and close the door softly behind me. Just then, the floodlights came on.

Shit.

I hadn't planned on that.

I took off running as fast as I could down the yard and to the rental. As soon as it came into view, it gave me the energy to run even faster.

When I got to the car, I threw my purse in and locked the door behind me. I started the car and immediately headed straight to the office.

I never turned around.

I never checked whether the outside lights woke Rodney. I couldn't bear the thought of seeing the living room lights come on and Rodney looking out the window.

I just kept going.

It was safe to say my heart never once slowed down. The amount of adrenaline that came over my body was nothing like I had ever felt.

I pulled into the office parking lot and ran up to the door and unlocked it. I went to the closet, grabbed my bags of clothing and other items I had stashed in there, and brought them to the car. This alone took me several trips, and I worried I was staying too long in case Rodney came looking for me.

Then I went to the desk, unlocked the bottom drawer, and pulled out my cash.

I was so thankful I had that cash set aside. It seemed to be the one thing helping me escape this mess. I got sidetracked for a few seconds and was taking one last glance around the office.

Amelia! I yelled to myself. Get moving!

I headed out of the office, locked it up behind me, and jumped back into the car.

I went to pull out of the lot and onto the main road. Something told me to take a side street to the interstate. I quickly made a right-hand turn, and as I drove down the narrow road, I looked up at the rearview mirror.

Rodney. His truck. I saw it quickly drive by.

He must have woken up after all from the floodlights coming on. It made complete sense that he would go to the office, too.

I started to speed down the narrow road, and after only a few more turns, I was on the interstate heading north.

Something in me knew I was now safe. There is no way he would even think about trying to find me on the interstate. And if so, he would probably pick the one that headed east towards the beach.

I loosened my grip on the steering wheel and took some deep breaths, which helped my heart rate return to normal.

I then felt tears streaming down my face.

The amount of relief I was already feeling was unimaginable.

Chapter 32

Everything in my plan worked out so well. Although I guess if I had stopped to turn around when running from the house, it could have thrown me off my focus. And thank goodness I snapped myself out of my last moments in the office when I slowed down to look around. I didn't even want to think about what would have happened if Rodney had pulled into the office.

I don't need to think about it.

I'm out.

I'm free.

I looked at the time – it was just after 11 pm. If I drove straight through, I would get to the city around 9 am. If I get tired, I can pull off at a rest area to take a nap, but doing that alone made me a little nervous. I didn't really want to check into a hotel either. I just wanted to get to the city and get my stuff into my new little apartment.

I turned on the radio and just drove. Since it was the middle of the night, there weren't many cars on the road, which made the drive relatively easy.

I was thankful to be in this car by myself, driving to my new life.

Away from Rodney.

No more pretending to enjoy his company. No more of him gaslighting me. I was still a bit shocked by how everything turned out. His behavior was so…bizarre to say the least. I am not sure I could ever describe to someone exactly what I went through.

Maybe I won't have to.

Maybe I can gloss over the last several years when I tell people I moved to Asheville for a bit.

I looked at the clock. It was almost 5 am, and I needed to stop for gas soon. If I didn't need gas, I'd have just kept going. Miraculously, I wasn't tired.

I saw an exit with several gas stations and found one with a lot of lights around it and other cars as well. I didn't take more than fifteen minutes to get gas, use the restroom, and buy myself a coffee and water. Then I was back on the road.

The rest of the time went quickly. It was a beautiful sunrise, and I couldn't help but feel that it was positive foreshadowing for my life. Eventually, the city came into view.

More tears came down my face.

I missed those buildings more than I realized.

I had looked up directions and memorized them for getting to my new apartment building.

It was a bit nerve-racking driving in Manhattan since I had never actually done it, but thinking about what I had just been through made me realize I would much rather be driving on the city streets than dealing with that nonsense again.

Once I turned onto the final street, I saw the apartment, and there was an unloading zone right in front of it.

Perfect.

I parked the car, got out, and looked up and down the street. It was the cutest neighborhood. It was not too far from where I had previously lived, so it already felt very comfortable to me.

I walked into the building and down a short corridor to a desk.

"Hi, I'm here to … well, move in."

The lady looked up from her computer and smiled at me.

"You must be Amelia!"

"Yes."

She got up, walked around the desk, and hugged me. "I'm Joy! I'm so glad you're here!"

"Oh, me too. You have no idea."

"Let me get your keys and show you around the building. First, though, are you okay?" She looked at me with concern.

"Yeah, I mean, I think I'm pretty tired. I drove straight from Asheville."

"You drove all night?" she asked.

"Yes… I had to leave when I had the chance. Then I just kept driving."

"I understand. You're very brave. I don't know what you've been through, but I can tell. How about we get the things from your car first so you can get settled. I can always show you around the building a bit later."

"Okay, that sounds good. Thank you."

We pulled the bags from my car. "I'm so sorry I packed my clothes in trash bags." I felt so embarrassed.

"Honey, don't be embarrassed. Fortunately, you were able to bring some clothing with you. Some women come here with nothing but the outfit they're wearing."

She made a good point and put me at ease.

We each grabbed a couple of bags, and she led me to my apartment.

"You're on the sixth floor, and you even have a nice view of the Hudson River."

"Oh, really? That's fantastic! My last view while living in the city was a brick wall." We both laughed.

She unlocked the door, and we went in. I loved it. It was small, but I didn't care.

"I love it! It seems to have really great energy in here," I said to Joy.

"Well, that would make sense because the last woman who stayed here was just a delight. She came from a complicated situation, but was always so positive and pleasant to everyone. She actually got herself a great job, so she just recently moved into a bigger apartment. She told me she wanted to free up this apartment for… someone who needed it more."

Joy and I smiled at each other.

I finished getting my things from the car and then drove it to the rental office to drop it off. It was only several blocks away, so I just walked back afterward. Once back in my new apartment, I lay down on my bed and fell asleep within seconds.

When I awoke, I suddenly remembered I was in New York. I replayed in my mind the escape from Rodney's house and the drive that followed.

Happy was an understatement. I was beyond thrilled and proud of myself, and best of all… I felt safe. I knew it would take some time to feel completely back to my old self, but I was determined to make that happen. I was excited to find a job and make new friends.

I sat up and looked around. I had bags of clothes everywhere, and I almost had to laugh a little. Who knew trash bags would be so convenient to move several states away? There was a nice-sized dresser that came with my apartment and a decent-sized closet – for Manhattan anyway. I decided to start unpacking and get organized.

Chapter 33

Over the coming days, everything was simply fantastic. My mood had lifted so much! I had followed up on two job interviews and was going to meet with both of them at the end of the week. I had even gone and gotten myself a cell phone and a small laptop.

I had met several women at the apartment building. While none of us had exchanged stories about how we ended up in the same building, there was a sense of peace and trust whenever I joined them for meals.

I spent a couple of days that week taking long runs along the river and also in Central Park. It was so fun to be back in the city. So many things to see, and the people-watching was so much better than in Asheville! I could sit in the park and be entertained for hours. I loved seeing all of the fashionable women and would take mental notes for some new outfits I could get for work…and dates.

Maybe next time I could get it right with a man. I clearly didn't want to repeat my past, but I was nowhere near ready to date. Besides, I just wanted to focus on myself, a new job, and making friends.

As I finished up dinner one evening, I felt like going out for a walk. I got dressed and decided I even felt like putting on some makeup and dressing up a bit. I grabbed my purse and headed out. I didn't know where I wanted to go, so I just picked a direction and started walking, enjoying all of the city sights.

As I walked, I started to think I should stop and get a glass of wine to celebrate my newfound freedom and fresh start. I walked a couple more blocks with nothing really catching my eye, until one place did. I saw a quaint little bar on a corner, so I thought I would stop in.

The bar had lots of books you could take to read. I guess it was a coffee bar in the morning. It was decently crowded, but there was a seat by the bar near the window. As I sat down and looked around, I felt like I was having déjà vu. Had I been here? I don't think so, but I had a really familiar feeling.

Just then, the bartender walked up to me. "Hi, miss! What would you like tonight? We have our famous cosmopolitans on special."

"That sounds fabulous!" I said with a smile.

Again. Why is this all feeling like I've been here before?

He set the cosmopolitan down in front of me, and I took a sip. It was delicious. I figured I might as well look around and do some people-watching.

As I glanced out the window, a building suddenly caught my attention. Red lights, it had red lights at the top.

Oh my God.

Hudson.

I wasn't having déjà vu. I had, in fact, been here before when I met Hudson! He was so nice to me, and I felt so comfortable with him. I started to remember more. He had seemed concerned about me and told me that if I ever needed anything, to go to the 23rd floor of that building and ask for him.

Should I?

Is that completely crazy?

Yes. It is. But then again, wasn't what I just went through actually crazy?

I remembered the night so vividly. I looked at my watch, and it was only 5:30 pm. Would he still be working? I mean, what are the chances he even still has the same job?

"Excuse me, sir? Can I have another Cosmo?"

As the bartender handed me my next drink, he smiled at me. "You know people love these drinks!"

I started drinking it and was very seriously contemplating whether to go to the building with the red lights. With each sip I took, the idea seemed less and less crazy. Then again, he probably isn't even there, and security would let me know that, and I would just go home.

I'm going. What have I got to lose?

I paid for my drinks and started to walk towards the building.

My heart started to race a bit, but really, this shouldn't be a big deal. I began to tell myself he wouldn't be there, and in no time, I'd be back in my apartment reading a book.

As I approached the building, I walked in through some revolving doors. I looked around for security and saw the desk to my right.

"Hello, I'm here to…" I stopped.

The security guard looked at me. "You're here to what, miss?"

"I'm here to see Hudson. On the 23rd floor."

"Do you have an appointment?"

"Uhh, no. Not exactly, I'm sorry," I said, worried he would turn me away.

"No worries, miss, let me call him. What's your name?"

"Amelia," I said, forcing myself to smile.

I heard the phone ring as the security guard called him. It rang several times, and I was beginning to think he had already left.

"This is Hudson."

He's still in his office.

"Good evening, sir. This is Bill at the front desk. I have a Miss Amelia here to see you."

There was silence on the other end. My heart felt like it was beating out of my chest.

"Sir? Are you there?" the guard asked.

I kept waiting for what felt like an eternity.

Just then, Hudson replied.

"Send her up."

About the Author

Chelsea Labzda grew up in Jupiter, Florida, and now resides in Raleigh, North Carolina. She finds joy in conversations with friends, shopping, and dreaming up her next travel adventure. Her writing is inspired by the beauty and transformation found in everyday life. This is her debut novel.

www.ingramcontent.com/pod-product-compliance
Lightning Source LLC
LaVergne TN
LVHW100519110826
845146LV00002B/699

* 9 7 9 8 9 9 4 7 6 4 5 1 0 *

1 Einleitung: Ein Fest für den Heiligen

> People ritualize their lives now as much as they ever have, not always in accepted religious fashion, but in some way: in hymns like John Philip Sousa's marches at the annual fireworks display on the Fourth of July; sermons like those given every four years by the candidates of each major party about to rally the faithful for a march to the White House; responsive readings like the antiphonal cheering between cheerleaders and crowd at the annual homecoming game; [...] I want only to shout as loudly as I may in favor of taking such things seriously as liturgies, that is, as acted-out rituals involving prescribed texts, actions, timing, persons, and things, all coming together in a shared statement of communal identity.[1]

1.1 Zeno und Verona

Mitten im Herzen der oberitalienischen Stadt Verona, etwa 100 Meter entfernt vom Ufer der Etsch, befindet sich ein Kleinod: Die winzige romanische Kirche San Zeno in Oratorio, die bei den Veronesern als ‚San Zenetto' bekannt ist.[2] Dieser verniedlichende Spitzname spielt nicht nur auf die bescheidene Größe und Ausstattung der Kirche an, sondern drückt auch die Vertrautheit und den liebevollen Umgang der Stadtbewohner mit diesem Gebäude aus. Die Kirche prägte sich vor allem deswegen so besonders in das Gedächtnis der Stadt ein, weil dort der Legende nach der Stein aufbewahrt liegt, auf dem Zeno, der heilige Bischof und Patron von Verona, saß, während er in der durch die Stadt fließenden Etsch fischte:[3] „Ille enim sedebat super lapidem, qui in proximo monasterii erat, et piscabatur in flumine [...].“[4]

Dieser Stein war auch für den mittelalterlichen Besucher der Kirche mehr als ein bloßes Memorabile. Nicht nur war er das konkrete Überbleibsel der Legende, er materialisierte auch im wahrsten Sinne des Wortes gewichtig die besondere Beziehung der Stadt Verona zu ihrem heiligen Patron. Die Bewohner der Stadt, zu deren Alltag das Fischen in der Etsch gehörte, waren mit Zeno zutiefst verbunden. Der Stein galt als unumstößlicher Beleg dafür, dass sie den Heiligen in dieser Tätigkeit an Ort und Stelle nachahmten.

Diese Anekdote veranschaulicht sehr plastisch, welches besondere Verhältnis Zeno und Verona – vom Mittelalter bis heute – verbindet. Die Figur des Zeno, wie sie von den mittelalterlichen Zeitgenossen konstruiert wurde, stand nämlich in einem konstitutiven Bezug zu Verona. Leben und Wirken des Heiligen entfal-

---

1 Lawrence A. Hoffman: Beyond the Text. A Holistic Approach to Liturgy (Jewish Literature and Culture 538), Bloomington 1987, S. 3.

2 Vgl. Mario Patuzzo: Verona: romana, medievale, scaligera, Verona [4]2013, S. 325–326.

3 Vgl. Luciano Rognini: Notizie storico-artistiche sulla chiesa di S. Zeno in Oratorio, in: Annuario storico zenoniano 6, 1989, S. 59–72, hier: S. 65.

4 Giuliano Sala: Il culto di S. Zeno nei secoli VIII e IX, in: Annuario storico zenoniano 7, 1990, S. 19–36, hier: S. 30.

teten sich in enger Verbindung mit dem physischen Raum der Stadt, der auch der Erfahrungsraum ihrer Bevölkerung war, die wiederum die Verehrergemeinschaft des Heiligen bildete.

Ein zentrales topographisches Merkmal dieses Raums ist der schon erwähnte Fluss, die Etsch. Sie umringt die Stadt von drei Seiten und beeinflusste wesentlich das Leben der mittelalterlichen Stadtbewohner, im Guten wie im Schlechten. Eine entsprechend zentrale und gleichzeitig ambivalente Rolle spielt der Fluss in der Geschichte von Zeno. Er war auf der einen Seite, wie in der Anekdote vom angelnden Bischof, Nahrungsquelle und gesegnete Präsenz in der Stadt.[5] Der fischende Zeno mit seinem wichtigsten Attribut, der Angelschnur, findet sich gleich an zwei Stellen auch im Kloster San Zeno Maggiore: einmal in einem der bronzenen Bildfelder auf der rechten Seite des Portals und einmal auf der Fassade, im unteren Band der Lunette, wo auch eine Inschrift angebracht ist: „Zeno fischt, ein Mensch kommt zum Stehen und der Teufel wird verjagt."[6] Damit konnten sich besonders die mittelalterlichen Veroneser identifizieren, die damals „mit dem Fluss geboren wurden und mit ihm lebten."[7]

Auf der anderen Seite konnte die Etsch aber gefährlich werden: dann wurde die Intervention des Heiligen nötig. Dies belegen eindrücklich zwei Wundererzählungen in der karolingischen Vita (BHL 9001). Laut der ersten rettete Zeno einen Bauern, dessen vom Teufel besessene Ochsen ihn nahezu in den Fluss gestürzt und so zum Ertrinken gebracht hätten:

> [...] als er die Augen erhob, sah er einen Menschen in einem Wagen entgegenkommen, vor den Ochsen gespannt waren und der fast in den Fluss versank. Das Gespann trug ihn nämlich mit einer solchen Geschwindigkeit, dass allen klar war, dass es mit dem Teufel zugehen musste. Und ja, der heilige Mann, als er die Augen erhebend dies sah, erkannte, dass dies vom Teufel bewirkt wurde. Er erhob die Hand, machte mehrere Male das Kreuzzeichen und sagte: ‚Kehr zurück, o Teufel, und zerstör nicht den Menschen, den Gott schuf'. Als der Teufel dieses Zeichen sah, verschwand er wie Rauch

5 S. dazu: Elisa Anti: Animali e ambiente nell'agiografia zenoniana, in: Annuario storico zenoniano, 1993, S. 25–34, hier: S. 27: „Die Gewässer spielten eine unersetzliche Rolle für den mittelalterlichen Menschen und sie waren für sein Überleben notwendig: Sie stellten oft die bequemsten Kommunikations- und Transportwege dar, sie versorgten die Mühlen mit Energie und vor allem lieferten sie Fisch, eines der Grundnahrungsmittel. Der Süßwasserfisch insbesondere, da er für alle in Griffnähe war, wurde sehr intensiv genutzt." Hier und im Folgenden Übersetzung durch die Autorin, soweit nicht anders angegeben. Das Originalzitat lautet: „Le acque [...] svolgevano [...] un ruolo insostituibile per l'uomo medievale, ed erano indispensabili per la sua sopravvivenza: costituivano spesso le più comode vie di comunicazione e di trasporto, fornivano energia per far girare i mulini, e soprattutto offrivano il pesce, uno degli alimenti basilari dell'alimentazione. Il pesce d'acqua dolce, in particolare, trovandosi alla portata di tutti i consumatori, era oggetto di uno sfruttamento intensissimo [...]."

6 „[...] Zeno piscatur. vir stat. demonque fugatur [...]". Zur Bronzetür siehe Alessandro Da Lisca: La basilica di San Zenone in Verona, Verona 1941, Tavola prima, ohne Seitenangabe. Zur Lunette siehe Giovanna Valenzano: La basilica di San Zeno in Verona: problemi architettonici, Vicenza 1993, S. 230, Zitat ebd.

7 „Nasceva[no] e viveva[no] sul fiume", Anti: Animali e ambiente, S. 29.

und mit Schreien und einem schrecklichen Geräusch, als ob er von einem hohen Felsen gestürzt wäre [...].[8]

In seinem berühmtesten Wunder, das unter anderen auch von Gregor dem Großen im dritten Buch seiner *Dialogi* referiert wird, zeigte Zeno seine über den Tod hinausreichende Wirkmächtigkeit, indem er die Bürger, die sich am Fest seines Todestages in einer Kirche versammelt hatten, vor einer Überschwemmung bewahrte:

> Der genannte Tribun erzählte nämlich, dass vor fast fünf Jahren, als in Rom der Tiber so sehr aus seinem Bett herausbrach und so groß war, dass seine Gewässer über die Mauern der Stadt flossen und den Großteil der Stadt überschwemmten, in Verona der Fluss Etsch bis zur Kirche des seligen Märtyrers und Bischofs Zeno anschwoll. Obwohl die Pforten dieser Kirche offen waren, drang kaum Wasser ein. Das Wasser stieg noch ein wenig, und kam bis zu den Fenstern der Kirche, die am nächsten unter der Decke lagen. Und so stand das Wasser und versperrte die Tür der Kirche, als ob das flüssige Element in eine harte Wand verwandelt worden wäre.[9]

Der Fluss wurde so vom Heiligen regelrecht gezähmt, sogar zum Nutzen der Bürger. Diese waren nun nicht mehr von der destruktiven Kraft des Wassers gefährdet (*et quasi aqua non erat ad invadendum locum*), sondern konnten vom süßen Flusswasser profitieren (*et aqua erat ad adiutorium*) und es trinken, solange sie in der Kirche eingeschlossen waren:

> Und da viele in die Kirche gekommen waren, sie aber, da die Kirche von allen Seiten durch das Wasser umgeben war, nicht herauskommen konnten, und sich fürchteten, vor Hunger und Durst zu sterben, kamen sie immer wieder zum Eingang der Kirche und tranken das Wasser, um den Durst zu löschen, und das Wasser, wie ich bereits gesagt habe, war bis zu den Fenstern angestiegen und floss trotzdem in keiner Weise in die Kirche hinein. Es konnte nämlich geschöpft werden, aber nicht wie Wasser fließen. Das Wasser stand nämlich vor der Tür der Kirche still, um allen die Verdienste des Märtyrers zu beweisen, und so war es da, um den Leuten zu helfen, und nicht, um in die Kirche einzudringen.[10]

---

8 „[...] erectis sursum oculis vidit de contra quemdam hominem in plaustro sedentem, bubus subiunctis, mergi in flumine. Tanta enim velocitate ferebatur, ut omnibus demonstraretur diaboli arte fuisse gestum. Et quidem sanctus vir, elevans oculos dum vidisset, cognovit hoc factum diaboli esse. Elevata sursum manu fecit sanctae crucis signum frequenti vice dicens: „Revertere retro Satanas, ne perimas hominem, quem Deus creavit". Quod signum diabolus ut vidit, evanuit velut fumus, ita ut clamoribus ac stridore nefando quasi de alta rupe inruperit [...]." aus: Sala: Il culto di Zeno nei secoli VIII–IX, S. 20.

9 „Praedictus etenim tribunus narravit dicens, quia ante hoc fere quinquennium, quando apud hanc Romanam urbem alveum suum Tiberis egressus est, tantumque crescens ut eius unda super muros urbis influeret atque in ea maximas regiones occuparet, apud Veronensem urbem fluvius Atesis excrescens ad beati Zenonis martyris atque pontificis ecclesiam venit. Cuius ecclesiae dum essent ianuae apertae, aqua in eam minime intravit. Quae paulisper crescens, usque ad fenestras ecclesiae quae erant tectis proximae pervenit, sicque stans aqua ecclesiae ianuam clausit, ac si illud elementum liquidum in soliditatem parietis fuisset inmutatum." aus: Gregor der Große: Dialogues – Livres I–III. Bd. 2, hrsg. von Adalbert d. Vogüé / Paul Antin. 3 Bde., Paris 1979, S. 346–348.

10 „Cumque essent multi interius inventi, sed, aquarum magnitudine ecclesia omni circumdata, qua possent egredi non haberent, ibique se siti ac fame deficere formidarent,

Über diese Erzählungen hinaus wird Zenos Leben im Allgemeinen durch seine Beziehung zum Stadtraum definiert. Der Heilige lebte zunächst asketisch und zurückgezogen in seinem *monasterium*: „Er lebte nämlich in einer Kirche in einem abgeschiedenen *Teil* in Verona und wandte sich beständig fastend in häufigem Gebet an Gott";[11] dann wurde er von Gallienus, dem heidnischen Kaiser, zum königlichen „palatium" gerufen.[12] Den Weg dahin konnte der Heilige auf wundersame Weise sehr zügig zurücklegen. Er erreichte die kaiserliche Residenz noch schneller als die königlichen Boten: „aber der Heilige erhob sich und begab sich zum Palast, und als der heilige Bischof den Weg ging, kam er früher dort an als die Soldaten, die gesandt worden waren."[13] Zeno rettete die vom Teufel besessene Tochter Gallienus' und durch den erfolgreichen Exorzismus konnte er sowohl den Kaiser als auch das bis dahin noch heidnische Veroneser Volk, das vor der Residenz zusammengeströmt war, zum Christentum bekehren: „Und er sah eine große Masse an Menschen, die sich beim Palast versammelt hatte, und sie glaubten an Jesus Christus, nachdem sie vom heidnischen Irrtum bekehrt worden waren."[14] Daraufhin konnte nun der Heilige in Verona die Götzenbilder zerstören, mit der Unterstützung des Kaisers christliche Kirchen bauen und als Bischof wirken: „Nachdem der Priester die Stadt Verona betrat, predigte er furchtlos, so dass im Namen Christi Kirchen gebaut wurden."[15] Nach seinem Tod wurde Zeno in einer zu seinen Ehren durch die kaiserliche Familie erbauten Basilika bestattet, wo sich die Bürger fortan jedes Jahr versammelten, um feierlich sein Fest zu begehen.[16]

Das Leben des Heiligen kann somit als sukzessives Eintreten in den Stadtraum erzählt werden: zuerst die Askese in seiner Zelle, abgeschottet vom städtischen Leben, dann der Ruf zum königlichen Palast und der siegreiche Einzug in die Stadt. Dort, im Stadtraum, entfaltete er sein Wirken, das wiederum als ein Sich-Einschreiben in die Topographie Veronas gesehen werden kann: Zeno

---

ad ecclesiae ianuam veniebant, ad bibendum hauriebant aquam, quae, ut praedixi, usque ad fenestras excreverat et tamen intra ecclesiam nullo modo defluebat. Hauriri itaque ut aqua poterat, sed defluere ut aqua non poterat. Stans autem ante ianuam ad ostendendum cunctis meritum martyris, et aqua erat ad adiutorium et quasi aqua non erat ad invadendum locum." Ebd., S. 348.

11 Meine Übersetzung gibt die Mehrdeutigkeit der Formulierung „in monasterio in secretiori parte in oppido Veronensis" wieder. Es ist nicht endgültig zu klären, worauf „in secretiori parte" zu beziehen ist: Ist „in einem abgeschiedenen Teil des Klosters" oder „der Stadt" gemeint? „Erat enim sedens in monasterio in secretiori parte in oppido Veronensi, continuis ieiuniis et crebris orationibus a Domino petens […]", aus: Sala: Il culto di Zeno nei secoli VIII–IX, S. 29.

12 Ebd., S. 30.

13 „[...] exsurgens vero sanctus […] perrexit ad palatium […] quo sanctus Dei episcopus, dum iter ageret, ante pervenit quam hi, qui missi fuerant milites", ebd., S. 31.

14 „Videns multitudo populi qui ad palatium convenerat, ab errore conversa gentili crediderunt in Christum Iesum […]", ebd.

15 „Ingressus sacerdos Veronam civitatem intrepidus praedicabat […] ut […] in Christi nomine construerentur ecclesiae", ebd.

16 Vgl. ebd.

zerstörte alle heidnischen Gebäude und baute stattdessen christliche Kirchen, in seinem Tun veränderte er das Antlitz der Stadt tiefgreifend und dauerhaft.

So entstand vor dem Hintergrund der Geschichte von Zeno ein Netz von Bezügen und Bedeutungen, das sich über die historische Stadt legte und sie verwandelte: Verona wurde zur ‚Zenostadt'.[17] Sharon Farmer beschreibt auf ähnliche Weise die Stadt Tours aufgrund des hier gepflegten Martinskultes als „Martinopolis".[18]

1.2 Zeno und die Forschung

Das ungebrochene Interesse, das Lokalhistoriker dem Kult des heiligen Bischofs bis in die heutige Zeit entgegenbringen, zeigt, dass Verona auch über das Mittelalter hinaus die Zenostadt blieb. Bereits im 16. Jahrhundert sammelten zwei gelehrte Priester aus Verona, Raffaele Bagatta und Battista Peretti, historisches Material, vor allem Inschriften, mit Bezug zu allen Heiligen, deren Reliquien sich in Verona befanden, darunter natürlich auch zu Zeno.[19] Auch im 18. Jahrhundert hielt die Begeisterung der Veroneser Historiker für die Geschichte ihrer Heiligen an. Scipione Maffei verfasste mehrere Werke zur Stadtgeschichte und interessierte sich besonders für Zeno, zu dessen Viten (BHL 9001 und BHL 9010) er Editionen vorbereitete. Den Gebrüdern Ballerini, die sich für Zeno vor allem als historische Person interessierten, verdanken wir nicht nur die Edition des Translationsberichtes der Reliquien von Zeno, sondern auch die erste Edition der Predigtsammlung *Tractatus*.[20]

Ein großer Teil der Forschung des 20. und 21. Jahrhunderts fußt auf diesen Vorarbeiten aus dem 18. Jahrhundert. Unter anderem gelten mangels einer modernen historisch-kritischen Edition immer noch die Editionen Maffeis und Ballerinis als

---

17 Zum ‚spatial turn' siehe zum Beispiel: Anne E. Lester u. a. (Hg.): Cities, Texts and Social Networks, 400–1500. Experiences and Perceptions of Medieval Urban Space, Florenz 2010. Zum besonderen Verhältnis von Heiligen und Raum, insbesondere unter Einbezug der performativen Aspekte der Liturgie siehe auch: Dieter Bauer u. a. (Hg.): Heilige – Liturgie – Raum (Beiträge zur Hagiographie 8), Stuttgart 2010; sowie Hans Bjur / Santillo B. Frizell (Hg.): Via Tiburtina. Space, Movement and Artefacts in the Urban Landscape, Rom 2005.

18 „Natural resources and geographical location alone do not go far in explaining the history of ‚Martinopolis'. For this town was, from its inception, a product of human artifice, institutions and imagination. [...] It was above all the Christian religion, and especially the cult of Saint Martin that contributed to the survival, the importance, and even the shape of medieval Tours", Sharon Farmer: Communities of Saint Martin. Legend and Ritual in Medieval Tours, Ithaca 1991, S. 13–14.

19 Vgl. Raffaele Bagatta / Battista Peretti (Hg.): Sanctorum episcoporum Veronensium antiqua monumenta et aliorum sanctorum quorum corpora, et aliquot, quorum ecclesiae habentur Veronae, Venedig 1576.

20 Vgl. Scipione Maffei: Istoria diplomatica, Mantua 1727; Pietro Ballerini / Girolamo Ballerini: Sancti Zenonis Episcopi Veronensis Sermones nunc primum, qui par erat, diligentia editi., Verona 1739. Historisch-kritische Edition des *Tractatus*: Zeno von Verona: Zenonis Veronensis tractatus, hrsg. von Bengt Löfstedt (Corpus Christianorum. Series Latina 22), Turnhout 1971.

Referenzwerke für die beiden Viten des Heiligen.[21] Gleichwohl ist das Interesse an Zeno und seinem Verhältnis zur Stadt auch in neuerer Zeit ungebrochen: Seit 1983 werden in der Zeitschrift *Annuario storico Zenoniano* Beiträge aus allen Disziplinen zur Geschichte Veronas, seiner kirchlichen Institutionen sowie Veroneser Heiligenkulte gesammelt.[22] Sehr wichtig ist darüber hinaus die historische Studie von Elisa Anti zum Kult des heiligen Zeno in Verona sowie ihr zusammenfassender Überblick über die handschriftliche Überlieferung der Viten von Zeno. Der große Wert der Studie liegt vor allem in der übersichtlichen Gesamtschilderung des Zenokultes in Verona, im Detail weist sie jedoch vielfältige Ungenauigkeiten auf und ist deswegen mit Vorbehalt zu verwenden und an einigen Stellen zu korrigieren.[23]

Während die Viten Zenos also eine vergleichsweise große Aufmerksamkeit erfahren haben, muss leider betont werden, dass dabei liturgisches Material weitestgehend außen vor blieb. Eine Ausnahme stellt in diesem Zusammenhang das Werk von Franco Segala dar, in dem überblicksartig die mittelalterliche Messeliturgie für Zeno behandelt wird.[24] Darüber hinaus wurden einige Texte aus dem Quellencorpus, die dem Gattungsbereich des Stundengebets zuzurechnen sind, von den Gebrüdern Ballerini transkribiert. Allerdings entsprechen die Arbeiten von Segala und den Brüdern Ballerini nicht modernen editorischen Maßstäben, was eine Neubearbeitung des Materials notwendig macht. Die Beschäftigung mit der liturgischen Überlieferung aus dem Kontext des Zenokultes bleibt weiterhin ein Desiderat, das mit der vorliegenden Untersuchung zumindest mit Bezug auf das Stundengebet geschlossen wird.

1.3 Zeno und seine Verehrer

Der Zenokult ist und war, wie erwähnt, in Verona und für seine Bewohner sehr präsent und durchdrang in materieller und symbolischer Form alle Bereiche des Sozialen und Politischen: Vom einzelnen Bürger, der seiner Verehrung für den Heiligen oft durch die Namenswahl für seine Nachkommen Ausdruck verlieh,[25] zu der einzelnen Patrizierfamilie, wie beispielsweise den Scaligeri, die auf der Glocke des von ihnen 1370 errichteten Turmes den eigenen Namen unter einer

21 Vgl. zum Beispiel in Sala: Il culto di Zeno nei secoli VIII–IX und ders.: Il culto di S. Zeno dal X al XII secolo, in: Annuario storico zenoniano 8, 1991, S. 15–32 sowie Gian P. Marchi: Le antiche storie di San Zeno, in: Gian P. Marchi u. a. (Hg.): Il culto di San Zeno nel Veronese, Verona 1972, S. 13–61, hier: S. 13–61.

22 Annuario storico zenoniano, Verona 1983–2021 (laufend).

23 Vgl. Elisa Anti: Verona e il culto di San Zeno tra IV e XII secolo, Verona 2009.

24 Franco Segala: Il culto di San Zeno nella liturgia medioevale, Verona 1982.

25 Ebd., S. 72–73: „[...] A partire dalla metà circa del secolo IX, il nome Zeno inizia ad attestarsi nell'onomastica cittadina. La sua diffusione si amplia sempre più nel secolo successivo, finché, nel Mille, Zeno (con la versione femminile Zena) diviene l'antroponimo probabilmente più diffuso nel Veronese, come dimostra il comparire in quasi tutti i documenti di almeno una persona con questo nome."

Darstellung des Bischofs mit der Angelschnur anbringen ließen,[26] hin zur sich verfestigenden Kommune, deren amtierende Funktionäre, wie der *Potestà*, expressis verbis vor Gott, Maria und Zeno schwören mussten: „Zu Ehre Gottes und seiner ruhmvollen Mutter und des seligen Zeno. Wir erfreuen uns an dem Trost seines hochheiligen Körpers und sind durch sein Patrozinium geschützt und haben die Obhut über die Stadt Verona."[27]

Vor dem Hintergrund einer teilweise imaginierten, teilweise historischen Topographie entstanden Institutionen an besonders bedeutungsvollen Orten in der Stadt, wo sich die Heiligenverehrung konkretisierte und sich das Netz von Bedeutungsbezügen verdichtete. Dort huldigten vor allem religiöse Gruppen und Gemeinschaften Zeno als symbolischer Leitfigur, die sie mit verschiedenen Praktiken verehrten. Bis ins hohe Mittelalter waren es vor allem zwei Gruppen, die sich wesentlich durch die Verehrung des heiligen Zeno konstituierten und auch durch ihre Verortung in der Sakraltopographie der Zenostadt einen besonderen Bezug zum Heiligen aufwiesen. Es handelt sich um die Gemeinschaft der Kleriker am Dom und die monastische Gemeinschaft des Klosters San Zeno Maggiore vor den Toren der Stadt.

Am Dom war nicht nur der Bischof, sondern auch eine Gruppe von Klerikern tätig, Priester und Diakone, die der seit dem frühen 9. Jahrhundert nachweisbaren „Schule der Priester und anderer Kleriker" zugerechnet werden können.[28] Dabei bezeichnet der Begriff „*schola*" sowohl das Domkapitel als Körperschaft als auch die dort angesiedelte Priesterschule.[29] Die Kleriker waren vor allem für das Aufrechterhalten des liturgischen Betriebes in der bischöflichen Kathedrale zuständig und dienten darin dem Bischof.[30] Wirtschaftlich und teilweise auch räumlich war das Kapitel hingegen bereits seit der Karolingerzeit vom Bischofshof getrennt und damit relativ unabhängig: Bischof Ratold hatte den Klerikern ein eigenes Einkommen zugesichert, das getrennt von der bischöflichen Kam-

---

26 Vgl. Lanfranco Franzoni: La campana di Cansignorino per la torre del Gadello (1370), in: Gian Maria Varanini (Hg.): Gli scaligeri 1277–1387. Saggi e schede pubblicati in occasione della mostra storico-documentaria allestita dal Museo di Castelvecchio di Verona (giugno–novembre 1988), Verona 1988, S. 322.

27 „Ad honorem Dei et gloriosissime eius genitricis Marie et beatissime Zenonis, cuius sacratissimi corporis consolatione gaudemus et patrocinio munimur et salvamentum civitatis Verone". Gino Sandri: Gli Statuti Veronesi del 1276, Venedig 1940, S. 21. Vgl. dazu auch: Andrea v. Hülsen-Esch: Romanische Skulptur in Oberitalien als Reflex der kommunalen Entwicklung im 12. Jahrhundert. Untersuchungen zu Mailand und Verona (Artefact 8), Berlin 1994, S. 178.

28 „schola sacerdotum ceterorumque clericorum", Vittorio Fainelli: Codice diplomatico Veronese. Bd. 1 Dalla caduta dell'impero romano alla fine del periodo carolingio. 2 Bde. (Monumenti storici. Nuova serie 1), Venedig 1940, Nr. 122, S. 161. Vgl. Cristina La Rocca: Pacifico di Verona. Il passato carolingio nella costruzione della memoria urbana, Rom 1995, S. 76.

29 Vgl. Giuseppe Forchielli: Collegialità di chierici nel veronese dall'VIII secolo all'etá comunale, in: Archivio veneto 58, 1928, S. 1–117, hier: S. 31–33.

30 Vgl. Pierpaolo Brugnoli: Le case del capitolo canonicale presso il duomo di Verona, Verona 1979, S. 44.

mer, von den Leitern des Kapitels, dem Erzdiakon und dem Erzpriester, verwaltet wurde. Außerdem hatte Ratold dem Kapitel eine eigene Kultstätte, die neben dem Dom gelegene Kirche San Giorgio e San Zeno (heute Sant'Elena), zu Verfügung gestellt.[31]

Diese erste Verehrergemeinschaft nahm den heiligen Zeno für sich in Anspruch, obwohl der Dom nicht die Grabkirche des Heiligen war. Auf der einen Seite konnte sich der Bischof auf Zeno als seinen Amtsvorgänger berufen und sich mit dem berühmten Prälaten in eine Traditionslinie setzten.[32] Dieser Versuch der Veroneser Bischöfe, an der Aura des Heiligen zu partizipieren wird bereits in der Benennung des Episkopiums als „*domus sancti Zenonis*", also als „Haus des heiligen Zeno", deutlich.[33] Auf der anderen Seite beriefen sich auch die Kleriker des Kapitels auf Zeno. Die früheste Vita des Heiligen, der sogenannte *Sermo de vita sancti Zenonis*, wurde von der neueren Forschung als Produkt eines Klerikers des Domkapitels erkannt.[34] Darin wird der Heilige als Priester („sacerdos") profiliert und in seinem gepriesenen Wirken als Vorbild der Kleriker und Berühmter Vertreter ihres Amtes vereinnahmt.

Während die Gemeinschaft am Dom nicht in Anspruch nehmen konnte, den Heiligen an seiner Grabstätte zu verehren, konnten sich hingegen die Benediktinermönche des Zenoklosters San Zeno Maggiore am westlichen Rand der Stadt als eigentliche Hüter der Reliquien Zenos profilieren. Hier waren die sterblichen Überreste des Heiligen begraben, markiert durch ein in Stein errichtetes Reliquiar,[35] das dem Heiligen physische Präsenz verlieh, und wo er seine anhaltende

---

31 Vgl. Forchielli: Collegialità di chierici, S. 36–42; außerdem Fainelli: Codice diplomatico Veronese, Nr. 101, 120–127.

32 Bereits aus zwei frühmittelalterlichen Quellen spricht die Idee, dass die dem Autor zeitgenössischen Bischöfe in der Tradition ihrer Amtsvorgänger und der Heiligen der Urkirche standen. Es handelt sich zum einen um das Lobgedicht für Verona *Versus de Verona*, in dem die frühen Bischöfe von Verona als Nachfolger der Märtyrer, Apostel, Doctores und Confessores präsentiert wurden und zum anderen um ein Altarparament, das sogenannte *Velo di Classe*, das im 8. Jhdt. den Altar der Kirche San Fermo in Verona schmückte und eine Liste der Prälaten von Verona bildlich darstellt. Zu dem *Versus de Verona* siehe Giovanni B. Pighi (Hg.): Versvs de Verona, Bologna 1960; zu *Velo di Classe* siehe Carlo Cipolla: Il velo di Classe, Verona 1972 und Jean-Charles Picard: Le souvenir des évêques. Sépultures, listes épiscopales et cultes des évêques en Italie du nord des origines au xe siècle (Bibliothèque des Ecoles Françaises d'Athènes et de Rome 268), Rom 1988, S. 515–518.

33 Vgl. Maureen C. Miller: The Formation of a Medieval Church. Ecclesiastical Change in Verona, 950–1150, Ithaca 1993, S. 123.

34 Vgl. Anti: Verona e il culto, S. 49–50 und Paolo Golinelli: Il Cristianesimo nella „Venetia" altomedievale. Diffusione, istituzionalizzazione e forme di religiosità dalle origini al sec. X, in: Andrea Castagnetti / Gian Maria Varanini (Hg.): Il Veneto nel medioevo. Dalla „Venetia" alla Marca Veronese, Verona 1989, S. 237–331, hier: S. 284. Der *Sermo de vita sancti Zenonis* wurde von Marchi: Le antiche storie, S. 17. als Produkt des Benediktinerklosters San Zeno Maggiore gesehen.

35 Vgl. Felix Heinzer: Poesie als politische Theologie. Texte und Kontexte der liturgischen Verehrung König Ludwigs des Heiligen, in: Francia 42, 2015, S. 73–92, hier: S. 80, der die Sainte-Chapelle als einen „monumentalen Reliquienschrein" für die Dornenkrone identifiziert.

Wirkmacht durch Mirakel manifestieren konnte. Die Mönche des Klosters hatten somit die Aufgabe, die Residuen des Heiligen zu verwahren und seine Memoria kultisch zu vollziehen. Dies taten sie jedes Jahr im Rahmen des Translationsfestes, anlässlich dessen das Grab des Heiligen in einer feierlichen Prozession in die Krypta aufgesucht und verehrt wurde.[36]

Am Beispiel des Zenokultes in Verona wird im Folgenden untersucht, wie religiöse Verehrergemeinschaften Heilige durch liturgische Performanz, durch die kultische Praxis, erst konstruierten und sich zu ihnen in ein Verhältnis setzten. Konkret wird diese Frage am Beispiel der Liturgie der Institutionen beantwortet, die sich in Verona auf den heiligen Zeno beriefen, nämlich des Veroneser Doms sowie des Klosters San Zeno Maggiore. Ein besonderer Fokus soll dabei auf dem Verhältnis liegen, das diese beiden Institutionen zum Heiligen und in der Folge auch untereinander entwickelten.

Die Beispiele bieten sich aus mehreren Gründen an. Zum einen erlaubt ihr Alter, den Formierungsprozess der Zenoliturgie von ihren Anfängen über einen längeren Zeitraum hinweg nachzuvollziehen. Spuren eines Zenokultes finden sich am Dom bereits im 5. Jahrhundert, im Kloster seit dem Frühmittelalter. Außerdem findet sich hier die umfassendste Überlieferung liturgischer Quellen aus Verona, die noch großteils vor Ort aufbewahrt wird und zugänglich ist. Zum anderen stellen diese Institutionen ein optimales Untersuchungsobjekt für die übergeordnete Frage, nämlich wie religiöse Verehrergemeinschaften Heilige durch liturgische Performanz konstruierten und sich zu ihnen in ein Verhältnis setzten, dar, weil sie in ihrer Bezugnahme auf den selben Heiligen in einem Konkurrenzverhältnis standen und so gezwungen waren, ein individuelles, abgrenzbares Profil des Heiligen zu konstituieren. Der zeitliche Rahmen der Untersuchung erstreckt sich vom Beginn des 9. Jahrhunderts, da aus dieser Zeit die frühesten liturgischen Zeugnisse stammen, bis zum Ende des 12. Jahrhunderts, als sich das liturgische Repertoire weitestgehend formiert hatte. Auch historische Gründe sprechen für diese Eingrenzung: Mit der Vermehrung der geistlichen Institutionen, die ab 1150 in Verona zu beobachten ist, bildete sich eine komplexe ekklesiastische Struktur aus, in der die Spannungsverhältnisse zwischen den einzelnen Institutionen nicht mehr deutlich nachzuvollziehen sind.[37]

Die vorliegende Studie ist wie folgt strukturiert: Nach dieser Einleitung werden in einem methodologischen Kapitel die Grundlagen der Untersuchung expliziert. Hier wird es um die Art und Weise gehen, in der Heiligkeit liturgisch konstruiert wurde und um die Frage, welche Schlüsse für die editorische Bearbeitung des Quellenmaterials daraus zu ziehen sind.

Diese Ergebnisse werden in Kapitel 3 angewandt, in dem das liturgische Material ediert und seine zeitgenössische Performanz rekonstruiert wird. Während

---

[36] Darüber gibt eine spätmittelalterliche Handschrift aus dem Kloster Auskunft, das Antiphonar Verona BC 739 I, auf fol. 107v.

[37] Vgl. Miller: The Formation of a Medieval Church, S. 11.

sich die nachfolgende Untersuchung auf die liturgischen Quellen aus Verona bis ins Hochmittelalter beschränkt, wird in dieser Edition das gesamte überlieferte liturgische Material zugänglich gemacht, um vergleichende Studien in der Zukunft zu ermöglichen. Da die Rekonstruktion der Performanz hingegen einer aufwendigen Analyse des handschriftlichen Materials bedarf und daher nur im Rahmen einer Fallstudie zu leisten ist, beschränkt sie sich auf die Verehrungskontexte in Verona.

In Kapitel 4 werden diese Verehrungskontexte, der Veroneser Dom und das Kloster San Zeno Maggiore, eingehender untersucht und historisch kontextualisiert. Diese Untersuchung erstreckt sich von den Anfängen des Kultes im 5. Jahrhundert über die Entstehung des frühesten liturgischen Materials im 9. und 10. Jahrhundert bis zur Verfestigung der Zenoliturgie im hohen Mittelalter. Dabei wird deutlich, dass Liturgie nicht nur wesentlich zur Profilierung und Identitätsbildung einer Verehrergemeinschaft führte, sondern in Verona auch zu einem Spannungsverhältnis zwischen den Institutionen beitragen konnte, die sich auf den gleichen Heiligen beriefen.

2 Methodische Grundlage der Arbeit

> Clearly, scholars have the right to study anything they want, and equally clearly, those who continue bringing to our attention more accurate recensions of ancient prayer material will also continue to receive the proper adulation of those who recognize that without these data we could say nothing at all of the communities who once composed them. But equally clearly, it is the obligation of others in the scholarly community to take the next step and postulate pictures of those communities.[1]

2.1 Von der Hagiographie *zur* Hagiopraxis

Gegen Ende der 1980er Jahre veröffentlichte der Historiker Peter Brown den viel beachteten Artikel *Society and the Supernatural: A Medieval Change*. Dort gibt er eine prägnante Beschreibung des Phänomens der Reliquienverehrung in Spätantike und Mittelalter: „[A]mong the many newly discovered or newly arrived pieces of dust, only the [human] group can make up its mind which is the holy dust."[2] Dieses Zitat trifft meines Erachtens auch den Kern der mittelalterlichen Heiligenverehrung. In beiden Fällen werden Wesen und Bedeutung von Objekten und Personen im Rahmen von kommunikativen Prozessen sozialer Gruppen konstituiert. Viel mehr als die tatsächliche und historische Biographie eines Heiligen sind es die sozialen Gruppen der Verehrer sowie die jeweils unterschiedlichen Verehrungssituationen, die den Heiligen als solchen konstituieren und über seine jeweilige Bedeutung und Funktion entscheiden: So wurde der Staub zur Reliquie, ein im 4. Jahrhundert verstorbener Bischof zum Heiligen.

Dieser kommunikative Vorgang kann mit Gewinn den theoretischen Grundlagen des Freiburger Sonderforschungsbereiches 948 ‚Helden – Heroisierungen – Heroismen' entsprechend als Heroisierung definiert werden, nämlich als:

> [...] der Prozess [...], in dem einer realen oder fiktiven Person heroische Qualitäten zugeschrieben werden und diese Person so zum gestalthaften Fokus einer Gemeinschaft (welcher Größe auch immer) avanciert. Die heroische Figur konstituiert sich in diesem sozialen und kommunikativen Prozess. Dessen Elemente sind die Zuschreibung von Eigenschaften, die Formierung und Artikulation in Ausdrucks- und Darstellungsmedien und die Etablierung der Verehrung.[3]

Dementsprechend kann auch mittelalterliche Heiligenverehrung als besondere Form einer solchen Heroisierung verstanden werden, in der dem von den Zeitgenossen als historische Person angesehenen Heiligen Eigenschaften zugeschrieben

---

1 Hoffman: Beyond the Text, S. 7.

2 Peter Brown: Society and the Holy in Late Antiquity 1989, S. 318.

3 SFB 948 (Hg.): Antrag auf Einrichtung und Förderung des Sonderforschungsbereichs 948 Helden – Heroisierungen – Heroismen. Transformationen und Konjunkturen von der Antike bis zur Moderne, S. 14.

werden, die ihn als außergewöhnlich und verehrungswürdig auszeichnen und nicht nur genuin „heroische" sein müssen, wie es das Zitat nahelegt.[4]

Nun stellt sich die Frage, wie dieser Zuschreibungsprozess genau vonstattenging, in welchen Quellen er fassbar wird und mit welchen Methoden er rekonstruiert werden kann. Der Großteil der aktuellen Forschung hat hierauf eine klare Antwort: Der Prozess der Konstruktion eines Heiligen hätte sich ausschließlich in hagiographischen Texten artikuliert, denen man sich heute mit einem geschichts- oder literaturwissenschaftlichen Interesse nähert.[5]

So ist Hagiographie in den Augen von Dolbeau und Philippart im Grunde ein Subgenre der Historiographie, mit dem Unterschied, dass im Zentrum dieser Texte der Heilige steht, dessen „mémoire historique"[6] darin konstruiert wurde. Aus ihrer Sicht handelt es sich bei der Hagiographie also um eine Form der Geschichtsschreibung, bei welcher der an sich historiographisch arbeitende Hagiograph durch liturgische Bedürfnisse dazu gezwungen ist, seine wissenschaftlichen Prinzipien hintanzustellen und sich in den Bereich des Wahrscheinlichen zu begeben, also Fiktives und Übernatürliches wie Wunder und Mirakel in seinen Bericht zu integrieren.[7]

Diese Auffassung scheint mir aus verschiedenen Gründen problematisch zu sein, vor allem führt sie aber zu einer Engführung des hagiographischen Genres, zu dem ausschließlich Viten, Passiones, Translations- und Mirakelberichte gezählt werden. Liturgische Quellen, also Gebete, Hymnen und so weiter werden weitestgehend exkludiert, da mit diesen Textgenres keine historischen Ansprüche verbunden seien:

---

4 Siehe dazu: Felix Heinzer u. a.: Einleitung: Relationen zwischen Sakralisierungen und Heroisierungen, in: Felix Heinzer u. a. (Hg.): Sakralität und Heldentum (Helden – Heroisierungen – Heroismen 6), Würzburg 2017, S. 9–18, hier: S. 11. Für die Wandlung der heroischen Semantik in der Spätantike siehe: Felix Heinzer: Hos multo elegantius, si ecclesiastica loquendi consuetudo pateretur, nostros heroas uocaremus – Sprachbilder im frühchristlichen Märtyrerdiskurs, in: Ralf von den Hoff u. a. (Hg.): Imitatio heroica. Heldenangleichung im Bildnis (Helden – Heroisierungen – Heroismen 1), Würzburg 2015, S. 119–136, hier: S. 131–132.

5 „Bei ihrer redaktionellen Arbeit waren die Hagiographen Schriftsteller wie die anderen. Im Sammeln und in der kritischen Überarbeitung der Quellen war ihre Arbeit gleich wie die der Historiographen" („Dans leur travail rédactionnel, les hagiographes étaient donc des écrivains comme les autres [...]. Dans la collecte et l'élaboration critique de leur documentation, leur tache s'apparentait à celle des historiographes"), in: François Dolbeau: Les hagiographes au travail: collecte et traitement des documents écrits (IX–XII siècles), in: Martin Heinzelmann (Hg.): Manuscrits hagiographiques et travail des hagiographes (Beihefte der Francia 24), Sigmaringen 1992, S. 49–76, hier: S. 50.

6 Guy Philippart: Introduction, in: Guy Philippart (Hg.): Hagiographies. Histoire internationale de la littérature hagiographique latine et vernaculaire en Occident des origines à 1550 (Corpus Christianorum. Hagiographies), Turnhout 1994–2006, S. 9–24.

7 „Die Ansprüche der Auftraggeber und die Bedürfnisse der Liturgie zwangen viele Hagiographen, ihre Einstellung zu ändern. Zwischen dem Wahren und dem Falschen öffnet sich das riesige Gebiet des Wahrscheinlichen." („Les exigences des commanditaires et les necessites liturgiques forcerent beaucoup d'hagiographes à prender une autre attitude. Entre le vrai et le faux, se déploie le champ immense du vraisemblable." Dolbeau: Les hagiographes au travail, S. 54–55.

Wir schliessen liturgische Traktate, Gebete, Predigten, Sprüche, Litaneien, Kalender, Orationen und Segnungen ausdrücklich aus unserem Projekt aus, nämlich alle jene meistens zweitrangigen Stücke der Hagiographie, die keine historischen Ansprüche haben.[8]

Die diesen Ausführungen zugrundeliegende Gleichsetzung von hagiographischem und historiographischem Schreiben wird von der jüngeren Forschung zunehmend in Frage gestellt. Ein Ergebnis dieser Diskussion ist die Charakterisierung der Hagiographie als eine Form pragmatischer Schriftlichkeit. 1997 hielt Hedwig Röckelein fest, dass „die mittelalterliche Hagiographie zu den ‚Formen der Schriftlichkeit [gehört], die unmittelbar zweckhaftem Handeln dienen oder die menschliches Tun und Verhalten durch Bereitstellung von Wissen anleiten wollen', und [dass sie] zu dem ‚Schriftgut [gehört], für dessen Entstehung und Nutzung Erfordernisse der Lebenspraxis konstitutiv waren'."[9]

Zwar lässt sich daraus folgern, dass Motivation sowie Funktion der hagiographischen Verschriftlichungen vielfältige, in der jeweiligen Lebenswelt der Autoren wurzelnde Gründe haben können. Diese werden von der Forschung jedoch weitestgehend im Bereich politischer Interessen und Ziele gesucht.[10] In der Tat zeigt auch die vorliegende Studie, dass politische und wirtschaftliche Gründe hagiographisches Schreiben motivieren konnten, allerdings ist eine Engführung auf diesen Bereich fragwürdig, da weitere, zweifelsfrei wichtige Aspekte der mittelalterlichen Hagiographie außer Acht bleiben, darunter Identitätsstiftung und genuin religiöse Motive. Vor allem ist kritisch festzuhalten, dass auch diese Forschungsansätze unter Hagiographie ausschließlich Viten, Translations- und Mirakelberichte verstehen.

Tatsächlich hat sich bereits um die Jahrtausendwende Klaus Herbers kritisch mit dieser Engführung auseinandergesetzt. Seiner Auffassung nach lässt sich Hagiographie nur dann verstehen, wenn sie im Rahmen ihrer handschriftlichen (Mit-)Überlieferung und ihres Entstehungs- und Nutzungskontextes als der Causa scribendi, legendi oder audiendi untersucht wird.[11] Als Folge sieht er die Exklu-

---

8 „[...] nous exclurons expressément de notre projet [...] les traités liturgiques, les prières, les serments [sic], les dictons, les litanies, les calendriers, les oraisons, les bénédictions, tout ces morceaux généralement mineurs d'hagiographiques, mais n'ont pas de prétentions historiques." Philippart: Introduction, S. 14.

9 Hedwig Röckelein: Zur Pragmatik hagiographischer Schriften im Frühmittelalter, in: Thomas Scharff (Hg.): Bene vivere in communitate. Beiträge zum italienischen und deutschen Mittelalter. Hagen Keller zum 60. Geburtstag überreicht von seinen Schülerinnen und Schülern, Münster 1997, S. 225–238, hier: S. 226.

10 Vgl. Bernhard Vogel: Das hagiographische Werk Lantberts von Deutz über Heribert von Köln, in: Dieter Bauer / Klaus Herbers (Hg.): Hagiographie im Kontext. Wirkungsweisen und Möglichkeiten historischer Auswertung (Beiträge zur Hagiographie 1), Stuttgart 2000, S. 117–129, hier: S. 124.

11 Vgl. Klaus Herbers: Hagiographie im Kontext – Konzeption und Zielvorstellung, in: Dieter Bauer / Klaus Herbers (Hg.): Hagiographie im Kontext. Wirkungsweisen und Möglichkeiten historischer Auswertung (Beiträge zur Hagiographie 1), Stuttgart 2000, S. IX–XXVIII, hier: XIV–XV.

sion des liturgischen Materials, das vielfach Teil dieser Kontexte war, äußerst kritisch:

> Folglich wären – so Dolbeau – vorwiegend narrative hagiographische Texte, wie Viten, Translationsberichte und Mirakel, von eher liturgischen Stücken in Kalendarien, Martyrologien, Offizien und Litaneien zu scheiden. Geht man davon aus, dass in der Regel – unabhängig, ob überliefert oder nicht – zunächst narrative Texte verfasst wurden, sodann diese Texte gegebenenfalls für liturgische oder andere Zwecke überarbeitet wurden, erscheint es durchaus plausibel, dass sich die hagiographische Forschung bisher eher den narrativen Texten angenommen hat. Von ganz ähnlichen Voraussetzungen gehen auch die ersten zwei des auf vier Bände geplanten Werkes ‚Hagiographies' von Guy Philippart aus. Die Integration dieser Texte, zum Beispiel in liturgische Bücher, gewinnt für die hier verfolgten Fragen an Gewicht, und zu diskutieren wäre, inwieweit die Trennung in narrative und weitere hagiographische Schriften aufrechterhalten und das bisher ungleichgewichtige Interesse künftig ausgeglichen werden sollte.[12]

Zu einem ähnlichen Schluss war De Gaiffier bereits in den 1970ern gekommen, der aber weitestgehend unbeachtet blieb:

> Wenn man von Hagiographie spricht, von hagiographischen Dokumenten, neigt man zu oft dazu, das Leben des Heiligen (Passio, Vita) in den Vordergrund zu stellen, und zwar meistens ausschließlich oder zumindest vorwiegend. Nun aber, die hagiographische Gattung erschöpft sich bei Weitem nicht in den Viten: man sollte auch die anderen Dokumente berücksichtigen, hauptsächlich: Kalender, Martyrologien, Inschriften, liturgische Bücher (Sakramentare und Brevieren), Litaneien, Hymnen, Ikonographie, ohne dabei die Translation der Reliquien und vor allem die Wunderberichte zu vergessen. Diesen ganzen Komplex benötigen wir, um die Geschichte eines Heiligen zu rekonstruieren.[13]

Diesen Forderungen, liturgische Quellen zur Gattung der Hagiographie zuzuordnen, ist insofern zuzustimmen, als dass Viten, Translations- und Mirakelberichte nicht isoliert verstanden werden können, sondern Teil eines größeren Kultarrangements waren, das auch andere Quellen, darunter etwa auch die für die liturgische Feier des Heiligen geschaffenen Texte, umfasste.

Die Erweiterung des Corpus hagiographischer Quellen um das liturgische Material ist zwar ein wichtiger Fortschritt bei der Erforschung mittelalterlicher Heiligenkulte, löst aber das eigentliche Problem nicht. Dieses liegt in der unterschiedlichen Auffassung darüber, wie und auf welcher medialen Ebene Heiligkeit konstruiert wurde. Die Vertreter der Hagiographie-Forschung sehen in dieser

---

12 Ebd., S. XI–XII.

13 „Quand on parle d'hagiographie, de documents hagiographiques, on a trop souvent la tendance de mettre à l'avant plan, et presque d'une manière exclusive ou tout au moins prépondérante, la Vie du Saint: Passio, Vita. Or, les Vitae ne constituent nullement tout le genre hagiographique: il faut tenir compte d'autres documents dont voici les principaux: calendriers, martyrologies, inscriptions, livres liturgiques (sacramentaires et bréviaires), litanies, hymnes, iconographie, sans oublier les translations et surtout les Miracula. Tout cet ensemble nous sert à rejoindre l'histoire d'un saint." Baudouin de Gaiffier d'Hestroy: Hagiographie et historiographie, in: La storiografia altomedievale (Settimane di studio del Centro Italiano di Studi sull'Alto Medioevo 17), Spoleto 1970, S. 139–166, hier: S. 140.

Konstruktionsleistung primär das Ergebnis narrativer Strategien eines literarisch tätigen Autors, dessen Zuschreibungen und Motive es zu rekonstruieren gelte. Daraus resultiert das Verständnis von Heiligen als Protagonisten narrativer Texte und daher als literarische Figuren.

Diese Auffassung basiert aber auf einem Missverständnis, das auf die enge, Heiligenviten fokussierende Gattungskonzeption von Hagiographie zurückzuführen ist. Viten, Translations- und Mirakelberichte eignen sich besonders für eine im breiten Sinne literarische Betrachtung, weil sie in sich geschlossene, textliche Produkte darstellen, die sich unabhängig von ihrem Gebrauch untersuchen lassen. Tatsächlich wurden Viten bereits im Mittelalter zu vielfältigen Zwecken verfasst und in unterschiedlichen Kontexten verwendet, wie zum Beispiel für die private Lesung in der Zelle[14] oder für die öffentliche Erbauung von Laien.[15] Die Vielfältigkeit der Motive zu betonen, Heiligenviten zu verschriftlichen und zu nutzen sowie die Tatsache, dass sich Viten, Translations- und Mirakelberichte dank ihrer literarischen Eigenheit auch getrennt vom liturgischen Heiligenkult untersuchen lassen, kann allerdings nicht einen viel evidenteren Aspekt verbergen, nämlich dass Heiligenviten in erster Linie Ausdruck eines liturgischen Kultes waren. So auch De Gaiffier:

> Die Hagiographie ist der Ausdruck des Kultes. Aber es reicht nicht aus, diese Reihe von Dokumenten aufzulisten; man sollte sich vielmehr dessen bewusst sein, dass diese aus einem einzigen Bedürfnis entstehen: einen Heiligenkult zu erwecken und ihn aufrecht- und wachzuhalten. Infolgedessen sollte man versuchen, zu verstehen, wie diese Dokumente, die oft wegen der Notwendigkeiten des Heiligenkultes entstanden, nicht überwiegend und ausschließlich als historische Quellen verfasst wurden, die uns Informationen über die Helden des Christentums liefern sollen. Vielmehr wurden sie verfasst, um deren Andenken innerhalb der christlichen Gemeinde aufrechtzuhalten, auch, auf der einen Seite, um deren Heiligkeit zu preisen und auf der anderen, um in den Gläubigen den Wunsch zu erwecken, die Heiligen nachzuahmen und deren Schutz zu erbitten.[16]

Ein solches Missverständnis, aufgrund dessen liturgische Quellen lediglich als literarische Produkte verstanden und untersucht werden, wurde am Ende der 1980er Jahre auch von dem Liturgiehistoriker Lawrence A. Hoffman konsta-

---

14 Wie Alkuin bezüglich seiner metrischen *Vita Willibrodi* behauptet, vgl. ders.: Etudes critiques d'hagiographie et d'iconologie (Subsidia Hagiographica 43), Brüssel 1967, S. 475.

15 Vgl. Pierre Riché: Les bibliothèques de trois aristocrates laics carolingiens, in: Le Moyen Âge 69, 1963, S. 87–104, hier: S. 93; 98; 102.

16 „L'hagiographie [...] est l'expression du culte. Mais il ne suffit pas d'aligner cette série de documents; il est indispensable de rappeler qu'ils proviennent principalement d'une seule et même exigence: susciter, maintenir et entretenir le culte des saints. Dès lors, il faut tacher de comprendre comment ces documents, nés souvent des nécessités du culte rendu aux saints, ont été élaborés non pas avant tout et exclusivement comme livres historiques destinés à nous fournir des renseignements sur les héros du christianisme, mais à maintenir leur souvenir dans la communauté chrétienne, afin, d'une part, d'en exalter la sainteté, et, d'autre part, d'inspirer aux fidèles le désir de les imiter et de solliciter leur protection." de Gaiffier d'Hestroy: Hagiographie et historiographie, S. 140–141.

tiert.[17] In seinem 1987 erschienenen Werk *Beyond the Text. A Holistic Approach to Liturgy* kritisiert Hoffman die philologischen und formanalytischen Ansätze der Untersuchungen liturgischer Quellen im 19. und 20. Jahrhundert. Die so orientierten Forschenden würden sich nach ihm nicht wirklich für Liturgie interessieren, sondern lediglich für deren literarische Überreste („literary remains").[18] Dies habe auch zur Folge, dass man sich auf „eine ewige Wiederherstellung von wissenschaftlich akkuraten Texten"[19] beschränke, ohne sich die viel wichtigere Frage zu stellen, nämlich „wie solche Texte, als gelebte liturgische Praxis, Auswirkungen auf die Menschen hatten, die sie verwendeten."[20]

Hoffman räumt ein, dass es bis zu einem gewissen Grad notwendig sei, sich auf die literarischen Produkte liturgischen Handelns zu fokussieren, besonders im Fall von vormodernen Gesellschaften, die sich nicht mehr empirisch beobachten lassen:

> Diese Textzentrierung mag offensichtlich und überhaupt notwendig für Disziplinen erscheinen, die die Antike untersuchen, da sie ihre Materialien aus den literarischen Resten – dem Einzigen, was übrig geblieben ist – von Kulturen sammeln, die vor langer Zeit von der Verwüstung der Geschichte zerstört wurden.[21]

Er besteht aber darauf, dass es sinnvoll sei, es bei der Untersuchung von Liturgie und ihren Quellen nicht bei einer solch ausschließlich philologischen Betrachtungsweise zu belassen: „Of course research must begin with the literature in which the evidence is embedded; that indeed is necessary. But both philology and form-criticism end with that literature as well; and that is not necessary at all."[22]

Im Gegensatz dazu betont auch Hoffman, dass liturgische Quellen nicht als rein literarische Erzeugnisse verstanden werden sollen, „als ob sie tote literarische *specimina* wären, die man von den betenden Akteuren trennen kann."[23] Vielmehr sei es notwendig, dass „[...] Forschende der Liturgie früher oder später mit der verstörenden Erkenntnis konfrontiert werden, dass auch wenn ihr Material aus der Vergangenheit im Wesentlichen literarisch ist, die menschliche Tätigkeit des Betens es nicht ist."[24] Somit wird deutlich, dass die Methoden der literarischen Analyse für die Untersuchung von Liturgie nicht ausreichen können. Hoffman fordert die Forschenden dagegen auf, eine eigene Methode zu entwickeln, um

---

17 Vgl. Hoffman: Beyond the Text.
18 Ebd., S. 3.
19 Ebd., S. 173: „[to] go beyond an eternal recreation of scientifically accurate texts [...]."
20 Ebd.: „[to] see how those texts, played out as lived liturgical practice, had consequences for the people who used them."
21 Ebd., S. 5: „This text-centeredness might seem obvious and even necessary in studies of antiquity, which must gather their evidence in literary remains, the only thing we have left, at times, of cultures long destroyed by the ravages of history."
22 Ebd.
23 Ebd., S. 7: „as if they were inert literary specimens separable from the praying actors."
24 Ebd., S. 6: „is not a literary matter in the first place. [...] Liturgists must eventually confront the disturbing recognition that though their evidence from the past is essentially literary, the human activity of worship is not."

Liturgie und ihre schriftlichen Quellen als solche zu untersuchen, ohne sich den Methoden anderer Disziplinen zu sehr zu verpflichten:

> [...] we liturgists must develop some context for handling prayer qua prayer, not just prayer qua literature. We will have to acknowledge the common-sense recognition that prayers are not readings, and prayer books are not literary specimens.[25]

Das Ziel Hoffmans ist somit weniger die philologische Auswertung von Textbeständen, sondern vielmehr die Untersuchung der Verehrungspraxis einer konkreten Gemeinschaft zu einer bestimmten Zeit und an einem bestimmten Ort, deren kontextspezifische Bedeutung es aufzuschließen gilt:

> The essential unknown, that which cries out for clarification [...] is not the texts; what little we know of them, they are at least before us and are amenable to restoration in a more or less accurate facsimile by virtue of manuscript evidence. It is the people about whom we know virtually nothing, at least insofar as they constituted worshiping communities in various ages of [...] history. We ought not to argue from the people to the texts, then, but from the texts to the people.[26]

Um eine derartige Untersuchung durchzuführen, müssen nach Hoffman drei Dimensionen berücksichtigt werden: Zunächst, logischerweise, der Inhalt der Liturgie, so wie er aus den Texten hervorgeht.[27] Dieser offenkundige Inhalt der Gebete („manifest content of the prayers") stellt eine von insgesamt drei Variablen, die zusammen genommen die Botschaft („liturgical message") ausmachen.[28]

Der zweite Aspekt, der als bedeutungstragendes Element in der Analyse von Liturgien unabdingbar miteinbezogen werden soll, ist das, was Hoffman die Choreographie oder die Art und Weise der Gestaltung der liturgischen Dienste nennt.[29] Als Beispiel dafür nennt er spezifische Aspekte der jüdischen liturgischen Praxis, doch der zugrundeliegende Gedanke lässt sich mühelos auf die christliche Liturgie übertragen, wie zum Beispiel auf die monastische Feier des Stundengebetes:

> The contrast between the eastern European shtetl and American Reform is instructive here. In the former, worship was characterized by ‚davening',[30] a particular brand of Hazzanut[31], and an intimacy among peers balanced by a seating arrangement that both reflected and supported class structure. The very pathos of the singsong sound of ‚davening,' and the ‚kvetch' of the small town Hazzan reflected the misery of shtetl existence. The small synagogues (or shtüblech) in which worshippers ‚davened' side by side, often packed together, each person apparently doing his own thing without disturbing the others, was the most intimate of services imaginable and testified to the closeness

25 Ebd.

26 Ebd., S. 8.

27 Vgl. ebd., S. 69–70.

28 Beide Zitate ebd., S. 71.

29 „the way services are conducted", ebd.

30 Das jiddische Wort für „beten".

31 Von hazzan oder chazzan, der Cantor. Hazzanut ist eine besondere Art der vokalen liturgischen jüdischen Performanz, vgl. Ronald Eisenberg: Dictionary of Jewish Terms. A Guide to the Language of Judaism, Lanham 2011, S. 168–169.

forced on the crowded Jewish communities of the Pale. But social class in the ghetto was maintained by the system of reserving seats by the eastern wall for those with status. How different all of this was from the highly decorous service in large, architecturally elaborate temples founded by the Reform movement in America! There, the organ, the German music so dependent on high European culture, or the stylized and, to some extent, Protestantized mode of worship carried a message for Jews who were part and parcel of Western enlightenment.[32]

Solche Aspekte, „the How of worship", sind laut Hoffman für die Bestimmung der Bedeutung von liturgischen Praktiken genauso wichtig wie etwa der Inhalt der Texte:

> [...] the ‚how' of worship in different times and places are just as significant as the meaning of the prayers themselves in defining [...] identity, and these two elements (choreography and content), along with the prayer book's structure, have combined to present a coherent message to the worshiper [...].[33]

Als drittes Element werden die jeweiligen Textträger oder Bücher genannt, die die rituellen Handlungen fixieren und wo sie, nach Bedarf, immer wieder modifizierbar waren.[34] Layout, Design, Struktur und Organisation, sprachliche Aufmachung und so weiter verfügen nämlich nach Hoffman über ein großes kommunikatives Potential, das in die Analyse miteinzubeziehen ist.[35] Dabei sind Hoffmans Beobachtungen einigen aktuellen Entwicklungen der mediävistischen Liturgieforschung überraschend ähnlich, wie sie von Hanns Peter Neuheuser thematisiert worden sind:

> Mit der Integration der seit den 90er Jahren des 20. Jahrhunderts stärker profilierten kulturhistorischen Ansätze in die Geisteswissenschaften – dem ‚Cultural Turn' – sind neben dem Entwurf völlig neuer Themenfelder auch neuartige Zugänge zu traditionellen Forschungsgebieten entwickelt worden. Es galt, die Artefakte erneut und kritisch zu befragen, ob sie etwa nur ihre eigene isolierte Geschichte dokumentieren oder auch den ‚Wandel ihrer Bedeutungen' respektive, ob mit ihrer Hilfe die werkimmanente ‚Faktengeschichte alten Stils' in eine Bedeutungsgeschichte überführt werden könne. [...] Bei der retrospektiven Erschließung kultureller und zivilisatorischer Überlieferungen gerieten insofern Medien in den Blick, welche – wie die liturgischen Bücher – zu den ältesten, typologisch geschlossenen Literaturgattungen überhaupt zählen. [...] Unterstützt wurde dieser Wandel durch die Erkenntnis, dass gottesdienstliche Vollzüge neben ihrer Primärbedeutung für die unmittelbar beteiligten Gläubigen zahlreiche anthropologisch aufschlussreiche Konstanten ausbildeten und qualitativ hoch stehende Kunsterzeugnisse, darunter neben Architektur, Einrichtungsgegenständen, Gefäßen, Geräten, Gewändern, Texten und Melodien etc. eben auch liturgische Bücher hervorgebracht haben: Eine umfassende kulturhistorische Betrachtung konnte sich sinnvollerweise diesem Komplex nicht auf Dauer entziehen.[36]

---

32 Hoffman: Beyond the Text, S. 71.

33 Ebd.

34 Vgl. ebd., S. 70.

35 Ebd.

36 Hanns P. Neuheuser: Liturgische Bücher als Gegenstände der kulturhistorischen Betrachtung. Tendenzen neuerer Publikationsformen, in: BIBLIOTHEK Forschung und Praxis 34, 2010, S. 238–258, hier: S. 239.

Im Sinne Hoffmans ist zunächst eine solche Gesamtbetrachtung aller drei Elemente nötig, um die liturgische Praxis einer Gemeinschaft wahrnehmen und sie anschließend interpretieren zu können.[37] Unterschiede und Modifikationen dieser drei Elemente, egal wie umfangreich, zeigen für ihn eine veränderte Identität der jeweiligen Gemeinschaften an, die sich wesentlich über die liturgische Verehrung definieren, eine Zuschreibung, die ja gerade für die religiösen Gemeinschaften des Mittelalters Gültigkeit beanspruchen kann.[38]

Mit Hoffmans Begriffen und Methoden lassen sich meines Erachtens auch mittelalterliche Heiligenkulte und ihre Quellen untersuchen. Schriftliche Zeugnisse des Heiligenkultes, darunter auch Viten, sind aus zwei Gründen für diese Untersuchung unverzichtbar: Zum einen geben sie über den Inhalt des Kultes und über die Profilierung der heiligen Figur Auskunft, und zum anderen verweisen sie auf den textexternen Prozess der Konstruktion des Heiligen. Dieser war ein sozialer und kommunikativer Prozess, in dessen Rahmen dem Heiligen durch eine Verehrergemeinschaft Eigenschaften zugeschrieben wurden. Der Heilige war somit eine soziale Figur, nicht bloß der Protagonist einer Erzählung.

Ein solcher Prozess muss aber, damit er stattfinden kann, medialisiert werden, das heißt in Ausdrucksmedien „des Körpers und seiner Praktiken“ oder „in Medien textueller / verbaler, bildlicher, musikalischer oder medial hybrider Darstellung“[39] artikuliert werden. Diese Medialisierungspraktiken fielen bei unterschiedlichen Verehrergemeinschaften unterschiedlich aus. Für solche außerhalb des regulierten kirchlichen Lebens im Mittelalter konnte der Konstruktionsprozess des Heiligen beispielsweise auch monetäre Praktiken (Spenden) einschließen oder durch eine an den Heiligen angelehnte Namensgebung artikuliert werden. In erster Linie wurde der Heilige aber von den religiösen Verehrergemeinschaften der Mönche und Kleriker durch eine bestimmte Art von Praktiken konstituiert, die als liturgische Performanz bezeichnet werden können. Dieser Begriff schließt zum Beispiel die Markierung einer für den Heiligen reservierten Zeit (das Heiligenfest) oder den Besuch seines Bestattungsortes in gemeinsamer Prozession ein, sowie das Vorlesen eines Berichtes über sein Leben und Sterben. Zwar konnte der Konstruktionsprozess des Heiligen durchaus durch das Schreiben über ihn (Hagiographie) medialisiert werden, er stellte letztlich aber das Ergebnis eines umfassenderen Prozesses dar, von dem Hagiographie ein Teil war. Die soziale und kommunikative Konstruktion des Heiligen möchte ich als Hagiopraxis bezeichnen und seine Medialisierungsform in der liturgischen Performanz und ihren Medien identifizieren. Im Folgenden wird dies überblickartig erklärt.

---

[37] Vgl. Hoffman: Beyond the Text, S. 71.

[38] Vgl. ebd., S. 72.

[39] SFB 948 (Hg.): Antrag des SFB 948, S. 15.

Den ersten Schritt in der kultischen Konstruktion eines Heiligen stellte die Markierung einer für ihn reservierten Zeit dar.[40] In Anlehnung an eine Tradition des spätantiken Märtyrerkultes steht auch im Mittelalter zunächst der Todestag eines Heiligen im Fokus der liturgischen Verehrung. Nach der christlichen Logik des Mittelalters repräsentierte der Todestag eines Märtyrers beziehungsweise eines Heiligen den Tag, an dem er ins wahre Leben geboren wurde, nämlich den Tag, an dem er das Saeculum verlassen durfte und im Himmel aufgenommen wurde.[41] So wurden neben den Festen, die jedes Jahr die wichtigsten Ereignisse der Biographie Jesu vergegenwärtigen sollten, auch besondere Termine eingeführt, zu denen die Heiligen, sozusagen die Nebenfiguren der Historia sacra, in den Vordergrund der Verehrung gerückt wurden. Neben dem Todestag wurden auch weitere Stationen der Biographie eines Heiligen liturgisch gefeiert, wie beispielsweise der Tag, an dem ein Heiliger zum Bischof geweiht wurde oder der Tag der Übertragung seiner körperlichen Überreste. Diese sogenannte Translation war besonders lokal relevant, da sie an den Orten und bei den Institutionen gefeiert wurde, an denen die Übertragung der Reliquien stattfand.[42]

An einem solch besonderen Tag eines Heiligen („dies sancti“[43]) wurde also ein Fest veranstaltet, um ihn zu ehren und seine Memoria zu pflegen. Für eine Gemeinschaft besonders wichtige Heilige wurden mit einem prächtig ausgestalteten Fest gefeiert: Ein wichtiger Heiliger, dessen Fest zum Beispiel in einem Kalender als Festum duplex identifiziert werden kann, wurde über 24 Stunden,

---

40 Vgl. Arnold Angenendt: Heilige und Reliquien. Die Geschichte ihres Kultes vom frühen Christentum bis zur Gegenwart, München 1994, S. 129–132.

41 Dazu zum Beispiel Hrabanus Maurus, der sich in seinem *De institutione clericorum* auf eine Passage aus Beda bezieht: „[...] mos obtinuit ecclesiasticus, ut dies beatorum martyrum sive confessorum Christi, quibus de saeculo transierunt, natales vocitemus eorumque solemnis non funebria, sed natalicia dicantur.“ Detlev Zimpel (Hg.): Hrabanus Maurus, De institutione clericorum – Über die Unterweisung der Geistlichen (Fontes Christiani 61), Turnhout 2006, S. 374; oder: Amalar von Metz, Liber officialis: „Natalitia sanctorum nativitates eorum monstrant quibus nascuntur in societatem novem ordinum angelorum, et in societatem sanctorum patrum naturalis legis, et legis litterae et Novi Testamenti.“ Eric Knibbs (Hg.): On the Liturgy, Amalar of Metz, Volume II, Books 3–4 (On the Liturgy / Amalar of Metz. Ed. and Transl. by Eric Knibbs), Cambridge / Mass 2014, S. 560. Außerdem: Vgl. Arnold Angenendt: Liturgie im Mittelalter, in: Patrizia Carmassi (Hg.): Präsenz und Verwendung der Heiligen Schrift im christlichen Frühmittelalter, Wiesbaden 2008, S. 211–238, hier: S. 225.

42 Vgl. Martin Heinzelmann: Translationsberichte und andere Quellen des Reliquienkultes (Typologie des sources du Moyen Âge occidental), Turnhout 1979, S. 114.

43 Angenendt: Heilige und Reliquien, S. 129. Das Thema wird auch vier Jahrhunderte später, in der zweiten Hälfte des 13. Jhdts., von Durandus von Mendes angesprochen, der das ganze siebte Buch seines *Rationale divinorum officiorum* den Heiligenfesten widmet und unter anderem die Gründe dafür erklärt, dass die Kirche Heiligenfeste feiert, vgl. A. Davril u. a. (Hg.): Guillelmi Duranti Rationale divinorum officiorum (Gvillelmi Dvranti Rationale divinorvm officiorvm / ed. A. Davril), Turnhout 2000, S. 9–130.

nämlich von der Vesper des Vortages bis zur Vesper des Festes selbst gefeiert.[44] Ein besonderer Indikator der Wichtigkeit eines Festes ist die Verwendung individualisierten Materials anstelle von Elementen des sogenannten Commune sanctorum, die auf alle Heiligen eines bestimmten Typus appliziert werden konnten.[45]

Es waren meistens lokal oder regional verehrte Heilige, zum Beispiel die Heiligen einer Stadt, eines Bischofssitzes oder eines Klosters, die mit einer vergleichsweise aufwendigen Liturgie gefeiert wurden. Sie galten als die „patroni loci", als diejenigen, die „über die einzelnen Orte wachten", während Gott, der „‚salvator mundi' [die Welt] beherrscht[e]."[46] Diese Zuschreibung, die in der spätantiken Tradition der Märtyrerverehrung wurzelte, welche primär mit der Grabstätte des Heiligen verbunden war, blieb für das ganze Mittelalter entscheidend. Auch wenn nach der Einführung eines für die ganze Christenheit gültigen Heiligenkalenders sowohl universelle als auch lokale Heilige gefeiert wurden,[47] erfuhren nach wie

---

44 Auch andere kalendarische Bezeichnungen wie: *festum simplex*, *semi-duplex* usw. bezeichnen die Höhe eines Feiertages. Siehe: John Harper: The Forms and Orders of Western Liturgy from the Tenth to the Eighteenth Century. A Historical Introduction and Guide for Students and Musicians, Oxford 1991, S. 57. Einstufen ließen sich diese auch anhand der Anzahl der vorgesehenen Lektionen der Matutin: bei wichtigen Festen im kanonikalen *cursus* waren neun Lesungen vorgesehen (*festum IX lectionum*), bei wichtigen Festen im monastischen *cursus* wurden zwölf Lesungen vorgetragen (*festum XII lectionum*), vgl. Daniel Sheerin: The Liturgy, in: Frank Anthony Carl Mantello / A. G. Rigg (Hg.): Medieval Latin: An Introduction and Bibliographical Guide 1996, S. 157–182, hier: S. 160. Bei besonders wichtigen Festen wurde auch eine sogenannte Oktav gefeiert, vgl. Pierre-Marie Gy: Le culte des saints dans la liturgie d'Occident entre le IXe et le XIIIe siècle, in: Robert Favreau (Hg.): Le culte des saints aux IXe-XIIIe siècles. Actes du Colloque tenu à Poitiers les 15–16–17 septembre 1993 (Civilisation médiévale 1), Poitiers 1995, S. 85–89, hier: S. 88.

45 Dies gilt auch für die Lesungen des Nachtgottesdienstes. So konnte Tjamke Snijders an hagiographischen Lesungen für die Matutin in Handschriften aus hochmittelalterlichen niederländischen Klöstern zeigen, dass bei unterschiedlichen Heiligenfesten große Unterschiede in Umfang, narrativer Kohärenz und Verarbeitung des hagiographischen Materials bestanden. Für Feiern zu Ehren von Klosterpatronen oder Heiligen, deren Reliquien das Kloster besaß, wurde der hagiographische Stoff vorsichtig ausgewählt und sorgfältig für die nächtliche Liturgie aufbereitet. Mit dem Ziel, das klösterliche Publikum über wichtige Heilige besser und ausführlich zu informieren, erarbeiteten liturgische Redakteure erzählerisch sehr kohärente Abfolgen von Lesungen. Bei Heiligen hingegen, zu denen die Klöster keine besondere Bindung hatten, wirkt die Auswahl und Aufbereitung der Lesungen eher unaufmerksam, so dass zum Teil sogar inkohärente oder unverständliche Heiligengeschichten ausgesucht und während der Matutin vorgelesen wurden. Im ersten Fall, folgert Snijders, ging es offensichtlich darum, das monastische Publikum gut und vollständig über den eigenen Klosterpatron zu informieren, im zweiten Fall waren die Inhalte der Lesungen weit weniger relevant als das gemeinsame Begehen des Festes. Vgl. Tjamke Snijders: Celebrating with Dignity: The Purpose of Benedictine Matins Reading, in: Steven Vanderputten (Hg.): Understanding Monastic Practices of Oral Communication (Western Europe Tenth–Thirteenth Centuries) (Utrecht studies in medieval literacy 21), Turnhout 2011, S. 115–136.

46 Angenendt: Heilige und Reliquien, S. 128.

47 Vgl. Gy: Le culte des saints, S. 85. Dass die Verehrung vor allem der Apostel und der ersten Märtyrer des Christentums, wie Stephanus und Laurentius, sich im ganzen mittelalterlichen Europa verbreitete, bezeugen auch die Bestattungslagen von Bischöfen zwischen dem 4. und 7. Jhdt. Wie Picard in Bezug auf Oberitalien zeigen konnte, ließen

vor bestimmte, für eine Verehrergemeinschaft äußerst bedeutende Figuren – wie Patrone –, dort vergleichsweise größere Verehrung. Dabei war zum einen die Idee entscheidend, dass insbesondere an dem Ort, an dem die körperlichen Überreste lagen, die thaumaturgische Kraft des Heiligen dauerhaft und intensiv wirken konnte.[48] Zum andern aber galt der gefeierte Märtyrer oder Heilige in gewisser Weise auch als Gründer eines Ortes und der dort ansässigen Gemeinschaft seiner Verehrer.[49] In dieser Hinsicht kann die spätantike und mittelalterliche Märtyrer- und Heiligenverehrung als eine Fortsetzung des privaten Totengedächtnisses verstanden werden: „[…] the cult of martyrs at the *memoriae* of their burial could be seen as a Christian perpetuation of the care for the dead members of their families that the living were expected to show towards them."[50]

In der Lebenswelt der Verehrergemeinschaft wurden nicht nur bestimmte Zeiträume, sondern spezielle Orte als mit den Heiligen in Verbindung stehend markiert. Da die irdische Präsenz von Heiligen, wie gerade geschildert, mit ihren körperlichen Spolien in Verbindung gebracht wurde, handelte es sich oft um Grabkirchen, Altäre oder Krypten, wo diese verwahrt wurden. Solche ihrerseits durch ihre Verbindung mit dem Heiligen ausgezeichneten Orte wurden auch liturgisch einbezogen, indem sie am Tag des Heiligenfestes, meistens nach den Laudes, vor der Messe oder nach der Vesper in feierlicher Prozession besucht wurden.[51] Zu diesen Anlässen wurden spezielle Gesänge vorgetragen (Hymnen, Responsorien und Antiphonen), die das Thema des Festes behandelten. Die Kanoniker des bayerischen Stiftes Sankt Zeno Reichenhall beispielsweise besuchten den dortigen Altar für Zeno zweimal im Jahr, am 9. Dezember für die Feier des Todestages und am 10. Juli für die Feier der Übertragung der Gebeine des Heiligen.[52] Dies wird durch einen liturgischen Codex des 14. Jahrhunderts, Kremsmünster BS CC31 belegt.[53] Dieses Prozessionale sieht für das Fest im Dezember eine feierliche Prozession zum Altar vor, die mit dem Singen einer Antiphon zu begleiten ist, sowie das Singen eines Responsoriums auf dem Weg zurück zum Chor. Auch für das Fest im Juli war eine Prozession mit dem begleitenden Gesang eines Responsori-

---

sich Bischöfe in dieser Zeit bevorzugt in Kirchen bestatten, wo Reliquien von Aposteln oder Märtyrern aufbewahrt wurden, siehe: Picard: Le souvenir des évêques, S. 251–310. Während der Karolingerzeit prägte sich diese Tendenz noch stärker aus: Heilige, deren Reliquien nun vermehrt transportiert, umgesiedelt und verteilt wurden, wurden multilokal, siehe dazu: Angenendt: Heilige und Reliquien, S. 204.

48 Vgl. ebd., S. 125–126.

49 Ebd., S. 125.

50 Robert A. Markus: The End of Ancient Christianity, Cambridge 1990, S. 147.

51 Vgl. Harper: The Forms and Orders, S. 127–129. Siehe außerdem: Peter Kritzinger: The Cult of Saints and Religious Processions in Late Antiquity and the Early Middle Ages, in: Peter A. V. Sarris u. a. (Hg.): An Age of Saints? Power, Conflict and Dissent in Early Medieval Christianity, Leiden 2011, S. 36–48.

52 Vgl. Johannes Lang: Das Erzbistum Salzburg. Teilband 2. Das Augustinerchorherrenstift St. Zeno in Reichenhall (Germania Sacra. Folge 3 9, 2), Berlin 2015, S. 355.

53 Vgl. Michel Huglo: Les manuscrits du processionnal. Bd. 1 Autriche à Espagne. 2 Bde. (Répertoire international des sources musicales 14,1), München 1999, S. 11–13.

ums vorgesehen.[54] Gegenstand aller dieser Gesänge war Zeno, in dessen Anwesenheit in Form von Reliquien das liturgische Geschehen stattfand.

Das Fest

Nach der Tradition spätantiker Märtyrerverehrung beging die Gemeinschaft am Todestag des Märtyrers eine Gedächtnisfeier. Diese bestand aus zwei Elementen: zum einen aus einer Nachtwache, einer *vigilia*, am Grab und zum zweiten aus einem feierlichen Mahl zu Ehren des gefeierten, toten Märtyrers.[55] Von einer solchen Nachtwache berichtet zum Beispiel Ambrosius in der Epistel 77, in der der Bischof seiner Schwester über die Auffindung der Reliquien des Märtyrerpaars Gervasius und Protasius berichtet:

> Was soll ich noch sagen? Wir richteten die Reliquien ordentlich her, wir überführten sie zu der Fausta-Basilika als der Abend schon begann; wir bewachten sie die ganze Nacht mit aufgelegter Hand. Am nächsten Tag verbrachten wir sie in die Basilika, die man Ambrosiana nennt.[56]

Auch der Brauch des Totenmahles ist in der Spätantike bezeugt, Augustinus war sogar dazu gezwungen, ihn gegenüber seinem heidnischen Gegner Faustus zu rechtfertigen, da diese angeblich christliche Tradition in den Augen des manichäischen Philosophen offensichtlich zu große Ähnlichkeiten mit genuin heidnischen Bräuchen aufwies. Das spätantike Symposion „durch eine Eucharistie [zu ersetzen]“[57] war nicht ohne weiteres möglich: die räumliche und zeitliche Nähe der eucharistischen zur Heiligenverehrung rief nicht nur andersgläubige Kritiker auf den Plan. Auch gegenüber Christen war diese Praxis differenziert zu erläutern, vor allem, um sie vom paganen Heroenkult abzugrenzen. Augustinus musste seiner eigenen Gemeinde erklären, dass das im Rahmen der Heiligenfeste dargebrachte Opfer niemals den Märtyrern selbst galt, sondern immer nur Gott. Der Brauch, an den Gedenkstätten der Märtyrer die Messe zu zelebrieren, sollte dem Kirchenvater zufolge ausschließlich der Erbauung des christlichen Volkes

---

[54] In Kremsmünster BS CC31, fol. 67r ist die Rubrik zu finden: „In translationem sancti Zenonis ad processionem cantatur Responsorium Iustum deduxit“ [...]. Auf fol. 67v findet man die Antiphon, die zur Station zum Zenoaltar im Dezember zu singen war und auf fol. 68r das Responsorium *Ingrediente sacerdote* [...], das mit der Rubrik „ad reditum“ gekennzeichnet ist.

[55] Vgl. Angenendt: Heilige und Reliquien, S. 130–132.

[56] „Quid multa? Condivimus integra ad ordinem, transtulimus vespere iam incumbente ad basilicam Faustae; ibi vigiliae tota nocte, manus impositio. Sequenti die transtulimus ea in basilicam quam appellant Ambrosianam.“ Ambrosius von Mailand: Sancti Ambrosii Opera. Epistularum liber decimus, Epistulae extra collectionem, Gesta Concilii Aquileiensis, hrsg. von Michael Petschenig / Michaela Zelzer (Corpus Scriptorum Ecclesiasticorum Latinorum 82,3), Wien 1982, Ep. 77, S. 126–140. Siehe dazu auch: Alan T. Thacker: „Loca sanctorum“: The Significance of Place in the Study of the Saints, in: Alan T. Thacker (Hg.): Local Saints and Local Churches in the Early Medieval West, Oxford 2002, S. 1–44, hier: S. 1–13.

[57] Angenendt: Heilige und Reliquien, S. 130.

dienen. Die Unterscheidung zwischen dem Cultus latriae, der nur Gott gebührt, und der Verehrung des Heiligen im Cultus duliae legitimierte das Gedenken an letzteren im Rahmen der Messfeier.[58]

In der mittelalterlichen Liturgiepraxis wurden diese spätantiken Formen der Heiligenverehrung im Wesentlichen in zwei Bereichen tradiert: im Rahmen der Messe, wo die Eucharistie das spätantike Totenmahl ersetzte,[59] und beim Stundengebet, wo bei Heiligenfesten mit umfangreichem nächtlichem Beten das Konzept der Nachtwache aufgenommen wurde.

Die Messe wurde in der Regel nach der Terz gefeiert. Wichtige Heilige wurden am Tag ihres Festes mit einer Missa propria geehrt: eine Messe, für die Serien von Gebeten (Orationes) verfasst wurden. Diese Serien umfassten drei Messgebete: Die Kollekt,[60] die Super oblata und die Oratio ad complendum. Diese speziell für einzelne Feste verfassten Gebete der Messe wurden üblicherweise in Sakramentaren – ab dem 12. Jahrhundert auch in sogenannten Missalien – überliefert.[61] In diesen Gebeten wurde der Heilige zwar memoriert, allerdings wurde er weniger

---

58 „Das christliche Volk aber feiert die Feste der Märtyrer mit religiöser Feierlichkeit, sowohl um das Nachahmen anzuregen, als auch damit wir an ihren Verdiensten teilhaben können und durch die Gebete Hilfe erfahren. Dennoch sollen wir niemals Altäre für die Märtyrer bauen, sondern für den Gott der Märtyrer selbst, auch wenn wir die Altäre an den Gräbern der Märtyrer bauen. Welcher Bischof nämlich, der die Messe an den Orten der Heiligen feiert, sagte jemals: ‚Wir bringen Dir Gaben, o Petrus oder Paulus oder Cyprianus?'. Vielmehr wird das was dargebracht wird, Gott dargebracht, der die Märtyrer krönte, bei den Altären derer, die er krönte, damit durch das Beispiel dieser Orte eine größere Bewegung der Seele entstehe, um die Liebe zu den Märtyrern zu steigern, die wir nachahmen können, und zu demjenigen, dem wir dabei helfen können. [...] Aber denjenigen Kult, der auf Griechisch λατρεία genannt wird, kann man nicht mit einem Wort auf Latein benennen. Da aber diese Verehrung nur der Gottheit zukommt, verehren wir nichts anderes und bringen wir das Verehren keinem anderen dar als Gott." („Populus autem christianus memorias martyrum religiosa sollemnitate concelebrat et ad excitandam imitationem et ut meritis eorum consocietur atque orationibus adiuvetur, ita tamen, ut nulli martyrum, sed ipsi Deo martyrum quamvis in memoriis martyrum constituamus altaria. Quis enim antistitum in locis sanctorum corporum adsistens altari aliquando dixit: ‚Offerimus tibi, Petre aut Paule aut Cypriane'? Sed quod offertur, offertur Deo, qui martyres coronavit, apud memorias eorum quos coronavit, ut ex ipsorum locorum admonitione maior adfectus exsurgat ad acuendam caritatem et in illos, quos imitari possumus, et in illum, quo adiuvante possimus. [...] At illo cultu, quae graece λατρεία dicitur, latine uno verbo dici non potest, cum sit quaedam proprie divinitati debita servitus, nec colimus nec colendum docemus nisi unum deum."), aus: Augustinus: Contra Faustum, hrsg. von Ioseph Zycha (Corpus Scriptorum Ecclesiasticorum Latinorum 25,1), Wien 1891, S. 562.

59 Vgl. Angenendt: Heilige und Reliquien, S. 130.

60 Vgl. Andrew Hughes: Medieval Manuscripts for Mass and Office. A Guide to their Organization and Terminology, Toronto [1]1982, S. 84.

61 Siehe dazu: Éric Palazzo: A History of Liturgical Books from the Beginning to the Thirteenth Century, Collegeville 1998, S. 107–110. In der Forschung zu diesen Sakramentarhandschriften wird zwischen einer gelasianischen und einer gregorianischen Form unterschieden, unter anderem anhand abweichender Messformulare. Die in weiten Teilen Europas mit der Ausnahme der ambrosianischen und mozarabischen Liturgie übliche gregorianische Form des Sakramentars sieht hier drei Gebete vor: Oratio, oft auch Oratio prima oder Oratio diei genannt, Super oblata und Ad complendum. Siehe dazu: ebd., S. 21–56. Auch die Bezeichnungen der Messegebete fallen je nach Typus

für seine individuellen Leistungen gepriesen, sondern vielmehr in seiner Rolle als Intercessor (Fürsprecher) angesprochen. Aus diesem Grund enthalten solche Orationen in der Regel[62] kaum bio- oder hagiographische Elemente,[63] sondern erschöpfen sich in eher unspezifischen Anrufungen.

Die Memorierung des Heiligen hingegen war im Rahmen der Lesungen der Messe verboten. Im Gegensatz zu den Lesungen des Stundengebets, für welche durchaus hagiographische Texte als Quellen herangezogen wurden, wurden aus den Leseteilen der Messe nach einer ersten kurzen Phase der Unklarheit alle nicht biblischen Quellen ausgesondert, zuallererst die Gesta sanctorum.[64]

Der gesungene Teil der Messe setzte sich aus mehreren Elementen zusammen, nämlich aus dem Ordinarium missae und dem Proprium missae. Während das Ordinarium (Kyrie, Gloria, Credo, Sanctus und Benedictus, Agnus Dei) in jeder Messe identisch blieb, wurde das Proprium missae (Introitus-Antiphon, Graduale, Alleluia-Vers, Offertorium und die Communio-Antiphon) nach Fest und Saison geändert. Allerdings bestanden die Gesänge des Propriums meistens aus Psalmzitaten und priesen selten den individuellen Heiligen.[65] So enthalten auch diese Gesänge dementsprechend wenig spezifisch hagiographisches Material.[66]

---

des Sakramentars unterschiedlich aus, siehe dazu: Cyrille Vogel: Medieval Liturgy. An Introduction to the Sources, Washington, DC 1986, S. 79.

62 Eine Ausnahme stellen die sogenannten ‚prefazi' der ambrosianischen Liturgie dar, die, wie Paredi beobachtet, reichlich hagiographisches Material rezipieren. Vgl. Angelo Paredi: I prefazi ambrosiani: contributo alla storia della liturgia latina, Mailand 1937, S. 215–216. Auch in der mozarabischen Liturgie werden hagiographische Quellen stärker berücksichtigt. Siehe dazu: Els Rose: Ritual Memory. The Apocryphal Acts and Liturgical Commemoration in the Early Medieval West (c. 500–1215) (Mittellateinische Studien und Texte), Leiden 2009, S. 90.

63 Daher werden in der Edition etliche Messformulare nicht berücksichtigt. Ausgewählte Formulare werden in die Analyse miteinbezogen. Dabei wird entweder direkt aus der jeweiligen handschriftlichen Quelle oder aus Segala: Il culto di San Zeno zitiert.

64 Vgl. Josef A. Jungmann: Missarum sollemnia. Bd. 1 Messe im Wandel der Jahrhunderte. Messe und kirchliche Gemeinschaft. Vormesse, Wien 1962, S. 504.

65 Vgl. Hughes: Medieval Manuscripts, S. 153–154.

66 Die liturgische Feier aber für Heilige, die für eine Verehrergemeinschaft eine besonders prominente Rolle spielten, wurde auch im Bereich der Messe durch zusätzliche Gesänge reichlicher ausgestaltet, nämlich mit dem sogenannten Tropus und mit der Sequenz. In beiden Fällen werden Gesänge, die zur Standardstruktur der Messe gehören – sowohl des variablen Teils der Messe, also des Propriums, als auch des festbleibenden Teils oder Ordinariums –, durch solche dichterischen und musikalischen Erweiterungen betont und dabei kommentiert. Beide Gesänge gehörten nicht zum ursprünglichen Bestandteil der Messliturgie, sondern wurden erst ab dem 9. Jhdt. entwickelt. Auch werden sie nicht regelmäßig und flächendeckend in der alltäglichen Liturgie eingesetzt: nur besonders wichtige Feste werden durch eine Sequenz oder durch Tropen ausgestaltet. Es sind meistens die wichtigsten Herrenfeste des liturgischen Jahres, die stärker ‚tropiert' wurden, doch finden sich auch Tropen und vor allem Sequenzen für Heiligenfeste. Insbesondere die gereimte Sequenz war im Spätmittelalter eine beliebte Form der Heiligenverehrung im Rahmen der Messe. Die narrative Lebensbeschreibung des Heiligen (die sogenannte Vita) stellt meistens den Subtext der Sequenz dar, in der das hagiographische Material dichterisch umgearbeitet wird. Durch die Erwähnung biographischer Episoden und der persönlichen ‚Leistungen' wird so die Möglichkeit der individualisierten Verehrung eines

Da die Messe wenig Raum für profilierte Hagiopraxis bot, wurde in dieser Arbeit von einer Edierung und tiefergehenden Analyse des liturgischen Materials für die Messe abgesehen.[67] Eingehend behandelt wird hingegen das Stundengebet, in welchem der Heilige individualisierte Verehrung erfuhr: Zum einen konnte im Stundengebet die Heiligenverehrung liturgisch ausführlicher entfaltet werden als bei der Messe, wo der Fokus auf der Eucharistie lag.[68] Zum andern erweisen sich Stundengebete inhaltlich und formal als wesentlich vielfältiger. Dies gilt, wie im Folgenden gezeigt wird, auch für Lokalheilige, die an einem Ort in mehreren Institutionen parallel verehrt wurden.

Heiligen im Rahmen der Messe und vor allem der gesungenen Teile, eröffnet. Zu diesem Themenkomplex siehe: Wulf Arlt: Neue Formen des liturgischen Gesangs: Sequenz und Tropus, in: Christoph Stiegemann / Matthias Wemhoff (Hg.): 799 – Kunst und Kultur der Karolingerzeit. Karl der Große und Papst Leo III. in Paderborn. Bd. 3 Beiträge zum Katalog der Ausstellung, Paderborn 1999. Handbuch zur Geschichte der Karolingerzeit, Mainz 1999, S. 732–740; außerdem David Hiley: Western Plainchant. A Handbook, Oxford 1993, S. 196–238; Giacomo B. Baroffio / Anastasia E. J. Kim: Cantemus domino gloriose. Introduzione al canto gregoriano, Cremona 2003, S. 95; Felix Heinzer hat darauf aufmerksam gemacht, dass die Funktion der Tropierung durch Tropus und Sequenz sich nicht in dem Ausschmücken erschöpfte, sondern dass es sich vielmehr um eine „reflektierte Aneignung durch Glossierung und Erläuterung", meistens im Sinne eines figural-typologischen Verhältnisses zum gregorianischen Bezugsgesang handelte: Felix Heinzer: *Figura* zwischen Präsenz und Diskurs. Das Verhältnis des gregorianischen Messgesangs zu seiner dichterischen Erweiterung, in: Christian Kiening / Katharina Mertens Fleury (Hg.): Figura. Dynamiken der Zeiten und Zeichen im Mittelalter, Würzburg 2013, S. 71–90, hier: S. 76.

67 Tatsächlich gibt es liturgisches Material, welches eine Profilierung des Heiligen auch im Bereich der Messe ermöglicht. Dabei handelt es sich um Tropen aus Pistoia (12.–13. Jhdt.), sowie Sequenzen aus Cividale und dem Süddeutschen Raum (14.–15. Jhdt.). Da es aber nicht zu dem hier untersuchten Kontext der Zenoverehrung in Verona gehört, wurde es nicht untersucht, soll aber im Rahmen weiterer Publikationen ediert und erschlossen werden.

68 Die Verehrung der Heiligen vor allem im Rahmen der Messe, in der eigentlich allein das Opfer Jesu am Kreuz im Vordergrund stehen soll, bedurfte stets der Erklärung, wie viele mittelalterliche Quellen bezeugen. Vgl. Irénée H. Dalmais u. a. (Hg.): Volume IV: The Liturgy and Time. The Church at Prayer. An Introduction to the Liturgy, Collegeville 1985, S. 129. Marc van Uytfanghe nennt hagiographische Quellen, wie die *Vita Faronis*, sowie Autoren des 9. Jhdts., wie Agobard von Lyon, den Bischof Claudius von Turin und Paschasius Radbertus, die das theologische Problem explizit thematisieren, welche Verehrung den Heiligen im Vergleich zu Gott gebührt. Dazu siehe: Marc van Uytfanghe: Le culte des saints et l'hagiographie face à l'écriture: les avatars d'une relation ambiguë, in: Santi e demoni nell'alto medioevo occidentale. (Secoli V–XI), Spoleto 1989, S. 155–202, hier: S. 170–172. Die erstaunliche Langlebigkeit dieser augustinischen Tradition zeigt auch die Tatsache, dass die Stelle noch in die Acta des tridentinischen Konzils Eingang fand. Dies fand zu einer Zeit statt, in der die römische Kirche hinsichtlich der Heiligenverehrung unter besonderem Rechtfertigungsdruck stand. Siehe dazu: Gerhard L. Müller: Gemeinschaft und Verehrung der Heiligen. Geschichtlich-systematische Grundlegung der Hagiologie, Freiburg 1986, S. 69–70.

Neben der Messe stellt das Stundengebet, Opus Dei oder Opus divinum[69] oder auch Liturgia horarum[70] die zentrale Beschäftigung von Mönchen und Klerikern dar.[71] Das Gebet wird in Form sogenannter Horen zu bestimmten Tages- und Nachtzeiten abgehalten und so über den ganzen Tag verteilt. Im Durchbeten von Tag und Nacht wurde nicht nur die natürliche Zeit der Schöpfung geheiligt,[72] sondern vor allem das biblische Ideal einer Laus perennis zumindest symbolisch umgesetzt.[73]

In der Spätantike waren im Westen zwei Typen des Stundengebetes verbreitet, aus denen die Grundformen der mittelalterlichen Liturgia horarum hervorgingen. Die kathedrale Form bestand aus einem durch den Bischof geleiteten Gebet, das ursprünglich nur an zwei Gebetszeiten im Laufe des Tages gehalten wurde und die Beteiligung der christlichen Laienbevölkerung vorsah: dem gemeinsamen Gebet am Morgen und am Abend.[74] Im klösterlichen Kontext war die Praxis des Stundengebetes weniger einheitlich formalisiert.[75] Diese asketisch-monastische Form wurde im Westen vor dem 8. Jahrhundert praktiziert, das heißt vor der flächendeckenden Ausbreitung der Benediktsregel.[76] Gemeinsames Merkmal aller monastischen Regeln war ein im Vergleich zur kathedralen Form umfangreicheres liturgisches Pensum: hier waren neben jenen zum Sonnenauf- und Untergang auch Gebete während des Tages, Prim, Terz, Sext und Non, sowie während der Nacht vorgesehen.[77] Aus der Verschmelzung von Elementen der kathedralen und der monastischen Form des Stundengebets entwickelten sich die Strukturen, die das tägliche Gebet von Mönchen und Klerikern außerhalb der Messe im Mittelalter regelten.[78]

---

69 Benedikt von Nursia: La Règle de Saint Benoît Bd. 2 Ch. VIII–LXXIII, hrsg. von Adalbert d. Vogüé / Jean Neufville. 7 Bde., Paris 1972, S. 524 und zusammengefasst S. 790–791.

70 Irénée H. Dalmais u. a. (Hg.): The Church at Prayer, S. 155.

71 Vgl. Heinzer: Poesie als politische Theologie, S. 76.

72 Vgl. Thomas O'Loughlin: The Monastic Liturgy of the Hours in the Nauigatio Sancti Brendani. A Preliminary Investigation, in: Irish Theological Quarterly 71, 2006, S. 113–126, hier: S. 114.

73 Wie zum Beispiel in Lk 18, 1: „oportet semper orare et non deficere". Dazu siehe auch Aimé G. Martimort: The Liturgy of the Hours, in: Irénée H. Dalmais u. a. (Hg.): Volume IV: The Liturgy and Time. The Church at Prayer. An Introduction to the Liturgy, Collegeville 1985, S. 151–256, hier: S. 155–156; 162–163.

74 Vgl. Irénée H. Dalmais u. a. (Hg.): The Church at Prayer, S. 171–172.

75 Siehe dazu: Joseph Pascher: Das Stundengebet der römischen Kirche, München 1954, S. 37–44.

76 Vgl. Joachim Wollasch: „Benedictus abbas Romensis": das römische Element in der frühen benediktinischen Tradition, in: Norbert Kamp / Joachim Wollasch (Hg.): Tradition als historische Kraft. Interdisziplinäre Forschungen zur Geschichte des früheren Mittelalters, Berlin 1982, S. 119–137, hier: S. 119–120.

77 Vgl. Irénée H. Dalmais u. a. (Hg.): The Church at Prayer, S. 173.

78 Vgl. Irénée H. Dalmais u. a. (Hg.): Volume IV: The Liturgy and Time. The Church at Prayer. An Introduction to the Liturgy, Collegeville 1985, S. 174; siehe dazu auch: Rose: Ritual Memory, S. 10–11. Da sie im Laufe dieser Arbeit verwendet werden, seien hier die technischen Bezeichnungen dieser zwei Formen des Stundengebets kurz erwähnt. Man unterscheidet dabei zwischen einem sogenannten cursus romanus, der für Priester, Kleriker und andere nicht-benediktinische geistliche Institutionen (wie Augustinerchorherren

Im Rahmen des Stundengebets wurden Heilige an ihren Feiertagen vor allem bei der liturgischen Lesung und dem antiphonalen und responsorialen Gesang ins Zentrum der Verehrung gerückt. Das Lesen während des Stundengebets ist passender als Vorlesen beschrieben, da es sich dabei um eine gemeinschaftliche Aktivität handelte: Ein Lector rezitierte die dafür vorgesehenen Abschnitte für die versammelte Gemeinschaft mit lauter Stimme und in einfacher melodischer oder Cantillationsform.[79]

Im Gegensatz zur Messe, in der ausschließlich Lesungen aus der Bibel gestatten waren, wurden für die Lesungen im Stundengebet oft Vitae, Passiones, Translationes und ähnliche Texte aus dem Bereich der narrativen Hagiographie eingesetzt. Es sind vor allem die für die nächtlichen Gebetsstunden vorgesehenen, umfangreichen Leseabschnitte,[80] in denen aus der Vita oder Passio eines Heiligen erzählt wurde. Hier ist anzumerken, dass es sich hierbei um die Tradition gallikanischer, afrikanischer und mozarabischer Gepflogenheiten handelte, die in Rom und Italien aber bis zur Karolingischen Liturgiereform durchaus fremd waren.[81] Hier überwog – in Rom sogar bis zum 9. Jahrhundert – ein gewisser ‚Ostrazismus' gegenüber den hagiographischen Lesungen.[82] Weder die Benediktinerregel[83] noch die altrömische Fassung des *Ordo romanus XIII* (sowohl *A* als auch *B*) sahen nämlich hagiographisches Material für die Messe oder das Stundengebet vor.[84] Erst ab dem 8. Jahrhundert, als sich neben Bestrebungen zu einer Romanisierung im Reich der Karolinger auch eine gewisse Frankisierung der römischen Bräu-

oder Bettelorden) galt, und einem cursus monasticus, der das Leben einer monastischen (meistens, aber nicht ausschließlich benediktinischen) Gemeinschaft regelte. Vgl. Peter Wagner: Ursprung und Entwicklung der liturgischen Gesangsformen bis zum Ausgange des Mittelalters, Leipzig [3]1911, S. 128–129.

79 Vgl. ebd., S. 130. Dazu auch: Solange Corbin: La cantillation des rituels chrétiens, in: Revue de musicologie 47, 1961, S. 3–36. Grundlegend zum Thema des Lesens oder Laut-Lesens in Antike und Mittelalter: József Balogh: „Voces Paginarum". Beiträge zur Geschichte des lauten Lesens und Schreibens, in: Philologus 82, 1927, S. 84.

80 Kürzere, oft auswendig rezitierte Lesungen wurden auch bei anderen Horen vorgetragen. Diese werden allerdings meistens als Capitulum verzeichnet, dazu: Harper: The Forms and Orders, S. 81.

81 Vgl. Baudouin de Gaiffier d'Hestroy: La lecture des Actes des martyrs dans la prière liturgique en Occident. A propos du passionaire hispanique, in: Analecta Bollandiana 72, 1954, S. 134–166, hier: S. 141.

82 Vgl. ebd., S. 139–142.

83 In der Benediktinerregel findet sich der Ausdruck „lectiones ad ipsum diem pertinentes dicantur", siehe: Benedikt von Nursia: La Règle, S. 522–523. Doch diese Formulierung findet sich auch in den Ordines der römischen Kirche, wo sie nicht auf die Lektüre aus hagiographischen Quellen hinweist, wie Andrieu unterstreicht: „Les autres lectures [...] seront des sermons ou des homélies patristiques: *sermones vel omelias catholicorum patrum ad ipsum diem pertinentes*. A aucun endroit de l'*Ordo*, il n'est question de *passiones* ou de *Vies* de saints", Michel Andrieu: Les Ordines Romani du haut moyen âge. Bd. 2 Les textes (Ordines I–XIII) (Spicilegium Sacrum Lovaniense: Etudes et documents), Löwen 1960, S. 478.

84 Vgl. De Gaiffier d'Hestroy: La lecture des Actes, S. 140.

che beobachten lässt,[85] kamen vermehrt hagiographische Texte für Lesungen des Stundengebets zum Einsatz.[86]

Nicht nur durch das Lesen über ihn, sondern auch im Gesang wurde der Heilige im Stundengebet verehrt. Den umfangreichsten Teil der cantoralen Liturgie bildete die Psalmodie, das Singen der Psalmen.[87] Während in einer monastischen Gemeinschaft das ganze Psalterium (150 Psalmen) innerhalb einer Woche gesungen werden musste,[88] wurde dieses Prinzip im kanonikalen System des Stundengebets aufgehoben. Aus diesem Grund sind die Psalmen im Cursus monasticus teilweise anders verteilt als im Cursus romanus.[89] Das Singen der Psalmen war während des Stundengebets eine der Hauptaufgaben für den Chor.[90] Sie wurden von den zwei Hälften des Chores gesungen, die sich, nachdem ein Solist den Beginn angestimmt hatte, Psalmvers für Psalmvers abwechselten.[91]

Die Auswahl der an Feiertagen, vor allem zu Laudes, Vesper und Matutin, gesungenen Psalmen orientierte sich am Typus des jeweils gefeierten Heiligen. Die Grundformen solcher Psalmenreihen sind bereits im Commune sanctorum – Sets von liturgischen Texten, die nach Heiligen-Typus (Märtyrer, Confessores, Jungfrauen und so weiter) gruppiert wurden – festgehalten: Das Fest eines Märtyrers im monastischen Cursus sah zum Beispiel für die Matutin die Psalmenreihe 1, 2, 3, 4 / 5, 8, 14, 20 / 23, 33, 64, 91 vor; eine Jungfrau etwa wurde nach dem Cursus romanus bevorzugt mit der Psalmenreihe 8, 18, 23 / 44, 45, 8 / 95, 96, 98 gefeiert.[92] Die mit solchen standardisierten Psalmenreihen implizierten Zuschrei-

---

85 Vgl. Theodor Klauser: Die liturgischen Austauschbeziehungen zwischen der römischen und fränkisch-deutschen Kirche vom achten bis zum elften Jahrhundert, in: Historisches Jahrbuch 53, 1933, S. 169–189, hier: S. 172; 183–184; auch dazu: Jungmann: Missarum sollemnia, S. 98–122.

86 Dies bestätigt nicht nur der *Ordo romanus XII*, sondern auch Papst Hadrian selbst, der in einem Brief an Karl den Großen diese Praxis auch für Rom bezeugt. Siehe dazu: De Gaiffier d'Hestroy: La lecture des Actes, S. 143–152.

87 Vgl. Wagner: Ursprung und Entwicklung, S. 6. Siehe außerdem: Joseph H. Dyer: Monastic Psalmody in the Middle Ages, in: Revue bénédictine 99, 1989, S. 41–74 und ders.: The Singing of Psalms in the Early Medieval Office, in: Speculum 64, 1989, S. 535–578.

88 Vgl. Petrus Nowack: Die Strukturelemente des Stundengebets der Regula Benedicti, in: Archiv für Liturgiewissenschaft 26, 1984, S. 253–304, hier: S. 254–255.

89 Entscheidend war hier vielmehr, dass die ausgewählten Psalmen der Spiritualität der einzelnen Hore entsprachen. Siehe dazu: Joseph Pascher: Die Methode der Psalmenauswahl im römischen Stundengebet (Sitzungsberichte / Bayerische Akademie der Wissenschaften), München 1967.

90 Die chorische Psalmodie stellt eine Neuerung der christlichen Liturgie um die Mitte des 4. Jhdts. dar. Vor dieser Zeit wurden die Psalmen von einem Solisten gesungen, wobei auch das Volk sich am Gesang einzelner Verse beteiligte. Vgl. Wagner: Ursprung und Entwicklung, S. 19–22.

91 Vgl. Harper: The Forms and Orders, S. 78. Siehe auch: Hiley: Western Plainchant, S. 58; ders.: Gregorian Chant, Cambridge 2009; Baroffio / Kim: Cantemus domino gloriose, S. 147–149.

92 Vgl. Pascher: Das Stundengebet, S. 198–203.; außerdem: Pascher: Die Methode der Psalmenauswahl.

bungen trugen zur entsprechenden Deutung des jeweils verehrten Heiligen bei.[93] Durch ad hoc-Modifizierungen festgelegter Abfolgen konnten die Feierlichkeiten speziell auf den einzelnen Heiligen zugeschnitten werden, indem man beispielsweise einen besonderen Aspekt seiner Legende hervorhob.[94]

In zwei weiteren gesungenen Elementen des Stundengebets konnte der Heilige besonders feierlich gepriesen werden, nämlich in den Antiphonen und Responsorien. Die Antiphonen rahmten Psalmen sowie Cantica ein,[95] um die Botschaft des begleiteten Elements zu betonen und sie zum jeweiligen Fest in Bezug zu setzen. Dabei waren dem Heiligen nicht nur die Antiphonen gewidmet, welche die Psalmodie der Matutin begleiteten, sondern auch die musikalisch feierlicher ausgestalteten Antiphonen zu den Cantica der Vesper und Laudes, sowie das sogenannte Invitatorium, das den täglich gesungenen Psalm 94 begleitete.[96]

Für das Singen der Antiphonen war vor allem der Chor zuständig. Es waren grundsätzlich zwei Formen des antiphonischen Vortrags möglich: Die Antiphon konnte im Ganzen entweder vor und nach dem Psalm gesungen oder nach jedem Psalmvers wiederholt werden. Die erste Form scheint sich durchgesetzt zu haben, während die zweite Form im Vortrag des Invitatoriums bewahrt wurde, bei dem die Antiphon nach jedem Vers des Psalms 94 (*Venite*) gesungen wurde. Im Laufe des Mittelalters wurde es in diesem liturgischen Kontext üblich, die Antiphon vor dem Psalm nur anzustimmen und sie nach dem Psalm komplett zu singen.[97]

Responsorien begleiteten hingegen immer eine Lesung.[98] Dem Wortsinne entsprechend stellten sie in der mittelalterlichen Liturgie sozusagen eine Antwort auf die Lesung dar.[99] Für die Untersuchung der liturgischen Verehrung der Heiligen sind vor allem die Responsorien der Matutin relevant.[100] Diese waren nicht nur umfangreicher als die Antiphonen, sondern auch musikalisch kunstvoller gestaltet und daher anspruchsvoller, nicht zuletzt, weil sie das reibungslose Zusammen-

---

93 Siehe dazu beispielsweise: Felix Heinzer: Die „heilige Königstochter" in der Liturgie: Zur Inszenierung Elisabeths im Festoffizium „Laetare Germania", in: Dieter Blume / Matthias Werner (Hg.): Elisabeth von Thüringen – eine europäische Heilige: Aufsätze, Petersberg 2007, S. 215–225, hier: S. 218.

94 Wie zum Beispiel bei Laurentius oder Agnes, bei deren Festen jeweils an einer Stelle ein passenderer Psalm ausgewählt wurde, Pascher: Das Stundengebet, S. 206.

95 *Cantica* waren alt- sowie neutestamentarische lyrische Lieder, wie zum Beispiel das aus dem Lukasevangelium entnommene *Magnificat* (Lk 1, 46–55), das jeden Tag während der Vesper gesungen wurde, oder das *Benedictus* (Lk 1, 68–79), das im Rahmen des morgendlichen Lobes, der Laudes, vorgetragen wurde. Vgl. Harper: The Forms and Orders, S. 83–84.

96 Vgl. Hiley: Western Plainchant, S. 98–99.

97 Vgl. Harper: The Forms and Orders, S. 78.

98 Vgl. Wagner: Ursprung und Entwicklung, S. 132.

99 Zusammengefasst in: Franz J. A. Antony: Archäologisch-liturgisches Lehrbuch des gregorianischen Kirchengesanges. Mit vorzüglicher Rücksicht auf die Römischen, Münsterschen und Erzstift Kölnischen Gesangsweisen, Münster 1829, S. 48, Fußnote; siehe auch: Hiley: Western Plainchant, S. 69–76.

100 Kürzere Antwort-Gesänge werden auch im Rahmen von Dialogen zwischen dem Zelebranten und dem Chor sowie nach Kurzlesungen, sogenannten capitula, vorgetragen. Vgl. Harper: The Forms and Orders, S. 82.

spiel des Solisten mit dem Chor erforderten.[101] Die am wenigsten elaborierte Form des Vortrages sah vor, dass nach dem Anstimmen durch einen Solisten der Chor das Responsorium sang. Anschließend wurde ein Vers solistisch vorgetragen und der Chor wiederholte nach dem Vers die zweite Hälfte des Responsoriums, die sogenannte Repetenda.[102]

Für Antiphonen und Responsorien wurden zunächst einzelne Psalmverse oder Passagen aus der Bibel intoniert.[103] Ab dem 9. und 10. Jahrhundert wurde es üblich, bei wichtigen Heiligenfesten die Psalmenreihen und die Lesungen mit besonderen Zyklen von Antiphonen und Responsorien zu verbinden. Diese bestanden nun nicht mehr zwingend aus einzelnen Psalmenversen, sondern wurden weiteren, nicht-biblischen Quellen entnommen.[104] Für Heiligenfeste stellte die Vita die meist verwendete Quelle für das Verfassen solcher Antiphonen- und Responsorienreihen dar, aber auch Hymnenfragmente, Inschriften und lyrische Texte wurden als Spolia dafür verwendet. Da Texte in Versform übernommen wurden, finden sich bereits in sehr frühen Offiziendichtungen einzelne versifizierte Elemente.[105] In der Regel aber wurden zunächst Offizien in Prosa gestaltet, erst ab dem 13. Jahrhundert wurden „‚durchkomponierte' Gebilde mit homogenen Vers- und Reimstrukturen"[106] gängig.

Die zeitgenössische Bezeichnung solcher Reihen von Antiphonen und Responsorien – oder Festoffizien – war Historia. Diese Begrifflichkeit verweist auf die Tatsache, dass solche Gesangsabfolgen narrativ verbunden und als einem einheitlichen Thema gewidmetes Ensemble erkennbar sind.[107] Wenn der Heilige mit einer solchen Historia besungen wurde, wurde er ausdrücklich zum Protagonisten der liturgischen Feier:

> Unter allen diesen ausdifferenzierten Formen und Ausdrucksweisen des Heiligenkultes bewirkt das Verfassen eines eigenen Offiziums, speziell für den Heiligen komponiert, auf der Grundlage seiner Vita oder Passio, dass dieser Heilige über die anderen erho-

---

101 Vgl. Hiley: Western Plainchant, S. 69.

102 Vgl. Harper: The Forms and Orders, S. 82–83. Die Beschreibungen von Amalar von Metz legen nahe, dass diese Vortragsform im 9. Jhdt. noch nicht üblich war. Sie muss sich daher später entwickelt haben, ist aber für das 12. und 13. Jhdt. belegt. Vgl. Hiley: Western Plainchant, S. 73–74.

103 Die Responsorien des *Temporale* zum Beispiel basierten auf dem Text der Lesungen, die sie begleiteten. Vgl. ebd., S. 70. Die Antiphonen, deren Text aus den Psalmen entnommen ist, bilden den ältesten Bestand an Gesängen der christlichen Kirche. Vgl. Wagner: Ursprung und Entwicklung, S. 152–153; Hiley: Western Plainchant, S. 88–102.

104 Siehe dazu insbesondere: Ritva Jonsson: Historia. Études sur la genèse des offices versifiés, Stockholm 1968, S. 177.

105 Ebd., S. 178. Darüber auch, Jonssons Ergebnisse zusammenfassend, Joachim Knape: Zur Benennung der Offizien im Mittelalter. Das Wort „historia" als liturgischer Begriff, in: Archiv für Liturgiewissenschaft 26, 1984, S. 305–320, hier: S. 307.

106 Heinzer: Die heilige Königstochter, S. 215.

107 Jonsson: Historia, S. 12. Ich benutze im Folgenden zwei Begriffe für Historia synonym, nämlich Historia und Offizium. Der Begriff Offizium ist allerdings umfassender und kann sich auch je nach Kontext auf die ganze liturgische Feier an einem Heiligentag beziehen.

ben und auf eine Stufe mit den universellen Heiligen des Römischen Kalenders gestellt wurde. Die Historia ist also die höchste Krönung seines Kultes.[108]

Darauf wird später nochmal zurückzukommen sein.

Ein weiteres Element konnte thematisch ganz dem Heiligen gewidmet werden, nämlich der an mehreren Stellen im Laufe des Stundengebets gesungene Hymnus.[109] Der Hymnus ist eine spätantike Gattung der liturgischen Poesie, als deren Erfinder Augustinus den Mailänder Bischof Ambrosius kolportiert. Ambrosius habe, so Augustinus, solche Lieder gedichtet und für den liturgischen Gebrauch in seiner Kirche vorgesehen.[110] Diese Zuschreibung blieb während des Mittelalters so wirkmächtig, dass für den Hymnus der Begriff *ambrosianum* Verbreitung fand.[111] Somit waren Hymnen von Anfang an deutlich als nicht-biblische Dichtungen markiert und fanden erst nach einer ersten Phase der Ablehnung, spätestens aber ab dem 11. Jahrhundert, in ganz Europa Eingang in die Liturgie.[112] Auch der Form nach waren Hymnen leicht vom übrigen liturgischen Material unterscheidbar, weil sie nie in Prosa, sondern stets metrisch komponiert wurden. Die beliebtesten Versmaße waren der jambische Dimeter (in Anlehnung an die Hymnen des Ambrosius) und die sapphische Strophe.[113]

In Bezug auf den Inhalt zeichnete sich der Hymnus durch eine große Vielfalt aus: Ausgehend von den ersten Hymnendichtungen, die meistens Episoden aus dem Leben Jesu thematisierten und anlässlich der wichtigen Herrenfeste gesungen wurden, wurde der Bestand auch durch die Aufnahme lokaler Kulttraditionen ständig erweitert.[114]

Die hier dargelegten Formen und Elemente des mittelalterlichen Konstruktionsprozesses von Heiligen bezeichne ich zusammenfassend als Hagiopraxis. Diese Bezeichnung soll in Abgrenzung zum Hagiographiebegriff deutlich machen, dass

---

108 „Ainsi, toutes ces formes et expressions différenciées du culte des saints, la composition d'un office propre, spécialment composé pour le saint à partir de la rédaction d'une vita ou d'une passio, permet de le distinguer du commun, de le placer à niveau égal avec les saints dits universel du calendrier romain. L'historia s'impose donc comme la consécration suprême de son culte." Jean-François Goudesenne: Les Offices historiques ou Historiae composés pour les fêtes des saints dans la province ecclésiastique de Reims (775–1030), Turnhout 2002, S. 29.

109 Zu den Anfängen der christlichen Hymnodie siehe: Alan Dunstan: Hymnody in Christian Worship, in: Cheslyn Jones (Hg.): The Study of Liturgy, London 1992, S. 507–519. Grundsätzlich zum Hymnus vgl. Andreas Haug u. a. (Hg.): Der lateinische Hymnus im Mittelalter. Überlieferung, Ästhetik, Ausstrahlung, Kassel 2004.

110 Vgl. Hiley: Western Plainchant, S. 140.

111 Wie zum Beispiel in der Benediktregel, vgl. Benedikt von Nursia: La Règle, S. 510.

112 Siehe: Michel Huglo u. a.: Gallican Chant, in: Stanley Sadie (Hg.): The New Grove Dictionary of Music and Musicians, London 2001, S. 458–472; Harper: The Forms and Orders, S. 80; Helmut Gneuss: Zur Geschichte des Hymnars, in: Andreas Haug u. a. (Hg.): Der lateinische Hymnus im Mittelalter. Überlieferung, Ästhetik, Ausstrahlung, Kassel 2004, S. 63–86; Donald A. Bullough: Texts, Chant, and the Chapel of Louis the Pious, in: Peter Godman / Roger Collins (Hg.): Charlemagne's Heir. New Perspectives on the Reign of Louis the Pious (814–840), Oxford 1990, S. 489–508

113 Vgl. Hiley: Western Plainchant, S. 141–142.

114 Vgl. Harper: The Forms and Orders, S. 80.

die Konstruktion des Heiligen nicht in einem Text, sondern viel mehr im sozialen und kommunikativen Handeln erfolgte: Religiöse Verehrergemeinschaften medialisierten ‚ihren' Heiligen in der liturgischen Praxis, indem sie für ihn Zeiten und Orte markierten und zu seinen Ehren Feste feierten, bei denen sein Leben und seine Taten memoriert und besungen wurden. Im Folgenden wird die Methodik der Erschließung der Hagiopraxis behandelt.

2.2 *Die Erschließung der liturgischen Hagiopraxis*

Mit dem Begriff Hagiopraxis soll hier der soziale und kommunikative Prozess, während dessen eine Verehrergemeinschaft durch liturgische Praktiken einen Heiligen konstruiert, verstanden werden. Die wissenschaftliche Erschließung der Hagiopraxis erweist sich als äußerst komplex. Einerseits sind nicht alle Bestandteile der Hagiopraxis in allen Einzelheiten rekonstruierbar. Darüber hinaus spielten dabei verschiedene Praktiken und Medien eine Rolle, die sich nicht mit einer einheitlichen Methode untersuchen lassen. Sie alle verlangen nach spezifischen Erschließungsmethoden und können somit weder von einzelnen Forschenden noch in den Grenzen einer einzigen Disziplin untersucht werden. Hagiopraxis eignet sich viel mehr als Gegenstand multidisziplinärer Untersuchungen unter Einbezug mediävistischer Fächer wie der lateinischen Philologie, der Musikologie, der Kunst- und Baugeschichte, der Theologie und der Liturgiewissenschaft.

Im Rahmen einer solchen multidisziplinären Untersuchung der Hagiopraxis kommt schriftlichen Quellen eine zentrale Stellung zu. Als solche ist alles schriftliche Material anzusehen, das für die Feier des Heiligenfestes verfasst oder kompiliert und im Rahmen der liturgischen Praxis verwendet wurde. Überliefert ist es auf materiellen Trägern, für das Mittelalter in Handschriften. Dieses Material, nämlich liturgische Quellen und liturgische Bücher, erweisen sich für die Untersuchung des Konstruktionsprozesses von Heiligen als fundamental, weil sie nicht nur auf eine Hagiopraxis hinweisen, sondern auch über deren Inhalt informieren und ferner teilweise erlauben, die liturgische Choreographie zu rekonstruieren.[115] Entgegen der bereits erwähnten Auffassung von Philippart, dass liturgische Quellen mindere Gattungen seien, sind sie für die Untersuchung der Hagiopraxis unabdingbar.[116]

Die Aufgabe der Erschließung der schriftlichen Quellen der Hagiopraxis kommt den Philologen oder „text historians"[117] zu. Diese sind allerdings mit der Herausforderung konfrontiert, die Quellen auf eine Art und Weise aufzubereiten, dass sie im Rahmen einer multidisziplinären Untersuchung der Hagiopraxis zum Tragen kommen können.

115 Siehe oben, S. 26.

116 Siehe oben, S. 20.

117 Gunilla Iversen: Problems in the Editing of Tropes, in: Text. An interdisciplinary annual of textual studies 1, 1981, S. 95–132, hier: S. 103.

Die bereits zur Verfügung stehenden Methoden der Aufbereitung und Erschließung der liturgischen Quellen werden im Folgenden zusammenfassend vorgestellt und auf ihre Anschlussfähigkeit im Rahmen einer Untersuchung der Hagiopraxis hin kritisch hinterfragt. Im Anschluss daran wird die Methode vorgestellt werden, die in der vorliegenden Arbeit eingesetzt wird.

Historische Ansätze im editorischen Umgang mit und für die Erschließung von liturgischen Quellen

Ein Abriss der bisher entwickelten Erschließungsmethoden für liturgische Quellen muss notwendigerweise im 19. Jahrhundert ansetzen, da zu dieser Zeit bis heute maßgebliche Erschließungsprinzipien und Fragestellungen etabliert wurden. Besonders zwei Projekte stehen hierfür paradigmatisch: Zum einen Prosper-Louis Guérangers Bemühungen um eine Restitution des gregorianischen Chorals. Guéranger, der 1837 zum Abt der wiedergegründeten französischen Abtei Solesmes ernannt wurde, gilt als Pionier und Initiator der charakteristisch gewordenen Beschäftigung der Solesmes-Mönche mit den Quellen zur mittelalterlichen Monodie.[118] Sein Lebensziel war es, das Klosterleben seiner Zeit wieder an mittelalterlichen monastischen Idealen zu orientieren. Dafür sah er es als entscheidend an, sich intensiv mit den Grundlagen des Gesangs der Mönche, der im Stundengebet eine so zentrale Rolle spielt, auseinanderzusetzen. Guéranger begann damit, mittelalterliche monastische Texte und Melodien zu suchen, um nach diesen Vorlagen den ‚richtigen' monastischen Gesang zu rekonstruieren. Dem Vorhaben entsprechend, eine möglichst reine mittelalterliche Musiktradition zu finden beziehungsweise herzustellen, wurden die handschriftlichen Quellen meistens in Form von Faksimile-Ausgaben herausgebracht.

1886 erschien in Leipzig der erste Band der *Analecta hymnica medii aevi*. Die Herausgeber der *Analecta* waren vor allem an Werken der christlich-lateinischen Poesie interessiert. Sie planten eine vollständige Sammlung aller Gattungen mittelalterlicher Dichtung (Hymnen, Sequenzen, Tropen, Reimoffizien et cetera). Diese sollte „durch Veröffentlichung des *unedierten* oder schwer zugänglichen und zerstreuten hymnologischen Materials die notwendige Grundlage für eine Geschichte und die rechte Würdigung der lateinischen Hymnodie"[119] liefern. Beides gelang den Editoren: nicht nur konnte mit den *Analecta hymnica* das Material zugänglich gemacht werden, um das Corpus konstituierte sich auch ein neues Forschungsfeld, das mittelalterliche liturgische Dichtung zum ersten Mal als Gegenstand wissenschaftlicher Untersuchung würdigte.

---

118 Vgl. Walther Lipphardt: Solesmes, in: Friedrich Blume (Hg.): Die Musik in Geschichte und Gegenwart, Berlin 2001, S. 835–839, hier: S. 836.

119 Clemens Blume: Vorwort und Einleitung, in: Clemens Blume u. a. (Hg.): Thesauri hymnologici hymnarium. Die Hymnen des 5.–11. Jahrhunderts und die irisch-keltische Hymnodie (Analecta Hymnica Medii Aevi 51), Leipzig 1908, S. V–XLVII, hier: S. V. [Kursivierung im Original].

Zweifellos steht dem Forscher durch die Veröffentlichungen aus der Reihe der *Analecta hymnica* ein unabdingbar gewordenes Repertorium zu Verfügung, der hier gepflegte, mittlerweile kanonisch gewordene Umgang mit den Quellen reflektiert allerdings sehr stark die Verfahren und Interessen des 19. Jahrhunderts. Gegenstand derselben waren Zeugnisse höchster Errungenschaften der lateinisch-christlichen Dichtung, und nicht liturgische Texte. Diese stellen lediglich das Terrain dar, auf dem man verstreut auch wertvolle Beispiele für Literatur und Dichtung, „liturgische Poesien“,[120] finden kann, sind aber an sich nicht Teil der Untersuchung.

Bereits die Strukturierung der *Analecta hymnica* dient dieser Herangehensweise. Das Material wird nicht nach dem liturgischen Anlass oder nach dem zelebrierten Heiligen, sondern nach der Gattung der Stücke angeordnet: Mehrere Bände der Sammlung sind allein den Hymnen, anderen den Sequenzen oder liturgischen Prosen,[121] wieder andere den Tropen und zuletzt den Reimoffizien gewidmet. Dieses Vorgehen ist im Rahmen einer historisch-kritischen Edition des Materials naheliegend, löst aber den Kontext seiner Verwendung in der liturgischen Performanz ein und derselben Feier völlig auf. Zwar spiegelt dies teilweise die Situation der handschriftlichen Überlieferung wieder, denn auch dort wurden, zumindest bis zum Aufkommen des Breviers und des Missale, die Gesangs-, Lese- oder Gebetselemente getrennt schriftlich fixiert, allerdings entzieht sich so das liturgische Ensemble dem nicht mehr mit den Strukturen mittelalterlicher Liturgie vertrauten Leser.

Die editorischen Grundsätze der *Analecta hymnica* lassen sich anhand derjenigen Bände exemplarisch veranschaulichen, die den liturgischen Reimoffizien, den „historiae rhythmatae et rimatae“,[122] gewidmet sind. Zum einen wird hier lediglich der Bestand an Antiphonen und Responsorien berücksichtigt. Die Gesänge und Texte, mit denen sie gemeinsam im Wechsel vorgetragen wurden, wie Hymnen, Psalmen und Lesungen, werden aus der Darstellung ausgeschlossen. Zum zweiten werden die Texte hier auf eine Art und Weise präsentiert, die den Eindruck erweckt, es handele sich um kontextlose Poesie. Zwar deuten Überschriften wie „*In primo nocturno*“, „*In secundo nocturno*“ auf den liturgischen Kontext hin, in den diese Antiphonen und Responsorien eingebettet waren, doch sie dienen hier lediglich der Strukturierung des Stoffes. Dadurch verschwindet eine komplexe Praxis hinter dem Edierten, das nur einen Bruchteil der liturgischen Elemente des Stundengebets wiedergibt.

Die Beschränkung der Editoren auf die aus ihrer Sicht literarisch wertvollsten Stücke führt teilweise sogar dazu, dass ganze Bestandteile von Reimoffizien

---

120 Guido M. Dreves: Einleitung, in: Guido M. Dreves (Hg.): Historiae rhythmicae. Liturgische Reimofficien des Mittelalters. Erste Folge. Aus Handschriften und Wiegendrucken (Analecta Hymnica Medii Aevi 5), Leipzig 1889, S. 5–16, hier: S. 5.

121 Vgl. ders.: Vorwort, in: Guido M. Dreves (Hg.): Sequentiae ineditae. Aus Handschriften und Frühdrucken (Analecta Hymnica Medii Aevi 8), Leipzig 1890, S. 5–8.

122 Dreves: Einleitung, S. 6.

von der Edition ausgeschlossen wurden. Hinweise auf nicht berücksichtigte Teile der Handschriften lauten oft lakonisch: „Alles prosaisch“[123] oder „In 2. Vesp. ad Magn. befindet sich eine prosaische Antiphon.“[124] Gänzlich prosaische Offizien sind aus den gleichen Gründen in den *Analecta* überhaupt nicht enthalten.

Handlungsleitend für den Umgang mit den Texten ist vor allem das Ziel der Editoren, eine „solche Textausgabe“ zu liefern, „[...] auf Grund welcher der ursprüngliche Text rekonstruiert und der rekonstruierte Text auf seine Zuverlässigkeit nachgeprüft werden kann und muss.“[125] Dementsprechend greifen Editoren so stark ein, dass der hergestellte Text oft keinem einzigen Original entspricht. Außerdem werden orthographische und lexikalische Varianten im Apparat verzeichnet, zusammen mit größeren Unterschieden im überlieferten Bestand. Diese Unterschiede betreffen oft mehrere Antiphonen oder Responsorien, teilweise sogar all die Elemente, die einer bestimmten Gebetszeit zugeordnet waren. Auf diese Weise werden sie aber als reine Abweichungen gedeutet und einem vom Editor bevorzugten, rekonstruierten Text untergeordnet. Infolgedessen können die Texte der einzelnen Überlieferungsträger aber nur mühsam oder sogar überhaupt nicht rekonstruiert werden, zum Beispiel in den oben genannten Fällen, bei denen bestimmte Textelemente aufgrund ihrer aus Sicht der Autoren mangelhaften Qualität nicht verzeichnet werden.[126]

Gleichwohl waren sich die Herausgeber der besonderen Schwierigkeiten bei der Edition liturgischer Texte bewusst: „Ein Umstand, der eine richtige Edierung mancher Reimofficien erschwert, ist die abweichende Einrichtung der verschiedenen liturgischen Handschriften“. So käme es häufig vor, dass ein kanonikales Offizium für die monastische Form ergänzt wurde und dass man es deswegen mit einem „interpolierten“, „mit Schlacken durchsetzen und in Unordnung geratenen Text“ zu tun habe, oder dass ein monastisches Offizium zu einem kano-

123 Guido M. Dreves (Hg.): Historiae rhythmicae. Liturgische Reimofficien des Mittelalters. Erste Folge. Aus Handschriften und Wiegendrucken (Analecta Hymnica Medii Aevi 5), Leipzig 1889, S. 39.

124 Ebd., S. 117.

125 Blume: Vorwort und Einleitung

126 Zu ganz ähnlichen Schlüssen kommt auch Gunilla Iversen in Bezug auf die in den *Analecta* edierten Tropen: „The editors of the Gloria tropes and prosulas in Analecta Hymnica vol. 47, Henry Marriot Bannister and Clemens Blume, established a normalised version of what they considered to be real verse, that is metric poetry, leaving out other texts and only giving some variant verses in the apparatus. The established text version is however very often not found in any of the manuscripts. Many manuscripts and regional versions are simply omitted, due to the basic ambition only to edit the original version of the author, although the ‚author‘, in the case of tropes as in the case of many other floating, compilated texts typical for the medieval literary culture, should more fittingly be seen as the ‚compilator‘. Entire trope complexes were omitted since, according to their opinion, a poetic text had to be metric, versified, structured in a specific way to be accepted for the edition.” aus Gunilla Iversen: Tropes and Prosulas Added to the Chant Gloria in excelsis in the Medieval Mass: Editorial Problems and Proposed Solutions, http://hdl.handle.net/1807/32257 [10. Mai 2018].

nikalen verkürzt wurde und dabei ein „lückenhafter und unvollständiger Text" entstanden sei.[127]

Doch trotz dieses Bewusstseins um die Heterogenität der Überlieferung wurden gerade diese Unterschiede nicht berücksichtigt:

> Vor mir liegt beispielweise ein Barbaraofficium, das ich bisher nur in nicht-monastischen und Cistercienser-Brevieren gefunden [habe]; ich bin aber überzeugt, daß die monastische Form des Benediktiner-Breviers die ursprüngliche und allein richtige ist [...]. Zur Herstellung der ursprünglichen Form fehlt jetzt nur noch eine Antiphon, die fünfte der ersten Vesper.[128]

Zusammenfassend scheint eine wie in den *Analecta hymnica* praktizierte, auf lachmannschen Prinzipien basierende Editionsmethode nicht mehr zeitgemäß: Nicht nur werden die Charakteristika der handschriftlichen Überlieferung vorschnell zu Gunsten eines durch die Editoren rekonstruierten Textes übergangen, auch wird ihre Eigenschaft als liturgische Quellen weitgehend ignoriert, weil das Interesse nicht der Liturgie, sondern ihren literarischen Produkten gilt. Auch wenn die *Analecta hymnica* bis heute das Standardwerk für die Beschäftigung mit liturgischen Quellen darstellen, werden ihre Leitprinzipien von der jüngeren Forschung zunehmend diskutiert.

Andrieus Ordines romani

Als wegweisend im Bereich der Editionstechnik liturgischer Quellen gilt das Werk über die Ordines romani von Michel Andrieu.[129] Ziel seiner Arbeit ist die Rekonstruktion der ursprünglichen römischen Versionen der Ordines,[130] also von Texten, die unterschiedliche liturgische Abläufe (von der Messe bis hin zur Dedikation einer Kirche) normativ beschreiben und die im Zuge der karolingischen Liturgiereform von Rom aus in das ganze fränkische Reich verbreitet wurden.[131]

Trotz seiner rekonstruierenden Vorgehensweise ist sich der Editor bewusst, dass liturgische Quellen lebendige Texte sind,[132] die bestimmte Bräuche und Traditionen fixieren, unabhängig von ihrem Verhältnis zu einer ursprünglichen Fassung. Demzufolge wäre nach Andrieu der Informationsverlust zu groß, würde

---

127 Guido M. Dreves (Hg.): Historiae rhythmicae, S. 9–10.

128 Dreves: Einleitung, S. 10–11.

129 Vgl. Michel Andrieu: Les Ordines Romani du haut moyen âge. 5 Bde. (Spicilegium Sacrum Lovaniense: Etudes et documents), Löwen 1931–1961.

130 Andrieu: Les Ordines Romani 2, S. VIII–IX: „Le rôle de l'éditeur est donc de rassembler tous les manuscrits de l'ouvrage, de les confronter et d'en dégager, à ses risques et périls, un texte qui se rapproche autant que possible de ce que fut l'original."

131 Ders.: Les Ordines Romani du haut moyen âge. Bd. 1 Les manuscrits (Spicilegium Sacrum Lovaniense: Etudes et documents), Löwen 1965, S. 467–485.

132 Andrieu: Les Ordines Romani 2, S. X: „Les écrits liturgique [...] sont en effet des textes vivants."

man nur den Archetypus edieren und spätere Modifikationen vernachlässigen[133]. So gibt Andrieu den für ihn besten, also dem Original am nahestehendsten Text wieder, er ediert ihn aber teilweise synoptisch[134] und liefert einen höchst detaillierten Apparat, der alle Varianten, auch die wenig bedeutsamen, wiedergibt.[135]

Zusammenfassend bleibt festzuhalten, dass in Andrieus Werk die Varianz der Quellen sowie die Hinweise der handschriftlichen Überlieferung ernst genommen und in der Edition wiedergegeben werden, auch wenn das übergeordnete Ziel seiner Arbeit an den mittelalterlichen Ordines eine Rekonstruktion der vorkarolingischen römischen Liturgie ist.

Die editorischen Methoden des Corpus troporum

Sehr interessante editorische Methoden werden seit den 1970er Jahren im Rahmen des in Stockholm angesiedelten Forschungsprojekts *Corpus troporum* erprobt.[136] In den Jahren 2008 bis 2015 wurde im Rahmen des *Corpus troporum*-Projekts das Programm *Ars edendi* durchgeführt, im Zuge dessen neben Tropen auch weitere liturgische[137] sowie sogenannte paraliturgische Gattungen[138] in die Untersuchung einbezogen wurden.

Die Überlegungen der Herausgeber der *Corpus troporum*-Bände betreffen vor allem zwei Bereiche, die beide für den Umgang mit mittelalterlichen liturgischen Quellen zentral sind. Zum einen wurde die Darstellungsweise des Materials reflektiert.[139] Es existieren unterschiedliche Typologien von Tropen, die sich jeweils unterschiedlich zum tropierten Element verhalten und die in der Liturgie entsprechend auf unterschiedliche Art und Weise vorgetragen wurden. Dies spiegelt sich in der handschriftlichen Überlieferung wieder, zum Beispiel im Seitenlayout

133 Ebd: „On s'exposerait donc à perdre d'importantes informations, si on laissât de côté la descendance de l'archétype."

134 Ebd., S. IX: „Le mieux est alors de reproduire, en colonnes parallèles, les textes irréductibles à un type commun."

135 Ebd., S. 36: „Il m' a donc paru impossible de déterminer *a priori* les variantes qui pourraient un jour servir. Aussi me suis-je finalement arrêté au parti le plus sûr, qui est de les reproduire toutes."

136 Siehe Ritva Jonsson (Hg.): Tropes du propre de la messe (Corpus Troporum 1), Stockholm 1975.

137 Wie zum Beispiel das hochmittelalterliche Lektionar der Kirche von Piacenza in: Brian Møller Jensen: Lectionarium Placentinum as a Challenge to the Editor, http://hdl.handle.net/1807/32260 [20. September 2018].

138 Vgl. die Edition der spätmittelalterlichen Sequenzenkommentare von Erika Kihlman: Expositiones sequentiarum. Medieval Sequence Commentaries and Prologues. Editions with Introductions (Acta Universitatis Stockholmiensis. Studia Latina Stockholmiensia 53), Stockholm 2006.

139 Vgl. Iversen: Problems in the Editing, S. 97: „The first [problem] is to find a method of presenting what I call the main structure of the troped chants. That is, to present all the different combinations of the separate verses, the so-called trope elements, that belong to the same trope, and also to demonstrate the way the trope elements and the base liturgical text are linked together."

und in der Auszeichnung der zu tropierenden Elemente, was auch in der Edition berücksichtigt werden sollte. Dafür wurden von den Editoren elaborierte Darstellungsformen entwickelt, die sehr genau die jeweils spezifischen Eigenschaften des zu edierenden Materials beachten. Sie sind daher auf der einen Seite sehr raffiniert und für Editoren von Tropen sehr nützlich, lassen sich aber auf der anderen Seite nur schwer bei Editionen anderer Gattungen liturgischer Texte verwenden.

Zum zweiten wurde im Rahmen dieses Projektes auch grundsätzlich über die Konstitution liturgischer Texte nachgedacht. Die Frage nach Versionen und Varianten, die man für die Textkonstitution auswählen soll, beantworten die Herausgeber folgendermaßen: „Das Kriterium der Authentizität darf nicht auf traditionelle Art und Weise für dieses Material angewendet werden, da jeder Text, der eine tatsächlich ausgeführte liturgische Praxis wiederspiegelt, als authentisch betrachtet werden muss.“[140] Demzufolge kann das Ziel des Editors nicht mehr die Erarbeitung eines Stemmas oder die Rekonstruktion eines Autorenoriginals sein, vielmehr sollte die akribische Wiedergabe aller überlieferten Textversionen, so wie sie in den unterschiedlichen Kontexten Anwendung fanden, im Mittelpunkt stehen.[141]

Zusammenfassend sind die im *Corpus troporum* erprobten editorischen Lösungen nicht ohne Weiteres auf andere Gattungen liturgischer Quellen übertragbar, da sie vornehmlich im Hinblick auf das europäische Tropenrepertoire vom 9. bis ins 12. Jahrhundert entwickelt wurden. Nichtdestotrotz können die leitenden Prinzipien der Edition im *Corpus troporum* auch für den Umgang mit anderen Arten liturgischer Quellen fruchtbar gemacht werden. Diese Prinzipien lauten:

1. Editionsform und Darstellungsmodus müssen sich grundsätzlich an den spezifischen Eigenschaften und der Beschaffenheit des Materials ausrichten;

2. Die Edition muss über alle verfügbaren Versionen des Textes Auskunft geben, denn jede Version ist als Zeugnis einer historischen Praxis an sich gültig;[142]

3. Die Hinweise der handschriftlichen Überlieferung müssen stärker berücksichtigt werden. Dies schließt unter anderem zahlreiche Abbildungen der Codices, Anhänge und ausführlichen Indizes ein;[143]

---

[140] Ebd., S. 97.

[141] Vgl. ebd., S. 97–102.

[142] Ähnlich sieht das auch Valerio Polidori: L'edizione delle fonti liturgiche greche: una questione di metodo, in: Bollettino della Badia Greca di Grottaferrata 10, 2013, S. 173–198.

[143] Vgl. Iversen: Problems in the Editing, S. 103: „We have found that indices of feasts, repertories, surveys of manuscripts as entities, and descriptions of traditions and text analysis are important for most scholars using the trope editions; but we have now abstained from special sections giving melody-examples and dealing with the music. We prefer to give a photographic plate of a trope where the music is important for the understanding of the text and where the relation between text and music is especially intricate.“

4. Die Form der Aufführung oder Performanz der jeweiligen Elemente kann nicht ignoriert, sondern muss in der Edition berücksichtig werden.

2010 lokalisierte auch Giacomo Bonifacio Baroffio eine Kluft zwischen dem begrifflichen und dem realen Raum der liturgischen Philologie. Diese Kluft entsteht nach Baroffio aus der Differenz zwischen den Methoden, die für die Untersuchung von liturgischen Texten eingesetzt werden, und der tatsächlichen, realen Situation der überlieferten liturgischen Quellen. Sie käme dadurch zu Stande, dass bei der Analyse liturgischer Quellen meist philologische Methoden Anwendung fänden. Diese reichten nach Baroffio aber nicht aus, um die Eigenheit der liturgischen Quellen zu fassen.[144] Dies sei allerdings, so weiterhin Baroffio, nicht der Unzulänglichkeit der Methoden selbst geschuldet, die sich wiederum für die Untersuchung anderer literarischer Gattungen hervorragend eignen würden. Vielmehr machen die spezifischen Verbreitungs- und Überlieferungsmodalitäten sowie einige mentalitätsgeschichtliche Eigenschaften der liturgischen Quellen eine traditionell verstanden philologische Methode für ihre Untersuchung inadäquat.

Zunächst sei es nach Baroffio aus verschiedenen Gründen wenig sinnvoll (und nahezu unmöglich), für liturgische Texte Stemmata zu erarbeiten. Da liturgische Texte ständig aktualisiert werden mussten, um auch angesichts sich verändernder Bräuche und kultischer Traditionen nutzbar zu bleiben,[145] wurden im Mittelalter weitaus mehr liturgische Bücher produziert als heute bekannt sind. Weil damit aber auch die Vernichtung obsolet gewordener Bücher einherging, sei es extrem schwierig, ein vollständiges und akkurates Bild der Überlieferung zu rekonstruieren. Somit sei auch die Erarbeitung eines Stemmas nahezu unmöglich. Aber auch intrinsische Eigenschaften liturgischer Quellen stehen der unreflektierten Anwendung philologischer Methoden auf liturgische Texte im Weg. Wenn ein liturgischer Text abgeschrieben wurde, sei es selten Ziel des Kopisten gewesen, ihn wortgetreu wiederzugeben. Vielmehr sei der Zweck der Anfertigung eines liturgischen Buches gewesen, Texte und Gesänge zu liefern, die dem Interesse, der Sensibilität, den Bedürfnissen und theologischen Auffassungen einer bestimmten Kommunität zu einer bestimmten Zeit und an einem bestimmten Ort entsprochen hätten:

> Im Rahmen der Übertragung literarischer Texte der Antike gaben sich die Kopisten Mühe, einen Text abzuschreiben, der so korrekt und mit der Vorlage identisch war, wie nur möglich. Wenn aber liturgische Texte übertragen wurden, versuchten die Kopisten, nicht nur einen Text zu redigieren, der die Vorlage aus der Vergangenheit widerspiegelte, sondern auch einen Text zu liefern, der Ausdruck des Glaubens einer bestimmten Kultgemeinschaft war, die in einem spezifischen historischen Kontext lebte und eine eigene Kultur und eine spezifische dichterische Sensibilität hatte. Der literarische Text aus der Antike ist authentisch, wenn er mit dem Original übereinstimmt. Der liturgi-

---

144 Vgl. Giacomo B. Baroffio: Lo spazio concettuale e reale della filologia liturgica, in: Rivista Internazionale di Musica Sacra 31, 2010, S. 169–192, hier: S. 169.

145 Vgl. ebd.

sche Text hingegen ist authentisch, wenn er den Glauben einer Gemeinschaft ausdrückt, die mit Leidenschaft ihr Bekenntnis auslebt.[146]

Damit könne nach Erika Kihlman die Mehrheit der liturgischen Texte als „fluid“ oder als „open text“ klassifiziert werden.[147] Diese Eigenschaften würden noch dadurch unterstrichen, so Baroffio, dass ein liturgischer Text in aller Regel in einem Umfeld abgefasst wurde, in dem der Kontakt mit dem biblischen Wort alltäglich war:

> Die Herstellung liturgischer Bücher geschah in einer Umgebung, in der das Wort Gottes keine abstrakte Präsenz war, sondern in der man eine reale Vertrautheit damit hatte, wie in mittelalterlichen Klöstern und Kathedralschulen. Das wird deutlich, wenn man die Kirchenväter liest. Ihr Duktus ist geprägt von biblischen Ausdrücken. Einzelne Wörter und ganze Sätze sind aus der Bibel entnommen, teilweise wörtlich, teilweise paraphrasiert, und den individuellen Bedürfnissen angepasst. Themen, Bilder, Wörter fluktuieren zwischen der Bibel, der persönlichen Reflexion, den spirituellen Werken und den Gebetsformeln. Das ganze Material in den liturgischen Handschriften ist durch Lesen und/oder Diktieren, teilweise im Gedächtnis überliefert. So jeder täglich, wöchentlich, jährlich und regelmäßig – wie die Texte während Advent und Ostern – gelesene oder gehörte Text. Diesen Kontakt gilt es zu bedenken, er hat am Ende großen Einfluss auf Individuen und liturgische Gemeinschaften.[148]

Zusammenfassend können zwei Aspekte des Forschungsdiskurses der letzten Jahrzehnte herausgearbeitet werden. Innerhalb der Disziplinen, die sich traditionell mit der Erschließung und Untersuchung liturgischer Quellen beschäftigen, wie die Lateinische Philologie des Mittelalters, die Musikologie und die Liturgiewissenschaft, wird zunehmend eine Diskrepanz zwischen den Untersuchungsmethoden und dem untersuchten Phänomen der Liturgie ausgemacht. Diese

---

[146] „Nella trasmissione dei testi letterari classici, l'impegno dei copisti è di scrivere un testo che sia il più possibile corretto e identico all'opera dell'autore. Nella trasmissione dei testi liturgici, la preoccupazione dei copisti è di redigere un testo che non solo rifletta il patrimonio giunto dal passato, ma sia soprattutto l'espressione della fede di un'assemblea che vive in un preciso contesto sociale con una sua cultura e una sua particolare sensibilità poetica. Il testo letterario ‚classico' è autentico quando combacia con l'originale. Il testo liturgico è autentico quando esprime nel modo meno inadeguato possibile la fede di una comunità che vive con passione il suo credo.“ Ebd.

[147] Vgl. Erika Kihlman: Editing Fluid Texts: The Case of the Sequence Commentaries, http://hdl.handle.net/1807/32263 (Stand: 20.09.2018).

[148] „La redazione del libro liturgico avviene in un ambiente dove non soltanto in casi ideali astratti, ma spesso – come nel medioevo succede nei monasteri e nelle scuole delle cattedrali – c'è una reale familiarità con la Parola di D-i-o. Ciò risulta evidente nella lettura dei padri medievali. Il loro discorrere personale si costruisce e si diffonde attraverso espressioni bibliche. Singoli vocaboli e intere frasi sono mutuate dalla Bibbia, a volte in modo letterario, spesso rielaborati e piegati alle esigenze del momento. C'è un moto continuo di fluire e rifluire di temi, immagini, parole tra il thesaurus biblico, la meditazione personale, i testi spirituali, le formule di preghiera. Tutto il materiale scritto nei codici è recepito attraverso la lettura e/o la dettatura, talora anche in base alla memoria. Testi letti ed ascoltati, a seconda dei casi, a scadenza giornaliera, settimanale, annuale e periodica (si pensi ai testi propri dei tempi forti come l'avvento e la quaresima). Si tratta di una sollecitazione notevole che finisce per lasciare la propria impronta sui singoli e sulle assemblee liturgiche.“ Baroffio: Lo spazio concettuale, S. 169–170.

Feststellung geht mit einer Problematisierung der bisher unreflektierten Übertragung philologischer Methoden auf liturgische Quellen einher sowie mit dem Ruf nach einer grundsätzlich interdisziplinären Herangehensweise.[149]

Gleichzeitig wuchs in der mediävistischen Forschung in den letzten 20 Jahren das Interesse an liturgischen Texten und Quellen. Methoden und Ansätze unterscheiden sich aber vom Herkömmlichen. Die zunehmende Säkularisierung der Geisteswissenschaften[150] hat hier in gewissem Sinne eine größere Distanz zwischen dem Untersuchungsobjekt und den Forschenden geschaffen und die Liturgieforschung für Impulse aus den Kulturwissenschaften empfänglich gemacht.[151]

Darüber hinaus mehren sich in der Mediävistik die Plädoyers nicht allein für eine verstärkte kulturwissenschaftliche Untersuchung von mittelalterlichen liturgischen Praktiken, sondern auch für ein gänzlich neues Verständnis von Liturgie.[152] So sollen Methoden und Instrumente der ethnographischen und kulturwissenschaftlichen Disziplinen stärker berücksichtigt werden, denn dies erlaube, liturgische Texte ritualtheoretisch zu untersuchen und sie somit weniger als Texte, sondern vielmehr als ‚*cultural sites*' wahrzunehmen:

> Liturgy needs to be understood as more than a script for church officials, a minutely detailed script whose complex development and difficult terminology too often cause our students to lose interest in the religious culture of the Middle Ages. To engage that interest and also to do justice to the historically complex realities of medieval liturgy, we need to begin viewing it as the cultural site for the most inclusive social and political as well as religious performance.[153]

Den oben formulierten Prinzipien entsprechend wird im Folgenden eine alternative Erschließungsform entwickelt. Zunächst wird der Inhalt der liturgischen Praxis am Feiertag des Heiligen durch eine Textedition herausgearbeitet. So wird ein zuverlässiger Textbestand erarbeitet, der die Differenzen zwischen den einzelnen Überlieferungsgruppen betont, anstatt sie einzuebnen.

Außerdem wird die Choreographie nachvollziehbar gemacht, in welche die Texte eingebettet waren und die für ihr Verständnis wesentlich ist. Um ein solch volatiles Artefakt einer wissenschaftlichen Analyse unterziehen zu können, ist

---

149 Dies diagnostizierte bereits Knud Ottosen: La problématique de l'édition des textes liturgiques latins, in: Otto S. Due u. a. (Hg.): Classica et mediaevalia. Francisco Blatt septuagenario dedicata, Kopenhagen 1973, S. 541–556.

150 Vgl. Clifford C. Flanigan u. a.: Liturgy as Social Performance: Expanding the Definitions, in: Thomas J. Heffernan / Ann E. Matter (Hg.): The Liturgy of the Medieval Church, Kalamazoo 2001, S. 635–652, hier: S. 635: „The study of the medieval liturgy has been, with a few notable exceptions, primarily an ecclesiastical subject, carried out most often by clerics or others with close connections to western liturgical churches. This is one reason that medieval liturgiology seldom has appeared in the secular university curriculum, apart from musicology, where attention is devoted almost exclusively to the musical as opposed to the verbal text."

151 Vgl. Neuheuser: Liturgische Bücher, S. 239.

152 Flanigan u. a.: Liturgy as Social Performance, S. 652: „Current working concepts about medieval liturgy need to be rethought."

153 Ebd.

es aber notwendig, „ein […] fixierbar- und tradierbares Korrelat zu schaffen“,[154] in anderen Worten ein Modell zu bauen und ein „Notationssystem“[155] zu entwickeln. Ergebnis ist eine Rekonstruktion, in der die Choreographie des Festes ebenso aus der Druckseite ersichtlich wird, wie alle im Rahmen desselben vorgetragenen Texte. Das schließt Elemente ein, die für den Heiligen komponiert wurden, aber auch feststehende Texte wie die Psalmen, die zwar biblisch sind, aber dem Fest angepasst und variiert wurden.

Dafür wurden die materiellen Träger der Texte, nämlich die liturgischen Handschriften, erschlossen. Zuerst wurden die einzelnen Objekte jeweils einem Kultkontext zugeordnet. Anschließend wurden die diesen Objekten entnommenen und edierten Texte zu Rekonstruktionen zusammengefügt. Diese Rekonstruktionen sind wiederum Gegenstand der abschließenden Analyse der Hagiopraxis.

Edition und Rekonstruktionen sind konzeptionell getrennt, weil hier verschiedene, jedoch zusammenhängende Erkenntnisinteressen verfolgt werden: während die Edition eine philologische Analyse der überlieferten Texte leistet und nicht kontextgebunden ist, sollen die Rekonstruktionen die Analyse der Hagiopraxis ermöglichen und sind stets kontextabhängig. Außerdem hätte das Zusammenführen von Edition und Rekonstruktion die Lesbarkeit der Darstellung stark eingeschränkt.

---

154 Erika Fischer-Lichte: Semiotik des Theaters. Die Aufführung als Text, Tübingen [5]2009, S. 112.

155 Vgl. ebd.

3 Editionen und Rekonstruktionen

3.1 Handschriften, die den Editionen zugrunde liegen

Im Folgenden werden die Handschriften aufgelistet, die der Edition zugrunde liegen. Die Handschriften sind alphabetisch geordnet. In der ersten Zeile werden Sigle, Signatur, Provenienz, Datierung und der Typ der liturgischen Handschrift benannt. In der zweiten Zeile werden die Inhalte angegeben, die sich auf den veronesischen Stadtheiligen Zeno beziehen. Dabei bedeutet: O-CR Offizium im Cursus romanus; O-CM Offizium im Cursus monasticus; Hy Hymnen; Le Lesungen mit Angabe der BHL-Nummer. In der letzten Zeile finden sich Hinweise auf weitere Literatur zu der jeweiligen Handschrift.

Aug	**Augsburg Staats- und Stadtbibliothek 2° 204**
	Augsburg, St. Ulrich und Afra (?), saec. 15
	Breviarium
Inh.	O-CM; Hy; Le-BHL9010–9011
Lit.	Spilling 1984,[1] S. 196–199
Civ¹	**Cividale Museo Archeologico Nazionale XII**
	Cividale (Dom), saec. 15 med.
	Passionarium
Inh.	Le-BHL9010d
Lit.	Scalon / Pani 1998,[2] S. 109–115
Civ²	**Cividale Museo Archeologico Nazionale XXI**
	Cividale (Dom), saec. 12 med.
	Passionarium
Inh.	Le-BHL9010d
Lit.	Scalon / Pani 1998, S. 135–139

1 Vgl. Herrad Spilling: Die Handschriften der Staats- und Stadtbibliothek Augsburg. Bd. 2 2° COD 101–250. Beschrieben von Herrad Spilling (Die Handschriften der Staats- und Stadtbibliothek Augsburg 2), Wiesbaden 1984, S. 185–187; 158–159. Im Folgenden: Spilling 1984.

2 Vgl. Cesare Scalon / Laura Pani: I codici della Biblioteca Capitolare di Cividale del Friuli (Biblioteche e archivi 1), Florenz 1998. Im Folgenden: Scalon / Pani 1998.

Civ^{3}	**Cividale Museo Archeologico Nazionale XVI**
	Cividale (Dom), saec. 13 med.
	Passionarium
Inh.	Le-BHL9001
Lit.	Scalon / Pani 1998, S. 123–126
Civ^{4}	**Cividale Museo Archeologico Nazionale XXX**
	Cividale (Dom), saec. 14/15 (vor 1433)
	Antiphonarium
Inh.	O-CR (unvollständig)
Lit.	Camilot-Oswald 1997,[3] S. 7–9 der Handschriftenbeschreibungen
	Scalon / Pani 1998, S. 153–154
Civ^{5}	**Cividale Museo Archeologico Nazionale XXXIV**
	Cividale (Dom), saec. 14 / 15 (vor 1433)
	Antiphonarium
Inh.	O-CR
Lit.	Camilot-Oswald 1997, S. 9–11 der Handschriftenbeschreibungen
	Scalon / Pani 1998, S. 158–159
Civ^{6}	**Cividale Museo Archeologico Nazionale XLVII**
	Cividale (Dom), saec. 15 (vor 1433)
	Antiphonarium
Inh.	O-CR
Lit.	Camilot-Oswald 1997, S. 17–20 der Handschriftenbeschreibungen
	Scalon / Pani 1998, S. 185–187
Kr	**Kremsmünster Stiftsbibliothek CC60**
	Verona (Abtei San Zeno Maggiore), saec. 15 (um 1467)
	Breviarium
Inh.	O-CM; Hy; Le-BHL9010–9011
Lit.	Fill 2000,[4] S. 301–308

3 Vgl. Raffaella Camilot-Oswald: Die liturgischen Musikhandschriften aus dem mittelalterlichen Patriarchat Aquileia (Monumenta Monodica Medii Aevi. Subsidia 2), Kassel 1997.

4 Vgl. Hauke Fill: Katalog der Handschriften des Benediktinerstiftes Kremsmünster. Teil 2 Zimeliencodices und spätmittelalterliche Handschriften nach 1325 bis einschliesslich CC 100. 2 Bde. (Denkschriften der philosophisch-historischen Klasse 270), Wien 2000.

Mü[1] **München BSB Clm 23143**
Bad Reichenhall (Augustinerchorherrenstift St. Zeno), saec. 14
Breviarium
Inh. O-CR; Hy; Le (keine BHL)
Lit. Halm 1881,[5] S. 56

Mü[2] **München BSB Clm 24882**
Bad Reichenhall (Augustinerchorherrenstift St. Zeno), a. 1458
Breviarium
Inh. O-CR; Hy; Le (keine BHL)
Lit. Halm 1881, S. 151

Mü[3] **München BSB Clm 16402**
Bad Reichenhall (Augustinerchorherrenstift St. Zeno), saec. 15
Sammelhandschrift (Augustinus, Orationes etc.)
Inh. Hy
Lit. Halm 1881, S. 64

Mü[4] **München BSB Clm 23147**
Bad Reichenhall (Augustinerchorherrenstift St. Zeno), saec. 14. Historia auf einer dazugebundenen Papierlage, saec. 16
Breviarium
Inh. O-CR; Hy
Lit. Halm 1881, S. 56

NovaraII **Novara Biblioteca Capitolare II**
Novara (Dom), saec. 11
Lectionarium sanctorum
Inh. Le-BHL9007
Lit. Mazzatinti 1896,[6] S. 78–79

NovaraLXIII **Novara Biblioteca Capitolare LXIII**
Novara (Dom), saec. 10
Lectionarium sanctorum
Inh. Le-BHL9007
Lit. Mazzatinti 1896, S. 74

5 Vgl. Karl Halm u. a.: Catalogus codicum latinorum Bibliothecae Regiae Monacensis. Codices num. 15121–21313 (Catalogus Codicum Manu Scriptorum Bibliothecae Regiae Monacensis 2,3), München 1878. Im Folgenden: Halm 1881.

6 Vgl. Giuseppe Mazzatinti: Inventari dei Manoscritti delle Biblioteche d'Italia Bd. 6, Forlì 1896. Im Folgenden: Mazzatinti 1896.

Vr[1]	**Verona Biblioteca Capitolare XCIV(89), ‚Carpsum'** Verona (Dom), saec. 11 med. Liber ordinarius
Inh.	O-CR; Hy
Lit.	Marchi / Spagnolo 1996,[7] S. 170–172; Meerssemann 1974,[8] S. 79–86; Venturini 1930,[9] S. 69–73, 116–118; Borders 1983,[10] S. 431–436
Vr[2]	**Verona Biblioteca Capitolare XCVI(90*)** Verona (OSB San Zeno Maggiore?), saec. 12 ex. Lectionarium sanctorum
Inh.	Le-BHL9010–9011
Lit.	Marchi / Spagnolo 1996, S. 174–176
Vr[3]	**Verona Biblioteca Capitolare XCVIII(92)** Verona (Dom), saec. 11 in./med. Antiphonarium
Inh.	O-CR
Lit.	Marchi / Spagnolo 1996, S. 179–180; Ropa 1972,[11] S. 23–24; Venturini 1930, S. 79–81; Borders 1983, S. 458–461; Hesbert 1963,[12] S. XXII–XXIII
Vr[4]	**Verona Biblioteca Capitolare CIII(96)** Verona (Dom), saec. 12/13
Inh.	O-CR (nur A für die kleine Horen. ‚Diurnale');
Lit.	Marchi / Spagnolo 1996, S. 184–186; Borders 1983, S. 465–467

7 Vgl. Silvia Marchi: I Manoscritti della Biblioteca Capitolare di Verona. Catalogo descrittivo redatto da don Antonio Spagnolo, Verona 1996. Im Folgenden: Marchi / Spagnolo 1996.

8 Vgl. Gilles G. Meersseman u. a.: L'orazionale dell'arcidiacono Pacifico e il Carpsum del cantore Stefano. Studi e testi sulla liturgia del duomo di Verona dal IX all'XI sec. (Spicilegium Friburgense 21), Freiburg 1974. Im Folgenden: Meerssemann 1974.

9 Vgl. Maria Venturini: Vita ed attività dello „scriptorium" veronese nel secolo XI, Verona 1930. Im Folgenden: Venturini 1930.

10 Vgl. James M. Borders: The Cathedral of Verona as a Musical Center in the Middle Ages. Its History, Manuscripts, and Liturgical Practice. 2 Bde., Chicago 1983. Im Folgenden: Borders 1983.

11 Vgl. Giampaolo Ropa: Liturgia, cultura e tradizione in Padania nei sec. XI–XII, in: Quadrivium 13, 1972, S. 17–156.

12 Vgl. René-Jean Hesbert: Corpus Antiphonalium Officii. Bd. 1 Manuscripti „cursus Romanus" (Rerum Ecclesiasticarum Documenta. Series Maior. Fontes 7), Rom 1963.

Vr⁵	**Verona Biblioteca Capitolare CIX(102)** Verona (OSB San Zeno Maggiore?), saec. 11 ex. Hymnarium
Inh.	Hy
Lit.	Marchi / Spagnolo 1996, S. 196–199; Stäblein 1956,[13] S. 597–606, 357–404; Borders 1983, S. 462–465

Vr⁶	**Verona Biblioteca Capitolare MLII** Verona (Dom), a. 1368 Antiphonarium
Inh.	O-CR
Lit.	Marchi / Spagnolo 1996, S. 736–738; Castiglioni 1988,[14] S. 421–426

Vr⁷	**Verona Biblioteca Capitolare MLIII** Verona (Dom), a. 1368 Antiphonarium
Inh.	O-CR
Lit.	Marchi / Spagnolo 1996, S. 736-738; Castiglioni 1988, S. 421–426

VrCiv¹	**Verona Biblioteca Civica 739 I** Verona (OSB San Zeno Maggiore), saec. 15 ex. Antiphonarium
Inh.	O-CM
Lit.	Biadego 1892,[15] S. 385; Castiglioni 1985,[16] S. 408–411

13 Vgl. Bruno Stäblein: 1: Hymnen. Die mittelalterlichen Hymnenmelodien des Abendlandes (Monumenta Monodica Medii Aevi 1), Kassel 1956.

14 Vgl. Gino Castiglioni: I corali tardotrecenteschi del capitolo veronese, in: Gian Maria Varanini (Hg.): Gli scaligeri 1277–1387. Saggi e schede pubblicati in occasione della mostra storico-documentaria allestita dal Museo di Castelvecchio di Verona (giugno–novembre 1988), Verona 1988, S. 421–426. Im Folgenden: Castiglioni 1988.

15 Vgl. Giuseppe Biadego: Catalogo descrittivo dei manoscritti della Biblioteca comunale di Verona, Verona 1892.

16 Vgl. Gino Castiglioni: Note sui codici quattrocenteschi del Monastero di San Zenone Maggiore nella Biblioteca Civica di Verona, in: Emanuela Sesti (Hg.): La miniatura italiana tra Gotico e Rinascimento: atti del II Congresso di Storia della Miniatura Italiana (Storia della miniatura 6) 1985, S. 389–413. Im Folgenden: Castiglioni 1985.

VrCiv[2]	**Verona Biblioteca Civica 745** Verona (OSB San Zeno Maggiore), saec. 15 med. Hymnarium
Inh.	Hy
Lit.	Castiglioni 2007,[17] S. 213–228; Castiglioni 1985, S. 397–398
Y	**Yale University Library Beinecke rare Book & Manuscript Library 744** Verona (OSB San Zeno Maggiore), saec. 15 (vor 1427 Babcock/1450 Castiglioni) Hymnarium
Inh.	Hy
Lit.	Castiglioni 2007, S. 213–228; Castiglioni 1985, S. 389–413; Babcock 1992,[18] S. 105–116

3.2 Editionsrichtlinien

Zweck der Edition ist es, einen lesbaren, standardisierten Text bereitzustellen, ohne die Varianz in der Überlieferung zu verdecken. Die für die einzelnen Textelemente herangezogenen Quellen werden eingangs der jeweiligen Edition aufgelistet. Die Siglen werden im vorangestellten, alphabetisch angeordneten Handschriftenkatalog aufgelöst.

Die edierten Texte werden tabellarisch präsentiert, geordnet nach den jeweiligen Sektionen des Stundengebets, bei denen sie zum Vortrag kamen. Beispielsweise wurden die Hymnen unterteilt und die Strophen jeweils der Vesper, Matutin oder Nokturn zugeordnet. Das gilt für den Text der Historia und der Hymnen, der in einer Tabelle ediert wurde, deren linke Spalte die Struktur und Elemente des Stundengebets abbildet. Die Elemente des Stundengebets sind auf Deutsch bezeichnet, weil die Bezeichnungen der Elemente in den Handschriften uneinheitlich sind. So wird der Überblick über den Ablauf des Heiligenfestes bewahrt. Dabei wurden folgende Abkürzungen verwendet: A: Antiphon, R: Responsorium, V: Vers, I: Invitatorium, M-A: Magnificat-Antiphon, L-A: Laudes-Antiphon, B-A: Benedictus-Antiphon. Auch die Lesungen werden den Angaben der Handschriften folgend in einer Tabelle wiedergegeben.

In den weiteren Spalten wird der edierte Text präsentiert. Bei einheitlicher Überlieferung in allen Zeugen, abgesehen von Varianten in der Schreibweise

17 Vgl. ders.: Tre salteri, un officio e qualche riflessione sulla miniatura veronese in età tardogotica, in: Rivista di storia della miniatura, 2007, S. 213–228. Im Folgenden: Castiglioni 2007.

18 Vgl. Robert G. Babcock / Walter Cahn: A New Manuscript from the Abbey of San Zeno at Verona, in: The Yale University Library Gazette 66, 1992, S. 105–116

der Wörter, der Hinzufügung der Doxologie oder eines Alleluias, wird nur eine Spalte verwendet:

	Omnes alii codd.
A1	Ab utero matris fuit sanctificatus beatus Zeno et a cunabulis benedictus.

Wo signifikante textliche Unterschieden zwischen einzelnen Überlieferungsträgern exisiteren, werden die entsprechenden Elemente parallel präsentiert:

	***Vr*^{1} *Vr*^{3} *Vr*^{6} *Vr*^{7} *Mü*^{1}**	***Civ*^{4} *Civ*^{5} *Civ*^{6}**	***Mü*^{2}**
M-A1	Dum Zeno pontificatus honore valde polleret, meritis non paucis existentibus, Gallieni caesaris filiam a ruinosa peste Dei virtute sanavit	Clementissime Christi confessor Domini beatissime Zeno, te suppliciter petimus, ne nos derelinquas, sed apud Dominum pius semper pro nobis intercessor existas, quo te opitulante ad gaudia eternae vitae pervenire mereamur	Beatus Christi confessor et pontifex Zeno digne veneratur hymnis et laudibus hominum qui ad consortium pertransit angelorum, eius precibus nobis indulgentia reddatur peccatoribus

Auch die Texte für monastische Lesungen werden in mehreren Spalten abgedruckt, um darzustellen, dass der Umfang der Lesungen sich auch bei gleichbleibendem Inhalt unterscheidet.

Offensichtliche Fehler wurden behoben (zum Beispiel wird aus einem Nominativ ein Akkusativ gemacht, wo die grammatikalische Struktur des Satzes danach verlangt). Der Wortlaut der Handschrift wird dann in der Fußnote wiedergegeben.

Die Schreibweise der Wörter orientiert sich aus pragmatischen Gründen am klassischen Latein. Orthographische Abweichungen in den unterschiedlichen handschriftlichen Zeugen werden der Einfachheit halber stillschweigend normalisiert. Dies betrifft vor allem die Schreibweise von -c und -t; -t und -d; -u, -w und -v; -i, -ii und -y; -x oder -c für -ch (zum Beispiel in: *christi*, *cristi*, *xristi*); -e oder -ę für -ae; -h für -o (zum Beispiel wird: *per hos puelle* in *per os puellae* vereinheitlich). Auch Doppelkonsonanten wie -ff oder -ss (*novisimus* für *novissimus*) und die Schreibung -in für -imm, -nm für -mm (*conmercia*, *commercia*), -nl für -ll (*conlaudo*, *collaudo*) wurden anhand der klassischen Orthographie einheitlich normalisiert.

Moderne Interpunktionen wurden dort eingesetzt, wo sie zur Sinnklärung beitragen. Die Groß- und Kleinschreibung von Eigen- und Ortsnamen wurde normalisiert und entsprechend der Interpunktion eingeführt. Der Notation in den Handschriften folgende Worttrennungen und -zusammenfügungen wurden nicht beibehalten, die Normalisierung orientiert sich hier an der Schreibweise von Georges.[19] Abkürzungen wurden stillschweigend aufgelöst. Abgekürzte Einzelworte sowie Termini wie *nomina sacra* (*Dominus*, *Deus*, *Christi* und so weiter)

19 Karl E. Georges: Ausführliches lateinisch-deutsches Handwörterbuch, Hannover ^{8}1913.

wurden aufgelöst. Ergänzungen durch die Editorin werden durch eckige Klammern ausgezeichnet.

Die prosaischen Elemente der Stundengebete, die die Mehrheit des edierten Materials ausmachen, sind anhand von grammatikalischen und syntaktischen Merkmalen gegliedert und mit entsprechender Interpunktion versehen. Gereimte oder versifizierte Elemente werden in passender Form (Vers- und Absatzgliederung) präsentiert. Ein Element, das in der Handschrift nur mit Incipit verzeichnet ist, ist am Ende des in der Handschrift zu findenden Satzes durch ... markiert. Folgende lateinische Abkürzungen wurden im Apparat eingesetzt:

add.:	fügte hinzu
add. sed cancell.:	fügte hinzu, aber löschte
antep.:	stellte davor
cf.:	vergleiche
coni.:	hat vermutet
corr. ex:	korrigierte aus
des.:	hört auf
exp.:	expungierte
hic des.:	hört hier auf
hic inc.:	hier beginnt
in ... corr.:	hat zu ... korrigiert
ex ... corr.:	hat aus ... korrigiert
in margine:	am Rande
inc.:	beginnt
legi nequit:	kann nicht gelesen werden
om.:	hat weggelassen
post rasuram:	nach der Rasur
postea suprascr.:	hat später darübergeschrieben
praem.:	hat vorangestellt
scr.:	schrieb
sub macula:	unter einem Fleck
super rasuram:	auf Rasur
suppl.:	hat ergänzt
suprascr.:	hat darübergeschrieben

3.3 Editionen

3.3.1 Historia

Zeno-*historia* Dum Zeno pontificatus honore (cursus romanus)

Basiert auf den Handschriften: Cividale MAN XXX (Civ^4), Cividale MAN XXXIV (Civ^5), Cividale MAN XLVII (Civ^6), München BSB Clm 23143 ($Mü^1$), München BSB Clm 24882 ($Mü^2$), Verona BC XCIV(89) (Vr^1), Verona BC XCVIII(92) (Vr^3), Verona BC CIII(96) (Vr^4), Verona BC MLII (Vr^6), Verona BC MLIII (Vr^7).

	Vr^1	Vr^3	Vr^6 Vr^7	Vr^4	Civ^4 Civ^5 Civ^6	$Mü^1$ $Mü^2$
FESTANLASS	Depositio sancti Zenonis episcopi	In natale sancti Zenonis	In festivitate[20] sancti Zenonis episcopi et confessoris	Sancti Zenonis	In festo sancti Zenonis	Historia in depositione sancti Zenonis

I. VESPER

	Civ^4 Civ^5 Civ^6	$Mü^1$ $Mü^2$	
A1	O Zeno...	Dum Zeno pontificatus honore valde polleret meritis et existeret Gallieni caesaris filiam a ruinosa[21] peste Dei virtute sanavit	
	Civ^4 Civ^5 Civ^6	$Mü^1$	$Mü^2$
RESPONSORIUM	Sancte Zeno...[22]	Ingrediente sacerdote Christi palatium et facto crucis signo[23] mox coepit daemon clamare dicens: „Tu, Zeno, expellis me et ego propter	O dilecte Dei praesul sanctissime Zeno ad te clamantes et festa tui celebrantes exaudi clemens cunctis

20 Festivitate] *om.* Vr^7.
21 Ruinosa] *sub macula* $Mü^2$.
22 Sancte Zeno...] *cf.* R9.
23 Signo] singno *cod.*

		tuam sanctitatem stare non possum V Etsi hinc abiero eo Veronam ibique invenies me. Et ego…“	suffragia praebens V Hi quicumque rei fuerint sua crimina questi. Exaudi…
	Mü^{1} Vr^{1} Vr^{3} Vr^{6} Vr^{7}	***Civ^{4} Civ^{5} Civ^{6}***	***Mü^{2}***
M-A1	Dum Zeno pontificatus honore valde polleret, meritis non paucis existentibus[24], Gallieni caesaris filiam[25] a ruinosa peste Dei virtute sanavit[26][27]	Clementissime Christi confessor Domini beatissime Zeno, te suppliciter petimus, ne nos derelinquas, sed apud Dominum pius semper pro nobis intercessor existas, quo te opitulante ad gaudia eternae vitae pervenire mereamur	Beatus Christi confessor et pontifex Zeno digne veneratur[28] hymnis et laudibus hominum, qui ad consortium pertransit angelorum, eius precibus nobis indulgentia reddatur peccatoribus
MATUTIN			
	Vr^{1} Vr^{3}		***Civ^{4} Civ^{5} Civ^{6} Mü^{1} Mü^{2} Vr^{6} Vr^{7}***
I	Confessorum regem…[29]		Aeternum trinumque Deum laudemus et unum[30]/ qui sibi Zenonem transvexit in[31] aethera sanctum[32]

24 Non paucis existentibus] et existeret *Mü^{1}*.
25 Filiam] filia *Vr^{3}*.
26 Sanavit] alleluia ALIA ANTIPHONA Confessor sancte sacerdos magne Zeno beate intercede pro nobis *add. Vr^{3}* alleluia *add. Vr^{6} Vr^{7}*.
27 Dum…sanavit] Dum Zeno… *Mü^{1}* Dum Zeno pontif *Vr^{1}*.
28 veneratur] venerator *Mü^{2}*.
29 Confessorum regem] regem conf *Vr^{1}*.
30 Unum] verum *Mü^{1}*.
31 In] ad *Mü^{1}Mü^{2}*.
32 Sanctum] alleluia *add. Vr^{6} Vr^{7}*.

I. Nokturn

A1 Ab utero matris fuit sanctificatus beatus Zeno et a cunabulis benedictus[33]

A2 Probitatis et[34] scientiae iugibus incrementis ad hoc pertingere meruit ut per sacerrimam[35] vitam pastor in populis[36] efficeretur[37]

A3 Continuis[38] ieiuniis et orationibus crebris a Domino petebat ut sibi aditum[39] praedicationis in populos[40] aperiret[41]

R1 Hic[42] est sacer antistes[43] Zeno quem gemina virtute Dominus[44] sanctitatis et[45] sapientiae[46] decoravit, cuius praeclara fulserunt in mundum[47] miracula et in caelis[48] adeptus est angelorum commercia[49]

V Iste est qui ante Deum magnas[50] virtutes operatus est et omnis terra doctrina eius repleta est[51]. Et in caelis...[52]

---

33 Ab…benedictus] Gloria Patri et Filio et Spiritui Sancto, sicut erat in principio et nunc et semper et in saecula saeculorum amen *add.* Civ^5 Ab utero matris Vr^1 alleluia *add.* Vr^3 Vr^6 Vr^7.
34 Et] *om.* $Mü^1$.
35 Sacerrimam] *corr. ex* acerrimam $Mü^1$.
36 Populis] populo $Mü^1$.
37 Probitatis…efficeretur] Gloria Patri et Filio et Spiritui Sancto, sicut erat in principio et nunc et semper et in saecula saeculorum amen *add.* Civ^5 probitatis Vr^1 alleluia *add.* Vr^3 Vr^6 Vr^7.
38 Continuis] *sub macula* $Mü^2$.
39 Petebat…aditum] *sub macula* $Mü^2$.
40 Populos] populo $Mü^1$ $Mü^2$.
41 Continuis…aperiret] Gloria Patri et Filio et Spiritui Sancto, sicut erat in principio et nunc et semper et in saecula saeculorum amen *add.* Civ^5 continuis Vr^1 alleluia *add.* Vr^3 Vr^6 Vr^7.
42 Hic…commercia] Hic est sacer Vr^1.
43 Antistes] antiste Vr^3.
44 Dominus] Domino $Vr.^3$
45 Et] *om.* $Mü^1$.
46 Sapientie] sapiencia Vr^3.
47 Mundum] mundo Civ^4 Civ^5 Civ^6 $Mü^1$ $Mü^2$.
48 Caelis] celo $Mü^1$.
49 Commercia] consortia Civ^4 Civ^5 Civ^6 alleluia *add.* Vr^3 Vr^6 Vr^7.
50 Magnas] magna Vr^3.
51 Iste…caelis] Iste est qui Vr^1.

R2 Ab utero sanctificatus beatus Zeno et a cunabulis[53] benedictus, ad hoc pertingere meruit ut pastor in populis per sacerrimam vitam[54] efficeretur[55]

V In omnem terram sonus exiit[56] conversationis[57] eius et sanctitas[58] luculenter emicuit[59]. Per sacerrimam...[60]

R3 In[61] secretiori parte[62] oratorii[63] continuis[64] ieiuniis et crebris[65] orationibus a Domino petebat ut sibi[66] dignaretur aditum[67] praedicationis in populos[68] aperiret[69]

V Ad convertendas in amore Christi animas hominum die noctuque[70] deditus erat[71]. Ut sibi...[72]

---

52 Et in caelis…] Cuius… *Civ*[4] *Civ*[5] *Civ*[6] *Mü*[1] *Mü*[2] *Vr*[6] *Vr*[7] alleluia *add. Vr*[1].

53 A cunabulis] *sub macula Mü*[2].

54 Ut pastor…vitam] ut per acerrimam vitam pastor in populo *Mü*[1] ut per sace[rrimam] vitam pastor in populo *Mü*[2].

55 Ab…efficeretur] Ab utero sanctificatus... *Vr*[1] alleluia alleluia *add. Vr*[3] *Vr*[6] *Vr*[7].

56 Sonus exiit] exivit sonus *Mü*[1] *Mü*[2].

57 In omnem...conversationis] *cf.* Ps 18, 5 *In omnem terram exivit sonus eorum, et in fines orbis terrae verba eorum.*

58 Sanctitas] eius *add. Mü*[1] *Mü*[2].

59 In…sacerrimam] In omne… *Vr*[1].

60 Per sacerrimam…] Ut… *Civ*[4] *Civ*[5] *Civ*[6] *Mü*[1] *Mü*[2] *Vr*[6] *Vr*[7] alleluia alleluia *add. Vr*[1].

61 In…aperiret] In secretiori… *Vr*[1] alleluia alleluia *add. Vr*[3] *Vr*[6] *Vr*[7].

62 Parte] partem *Vr*[3].

63 Oratorii] *hic des. Civ*[4] oratori *Vr*[3].

64 Continuis] *om. Mü*[2] *corr. ex* continuiis *Vr*[6].

65 Crebris] *om. Mü*[1] *Mü*[2].

66 Petebat…sibi] *sub macula Mü*[2]

67 Aditum] additum *Mü*[1].

68 Populos] populo *Mü*[1] *sub macula Mü*[2].

69 Aperiret] aperire *Civ*[5] *Civ*[6] *Mü*[1] *Vr*[6] *Vr*[7] *sub macula Mü*[2].

70 Hominum…noctuque] *sub macula Mü*[2].

71 Ad…sibi] Ad conver... *Vr*[1].

72 Ut sibi…] alleluia alleluia *add. Vr*[1].

A4 Affabilis ita[73] erat in sermonibus et in[74] habitu mitis ut[75] Deus in ipso conlaudaretur ab omnibus venientibus ad se[76][77]

A5 Dum exercitio piscationis fungeretur[78] in fluvio[79] vidit quendam hominem in plaustro sedentem per praeceps[80] in amnem[81] demergi[82]

A6 Vir Dei, elevata sursum manu[83], fecit signum crucis dicens: „Revertere retro Sathanas, ne perimas hominem quem Deus creavit“ [84]

	***Mü*^{1} *Mü*^{2} *Vr*^{1} *Vr*^{3} *Vr*^{6} *Vr*^{7}**	***Civ*^{5} *Civ*^{6}**
R4	Affabilis ita erat in sermonibus et mansuetudine[85] atque habitu mitis ut Deus in ipso conlaudaretur ab omnibus[86] ad se venientibus[87] V Ita existebat alacer ut mox ad[88] eum properantes[89] relictis idolis	Iuxta Athesis fluvium iussit beatus confessor Zeno construi oratorium ubi post modum quievit in Domino

73 Ita] itaque *Mü*^{1} *Mü*^{2}.
74 In] *om.* *Mü*^{1}*Mü*^{2}.
75 Mitis ut] *sub macula Mü*^{2}.
76 Venientibus ad se] ad se *sub macula Mü*^{2} ad se venientibus *Vr*^{6} *Vr*^{7}.
77 Affabilis…se] Gloria Patri et Filio et Spiritui Sancto, sicut erat in principio et nunc et semper et in saecula saeculorum amen *add.* *Civ*^{5} afabilis ita *Vr*^{1} alleluia *add.* *Vr*^{3} *Vr*^{6} *Vr*^{7}.
78 Fungeretur] *sub macula Mü*^{2}.
79 Fluvio] flumine *Civ*^{5} *Civ*^{6}.
80 Praeceps] precipitante *Mü*^{1}*Mü*^{2} preces *Vr*^{3}.
81 Amnem] Gloria Patri et Filio et Spiritui Sancto, sicut erat in principio et nunc et semper et in saecula saeculorum amen *add.* *Civ*^{5} amne *Mü*^{2}.
82 Dum…demergi] Dum exercitio *Vr*^{1} alleluia *add.* *Vr*^{3} *Vr*^{6} *Vr*^{7}.
83 Manu] manus *Vr*^{3}.
84 Vir…creavit] Vir Dei ele *Vr*^{1} alleluia *add.* *Vr*^{3} *Vr*^{6} *Vr*^{7}.
85 Mansuetudine] *sub macula Mü*^{2} mansuetudinem *Vr*^{3}.
86 Conlaudaretur ab omnibus] *sub macula Mü*^{2}.
87 Afabilis…venientibus] Afabilis ita *Vr*^{1} alleluia alleluia *add.* *Vr*^{3} *Vr*^{6} *Vr*^{7}.

	Domino crederent Iesu[90] Christo[91]. Ut Deus…[92]	V Ibique sepultus corpore et in caelo spiritus eius. Quievit…
	Mü^{1} Mü^{2} Vr^{1} Vr^{3} Vr^{6} Vr^{7}	***Civ^{5} Civ^{6}***
R5	Dum in fluvio Athesis[93] piscationis exercitio fungeretur, erectis sursum oculis, vidit quendam hominem in plaustro sedentem, bubus[94] subiunctis, in amnem[95] dimergi[96] V Tanta enim velocitate ferebatur ut cunctis ostenderetur[97] antiqui hostis arte peractum.[98] Vidit…[99]	Affabilis ita erat in sermonibus et mansuetudine atque habitu mitis ut Deus in ipso collaudaretur ab omnibus ad se venientibus V Ita existebat alacer ut mox ad eum properantes relictis idolis domino crederent Iesu Christo. Ut Deus…[100]
	Mü^{1} Mü^{2} Vr^{1} Vr^{3} Vr^{6} Vr^{7}	***Civ^{5} Civ^{6}***
R6	Elevata sursum manu beatus Zeno fecit sanctae[101] crucis signum[102] frequenti vice[103] et dixit: „Revertere retro Sathanas, ne perimas[104] hominem[105] quem Deus creavit.“[106]	Dum in fluvio Athesis piscatione fungeretur erectis sursum oculis vidit quendam hominem in plaustro sedentem bubus subiunctis in amnem dimergi

88 Ut mox ad] *sub macula Mü^{2}*.
89 Properantes] properaret *Vr^{3}*.
90 Crederent Iesu] *sub macula Mü^{2}*.
91 Ita…Christo] Ita existe *Vr^{1}*.
92 Ut Deus in…] *om. Mü^{1}* alleluia alleluia *add. Vr^{1}*.
93 Athesis] Athesi *Vr^{6} Vr^{7}*.
94 Bubus] bobos *Mü^{2}*.
95 Amnem] amne *Mü^{1}* annem *Vr^{7}*.
96 Dum…dimergi] Dum in fluvio *Vr^{1}* alleluia alleluia *add. Vr^{3} Vr^{6} Vr^{7}*.
97 Ostenderetur] videretur *Mü^{1} Mü^{2}*.
98 Tanta…peractum] Tanta enim *Vr^{1}*.
99 Vidit…] alleluia alleluia *add. Vr^{1}*.
100 Affabilis...Iesu Christo] *cf.* R4 *in Mü^{1} Mü^{2} Vr^{1} Vr^{3} Vr^{6} Vr^{7}*.

	V Quod signum ut vidit daemon evanuit velut fumus cum clamoribus ac stridore nefando.[107] „Revertere…[108]	V Tanta enim velocitate ferebatur ut cunctis ostenderetur antiqui hostis arte peractum. Erectis… Gloria patri et filio et spiritui sancto. Vidit…

III. Nokturn

A7	Beatus Zeno dixit: „Non te permittit Dominus aliquid agere adversus servum[109] suum.“[110]
A8	Miserabilis pater totaque[111] domus regia maerore affligebatur eo quod acriter puella suffocaretur[112]
A9	Sacerdos Dei Zeno sedebat super lapidem et artis apostolicae documenta sequens piscabatur in flumine[113]

101 Sancte] *om.* *Mü*^{1} *Mü*^{2}.
102 Signum] signo *Vr*^{3}.
103 Vice] voce *Vr*^{3}.
104 Perimas] punias *Mü*^{1}.
105 Hominem] *om.* *Mü*^{2}.
106 Elevata…creavit] Elevata sur *Vr*^{1} alleluia alleluia alleluia *add.* *Vr*^{3} alleluia *add.* *Vr*^{6} *Vr*^{7}.
107 Quod…revertere] Quod signum *Vr*^{1}.
108 Revertere] alleluia alleluia alleluia *add.* *Vr*^{1} *Vr.*^{7}
109 Servum] sanctum *Civ*^{5} *Civ*^{6}.
110 Beatus…suum] Gloria Patri et Filio et Spiritui Sancto, sicut erat in principio et nunc et semper et in saecula saeculorum amen *add.* *Civ*^{5} Beatus Zeno dixit *Vr*^{1} alleluia *add.* *Vr*^{3} *Vr*^{6} *Vr*^{7}.
111 Totaque] simulque tota *Mü*^{1} *Mü*^{2}.
112 Miserabilis…suffocaretur] Gloria Patri et Filio et Spiritui Sancto, sicut erat in principio et nunc et semper et in saecula saeculorum amen *add.* *Civ*^{5} Miserabilis pater *Vr*^{1} alleluia *add.* *Vr*^{3} *Vr*^{6} *Vr*^{7}.
113 Sacerdos…flumine] Gloria Patri et Filio et Spiritui Sancto, sicut erat in principio et nunc et semper et in saecula saeculorum amen *add.* *Civ*^{5} Sacerdos Dei Zeno *Vr*^{1} alleluia *add.* *Vr*^{6} *Vr*^{7}.

	***Mü*^{1} *Mü*^{2} *Vr*^{1} *Vr*^{3} *Vr*^{6} *Vr*^{7}**	***Civ*^{5} *Civ*^{6}**
R7	Festinans itaque daemon ingressus est palatium caesaris Gallieni et comprehensam eius unicam filiam[114] coepit eam[115] crudeliter vexare[116, 117] V Miserabilis pater simulque tota[118] domus eius[119] cruciatu et maerore[120] affligebatur[121]. Et comprehensam…[122]	Elevata sursum manu beatus Zeno fecit sanctae crucis signum frequenti vice et dixit: „Revertere retro Sathanas ne perimas hominem quem Deus creavit.“ V Quod signum ut vidit daemon evanuit velut fumus cum clamoribus ac stridore nefando. Revertere...
	***Mü*^{1} *Mü*^{2} *Vr*^{1} *Vr*^{3} *Vr*^{6} *Vr*^{7}**	***Civ*^{5} *Civ*^{6}**
R8	Ingrediente Christi[123] sacerdote[124] palatium et facto crucis signo, mox coepit daemon clamare dicens: „Tu, Zeno, expellis me et ego propter tuam sanctitatem[125] stare non possum.[126]	Beatissimus Christi confessor Zeno petiit a rege ut in urbe Verona destruerentur omnia manufacta idola et conderetur cum omni honore Iesu Christi catholica ecclesia

[114] Comprehensam…filiam] comprehensa eius unica filia *Mü*^{1} *Mü*^{2}.
[115] Eam] *om. Vr*^{6}.
[116] Vexare] vexaret *Vr*^{1} *Vr*^{3}.
[117] Festinans…vexare] Festinans itaque *Vr*^{1} alleluia alleluia *add. Vr*^{3} *Vr*^{6} *Vr*^{7}.
[118] Simulque tota] totaque *Vr*^{6} *Vr*^{7}.
[119] Eius] regia *Mü*^{1} *Mü*^{2} *Vr*^{6} *Vr*^{7}.
[120] Cruciatu et maerore] a *antep. Vr*^{6}.
[121] Miserabilis…affligebatur] Miserabilis *Vr*^{1}.
[122] Et comprehensam…] alleluia alleluia *add. Vr*^{1}.
[123] Christi] *om. Mü*^{1}.
[124] Christi sacerdote] sacerdote Christi *Mü*^{2}.
[125] Sanctitatem] sanctitate *Vr*^{3}.
[126] Ingrediente…possum] Ingrediente sacerdote UT SUPRA *Mü*^{1} stare non possum *sub macula Mü*^{2} Ingrediente *Vr*^{1} alleluia alleluia alleluia *add. Vr*^{3} alleluia alleluia *add. Vr*^{6} *Vr*^{7}.

V Etsi[127] hinc[128] abiero eo Veronam ubique[129] invenies me[130]. Et ego…“[131]

V Cumque sanasset[132] filiam regis petiit a rege ut in urbe Verona destruerentur…

R9 Sancte Zeno Christi confessor, audi rogantes[133] servulos et impetratam[134] caelitus tu defer indulgentiam[135] [136]

V O sancte Zeno, sidus[137] aureum Domini[138] gratia servorum[139] gemitus solita suscipe clementia[140]. Et impetratam...[141]

LAUDES

A1 Dominus Iesus Christus omnipotens est, oportet enim[142] ut mirabilia Dei[143] omnibus manifestentur[144]

A2 Exurgens[145] beatus sacerdos fecit orationem perrexitque ad palatium ubi affligebatur pro sua filia rex[146]

---

127 Etsi…me] Etsi hinc *Vr¹*.
128 Etsi hinc] *sub macula Mü²* hic *Vr⁷*.
129 Ubique] ibique *Mü² Vr³ Vr⁶ Vr⁷*.
130 Invenies me] *sub macula Mü²*.
131 Et ego…] alleluia alleluia *add. Vr¹*.
132 Sanasset] sanascet *Civ⁵*.
133 Audi rogantes] *sub macula Mü²*.
134 Impetratam] impetrata *Civ⁵*.
135 Defer indulgentiam] def[er indul]gentiam *Mü²*.
136 Sancte…indulgentiam] Sancte Zeno *Vr¹* Sancte Zeno REQUIRATUR IN SANCTI MARTINI *Vr³* alleluia *add. Vr⁶ Vr⁷*.
137 Sidus] *postea suprascr. Mü¹*.
138 Domini] *sub macula Mü²*.
139 Servorum] servuorum *Mü¹*.
140 O…clementia] cleme[ntia] *Mü²* O sancte Zeno *Vr¹* .
141 Et…] Gloria Patri et filio et spiritui sancto Tu defer... *Civ⁵ Civ⁶ Vr⁷* om. *Mü¹* Tu defer... *Mü²* alleluia alleluia *add. Vr¹* Gloria patri et filio et spiritui sancto alleluia *add. Vr⁶*.
142 Enim] eim *Vr⁶*.
143 Dei] eius *Mü¹Mü² Vr⁶ Vr⁷*.
144 Dominus…manifestentur] Gloria Patri et Filio et Spiritui Sancto, sicut erat in principio et nunc et semper et in saecula saeculorum amen *add. Civ⁵* Dominus Ihesus Christus *Vr¹* alleluia *add. Vr³ Vr⁶ Vr⁷*.

A3	Ingrediente Christi confessore palatium[147] facto crucis signo[148] per os[149] puellae daemon clamavit[150] dicens: „Tu, Zeno, venisti[151] ad expellendum me et[152] propter tuam sanctitatem stare non possum.“[153]
A4	Tenens beatus Zeno manum puellae dicens[154]: „In nomine Domini mei Iesu Christi praecipio tibi exi ab ea[155] daemon.“[156]
A5	Christi namque sacerdos ab omni daemoniacae[157] incursionis[158] ludificatione[159] sanam restituit filiam regis[160]
BENEDICTUS-A	Acceptam[161] beatus Zeno coronam a rege[162] distribuit pauperibus dicens: „Si Dominus operatur[163] excelsa, ipsi perpetuae laudes referantur[164] et gloria.“[165]

---

145 Exurgens…rex] Gloria Patri et Filio et Spiritui Sancto, sicut erat in principio et nunc et semper et in saecula saeculorum amen *add.* *Civ*^{5} Exurgens beauts *Vr*^{1} alleluia *add.* *Vr*^{3} *Vr*^{6} *Vr*^{7}.

146 Pro…rex] pro sua rex filia *Mü*^{1} *Mü*^{2}.

147 Palatium] palatio *Vr*^{1}*Vr*^{3} *Vr*^{6}.

148 Crucis signo] signo crucis *Mü*^{1} *Mü*^{2}.

149 Os] hos *Vr*^{3}.

150 Daemon clamavit] demon clavit *Mü*^{1} clamavit demon *Mü*^{2}.

151 Venisti] advenisti *Mü*^{2}.

152 Et] ego *add.* *Mü*^{1} *Mü*^{2}.

153 Ingrediente…possum] Gloria Patri et Filio et Spiritui Sancto, sicut erat in principio et nunc et semper et in saecula saeculorum amen *add.* *Civ*^{5} Ingrediente *Vr*^{1} alleluia *add.* *Vr*^{3} *Vr*^{6} *Vr*^{7}.

154 Dicens] dixit *Civ*^{5} *Civ*^{6} *Mü*^{1} *Mü*^{2} *Vr*^{6} *Vr*^{7}.

155 Ea] hac puella *Mü*^{1} *Mü*^{2}.

156 Tenens…daemon] Gloria Patri et Filio et Spiritui Sancto, sicut erat in principio et nunc et semper et in saecula saeculorum amen *add.* *Civ*^{5} Tenens beatus Zeno *Vr*^{1} alleluia *add.* *Vr*^{3} *Vr*^{6} *Vr*^{7}.

157 Daemoniacae] demonice *Vr*^{3} *Vr*^{6} *Vr*^{7} *Vr*^{4} demo *suprascr.* *Vr*^{7}.

158 Incursionis] *corr. ex* incursiones *Vr*^{3}.

159 Ludificatione] ludificacionem *Vr*^{3}.

160 Christi…regis] Gloria Patri et Filio et Spiritui Sancto, sicut erat in principio et nunc et semper et in saecula saeculorum amen *add.* *Civ*^{5} Christi namque sacerdos *Vr*^{1} alleluia *add.* *Vr*^{3} *Vr*^{6} *Vr*^{7}.

161 Acceptam…gloriam] Gloria Patri et Filio et Spiritui Sancto, sicut erat in principio et nunc et semper et in saecula saeculorum amen *add.* *Civ*^{5} Acceptam beatus *Vr*^{1} alleluia *add.* *Vr*^{3} *Vr*^{7}.

162 Coronam a rege] a rege coronam *Mü*^{1} *Mü*^{2}.

163 Operatur] *postea suprascr.* *Mü*^{1}.

164 Laudes referantur] laudis referatur *Civ*^{6} *Civ*^{2} *Civ*^{5} Vr^{1} *Vr*^{3} *Vr*^{4} *Vr*^{6} *Vr*^{7}.

Vr⁴

PRIM

A Dominus Iesus Christus omnipotens est oportet enim ut mirabilia eius omnibus manifestentur[166]

TERZ

A Exurgens beatus sacerdos fecit orationem perrexitque ad palatium ubi affligebatur pro sua filia rex[167]

SEXT

A Ingrediente Christi confessore palatium facto crucis signo per os puellae daemon clamavit dicens: „Tu, Zeno, venisti ad expellendum me et propter tuam sanctitatem stare non possum[168].“

NON

A Christi namque sacerdos ab omni daemonicae incursionis ludificatione sanam restituit filiam regis[169]

II. VESPER

Vr⁶ Vr⁷

A1 Dominus Iesus Christus...[170]

---

165 Et gloria] gloria *Mü¹* Et gloriam *Vr¹ Vr.³*
166 Manifestentur] alleluia *add. Vr⁴*.
167 Rex] alleluia *add. Vr⁴*.
168 Possum] alleluia *add. Vr⁴*.
169 Regis] alleluia *add. Vr⁴*.
170 CUM RELIQUIS Dixit dominus CUM RELIQUIS IN FINE PSALMUS Memento domine *Vr⁶ Vr⁷*.

	Mü¹ Mü² Vr¹ Vr³ Vr⁶ Vr⁷	***Civ⁵ Civ⁶***
MAGNIFICAT-A	Sancte confessor Zeno, pastor Domini[171] gregis, te deprecamur: intercede pro nobis ut mereamur tecum esse[172] in caelis[173]	Beatum et gloriosum antistitem sanctum Zenonem qui flore mentis et documento fidei sanctam illustravit ecclesiam precamur ut suis precibus liberemur nostris a criminibus[174]
ZUSATZ-GESANG		Exultet magno gaudio Veronensis ecclesia tali freta subsidio et fulcita clementia. Gloria Patri et Filio et Spiritui Sancto, sicut erat in principio et nunc et semper et in saecula saeculorum amen
ZUSATZ-GESANG		O Zeno sanctissime forma sanctitatis, speculum munditiae, lima pravitatis plebem tuam respice iunge nos beatis. Gloria Patri et Filio et Spiritui Sancto, sicut erat in principio et nunc et semper et in saecula saeculorum amen

171 Domini] nostri *add. Mü¹* nostri *Mü²*.
172 Tecum esse] *sub macula Mü²*.
173 Sancte…caelis] Sancte confessor Zeno *Vr¹* alleluia alleluia alleluia *add. Vr³ Vr⁶ Vr⁷*.
174 A criminibus] saeculorum amen Gloria Patri et Filio et Spiritui Sancto, sicut erat in principio et nunc et semper et in saecula saeculorum amen *add. Civ⁵*.

Zeno-*historia Dum Zeno pontificatus honore* (*cursus monasticus*)

Basiert auf den Handschriften: Augsburg StStadtB 2° 204 (*Aug*), Kremsmünster SB CC60 (*Kr*), Verona BCi 739 I (*VrCiv*[1])

FESTANLASS	***Aug*** In ordinatione sancti Zenonis	***VrCiv*[1]** In translatione sancti Zenonis episcopi et martiris[175]	***Kr*** In ordinatione sancti Zenonis episcopi et confessoris

I. VESPER

	Omnes codd.
A1	Dominus Iesus Christus...[176]
RESPONSORIUM	Summe Dei praesul beate Zeno tuam catervam protege namque credimus tuis laudibus nos semper esse salvandos.[177] V Qui filiam Gallieni caesaris a daemonio liberasti tuis laudibus instantem conserva plebem. Namque...[178]
MAGNIFICAT-A	Clementissime Christi confessor[179] Domini beatissime Zeno te suppliciter petimus ne nos[180] derelinquas sed apud Dominum pius semper pro nobis intercessor existas quo te opitulante ad gaudia aeternae vitae pervenire mereamur[181]

175 Martiris] *super rasuram ms.*
176 CUM RELIQUIS DE LAUDIBUS PS Dixit dominus CUM RELIQUIS *Aug Kr VrCiv*[1].
177 Salvandos] alleluia *add. VrCiv*[1].
178 Namque] V Ora pro nobis… *add. Aug* V Gloria patri et filio et spiritui sancto. Salvandos… *add. VrCiv*[1].
179 Confessor] martir *super rasuram VrCiv*[1].
180 Nos] ne *add. sed cancell. Kr.*
181 Mereamur] alleluia R Sancte Zeno... *add. VrCiv*[1].

MATUTIN

INVITATORIUM	Aeternum trinumque Deum laudemus et unum/ qui sibi Zenonem transvexit in aethera sanctum
I. NOKTURN	
A1	Ab utero matris[182] fuit sanctificatus beatus Zeno et a cunabulis[183] benedictus[184]
A2	Probitatis et scientiae iugibus incrementis ad hoc pertingere meruit ut per sacerrimam vitam pastor in populis efficeretur[185]
A3	Continuis ieiuniis et orationibus crebris a Domino petebat ut sibi aditum praedicationis in populos aperiret[186]
A4	Affabilis ita erat in sermonibus et in habitu mitis ut Deus in ipso collaudaretur ab omnibus venientibus ad se[187]
A5	Cum exercitio piscationis fungeretur in flumine vidit quendam hominem in plaustro sedentem per praeceps in amnem dimergi[188]
A6	Vir Dei elevata sursum manu fecit signum crucis dicens: „Revertere retro Sathanas ne perimas hominem quem Deus creavit.“[189]

182 Matris] sue *add. Aug.*
183 A cunabulis] accunabilis *Kr.*
184 Benedictus] alleluia *add. VrCiv*[1].
185 Efficeretur] alleluia *add. VrCiv*[1].
186 Aperiret] alleluia *add. VrCiv*[1].
187 Se] alleluia *add. VrCiv*[1].
188 Dimergi] alleluia *add. VrCiv*[1].
189 Creavit] alleluia *add. VrCiv*[1].

R1	Hic est[190] sacer antistes Zeno quem gemina virtute Dominus sanctitatis et sapientiae decoravit cuius praeclara fulserunt in mundo miracula et in caelis adeptus est angelorum consortia[191] V Iste est qui ante Deum magnas virtutes operatus est et omnis terra doctrina eius repleta est. Cuius…
R2	Ab utero sanctificatus beatus Zeno et[192] a cunabulis benedictus ad hoc pertingere meruit ut pastor in populis per sacerrimam vitam efficeretur V In omnem terram sonus[193] exiit conversationis eius et sanctitas luculenter emicuit. Ut pastor…
R3	In secretiori parte oratorii continuis ieiuniis et crebris orationibus a Domino petebat ut sibi dignaretur aditum praedicationis in populos aperire[194] V Ad convertendas in amore[195] Christi animas hominum die noctuque deditus erat. Ut sibi…
R4	Iuxta Athesis fluvium iussit beatus confessor[196] Zeno construi oratorium ubi post modum quievit in Domino[197] V Ibique sepultus corpore et in caelo spiritus eius. Quievit…[198]

190 Est] *om. Aug.*
191 Consorcia] alleluia *add. VrCiv¹*.
192 Et] *om. Kr.*
193 Sonus] *om. Kr.*
194 Iste…aperire] *om. et super rasuram posterior manus scr.* Iacob autem genuit Ioseph virum Mariae de qua natus est Iesus qui vocatus Christus alleluia seculorum amen Missus est angelus Gabriel a Deo in civitatem Galileae cui nomen Nazareth ad virginem desponsatam viro cui nomen erat Ioseph alleluia seculorum amen Ascendit autem Ioseph a Gelilaea de civitate Nazareth in Iudeam in civitatem David quae vocatur Bethlehem alleluia seculorum amen Et ipse Iesus erat incipiens quasi annorum triginta ut putabatur filius Ioseph alleluia seculorum amen Ad Magnificat Fili quid fecisti nobis sic ecce pater tuus et ego dolentes quaerebamus te alleluia seculorum amen Pro commune dominice tertie per Paskam Amen dico vobis quia plorabitis et flebitis vos mundus autem gaudebit vos vero contristabimini sed tristitia vestra vertetur in gaudium alleluia *VrCiv¹*.
195 Amore] amorem *VrCiv¹*.
196 Confessor] martir *super rasuram VrCiv¹*.
197 Domino] alleluia *add. VrCiv¹*.
198 Quievit…] V Gloria patri… Quievit… *add. Kr.*

II. Nokturn

A7	Beatus Zeno dixit: „Non te permittit Dominus aliquid agere adversus servum[199] suum.“[200]
A8	Miserabilis pater[201] totaque domus regia maerore affligebatur eo quod[202] acriter puella suffocaretur[203]
A9	Sacerdos Dei Zeno sedebat super lapidem et artis apostolicae documenta sequens piscabatur in flumine[204]
A10	Beate[205] Zeno praesul qui regis unicam salvasti filiam a daemonum potestate nos te rogantes et deprecantes libera[206]
A11	Coepitque beatus pontifex in Verona destruere omnia idola et fabricare Christi ecclesias[207]
A12	Iuxta Athesis[208] fluvium iussit beatus Zeno construi oratorium in quo quievit in Domino[209]
R5	Affabilis ita erat in sermonibus et mansuetudine atque habitu mitis ut Deus in ipso collaudaretur ab omnibus ad se venientibus[210] V Ita existebat alacer ut mox ad eum properantes relictis idolis Domino crederent Iesu Christo. Ut Deus…

---

199 Servum] *add. in margine Aug.*
200 Suum] alleluia *add. VrCiv¹*.
201 Pater] *om. Aug.*
202 Quod] quo *VrCiv¹*.
203 Suffocaretur] alleluia *add. VrCiv¹*.
204 Flumine] alleluia *add. VrCiv¹*.
205 Beate] beato *Aug.*
206 Libera] alleluia *add. VrCiv¹*.
207 Ecclesias] alleluia *add. VrCiv¹*.
208 Athesis] Athasi *Aug.*
209 Domino] alleluia *add. VrCiv¹*.
210 Venientibus] alleluia alleluia *add. VrCiv¹*.

R6	Dum in fluvio Athesis[211] piscationis exercitio[212] fungeretur erectis sursum oculis vidit quendam hominem in plaustro sedentem bubus subiunctis in amnem dimergi[213] V Tanta enim velocitate ferebatur ut cunctis ostenderetur antiqui hostis arte peractum. Erectis sursum…
R7	Elevata sursum manu beatus Zeno fecit sanctae crucis signum frequenti vice et[214] dixit: „Revertere retro Sathanas ne perimas hominem quem Deus creavit.“[215] V Quod[216] signum ut vidit daemon[217] evanuit velut fumus cum clamoribus[218] ac stridore nefando. „Revertere…
R8	Beatissimus Christi confessor[219] Zeno petiit a rege ut in urbe Verona destruerentur omnia manufacta idola et conderetur[220] cum omni honore Iesu Christi catholica ecclesia[221] V Cumque sanasset filiam regis petiit a rege ut in urbe Verona. Destruerentur…

III. Nokturn

A13	Iste est de sublimibus caelorum praepotentibus unus quem manus Domini[222] consecravit matris in visceribus cuius nos precibus adiuvari supplices deposcimus[223]

---

211 Athesis] Athasi *Aug.*
212 Exercitio] *om. Aug VrCiv[1]*.
213 Dimergi] alleluia alleluia *add. VrCiv[1]*.
214 Et] *om. Kr.*
215 Creavit] alleluia alleluia alleluia *add. VrCiv[1]*.
216 Quod] Quot *Aug.*
217 Daemon] demun *Kr.*
218 Clamoribus] clamore *Aug.*
219 Confessor] martir *super rasuram VrCiv[1]*.
220 Et conderetur] et conterentur et conderetur *scr. Aug.*
221 Ecclesia] alleluia alleluia alleluia *add. VrCiv[1]*.
222 Domini] in i *add. sed cancell. Kr.*
223 Iste est...deposcimus] alleluia *add. VrCiv[1]*; *cf.* CAO 3420.

R9	Festinans itaque daemon ingressus est palatium caesaris Gallieni et comprehensam eius unicam filiam coepit eam crudeliter vexare[224] V Miserabilis pater totaque domus regia cruciatu[225] et maerore affligebatur. Et comprehensam...
R10	Ingrediente Christi sacerdote palatium et facto crucis signo mox coepit daemon clamare dicens: „Tu, Zeno, expellis me et ego propter tuam sanctitatem stare non possum[226] V Etsi hinc abiero eo Veronam ibique invenies me. Et ego…“
R11	Sacerdos Dei altissimi Zeno interveni pro delictis nostris in conspectu Domini[227] V Ut vitae presentis et futurae percipiamus consolationem. In conspectu...
R12	Sancte Zeno Christi confessor, [228, 229] audi rogantes servulos et impetratam[230] caelitus tu defer indulgentiam[231] V O sancte Zeno, sidus aureum Domini gratia servorum gemitus solita suscipe clementia. Et impetratam…[232]

LAUDES

A1	Dominus Iesus Christus omnipotens est oportet enim ut mirabilia Dei omnibus manifestentur[233]

---

224 Vexare] alleluia alleluia *add. VrCiv¹*.
225 Cruciatu] a *praem. VrCiv¹*.
226 Possum] alleluia alleluia *add. VrCiv¹*.
227 Domini] alleluia *add. VrCiv¹*.
228 Confessor] martir *super rasuram VrCiv¹*.
229 Sancte…confessor] Sancte confessor Zeno Christi *Kr*.
230 Impetratam] impetrata *Aug*.
231 Indulgentiam] alleluia *add. VrCiv¹*.
232 Impetratam] V Gloria patri et filio et spiritui sancto alleluia *add. VrCiv¹*.
233 Manifestentur] alleluia *add. VrCiv¹*.

A2	Exurgens beatus sacerdos fecit orationem perrexitque[234] ad palatium ubi affligebatur pro sua filia rex[235]
A3	Ingrediente Christi confessore[236] palatium facto crucis signo per os puellae daemon clamavit[237] dicens: „Tu, Zeno, venisti ad expellendum me et propter tuam sanctitatem stare non possum."[238]
A4	Tenens beatus Zeno manum puellae dixit: „In nomine Domini mei Iesu Christi praecipio tibi[239] exi ab ea daemon."[240]
A5	Christi namque sacerdos ab omni daemoniacae incursionis ludificatione sanam restituit filiam regis[241]
BENEDICTUS-A	Acceptam beatus Zeno coronam a rege distribuit pauperibus dicens: „Si Dominus operatur excelsa ipsi perpetuae laudes referantur[242] et gloria."[243]
PRIM	
A	Dominus Iesus Christus omnipotens est oportet enim ut mirabilia Dei omnibus manifestentur
TERZ	
A	Exurgens beatus sacerdos fecit orationem perrexitque ad palatium ubi affligebatur pro sua filia rex
SEXT	
A	Ingrediente Christi confessore palatium facto crucis signo per os puellae daemon clamavit dicens: „Tu, Zeno, venisti ad expellendum me et propter tuam sanctitatem stare non possum."

234 Perrexitque] perrexit *Aug*.
235 Rex] alleluia *add. VrCiv¹*.
236 Confessore] martire *super rasuram VrCiv¹*.
237 Clamavit] clamat *Aug*.
238 Possum] alleluia *add. VrCiv¹*.
239 Tibi] te *Aug*.
240 Daemon] alleluia *add. VrCiv¹*.
241 Regis] alleluia *add. VrCiv¹*.
242 laudes referantur] laudis referatur *Aug Kr VrCiv¹*.
243 Gloria] alleluia *add. VrCiv¹*.

NON	
A	Christi namque sacerdos ab omni daemoniace incursionis ludificatione sanam restituit filiam regis
II. VESPER	
A1	Dominus Iesus Christus...[244]
MAGNIFICAT-A	O beatum et gloriosum antistitem sanctum Zenonem qui flore meriti et documento fidei sanctam illustravit ecclesiam precamur ut suis precibus liberemur nostris a[245] criminibus[246]

---

244 CUM RELIQUIS DE LAUDIBUS PS Dixit dominus CUM RELIQUIS *Aug Kr VrCiv*[1].
245 A] *suprascr. Kr.*
246 Criminibus] V Ora pro nobis…*add. Kr.*

3.3.2 Hymnen

Hymnen aus San Zeno Maggiore
***Zeno pontifex inclite*[247], *Iesu redemptor omnium*[248], *Deus tuorum militum*[249]**
Basiert auf der Handschrift Verona BC CIX(102) (*Vr*[5])

Festanlass	In sancti Zenonis episcopi
Ad vesperum ymnus	Zeno pontifex inclite, Christi athleta splendide adesto nostris vocibus, quas[250] pie tibi fundimus.
	O gloriose patrone, nostrae salutis opifex ut digne demus cantica nostra dirumpe crimina.
	Adesse tuis famulis dignare dux amabilis, sentiant nostra pectora semperque tua numina.
	Tu es nostrum refugium, tu robur potentissimum, tu salus et protectio nostraque iubilatio.
	O pastor pie et clare, nobis benigne succurre nosque supplices respice vota servorum suscipe.
	Deo patri sit gloria eiusque soli filio cum spiritu paraclito et nunc et in perpetuum.[251] Amen.

---

[247] *cf.* AH 22, Nr. 496, S. 291–292.
[248] *cf.* AH 2, Nr. 110, S. 76.
[249] *cf.* AH 2, Nr. 99, S. 76.
[250] Quas] quae *coni.* AH 22, Nr. 496, S. 291.
[251] Perpetuum] *hic des.* AH 22, Nr. 496, S. 292.

Ad nocturnum ymnus	Iesu redemptor omnium...[252]

In laudibus ymnus	Deus tuorum militum[253]
corona, spes et praemium
attende pronis auribus
indignis nostris vocibus,

Qui Zenonem episcopum
ab omni purum crimine
eductum carnis cavea
locasti super aethera.

Ob eius alma merita
nostra relaxa crimina,
hic libera de noxiis
et in futuris saeculis.

Te cuncta laudant pariter
summe cunctorum arbiter
est, cuius regnum stabile
per aevum sine tempore. Amen

Effulget orbis speculum,[254] ***Post haec curavit,***[255] ***Praesulis sancti***[256]
Basiert auf den Handschriften: Augsburg StStadt 2° 204 (*Aug*), Kremsmünster SB CC60 (*Kr*), München BSB Clm 23143 (*Mü¹*), Verona BCi 739 I (*VrCiv¹*), Verona BCi 745 (*VrCiv²*), Yale BeineckeL 744 (*Y*)

Ad Vesperas Hymnus	Effulget orbis[257] speculum[258]
Zeno praesul mirificus,
cuius festa solemnia
anni nobis fert orbita.

---

252 Omnium...] Requiratur in natale confessorum *ms.*; cf. AH 51, Nr. 117, S. 133–134.
253 *cf.* AH 19, Nr. 323, S. 184-185 De sancto Luca (basiert ebenso aus *Vr⁵*).
254 *cf.* AH 22, Nr. 497, S. 292.
255 *cf.* AH 22, Nr. 498, S. 292.
256 *cf.* AH 22, Nr. 499, S. 292–293.
257 Orbis] orbi *Mü¹*.
258 Effulget...speculum] Effulget orbis speculum et cetera *VrCiv¹*.

Qui Christi[259] fide fervidus
hoc[260] praesens spernens saeculum
flore virtutum praeditus
caeli possedit praemium.

Hic onus carnis baiulans
plura fecit miracula,
ut floret lux clarissima
caecas fugavit tenebras.

Nempe piscans[261] in flumine
vidit plaustro praecipitem[262]
cum bubus[263] suis rusticum
ad amnis ima mergere.

Quod hostis hoc nequissimus
patrasset cernens vir pius
preces fudit ad Dominum
eius poscens auxilium.

Subvenit Christi gratia,
quae se credentes munerat
ac[264] liberavit hominem
reddens[265] saluti pristinae.[266]

Ad nocturnum Hymnus

Post haec[267] curavit[268] filiam
imperatoris unicam,
quam fecerat hospitium
daemon tunc sibi[269] pessimus.

---

259 Christi] Christu *corr. ex* Christus *Mü¹*.
260 Hoc] hac *Aug* ac *Kr Mü¹* ac *corr. ex* hac *VrCiv² Y*.
261 piscans] piscas *Kr*.
262 Praecipitem] precipite, *corr. ex* precipitem *Y*.
263 bubus] bubis *Kr*.
264 Ac] *corr. ex* hac *Y*.
265 Reddens] d *suprascr. VrCiv²*.
266 Pristinae] Deo patri… V Ora pro nobis… *add. Aug* Deo patri sit gloria… V Ora pro nobis sancte Zeno *add. Kr*. Versus Ora pro nobis beate Zeno *add. VrCiv¹* Deo patri sit gloria… *add. VrCiv² Y*.
267 Haec] hoc *Mü¹*.
268 Post…curavit] Post hec curavit… *VrCiv¹*.
269 Tunc sibi] sibi tunc *VrCiv² Y*.

Athesis[270] amnis alveus
excrescens ultra solitum
conscendit ad eximium
ecclesiae fastigium.

Confestim fulgent merita
viri sancti dignissima,
nam mansit aqua solida
cum sit natura fluida.

Precamur ergo supplices,
Zeno praesul sanctissime,
ut caeli nobis Dominum
efficias propitium.

Quo post abluta crimina
fruamur eius gloria
habituri felicia
in aeternum solemnia.
Praesta pater piissime...[271]

AD LAUDES HYMNUS

Praesulis[272] sancti[273] reddeunt colenda
festa Zenonis Dominum[274] sequentis,[275]
qui diem nobis celebrem sacravit
fine beato.

Magnus[276] excelsus[277] fuerat sacerdos
praedicans gentes bene transmarinas[278]
inde Veronam hunc ad urbem Deus[279]
mittere curavit.[280]

---

270 Athesis] Atthasis *Y.*
271 Piissime] et cetera amen *add. Mü*[1].
272 Praesulis] presul *Mü*[1] presul *post rasuram Y.*
273 Praesulis sancti] Praesulis sancti… *VrCiv*[1].
274 Dominum] Deum *Mü*[1].
275 Sequentis] sequentes *Mü*[1] *Y.*
276 Magnus] agnus *scr. Mü*[1].
277 Excelsus] excelsi *Mü*[1].
278 bene transmarinas] penetrans marinas *Aug Kr VrCiv*[2] *Y* bene transmarinos *Mü*[1].
279 Hunc ad urbem Deus] Deus hunc ad urbem *postea scr. VrCiv*[2] *Y.*
280 Curavit] curat *Aug VrCiv*[2] *Mü*[1] *Y.*

Qua Deo multum populum lucratus
instruit verbis, solidavit actis
in Deo tum[281] patiendo mortem
vivit in aevum.

Nunc[282] in aeternis meritis corruscat
clarus et mundo[283] manifestus omni,
qui[284] Deo[285] soli studuit placere
corpore vivens.

Pastor aeterno radians triumpho
servulos audi tibi supplicantes,
praemium iustis veniam deposce[286]
crimine lapsis.

Quo Dei magna miseratione
ordinem[287] caeli decimum[288] replentes
ipsius[289] vultum videamus omni
tempore saeculi
amen.[290]

Hymnus aus Bad Reichenhall

Summe rex regno[291]
Basiert auf den Handschriften: München BSB Clm 16402 (*Mü³*), München BSB Clm 23147 (*Mü⁴*)

Summe[292] rex regno dominans superno[293]
rector et celsi sapiens Olympi
lege qui vastum stabili per orbem
cuncta gubernas.

---

281 Tum] tamen *Kr* tamen *suprascr. Mü¹* tandem (dem *suprascr.*) *VrCiv² Y*.
282 Nunc] hunc *Mü¹*.
283 mundo] mirificus *add Mü¹*.
284 Omni qui] omnique *Mü¹*.
285 Deo] *hic des. Mü¹*.
286 Deposce] deposce veniam iustis *Aug* de *suprascr. VrCiv²*.
287 Ordinem] ordine *Aug Kr*.
288 Decimum] ci *suprascr. VrCiv²*.
289 Ipsius] ipsum *Aug*.
290 Amen] V Ora pro nobis beate Zeno *add. Kr* V Ora pro nobis… *add. VrCiv¹*.
291 *Cf.* AH 4, Nr. 499, S. 263–264.
292 Summe] Carmen saphicum in divi Zenonis laudem editum ab Andrea Svevulo canonico huius cenobii sancti Zenonis *antep. Mü³*.
293 superno] supremo *Mü⁴ AH*.

Tu Cephe navi pelago natanti
provides nautas maris[294] alta doctos
hanc tuo qui ne pereat procellis
flamine ducunt.

Munus ad tantum fideique transtra
atque Zenonem dederis locandum
quem parens quando[295] peperit sacrasti
ventris ab umbra.

Hostis ut novit puerum nephandus
indolis sanctae rapit hunc Veronae
matre de cara Medioquelani
vexit in arces.

At tuo tutus clipeo beatus
ne sacros daemon laniaret artus
exteras exul subiit nutrices
lacte ducandus.

Cumque discernens veniebat aetas
litteras morum radians decore
hausit ac annis iter a tenellis
flexit ad astra.

Patrias tandem remeans in oras[296]
ad sacrum felix ubi praesulatus
culmen ascendit populique factus
pastor amatus.

Grex ut aeternis fruiturus esset
pascuis verbum servit salutis
fulgido firmans operum bonorum
lumine dicta.

Te Deum laudant sua mira magnum
morte nam victis animas reduxit
daemonum turbas domuit tuoque
numine pellit.

---

294 maris] navis *AH*.
295 quando] *quondam Mü*[4] *AH*.
296 oras] *horas Mü*[3].

Unde per mundi mare navigantes
nos iuva ventis placidis ut ipsi
eius ad portum meritis vehamur
aetheris altum.

Laus honor summo tibi sit parenti
gloriae splendor genitoque verbo
pneumati sancto decus atque virtus
nunc et in aevum.[297]

3.3.3 Lesungen

Lesungen der Zenoliturgie am Veroneser Dom (BHL 9007)
Basiert auf den Handschriften: Novara BC II (*NovaraII*) und Novara BC II LXIII (*NovaraLXIII*)

INCIPIT PROLOGUS DE VITA BEATI ZENONIS.[298]
Pontificum splendor, iustorum norma virorum
   Aequilibra Zeno trames et ordo boni.
Acta viri cuius totum respersa per orbem,
   Quanta nequit dextra scribere lingua loqui.
Sed tamen e multis perstringam pauca legenti,
   In quibus antistes fulserit ille sacer.
Pro dolor!, antiquo quidam correptus ab hoste
   In fluvium sese precipitando ruit.
Tunc crucis efficiens sacratae signa subinde,
   Mortis ab articulo sustulit ipse pater.
Ipse domum petit Gallieni caesaris, in qua
   Nata iacet gravibus exagitata malis.
Illam namque taeter vexabat spiritus, unde
   In luctum mater vertitur atque pater.
Sed Domini veniens ad regis[299] iussa sacerdos
   Cum iubet obsessam deserit alta gemens.
Hoc etiam minitans quod non post multa Veronae,
   Impedimenta sui sint subeunda sibi.
Cuius amore stilo depinximus ista redemptor,
   Illius munda crimina nostra prece.

---

[297] aevum] Hoc carmen reverendissimus in Christo pater dominus Ludovicus Ebmer episcopus chiemensis concessit atque autorizavit ut in ecclesia nostra in festis divi Zenonis pro ymno cantetur anno Domini 1498 *add. Mü^3*.
[298] Incipit prologus de vita beati Zenonis] Vita beati *NovaraII.*
[299] regis] *suprascr. NovaraLXIII.*

Incipit vita et actus beatissimi Zenonis episcopi VI Idus decembris.[300] [I][301] Olim peritissimorum disciplinabilis mos extitit virorum indagatione diligenti sanctorum vitas exquirere earumque seriem stili officio sollicite ac rationabiliter memoriae posteritati[302] assignare, quatenus ob suae studium doctrinae ipsorum in orbe imitatione potirentur et eorum quandoque consortio in perhennis vitae gloria fruerentur. Sic etenim instat sapientis mens ad investigandas sanctorum vitas, tamquam si aliquis sitiens ardore solis adustus, avide fontium concupiscat fluenta, vel etiam si quis desideratissimum ex remota regione audire ambiat nuntium, aut certe si quilibet[303] deliciarum dapibus enutritus, in quodam longinquo itinere positus esuriens, ad solitam sui cupiat ventris pervenire satietatem.

II Nos itaque licet eis, qui talia conscripsere, simus scientia impares, et penitus ad exprimenda, quae gestimus inefficaces, quoniam rei materiam verborum compositio non aequiperat, ea tamen, quae de beati Zenonis virtutibus vel scriptis vel faminibus ediscere valuimus disseramus. In diebus imperatoris Gallieni, qui per successiones caesarum vigesimus septimus in eorum est catalogo subrogatus, quo etiam tempore, Dionisius vir reverentissimus a beato Petro apostolo vigesimus tertius Romanae praesidebat ecclesiae, in provincia Italia in civitate Verona beati Zenonis acta claruentur. Cuius viri virtutes ad liquidum, quas in conversatione vel in miraculis peregit, explicare non sufficientes, aliquas tamen iuxta quod attingere possumus, ennarrare veridica ratione conamur.

III Fuit quippe a matris utero sanctificatus, et a cunabulis benedictus, ut assertione divina in eo repeti videretur, quod Hieremiae dictum est: „Priusquam te formarem in utero, novi te et antequam exires de ventre sanctificavi te."[304] Denique probitatis atque scientiae iugibus incrementis ad hoc pertingere meruit, ut per sacerrimam vitam fieri pastor in populo mereretur. Nempe audiant populi omnes, qui eius cupiunt nosse miracula, quia in omnem terram sonus exiit conversationis eius et sanctitas luculenter emicuit. Erat enim sedens in monasterio in secretiori parte oppidi Veronensis, continuis ieiuniis et orationibus crebris a Domino petens, ut sibi dignaretur aditum melliferae praedicationis in populos aperire. Igitur ad convertendas in amorem Christi animas hominum die noctuque deditus erat. Revera quoniam sanctus ei spiritus purarum illuminator mentium doctor existebat, sicut ipsa veritas loquitur dicens: „Non enim vos estis, qui loquimini, sed spiritus patris vestri, qui loquitur in vobis."[305] [IV] Ita sane affabilis erat in sermone, et in mansuetudine, seu in habitu mitis, ut iure Deus in ipso collaudaretur ab omnibus venientibus ad se, ita alacer et splendifico[306] nitore facundiae vividus, ut mox ad eum properantes relictis idolis et pravitate

---

300 Incipti vita et actus beatissimi Zenonis episcopi VI Idus decembris] Vita beati Zenonis *NovaraII.*

301 Die Teilung der Lesungen entspricht *NovaraII*, da sie nur dort vollständig angegeben ist.

302 posteritati] posteritatis *NovaraII NovaraLXIII.*

303 quilibet] quislibet *NovaraII NovaraLXIII.*

304 Priusquam ... te] *cf.* Ier 1, 5.

305 Non ... vobis] *cf.* Mt 10, 20.

306 splendifico] splendidifico *scr. NovaraLXIII.*

gentilitatis exempti Domino crederent Iesu Christo. Per idem tempus iuxta urbem Veronam, dum egrediens idem vir a monasterio in Atesi fluvio piscationis exercitio fungeretur erectis sursum oculis vidit ex adverso quendam hominem in plaustro sedentem bobus subiunctis per praeceps in amnem dimergi. Tanta quippe miserabilis velocitate ferebatur, ut palam cunctis cernentibus daretur intellegi, hoc diaboli arte fuisse peractum. Sanctus itaque vir, dum intentis luminibus hoc a longe prospiceret, cognovit lymphaticam viri ruinam factum diaboli esse. Interea vir Dei elevata sursum manu fecit sanctae crucis signum frequenti vice et dixit: „Revertere retro Sathana, ne perimas hominem quem Deus creavit." Quod videlicet signum ut diabolus aspexit, velut fumus vento raptatus[307] evanuit et clamoribus nimiis ac stridore nefando, quasi de alta rupe cum impetu decideret ait: „Etsi non hic me permittis animas hominum mea obsessione lucrari, tamen paratus sum in patrias notas circumquaque sitas, ad tuum perniciter abire impedimentum."

V Sanctus autem Dei Zeno dixit: „Non te permittit Dominus dire aliquid agere adversus servum suum." His ita peractis, cum detestabili ululatu et clamore discessit. Festinans itaque daemon ingressus est concite palatium caesaris Gallieni arreptamque filiam eius, quae tunc temporis unica parentibus erat, coepit crudeliter vexare. Miserabilis ergo pater simulque tota domus regia in tristiam versa, cruciatu et maerore[308] ingenti affligebantur, eo quod tam acriter puella suffocaretur. Quae dum crudeli vexatione corriperetur, coepit per os infantulae regis filiae daemon clamare dicens: „Non egrediar a corpore isto, nisi Zeno venerit episcopus, ac per ipsius imperium coactus migrabo." Mox itaque ut hoc regi Gallieno innotuit, missis apparitoribus sollicita intentione coepit investigare, sic ubi sanctum potuisset invenire virum. Ex iussu autem regis milites velocibus ad virum Dei gressibus pergunt. Ille vero sedebat super lapidem, qui in proximo erat monasterii, et artis apostolicae documenta proficiens, ex more piscabatur in flumine. Venientes ergo milites, quoniam ignotus eis erat, coeperunt sollicite sanctum Dei sacerdotem interrogare dicentes: „Quis es tu, homo Dei? Indica nobis, si vidisti Zenonem episcopum, quem nos ex iussu regis perquirimus." At ille repondit: „Ad quod missi estis edicite. Ego enim quamvis tantillus servus Christi, tamen Zeno vocor."

VI Igitur conferentes ad invicem milites dicebant inter se: „Quid multa colloquimur? Indicemus, pro qua re istum destinati sumus ad virum." Tunc patenter intimantes beato sacerdoti dixerunt: „Rogat te rex venire ad se, quia vult faciem tuam videre." Zeno respondit: „Quid meam rex vult humilitatem cernere, qui omnium Christianorum manifestis indiciis inimicus esse non desinit?" At illi[309] respondentes dixerunt: „Obsecrat enim te rex, ut filiam ipsius, quae immani atrocitate a daemonio vexatur, sanitati restituas, quia unica illi est." Ille vero dixit eis: „Dominus Iesus Christus omnipotens est. Ite", inquit, „ecce ego paulatim subsequor vos. Oportet enim ut mirabilia Dei luce clarius omnibus

---

[307] raptatus] *in* raptus *corr. NovaraII.*
[308] cruciatu et maerore] *cf.* Cic. Verr. 2,5,123.
[309] illi] *ex* ille *corr. NovaraII.*

manifestentur.“ Quo dicto milites viam, qua venerant, repedarunt. Exurgens vero beatus sacerdos, ne diutius „absconderetur civitas supra montem domus Domini posita“[310], fecit orationem perrexitque ad palatium, ubi cruciabatur et lamentabiliter affligebatur pro sua filia rex. Sanctus quoque Dei episcopus Zeno, dum celeri peragratione iter ageret, ante eo pervenit, quam hi qui missi fuerant milites. Ingrediente siquidem Christi sacerdote palatium et facto crucis signo coepit confestim per os infantulae daemon clamare dicens: „Ecce tu, Zeno, venisti ad expellendum me et ego propter tuae pavorem sanctitatis hic stare non possum.“

VII His quidem auditis tenens sacerdos manum puellae dixit: „In nomine Domini nostri Iesu Christi praecipio tibi: „Exi ab ea, daemon!“ At ille publica coepit et horribili voce clamare dicens: „Etsi hinc a te expulsus fuero eo Veronam ibique invenies me et eos in quibus habitem stantes in platea expectantes te.“ Christi namque sacerdos sanam mox ab omni daemonicae incursionis ludificatione restituit filiam regis. Protinus autem ut rex Gallienus vidit hoc factum, attonitus admiratione coronam regalem, quam capite gestabat, sancto sacerdoti obtulit dicens: „Tam salutifero medico qui sanam unicam filiam meam restituit, nullis muneribus aliis placere possum, nisi ipsam ei quam habeo meam offeram coronam.“ Cumque hoc gestum multitudo vidisset populi, quae ad palatium convenerat, a tenebris infidelitatis et errore conversa gentili, crediderunt unanimiter in Iesum Christum Dominum nostrum, obsecrantes sacerdotem Christi, ut docerentur viam salutis et baptismum mererentur in remissionem percipere delictorum.

VIII At ubi sacerdos coronam accepit a rege, statim in partes divisam distribuit pauperibus dicens: „Si Dominus operatur excelsa, ipsi perpetuae laudes referantur et gloria.“ His ita gestis, petiit beatissimus Zeno, ut ei licentia tribueretur omnia idola destruendi et basilicas in Christi nomine fabricandi. Cuius almificis precibus adquievit rex affatim in omnibus, quae ille poposcerat. Nempe talibus et his similibus incedebat opinatus virtutibus, ut compleretur in eo, quod Dominus apostolis ait: „Ecce dedi vobis potestatem calcandi supra serpentes et scorpiones et omnem virtutem inimici.“[311] Post haec igitur ingressus sacerdos civitatem Veronam, intrepidus praedicabat in Christi nomine verbum et hoc instanter agebat, ut funditus idola destruerentur et in honorem Domini aedificarentur ecclesiae.

VIIII Denique, dum haec agerentur, multitudo populi paganorum saeviens incessanter moliebatur, ut impedimentum Christi famulus pateretur. Sed vigilante in servis suis Christo vincebatur mendacium, quod pura et rectissima fides ab infidelium cordibus abigebat. His equidem ita patratis sacrosancta agebat antistes pro populi intercessione salutaria, seu ab ineunte aetate in Christi amore solitus erat. Qui nimirum dum haec indesinenter ageret operante manu voluntatis Dei, cuius in omni vitae transeuntis tempore nutui oboedierat non multo post in pace receptus est. Porro quia in virtutibus exhibitae sanctitatis[312] veluti

---

[310] absconderetur ... posita] *cf.* Mt 5, 14.
[311] Ecce ... inimici] *cf.* Lc 10, 19.
[312] sanctitatis] sanitatis *NovaraII NovaraLXIII.*

fulgidissimum sidus omni populo claruit, in honore Dei et ipsius sancti sacerdotis quidam ex genere Gallieni fecit reverendo eius nomini basilicam, haud procul a fluvio, ubi longo tempore corpus ipsius requievit. Qui etiam venerabilis locus in recta ineffabilis ac beatae Trinitatis confessione signis et miraculis coruscat.

LECTIO SANCTI GREGORII DE MIRABILIBUS BEATI ZENONIS EPISCOPI[313]

Quando apud Romanam urbem alveum suum Tiberis egressus est, tantumque crescens, ut unda eius super muros urbis influeret atque in ea maximas regiones occuparet apud Veronensem urbem fluvius Athesis excrescens ad beati Zenonis martyris atque pontificis ecclesiam venit. Cuius ecclesiae, dum essent ianuae apertae, aqua in eam minime intravit. Quae paulisper crescens usque ad fenestras ecclesiae, quae erant tectis proximae, pervenit. Siquidem stans aqua ecclesiae ianuam clausit ac si illud elementum liquidum in soliditatem parietis fuisset immutatum cumque essent multi interius inventi, sed aquarum multitudine ecclesia omni circumdata, qua possent egredi non haberent ibique siti ac fame deficere formidarent, ad ecclesiae ianuam veniebant. Ad bibendum hauriebant aquam, quae – ut praedixi – usque ad fenestras excreverat et tamen intra ecclesiam nullo modo defluebat.[314] Hauriri itaque ut aqua poterat, sed defluere ut aqua non poterat. Stans autem ante ianuam ad ostendendum cunctis meritum martyris et aqua erat ad adiutorium et quasi aqua non erat ad invadendum locum.

Lesungen der Zenofeste aus San Zeno Maggiore (BHL 9010–9011)

Basiert auf den Handschriften: Augsburg StStadtB 2° 204 (*Aug*), Kremsmünster SB CC60 (*Kr*), Verona BC CXVI(90*) (*Vr*²)

Vita sancti Zenonis episcopi[315]

Eo tempore quo Valerianus cum filio suo[316] Gallieno fasces Romani[317] imperii suscepit prima fronte regiminis humanus et benignus existitit erga famulos Dei quia mitissima sors regnorum solet esse sub novo rege.[318] Sed[319] postquam vetustari coepit in regno depravatus est et a veritate deiectus per quendam doctorem pessimum magistrum et principem Aegyptiorum magorum, ut iustos et sanctos viros interemi iuberet. Tamquam qui[320] adversarentur magicis artibus quibus ipse[321] sordebat.[322] Fuso[323] per omnem Romani regni latitudinem sanctorum

---

313 Lectio...episcopi] miraculum beati Zenonis *NovaraII.*

314 defluebat] defluebit *NovaraII.*

315 Vita sancti Zenonis episcopi] Vita beati Zenonis Veronensis episcopi *Aug* In ordinatione sancti Zenonis episcopi et confessoris *add. Kr.*

316 Suo] *om. Vr*².

317 Romani] romano *Kr.*

318 Rege] Tu au *add. Kr, hic des. lectio I Kr.*

319 Sed] *hic inc. lectio II Kr.*

320 Qui] *om. Kr.*

321 Ipse] *om. Kr.*

322 Sordebat] *hic des. lectio II Kr Vr*².

323 Fuso] *hic inc. lectio III Kr Vr*².

sanguine[324] Valerianus illico nefarii[325] auctor edicti. A Sapore[326] rege Persarum captus imperator populi Romani ignominiosa servitute apud Persas consenuit, hoc infamis[327] officii continua donec vixit damnatione sortitus ut ipse a clinis[328] humi regem semper ascensurum equum non manu sed dorso attolleret.[329] Ac[330] Gallienus claro Dei iudicio territus et tam misero college permotus exemplo pacem ecclesiis[331] trepida satisfactione restituit, quo adhuc septra Romana regente[332] Dyonisius vir reverentissimus apostolicae sedis apicem ascenderat.[333] Eodem[334] temporis curriculo[335] Zeno egregius pastor ac praestantissimus tam opere quam sermone in urbe Verona fuit intronizatus et populi magnitudine et aedificiorum altitudine et reliquis incrementis et ornamentis urbanis inter alias[336] Italiae civitates florebat.[337]

Sed[338] Veronensis fidei radicem hic orthodoxae fidei doctor firmavit et omnia deliramenta paganorum velut clara lux tenebras ab urbe sua fugavit[339] et populum adhuc informem sigillo formae Dei imaginavit.[340] Fuit[341] quippe a matris[342] utero sanctificatus et a cunabulis benedictus ut assertione[343] divina in eo repeti videretur quod Hieremiae dictum est: „Priusquam te formarem in utero novi te et antequam exires de ventre sanctificavi te[344].“[345]

Denique[346] probitatis atque scientiae iugibus incrementis ad hoc pertingere meruit ut per sacerrimam vitam fieri pastor in populo mereretur.[347] Nempe audiant populi omnes qui eius cupiunt nosse[348] miracula. Quia in omnem terram sonus exiit conversationis eius[349] et sanctitas luculenter emicuit.[350] Erat enim

---

324 Sanguine] saguine *Aug.*
325 Nefarii] nefari *Kr.*
326 Sapore] sopore *Aug.*
327 Infamis] infavus *Aug.*
328 A clinis] acclinis *Aug.*
329 Attolleret] *hic des. lectio III Kr.*
330 Ac] at *Vr²* *hic inc. lectio IV Kr.*
331 Ecclesiis] ecclesis *Aug Vr²*.
332 Regente] gerente *Vr²*.
333 Ascenderat] *hic des. lectio IV Kr, hic des. lectio II Vr²*.
334 Eodem] *hic inc. lectio V Kr, hic inc. lectio III Vr²*.
335 Curriculo] circulo *Kr.*
336 Alias] *om. Vr²*.
337 Florebat] *hic des. lectio V Kr.*
338 Sed] *hic inc. lectio VI Kr.*
339 Fugavit] fugat *Aug.*
340 Et…imaginavit] *om. Aug hic des. lectio VI Kr.*
341 Fuit] *hic inc. lectio VII Kr.*
342 Matris] matre *Kr.*
343 Assertione] a sermone *Aug.*
344 Priusquam ... te] *cf.* Ier 1, 5.
345 Te] *hic des. lectio VII Kr, hic des. lectio III Vr²*.
346 Denique] *hic inc. lectio VIII Kr, hic inc. Lectio IV Vr²*.
347 Mereretur] re *in margine suppl. Aug.*
348 Nosse] nosce *Kr.*
349 in...eius] *cf.* Ps 18, 5 *in omnem terram exivit sonus eorum et in fines orbis terrae verba eorum.*
350 Emicuit] *hic desunt lectiones Kr.*

sedens in monasterio in secretiori parte oppidi Veronensis continuis ieiuniis et orationibus crebris a Domino petens ut sibi dignaretur aditum mellifluae[351] praedicationis in populos aperire. Igitur ad convertendas in amore[352] Christi animas hominum die noctuque deditus erat. Revera quondam sanctus ei spiritus[353] purarum illuminator mentium doctor assistebat,[354] sicut ipsa veritas loquitur dicens: „Non enim vos estis qui loquimini sed spiritus patris vestri qui loquitur in vobis.“[355] Ita sane affabilis erat in sermone et in[356] mansuetudine seu in habitu mitis ut iure Deus in ipso esse crederetur ab omnibus venientibus ad se. Ita alacer et splendifico nitore[357] facundiae vividus ut mox ad eum properantes relicits idolis et pravitate[358] gentilitatis exempti Domino crederent Iesu Christo.[359] Per idem[360] tempus iuxta urbem Veronam egrediens idem vir a monasterio dum[361] in Athesi fluvio piscationis exercitio fungeretur, erectis sursum oculis vidit ex adverso[362] quendam hominem in plaustro sedentem bubus subiunctis per praeceps in amnem dimergi.[363] Tanta[364] quippe miserabilis velocitate[365] ferebatur ut palam cunctis cernentibus daretur intelligi hoc diaboli arte fuisse peractum.[366] Sanctus itaque vir dum intentis luminibus hoc a longe prospiceret cognovit lymphaticam viri ruinam factum diaboli esse. Interea vir Dei elevata sursum manu fecit sanctae crucis signum, frequenti vice et dixit: „Revertere retro Sathana ne perimas hominem quem Deus creavit.“ Quot videlicet signum ut[367] diabolus aspexit velut fumus vento raptus evanuit et clamoribus nimiis ac stridore horribili, quasi de alta rupe praecipitans ait: „Etsi non hic[368] permittis animas hominum mea obsidione lucrari, tamen[369] paratus sum in patrias notas circumquaque sitas ad tuum perniciter abire impedimentum.“[370] Sanctus[371] autem

---

351 Mellifluae] melluflue *Aug* mellifere *Vr²*.
352 Amore] amorem *Vr²*.
353 Sanctus…spiritus] spiritus ei sanctus *Vr²*.
354 Assistebat] existebat *Vr²*.
355 Non...vobis] *cf.* Mt 10, 20.
356 In] *om. Aug.*
357 Nitore] sermone *Aug.*
358 Pravitate] pravitates *Aug.*
359 Christo] *hic des. lectio IV Vr²*.
360 Per idem] *hic inc. lectio V Vr²*.
361 Dum] ut *Aug.*
362 Adverso] averso *Aug.*
363 Suum] alleluia *add. VrCiv¹*.
364 Tanta] *hic inc. lectio VI Vr²*.
365 Miserabilis velocitate] velocitate miserabilis *Aug.*
366 hoc...peractum] om. *Aug.*
367 Ut] *om. Aug.*
368 Non hic] hic me non *Aug.*
369 Tamen] tum *Aug.*
370 Impedimentum] *hic des. lectio VI Vr²*.
371 Sanctus] *hic inc. lectio VII Vr²*.

Dei[372] Zeno dixit: „Non te permittit Deus[373] dire[374] aliquid agere adversus servum suum." His ita transactis cum detestabili ululatu et clamore discessit. Festinans itaque daemon ingressus est concite palatium caesaris Gallieni arreptamque filiam eius,[375] quae tunc temporis unica parentibus erat, coepit crudeliter vexare. Miserabilis ergo pater simulque tota domus regia in tristitiam versa cruciatu et maerore[376] ingenti affligebantur. Eo quod tam acriter puella suffocaretur. Quae dum crudeli vexatione corriperetur, coepit per os infantulae regis filiae daemon clamare dicens: „Non egrediar a corpore isto nisi Zeno venerit episcopus, tunc per ipsius imperium coactus migrabo." Mox itaque ut hoc regi innotuit Gallieno[377] missis apparitoribus sollicita intentione coepit investigare sic ubi sanctum potuisset invenire[378] virum.[379] Ex[380] iussu autem regis milites velocius[381] ad virum Dei gressibus pergunt. Ille vero sedebat super lapidem qui in proximo erat monasterii et artis apostolicae[382] baiulans instrumenta[383] ex more piscabatur in flumine. Venientes ergo milites quoniam[384] ignotus eis erat[385] coeperunt sollicite sanctum Dei sacerdotem interrogare dicentes: „Quis es tu, homo Dei? Indica nobis si vidisti Zenonem episcopum quem nos ex iussu regis perquirimus." At ille respondit: „Ad quod missi estis dicite. Ego enim quamvis tantillus servus tamen Christi Zeno vocor." Igitur conferentes ad invicem milites dicebant inter se: „Quid multa colloquimur? Indicemus istum pro quare[386] destinati sumus ad virum." Tunc patenter intimantes beato sacerdoti dixerunt: „Rogat te rex venire ad se quia vult faciem tuam videre." Quibus Zeno respondit: „Quid meam rex vult humilitatem cernere qui omnium Christianorum manifestis indiciis inimicus esse non desinit?" At illi respondentes dixerunt: „Obsecrat enim te rex ut filiam ipsius, quae immani atrocitate a daemonio vexatur,[387] sanitati restituas quia unica illi est." Ille vero dixit eis: „Dominus Iesus Christus[388] omnipotens est. Ite", inquit, „ecce ego paulatim subsequor vos. Oportet enim ut mirabilia Dei luce clarius omnibus manifestentur." Mox ex piscatura quam ceperat legatis regis Gallieni tres sumere iussit. Dum illi numero contempto unum plus piscem raperent et quattuor in ferventis aquae dolium mitterent. Tribus datis decoctis ad epulas quartus

---

372 Dei] *om. Aug.*
373 Deus] Dominus *Aug.*
374 Dire] *om. Aug.*
375 Eius] *om. Vr²*.
376 cruciatu et maerore] *cf.* Cic. Verr. 2,5,123.
377 Innotuit Gallieno] Gallieno innotuit *Vr²*.
378 Potuisset invenire] potuit investigare *Aug.*
379 Virum] *hic des. lectio VII Vr²*.
380 Ex] *hic inc. lectio VIII Vr²*.
381 Velocius] velocibus *Vr²*.
382 Artis apostolicae] arte apostolicis *Aug.*
383 Baiulans instrumenta] instrumenta baiulans *Vr²*.
384 Quoniam] quam *Aug.*
385 Erat] esset *Aug.*
386 Istum pro quare] pro quare istum *Vr²*.
387 Vexatur] ut *add. Aug.*
388 Christus] *om. Vr²*.

raptus crudus et velut illaesus in vase natabat[389] quasi commonens[390] ut illicitum redderent et licitos comederent. Illi rubore perfusi vitium rapinae sentientes obesse naturae iniuste acceptum sancto piscatori piscem[391] reddunt. Vir autem Dei et piscem eis concessit et culpam indulsit. Hoc visum, fidem videntibus[392] adhibuit ut si Romam pergeret natam Domini sui a daemone liberaret. Quo facto milites viam[393] qua venerant remeaverunt.[394] Exsurgens vero beatus sacerdos ne diutius absconderetur civitas supra montem Domini posita,[395] fecit orationem perrexitque[396] ad palatium ubi cruciabatur[397] et lamentabiliter affligebatur pro sua filia rex. Sanctus quoque Dei episcopus dum celeriter iter ageret ante eos[398] pervenit quam hi qui missi fuerant milites. Ingrediente siquidem Christi sacerdote palatium et facto crucis signo coepit confestim[399] per os infantulae daemon clamare dicens: „Ecce tu, Zeno, venisti ad expellendum me et ego propter pavorem tuae[400] sanctitatis hic[401] stare non possum." His quidem auditis tenens sacerdos manum puellae dixit: „In nomine Domini nostri[402] Iesu Christi praecipio tibi, exi ab ea daemon." At ille publica voce coepit et horribile clamare dicens:[403] „Etsi hinc a te fuero expulsus eo Veronam, ibi[404] invenies me et mea zizania sanctum populum, quem lucrari conaris, ludificabit."[405] Christi namque sacerdos sanam mox ab omni daemoniace incursionis ludificatione restituit filiam regis. Protinus autem ut rex Gallienus vidit hoc factum attonitus admiratione coronam regalem quam capite gestabat sancto sacerdoti obtulit dicens: „Tam salutifero medico qui sanam unicam meam filiam[406] restituit nullis muneribus aliis placere[407] possum nisi meam coronam offeram."[408] Cumque hoc gestum multitudo vidisset populi quae ad palatium convenerat,[409] a tenebris infidelitatis et errore conversa gentili crediderunt unanimiter in Dominum nostrum Iesum Christum.[410] Obsecrantes

389 Natabat] nataverat (ta *suprascr.*) *Aug.*
390 Quasi commonens] *om. Aug.*
391 Piscem] *om. Aug.*
392 Videntibus] videndo *Aug.*
393 Viam] via *Vr*^{2}.
394 Remeaverunt] remearunt *Aug Vr*^{2}.
395 absconderetur...posita] *cf.* Mt 5, 14.
396 Perrexitque] que *suprascr. Aug.*
397 Cruciabatur] cruciebatur *Vr*^{2}.
398 Eos] eo *Vr*^{2}.
399 Confestim] *om. Aug.*
400 Pavorem tue] tue pavorem *Vr*^{2}.
401 Hic] *om. Aug.*
402 Nostri] *om. Vr*^{2}.
403 At...dicens] At ille publica cepit et horribile voce clamare dicens *Vr*^{2}.
404 Ibi] ibique *Vr*^{2}.
405 Et...ludificabit] Et meae zizaniae semen populum, quem lucrari conaris, ludificabo *Aug.*
406 Sanam...filiam] sanam unicam filiam meam *Vr*^{2}.
407 Placere] placare *Aug.*
408 Coronam offeram] offero coronam *Vr*^{2}.
409 Convenerat] convenerant *Aug.*
410 Dominum...Christum] Iesum Christum Dominum nostrum *Vr*^{2}.

sacerdotem Christi ut docerentur viam salutis et baptismum mererentur[411] in remissionem percipere peccatorum. At ubi sacerdos coronam a rege accepit[412] statim in partes divisam distribuit pauperibus dicens: „Si Dominus operatur excelsa ipsi perpetuae laudes referantur[413] et gloria."[414]

Eodem[415] die sanctissimi Zenonis episcopi qui inter procellas persecutionis Veronensem urbem mirabiliter rexit. His itaque gestis petiit beatus Zeno ut ei licentiam tribueretur omnia idola destruendi et basilicas in Christi nomine fabricandi cuius almificis precibus adquievit rex in omnibus affatim quae ipse poposcerat. Nempe talibus et his similibus incedebat opinatus virtutibus ut compleretur in eo quod Dominus apostolis ait: „Ecce dedi vobis potestatem calcandi supra serpentes et scorpiones et omnem virtutem inimici."[416] Post haec igitur ingressus sacerdos sanctus Zeno in civitatem Veronam intrepidus praedicabat in Christi nomine verbum et instanter agebat ut funditus idola destruerentur et in honore Domini ecclesiae aedificarentur. Denique cum haec agerentur multitudo populi paganorum saeviens incessanter moliebatur ut impedimentum Christi famulus pateretur. Sed vigilante in servis suis Christo vincebatur mendacium quod pura et rectissima fides ab infidelium cordibus ambigebat. Mox multitudo profana magis ad argumentum ridiculi quam ad propositum alicuius proficui cadaver eiectum in flumine ante viri Dei faciem obtulit dicens: „Si hoc ad invocationem Dei tui animaveris nostram deferentes et[417] quam praedicas doctrinam imitabimur." Vir Dei pro missione gavisus pro vita ex animis Christum precatur. Sed quo oratio ascendit illinc impetratio descendit quae quaerentibus hominem restituit vociferantem: „Verus Deus est quem iste praedicat." Illi duplici capti animo tum fidele promissionis tum spectaculo visionis clamarunt: „Credamus, credamus et idola fallacia dimittamus."[418] Sic falsa deserentes veritati adhaerentes Christo crediderunt.

His equidem ita patratis sacrosancta agebat antistes pro populi intercessione salutaria. Seu[419] ab ineunte aetate in Christi amore solitus erat atque ibidem urbanam invitationem baptismatis populo peregit huic etiam de gravitate patientiae alteras annexit quas, quia breves et utiles sunt, non dubitamus inserere: „Eia quid statis fratres? Vestram quos per fidem genitalis unda concipit per sacramentam iam parturit ad desiderata quantocius[420] festinate. Ecce vox infantium et dulcis vagitus auditur, ecce parturientis uno de ventre clarissima

---

411 Mererentur] merentur *Aug.*

412 A…accepit] acceperit a rege *Vr*^{2}.

413 *cf.* AH 19, Nr. 323, S. 184-185 De sancto Luca (basiert ebenso aus *Vr*^{5}).

414 Omelia de confessoribus pontificis cum evangelio Nemo accendit lucernam *add. Kr* Omelia Vos estis sal terre *add. Aug.*

415 Depositio sancti Zenonis episcopi et confessoris Residuum de vita beati Zenonis episcopi et confessori *add. Aug* Depositio Zenonis add. *Kr.*

416 Ecce...inimici] *cf.* Lc 10, 19.

417 et] om. *Aug.*

418 Dimittamus] dmittamus *Aug.*

419 Seu] ceu *Aug.*

420 Quantocius] quantocicius *Aug.*

turba procedit. Nova res ut in re spirituali unusquisque nascatur. Ultro currite ad matrem quae tunc non laborat cum parit. Intrate, intrate ergo felices omnes simul subito futuri lactantes. Vetus homo vester feliciter quod condemnatur et sacri gurgitis unda sepelitur ut absolvatur et sepulcri nido vivificatur resurrectionis iura degustat. O magna providentia Dei nostri, o bone matris caritas pura quae unam nativitatem, unum lac, unum stipendium, unam[421] spiritus sancti praestat omnibus dignitatem. Quam speciosum est, fratres, ut quem cupidum semper horrueris stupeas passim in pauperes et egenos sua bona universa fundentem. Postremo quem noveris idolatriae fanum gaudeas Dei templum. Itaque beatus est semper qui meminit quod renatus est, beatius qui non meminerit esse quod fuit antequam renatus sit; beatissimus qui infantiam suam provectu temporis non mutaverit."

Praeterea sic de patientia sic disputat: „Etsi beata diversis vita virtutibus quaeritur cuius cupidine flagrans humanitas per momenta suspirat. Tamen omnes uno eodemque consensu quasi quendam patientiae deferuntur in portum sine qua nec audiri nec concipi nec disci quidquam poterit nec doceri nam profecto sola est ad quam prorsus[422] res omnis spectet. Dubium quippe eum non sit spem, fidem, iustitiam, humilitatem, castitatem, probitatem, concordiam, caritatem, omnes artes omnesque virtutes ipsa quoque elementa constare non posse sine eius eruditione vel freno. Est enim patientia matura semper, humilis, cauta, prudens, provida, omni necessitate contenta, quamvis turbationum tempestate tranquilla, serenitatem suam nobilis turbulentare non novit. Paenitentiam nescit, altercatio quid sit ignorat, omnes aut devitat autem portat[423] iniurias. Incertum est utrum impassibilis indicetur cum aliquid passa quasi nihil passa sit invenitur. Postremo impossibile est, fratres, eius estimare virtutem cuius vinci victoria est. Non illam loco vis ulla detorquet non labor, non fames, non nuditas, non persecutio, non metus, non periculum, non mors, non tormenta, semper immobilis manet. Sed o quam vellem te si possim rerum omnium regina patientia magis moribus concelebrare morte ipsa graviora, non potestas, non ambitio, non felicitas semper immobilis stat. Scio enim quia libentius in tuis moribus, tuis fundamentis tuisque consiliis quam in alienis nudisque sermonibus conquiescis neque tantam in multiplicandis virtutibus laudem ponis quanta in finiendis. Tu virginitati praestas ne flos eius ullo morbo ullo tempore deflorescat. Tu variarum semper in tempestatum crebris turbinibus constitute fidissimus viduitatis es portus. Tu sanctissimo coniugali iugo rudi cervice binos subeuntes innisum laboris vel amoris aequalem retinaculis blandis quasi quidam peritis auriga componis. Tu servituti unica ac fortissima consolatio, saepe libertatem paris. Tu paupertati praestas ut habebat totum sui contenta cum sustinet totum. Tu prophetas provexisti, tu Christo apostolos glutinasti, tu cottidiana martyrum

---

421 Unam] una *Aug.*
422 Prorsus] prossus *Aug.*
423 Portat] *legi nequit Aug.*

et mater es et corona. Tu murus fidei, fructus spei, amica caritatis. Tu specialiter omnem populum divinasque virtutes quasi crines effusos in unius verticis nodum, honorem decoremque conducis. Felix est qui semper te habuerit in se." Sic sanctus Zeno episcopus de doctrina baptismatis et patientiae finierat.

Ad huiusmodi et altia vestigia virtutum instigabat populi adquisitum; cuius lingua[424] velut fons indeficiens per exercitia divini dogmatis effluebat et omnem contagionem priusquam adolesceret expurgabat. Et parum credebat esse actum cum aliquid superesset agendum. Neque amor saecularis genitoris tantum aestuat in agenda facultate parvulorum dum timet ne penuria fatigentur, quantum Zeno vir paterni pectoris circa filios adoptionis flagrabat, ne inopia verbi divini tabescerent. Quos luculenta oratione et affabili affectione importune et opportune saginabat et non parvum [ardorem] amoris eis impectorabat. Unde patrem et natos tantae dilectionis foedus coniunxerat ut fere ambiguum esset an [pater] illos, an illi patrem plus diligerent. Sed diabolus doctrinae felicitate torquebatur quae non exiguis ecclesiam opibus ditabat, praestigiator insatiabilis mille formas nocendi accipit et explorat velut latro non modo infirmos et titubantes, verum etiam viros excellentes et robustos ut accepta occasione latrocinium exerceat. Nam a quo dolos suos contineat, qui ipsum Dominum tripliciter temptare praesumpsit. Hic artifex fraudolentus idolatriae magistros eorumque discipulos multis argumentis contra sancti Zenonis tyrones adhuc rudes infestabat. At Deus qui dedit illis se nosse auxit et posse ut ante signum miraculorum Zenonem sequentes gloriosam victoriam triumphantis hostibus reportarent. Ipse vero sanctus accepta palma non proiecit arma neque suos proicere permisit sed esse paratissimos ad resistendum eisdem hostibus persuasit nec nudis verbis sed factorum exemplis illos exagitabat. Nam vigilando, orando, ieiunando, elemosinando miraculis coruscando magnum robur constantiae illis inculcavit et ut certatim fortiores essent in residua pugna indulcavit. Et iustus Zeno ut palma in domo Dei florebat et sua plantatio in eadem aula et in atriis domus Dei vehementer crescebat[425].

Sed tempus instabat ut legitimi certaminis coronam acciperet et animam ex corruptione exutam incorruptioni redderet. Quod virum Dei plenum non latuit. Mox gregem multo labore et sudore quaesitum quo iacebat vocari praecepit quibus inspectis[426] ait: „Filii carissimi diutius vobiscum esse mallem sed Dominus ergastulum animae pulsat et quam dedit ad se vocat. Nunc vestrae fidei, spei et caritati ecclesiam Dei commendo, quam ille non quovis pretio sed proprio sanguine quaesivit ut eam doctrinae lumine illustretis et exemplorum fultu roboretis. Vigilate in fide, viriliter agite, confortamini in Domino et omnia vestra in caritate fiant. Scitis, qui legitime certaverit, coronabitur. Hic certate, hic pugnate, hic contra vitiorum aciem dimicate ut coronam non tabentibus floribus aut lauro fluitura textam capiatis. Sed gemmis perenniter fulgentibus et

---

424 Lingua] ligwa *Aug.*

425 ut palma...crescebat] *cf.* Ps 91, 13–14 *iustus ut palma florebit, ut cedrus Libani multiplicabitur, plantati in domo Domini in atriis Dei nostri florebunt.*

426 Inspectis] inspecis *Aug.*

auro numquam perituro Dei digito fabricatam possideatis[427]." Post multiplices et elegantes sermones mysterium tali aptum negotio sumpsit et osculum singulis – velut iturus Ierusalem – dedit. Post haec signavit eos et benedixit. Mox sanctam animam creatori suo reddidit.

Pridie idus Aprilis quod omnem populum quasi unum hominem congregat. Videntes senes et iuvenes atque infantulos et alterum sexum eiusdem aetatis circa corpus redolens velut omni genere odoris aspersum ingentem clamorem facere ac sicut omnium patres et matres eo momento morerentur plorare: „Cui nos reliquisti pater? Quis maestos consolabitur? Quis aegros tam celeriter medicabitur? Quis egenis tantum dederit? Quis famelicos tam bene satiaverit? Si optio nobis daretur tuam vitam nostra morte commercaremur!" Haec vota animi omnis aetas fundebat et pro amore eius boni pastoris eiulabat. Cui dignas exequias persolverunt sepelientes non longe ab urbe Verona ubi deo feliciter sacrificare consueverat. Multiplices et varie mirabilium species repente circa tumulum eius apparuerunt.

Sed ex Gallieni genere religiosi viri memores consanguineae daemonio liberatae, eo loco, ubi tanta margarita quieverat, templum construxerunt. A quo quamplures non venientes redierunt, in quo non videntes viderunt, cuius beneficia nonnulli aegroti ad huc et olim senserunt. Sed die natalicii sui aqua fluminis intemperie acria intumuit et circumquaque superficiem terrae subito operuit. Hoc enim primo mane factum est cum frequens multitudo inerat quantam vix ecclesiae sinus acceperat. Ecce Athesis undique voragine basilica obsidebatur et usque ad fenestras illius impetus infremuit atque aditum ecclesiae clausit et stetit ac si illud elementum liquidum in solidum parietem fuisset immutatum. Quod ut viderunt prius exanimati sunt confortati[428] sed inclusi mirabili obsidione iam plus famis quam fluminis periculum formidabant. Illi laborantes siti primo diluvii timore deinde densitatis calore. Venientes ad ianuam sitis habuere praesidium quod estimaverunt esse exitium. Hauriri ut aqua poterat sed diffluere ut aqua non poterat. Stans autem ante ianuam ad ostendendum sancti meritum et aqua erat ad adiutorium et quasi aqua non erat ad invadendum locum. Mox constituti inter spem et metum maerorem et gaudium stantes quia iacentes non valebant rogabant ut qui aquam qui compescuit ne ingrederetur idem cogeret ut ad alveum suum regrederetur. Statim Athesis, velut hostis persequeretur, aufugit et obsidionem timidus[429] deseruit. Tunc divino mysterio attentius et religiosius acto omnes in via, aqua venerant hilares redierunt, sed aliqua pars muri civitatis ea coruscatione dirupta fuit et quae per apertam ianuam intrare non valuit firmissima propugnacula diminuit. Haec fama longe diffusa Gregorii calamum movit et Petro suo dialogice edidit et multi prius insolventes et renitentes effecti sunt religionis milites.

---

427 Possideatis] possidereatis *Aug.*
428 Confortati] conforati *Aug.*
429 Timidus] tumulus *Aug.*

Nunc[430] necessarium nobis videtur translationis[431] beati Zenonis seriem notificare, quia in gestione huius negotii, queadam[432] memoratu digna claruerunt. Quae tanslatio acta est cum[433] Rotaldus vir attributis personae praestantissimus pastoralem curam Veronae gerebat et Pippinus rex Karoli filius, quem Adrianus papa baptizavit, regnum Italicum regebat. Rex vero Veronam regali situ praeditam plus ceteris urbibus diligebat et cum episcopo sibi dilecto frequens colloquium habebat, qui dum quadam die pariter sancti Zenonis aedem ingrederentur et tam de auditis quam de visis mirabilibus huius loquerentur rationabiliter et digne proposuerunt ut magnum thesaurum humilius[434] quam oporteret positum decentius et sublimius locarent et ecclesiae angustiam[435] dilatarent. Aedificantes ecclesiam antrum opacum columnis subnixum et lapidibus pavimentatum[436] construxerunt. Ubi eminentem aggerem ex politis marmoribus ediderunt quem sacrosancti[437] tumulum corporis[438] devoverunt. Deinde rex cum praesule congregatis sacerdotibus et aliis sacris ordinibus in quibus respectu[439] bonitatis speraverant per multimodas orationes sanctum prius demulcentes ne illis motus irasceretur cum ingenti timore cubiculum aperuerunt. Qui adeo perterrefacti ut nullus tanti collegii tangere ossa praesumeret. Nam divinum quiddam[440] et valde timendum videbatur inde exalare quod horrorem inspiraverat et omnes circumstantes exanimaverat. Mox claudentes sepulcrum abierunt. Cumque[441] rex et pontifex quid acturi essent ambigerent ex multis quas ventilabant coniecturis haec[442] placuit, ut per quadraginta dies ter in ebdomada[443] omnis ordo utriusque sexus saecularis et ecclesiasticus cum ipso rege et episcopo ad specum sanctum reverenter ac sollemniter convenirent et Dei ac[444] confessoris clementiam uno voto efflagitarent ut cui tam reverenda motio conveniret[445] instillaret.

---

430 Translatio sancti Zenonis episcopi confessoris Ipso die aput Veronam translatio sancti Zenonis episcopi et confessoris *add. Aug* In translatione sancti Zenonis episcopi et confessoris Omnia dicuntur sicut in festo in mense december praeter VIII lectiones et excepto oratione *add. Kr.*
431 Translationis] translatio *Aug.*
432 Quaedam] omnia *Aug.*
433 Cum] tum *Aug.*
434 Humilius] *legi nequit Aug.*
435 Angustiam] angustam *corr. ex* angustiam *Aug.*
436 Pavimentatum] pavimentum *Aug.*
437 Sacrosancti] sacrosanctum *Kr.*
438 Corporis] corpori *Kr.*
439 Respectu] respectum *Aug.*
440 Quiddam] quidam *Kr.*
441 Cumque] cum *Aug.*
442 Haec] hoc *Aug.*
443 Ebdomada] ebdomoda *Kr.*
444 Ac] atque *Kr.*
445 Conveniret] convenirent *Kr.*

Dum[446] haec diligenti cura agerentur fama cuiusdam solitarii viri herbusculis et aqua paucoque pane pasti regi innotuit quod dum alacriter audivit episcopum vocavit celeriter. Elegerunt nuntios industrios[447] et providos, quibus hanc curam committerent. Qui venientes ad lacum qui Benacus dicitur ad remoti viri latibulum in eminenti specula situm angusto et periculoso calle aspirarunt.[448] Intuentes[449] autem virum Benignum nomine et discipulum eius qui Carus vocabatur, gavisi sunt gaudio magno. Audita legatione regis et episcopi ait legatis: „Revertimini in pace resalutantes[450] dominos vestros, carissime. Ego non parum tripudio quod ad illam sollemnitatem vocor et post paululum vos subsequor."[451] Mox[452] aediculam oraculi ingressus auxilium divinum imploravit, deinde ad itineris exercitium[453] se expedivit. Cum autem non longe a cellula progrederetur ecce merula alis coepit strepere, voce zinzulare et saepissime callem transvolitare et quasi sinistrum omen significare, ut virum Dei ab incepto revocaret.[454] Sed[455] vir ille, non ignorans hoc esse apparatum daemonis, merulam adiuravit ut nullum motum faceret donec ipse rediret. Ibi merula stetit immobilis velut esset insensibilis. Cum autem appropinquaret et rex cum episcopo et honestis viris illi obviaret honorifice susceptus, quid rex vellet audivit. Tunc ait: „Cum vota vestra a iusto proposito pendeant[456] Deum invenietis placabilem et successum bone petitionis ferentem."[457] Tunc ipsi cum electis aditum introeuntes lapidem removerunt. Nullus orationibus parcebat et eorum qui intus aderant et qui prae foribus manserant, sed eremita quamvis suis meritis et omnium adiutus precibus tamen tremebundus intravit et ossa beatissima baiolavit atque in mundissimo locello tale usui praeparato singula ordinabiliter posuit. Tanta vis odoris flagraverat ut nemo illorum tam suavem ante persenserat. Tunc rex sua et suorum instigatione permotus reliquiarum aliquid postulavit quod episcopus fieri denegavit at rex magis ac magis insistere et magna munera promittere tandem praesul non paucis neque parvis precibus victus acquievit. Integritate membrorum servata, nervorum et cineris ac vestimentorum particulas tribuit. Alia autem firmiter circumsepta annuloque sigillata condidit. Ad vocem psallentium Athesis litus resonuit intonuere campestria et ipsam aulam omnipotentis credimus esse gavisam. Dum circa ecclesiam gestaretur ut fieri solet praedicta praeconia resultabant. Multi languores corpora diu obsessa reliquerant. Ingens laetitia orta est die illa cuius similem nullus illius temporis viderat quia omnigenum curationum genera brevi

[446] Dum] *hic inc. lectio V Kr.*
[447] Industrios] industros *Kr.*
[448] Aspirarunt] *hic des. lectio V Kr.*
[449] Intuentes] *hic inc. lectio VI Kr.*
[450] Resalutantes] resultantes *Kr.*
[451] Subsequor] *hic des. lectio VI Kr.*
[452] Mox] *hic inc. lectio VII Kr.*
[453] Ad...exercitium] ad exercitium itineris *Kr.*
[454] Revocaret] *hic des. lectio VII Kr.*
[455] Sed] *hic inc. lectio VIII Kr.*
[456] Pendeant] pendent *Aug.*
[457] Ferentem] *hic desunt lectiones Kr.*

acta sunt tempore et prolixior facta processio fuit pro visione signorum. Sed rex et episcopus atque rupis incola pavidi sancta membra introduxerunt et in parato mausuleo[458] posuerunt.

Postquam pontifex reverenter missam celebrat, rex dote nobili Dei sponsam ditavit: Dedit ei proprietario iure monasterium sancti Petri qui Mauriatica dicitur cum omnibus possessionibus inibi pertinentibus; ecclesiam quoque sancti Andreae apostoli quae Incavi[459] nuncupatur cum familiis, montibus et silvis, pratis et vineis, arvis et sationalibus[460] et cunctis appendicibus, nec non et ecclesiam sancti Zenonis, quae iuxta lacum posita erat cum omnibus redditibus subiecit, Silvam quoque Mantico[461] tradidit. Vasorum argenteorum et aureorum anaglypha plurima, evangelium gemmarum atque margaritarum compositura et speciosa auri celatura editum donavit et alia quibus regalis dignitas effluebat. Cuius exempli sequaces nostri imperatores praefatum locum dilexerunt ac sua munera obtulerunt. Rotaldus praesul dives possessionum suis omnibus ecclesiam hereditavit nam et nobilium plurimi magnas portiones suarum facultatum certatim adhibuerunt. Unde antequam sol occumberet illa ecclesia ditissima facta est.

At vir Dei, avidus redeundi ad heremum, iter suum accelerabat. Hic dum domicilio appropinquaret vidit merulam in praecisa rupe iacentem, quam ratus quiescere et suum adventum praestolari accessit ut excitaret et eundi licentiam daret at illa iam exspiraverat. Vir bonus compatiens ei dixit: „Haec avicula daemonis instructu deliquit et quia irrationabilis erat ignoranter offendit. Venia, non morte digna fuit." Unde aerea imago merulea fusuli artefacta ibi huc usque dependet.

Videntes rex et pontifex virtutes Zenonis increbrescere et res eius velut amnis liquefacta nive crescere ut tutores et fidi procuratores summa ope nitebantur, ne locus fortunatus copia fieret macilentus orationis inopia. Ergo pari voto ut gemelli fratres monasterium olim actum augere sanxerunt. Erat illis communis cura probate vitae monachos ibi habitantes ad meliora provehere sicut artifex coronam acturus praestantes gemmas ac margaritas exornat, quibus opus ceptum perficiat. Non multo post Deo clavum gubernante seniores illos cum abbate eadem institutio et moralis gravitas tales exhibuit, quibus gubernaculum coenobiale regule mirifice servaretur et formula atque speculum sequacibus essent et ut boni patres bonos heredes efficerent. Iocundatur rex, iocundatur episcopus pullulantis segetis uberem fructum spectantes. Urbs et suburbana communiter huiusmodi contubernio gaudebant. Unde plures fallacis saeculi umbratilem auram vitantes ut couterini tantorum virorum fierent satagebant, quos non penuria id facere cogebat sed esuries et sitis sanctae conversationis inhiantes non minimas opes Zenoni ferentes monasticum habitum induerunt. Hoc modo locus

[458] Mausuleo] manseolo *Aug.*
[459] Incavi] Nycavi *Aug.*
[460] Sationalibus] sationabilibus *Aug.*
[461] Mantico] Mantyci *Aug.*

ille fortunatior et religiosior factus sub cuiusque Caesaris alis protectus est. Sed beatissimus confessor vires a Domino datas quam sepe excitans, multa memoratu, digna perficiens ex longinquis regionibus plures vocaverat; alios religione motos, alios aegritudinis necessitate coactos. Sed pretereamus omnia suorum per hoc opusculum diseramus aliqua.[462]

Quendam Tridentinum daemon ingressus, corporis et animi sibi vires vendicavit; nam nullum membrorum officium suum exercebat, cuius spumosum os non hominem sonabat et apertis oculis non videbat: ad quos cum hostis saeviens evolabat, sanguineos reddebat et horribiles. Occulta hominum fatebatur et multa, quae humanitas non erant, operebatur: erat omnibus mirabile spectaculum. Quem dum presbyter, ut moris est, adiuvarit, daemon eunuchum illum appellavit, quod vitium nondum notum erat circumstantibus. Tunc ille turpitudine inlati improperii erubuit et exivit. Ecce quidam diaconus daemonem adivit, et quasi ad ultionem presbyteri eum gravius adiuravit. Hunc daemon quasi notissimus agnovit et ex nomine vocavit et, ridiculus proditor, plura, quae levita commiserat, indicavit: unde aliquot sibi conscii non audebant accedere. Sic daemon quasi victoriosus sua ludibria excitabat. Mox quidam Zeno praepositus monasterii, quem ob religionis et sapientiae meritum Salomonem agnominabant, non ferens daemonis superbiam, dolens proditionis contumeliam, plus etiam invasi plasmatis iniuriam, aram sancti Zenonis amplexus, visceribus commotus, lacrimis irrigatus, orationem fudit, ne daemoniaca insultatio impunita transiret. Protinus daemon vim orationis persensit, et vas diu iniuratum invitus reliquit. Homo ille ingentes et illustres Deo ac sancto Zenoni gratias referens, damnosum hospitem fugatum esse gaudebat.

Praeterea Wilielmus, aridus et contractus, qui sicut quadrupes pronus manibus terram calcaverat, postquam praeconia multiplicis curaturae audivit, lectica illuc se vehere rogavit. Dum appropinquaret vestibulo templi, alienis susceptus ulnis humi depositus est. Pectus pugnis tundebat, vocem singultibus implebat, deterius dignus se esse dicebat. Tunc luminaria fecit accendere, et curvus ut bestia, quia rectus non valebat, genibus et palmis adversum altare coepit repere. Protinus divina virtus et ossa et nervos eius ingressa, artecticum morbum tetigit. Ille velut exanimis in terram corruit et diutius quasi sine spiritu iacuit ut iam crederetur mortuus. Repente consolidata sunt lineamenta corporis et flexurae et bases nodique omnes restituti. Confestim erigitur et ad aram cito proficiscitur. Fit consursus popularis, fit laus ac iubilatio spiritalis. Deo refertur gloria et omnipotentia, et inclito Zenoni clementia et magnificentia.

Cum fama virtutis nuntia circumquaque abiret, undique turba non minima maturabat, ceu greges ad agrum compascuum ubertatis plenum solent. Duo viri, unus erat Ioannes, alter erat Calvus, huc devecti, paralytici iacebant, socii itineris, socii passionis et curationis, quos diutina mora iam notos pluribus commendabat. Hi assidui ianuas ecclesiae observabant et sancti Zenonis nunc communibus, nunc

462 OMELIA Ego sum vitis vera *add. Aug* EVANGELIUM Ego sum vitis vera *Kr.*

alternis precibus auxilium implorabant. Illos dum nox et somnum opprimeret, pariter viderunt senem aspectus pulcherrimi, coloris vividi, quem canities instar nivis illustrabat, ex interioris templi aditu exeuntem virgamque in manu ferentem quam erexit, ambosque pulsavit et ait: „Satis diu in his cubiculis iacuistis; surgite et Deum salvatorem laudate." Mox abiit. Evigilantes mutua narratione quod viderant invicem conferebant. Confestim se sanitari redditos consenserunt. Protinus velociter surgentes, grandisonis laudibus Deo iubilarunt; qui timentes, si cito redirent, ne Deus illis ingratitudinem imputaret, diebus aliquot remanserunt, et quod illis evenerat fideliter notificabant.

Nec quoddam memorabile praeteribimus, quod Alberto Cenedensi contigit. Hunc dum feroces caperent hostes, daemon non capturae contenti gloria, nec aliis satiati flagitiis contra ius et fas inlatis, ignito ferro lumina combusserunt. Orbatus luce sedebat in tenebris repentinae privationis querulus, importunus nocte dieque Deum iudicem plorando implorabat. Dum consuetudo mali iam verecundiam minueret, a latebris prodire coepit, alieno ductus regimine, et non parvo tempore suum sequebatur ducem. Iam erat gravis atque odibilis suis, ut saepe Deum rogaret, ut sibi infelicem vitam truncaret. Cui repente fuit cordi ad sancti Zenonis praesidium festinare, tunc a cognatis et amicis subsidium itineris exigebat. At illi eum amentem vocabant, et ei pro tali petitione insultabant. Omissis reliquis, praevium suum, olim sibi pedagogum, misericorditer rogavit ut suis coeptis annueret. Mox ille paruit et quod herus suus vellet, se acturum spopondit. Incipit iter hilaris, sed alii ex suis, humaniter agentes, secum profecti sunt. Ductus est ad antrum, in quo prius Zeno quievit. Stratus humi flebilibus modis invocat ad quem venerat, ut consuetae medicinae iuvamen praeberet. Cum: „Miserere!" frequenter iteraret, inopinate circumstantes vidit. Repente se videre clamavit. Cumque qui secum venerant non crederent, alter alterum praesentabat, et quis esset et quid indueret explorabat. Dum index inquisitorum esset, omnes coeperunt plaudere et Deum et fidelem eius Zenonem laudare. Hoc audientes tortores illius, ducti poenitentia, eum audacter aggressi sunt, ut pro eius amore illis daret veniam, a quo et ipse consecutus est misericordiam. Ille impiger pepercit culpam nullamque recepit multam. Abbatem sancti Zenonis adiit, et loricam sancti Benedicti induit, ibique per quatuor lustra fideliter militavit.

Neque te silebo, Wezilla, daemone capta adhuc puella, quo sub teneris membris modo latente, modo fuerente facta es iuvencula. Haec parentibus debuerat esse solatium, sed erat illis inconsolabile spectaculum: quos daemon saepe fefellerat, se exiturum iurans, si ad illius aut illius sancti duceretur aram. Sic multo tempore spem illorum luserat et eorum studiosam curam fatigaverat. Sed ea tempestate, qua Sanguis Christi Mantuae inventus esse ferebatur, dum illuc a parentibus duceretur, digressionem ad Zenonis aedem fecerunt. Dum ingrederetur, daemon atrocius solito puellam concutiebat, velut eurus arbusculam et, ut erat terminus rogatium, magnus illuc populus psallendo praecedebat. Qui cum cerneret caput rotare, capillos volitare, manus et brachia vibrare, pedes saltare plures viros in una muliercula tenenda laborare, palmis erectis in aera omnes uno ore „Auxiliare Deus!“ clamarunt. Nullus tantae multitudinis huiusmodi studii abstinebat: videres alios pronos orare, alios misericorditer plorare, alios sacerdotes ad officium instigare, qua commotione omnis regia intonuit. Confestim fortior armatus venit et a domo propria abusivum eliminavit. O daemon, cum quanto dolore et quam magno clamore et quam sulphureo foetore lapsus es! Stetit in medio populi puella, pallida, perterrita, tremula, fatigata. Vix fari poterat, quae dudum omnes voce superbat; pedibus et omnibus membris vacillabat, quae dudum fortes viros fatigabat. Aberat ille qui vexavit et vires ingentes inspiravit. O quam magna laus et gloria et quanta ibi edita sunt praeconia!

Cum ille iniquus spiritus abiret, circumiens quem devoret, videt monachum manentem iuxta celsam turrim quae tunc aedificabatur, super quem de eminenti pinna lapidem devolvit et in vertice graviter vulneravit. Inde quasi mortuus a fratribus est sublatus et hoc habetur memoriale quod tam patens vulnus non fuit exitiale. Protinus velut sagitta praecipitavit se in mensam cuiusdam indigenae et quidquid erat in ea eminus, velut nimbosus turbo, dispersit. Deinde citius dicto irruit in plaustrum onustum spinis, quod nec ullum animal movebat, nec venti ulla visa erat. Tum perversus auriga huc rotabat, illuc exagitabat, ac si feroces tauri et indomiti iuncti iugo forent. His actis ludibriis illico impulit gubernatorem navis trasvehentis lapides ad spectabile aedificium sancti Zenonis, ratus et hominem in flumine demergere, et navim naufragare. At ille infra puppim ruit et navis sine iactura portum tenuit. Eodem momento ab Athesi ad amnem, qui Flubius dicitur, se intulit, aratoribus prope amoenam ripam meridiantibus; ubi dum pacifice sua tractarent nihilque rixarum apud illos esset, Satan illorum praecordia titillare coepit, unde quidam illorum insolenter locuti et arroganter, socios et familiares amicos ad contumeliam verba exagitarunt. Extemplo hostiliter animati, baculis graviter conflixerunt et, si militaria arma praesto forent, mutua strage perirent. Sed forte sacerdotes ibi aderant, qui mediastini atrociter saucios dirimerunt. In se reversi, alter alterius vulnera adhuc stillantia, quae ipsi fecerant, lavabant, et ex vestibus ligatures praecidentes, cum caritate et lacrimis plagas vinciebant. Deinde clam magis quam palam artifex dirus nocuit, qui magis dolis et technis quam viribus confidit. Protinus sacerdotes apertis indiciis Satan inter filios Dei venisse cognoverunt.

Lesungen der Zenoliturgie aus Cividale

Basiert auf den Handschriften: Cividale MAN XXI (*Civ²*), Cividale MAN XII (*Civ¹*), Civividale MAN XVI (*Civ³*)

Incipit vita sancti Zenonis confessoris[463]

Civ² Civ¹	*Civ³*
	In diebus Gallieni imperatoris in provincia Italia in civitate Verona beati Zenonis acta claruerunt. Sic enim est humana mentis ad investigandas sanctorum vitas tanquam quis sitiens ardore solis adustus concupiscat fontium fluenta, aut quis desiderantissimus nuntium audire cupiat vel etiam quis deliciarum epulis enutritus in quondam longiquo itinere positus ad solitam pervenire sui ventris satietatem cupiat. Ita et ego tanti virtutes quam vis ad omnia, quae egit vel in conversatione vel etiam in miraculis, explere non valeo. Attamen vel quod attingere pro parte possum enarrare non desisto. Et ne quis ille lector deroget aut audiens legentem desidioso animo detrahat cum scriptum sit „Qui retribuunt michi mala pro bonis, detrahunt michi."[464] Et quia ipse Dominus dixit bona operantibus „Priusquam te formarem in utero novi te et antequam exires de ventre sanctificavi te."[465]

Igitur Zenon[466] a cunabulis benedictus et[467] a ventre sanctificatus erat et ad hoc pertingere meruit ut vita sancta[468] pastor in populo esse mereretur et ideo quia

[463] Incipit…confessoris] Legenda sancti Zenonis episcopi confessoris *Civ¹* Vita sancti Zenonis episcopi et confessoris veronensis *in marg. paginae manu saec. XV Civ³*.

[464] qui...michi] *cf.* Ps. 37, 21: Qui retribuunt mala pro bonis, detrahebant mihi: quoniam sequebar bonitatem.

[465] priusquam...te] *cf.* Ier 1, 5.

[466] Igitur Zenon] ille *Civ³*.

[467] et] *om. Civ¹ Civ²*.

[468] vita sancta] per vitam sanctam *Civ³*.

in omnem terram exiit[469] sonus conversationis eius et sanctitas emicuit audiant populi eius qui[470] cupiunt miracula. Erat enim sedens in monastero in secretiori parte in opido veronensi[471] continuis ieiuniis et crebris orationibus a Domino petens, ut sibi dignaretur aditum praedicationis in populo aperire. Denique ad convertendas in Christi amore[472] animas hominum de die in diem deditus erat.[473] Revera quia in ipso spiritus sanctus doctor erat sicut[474] ipsa veritas per se loquitur dicens „Non enim estis vos qui loquimini“[475] et reliqua[476] et ut[477] illud „Ego sum pastor bonus“[478] et cetera.[479] Ita ergo in sermone[480] affabilis erat[481] et in habitu mitis ut Deus in ipso a quibus poterat videri collaudaretur at omnibus parentibus et venientibus ad se.[482] Ita alacer erat[483] ut mox relictis idolis Domino Ihesu Christo crederent. T[u autem…][484]

II Eodem vero tempore[485] cum iuxta eandem[486] civitatem Veronam, quae in propinquo erat itinere, egrediente eodem viro[487] Dei[488] a monasterio in fluvio Atesi piscationem dum ageret, erectis sursum oculis,[489] vidit de contra quendam hominem in plaustro[490] bobus subiecto[491] mergi in flumine. Tanta enim velocitate ferebatur, ut omnibus demonstraretur diaboli arte fuisse gestum.[492] Et quidem cum sanctus Dei vidisset[493] hoc factum diaboli esse, elevata sursum manu,[494] fecit[495] crucis signum[496] frequenti vice[497] dicens: „Revertere retro, Satanas, ne perdas animam, quam[498] Deus creavit.“ Quod signum diabolus ut vidit, evanuit velut fumus ita ut

---

469 exiit] exivit *Civ*^{3}.
470 eius qui] qui eius *Civ*^{1} *Civ*^{3}.
471 in oppido veronensi] oppidi veronensis *Civ*^{3}.
472 amore] amorem *Civ*^{3}.
473 erat] *om. Civ*^{3}.
474 sicut] in *add. Civ*^{3}.
475 non...loquimini] cf. Mt 10, 20.
476 et reliqua] sed spiritus patris vestri qui loquitur in vobis *Civ*^{3}.
477 ut] *om. Civ*^{1}.
478 ego...bonus] cf. Io 10, 14.
479 cetera] animam meam pono pro ovibus meis *Civ*^{3}.
480 sermone] sermonibus *Civ*^{3}.
481 erat] et in mansuetudine *add. Civ*^{3}.
482 a quibus…ad se] conlaudaretur ab hominibus venientibus ad se et *Civ*^{3}.
483 erat] *om. Civ*^{3}.
484 T[u autem]…] *om. Civ*^{1} *Civ*^{3}.
485 Eodem vero tempore] per idem vero tempus *Civ*^{3}.
486 eandem] *om. Civ*^{3}.
487 egrediente eodem viro] egrediens idem vir *Civ*^{3}.
488 Dei] *om. Civ*^{3}.
489 sursum oculis] oculis sursum *Civ*^{3}.
490 in plaustro] plaustro sedentem *Civ*^{3}.
491 subiecto] subiunctis *Civ*^{3}.
492 fuisse gestum] gestum fuisse *Civ*^{1}.
493 cum…vidisset] sanctus vir elevans oculos dum vidisset cognovit *Civ*^{3}.
494 elevata manu] levataque sursum manu *Civ*^{3}.
495 fecit] sancte *add. Civ*^{3}.
496 crucis signum] signum crucis *Civ*^{1}.
497 frequenti vice] frequenter *Civ*^{1}.
498 perdas…creavit] perimas hominem quem Deus creavit *Civ*^{3}.

cum[499] clamoribus ac stridore nefando quasi de alta rupe inrumperet[500] dicens: „Et siquidem nunc me non permittis[501] animas[502] hominum lucrari, tamen[503] paratus sum ire[504] in patrias mihi[505] notas quae circumquaque[506] sunt[507] ad impedimentum tuum.“ Tunc sanctus Dei Zenon ait: „Non te permittet[508] Dominus agere[509] adversus servum suum tamen conare quae[510] vis.“ T[u autem…][511]

III His ita actis, cum ululatu[512] et clamore discessit et[513] festinans daemon ingressus[514] palatium Gallieni, comprehensa[515] filia[516] eius, quae viro tunc in tempore erat tradenda et[517] parentibus unica erat, coepit crudeliter eam[518] vexare. Tunc miserabilis pater simulque tota regia domus[519] in tristitiam versa cruciatu affligebatur eo quod sic crudeliter suffocaretur.[520] Quae dum crudeli et continua[521] vexatione arrepta esset, coepit per os infantulae regis filiae daemon clamare dicens: „Non egrediar de[522] corpore isto, nisi Zenon[523] episcopus venerit et eam salvam reddat[524] ac per ipsius imperium egrediar.“ Mox vero ut hoc[525] rex Gallienus audivit missis apparitoribus ad perquirendum sanctum virum coepit sollicite ei demandare.[526] Tunc ex[527] iussu regis milites pergunt ad virum Dei. Ille enim sedebat super lapidem, qui proximus monasterio[528] erat et piscabatur in flumine. Venientes vero milites, quia inscii illius erant,[529] coeperunt sollicite interrogare sanctum Dei sacerdotem dicentes: „Quis es tu, homo Dei? Indica

---

499 cum] *om. Civ^3*.
500 inrumperet] irrumperet *Civ^1* irruperit *Civ^3*.
501 me non permittis] permittis me non hic *Civ^3*.
502 animas] peccatorum *add. Civ^3*.
503 tamen] tum *Civ^1*.
504 ire] *om. Civ^3*.
505 mihi] *om. Civ^3*.
506 circumquaque] circa quaque *Civ^3*.
507 sunt] ire *add. Civ^3*.
508 permittet] permittit *Civ^3*.
509 agere] aliquid *Civ^3*.
510 conare quae] certa quod *Civ^3*.
511 T[u autem]…] *om. Civ^1 Civ^3*.
512 ululato] *exp. et suprascr. alia manus* ullulatu *Civ^3*.
513 et] *om. Civ^3*.
514 ingressus] est demun *add. Civ^3*.
515 comprehensa] comprehensaque *Civ^3*.
516 filia] filiam *Civ^3*.
517 viro…et] *om. Civ^3*.
518 eam] *om. Civ^3*.
519 regia domus] domus regia *Civ^3*.
520 suffocaretur] et versaretur *add. Civ^3*.
521 et continua] *om. Civ^3*.
522 de] a *Civ^3*.
523 Zenon] Zeno *Civ^3*.
524 et reddat] *om. Civ^3*.
525 hoc] *om. Civ^3*.
526 ei demandare] investigare *Civ^3*.
527 ex] *sub macula Civ^2*.
528 qui proximus monasterio] qui in proximo monasterii *Civ^3*.
529 inscii illius erant] inscius illis erat *Civ^3*.

nobis si vidisti Zenonem episcopum, quem nos ex iussu regis perquirimus.“ At ille respondit eis[530] dicens: „Quamvis plura sint nomina in monasterio[531] de nomine isto quod vos inquiritis,[532] tamen cur[533] missi estis dicite. Ego enim quamvis tantillus servus tamen Christi sum Zenon.“[534] Tunc vero conferentes milites ad invicem dicebant:[535] „Quid multa colloquimur? Indicemus pro quo[536] missi sumus ad virum istum.“ Respondentes vero dixerunt: „Rogat te rex et te vult videre.“ Respondit Zenon:[537] „Quid meam vult humilitatem[538] rex, qui omnium christianorum inimicus esse non desistit?“ At illi dixerunt: „Ita enim rogat rex, ut filiam ipsius, quae a daemonio vexatur, sanam reddas, quia unica illi est.“ Ille vero dixit eis: „Dominus Ihesus Christus omnipotens est. Ite“ inquit, „en[539] ego subsequar[540] vos, quia Dei mirabilia oportet, ut omnibus manifestentur.“ Quo dicto abierunt milites.[541] Postea[542] vero exurgens sanctus sacerdos fecit orationem et perrexit[543] ubi cruciabatur rex[544] et affligebatur pro sua filia.[545] Qui sanctus Dei episcopus dum iter ageret ante pervenit, quam hi[546] qui missi fuerant milites. T[u autem...][547]

IIII Facto vero crucis signo ingrediente sacerdote palatium coepit mox per os infantulae daemon clamare dicens: „Ecce tu, Zenon[548], ad hoc[549] venisti ad expellendum me et ego stare[550] propter tuam sanctitatem non possum.“ Quo dicto tenens sacerdos manum puellae[551] dixit: „In nomine[552] Ihesu Christi[553] exi[554]

---

530 eis] *om. Civ³*.
531 monasterio] nostro *add. Civ³*.
532 inquiritis] dicitis *Civ³*.
533 cur] ad quod *Civ³*.
534 Zenon] Zeno vocor *Civ³*.
535 dicebant] intra se *add. Civ³*.
536 quo] quare *Civ³*.
537 Zenon] Zeno *Civ³*.
538 humilitatem] li *suprascr. Civ¹* videre *add. Civ³*.
539 en] ecce *Civ³*.
540 subsequar] subsequor *Civ³*.
541 abierunt milites] milites abierunt *Civ³*.
542 Postea] et *Civ³*.
543 perrexit] ad palacium *add. Civ³*.
544 rex] *om. Civ³*.
545 filia] rex *add. Civ³*.
546 hi] hii *Civ¹ Civ³*.
547 T[u autem]...] *om. Civ¹ Civ³*.
548 Zenon] Zeno *Civ³*.
549 ad hoc] *om. Civ³*.
550 stare propter tuam sanctitatem non possum] propter tuam sanctitatem stare non possum *Civ³*.
551 tenens sacerdos manum puellae] tenens manum puelle sacerdos *Civ³*.
552 nomine] domini *add. Civ³*.
553 christi] preacipio tibi] *add. Civ³*.
554 exi] ab ea *add. Civ³*.

daemon.“ At ille[555] respondit dicens publica voce[556]: „Etsi hinc[557] a[558] te[559] expulsus fuero, ecce[560] Veronam veniens[561] invenies me et eos qui presentes sunt impii[562] stantes in platea et expectantes te.“ Sanam vero reddens[563] [564] restituit regi[565] filiam. Quod vero factum ut vidit rex Gallienus admiratione comprehensus coronam regalem, quam in suo[566] capite habebat,[567] sancto sacerdoti obtulit dicens: „Tali medico qui sanam unicam filiam[568] meam restituit nullis[569] muneribus placere possum, nisi ut tota voluntate ipsam quam habeo coronam offeram ei.“[570] Quod factum dum gereretur audens[571][572] multitudo populi qui[573] ad palatium convenerant[574] ab errore conversi gentili crediderunt in Christum Ihesum Dominum nostrum petentes sacerdotem Christi ut docerentur[575] viam salutis et[576] baptismum[577] in[578] remissionem perciperent peccatorum et idola destruerentur et in Christi nomine construerentur basilicae.[579]

---

555 ille] illa *Civ³*.
556 respondit dicens puplica voce] publica voce cepit clamare *Civ³*.
557 hinc] huic *Civ³*.
558 a] ad *scr. sed exp.* d *Civ³*.
559 a te] ait *Civ¹*.
560 ecce] eo *Civ³*.
561 veniens] cum veneris illuc invenies me *Civ³*.
562 qui presentes sunt impii] in quibus habitem *Civ³*.
563 reddens] *om. Civ¹*.
564 sanam ...reddens] Christi itaque sacerdos sanam *Civ³*.
565 regi] regis *Civ³*.
566 in suo] *om. Civ³*.
567 habebat] gestabat *Civ³*.
568 filiam] *suprascr.* m_1 *Civ²*.
569 nullis] aliis *add. Civ³*.
570 ut tota voluntate ipsam quam habeo coronam offeram ei] ei ipsam quam habeo coronam meam offeram *Civ³*.
571 audens] audiens *Civ¹*.
572 Quod factum dum gereretur audens] Quod factum videns *Civ³*.
573 qui] que *Civ³*.
574 convenerant] convenerunt *Civ¹* convenerat *Civ³*.
575 docerentur] doceret eos *Civ³*.
576 et] ut *Civ³*.
577 baptismum] penitentie add. *Civ³*.
578 et] in *Civ³*.
579 et idola...basilice] *om. Civ³*.

Civ^{2} *Civ*^{1}

Rumor etiam populi pagani super eum saeviens ut impedimentum pateretur insultabat sed vigilans in servis suis Christus vincebat mendacia quia puram fidem tenebat in corde. T[u autem...][580]

Civ^{3}

At ubi sacerdos accepit coronam a rege statim distribuit pauperibus dicens: „Si Dominus operatur excelsa ipsi referatur et gloria.“ His ita gestis petiit beatus Zeno ut ei licentia tribueretur omnia ydola destruendi et in Christi nomine ecclesias fabricandi. Cuius precibus acquievit rex in omnibus quae ille poposcerat. Post hec ingressus sacerdos civitatem Veronam intrepidus praedicabat in Christi nomine vernum ut diaboli ydola destruerentur et in Christi nomine construerentur ecclesiae. Quo facto multitudo populi paganorum saeviens incessanter agebat, ut impedimentum Christi famulus pateretur sed vigilante in suis servis Christo vincebatur[581] mendacium, quod pura fides ab infidelium corde abgebat.

V Perfectis igitur his[582] revertens ad monasterium agebat[583] salutaria pro populi intercessione quod ab ineunte aetate in Christi amore[584] sollicitus fuerat.[585] Qui dum hoc iuxta Dei adiutorium ageret Dei voluntati quando placuit non post longum tempus[586] receptus est in pace.[587] Ob hoc[588] quia in miraculis omni populo claruit in honorem[589] Dei et[590] ipsius sancti sacerdotis quidam ex genere Gallieni fecit sancto nomini ipsius basilicam iuxta fluvium, quae[591] etiam nunc eminet[592] ubi nunc sanctum ipsius corpus requiescit qui etiam venerabilis locus in

580 T[u autem]...] *om. Civ*^{1}.
581 vincebatur] d *add. sed exp. manus*^{1}.
582 his] hiis *Civ*^{1}.
583 agebat] augebat *Civ*^{3}.
584 amore] agere *add. Civ*^{3}.
585 fuerat] erat *Civ*^{3}.
586 iuxta...tempus] instanter ageret Dei voluntati quando placuit non multo post *Civ*^{3}.
587 est in pace] in pace est *Civ*^{3}.
588 ob hoc] et *Civ*^{3}.
589 honorem] honore *Civ*^{3}.
590 et] in *add. Civ*^{3}.
591 quae] qui *Civ*^{2}.
592 iuxta fluvium...eminet] haud procul a fluvio *Civ*^{3}.

nomine Ihesu Christi[593] miraculis coruscat. Post vero aliquod tempus[594] dum die sancti natalicii ipsius devote populus una cum clero vel sacerdotibus ad missarum sollemnia cumvenissent fluvius ipse[595] ubi super ripam[596] reconditum esse dinoscitur[597] corpus subito tanta inundatione crevit,[598] ut aqua fluminis usque ad fenestras vel tectum excrevisset.[599]

Civ² *Civ¹*

Quod etiam factum videns populus admiratione comprehensus qui illic ad honorem Dei sancti sacerdotis convenerant fame sitique se perire clamabant T[u autem…][600]

VI Et cum tanta inundatione aquae velut murus circumquaque basilicae erectus esset intro aqua minime ingrediebatur. Tantum enim virtus orationis ipsius apud Deum obtinere poterat, ut quamvis aqua in speciem muri erecta esset, ingredi locum venerabilem non auderet.

Civ³

Cuius ecclesiae dum essent ianuae apertae aqua in eam minime intravit. Sicque stans aqua ecclesiae ianuam clausit ac si illud elementum liquidum in soliditatem parietis fuisset inmutatum. Quod etiam factum videns populus admiratione comprehensus, qui illic ad honorem Dei et sancti sacerdotis convenerat, „Fame sitique super me“ acclamabat. Cum ergo essent multi interius inventi et aquarum multitudine ecclesia omnis circumdata esset et ipsi unquam[601] possint partem egredi non haberent ibique, se siti et fame deficere formidarent ad ecclesiae ianuam veniebant et ad bibendum hauriebant aquam quae, ut praedixi, usque ad fenestras excreverat et tamen intra ecclesiam nullo modo diffluebat. Hauriri itaque ut aqua poterat, sed diffluere ut aqua non poterat, stans autem ante ianuam ad ostendendum cunctis meritum confessoris. Et aqua erat ad adiutorium et quasi non erat ad invadendum locum.

---

593 in nomine Ihesu Christi] in Christi nomine *Civ³*.
594 tempus] apud eadem urbem veronensem *add. Civ³*.
595 ipse] Athesis *Civ³*.
596 ripam] eius *add. Civ³*.
597 dinoscitur] dignoscitur *Civ¹*.
598 crevit] excrevit *Civ³*.
599 excrevisset] ascenderet *Civ³*.
600 T[u autem]…] *om. Civ¹*.
601 ipsi unquam] ipsum inquam *scr. Civ³*.

Et dum tanta esset inundatio, ut velut murus circum ianuas ecclesiae erectus esset, intus aqua minime ingrediebatur. Quanta enim putamus virtus orationis ipsius apud Deum optinere poterat cum et aqua in specie muri erecta erat et ingredi locum venerabilem non audebat.

Unde adcrevit veneratio et timor in[602] Christi sacerdotem, ut etiam, si fides exigat, infirmi curentur, daemoniaci veniant et liberentur, etsi quis ex vera fide[603] sanctum nomen eius[604] invocaverit[605] sine dubio eius petitio[606] adnuitur. Multi etenim[607] de longinquis[608] regionibus venientes obsessaque infirmitatum corpora habentes[609, 610] ad eius sanctum[611] sepulchrum iacentes per ipsius sancti sacerdotis[612] intercessionem ad propria cum sanitate et gaudio revertuntur.

Civ² Civ¹	*Civ³*
Ecce de multis eius miraculis ego inutilis coronatus notarius quod compertum tenui in parvo conclusi ne legentibus vel audientibus fastidium generarem quod tamen fulget agitur in veronensi[613] urbe migrante ipso ad Dominum	prestante Domino nostro Ihesu Christo

cui est honor et gloria in saecula saeculorum amen.

602 in] circa *Civ³*.
603 fide] inde *Civ³*.
604 nomen eius] eius nomen *Civ³*.
605 invocaverit] invocaverunt *Civ³*.
606 peticio] peticioni *Civ¹ Civ³*.
607 etenim] enim *Civ³*.
608 longinquis] longuinquis *scr. sed* u *exp. Civ³*.
609 obsessaque… habentes] obsessi infirmitate corpore *ex* corpora *corr.* corpore *et suprascr.* e *altera manus Civ³*.
610 habentes] et *add. Civ³*.
611 sanctum] *om. Civ³*.
612 sancti sacerdotis] *om. Civ³*.
613 veronensi] veronense *Civ²*.

Lesungen der Zenoliturgie in Bad Reichenhall
Basiert auf den Handschriften: München BSB Clm 23143 (*Mü¹*), München BSB Clm 24882 (*Mü²*)

Historia in depositione sancti Zenonis

I Tempore venerabilis Zenonis archiepiscopi mediolanensis[614] ecclesiae erat vir generosus praepotens et dives valde[615] stipatusque multa familia et omni honestate saeculari[616] in civitate Verona, qui usitatiori nobilitatis divitiarum et virtutum titulo vulgari dictus est magnus Zeno Veronensis et ille devotarum orationum frequentia una cum coniuge sua preclarissima filium a Deo heredem ut Anna Elchie[617] Samuelem impetraverunt. Quo concepto et nato ab utero matris est sanctificatus et in cunabulis a Deo benedictus. Et hunc beatissimum puerum Zenonem pro salute fidelium suorum, ne eis inimici praevaleret iniquitas aut ulla imminentium peccatorum seu periculorum vastitas elegit dignum pastorem et pium patronum atque de gentium potissimum tutorem. Tu [autem...][618]

II Hunc itaque infantulum ipse antiquus serpens diabolus humani generis inimicus a materno sinu in puerperio in principio suae nativitatis rapere et asportare una cum cunabulis et etiam auferre praesumpsit. Sed divina eum protegente gratia futurum Dei famulum dignum salutis nostrae intercessorem nullo modo laedere potuit. Sed Mediolanum[619] et ibidem intra septa ecclesiae cathedralis iuxta aulam archiepiscopalem vagientem infantem loco in abdito in cunabulis exsulem expositum reliquit. Haec autem sua cunabula metallis[620] et lapidibus praetiosis erant intexta et subtili[621] opere fabricata a patris magnificentia titulo[622] marginibus et fastiis insculpta tali: Hic est filius[623] magni Zenonis incolae nobilis Veronensis.[624] T[u autem...][625]

III Porro ipse diabolus se ipsum fraudulenter mille artifex simulans filium a Deo datum et a patre petitum pro eodem nuper nato puero et, ut supra dictum est, alienato vice sinui materno ingessit cunabulis, ut praemittitur pariter, et infantulo asportatis. Ille autem deceptor vorago et insatiabilis cruenta bestia et non homo, sed diabolus maternis uberibus pariter et nutricum plurimarum lactis alimonia nec studiosissima contrectatione seu custodia nec uberrima provisione contentus, sed frequenter eiulans, fremens, mordens ac stridens ac naturae suae

614 Mediolanensis] *sub macula Mü²*.
615 Valde] *sub macula Mü²*.
616 Saeculari] *sub macula Mü²*.
617 Elchie] sic *Mü¹ Mü²*.
618 Tu autem...] *om. Mü²*.
619 Mediolanum] vexit *suprascr. Mü²*.
620 Cunabula metallis] *sub macula Mü²*.
621 Intexta et subtili] *sub macula Mü²*.
622 Magnificentia titulo] *sub macula Mü²*.
623 Hic est filius] *sub macula Mü²*.
624 Veronensis] *sub macula Mü²*.
625 Tu autem...] *om. Mü²*.

diabolicae impetu inquietus totius regionis copiam lactis in infantium pariter per temporum momenta carnes caprarum, vaccarum et omnium caeterorum brutorum universas tamquam, qui initiaverunt Beelphegor et comederunt sacrificia mortuorum[626] mirando appetitu immoderatissime devorabat. Itaque ut generosi parentes divites maestissime facti aggravati et depauperati in rerum suorum facultate deficere vicissim coeperunt. T[u autem...][627]

IV Et in hoc eventu spiritu tribulationis et maeroris inenarrabilium gemituum patientia divinam consolationem praestolantes venditis sigillatim omnium rerum suarum facultatibus civitatibus villarum et praediorum universorum et impensis atque consumptis auro et argento pro ipsius[628] fere educatione, qui nec mori potuit nec vivendo profecit, sed deformior specie crudelior more tortuosior habitudine est insolentior detestabili, mansuetudine tam aetate quam saevitia peior crevit, pessimus permansit. Ad tantam irrecuperabilem egestatem et inopiam praemissa deceptoris[629] inaudita voracitate devenerunt, ut etiam in opprobrium et disputationem[630] et contemptum consanguineis sicuti beatus Iob uxori et amicis aut Tobias de operibus pietatis et sepultura mortuorum inciderunt. Ac tandem in omnis plebis abiectionem, ut in rure vili tugurio urgerentur lamentabiliter egere et mendicando pro se et deceptore educando comportare necessaria. Tu [autem...]

V Ambulans autem[631] venerabilis pater Zeno archiepiscopus praefatus secundum consuetudinem suae laudabilis devotionis oraturus[632] pro populi salute et omni fidelium animarum requie et luce perpetua iuxta locum et in loco dedicato, quo beatus infans a diabolo in cunis erat relictus vagientis ipsius pueri balatum audivit, qui tanta[633] voce[634] rimatur et deprehendit humanam et locum exploret animosius accessit puerum vagientem[635] elegantem in[636] insolito loco expositum invenit et excepit sculptura[637] quoque cunabulorum pretiosorum quis puer sit sufficienter edoceret[638] gaudet et sub sua cura[639] sollicite, ut Samaritanus vulneratum semivivum relictum stabulario. [Tu autem...]

---

626 initiaverunt...mortuorum] *cf.* Ps 105, 28 et initiati sunt Beelphegor et comederunt sacrificia mortuorum.

627 Tu autem...] *om. Mü²*.

628 Ipsius] pessime *suppl. in marg. Mü²*.

629 Deceptoris] praeceptoris *Mü²*.

630 Et disputationem] *om Mü²*.

631 Ambulans autem] *super rasuram Mü¹*.

632 Oraturus] *sub macula Mü²*.

633 Tanta] tante *Mü¹*.

634 Voce] vocem *Mü²*.

635 Vagientem] *om. Mü¹*.

636 In] *suprascr. Mü²*.

637 Sculptura] l *suprascr. Mü¹*.

638 Edoceret] edocet *Mü²*.

639 Cura] *om. Mü¹*.

VI Sic ille nutrici puerum studiose lactandum favendum[640] commisit et educandum.[641] Tandem[642] litterarum studio abilem applicuit ita ut perficiens trivio et quadrivio pariter nigromantiae peritia super omnes docentes se in studio quatuor annorum tempore pluribus suis consortibus praeferebatur, inter quos talem se tum exibuit, ut ab omnibus amaretur. Reversus[643] itaque a studio laetus a venerabili praesule Zenone[644] archiepiscopo suscipitur et quia sapientia et scientia[645] pariter consiliorum maturitate morum atque virtutum[646] disciplina, fide, constantia et omni discretione in agendis[647] pollebat praeclarus valde curiae archiepiscopi praeficitur[648] dispensator. Medio itaque[649] tempore contigit beatum adolescentem cum pueris nobilibus Veronam[650] terrae qui[651] curiae et[652] disciplinae ipsius archiepiscopi clientuli[653] bonis moribus et virtutibus imbuendi fuerunt commissi lusibus et iocis curiosior immorari. T[u autem...][654]

3.4 Rekonstruktionen

3.4.1 Rekonstruktion 1: Das Zeno-Offizium am Veroneser Dom ab dem Ende des 10. Jahrhunderts

Die folgende tabellarische Darstellung macht das Offizium für Zeno nicht nur als Konvolut von Texten, sondern auch als aufgeführtes Ganzes nachvollziehbar. Hierfür werden in der linken Spalte neben den Texten die Struktur des Stundengebets durch die Benennung der Gebetszeiten (Vesper, Matutin, Laudes und so weiter) und die Elemente des Ritus (wie Versikel, Antiphonen, Responsorien) aufgelistet. In der mittleren Spalte werden diejenigen textlichen Bausteine abgedruckt, die nicht veränderlich sind. Einige wurden tagtäglich bei der Feier des Stundengebets rezitiert, andere, wie zum Beispiel die Psalmen, wurden dem jeweiligen Fest angepasst. Da es sich hierbei um biblische und daher feststehende Texte handelt, werden diese auch in der mittleren Spalte abgedruckt. Der Text der Elemente in dieser mittleren Spalte wird beim ersten Vorkommen ganz abge-

640 Favendum] fovendum *Mü*2.
641 educandum] *hic des. lectio V Mü*2.
642 Tandem] *hic inc. lectio VI Mü*2.
643 Reversus] *sub macula Mü*2.
644 Venerabilis...Zenone] *sub macula Mü*2.
645 Sapientia et sciencia] *sub macula Mü*2.
646 Virtutum] *sub macula Mü*2.
647 In agendis] *sub macula Mü*2.
648 Praeficitur] *sub macula Mü*2.
649 Itaque] a *suprascr. Mü*1.
650 Veronam] Varonum *Mü*1.
651 Qui] *sub macula Mü*2.
652 Et] *om. Mü*1 *suprascr. Mü*2.
653 Clientuli] cleenculi *Mü*1.
654 Evangelium quaere in festo sancti Nicolai *Mü*1 Evangelium de confessore et pontifice *Mü*2.

druckt, bei allen weiteren aus Platzgründen nur durch Incipit angegeben. In der rechten Spalte befinden sich die Texte, die spezifisch auf Zeno zugeschnitten sind. Diese wurden entweder für das Zeno-Offizium neu verfasst oder aus Offizien für andere Heilige, aber auch aus dem Commune entnommen und mit Bezug auf Zeno – zum Beispiel durch Namensnennung – angepasst.

Für diese Rekonstruktion wurden, wie oben erwähnt, unterschiedliche liturgische Handschriften konsultiert: zum einen der Veroneser Liber ordinarius oder *Carpsum*, die Handschrift Verona BC XCIV(89). Dieser gibt im Großen und Ganzen, wie oben schon gezeigt wurde, die Liturgie des Veroneser Doms des späten 10. und 11. Jahrhunderts wieder, auch wenn er erst gegen Mitte des 11. Jahrhunderts verfasst wurde. Hier ist der Text jedoch nur unvollständig überliefert: Der Liber ordinarius gibt, wie für diese Textgattung üblich, nur die Incipits der Gesänge wieder. Deswegen wurde die Handschrift Verona BC XCVIII(92), ein Antiphonar des frühen 11. Jahrhunderts, hinzugezogen, die ein vollständiges Zeno-Offizium bietet. Auf diesen zwei Handschriften basiert nicht nur die Rekonstruktion der Texte von Antiphonen, Responsorien und Versikeln, sondern auch die der Psalmenreihe der Matutin für das Zenofest, da diese im *Carpsum* und im Antiphonar explizit angegeben wird. Der Text der Psalmen wurde gemäß der Vulgata ergänzt.

Für die Lesungen wurde der Text von BHL 9007 abgedruckt, und zwar in seiner frühesten Textfassung, die in den Handschriften aus Novara (Novara BC II und Novara BC LXIII) überliefert ist. Der Text wird in der Rekonstruktion nach den Angaben von Novara BC LXIII gegliedert, da er hier vollständig überliefert ist und darüber hinaus mit einem weiteren hagiographischen Lektionar (Paris BN Lat. 9739) nahezu perfekt übereinstimmt, das sicherlich aus Verona stammt, wie die Tatsache belegt, dass neben den Lesungen für das Zenofest auch die Lesungen für das Fest der Märtyrer Firmus und Rusticus auf 82r–88r überliefert sind. Bemerkenswert ist in diesem Zusammenhang die Tatsache, dass in Verona auch der Prolog für die Lesung der Matutin vorgesehen war, und zwar als erste Lesung der ersten Nokturn. Dies umso mehr, weil der Prolog keine Informationen über das Leben des Heiligen enthält, sondern die Arbeitsweise des Autors thematisiert.[655] Die Verteilung des Lesestoffs beginnt mit dem Prolog. Anschließend ist der ganze Vitatext auf die neun Lesungen verteilt.[656] Nach dem Prolog sind bis einschließlich Lesung 5 und Responsorium 5 die Leseabschnitte thematisch an das darauffolgende Responsorium angepasst. Ab der Lesung 6 ergibt sich eine kleine Verschiebung, so dass die Lesungen im Verhältnis zu den Responsorien einen Schritt voran sind und Episoden des Lebens Zenos erzählen, die nicht im unmittelbar folgenden Responsorium besungen werden. So wird zum Beispiel

655 Vgl. Snijders: Celebrating with Dignity, S. 123.

656 Damit handelt der Redaktor und Gestalter des Zeno-Offiziums in Linie mit der üblichen Praxis: Eine Untersuchung von hochmittelalterlichen hagiographischen Lektionaren und liturgischen Vitensammlungen aus benediktinischen Klöstern des flandrischen und nordfranzösischen Raums zeigte, dass in den meisten Handschriften die Heiligenviten auf identische Weise wie in Verona als Lesungen aufbereitet wurden. Vgl. ebd., S. 121.

der zweite Teil der Teufelsvertreibung und der Rettung des Bauern gegen Ende der Lesung 5 erzählt, besungen wird sie erst im Responsorium 6, während Responsorium 5 noch beim ersten Teil der Geschichte verweilt. Ebenso wird die Rettung der Tochter des Gallienus in Lesung 7 gehört, aber sie wird erst im Responsorium 8 besungen. Vom Tod von Zeno und dem Bau einer Basilika, in der er bestattet wurde, wird in den Lesungen erzählt, er wird aber in keinem Responsorium der Historia im kanonikalen Cursus erwähnt. Dieses vielfältige Abrufen von Themen und Formulierungen zwischen Lesungen und Responsorien erzeugt einen wichtigen Resonanzeffekt in der Performanz des Offiziums, der hier durch die Rekonstruktion nachvollziehbar wird.

Basiert auf den Handschriften: Verona BC XCIV(89), Verona BC XCVIII(92), Novara BC LXIII

Gebetszeiten und Elemente des Ritus	**Feststehende Bestandteile**	**Individuelle Bestandteile**
Festanlass		**Depositio/Natale sancti Zenonis episcopi**
I Vesper		
Eröffnungsversikel	V. *Deus in adiutorium meum intende* R. *Domine ad adiuvandum me festina* *Gloria patri et filio et spiritui sancto, sicut erat in principio et nunc et semper et in saecula saeculorum. Amen* *alleluia*[657] / *Laus tibi Domine rex aeterne gloriae*	
5 Antiphone – 5 Psalmen		[nicht überliefert, wahrscheinlich aus dem Commune sanctorum]
Kurzlesung + Responsorium		[nicht überliefert, wahrscheinlich aus dem Commune sanctorum]
Hymnus		[nicht überliefert, wahrscheinlich aus dem Commune sanctorum]
Versikel		[nicht überliefert, wahrscheinlich aus dem Commune sanctorum]

[657] Das Alleluia wird während der Fastenzeit zwischen Septuagesima und Ostern nicht gesungen. Es wird in dieser Zeit im Eröffnungsteil des Offiziums durch *Laus tibi Domine* ersetzt. Vgl. Harper: The Forms and Orders, S. 78.

M-A1		Dum Zeno pontificatus honore valde polleret, meritis non paucis existentibus, Gallieni caesaris filiam a ruinosa peste Dei virtute sanavit.
Magnificat (Lc 1, 46-55)	*Magnificat anima mea Dominum, et exsultavit spiritus meus in Deo salutari meo. Quia respexit humilitatem ancillae suae. Ecce enim ex hoc beatam me dicent omnes generationes. Quia fecit mihi magna, qui potens est, et sanctum nomen eius. Et misericordia eius a progenie in progenies timentibus eum. Fecit potentiam in brachio suo, dispersit superbos mente cordis sui. Deposuit potentes de sede et exaltavit humiles. Esurientes implevit bonis et divites dimisit inanes. Suscepit Israel puerum suum, recordatus misericordiae suae. Sicut locutus est ad patres nostros, Abraham et semini eius in saecula.*	
Kyrie	*Kyrie eleison. Christe eleison. Kyrie eleison.*	
Pater noster	*Pater noster, qui es in caelis, sanctificetur nomen tuum; adveniat regnum tuum. Fiat voluntas tua sicut in caelo et in terra. Panem nostrum quotidianum da nobis hodie et dimitte nobis debita nostra, sicut et nos dimittimus debitoribus nostris.* V. *Et ne nos inducas in tentationem;* R. *Sed libera nos a malo.* [*Quia tuum est regnum et potentia et gloria in saecula saeculorum*] *Amen.*	
Preces		[nicht überliefert]

Oratio	*Oremus…Amen*	[nicht überliefert]
Entlassung: Segnung und Antwort	V. *Dominum vobiscum* R. *Et cum spiritu tuo* V. *Benedicamus Domino* R. *Deo gratias*	
Matutin		
Eröffnung	V. *Domine labia mea...* R. *Et os meum...* *V. Deus in adiutorium... R. Domine ad adiuvandum Gloria patri...in saecula saeculorum. Amen.* *Alleluia* (von Septuagesima bis Osterwoche: *Laus tibi Domine*)	
I		Regem confessorum adoremus, qui caelestis regni meritum et gloriam contulit sancto suo Zenoni.
Psalm 94	*Venite, exsultemus Domino; iubilemus Deo salutari nostro; praeccupemus faciem eius in confessione, et in psalmis iubilemus ei quoniam Deus magnus Dominus, et rex magnus super omnes deos; quia in manu eius sunt omnes fines terrae, et altitudines montium ipsius sunt; quoniam ipsius est mare, et ipse fecit illud, et siccam manus eius formaverunt. Venite, adoremus, et procidamus, et ploremus ante Dominum qui fecit nos, quia ipse est Dominus Deus noster, et nos populus pascuae eius, et oves manus eius. Hodie si vocem eius audieritis, nolite obdurare corda vestra sicut in irritatione, secundum diem tentationis in deserto, ubi tentaverunt me patres vestri, probaverunt me, et viderunt opera mea. Quadraginta annis offensus fui generationi illi; et dixi: Semper hi errant corde. Et isti non*	

	cognoverunt vias meas: ut iuravi in ira mea, si introibunt in requiem meam.	
Hymnus		[nicht überliefert]
I. Nokturn		
A1		Ab utero matris fuit sanctificatus beatus Zeno et a cunabulis benedictus.
Psalm	[Ps. 1] *Beatus vir qui non abiit in consilio impiorum, et in via peccatorum non stetit, et in cathedra pestilentiae non sedit, sed in lege Domini voluntas eius, et in lege eius meditabitur die ac nocte. Et erit tamquam lignum quod plantatum est secus decursus aquarum, quod fructum suum dabit in tempore suo et folium eius non defluet; et omnia quaecumque faciet prosperabuntur. Non sic impii, non sic; sed tamquam pulvis quem projicit ventus a facie terrae. Ideo non resurgent impii in iudicio, neque peccatores in concilio iustorum, quoniam novit Dominus viam iustorum; et iter impiorum peribit.*	
A2		Probitatis et scientiae iugibus incrementis ad hoc pertingere meruit ut per sacerrimam vitam pastor in populis efficeretur.
Psalm	[Ps. 2] *Quare fremuerunt gentes, et populi meditati sunt inania? Astiterunt reges terrae, et principes convenerunt in unum adversus Dominum, et adversus Christum eius. Dirumpamus vincula eorum et projiciamus a nobis iugum ipsorum. Qui habitat in caelis irridebit eos, et*	

	Dominus subsannabit eos. Tunc loquetur ad eos in ira sua, et in furore suo conturbabit eos. Ego autem constitutus sum rex ab eo super Sion, montem sanctum eius, praedicans praeceptum eius. Dominus dixit ad me: Filius meus es tu; ego hodie genui te. Postula a me, et dabo tibi gentes haereditatem tuam, et possessionem tuam terminos terrae. Reges eos in virga ferrea, et tamquam vas figuli confringes eos. Et nunc, reges, intelligite; erudimini, qui iudicatis terram. Servite Domino in timore, et exsultate ei cum tremore. Apprehendite disciplinam, nequando irascatur. Dominus, et pereatis de via iusta. Cum exarserit in brevi ira eius, beati omnes qui confidunt in eo.	
A3		Continuis ieiuniis et orationibus crebris a Domino petebat ut sibi aditum praedicationis in populos aperiret.
Psalm	[Ps. 3] *Domine, quid multiplicati sunt qui tribulant me? Multi insurgunt adversum me; multi dicunt animae meae: Non est salus ipsi in Deo eius. Tu autem, Domine, susceptor meus es, gloria mea, et exaltans caput meum. Voce mea ad Dominum clamavi; et exaudivit me de monte sancto suo. Ego dormivi, et soporatus sum; et exsurrexi, quia Dominus suscepit me. Non timebo millia populi circumdantis me. Exsurge, Domine; salvum me fac, Deus meus. Quoniam tu percussisti omnes adversantes mihi sine causa; dentes peccatorum contrivisti. Domini est salus; et super populum tuum benedictio tua.*	

Versikel		Voce mea ad Dominum clamavi, et exaudivit me de monte sancto suo.
Responsio		[nicht überliefert]
Pater noster	*Pater noster, qui es in caelis...*	
Absolution		[nicht überliefert]
Segnung		[nicht überliefert]
L1		Olim peritissimorum disciplinabilis mos extitit virorum indagatione diligenti sanctorum vitas exquirere earumque seriem stili officio sollicite ac rationabiliter memoriae posteritati assignare, quatenus ob suae studium doctrinae ipsorum in orbe imitatione potirentur et eorum quandoque consortio in perhennis vitae gloria fruerentur. Sic etenim instat sapientis mens ad investigandas sanctorum vitas, tamquam si aliquis sitiens ardore solis adustus, avide fontium concupiscat fluenta, vel etiam si quis desideratissimum ex remota regione audire ambiat nuntium, aut certe si quilibet deliciarum dapibus enutritus, in quodam longinquo itinere positus esuriens, ad solitam sui cupiat ventris pervenire satietatem.
R1		Hic est sacer antistes Zeno quem gemina virtute Dominus sanctitatis et sapientiae decoravit, cuius praeclara fulserunt in mundum miracula et in celis

		adeptus est angelorum commercia alleluia V Iste est qui ante Deum magna virtutes operatus est et omnis terra doctrina eius repleta est. Et in celis adeptus est angelorum commercia.
Segnung		[nicht überliefert]
L2		Nos itaque licet eis, qui talia conscripsere, simus scientia impares, et penitus ad exprimenda, quae gestimus inefficaces, quoniam rei materiam verborum compositio non aequiperat, ea tamen, quae de beati Zenonis virtutibus vel scriptis vel faminibus ediscere valuimus disseramus. In diebus imperatoris Gallieni, qui per successiones caesarum vigesimus septimus in eorum est catalogo subrogatus, quo etiam tempore, Dionisius vir reverentissimus a beato Petro apostolo vigesimus tertius Romanae praesidebat ecclesiae, in provincia Italia in civitate Verona beati Zenonis acta claruentur. Cuius viri virtutes ad liquidum, quas in conversatione vel in miraculis peregit, explicare non sufficientes, aliquas tamen iuxta quod attingere possumus, ennarrare veridica ratione conamur.
R2		Ab utero sanctificatus beatus Zeno et a cunabulis benedictus, ad hoc pertingere meruit ut pastor in populis per sacerrimam vitam efficeretur alleluia alleluia.

		V In omnem terram sonus exiit conversationis eius et sanctitas luculenter emicuit. Per sacerrimam vitam efficeretur.
Segnung		[nicht überliefert]
L3		Fuit quippe a matris utero sanctificatus, et a cunabulis benedictus, ut assertione divina in eo repeti videretur, quod Hieremiae dictum est: „Priusquam te formarem in utero, novi te et antequam exires de ventre sanctificavi te.“ Denique probitatis atque scientiae iugibus incrementis ad hoc pertingere meruit, ut per sacerrimam vitam fieri pastor in populo mereretur. Nempe audiant populi omnes, qui eius cupiunt nosse miracula, quia in omnem terram sonus exiit conversationis eius et sanctitas luculenter emicuit. Erat enim sedens in monasterio in secretiori parte oppidi Veronensis, continuis ieiuniis et orationibus crebris a Domino petens, ut sibi dignaretur aditum melliferae praedicationis in populos aperire. Igitur ad convertendas in amorem Christi animas hominum die noctuque deditus erat. Revera quoniam sanctus ei spiritus purarum illuminator mentium doctor existebat, sicut ipsa veritas loquitur dicens: „Non enim vos estis, qui loquimini, sed spiritus patris vestri, qui loquitur in vobis.“
R3		In secretiori parte oratorii continuis ieiuniis et crebris orationibus a Domino petebat ut sibi

		dignaretur aditum praedicationis in populos aperiret alleluia alleluia. V Ad convertendas in amore Cristi animas hominum die noctuque deditus erat. Ut sibi dignaretur aditum praedicationis in populos aperire.
II. Nokturn		
A4		Affabilis ita erat in sermonibus et in habitu mitis ut Deus in ipso conlaudaretur ab omnibus venientibus ad se.
Psalm	[Ps. 4] *Cum invocarem exaudivit me Deus, iustitiae meae in tribulatione dilatasti, mihi miserere mei et exaudi orationem meam. Filii hominum usquequo gravi corde ut quid diligitis vanitatem et quaeritis mendacium. diapsalma et scitote quoniam mirificavit Dominus sanctum suum. Dominus exaudiet me cum clamavero ad eum. Irascimini et nolite peccare quae dicitis in cordibus vestris in cubilibus vestris conpungimini. Sacrificate sacrificium iustitiae et sperate in Domino multi dicunt quis ostendet nobis bona. Signatum est super nos lumen vultus tui domine dedisti laetitiam in corde meo. A fructu frumenti et vini et olei sui multiplicati sunt. In pace in id ipsum dormiam et requiescam. Quoniam tu, Domine, singulariter in spe constituisti me.*	
A5		Dum exercitio piscationis fungeretur in fluvio vidit quendam hominem in plaustro sedentem per preces in amnem dimergi.

Psalm	[Ps. 5] *Verba mea auribus percipe, Domine, intellege clamorem meum. Intende voci orationis meae rex meus et Deus meus, quoniam ad te orabo: Domine mane exaudies vocem meam. Mane adstabo tibi et videbo quoniam non Deus volens iniquitatem tu es. Neque habitabit iuxta te malignus neque permanebunt iniusti ante oculos tuos. Odisti omnes qui operantur iniquitatem perdes omnes; qui loquuntur mendacium, virum sanguinum et dolosum abominabitur Dominus ego autem in multitudine misericordiae tuae. Introibo in domum tuam adorabo ad templum sanctum tuum in timore tuo. Domine deduc me in iustitia tua propter inimicos meos dirige in conspectu meo viam tuam. Quoniam non est in ore eorum veritas cor eorum vanum est. Sepulchrum patens est guttur eorum linguis suis dolose agebant iudica illos Deus. Decidant a cogitationibus suis secundum multitudinem impietatum eorum expelle eos quoniam inritaverunt te Domine. Et laetentur omnes qui sperant in te, in aeternum exultabunt et habitabis in eis. Et gloriabuntur in te omnes qui diligunt nomen tuum quoniam tu benedices iusto. Domine ut scuto bonae voluntatis coronasti nos.*	
A6		Vir Dei, elevata sursum manu, fecit signum crucis dicens: „Revertere retro Sathanas, ne perimas hominem quem Deus creavit.“
Psalm	[Ps. 8] *Domine Dominus noster quam admirabile est nomen tuum in universa terra! Quoniam elevata est magnificentia tua super caelos. Ex ore infantium et*	

	lactantium perfecisti laudem propter inimicos tuos, ut destruas inimicum et ultorem. Quoniam videbo caelos tuos; opera digitorum tuorum, lunam et stellas quae tu fundasti. Quid est homo quod memor es eius? aut filius hominis quoniam visitas eum? Minuisti eum paulo minus ab angelis, gloria et honore coronasti eum et constituisti eum super opera manuum tuarum. Omnia subiecisti sub pedibus eius, oves et boves universas, insuper et pecora campi, volucres caeli et pisces maris qui perambulant semitas maris. Domine Dominus noster quam admirabile est nomen tuum in universa terra!	
Versikel		Posuisti, Domine, super caput eius coronam de lapide pretioso.
Responsio		[nicht überliefert]
Pater noster	*Pater noster, qui es in caelis...*	
Absolution		[nicht überliefert]
Segnung		[nicht überliefert]
L4		Ita sane affabilis erat in sermone, et in mansuetudine, seu in habitu mitis, ut iure Deus in ipso collaudaretur ab omnibus venientibus ad se, ita alacer et splendifico nitore facundiae vividus, ut mox ad eum properantes relictis idolis et pravitate gentilitatis exempti Domino crederent Iesu Christo. Per idem tempus iuxta urbem Veronam, dum egrediens idem vir a monasterio in Atesi fluvio

		piscationis exercitio fungeretur erectis sursum oculis vidit ex adverso quendam hominem in plaustro sedentem bobus subiunctis per praeceps in amnem dimergi. Tanta quippe miserabilis velocitate ferebatur, ut palam cunctis cernentibus daretur intellegi, hoc diaboli arte fuisse peractum. Sanctus itaque vir, dum intentis luminibus hoc a longe prospiceret, cognovit limphaticam viri ruinam factum diaboli esse. Interea vir Dei elevata sursum manu fecit sanctae crucis signum frequenti vice et dixit: „Revertere retro Sathana, ne perimas hominem quem Deus creavit.“ Quod videlicet signum ut diabolus aspexit, velut fumus vento raptatus evanuit et clamoribus nimiis ac stridore nefando, quasi de alta rupe cum impetu decideret ait: „Etsi non hic me permittis animas hominum mea obsessione lucrari, tamen paratus sum in patrias notas circumquaque sitas, ad tuum perniciter abire impedimentum.“
R4		Affabilis ita erat in sermonibus et mansuetudinem atque habitu mitis ut Deus in ipso conlaudaretur ab omnibus ad se venientibus. V Ita existebat alacer ut mox ad eum properarent relictis idolis Domino crederent Iesu Christo. Ut Deus in ipso conlaudaretur ab omnibus ad se venientibus.
Segnung		[nicht überliefert]

L5		Sanctus autem Dei Zeno dixit: „Non te permittit Dominus dire aliquid agere adversus servum suum.“ His ita peractis, cum detestabili ululatu et clamore discessit. Festinans itaque daemon ingressus est concite palatium caesaris Gallieni arreptamque filiam eius, quae tunc temporis unica parentibus erat, coepit crudeliter vexare. Miserabilis ergo pater, simulque tota domus regia in tristiam versa, cruciatu et maerore ingenti affligebantur, eo quod tam acriter puella suffocaretur. Quae dum crudeli vexatione corriperetur, coepit per os infantulae regis filiae daemon clamare dicens: „Non egrediar a corpore isto, nisi Zeno venerit episcopus, ac per ipsius imperium coactus migrabo.“ Mox itaque ut hoc regi Gallieno innotuit, missis aparitoribus sollicita intentione coepit investigare, sic ubi sanctum potuisset invenire virum. Ex iussu autem regis milites velocibus ad virum Dei gressibus pergunt. Ille vero sedebat super lapidem, qui in proximo erat monasterii, et artis apostolicae documenta proficiens, ex more piscabatur in flumine. Venientes ergo milites, quoniam ignotus eis erat, coeperunt sollicite sanctum Dei sacerdotem interrogare dicentes: „Quis es tu, homo Dei? Indica nobis, si vidisti Zenonem episcopum, quem nos ex iussu regis perquirimus.“ At ille repondit: „Ad quod missi estis edicite. Ego enim quamvis tantillus servus Christi, tamen Zeno vocor.“

R5		Dum in fluvio Athesis piscationis exercitio fungeretur, erectis sursum oculis, vidit quendam hominem in plaustro sedentem, bubus subiunctis, in amnem dimergi. V Tanta enim velocitate ferebatur ut cunctis ostenderetur antiqui hostis arte peractum. Vidit quendam hominem in plaustro sedentem, bubus subiunctis, in amnem dimergi.
Segnung		
L6		Igitur conferentes ad invicem milites dicebant inter se: „Quid multa colloquimur? Indicemus, pro qua re istum destinati sumus ad virum.“ Tunc patenter intimantes beato sacerdoti dixerunt: „Rogat te rex venire ad se, quia vult faciem tuam videre.“ Zeno respondit: „Quid meam rex vult humilitatem cernere, qui omnium Christianorum manifestis indiciis inimicus esse non desinit?“ At illi respondentes dixerunt: „Obsecrat enim te rex, ut filiam ipsius, quae immani atrocitate a daemonio vexatur, sanitati restituas, quia unica illi est.“ Ille vero dixit eis: „Dominus Iesus Christus omnipotens est. Ite“, inquit, „ecce ego paulatim subsequor vos. Oportet enim ut mirabilia Dei luce clarius omnibus manifestentur.“ Quo dicto milites viam, qua venerant, repedarunt. Exurgens vero beatus sacerdos, ne diutius absconderetur civitas supra montem

		domus Domini posita, fecit orationem perrexitque ad palatium, ubi cruciabatur et lamentabiliter affligebatur pro sua filia rex. Sanctus quoque Dei episcopus Zeno, dum celeri peragratione iter ageret, ante eo pervenit, quam hi qui missi fuerant milites. Ingrediente siquidem Christi sacerdote palatium et facto crucis signo coepit confestim per os infantulae daemon clamare dicens: „Ecce tu, Zeno, venisti ad expellendum me et ego propter tuae pavorem sanctitatis hic stare non possum.“
R6		Elevata sursum manu beatus Zeno fecit sanctae crucis signum frequenti voce et dixit: „Revertere retro Sathanas, ne perimas hominem quem Deus creavit.“ Alleluia alleluia alleluia. V Quod signum ut vidit daemon evanuit velut fumus cum clamoribus ac stridore nefando. „Revertere retro Sathanas, ne perimas hominem quem Deus creavit.“
III. Nokturn		
A7		Beatus Zeno dixit: „Non te permittit Dominus aliquid agere adversus servum suum.“
Psalm	[Ps. 14] *Domine quis habitabit in tabernaculo tuo aut quis requiescet in monte sancto tuo? Qui ingreditur sine macula et operatur iustitiam; qui loquitur veritatem in corde suo; qui non egit dolum in lingua sua, nec fecit proximo suo malum et obprobrium non accepit adversus*	

	proximos suos. Ad nihilum deductus est in conspectu eius malignus; timentes autem Dominum glorificat. Qui iurat proximo suo et non decipi; qui pecuniam suam non dedit ad usuram et munera super innocentes non accepit; qui facit haec non movebitur in aeternum.	
A8		Miserabilis pater totaque domus regia maerore affligebatur eo quod acriter puella suffocaretur.
Psalm	[Ps. 20] *Domine in virtute tua laetabitur rex et super salutare tuum exultabit vehementer. Desiderium animae eius tribuisti ei et voluntate labiorum eius non fraudasti eum. Quoniam praevenisti eum in benedictionibus dulcedinis; posuisti in capite eius coronam de lapide pretioso. Vitam petiit a te et tribuisti ei longitudinem dierum in saeculum et in saeculum saeculi. Magna gloria eius in salutari tuo; gloriam et magnum decorem inpones super eum. Quoniam dabis eum benedictionem in saeculum saeculi; laetificabis eum in gaudio cum vultu tuo. Quoniam rex sperat in Domino et in misericordia Altissimi non commovebitur. Inveniatur manus tua omnibus inimicis tuis, dextera tua inveniat omnes qui te oderunt. Pones eos ut clibanum ignis in tempore vultus tui: Dominus in ira sua conturbabit eos et devorabit eos ignis. Fructum eorum de terra perdes et semen eorum a filiis hominum, quoniam declinaverunt in te mala; cogitaverunt consilia quae non potuerunt stabilire; quoniam pones eos dorsum; in reliquis tuis*	

	praeparabis vultum eorum. Exaltare Domine in virtute tua, cantabimus et psallemus virtutes tuas.	
A9		Sacerdos Dei Zeno sedebat super lapidem et artis apostolicae documenta sequens piscabatur in flumine.
Psalm	[Ps. 23] *Domini est terra et plenitudo eius, orbis terrarum et universi qui habitant in eo. Quia ipse super maria fundavit eum et super flumina praeparavit eum. Quis ascendit in montem Domini aut quis stabit in loco sancto eius? Innocens manibus et mundo corde qui non accepit in vano animam suam nec iuravit in dolo proximo suo. Hic accipiet benedictionem a Domino et misericordiam a Deo salvatore suo haec est generatio quaerentium eum quaerentium faciem Dei Iacob. Adtollite portas principes vestras et elevamini portae aeternales et introibit rex gloriae. Quis est iste rex gloriae Dominus fortis et potens Dominus potens in proelio. Adtollite portas principes vestras et elevamini portae aeternales et introibit rex gloriae Quis est iste rex gloriae? Dominus virtutum ipse est rex gloriae.*	
Versikel		Amavit eum Dominus et ornavit eum, stolam gloriae induit eum, et ad portas paradisi coronavit eum.
Responsio		[nicht überliefert]
Pater noster	*Pater noster, qui es in caelis...*	
Absolution		[nicht überliefert]

Segnung		[nicht überliefert]
L7		His quidem auditis tenens sacerdos manum puellae dixit: „In nomine Domini nostri Iesu Christi praecipio tibi: „Exi ab ea, daemon!“ At ille publica coepit et horribili voce clamare dicens: „Etsi hinc a te expulsus fuero eo Veronam ibique invenies me et eos in quibus habitem stantes in platea expectantes te.“ Christi namque sacerdos sanam mox ab omni daemonicae incursionis ludificatione restituit filiam regis. Protinus autem ut rex Gallienus vidit hoc factum, attonitus admiratione coronam regalem, quam capite gestabat sancto sacerdoti obtulit dicens: „Tam salutifero medico qui sanam unicam filiam meam restituit, nullis muneribus aliis placere possum, nisi ipsam ei quam habeo meam offeram coronam.“ Cumque hoc gestum multitudo vidisset populi, quae ad palatium convenerat, a tenebris infidelitatis et errore conversa gentili, crediderunt unanimiter in Iesum Christum Dominum nostrum, obsecrantes sacerdotem Christi, ut docerentur viam salutis et baptismum mererentur in remissionem percipere delictorum.
R7		Festinans itaque daemon ingressus est palatium caesaris Gallieni et comprehensam eius unicam filiam coepit eam crudeliter vexare alleluia alleluia.

		V Miserabilis pater simulque tota domus eius cruciatu et maerore affligebatur. Et comprehensam eius unicam filiam coepit eam crudeliter vexare.
L8		At ubi sacerdos coronam accepit a rege, statim in partes divisam distribuit pauperibus dicens: „Si Dominus operatur excelsa, ipsi perpetuae laudes referantur et gloria.“ His ita gestis, petiit beatissimus Zeno, ut ei licentia tribueretur omnia idola destruendi et basilicas in Christi nomine fabricandi. Cuius almificis precibus adquievit rex affatim in omnibus, quae ille poposcerat. Nempe talibus et his similibus incedebat opinatus virtutibus, ut compleretur in eo, quod Dominus apostolis ait: „Ecce dedi vobis potestatem calcandi supra serpentes et scorpiones et omnem virtutem inimici.“ Post haec igitur ingressus sacerdos civitatem Veronam, intrepidus praedicabat in Christi nomine verbum et hoc instanter agebat, ut funditus idola destruerentur et in honorem Domini aedificarentur ecclesiae.
R8		Ingrediente Christi sacerdote palatium et facto crucis signo, mox coepit daemon clamare dicens: „Tu, Zeno, expellis me et ego propter tuam sanctitatem stare non possum. V Etsi hinc abiero eo Veronam ibique invenies me. Et ego propter tuam sanctitatem stare non possum.“

L9		Denique, dum haec agerentur, multitudo populi paganorum saeviens incessanter moliebatur, ut impedimentum Christi famulus pateretur. Sed vigilante in servis suis Christo vincebatur mendacium, quod pura et rectissima fides ab infidelium cordibus abigebat. His equidem ita patratis sacrosancta agebat antistes pro populi intercessione salutaria, seu ab ineunte aetate in Christi amore solitus erat. Qui nimirum dum haec indesinenter ageret operante manu voluntatis Dei, cuius in omni vitae transeuntis tempore nutui oboedierat non multo post in pace receptus est. Porro quia in virtutibus exhibitae sanctitatis veluti fulgidissimum sidus omni populo claruit, in honore Dei et ipsius sancti sacerdotis quidam ex genere Gallieni fecit reverendo eius nomini basilicam, haud procul a fluvio, ubi longo tempore corpus ipsius requievit. Qui etiam venerabilis locus in recta ineffabilis ac beatae Trinitatis confessione signis et miraculis coruscat. LECTIO SANCTI GREGORII DE MIRABILIBUS BEATI ZENONIS EPISCOPI Quando apud Romanam urbem alveum suum Tiberis egressus est, tantumque crescens, ut unda eius super muros urbis influeret atque in ea maximas regiones occuparet apud Veronensem urbem fluvius Athesis excrescens ad beati Zenonis martyris atque pontificis ecclesiam venit. Cuius ecclesiae, dum

		essent ianuae apertae, aqua in eam minime intravit. Quae paulisper crescens usque ad fenestras ecclesiae, quae erant tectis proximae, pervenit. Siquidem stans aqua ecclesiae ianuam clausit ac si illud elementum liquidum in soliditatem parietis fuisset immutatum cumque essent multi interius inventi, sed aquarum multitudine ecclesia omni circumdata, qua possent egredi non haberent ibique siti ac fame deficere formidarent, ad ecclesiae ianuam veniebant. Ad bibendum hauriebant aquam, quae – ut praedixi – usque ad fenestras excreverat et tamen intra ecclesiam nullo modo defluebat. Hauriri itaque ut aqua poterat, sed defluere ut aqua non poterat. Stans autem ante ianuam ad ostendendum cunctis meritum martyris et aqua erat ad adiutorium et quasi aqua non erat ad invadendum locum.
R9		Sancte Zeno Christi confessor, audi rogantes servulos et impetratam tu celitus defer indulgentiam. V O sancte Zeno, sidus aureum Domini gratia servorum gemitus solita suscipe clementia. Et impetrata, tu celitus defer indulgentiam.[658]
Te Deum / R9[659]	*Te Deum laudamus. Te Dominum confitemur. Te aeternum patrem omnis terra veneratur. Tibi omnes Angeli, tibi caeli et universae potestates: Tibi cherubim et*	

[658] *Sancte Zeno* REQUIRATUR IN SANCTI MARTINI Verona BC XCVIII(92) (CAO 7580).
[659] Während der Adventszeit und von Septuagesima bis Ostern wurde das Responsorium 9 wiederholt.

	seraphim incessabili voce proclamant: Sanctus, Sanctus, Sanctus Dominus Deus Sabaoth. Pleni sunt caeli et terra maiestatis gloriae tuae. Te gloriosus Apostolorum chorus. Te prophetarum laudabilis numerus. Te martyrum candidatus laudat exercitus. Te per orbem terrarum sancta confitetur Ecclesia. Patrem immensae maiestatis. Venerandum tuum verum, et unicum Filium. Sanctum quoque Paraclitum Spiritum. Tu Rex gloriae, Christe. Tu Patris sempiternus es Filius. Tu ad liberandum suscepturus hominem, non horruisti Virginis uterum. Tu devicto mortis aculeo, aperuisti credentibus regna caelorum. Tu ad dexteram Dei sedes, in gloria Patris. Iudex crederis esse venturus. Te ergo quaesumus, tuis famulis subveni, quos pretioso sanguine redemisti. Aeterna fac cum sanctis tuis in gloria numerari. Salvum fac populum tuum Domine, et benedic haereditati tuae. Et rege eos, et extolle illos usque in aeternum. Per singulos dies, benedicimus te. Et laudamus nomen tuum in saeculum, et in saeculum saeculi. Dignare Domine, die isto sine peccato nos custodire. Miserere nostri, Domine, miserere nostri. Fiat misericordia tua Domine, super nos, quemadmodum speravimus in te. In te, Domine, speravi: non confundar in aeternum.	

Laudes		
Versikel		
Responsio		
Eröffnung	V. *Deus in adiutorium meum intende* R. *Domine ad adiuvandum me festina* *Gloria patri et filio et spiritui sancto, sicut erat in principio et nunc et semper et in saecula saeculorum. Amen* *alleluia / Laus tibi Domine rex aeterne gloriae*	
L-A1		Dominus Iesus Christus omnipotens est oportet enim ut mirabilia Dei omnibus manifestentur.
Psalm	[Ps. 92] *Dominus regnavit, decorem indutus est: indutus est Dominus fortitudinem, et praecinxit se. Etenim firmavit orbem terrae, qui non commovebitur. Parata sedes tua ex tunc; a saeculo tu es. Elevaverunt flumina, Domine, elevaverunt flumina vocem suam, elevaverunt flumina fluctus suos, a vocibus aquarum multarum. Mirabiles elationes maris; mirabilis in altis Dominus. Testimonia tua credibilia facta sunt nimis; domum tuam decet sanctitudo, Domine, in longitudinem dierum.*	
L-A2		Exurgens beatus sacerdos fecit orationem perrexitque ad palatium ubi affligebatur pro sua filia rex.
Psalm	[nicht überliefert]	

L-A3		Ingrediente Christi confessore palatio facto crucis signo per os puellae daemon clamavit dicens: „Tu, Zeno, venisti ad expellendum me et propter tuam sanctitatem stare non possum.“
Psalm	*[Ps. 62-66] Deus, Deus meus, ad te de luce vigilo. Sitivit in te anima mea; quam multipliciter tibi caro mea! In terra deserta, et invia, et inaquosa, sic in sancto apparui tibi, ut viderem virtutem tuam et gloriam tuam. Quoniam melior est misericordia tua super vitas, labia mea laudabunt te. Sic benedicam te in vita mea; et in nomine tuo levabo manus meas. Sicut adipe et pinguedine repleatur anima mea, et labiis exsultationis laudabit os meum. Si memor fui tui super stratum meum, in matutinis meditabor in te. Quia fuisti adjutor meus, et in velamento alarum tuarum exsultabo. Adhæsit anima mea post te; me suscepit dextera tua. Ipsi vero in vanum quæsierunt animam meam: introibunt in inferiora terræ; tradentur in manus gladii; partes vulpium erunt. Rex vero lætabitur in Deo; laudabuntur omnes qui jurant in eo, quia obstructum est os loquentium iniqua.*	
L-A4		Tenens beatus Zeno manum puellae dicens: „In nomine Domini mei Iesu Christi precipio tibi exi ab ea daemon.“
Alttestamentarisches Canticum		[nicht überliefert]

L-A5		Christi namque sacerdos ab omni daemonicae incursionis ludificatione sanam restituit filiam regis.
Psalm	[Ps. 148-150]	
Kurzlesung + *Deo gratias*		
Hymnus		[nicht überliefert]
Versikel		Super caput eius Dominus…[660]
B-A		Acceptam beatus Zeno coronam a rege distribuit pauperibus dicens: „Si Dominus operatur excelsa ipsi perpetuae laudes referantur et gloria alleluia.“
Benedictus (Lc 1, 68-79)	*Benedictus Dominus Deus Israel, quia visitavit et fecit redemptionem plebis suae et erexit cornu salutis nobis, in domo David pueri sui, sicut locutus est per os sanctorum, qui a saeculo sunt, prophetarum eius, salutem ex inimicis nostris, et de manu omnium, qui oderunt nos; ad faciendam misericordiam cum patribus nostris, et memorari testamenti sui sancti. Ius iurandum, quod iuravit ad Abraham patrem nostrum, daturum se nobis, ut sine timore, de manu inimicorum nostrorum liberati, serviamus illi in sanctitate et iustitia coram ipso, omnibus diebus nostris. Et tu, puer, propheta altissimi vocaberis: praeibis enim ante faciem Domini parare vias eius, ad dandam scientiam salutis plebi eius, in*	

[660] *Elegite* Verona BC XCVIII(92).

	remissionem peccatorum eorum, per viscera misericordiae Dei nostri, in quibus visitavit nos oriens ex alto, illuminare his, qui in tenebris et in umbra mortis sedent, ad dirigendos pedes nostros in viam pacis.	
Kollekt		[nicht überliefert]
Benedicamus Domino...		
Prim		
Terz		
Messe		
Sext		
Non		
II. Vesper		
Eröffnungsversikel	V. *Deus in adiutorium...* *Gloria Patri...* *Alleluia...*	
5 Antiphone – 5 Psalmen		[nicht überliefert]
Kurzlesung + Responsorium		[nicht überliefert]
Hymnus		[nicht überliefert]
Versikel		[nicht überliefert]

M-A2		Sancte confessor Zeno, pastor Domini gregis, te deprecamur: intercede pro nobis ut mereamur tecum esse in caelis, alleluia alleluia alleluia.[661]
Magnificat (Lc 1,46-55)	*Magnificat anima mea Dominum...*	
Kyrie	*Kyrie eleison. Christe eleison. Kyrie eleison.*	
Pater noster	*Pater noster, qui es in caelis...*	
Preces		[nicht überliefert]
Oratio	*Oremus…Amen*	[nicht überliefert]
Entlassung: Segnung und Antwort	V. *Dominum vobiscum* R. *Et cum spiritu tuo* V. *Benedicamus Domino* R. *Deo gratias*	

[661] CAO 4709.

3.4.2 Rekonstruktion 2: Das Zeno-Offizium in der zweiten Hälfte des 12. Jahrhunderts im Kloster San Zeno Maggiore

Bei der Rekonstruktion der liturgischen Feiern für Zeno, die ab der zweiten Hälfte des 12. Jahrhunderts in San Zeno Maggiore abgehalten wurden, ergibt sich die besondere Schwierigkeit, dass, wie bereits erwähnt, die Überlieferung erst im Spätmittelalter einsetzt. Als zeitgenössisches Zeugnis für die Anfänge des monastischen Offiziums kann lediglich ein hagiographischer Lektionar Verona BC XCVI(90*) aus dem späten 12. Jahrhundert gelten. Allerdings konnte im Rahmen einer philologischen Analyse der Entstehungskontext dieser Texte nachvollzogen werden und, daran anknüpfend, eine belastbare Rekonstruktion geleistet werden.

Die handschriftlichen Zeugen belegen, dass Zeno in San Zeno Maggiore drei Mal im Jahr gefeiert wurde: an seinem Todestag (Fest der Depositio am 12. April), am Tag der Überführung seiner Reliquien (Fest der Translatio am 21. Mai) und am Jahrestag seiner Bischofsweihe (Fest der Ordinatio am 8. Dezember). Die Quellen geben auch einheitlich darüber Auskunft, dass bei allen Festen die gleiche Zeno-Historia und Hymne verwendet und lediglich die Inhalte der Lesungen verändert wurden. Diesen liegt der Text von BHL 9010–11 zugrunde, der je nach Anlass des Festes angepasst wurde. Dementsprechend finden sich in der Rekonstruktion anstatt einer einzigen Spalte im Fall der Lesungen drei Spalten, bezeichnet mit IN DEPOSITIONE, IN TRANSLATIONE und IN ORDINATIONE, in denen jeweils die Lesungen abgedruckt worden sind.

Nun zu den einzelnen Handschriften, die das Material für meine Rekonstruktion liefern. Die Antiphonen- und Psalmenreihen für die beiden Vespern, Matutin und Laudes sind dem Antiphonar Verona BCi 739 I entnommen. Dieser Codex gibt, ähnlich wie ein Brevier, durch Incipits über weitere Elemente der Feier Auskunft, nämlich Kurzlesungen und dazugehörige Responsorien, Versikel und Hymnen. Die Rekonstruktion folgt in diesen Fällen den Angaben dieser Handschrift, da es sich um einen Codex für den Gebrauch im Chor handelt. Für die Hymnen wurden die Handschriften Verona BCi 745 und Yale BeineckeL 744 herangezogen, die identisch sind und jeweils gleichzeitig von jeweils einer Hälfte des Chores eingesehen wurden. Die Angaben dieser Hymnare stimmen mit den im Antiphonar 739 I angegebenen Incipits der Hymnen überein.

Die Texte der Lesungen wurden dem Lektionar Verona BC CXVI(90*) entnommen. Marginalnotizen einer hochmittelalterlichen Hand teilen den hier überlieferten Text von BHL 9010–9011 nicht nur in Lesungen, sondern verteilen ihn auch auf die unterschiedlichen Zenofeste. Beim Translationsfest wurde der Text der *Translatio* (BHL 9011) – beginnend mit *Nunc necessarium* (siehe Edition, S. 185) – gelesen, wie die Randnotiz auf S. 281 „In translatione sancti Zenonis episcopi" belegt. Eine weitere Marginalnotiz verdeutlicht, dass am Todestag Zenos mit den Lesungen mitten im Text von BHL 9010 begonnen wurde. Auf S. 278 dieser Handschrift notiert die gleiche Hand „In deposicione sancti Zenonis".

Auch die Einteilung der Leseabschnitte ist aus dieser Handschrift nachzuvollziehen, leider aber unvollständig. Es sind nur noch die Marginalia im ersten Teil des Textes zu lesen. Hier lassen sich acht Sektionen identifizieren. Das ist üblich, da anlässlich eines Heiligenfestes die ersten acht Leseabschnitte aus der Heiligenvita entnommen wurden, während die übrigen vier Lesungen der dritten Nokturn traditionell aus einer Predigt stammten. So wurden meistens Abschnitte der Kirchenväter vorgelesen, die die Evangeliumslesung der Messe am selben Tag kommentierten.[662] Dazu gibt das hagiographische Lektionar aus dem 12. Jahrhundert keinen Hinweis, es liefert den kompletten Text der Vita (BHL 9010–9011). Eine Untersuchung der spätmittelalterlichen Breviere (Augsburg StStadtB 2° 204 und Kremsmünster SB CC60) erbrachte aber Einsicht in die Gepflogenheiten der Abtei: Für das Fest der Ordinatio gibt Kremsmünster SB CC60 an, man solle zu einer Passage aus dem Lukasevangelium (Luc 11, 33) die Homilie aus dem Commune eines Bekenners und Bischofs lesen, nämlich aus Bedas Auslegung des Lukasevangeliums.[663] Für das Translationsfest findet sich hier auch der Hinweis, dass zur dritten Nokturn aus dem Evangelium von Johannes, Kapitel 15 *Ego sum vitis vera* zu lesen sei.[664] Eine Angabe über die zu lesende Homilie findet man an dieser Stelle nicht. Diese Passage aus dem Johannesevangelium wurde zusammen mit ihrer Auslegung durch Augustinus (Predigt LXXX[665]) aber bereits im Homiliar von Paulus Diaconus für das Commune eines Apostels vorgesehen. Da das Brevier des Zenoklosters Kremsmünster SB CC60 ebenso bezüglich des Ordinationsfestes mit den Angaben von Paulus Diaconus übereinstimmt,[666] ist daher wahrscheinlich, dass auch in San Zeno Maggiore im 12. Jahrhundert diese traditionelle Kombination (Johannesevangelium *Ego sum vitis vera* + Augustinus' Auslegung) gewählt wurde. Diese habe ich entsprechend vervollständigt. Für die Lesungen der dritten Nokturn des Festes am 12. April (Depositio) sind leider keine Angaben zu finden.

662 Harper, The Forms and Orders ebd., S. 87. Zu den homiletischen Lesungen der dritten Nokturn siehe auch: Nils H. Petersen: Theological Construction in the Offices in Honour of St Knud Lavard, in: Plainsong and Medieval Music 23, 2014, S. 71–96, hier: S. 75–90.

663 Beda venerabilis: In Lucae evangelium expositio 120, S. 239–240.

664 Auch Augsburg StStadtB 2° 204 gibt den gleichen Hinweis.

665 Augustinus: In Iohannis evangelium tractatus CXXIV, hrsg. von Radbodus Willems (Corpus Christianorum. Series Latina 36), Turnhout 1954, S. 527–528.

666 Auch Paulus Diaconus sieht für das Fest eines Bekenners die Lesungen aus dem Lukasevangelium und die Auslegung von Beda vor, vgl. Paulus Diaconus: Homiliarius, hrsg. von Jacques P. Migne (Patrologia Latina 95), Paris 1851, 1560.

Basiert auf den Handschriften: Verona BC CXVI(90*) (***Vr2***), Verona BCi 739 I (*VrCiv*[1]), Verona BCi 745 (*VrCiv*[2]), Yale BeineckeL 744 (*Y*), Kremsmünster SB CC60 (*Kr*)

Gebetszeiten und Elemente des Ritus	**Feststehende Bestandteile**	
Festanlass		**In depositione/translatione/ordinatione sancti Zenonis episcopi**
I. Vesper		
Eröffnungsversikeln	V. *Deus in adiutorium meum intende* R. *Domine ad adiuvandum me festina* *Gloria patri…* *Alleluia*	
A1		Dominus Iesus Christus omnipotens est oportet enim ut mirabilia Dei omnibus manifestentur.
Psalm	[Ps. 109] *Dixit Dominus Domino meo: Sede a dextris meis, donec ponam inimicos tuos scabellum pedum tuorum. Virgam virtutis tuae emittet Dominus ex Sion: dominare in medio inimicorum tuorum. Tecum principium in die virtutis tuae in splendoribus sanctorum; ex utero, ante luciferum, genui te. Iuravit*	

	Dominus, et non poenitebit eum: Tu es sacerdos in aeternum secundum ordinem Melchisedech. Dominus a dextris tuis; confregit in die irae suae reges. Iudicabit in nationibus; implebit ruinas, conquassabit capita in terra multorum, de torrente in via bibet; propterea exaltabit caput.	
A2		Exurgens beatus sacerdos fecit orationem perrexitque ad palatium ubi affligebatur pro sua filia rex.
Psalm	[Ps. 110] *Confitebor tibi, Domine, in toto corde meo, in consilio iustorum, et congregatione. Magna opera Domini, exquisita in omnes voluntates eius. Confessio et magnificentia opus eius; et iustitia eius manet in saeculum saeculi. Memoriam fecit mirabilium suorum, misericors et miserator Dominus. Escam dedit timentibus se; memor erit in saeculum testamenti sui. Virtutem operum suorum annuntiabit populo suo, ut det illis haereditatem gentium. Opera manuum eius veritas et iudicium; fidelia omnia mandata*	

	eius, confirmata in saeculum saeculi, facta in veritate et aequitate. Redemptionem misit populo suo; mandavit in aeternum testamentum suum. Sanctum et terribile nomen eius. Initium sapientiae timor Domini; intellectus bonus omnibus facientibus eum, laudatio eius manet in saeculum saeculi.	
A3		Ingrediente Christi confessore palatium facto crucis signo per os puellae daemon clamavit dicens: „Tu, Zeno, venisti ad expellendum me et propter tuam sanctitatem stare non possum.“
Psalm	[Ps. 111] *Beatus vir qui timet Dominum, in mandatis eius volet nimis. Potens in terra erit semen eius; generatio rectorum benedicetur. Gloria et divitiae in domo eius, et iustitia eius manet in saeculum saeculi. Exortum est in tenebris lumen rectis, misericors, et miserator, et iustus. Iucundus homo qui miseretur et commodat, disponet Sermones suos in iudicio; quia in aeternum non commovebitur. In memoria aeterna erit iustus; ab auditione mala non timebit. Paratum cor eius*	

	sperare in Domino, confirmatum est cor eius; non commovebitur donec despiciat inimicos suos. Dispersit, dedit pauperibus; iustitia eius manet in saeculum saeculi; cornu eius exaltabitur in gloria. Peccator videbit, et irascetur, dentibus suis fremet et tabescet; desiderium peccatorum peribit.	
A4		Tenens beatus Zeno manum puellae dixit: „In nomine Domini mei Iesu Christi praecipio tibi exi ab ea daemon.“
Psalm	[Ps. 112] *Laudate pueri Dominum, laudate nomen Domini. Sit nomen Domini benedictum ex hoc nunc et usque in saeculum. A solis ortu usque ad occasum laudabile nomen Domini. Excelsus super omnes gentes Dominus, et super caelos gloria eius. Quis sicut Dominus Deus noster, qui in altis habitat, et humilia respicit in caelo et in terra? Suscitans a terra inopem, et de stercore erigens pauperem: ut collocet eum cum principibus, cum principibus populi sui. Qui*	

	habitare facit sterilem in domo, matrem filiorum laetantem.	
Kurzlesung + *Deo gratias*	[Ecclesiasticus 31, 8-11] *Beatus vir qui inventus est sine macula, et qui post aurum non abiit, nec speravit in thesauris pecuniae; ideo stabilita sunt bona illius in Domino.*	
Responsorium		Summe Dei praesul beate Zeno tuam catervam protege namque credimus tuis laudibus nos semper esse salvandos alleluia. V Qui filiam Gallieni caesaris a daemonio liberasti tuis laudibus instantem conserva plebem. Namque... V Gloria patri et filio et spiritui sancto. Salvam...
Hymnus		Effulget orbis speculum Zeno praesul mirificus, cuius festa solemnia anni nobis fert orbita. Qui Christi fide fervidus hoc praesens spernens saeculum flore virtutum praeditus caeli possedit praemium. Hic onus carnis baiulans plura fecit miracula, ut floret lux clarissima caecas fugavit tenebras.

		Nempe piscans in flumine vidit plaustro praecipitem cum bubus suis rusticum ad amnis ima mergere. Quod hostis hoc nequissimus patrasset cernens vir pius preces fudit ad Dominum eius poscens auxilium. Subvenit Christi gratia, quae se credentes munerat ac liberavit hominem reddens saluti pristinae.
Versikel + *responsio*		Ora pro nobis beatus Zeno + Ut digni efficiatur...
M-A1		Clementissime Christi confessor Domini beatissime Zeno te suppliciter petimus ne nos derelinquas sed apud Dominum pius semper pro nobis intercessor existas quo te opitulante ad gaudia aeterna vitae pervenire mereamur.
Magnificat (Lc 1, 46-55)	*Magnificat anima mea Dominum: et exsultavit spiritus meus in Deo salutari meo. Quia respexit humilitatem ancillae suae: ecce enim ex hoc beatam me dicent omnes generationes, quia fecit mihi magna qui potens est: et sanctum*	

	nomen eius, et misericordia eius a progenie in progenies timentibus eum. Fecit potentiam in brachio suo: dispersit superbos mente cordis sui. Deposuit potentes de sede, et exaltavit humiles. Esurientes implevit bonis: et divites dimisit inanes. Suscepit Israel puerum suum, recordatus misericordiae suae: sicut locutus est ad patres nostros, Abraham et semini eius in saecula.	
Kyrie	*Kyrie eleison. Christe eleison. Kyrie eleison.*	
Pater noster	*Pater noster, qui es in caelis, sanctificetur nomen tuum; adveniat regnum tuum. Fiat voluntas tua sicut in caelo et in terra. Panem nostrum quotidianum da nobis hodie et dimitte nobis debita nostra, sicut et nos dimittimus debitoribus nostris.* V. *Et ne nos inducas in tentationem;* R. *Sed libera nos a malo.* *[Quia tuum est regnum et potentia*	

	et gloria *in saecula saeculorum*] *Amen.*	
Kollekt		[unbekannt]
		NOTA QUOD ULTIMA ORATIO NON DEBET CONCLUDI PER DOMINUM...SED ANTE PER DOMINUM DEBENT CANTORES INCIPERE RESPONSORIUM SANCTE ZENO...ET FIT PROCESSIO SUBTUS AD ALTARE SANCTI ZENONIS SICUT CONTINETUR IN QUATERNIS DE PROCESSIONE.[667]
Entlassung: Segnung und Antwort	*V. Benedicamus Domino R. Deo gratias*	
KOMPLET		[unbekannt]
MATUTIN		
Eröffnung	V. *Deus in adiutorium meum intende* R. *Domine ad adiuvandum me festina* *Gloria patri…* *(Alleluia)* V. *Domine labia mea aperies* R. *Et os meum adnuntiabit laudem tuam (3x)*	
Ps. 3	*Domine, quid multiplicati sunt qui tribulant me? Multi insurgunt*	

[667] Diese Angabe findet sich an dieser Stelle, nach dem Abschluss der ersten Vesper in *VrCiv*[1].

	adversum me; multi dicunt animae meae: Non est salus ipsi in Deo eius. Tu autem Domine, susceptor meus es, gloria mea, et exaltans caput meum. Voce mea ad Dominum clamavi; et exaudivit me de monte sancto suo. Ego dormivi, et soporatus sum; et exsurrexi, quia Dominus suscepit me. Non timebo millia populi circumdantis me. Exsurge, Domine; salvum me fac, Deus meus. Quoniam tu percussisti omnes adversantes mihi sine causa; dentes peccatorum contrivisti. Domini est salus; et super populum tuum benedictio tua.	
I		Aeternum trinumque Deum laudemus et unum qui sibi Zenonem transvexit in aethera sanctum.
Ps. 94	*Venite, exsultemus Domino; iubilemus Deo salutari nostro; praeoccupemus faciem eius in confessione, et in psalmis iubilemus ei: quoniam Deus magnus Dominus, et rex magnus super omnes deos; quia in manu eius sunt omnes fines terrae, et altitudines montium ipsius sunt; quoniam*	

	ipsius est mare, et ipse fecit illud, et siccam manus eius formaverunt. Venite, adoremus, et procidamus, et ploremus ante Dominum qui fecit nos; quia ipse est Dominus Deus noster, et nos populus pascuae eius, et oves manus eius. Hodie si vocem eius audieritis, nolite obdurare corda vestra sicut in irritatione, secundum diem tentationis in deserto, ubi tentaverunt me patres vestri, probaverunt me, et viderunt opera mea. Quadraginta annis offensus fui generationi illi; et dixi: Semper hi errant corde. Et isti non cognoverunt vias meas: ut iuravi in ira mea: Si introibunt in requiem meam.	
Hymnus		Post haec curavit filiam, imperatoris unicam quam fecerat hospitium daemon tunc sibi pessimus.

		Athesis amnis alveus excrescens ultra solitum conscendit ad eximium ecclesiae fastigium. Confestim fulgent merita viri sancti dignissima, nam mansit aqua solida cum sit natura fluida. Precamur ergo supplices, Zeno praesul sanctissime, ut caeli nobis Dominum efficias propitium. Quo post abluta crimina fruamur eius gloria habituri felicia in aeternum solemnia. Praesta pater piissime...
I. Nokturn		
A1		Ab utero matris fuit sanctificatus beatus Zeno et a cunabulis benedictus.
Psalm	[Ps. 1] *Beatus vir qui non abiit in consilio impiorum, et in via peccatorum non stetit, et in cathedra pestilentiae non sedit; sed*	

	in lege Domini voluntas eius, et in lege eius meditabitur die ac nocte. Et erit tamquam lignum quod plantatum est secus decursus aquarum, quod fructum suum dabit in tempore suo: et folium eius non defluet; et omnia quaecumque faciet prosperabuntur. Non sic impii, non sic; sed tamquam pulvis quem projicit ventus a facie terrae. Ideo non resurgent impii in iudicio, neque peccatores in concilio iustorum, quoniam novit Dominus viam iustorum; et iter impiorum peribit.	
A2		Probitatis et scientiae iugibus incrementis ad hoc pertingere meruit ut per sacerrimam vitam pastor in populis efficeretur.
Psalm	[Ps. 2] *Quare fremuerunt gentes, et populi meditati sunt inania? Astiterunt reges terrae, et principes convenerunt in unum adversus Dominum, et adversus Christum eius. Dirumpamus vincula eorum, et projiciamus a nobis iugum ipsorum. Qui habitat in caelis irridebit eos, et Dominus subsannabit eos. Tunc loquetur ad*	

	eos in ira sua, et in furore suo conturbabit eos. Ego autem constitutus sum rex ab eo super Sion, montem sanctum eius, praedicans praeceptum eius. Dominus dixit ad me: Filius meus es tu; ego hodie genui te. Postula a me, et dabo tibi gentes haereditatem tuam, et possessionem tuam terminos terrae. Reges eos in virga ferrea, et tamquam vas figuli confringes eos. Et nunc, reges, intelligite; erudimini, qui iudicatis terram. Servite Domino in timore, et exsultate ei cum tremore. Apprehendite disciplinam, nequando irascatur Dominus, et pereatis de via iusta. Cum exarserit in brevi ira eius, beati omnes qui confidunt in eo.	
A3		Continuis ieiuniis et orationibus crebris a Domino petebat ut sibi aditum praedicationis in populos aperire.
Psalm	[Ps. 4] *Cum invocarem exaudivit me Deus iustitiae meae, in tribulatione dilatasti mihi. Miserere mei, et exaudi orationem meam. Filii hominum, usquequo*	

	gravi corde? Ut quid diligitis vanitatem, et quaeritis mendacium? Et scitote quoniam mirificavit Dominus sanctum suum; Dominus exaudiet me cum clamavero ad eum. Irascimini, et nolite peccare; quae dicitis in cordibus vestris, in cubilibus vestris compungimini. Sacrificate sacrificium iustitiae, et sperate in Domino. Multi dicunt: Quis ostendit nobis bona? Signatum est super nos lumen vultus tui, Domine: dedisti laetitiam in corde meo. A fructu frumenti, vini, et olei sui, multiplicati sunt. In pace in idipsum dormiam, et requiescam; quoniam tu, Domine, singulariter in spe constituisti me.	
A4		Affabilis ita erat in sermonibus et in habitu mitis ut Deus in ipso collaudaretur ab omnibus venientibus ad se.
Psalm	[Ps. 5] *Verba mea auribus percipe, Domine; intellige clamorem meum. Intende voci orationis meae, rex meus et Deus meus. Quoniam ad te orabo, Domine, mane exaudies*	

	vocem meam. Mane astabo tibi, et videbo quoniam non Deus volens iniquitatem tu es. Neque habitabit iuxta te malignus, neque permanebunt iniusti ante oculos tuos. Odisti omnes qui operantur iniquitatem; perdes omnes qui loquuntur mendacium. Virum sanguinum et dolosum abominabitur Dominus. Ego autem in multitudine misericordiae tuae introibo in domum tuam; adorabo ad templum sanctum tuum in timore tuo. Domine, deduc me in iustitia tua: propter inimicos meos dirige in conspectu tuo viam meam. Quoniam non est in ore eorum veritas; cor eorum vanum est. Sepulchrum patens est guttur eorum; linguis suis dolose agebant, iudica illos, Deus. Decidant a cogitationibus suis; secundum multitudinem impietatum eorum expelle eos, quoniam irritaverunt te, Domine. Et laetentur omnes qui sperant in te; in aeternum exsultabunt, et habitabis in eis. Et gloriabuntur in te omnes qui	

	diligunt nomen tuum, quoniam tu benedices iusto. Domine, ut scuto bonae voluntatis tuae coronasti nos.	
A5		Cum exercitio piscationis fungeretur in flumine vidit quendam hominem in plaustro sedentem per praeceps in amnem dimergi.
Psalm	[Ps. 8] *Domine, Dominus noster, quam admirabile est nomen tuum in universa terra. Quoniam elevata est magnificentia tua super caelos. Ex ore infantium et lactentium perfecisti laudem propter inimicos tuos, ut destruas inimicum et ultorem. Quoniam videbo caelos tuos, opera digitorum tuorum, lunam et stellas quae tu fundasti. Quid est homo, quod memor es eius? aut filius hominis, quoniam visitas eum? Minuisti eum paulo minus ab angelis; gloria et honore coronasti eum; et constituisti eum super opera manuum tuarum. Omnia subjecisti sub pedibus eius, oves et boves universas, insuper et pecora campi, volucres caeli, et pisces maris qui perambulant semitas maris. Domine, Dominus*	

	noster, quam admirabile est nomen tuum in universa terra.	
A6		Vir Dei, elevata sursum manu, fecit signum crucis dicens: „Revertere retro Sathanas ne perimas hominem quem Deus creavit.“
Psalm	[Ps. 10] *In Domino confido; quomodo dicitis animae meae: Transmigra in montem sicut passer? Quoniam ecce peccatores intenderunt arcum; paraverunt sagittas suas in pharetra, ut sagittent in obscuro rectos corde; quoniam quae perfecisti destruxerunt; iustus autem quid fecit? Dominus in templo sancto suo; Dominus in caelo sedes eius. Oculi eius in pauperem respiciunt, palpebrae eius interrogant filios hominum. Dominus interrogat iustum et impium; qui autem diligit iniquitatem, odit animam suam. Pluet super peccatores laqueos; ignis et sulphur, et spiritus procellarum, pars calicis eorum. Quoniam iustus Dominus, et iustitias dilexit: aequitatem vidit vultus eius.*	

Versikel + Responsio		Versiculi de commune confessoris pontificis		
Pater noster				
Segnung				
		In depositione	In translatione	In ordinatione
L1		Neque tantam in multiplicandis virtutibus laudem ponis, quantam in fruendis. Tu virginitati praestas, ne flos eius ullo, morbo ullo tempore deflorescat; tu variarum semper in tempestatum crebris turbinibus constitutae fidissimus viduitatis es portus; tu sanctissimo coniugali iugo rudi cervice binos subeuntes, in nisum laboris, vel amoris aequalem retinaculis blandis, quasi quidam peritus auriga, componis; tu servituti unica ac fortissima consolatio saepe libertatem paris; tu paupertati praestas, ut	Nunc necessarium nobis videtur translationis beati Zenonis seriem notificare, quia in gestione huius negotii, queadam memoratu digna claruerunt. Quae tanslatio acta est cum Rotaldus vir attributis personae praestantissimus pastoralem curam Veronae gerebat et Pippinus rex Karoli filius, quem Adrianus papa baptizavit, regnum Italicum regebat. Rex vero Veronam regali situ praeditam plus ceteris urbibus diligebat et cum episcopo sibi dilecto frequens colloquium	Eo tempore quo Valerianus cum filio Gallieno fasces Romani imperii suscepit, prima fronte regiminis humanus et benignus existitit erga famulos Dei quia mitissima sors regnorum solet esse sub novo rege. Sed postquam vetustari coepit in regno depravatus est et a veritate deiectus per quendam doctorem pessimum magistrum et principem Aegyptiorum magorum, ut iustos et sanctos viros interemi iuberet. Tamquam qui adversarentur magicis artibus quibus ipse sordebat.

		habeat totum sui contenta, cum substinet totum; tu prophetas provexisti; tu Christo apostolos glutinasti; tu cottidiana martyrum et mater es et corona. Tu murus fidei, fructus spei, amica caritatis. Tu specialiter omnem populum divinasque virtutes, quasi crines effusos in unius verticis nodum, honorem, decoremque conducis. Felix est qui semper te habuerit in se.	habebat, qui dum quadam die pariter sancti Zenonis aedem ingrederentur et tam de auditis quam de visis mirabilibus huius loquerentur rationabiliter et digne proposuerunt ut magnum thesaurum humilius quam oporteret positum decentius et sublimius locarent et ecclesiae angustiam dilatarent. Aedificantes igitur ecclesiam antrum opacum columnis subnixum et lapidibus pavimentatum construxerunt. Ubi eminentem aggerem ex politis marmoribus ediderunt quem sacrosancti tumulum corporis devoverunt.	
R1		Hic est sacer antistes Zeno quem gemina virtute Dominus sanctitatis et sapientiae decoravit, cuius praeclara fulserunt in mundo miracula et in caelis adeptus est angelorum consortia.		

		V Iste est qui ante Deum magnas virtutes operatus est et omnis terra doctrina eius repleta est. Cuius…		
		IN DEPOSITIONE	IN TRANSLATIONE	IN ORDINATIONE
L2		Sic sanctus Zeno episcopus de doctrina baptismatis et patientiae finierat. Ad huiusmodi et alia vestigia virtutum instigabat populum adquisitum; cuius lingua velut fons indeficiens per exercitia divini dogmatis effluebat, et omnem contagionem, priusquam adolesceret expurgabat, et parum credebat esse actum cum aliquid superesset agendum. Neque amor saecularis genitoris tantum aestuat in augenda facultate parvulorum dum timet ne penuria fatigentur, quantum Zeno vir paterni pectoris circa filios adoptionis flagrabat, ne inopia verbi	Deinde rex cum praesule congregatis sacerdotibus et aliis sacris ordinibus in quibus respectu bonitatis speraverant per multimodas orationes sanctum prius demulcentes ne illis motus irasceretur cum ingenti timore cubiculum aperuerunt. Qui adeo perterrefacti ut nullus tanti collegii tangere ossa praesumeret. Nam divinum quiddam et valde timendum videbatur inde exalare quod horrorem inspiraverat et omnes circumstantes exanimaverat. Mox claudentes sepulcrum abierunt. Cumque rex et pontifex quid acturi	Fuso per omnem Romani regni latitudinem sanctorum sanguine Valerianus illico nefarii auctor edicti. A Sapore rege Persarum captus imperator populi Romani ignominiosa servitute apud Persas consenuit, hoc infamis officii continua donec vixit damnatione sortitus ut ipse a clinis humi regem semper ascensurum equum non manu sed dorso attolleret. At Gallienus claro Dei iudicio territus et tam misero college permotus exemplo pacem ecclesis trepida satisfactione restituit, quo adhuc septra romana

		divini tabescerent; quos luculenta oratione, et affabili affectione, importune et opportune saginabat et non parvum ardorem amoris eis impectorabat. Unde patrem et natos tantae dilectionis foedus coniunxerat ut fere ambiguum esset, an pater illos, an illi patrem plus diligerent.	essent ambigerent ex multis quas ventilabant coniecturis haec placuit, ut per quadraginta dies ter in ebdomada omnis ordo utriusque sexus saecularis et ecclesiasticus cum ipso rege et episcopo. Ad specum sanctum reverenter ac sollemniter convenirent et Dei ac confessoris clementiam uno voto efflagitarent ut cui tam reverenda motio conveniret instillaret.	gerente Dyonisius vir reverentissimus apostolicae sedis apicem ascenderat.
R2		Ab utero sanctificatus beatus Zeno et a cunabulis benedictus ad hoc pertingere meruit ut pastor in populis per sacerrimam vitam efficeretur. V In omnem terram sonus exiit conversationis eius et sanctitas luculenter emicuit. Ut pastor…		
		IN DEPOSITIONE	IN TRANSLATIONE	IN ORDINATIONE
L3		Sed diabolus doctrinae felicitate torquebatur, quae non exiguis ecclesiam opibus ditabat, et praestigiator insatiabilis mille formas	Dum haec diligenti cura agerentur fama cuiusdam solitarii viri herbusculis et aqua paucoque pane pasti regi innotuit quod dum alacriter	Eodem temporis curriculo Zeno egregius pastor ac praestantissimus tam opere quam sermone in urbe Verona fuit

		nocendi accipit, et explorat velut latro, non modo infirmos, et titubantes verum etiam viros excellentes et robustos, ut accepta occasione latrocinium exerceat. Nam a quo dolos suos contineat, qui ipsum Dominum tripliciter temptare praesumit. Hic artifex fraudolentus idololatriae magistros, eorumque discipulos multis argumentis contra sancti Zenonis tyrones adhuc rudes infestabat. At Deus, quid dedit illis se nosse, auxit et posse, ut ante signum miraculorum Zenonem sequentes, gloriosam victoriam triumphatis hostibus reportare.	audivit episcopum vocavit celeriter. Elegerunt nuntios industrios et providos, quibus hanc curam committerent. Qui venientes ad lacum qui Benacus dicitur ad remoti viri latibulum in eminenti specula situm angusto et periculoso calle aspirarunt. Intuentes autem virum Benignum nomine et discipulum eius qui Carus vocabatur, gavisi sunt gaudio magno. Audita legatione regis et episcopi ait legatis: „Revertimini in pace resalutantes dominos vestros carissime. Ego non parum tripudio quod ad illam sollemnitatem vocor et post paululum vos subsequor.“ Mox aediculam oraculi	intronizatus et populi magnitudine et aedificiorum altitudine et reliquis incrementis et ornamentis urbanis inter Italiae civitates florebat. Sed Veronensis fidei radicem hic orthodoxae fidei doctor firmavit et omnia deliramenta paganorum velut clara lux tenebras ab urbe sua fugavit et populum adhuc informem sigillo formae Dei imaginavit. Fuit quippe a matris utero sanctificatus et a cunabulis benedictus ut assertione divina in eo repeti videretur quod Hieremiae dictum est: „Priusquam te formarem in utero novi te et antequam exires de ventre sanctificavi te.“

			ingressus auxilium divinum imploravit, deinde ad itineris exercitium se expedivit. Cum autem non longe a cellula progrederetur ecce merula alis coepit strepere, voce zinzulare et saepissime callem transvolitare et quasi sinistrum omen significare. Ut virum Dei ab incepto revocaret.	
R3		In secretiori parte oratorii continuis ieiuniis et crebris orationibus a Domino petebat ut sibi dignaretur aditum praedicationis in populos aperire. V Ad convertendas in amore Christi animas hominum die noctuque deditus erat. Ut sibi…		
		IN DEPOSITIONE	IN TRANSLATIONE	IN ORDINATIONE
L4		Ipse vero sanctus accepta palma non proiecit arma, neque suos proicere permisit, nec nudis verbis, sed factorum exemplis illos exagitabat. Nam vigilando, orando, ieiunando, elemosinando, miraculis	Sed vir ille non ignorans hoc esse apparatum daemonis merulam adiuravit ut nullum motum faceret donec ipse rediret. Ibi merula stetit immobilis velut esset insensibilis. Cum autem appropinquaret et	Denique probitatis atque scientiae iugibus incrementis ad hoc pertingere meruit ut per sacerrimam vitam fieri pastor in populo mereretur. Nempe audiant populi omnes qui eius cupiunt nosse

		coruscando, magnum robur constantiae illis inculcavit, et ut certatim fortiores essent in residua pugna indulcavit. Iustus Zeno, ut palma in Dei domo florebat, et sua plantatio in eadem aula, et in atriis domus Dei vehementer crescebat. Sed tempus instabat, ut legitimi certaminis coronam acciperet, et animam corruptione exutam incorruptioni redderet.	rex cum episcopo et honestis viris illi obviaret honorifice susceptus, quid rex vellet audivit. Tunc ait: „Cum vota vestra a iusto proposito pendeant Deum invenietis placabilem et successum bone petitionis ferentem.“ Tunc ipsi cum electis aditum introeuntes lapidem removerunt. Nullus orationibus parcebat et eorum qui intus aderant et qui prae foribus manserant, sed eremita quamvis suis meritis et omnium adiutus precibus tamen tremebundus intravit et ossa beatissima baiolavit atque in mundissimo locello tale usui praeparato singula ordinabiliter posuit. Tanta vis odoris flagraverat ut nemo	miracula. Quia in omnem terram sonus exiit conversationis eius et sanctitas luculenter emicuit. Erat enim sedens in monasterio in secretiori parte oppidi Veronensis continuis ieiuniis et orationibus crebris a Domino petens ut sibi dignaretur aditum mellifere praedicationis in populos aperire. Igitur ad convertendas in amorem Christi animas hominum die noctuque deditus erat. Revera quondam spiritus ei sanctus purarum illuminator mentium doctor existebat, sicut ipsa veritas loquitur dicens: „Non enim vos estis qui loquimini sed spiritus patris vestri qui loquitur in vobis.“

			illorum tam suavem ante persenserat.	
R4		Iuxta Athesis fluvium iussit beatus confessor Zeno construi oratorium ubi post modum quievit in Domino alleluia. V Ibique sepultus corpore et in caelo spiritus eius. Quievit… V Gloria patri… Quievit.		
II. Nokturn				
A7		Beatus Zeno dixit: „Non te permittit Dominus aliquid agere adversus servum suum.“		
Psalm	[Ps. 14] *Domine, quis habitabit in tabernaculo tuo? aut quis requiescet in monte sancto tuo? Qui ingreditur sine macula, et operatur iustitiam; qui loquitur veritatem in corde suo; qui non egit dolum in lingua sua; nec fecit proximo suo malum, et opprobrium non accepit adversus proximos suos. Ad nihilum deductus est in conspectu eius malignus; timentes autem Dominum glorificat. Qui iurat proximo suo, et non decipit; qui pecuniam suam non dedit ad usuram, et munera super innocentem non accepit. Qui facit haec non movebitur in aeternum.*			

A8		Miserabilis pater totaque domus regia maerore affligebatur eo quod[668] acriter puella suffocaretur alleluia.
Psalm	[Ps. 20] *Domine, in virtute tua laetabitur rex, et super salutare tuum exsultabit vehementer. Desiderium cordis eius tribuisti ei, et voluntate labiorum eius non fraudasti eum. Quoniam praevenisti eum in benedictionibus dulcedinis; posuisti in capite eius coronam de lapide pretioso. Vitam petiit a te, et tribuisti ei longitudinem dierum in saeculum, et in saeculum saeculi. Magna est gloria eius in salutari tuo; gloriam et magnum decorem impones super eum. Quoniam dabis eum in benedictionem in saeculum saeculi; laetificabis eum in gaudio cum vultu tuo. Quoniam rex sperat in Domino; et in misericordia Altissimi non commovebitur. Inveniatur manus tua omnibus inimicis tuis; dextera tua inveniat omnes qui te oderunt. Pones eos ut clibanum ignis in tempore vultus*	

668 Quod] quo *VrCiv*[1].

	tui: Dominus in ira sua conturbabit eos et devorabit eos ignis. Fructum eorum de terra perdes, et semen eorum a filiis hominum, quoniam declinaverunt in te mala; cogitaverunt consilia quae non potuerunt stabilire. Quoniam pones eos dorsum; in reliquiis tuis praeparabis vultum eorum. Exaltare, Domine, in virtute tua; cantabimus et psallemus virtutes tuas.	
A9		Sacerdos Dei Zeno sedebat super lapidem et artis apostolicae documenta sequens piscabatur in flumine alleluia.
Psalm	[Ps. 23] *Domini est terra, et plenitudo eius; orbis terrarum, et universi qui habitant in eo. Quia ipse super maria fundavit eum, et super flumina praeparavit eum. Quis ascendet in montem Domini? aut quis stabit in loco sancto eius? Innocens manibus et mundo corde, qui non accepit in vano animam suam, nec iuravit in dolo proximo suo. Hic accipiet benedictionem a Domino, et misericordiam a Deo*	

	salutari suo. Haec est generatio quaerentium eum, quaerentium faciem Dei Iacob. Attollite portas, principes, vestras, et elevamini, portae aeternales, et introibit rex gloriae. Quis est iste rex gloriae? Dominus fortis et potens, Dominus potens in praelio. Attollite portas, principes, vestras, et elevamini, portae aeternales, et introibit rex gloriae. Quis est iste rex gloriae? Dominus virtutum ipse est rex gloriae.	
A10		Beate Zeno praesul qui regis unicam salvasti filiam a daemonum potestate nos te rogantes et deprecantes libera alleluia.
Psalm	[Ps. 63] *Exaudi, Deus, orationem meam cum deprecor; a timore inimici eripe animam meam. Protexisti me a conventu malignantium, a multitudine operantium iniquitatem. Quia exacuerunt ut gladium linguas suas; intenderunt arcum rem amaram, ut sagittent in occultis immaculatum. Subito sagittabunt eum, et non timebunt; firmaverunt sibi sermonem*	

	nequam. Narraverunt ut absconderent laqueos; dixerunt: Quis videbit eos? Scrutati sunt iniquitates; defecerunt scrutantes scrutinio. Accedet homo ad cor altum; et exaltabitur Deus. Sagittae parvulorum factae sunt plagae eorum; et infirmatae sunt contra eos linguae eorum. Conturbati sunt omnes qui videbant eos; et timuit omnis homo. Et annuntiaverunt opera Dei; et facta eius intellexerunt. Laetabitur iustus in Domino, et sperabit in eo; et laudabuntur omnes recti corde.	
A11		Coepitque beatus pontifex in Verona destruere omnia idola et fabricare Christi ecclesias alleluia.
Psalm	[Ps. 64] *Te decet hymnus, Deus, in Sion, et tibi reddetur votum in Ierusalem. Exaudi orationem meam; ad te omnis caro veniet. Verba iniquorum praevaluerunt super nos, et impietatibus nostris tu propitiaberis. Beatus quem elegisti et assumpsisti: inhabitabit in atriis tuis. Replebimur in bonis*	

	domus tuae; sanctum est templum tuum, mirabile in aequitate. Exaudi nos, Deus, salutaris noster, spes omnium finium terrae, et in mari longe. Praeparans montes in virtute tua, accinctus potentia; qui conturbas profundum maris, sonum fluctuum eius. Turbabuntur gentes, et timebunt qui habitant terminos a signis tuis; exitus matutini et vespere delectabis. Visitasti terram, et inebriasti eam; multiplicasti locupletare eam. Flumen Dei repletum est aquis; parasti cibum illorum; quoniam ita est praeparatio eius. Rivos eius inebria, multiplica genimina eius; in stillicidiis eius laetabitur germinans. Benedices coronae anni benignitatis tuae, et campi tui replebuntur ubertate. Pinguescent speciosa deserti, et exsultatione colles accingentur. Induti sunt arietes ovium, et valles abundabunt frumento; clamabunt, etenim hymnum dicent.	
A12		Iuxta Athesis fluvium iussit beatus Zeno construi oratorium in quo quievit in Domino alleluia.

Psalm	[Ps. 91] *Bonum est confiteri Domino, et psallere nomini tuo, Altissime. Ad annuntiandum mane misericordiam tuam, et veritatem tuam per noctem; in decachordo, psalterio, cum cantico, in cithara. Quia delectasti me, Domine, in factura tua; et in operibus manuum tuarum exsultabo. Quam magnificata sunt opera tua, Domine! Nimis profundae factae sunt cogitationes tuae. Vir insipiens non cognoscet, et stultus non intelliget haec. Cum exorti fuerint peccatores sicut foenum, et apparuerint omnes qui operantur iniquitatem, ut intereant in saeculum saeculi; tu autem Altissimus in aeternum, Domine. Quoniam ecce inimici tui, Domine, quoniam ecce inimici tui peribunt; et dispergentur omnes qui operantur iniquitatem. Et exaltabitur sicut unicornis cornu meum, et senectus mea in misericordia uberi. Et despexit oculus meus inimicos meos, et in insurgentibus in me malignantibus*	

	audiet auris mea. Iustus ut palma florebit; sicut cedrus Libani multiplicabitur. Plantati in domo Domini, in atriis domus Dei nostri florebunt. Adhuc multiplicabuntur in senecta uberi, et bene patientes erunt: ut annuntient quoniam rectus Dominus Deus noster, et non est iniquitas in eo.			
Versikel + Responsio				
Pater noster				
Segnung				
		IN DEPOSITIONE	IN TRANSLATIONE	IN ORDINATIONE
L5		Quod virum Dei plenum non latuit. Mox gregem multo labore, et sudore quaesitum, quo iacebat, vocari praecepit, quibus inspectis ait: „Filii carissimi, diutius vobiscum esse mallem, sed Dominus ergastulum animae pulsat, et quam dedit, ad se vocat. Nunc	Tunc rex sua et suorum instigatione permotus reliquiarum aliquid postulavit quod episcopus fieri denegavit at rex magis ac magis insistere et magna munera promittere tandem praesul non paucis neque parvis precibus victus acquievit.	Ita sane affabilis erat in sermone et in mansuetudine seu in habitu mitis ut iure Deus in ipso esse crederetur ab omnibus venientibus ad se. Ita alacer et splendifico nitore facundiae vividus ut mox ad eum properantes relicits idolis et pravitates

		vestrae fidei, spei, et caritati ecclesiam Dei commendo, quam ille non quovis pretio, sed proprio sanguine quaesivit, ut eam doctrinae lumine illustretis, et exemplorum fultu roboretis. Vigilate in fide, viriliter agite, confortamini in Domino, omnia vestra in caritate fiant. Scitis qui legitime certaverit, coronatur: hic certate, hic pugnate, hic contra vitiorum aciem dimicate, ut coronam non tabentibus floribus, aut lauro fluitura textam capiatis, sed gemnis perenniter fulgentibus, et auro nunquam perituro Dei digito fabricatam possideatis.“	Integritate membrorum servata nervorum et cineris ac vestimentorum particulas tribuit. Alia autem firmiter circumsepta annuloque sigillata condidit. Ad vocem psallentium Athesis litus resonuit intonuere campestria et ipsam aulam omnipotentis credimus esse gavisam. Dum circa ecclesiam gestaretur ut fieri solet praedicta praeconia resultabant. Multi languores corpora diu obsessa reliquerant. Ingens laetitia orta est die illa cuius similem nullus illius temporis viderat quia omnigenum curationum genera brevi acta sunt tempore et prolixior facta processio fuit pro visione signorum.	gentilitatis exempti Domino crederent Iesu Christo. Per idem tempus iuxta urbem Veronam egrediens idem vir a monasterio dum in Athesi fluvio piscationis exercitio fungeretur, erectis sursum oculis vidit ex adverso quendam hominem in plaustro sedentem bubus subiunctis per praeceps in amnem dimergi.

R5		Affabilis ita erat in sermonibus et mansuetudine atque habitu mitis ut Deus in ipso collaudaretur ab omnibus ad se venientibus. V Ita existebat alacer ut mox ad eum properantes relictis idolis Domino crederent Iesu Christo. Ut Deus…		
		IN DEPOSITIONE	IN TRANSLATIONE	IN ORDINATIONE
L6		Post multiplices, et elegantes sermones mysterium tali aptum negotio sumpsit, et osculum singulis – velut iturus Ierusalem – dedit. Post haec signavit eos, et benedixit. Mox sanctam animam creatori suo reddidit. Pridie idus Aprilis quod omnem populum quasi unum hominem congregavit. Videntes senes et iuvenes, atque infantulos, et alterum sexum eiusdem aetatis circa corpus redolens, velut omni genere odoris aspersum, ingentem clamorem facere, ac sicut omnium patres, et	Sed rex et episcopus atque rupis incola pavidi sancta membra introduxerunt et in parato mausuleo posuerunt. Postquam pontifex reverenter missam celebrat rex dote nobili Dei sponsam ditavit: Dedit ei proprietario iure monasterium sancti Petri qui Mauriatica dicitur cum omnibus possessionibus inibi pertinentibus; ecclesiam quoque sancti Andreae apostoli quae Incavi nuncupatur cum familiis, montibus et silvis, pratis et vineis, arvis et sationalibus et cunctis	Tanta quippe miserabilis velocitate ferebatur ut palam cuncits cernentibus daretur intelligi. Sanctus itaque vir dum intentis luminibus hoc a longe prospiceret cognovit lymphaticam viri ruinam factum diaboli esse. Interea vir Dei elevata sursum manu fecit sanctae crucis signum, frequenti vice et dixit: „Revertere retro Sathana ne perimas hominem quem Deus creavit.“ Quot videlicet signum ut diabolus aspexit velut fumus vento raptus evanuit et clamoribus nimiis ac stridore

		matres eo momento morerentur, plorare: „Cui nos reliquisti pater? Quis maestos consolabitur? Quis aegros tam celeriter medicabit? Quis egenis tantum dederit? Quis famelicos tam bene satiaverit? Si optio nobis daretur, tuam vitam nostra morte commercaremur.“	appendicibus. Nec non et ecclesiam sancti Zenonis quae iuxta lacum posita erat cum omnibus redditibus subiecit. Silvam quoque Mantico tradidit. Vasorum argenteorum et aureorum anaglypha plurima, evangelium gemmarum atque margaritarum compositura et speciosa auri celatura editum donavit et alia quibus regalis dignitas effluebat. Cuius exempli sequaces nostri imperatores praefatum locum dilexerunt ac sua munera obtulerunt.	horribili, quasi de alta rupe praecipitans ait: „Etsi non hic permittis animas hominum mea obsidione lucrari, tamen paratus sum in patrias notas circumquaque sitas ad tuum perniciter abire impedimentum.“
R6		Dum in fluvio Athesis piscationis exercitio fungeretur erectis sursum oculis vidit quendam hominem in plaustro sedentem bubus subiunctis in amnem dimergi. V Tanta enim velocitate ferebatur ut cunctis ostenderetur antiqui hostis arte peractum. Erectis sursum…		

		IN DEPOSITIONE	IN TRANSLATIONE	IN ORDINATIONE
L7		Haec vota animi omnis aetas fundebat, et pro amore eius boni pastoris eiulabat, cui dignas exequias persolverunt, sepelientes non longe ab urbe, ubi Deo feliciter sacrificare consueverat. Multiplices et variae mirabilium species repente circa tumulum eius apparuerunt. Sed ex Gallieni genere religiosi viri, memores consanguinae a daemonio liberatae, eo loci, ubi tanta margarita quieverat, templum construxerunt, a quo quamplures non venientes redierunt, in quo non videntes viderunt, cuius beneficia nonnulli aegroti adhuc, et olim senserunt.	Rotaldus praesul dives possessionum suis omnibus ecclesiam hereditavit nam et nobilium plurimi magnas portiones suarum facultatum certatim adhibuerunt. Unde antequam sol occumberet illa ecclesia ditissima facta est. Ad vir Dei avidus redeundi ad heremum iter suum accelerabat. Hic dum domicilio appropinquaret vidit merulam in praecisa rupe iacentem, quam ratus quiescere et suum adventum praestolari accessit ut excitaret et eundi licentiam daret at illa iam exspiraverat. Vir bonus compatiens ei dixit: „Haec avicula daemonis instructu deliquit et quia	Sanctus autem Dei Zeno dixit: „Non te permittit Deus dire aliquid agere adversus servum suum.“ His ita transactis cum detestabili ululatu et clamore discessit. Festinans itaque daemon ingressus est concite palatium caesaris Gallieni arreptamque filiam eius, quae tunc temporis unica parentibus erat, coepit crudeliter vexare. Miserabilis ergo pater simulque tota domus regia in tristitiam versa cruciatu et maerore ingenti affligebantur. Eo quod tam acriter puella suffocaretur. Quae dum crudeli vexatione corriperetur, coepit per os infantulae regis filiae daemon clamare dicens: „Non egrediar a corpore

			irrationabilis erat ignoranter offendit. Venia non morte digna fuit.“ Unde aerea imago merulae fusuli artefacta ibi huc usque dependet. Videntes rex et pontifex virtutes Zenonis increbrescere et res eius velut amnis liquefacta nive crescere ut tutores et fidi procuratores summa ope nitebantur ne locus fortunatus copia fieret macilentus orationis inopia.	isto nisi Zeno venerit episcopus, tunc per ipsius imperium coactus migrabo.“ Mox itaque ut hoc regi innotuit Gallieno innotuit missis apparitoribus sollicita intentione coepit investigare sic ubi sanctum potuisset invenire virum.
R7		Elevata sursum manu beatus Zeno fecit sanctae crucis signum frequenti vice et dixit: „Revertere retro Sathanas ne perimas hominem quem Deus creavit.“ V Quod signum ut vidit daemon evanuit velut fumus cum clamoribus ac stridore nefando. Revertere…		
		IN DEPOSITIONE	IN TRANSLATIONE	IN ORDINATIONE
L8		Sed die natalicii sui aqua fluminis intemperie acri intumuit, et circumquaque superficiem terrae subito operuit. Hoc enim primo	Ergo pari voto ut gemelli fratres monasterium olim actum augere sanxerunt. Erat illis communis cura probate vitae monachos ibi	Ex iussu autem regis milites velocibus ad virum Dei gressibus pergunt. Ille vero sedebat super lapidem qui in proximo erat monasterii

		mane fatum est, cum frequens multitudo inerat, quantum vix ecclesiae sinus acceperat: ecce undique Athesis voragine basilica obsidebatur et usque ad fenestras impetus illius infremuit, atque aditum ecclesiae clausit, et stetit, ac si illud elementum liquidum in solidum parietem fuisset immutatum: quod, ut viderunt, prius exanimati sunt, confortati; sed inclusi mirabili obsidione iam plus famis, quam fluminis periculum formidabant: illi laborantes siti, primo diluvii timore, deinde densitatis calore, venientes ad ianuam, sitis habuere praesidium, quod aestimaverant esse exitium. Hauriri ut aqua poterat, sed diffluere ut	habitantes ad meliora provehere sicut artifex coronam acturus praestantes gemmas ac margaritas exornat, quibus opus ceptum perficiat. Non multo post Deo clavum gubernante seniores illos cum abbate eadem institutio et moralis gravitas tales exhibuit, quibus gubernaculum coenobiale regule mirifice servaretur et formula atque speculum sequacibus essent et ut boni patres bonos heredes efficerent. Iocundatur rex, iocundatur episcopus pululantis segetis uberem frucutm spectantes. Urbs et suburbana communiter huiusmodi contubernio gaudebant. Unde plures fallacis saeculi umbratilem	et artis apostolicae instrumenta baiulans ex more piscabatur in flumine. Venientes ergo milites quoniam ignotus eis erat coeperunt sollicite sanctum Dei sacerdotem interrogare dicentes: „Quis es tu, homo Dei? Indica nobis si vidisti Zenonem episcopum quem nos ex iussu regis perquirimus.“ At ille respondit: „Ad quod missi estis dicite. Ego enim quamvis tantillus servus tamen Christi Zeno vocor.“ Igitur conferentes ad invicem milites dicebant inter se: „Quid multa colloquimur? Indicemus pro quare istum destinati sumus ad virum.“ Tunc patenter intimantes beato sacerdoti dixerunt: „Rogat te rex venire ad se quia vult faciem tuam

		aqua non poterat. Stans autem ante ianuam, ad ostendendum sancti meritum, et aqua erat adiutorium, et quasi aqua non erat ad invadendum locum. Mox constituti inter spem, et metum, maerorem, et gaudium, stantes, quia iacentes non valebant, rogabant, ut qui aquam compescuit ne ingrederetur, idem cogeret ut ad alveum suum regrederetur: statim Athesis, velut hostis persequeretur, aufugit, et obsidionem timidus deseruit. Tunc divino mysterio attentius, et religiosius acto, omnes via, qua venerant, hilares redierunt. Sed aliqua pars muri civitatis ea coruscatione dirupta fuit, et quae per apertam	auram vitantes ut couterini tantorum virorum fierent satagebant, quos non penuria id facere cogebat sed esuries et sitis sanctae conversationis inhiantes non minimas opes Zenoni ferentes monasticum habitum induerunt. Hoc modo locus ille fortunatior et religiosior factus sub cuiusque Caesaris alis protectus est. Sed beatissimus confessor vires a Domino datas quam sepe excitans, multa memoratu, digna perficiens ex longinquis regionibus plures vocaverat; alios religione motos, alios aegritudinis necessitate coactos. Sed pretereamus omnia suorum per hoc opusculum diseramus aliqua.	videre.“ Quibus Zeno respondit: „Quid meam rex vult humilitatem cernere qui omnium Christianorum manifestis indiciis inimicus esse non desinit?“ At illi respondentes dixerunt: „Obsecrat enim te rex ut filiam ipsius, quae immani atrocitate a daemonio vexatur, sanitati restituas quia unica illi est.“ Ille vero dixit eis: „Dominus Iesus omnipotens est. Ite“, inquit, „ecce ego paulatim subsequor vos. Oportet enim ut mirabilia Dei luce clarius omnibus manifestentur.“ Mox ex piscatura quam ceperat legatis regis Gallieni tres sumere iussit. Dum illi numero contempto unum plus piscem raperent et

		ianuam intrare non valuit, firmissima propugnacula diminuit. Haec fama longe diffusa, Gregorii calamum movit, et Petro suo dialogice edidit, et multi prius insolentes, et renitentes, effecti sunt religionis milites.		quattuor in ferventis aquae dolium mitterent. Tribus datis decoctis ad epulas quartus raptus crudus et velut illaesus in vase natabat quasi commonens ut illicitum redderent et licitos comederent. Illi rubore perfusi vitium rapinae sentientes obesse naturae iniuste acceptum sancto piscatori piscem reddunt. Vir autem Dei et piscem eis concessit et culpam indulsit. Hoc visum, fidem videntibus adhibuit ut si Romam pergeret natam Domini sui a daemone liberaret. Quo facto milites viam qua venerant remeaverunt. Exsurgens vero beatus sacerdos ne diutius absconderetur civitas supra montem Domini posita, fecit orationem perrexitque ad

				palatium ubi cruciabatur et lamentabiliter affligebatur pro sua filia rex. Sanctus quoque Dei episcopus dum celeriter iter ageret ante eos pervenit quam hi qui missi fuerant milites. Ingrediente siquidem Christi sacerdote palatium et facto crucis signo coepit confestim per os infantulae daemon clamare dicens: „Ecce tu, Zeno, venisti ad expellendum me et ego propter pavorem tuae sanctitatis hic stare non possum.“ His quidem auditis tenens sacerdos manum puellae dixit: „In nomine Domini nostri Iesu Christi praecipio tibi exi ab ea daemon.“ At ille publica voce coepit et horribile clamare dicens: „Etsi hinc a te fuero expulsus eo Veronam, ibi

				invenies me et mea zizania sanctum populum, quem lucrari conaris, ludificabit.“ Christi namque sacerdos sanam mox ab omni daemoniacae incursionis ludificatione restituit filiam regis. Protinus autem ut rex Gallienus vidit hoc factum attonitus admiratione coronam regalem quam capite gestabat sancto sacerdoti obtulit dicens: „Tam salutifero medico qui sanam unicam meam filiam restituit nullis muneribus aliis placere possum nisi meam coronam offeram.“ Cumque hoc gestum multitudo vidisset populi quae ad palatium convenerat, a tenebris infidelitatis et errore conversa gentili crediderunt unanimiter

				in Dominum nostrum Iesum Christum. Obsecrantes sacerdotem Christi ut docerentur viam salutis et baptismum mererentur in remissionem percipere peccatorum. At ubi sacerdos coronam a rege accepit statim in partes divisam distribuit pauperibus dicens: „Si Dominus operatur excelsa ipsi perpetuae laudes referantur et gloria.“
R8		Beatissimus Christi confessor Zeno petiit a rege ut in urbe Verona destruerentur omnia manufacta idola et conderetur cum omni honore Iesu Christi catholica ecclesia. V Cumque sanasset filiam regis petiit a rege ut in urbe Verona. Destruerentur…		

III. Nokturn				
A13		Iste est de sublimibus caelorum praepotentibus unus quem manus Domini consecravit matris in visceribus cuius nos precibus adiuvari supplices deposcimus.		
3 Cantica		[unbekannt]		
Versikel + Responsio		[unbekannt]		
Pater noster				
Segnung				
		In depositione	In translatione	In ordinatione
Vers aus dem Evangelium des Tages		[unbekannt]	In illo tempore dixit Iesus discipulis: „Ego sum vitis vera, et pater meus agricola est."[669]	In illo tempore dixit Iesus discipulis: „Nemo lucernam accendit et in abscondito ponit, neque sub modio sed super candelabrum."[670]
L9		[unbekannt]	Iste locus evangelicus, fratres, ubi se dicit	Omelia venerabilis Bede LIX De se ipso Dominus haec loquitur ostendens etsi

[669] Nach den Angaben des portablen Breviers der Abtei, Handschrift *Kr*: Evangelium Ego sum vitis vera (Joh 15). Die gleiche Angabe findet sich in *Aug*.

[670] Nach den Angaben des portablen Breviers der Abtei, Handschrift *Kr*: Omelia de confessoribus pontificis cum evangelio Nemo accendit lucernam (Luk 11, 33).

			Dominus vitem, et discipulos suos palmites, secundum hoc dicit quod est caput ecclesiae, nosque membra eius, mediator Dei et hominum homo Christus Iesus. Unius quippe naturae sunt vitis et palmites; propter quod cum esset Deus, cuius naturae nos sumus, factus est homo, ut in illo esset vitis humana natura, cuius et nos homines palmites esse possemus.	supra dixerit nullum generationi nequam nisi signum Ionae dandum nequaquam tamen lucis suae claritatem fidelibus occultandam. Ipse quippe lucernam accendit qui testam humanae naturae flamma suae divinitatis implevit. Quam profecto lucernam nec credentibus abscondere nec modio supponere, hoc est sub mensura legis includere vel intra unius Iudaeae gentis terminos voluit cohibere.
R9		Festinans itaque daemon ingressus est palatium caesaris Gallieni et comprehensam eius unicam filiam coepit eam crudeliter vexare. V Miserabilis pater totaque domus regia cruciatu et maerore affligebatur. Et comprehensam...		
		IN DEPOSITIONE	IN TRANSLATIONE	IN ORDINATIONE
L10		[unbekannt]	Quid ergo est: ego sum vitis vera? Numquid ut adderet vera, hoc ad eam	Sed supra candelabrum, inquit, ut qui ingrediuntur lumen

			vitem retulit, unde ista similitudo translata est? Sic enim dicitur vitis, per similitudinem, non per proprietatem, quemadmodum dicitur ovis, agnus, leo, petra, lapis angularis, et cetera huiusmodi, quae magis ipsa sunt vera, ex quibus ducuntur istae similitudines, non proprietates.	videant. Candelabrum ecclesiam dicit cui lucernam superposuit quia nostris in frontibus fidem suae incarnationis adfixit ut qui ecclesiam fideliter ingredi voluerint lumen veritatis palam queant intueri. Qua sententia Iudaeorum quoque proceres condemnat qui signa quaerentes exterius apertam lucis ianuam noluerint intrare credendo.
R10		Ingrediente Christi sacerdote palatium et facto crucis signo mox coepit daemon clamare dicens: „Tu, Zeno, expellis me et ego propter tuam sanctitatem stare non possum.“ V Etsi hinc abiero eo Veronam ibique invenies me. Et ego…		
		In depositione	In translatione	In ordinatione
L11		[unbekannt]	Sed cum dicit: ego sum vitis vera, ab illa se utique discernit cui dicitur: quomodo conversa es in amaritudinem, vitis	Denique praecipit ne opera tantummodo sed et cogitationes et ipsas etiam cordis intentiones mundare et castigare meminerint nam

			aliena? Nam quo pacto est vitis vera, quae exspectata est ut faceret uvam, fecit autem spinas? Ego sum, inquit, vitis vera. Et pater meus agricola est. Omnem palmitem in me non ferentem fructum, tollet eum; et omnem qui fert fructum, purgabit eum, ut fructum plus afferat.	sequitur: lucerna corporis tui est oculus tuus. Corpus quippe dicit opera quae palam cunctis apparent oculum vero ipsam mentis intentionem qua operatur et de cuius merito eadem opera lucis an tenebrarum sint opera discernuntur sicut ipse consequenter exposuit dicens.
R11		Sacerdos Dei altissimi Zeno interveni pro delictis nostris in conspectu Domini. V Ut vitae presentis et futurae percipiamus consolationem. In conspectu...		
		IN DEPOSITIONE	IN TRANSLATIONE	IN ORDINATIONE
L12		[unbekannt]	Numquid unum sunt agricola et vitis? Secundum hoc ergo vitis Christus, secundum quod ait: Pater maior me est; secundum autem id quod ait: Ego et pater unum sumus, et ipse agricola est. Nec talis quales sunt, qui extrinsecus operando	Si oculus tuus fuerit simplex, totum corpus tuum lucidum erit; si autem nequam fuerit, etiam corpus tuum tenebrosum erit. Si, inquit, pura rectaque intentione quae potes agere bona studueris, lucis profecto sunt opera quae facis, etiamsi coram

			exhibent ministerium; sed talis ut det etiam intrinsecus incrementum. Nam neque qui plantat est aliquid, neque qui rigat; sed qui incrementum dat Deus.	hominibus imperfectionis aliquid habere videantur quoniam diligentibus Deum omnia cooperantur in bonum his qui secundum propositum vocati sunt sancti.
R12		Sancte Zeno Christi confessor audi rogantes servulos et impetratam caelitus tu defer indulgentiam. V O sancte Zeno sidus aureum Domini gratia servorum gemitus solita suscipe clementia. Et impetratam…		
Te Deum laudamus	*Te Deum laudamus. Te Dominum confitemur. Te aeternum patrem omnis terra veneratur. Tibi omnes Angeli, tibi caeli et universae potestates: Tibi cherubim et seraphim incessabili voce proclamant: Sanctus, Sanctus, Sanctus Dominus Deus Sabaoth. Pleni sunt caeli et terra maiestatis gloriae tuae. Te gloriosus Apostolorum chorus. Te prophetarum laudabilis numerus. Te martyrum candidatus laudat exercitus. Te per orbem terrarum*			

	sancta confitetur Ecclesia. Patrem immensae maiestatis. Venerandum tuum verum, et unicum Filium. Sanctum quoque Paraclitum Spiritum. Tu Rex gloriae, Christe. Tu Patris sempiternus es Filius. Tu ad liberandum suscepturus hominem, non horruisti Virginis uterum. Tu devicto mortis aculeo, aperuisti credentibus regna caelorum. Tu ad dexteram Dei sedes, in gloria Patris. Iudex crederis esse venturus. Te ergo quaesumus, tuis famulis subveni, quos pretioso sanguine redemisti. Aeterna fac cum sanctis tuis in gloria numerari. Salvum fac populum tuum Domine, et benedic haereditati tuae. Et rege eos, et extolle illos usque in aeternum. Per singulos dies, benedicimus te. Et laudamus nomen tuum in saeculum, et in saeculum saeculi. Dignare Domine, die isto sine peccato nos custodire. Miserere nostri, Domine, miserere nostri. Fiat misericordia tua Domine, super nos, quemadmodum	

	speravimus in te. In te, Domine, speravi: non confundar in aeternum.			
		IN DEPOSITIONE	IN TRANSLATIONE	IN ORDINATIONE
Evangelium des Tages			In illo tempore dixit Iesus discipulis: „Ego sum vitis vera, et pater meus agricola est.“[671]	In illo tempore dixit Iesus discipulis: „Nemo lucernam accendit et in abscondito ponit, neque sub modio sed super candelabrum.“
Te decet laus	*Te decet laus, te decet hymnus; tibi gloria Deo Patri, et Filio, cum Sancto Spiritu in saecula saeculorum. Amen.*			
Kyrie, Pater noster, Preces				
Kollekt		[unbekannt]		

[671] Nach den Angaben des portablen Breviers der Abtei, Handschrift *Kr*: EVANGELIUM Ego sum vitis vera (Joh 15). Die gleiche Angabe findet sich in *Aug*.

LAUDES		
V. *Deus in adiutorium meum intende* R. *Domine ad adiuvandum me festina* *Gloria patri…* *(Alleluia)*		
L-A1		Dominus Iesus Christus omnipotens est, oportet enim ut mirabilia Dei omnibus manifestentur.
Psalm	[Ps. 92] *Dominus regnavit, decorem indutus est: indutus est Dominus fortitudinem, et praecinxit se. Etenim firmavit orbem terrae, qui non commovebitur. Parata sedes tua ex tunc; a saeculo tu es. Elevaverunt flumina, Domine, elevaverunt flumina vocem suam, elevaverunt flumina fluctus suos, a vocibus aquarum multarum. Mirabiles elationes maris; mirabilis in altis Dominus. Testimonia tua credibilia facta sunt nimis; domum tuam decet sanctitudo, Domine, in longitudinem dierum.*	

L-A2		Exurgens beatus sacerdos fecit orationem perrexitque ad palatium ubi affligebatur pro sua filia rex.
Psalm	[Ps. 99] *Iubilate Deo omnis terra; servite Domino in laetitia. Introite in conspectu eius in exsultatione. Scitote quoniam Dominus ipse est Deus; ipse fecit nos, et non ipsi nos; populus eius, et oves pascuae eius. Introite portas eius in confessione, atria eius in hymnis; confitemini illi. Laudate nomen eius, quoniam suavis est Dominus; in aeternum misericordia eius, et usque in generationem et generationem veritas eius.*	
L-A3		Ingrediente Christi confessore palatium facto crucis signo per os puellae daemon clamavit dicens: „Tu, Zeno, venisti ad expellendum me et propter tuam sanctitatem stare non possum.“
Psalm	[Ps. 62] *Deus, Deus meus, ad te de luce vigilo. Sitivit in te anima mea; quam multipliciter tibi caro mea! In terra deserta, et invia, et inaquosa, sic in sancto apparui tibi, ut viderem virtutem tuam et gloriam tuam. Quoniam melior est misericordia tua super vitas, labia mea laudabunt te. Sic*	

	benedicam te in vita mea; et in nomine tuo levabo manus meas. Sicut adipe et pinguedine repleatur anima mea, et labiis exsultationis laudabit os meum. Si memor fui tui super stratum meum, in matutinis meditabor in te. Quia fuisti adjutor meus, et in velamento alarum tuarum exsultabo. *Adhaesit anima mea post te; me suscepit dextera tua. Ipsi vero in vanum quaesierunt animam meam: introibunt in inferiora terrae; tradentur in manus gladii; partes vulpium erunt. Rex vero laetabitur in Deo; laudabuntur omnes qui jurant in eo, quia obstructum est os loquentium iniqua* [Ps. 66] *Deus misereatur nostri, et benedicat nobis; illuminet vultum suum super nos, et misereatur nostri; ut cognascamus in terra viam tuam, in omnibus gentibus salutare tuum. Confiteantur tibi populi, Deus, confiteantur tibi populi omnes. Laetentur et exsultent gentes, quoniam iudicas*	

	populos in aequitate, et gentes in terra dirigis. Confiteantur tibi populi, Deus, confiteantur tibi populi omnes. Terra dedit fructum suum: benedicat nos Deus, Deus noster! Benedicat nos Deus, et metuant eum omnes fines terrae.	
L-A4		Tenens beatus Zeno manum puellae dixit: „In nomine Domini mei Iesu Christi praecipio tibi exi ab ea daemon.“
Alttestamentarisches Canticum	[Dan 3, 56-88, 56] *Benedicite omnia opera Domini, Domino: laudate et superexaltate eum in saecula. Benedicite, angeli Domini, Domino: laudate et superexaltate eum in saecula. Benedicite, caeli, Domino: laudate et superexaltate eum in saecula. Benedicite, aquae omnes, quae super caelos sunt, Domino: laudate et superexaltate eum in saecula. Benedicite, omnes virtutes Domini, Domino: laudate et superexaltate eum in saecula. Benedicite, sol et luna, Domino: laudate et superexaltate eum in saecula. Benedicite, stellae caeli, Domino: laudate et superexaltate eum in*	

	saecula. Benedicite, omnis imber et ros, Domino: laudate et superexaltate eum in saecula. Benedicite, omnes spiritus Dei, Domino: laudate et superexaltate eum in saecula. Benedicite, ignis et aestus, Domino: laudate et superexaltate eum in saecula. Benedicite, frigus et aestus, Domino: laudate et superexaltate eum in saecula. Benedicite, rores et pruina, Domino: laudate et superexaltate eum in saecula. Benedicite, gelu et frigus, Domino: laudate et superexaltate eum in saecula. Benedicite, glacies et nives, Domino: laudate et superexaltate eum in saecula. Benedicite, noctes et dies, Domino laudate et superexaltate eum in saecula. Benedicite, lux et tenebrae, Domino: laudate et superexaltate eum in saecula. Benedicite, fulgura et nubes, Domino: laudate et superexaltate eum in saecula. Benedicat terra Dominum: laudet et superexaltet eum in saecula. Benedicite,	

	montes et colles, Domino: laudate et superexaltate eum in saecula. Benedicite, universa germinantia in terra, Domino: laudate et superexaltate eum in saecula. Benedicite, fontes, Domino: laudate et superexaltate eum in saecula. Benedicite, maria et flumina, Domino: laudate et superexaltate eum in saecula. Benedicite cete, et omnia quae moventur in aquis, Domino: laudate et superexaltate eum in saecula. Benedicite, omnes volucres caeli, Domino: laudate et superexaltate eum in saecula. Benedicite, omnes bestiae et pecora, Domino: laudate et superexaltate eum in saecula. Benedicite, filii hominum, Domino: laudate et superexaltate eum in saecula. Benedicat Israel Dominum: laudet et superexaltet eum in saecula. Benedicite, sacerdotes Domini, Domino: laudate et superexaltate eum in saecula. Benedicite, servi Domini, Domino: laudate et superexaltate eum in saecula. Benedicite, spiritus	

	et animae iustorum, Domino: laudate et superexaltate eum in saecula. Benedicite, sancti et humiles corde, Domino: laudate et superexaltate eum in saecula. Benedicite, Anania, Azaria, Misaël, Domino: laudate et superexaltate eum in saecula: quia eruit nos de inferno, et salvos fecit de manu mortis: et liberavit nos de medio ardentis flammae, et de medio ignis eruit nos.	
L-A5		Christi namque sacerdos ab omni daemoniacae incursionis ludificatione sanam restituit filiam regis.
Psalmen 148–150	[Ps. 148] *Laudate Dominum de caelis; laudate eum in excelsis. Laudate eum, omnes angeli eius; laudate eum, omnes virtutes eius. Laudate eum, sol et luna; laudate eum, omnes stellae et lumen. Laudate eum, caeli caelorum; et aquae omnes quae super caelos sunt, laudent nomen Domini. Quia ipse dixit, et facta sunt; ipse mandavit, et creata sunt. Statuit ea in aeternum, et in saeculum saeculi; praeceptum posuit, et non*	

	praeteribit. Laudate Dominum de terra, dracones et omnes abyssi; ignis, grando, nix, glacies, spiritus procellarum, quae faciunt verbum eius; montes, et omnes colles; ligna fructifera, et omnes cedri; bestiae, et universa pecora; serpentes, et volucres pennatae; reges terrae et omnes populi, principes et omnes iudices terrae; iuvenes et virgines, senes cum iunioribus laudent nomen Domini, quia exaltatum est nomen eius solius. Confessio eius super caelum et terram; et exaltavit cornu populi sui. Hymnus omnibus sanctis eius; filiis Israel, populo appropinquanti sibi. [Ps. 149] *Cantate Domino canticum novum; laus eius in ecclesia sanctorum. Laetetur Israel in eo qui fecit eum, et filii Sion exsultent in rege suo. Laudent nomen eius in choro, in tympano et psalterio psallant ei. Quia beneplacitum est Domino in populo suo, et exaltabit mansuetos in salutem. Exsultabunt sancti in gloria, laetabuntur in cubilibus*	

	suis. Exaltationes Dei in gutture eorum: et gladii ancipites in manibus eorum: ad faciendam vindictam in nationibus, increpationes in populis; ad alligandos reges eorum in compedibus, et nobiles eorum in manicis ferreis; ut faciant in eis judicium conscriptum: gloria haec est omnibus sanctis eius. [Ps. 150] *Laudate Dominum in sanctis eius; laudate eum in firmamento virtutis eius. Laudate eum in virtutibus eius; laudate eum secundum multitudinem magnitudinis eius. Laudate eum in sono tubae; laudate eum in psalterio et cithara. Laudate eum in tympano et choro; laudate eum in chordis et organo. Laudate eum in cymbalis benesonantibus; laudate eum in cymbalis jubilationis. Omnis spiritus laudet Dominum! Alleluia*	
Kurzlesung		Beatus vir...
Kurzes Responsorium		Posuisti, Domine, super caput eius coronam de lapide pretioso. Vitam petiit a te, tribuisti ei in saeculum saeculi.

Hymnus		Praesulis sancti reddeunt colenda festa Zenonis Dominum sequentis, qui diem nobis celebrem sacravit fine beato. Magnus excelsus fuerat sacerdos praedicans gentes bene transmarinas inde Veronam hunc ad urbem Deus mittere curavit. Qua Deo multum populum lucratus instruit verbis solidavit actis in Deo tum patiendo mortem vivit in aevum. Nunc in aeternis meritis corruscat clarus et mundo manifestus omni, qui Deo soli studuit placere corpore vivens. Pastor aeterno radians triumpho servulos audi tibi supplicantes, praemium iustis veniam deposce crimine lapsis.

		Quo Dei magna miseratione ordinem caeli decimum replentes ipsius vultum videamus omni tempore saeculi amen.
Versikel + Antwortgesang		Ora pro nobis...
B-A		Acceptam beatus Zeno coronam a rege distribuit pauperibus dicens: „Si Dominus operatur excelsa ipsi perpetuae laudes referantur et gloria.“
Benedictus (Lc 1, 68–79)	*Benedictus Dominus Deus Israel, quia visitavit et fecit redemptionem plebi suae et erexit cornu salutis nobis, in domo David pueri sui, sicut locutus est per os sanctorum, qui a saeculo sunt, prophetarum eius, salutem ex inimicis nostris, et de manu omnium, qui oderunt nos; ad faciendam misericordiam cum patribus nostris, et memorari testamenti sui sancti, ius iurandum, quod iuravit ad Abraham patrem nostrum, daturum se nobis, ut sine timore, de manu inimicorum liberati, serviamus illi in sanctitate et iustitia coram ipso omnibus diebus*	

	nostris. Et tu, puer, propheta Altissimi vocaberis: praeibis enim ante faciem Domini parare vias eius, ad dandam scientiam salutis plebi eius in remissionem peccatorum eorum, per viscera misericordiae Dei nostri, in quibus visitabit nos oriens ex alto, illuminare his, qui in tenebris et in umbra mortis sedent, ad dirigendos pedes nostros in viam pacis.	
Kyrie		
Pater noster		
Kollekt		[unbekannt]
Benedicamus Dominus		
LAUDES		
PRIM/TERZ/MESSE/ SEXT/NON		[unbekannt], außer für die Antiphonen: es werden die Laudes-Antiphonen gesungen.
II VESPER		siehe I Vesper

4 Zeno und seine historischen Verehrergemeinschaften im Spiegel der liturgischen Überlieferung

4.1 *Die Geburt des Heiligen*

Die vorliegende Arbeit versteht Heiligkeit als Konstruktionsprozess, bei dem aus einer bedeutenden Person ein Heiliger gemacht wird. Dieser Prozess erfolgt im Wesentlichen durch die Verehrung des Heiligen durch eine Gemeinschaft, die sich um diese Person, vielleicht am Ort ihres Wirkens oder Sterbens, konstituiert. Heilige sind daher nicht von Beginn an heilig, Heilige entstehen in postumer Idealisierung. Zwar handelt es sich in der Regel um historische Persönlichkeiten, zu Heiligen werden diese aber erst, wenn sie zugleich Objekte retrospektiver Zuschreibungen und liturgischer Verehrung werden. Das folgende Kapitel verfolgt die Spuren der Geburt des Heiligen Zeno. Dabei werden zunächst die wenigen bekannten Nachrichten über die historische Person sowie die ersten Zeugnisse ihrer kultischen Verehrung von der ausgehenden Spätantike über die Langobardenzeit gesammelt. Anschließend wird die Etablierung Zenos als Heiliger mit und durch feste Verehrergemeinschaften im karolingischen Verona beschrieben.

4.1.1 *Spuren des heiligen Zeno: von der historischen Person bis zu den Anfängen seiner Verehrung*

Nur wenig ist über den historischen Veroneser Bischof mit dem Namen Zeno bekannt. Der spätere Heilige lebte in der zweiten Hälfte des 4. Jahrhunderts, über die Zeit seiner Geburt sind wir nicht unterrichtet. Auch seine Herkunft ist nicht gesichert, allerdings lässt sich aus dem Inhalt einer ihm zugeschriebenen Predigtsammlung unter der Bezeichnung *Tractatus*[1] auf einen nordafrikanischen Hintergrund deuten:

> Es ist möglich, dass der Verfasser unserer Predigten aus Afrika stammt. Davon zeugt in erster Linie der Umstand, dass in die Sammlung die Passio des Heiligen Archadius mit

---

1 Dolbeau untersuchte die Verbreitung des *Tractatus* und kam zu folgendem Schluss: „les oeuvres de Zénon circulaient en Gaule du Sud, durant la première moitié de VIe siècle. [...] les Tractatus, loin d'etre confinés à la région de Vérone, ont connu une diffusion nettement plus large qu´on n le pensait naguère", vgl. François Dolbeau: Zenoniana. Recherches sur le texte et sur la tradition de Zénon de Vérone, in: Recherches Augustiniennes et Patristiques 20, 1985, S. 3–34, hier: S. 14. Auch in Nordirland muss das Werk von Zeno im 7. Jhdt. bekannt gewesen sein, wie ein Eintrag im sogenannten Antiphonar von Bangor zeigt. Hier ist ein Gebet überliefert, das eine Passage aus der Predigt XXII der Sammlung wiedergibt, vgl. André Galli: Zénon de Vérone dans l'antiphonaire de Bangor, in: Revue bénédictine 93, 1983, S. 293–301.

aufgenommen worden ist [...]; ich glaube, dass sie von demselben Autor wie die Predigten stammt, und es liegt nahe, anzunehmen, dass ein Afrikaner die Leidensgeschichte dieses sonst wenig bekannten Märtyrers geschrieben hat [...].[2]

Ebenfalls lässt sich Zenos Wirken anhand dieser Predigtsammlung geographisch und zeitlich verorten. Nicht nur benennen ihn die Handschriften, welche die Sammlung überliefern, als heiligen oder seligen Bischof von Verona.[3] Tatsächlich ergibt sich der Bezug zur Stadt auch aus den Inhalten der Predigten selbst. Die Tatsache, dass eine dieser Predigten anlässlich der Weihe einer umgebauten Kirche gehalten wurde, legt zusammen mit archäologischen Befunden nahe, dass Zeno als Erbauer einer Vorgängerkirche des heutigen Doms in Erscheinung trat.[4] Die Kirchweihe war ausdrücklich dem Bischof vorbehalten, womit gleichzeitig Zenos Inhaberschaft dieses Amtes bewiesen wäre.[5] Außerdem behandeln zahlreiche Predigten mit der Taufe und dem Osterfest wichtige liturgische Anlässe, die ebenfalls in den Aufgabenbereich des Bischofs fielen.[6] Um den Prediger herum war außerdem auch eine organisierte Gemeinschaft tätig, wie eine Passage in einer der Predigten (*Tractatus* I 41)[7] nahelegt, in der von einer Gruppe von Personen, den *operarii*, die Rede ist, die üblicherweise einem Bischof zuarbeiteten. Somit ist es möglich, dass nicht nur der Bischof, sondern auch die Gruppe der Kleriker, die ihm liturgisch dienten, auf die Spätantike zurückgeht. Auch die Lokalisierung in Verona wird durch die Predigten unterstrichen, die häufig einen Bezug zur Stadt aufweisen.[8] Textimmanent ist außerdem ein Terminus post quem für Zenos Wirken in der oberitalienischen Stadt: Er bezieht sich in einer seiner Predigten auf den Psalmenkommentar des Hilarius und daher, dies schlussfolgert der Editor des *Tractatus*, kann Zeno sein Werk nicht vor 360 verfasst haben.[9]

Ebenso wie die Umstände seiner Geburt bleibt auch Zenos Tod weitestgehend im Dunkeln. Lediglich ein Briefwechsel aus der Zeit von 380 bis 396 zwischen Ambrosius von Mailand und dem damaligen Veroneser Bischof Siagrio gibt Hinweise auf das Ableben Zenos, da dort bereits von seinem heiligen Andenken („sancta memoria") die Rede ist.[10] Dass seine Tätigkeit als Bischof ihm offenbar auch außerhalb Veronas ein gewisses Ansehen einbrachte, zeigt neben dem Ambrosiusbrief auch eine Passage in den *Dialogi* Gregors des Großen. Darin widmete dieser Zeno eine kurze Passage im Kapitel 19 des dritten Buches, womit wir den Boden

---

2 Zeno von Verona: Zenonis Veronensis tractatus, 6*–7*.

3 „sanctus (Beatus, Divus) Zeno, episcopus (presul) Veronensis", ebd., 5*.

4 Vgl. Silvia Lusuardi Siena: Puntualizzazioni archeologiche sulle due chiese paleocristiane, in: Pierpaolo Brugnoli (Hg.): La Cattedrale di Verona nelle sue vicende edilizie dal secolo IV al secolo XVI, Venedig 1987, S. 26–78, hier: S. 55.

5 Vgl. Zeno von Verona: Zenonis Veronensis tractatus, S. 7.

6 Vgl. ebd.

7 Vgl. ebd., 112.

8 ebd., 7*–8*.

9 Vgl. ebd., S. 8.

10 Vgl. Ambrosius von Mailand: Sancti Ambrosii Opera. Epistularvm libri VII–VIIII, hrsg. von Otto Faller (Corpus Scriptorum Ecclesiasticorum Latinorum 82,2), Wien 1990, S. 84.

der historisch gesicherten Tatsachen verlassen und den Bereich der Heiligenverehrung betreten. Gregor berichtet von der Wundertätigkeit Zenos, der hier als „beatus“, „pontifex“ und fälschlicherweise auch als „martyr“ beschrieben wird: Als sich die Verehrer Zenos zu dessen Ehren in seiner Kirche versammelt hätten, sei es zu einer Überschwemmung durch die Etsch gekommen. Durch das Eingreifen des Heiligen stoppte das Wasser vor dem Eingang der Kirche und bewahrte die Eingeschlossenen so auch vor dem Verdursten.[11] Diese Episode wird später zum wesentlichen Bestandteil der biographischen Erzählungen über Zeno und kommt ab dem 9. Jahrhundert in vielen Versionen seiner Vita in leicht abgeänderter Form vor. Relevant ist weiterhin, dass Gregor neben der Wundererzählung auch von einer dem Heiligen gewidmeten Kirche berichtet – und dies nicht als Einziger.

Auch zwei Predigten eines gewissen Petronius, die in einer Handschrift als *Predigt des Bischofs Petronius von Verona für den Todestag des heiligen Zeno* (*Sermo Petronii episcopi veronensis in natale sancti Zenonis*) und *Predigt über das gleiche Thema wie oben, am Tag der bischöflichen Weihe oder am Todestag des Bischofs* (*Sermo de cuius supra in die ordinationis vel natale episcopi*) bezeichnet werden,[12] bezeugen eine Verehrung Zenos sowie eine dem Heiligen gewidmete Kirche in Verona im 5. Jahrhundert. Zwar war die Identität des Autors dieser Predigten trotz der eindeutigen Nennung im ältesten handschriftlichen Zeugnis lange umstritten,[13] heute herrscht allerdings Konsens darüber, dass die zwei Predigten tatsächlich einem Veroneser Bischof namens Petronius aus dem 5. Jahrhundert (425–450) zuzuschreiben sind.[14] Petronius erwähnt in einer der Predigten, dass Zeno von

---

11 Siehe Einleitung, S. 11.

12 Hier gebe ich den Wortlaut der Überschriften der Handschrift wieder: Clm 14386, Homiliar aus Regensburg oder Umgebung; letztes Drittel des 9. Jhdts. Die Sermones des Petronius für Zeno sind auf fol. 31r–32v. Die Handschrift ist Online verfügbar unter: https://www.digitale-sammlungen.de/de/view/bsb00046516?page=65. [14. Juli 2021]. Übrigens ist zu den vier in der Forschung bekannten Handschriften, nämlich München BSB Clm 14386, Homiliarium, Regensburg oder Umgebung, letztes Drittel des 9. Jhdts.; Wien ÖNB 1557, Homiliarium, Mondsee, 10. Jhdt.; Wien ÖNB 1013, 13. Jhdt.1; Admont BS 120, Homiliarium, erste Hälfte des 12. Jhdts., eine fünfte hinzuzufügen, nämlich Innsbruck UB 243, Homiliarium, 1. Hälfte des 12. Jhdts.

13 Vgl. Enzo Lodi: Le due omelie di San Petronio vescovo di Bologna. Saggio critico-storico, in: Miscellanea liturgica in onore di Sua Eminenza il Cardinale Giacomo Lercaro, Rom 1967, S. 263–302, hier: S. 293–294. Vgl. Germain Morin: Deux petits discours d'un évêque Pétronius, du V e siècle, in: Revue bénédictine 14, 1897, S. 3–8, hier: S. 8. (Morin ist für eine Zuschreibung zu Petronius von Bologna und nicht, wie Anti schreibt, zu Petronius von Verona).

14 Vgl. Guglielmo Ederle / Dario Cervato: I vescovi di Verona: dizionario storico e cenni sulla Chiesa veronese, Verona 2002, 20–21. Die Veroneser Lokalforschung war bereits seit dem 18. und 19. Jhdt. überzeugt, dass die zwei Reden einem Petronius, Bischof von Verona, zuzuschreiben seien, auch wenn diese These zunächst eher patriotisch motiviert gewesen war. Vgl. Giuseppe Venturi: Compendio della storia sacra e profana di Verona 1825, VII. Siehe außerdem: Angelo Orlandi: Il culto dei vescovi veronesi: origine, sviluppo, testimonianze, in: Bollettino della diocesi di Verona 66, 1979, S. 199–213 und Guido Vitacchio: I vescovi pre-zenoniani, in: Zenonis Cathedra. Miscellanea di studi in onore di S.E.

seinem Grab aus Wunder bewirke: „das, was er während seines Amtes bewirkte, vermehrt er nun aus seinem Grab. Die großen Wunder, die der sehr selige Bischof lebendig bewirken konnte, bewirkt er heute aus seinem Grab.“[15] Petronius und die Gemeinde, der er predigte, befanden sich aber wahrscheinlich nicht am Grab Zenos, sondern in einer Kirche des Heiligen an einem anderen Ort. Einen Hinweis darauf gibt der Bericht in den Quellen von der „Schönheit dieser vergrößerten Kirche, die den Wohlgeruch ihrer Lieblichkeit überall ausstreut.“[16] Dieser Hinweis auf den Ausbau einer Zenokirche kann helfen, ihren genauen Ort zu bestimmen. Archäologische Funde belegen, dass während Petronius' Episkopat verschiedene Kirchen erbaut und umgebaut wurden. So wurde die Kirche Santo Stefano am nördlichen Ufer der Etsch neu errichtet[17] und die städtische Kathedrale renoviert. Archäologische Untersuchungen um die Kathedrale Santa Maria Matricolare, bei denen Reste eines Bodenmosaiks sowie frühchristliche Inschriften entdeckt wurden,[18] ergaben, dass sich hier zwei frühchristliche Kirchen befanden (die sogenannten ‚Chiesa A‘ und ‚Chiesa B‘). Während die ‚Chiesa A‘ zur Zeit des Episkopats von Zeno (ca. 360–380) gebaut wurde, wurde in der ersten Hälfte des 5. Jahrhunderts eine größere ‚Chiesa B‘ errichtet, die den alten Bau ersetzte und durchaus als Renovierung und Erweiterung bezeichnet werden kann.[19] Es liegt daher nahe, die von Petronius erwähnte und erweiterte Kirche Zenos mit dem Dom zu identifizieren, der damit bereits im 5. Jahrhundert als Ort einer ersten Verehrergemeinschaft des Heiligen fassbar wird. Es wurde auch ein Zusammenhang zwischen der baulichen Erweiterung und der zunehmenden Popularität des Kults um den heiligen Bischof vermutet.[20]

Über die Praktiken der Verehrung Zenos zu dieser Zeit ist wenig greifbar. Deutlich wird die Existenz einer Feier durch die Predigten des Petronius, die sich an eine wie auch immer geartete Gemeinde richteten. Belegbar ist allerdings das Datum dieser Feier, über die in den Predigten gesagt wird, dass sie zur Eröffnung der Adventszeit stattfände.[21] Damit war sehr wahrscheinlich das Fest am 8.

---

l'arcivescovo mons. Giovanni Urbani (Nova historia. Numero speciale 7/III–IV), Verona 1955, S. 15–21.

15 „quod in sacerdotio gessit, multiplicat in sepulchro. […] Ideoque quas beatissimus vates in corpore constitutus potuit exercere virtutes, hodie magnas suo operatur in tumulo.“ Morin: Deux petits discours, S. 4.

16 „[…] hac aedis istius ampliata sublimitas, quae [...] fragrantiam suavitatis eius longe lateque dispergit.“ Ebd.

17 Vgl. Pierpaolo Brugnoli (Hg.): La Cattedrale di Verona nelle sue vicende edilizie dal secolo IV al secolo XVI, Venedig 1987, S. 8. Siehe außerdem: Alessandro Da Lisca: La basilica di S. Stefano in Verona, in: Atti e memorie dell'Accademia di Agricoltura, Scienze e Lettere di Verona 14, 1936, S. 45–119

18 Vgl. Pierpaolo Brugnoli (Hg.): La Cattedrale di Verona, S. 26–36.

19 Ebd., S. 37–78.

20 Ebd., S. 7.

21 „Nun aber lass uns die Kirche Gottes mit einer Predigt, mit Gesängen honorieren: und lasst uns um das Gesicht der Braut für den himmlischen Bräutigam zu beleuchten, den Advent eröffnen“ („Nunc vero honoremus ecclesiam Dei sermonis officio, vocalibus can-

Dezember gemeint, das als einziges Zenofest in der Folgezeit bis in die Karolingerzeit bekannt war.[22]

Wer genau an diesem Datum in der Kathedrale versammelt war, lässt sich nur indirekt erschließen. Neben Laien, die so zahlreich die Kirche Zenos besuchten, dass der Dom renoviert werden musste, gibt es Hinweise auf eine Gruppe von Klerikern, die einen liturgischen Dienst versahen und den Bischof bei der Zeremonie unterstützten. Über eine solche Gruppe von Klerikern am Dom gibt 517 die berühmte Subscriptio des Ursicinus Auskunft, der sich in seiner Abschrift der *Vita Martini* und der *Vita Pauli* namentlich verewigte und sich dabei als Lector der Veroneser Kirche bezeichnete. Dieser Titel bezeichnet einen der niederen Weihegrade und zugleich eine bestimmte Funktion im liturgischen Dienst, nämlich die des Vorlesers der heiligen Schriften.[23] Dass der Codex auch im Rahmen eines gemeinsam geleisteten liturgischen Dienstes verwendet wurde, bezeugt das darin verwendeten Gliederungs- und Interpunktionssystem.[24]

Ob zum Fest des heiligen Zeno neben einer Messe, in der die Predigten des Petronius gehalten wurden, auch weitere liturgische Dienste gehörten, etwa die in der Einleitung erwähnte Nachtwache, ist nicht belegbar. Auch bleibt ungewiss, ob zu diesem Zeitpunkt biographische Texte oder gar eine regelrechte Vita des Heiligen existierten, die bei einem solchen liturgischen Dienst hätten gelesen werden können. Die wenigen Informationen über Zeno, die Petronius in seiner Predigt erwähnt, lassen eher darauf schließen, dass zu dieser Zeit noch kein spezifisch auf die Figur des heiligen Zeno zugeschnittenes Material zirkulierte. Die Predigten heben lediglich seine bischöfliche Funktion hervor und preisen sein Wirken als solcher und seine Wundertätigkeit als Heiliger: „So wird der vornehme Bischof Zeno mit Wundern bestätigt: das, was er während seines Amtes bewirkt, vermehrt er aus dem Grab.“[25] Zentraler Ort dieser ansonsten unspezifischen Verehrung Zenos war zum Ausgang der Spätantike auf jeden Fall der Dom.

Für die folgenden Jahrhunderte bleibt die weitere Entwicklung des Zenokultes weitgehend im Dunkeln. Dass er bis ins 8. Jahrhundert und damit über die Langobardenzeit hinweg bestehen blieb, wird durch das sogenannte Sakramentar von Prag (Prag, Bibliothek des Metropolitankapitels, Cod. 083) aus der Zeit vor 794 angedeutet, in welchem das Zenofest für den 8. Dezember notiert ist. Zur Feier war dort eine Messe vorgesehen, deren Wortlaut nach Gamber gallikani-

---

tilenis; et ad inluminandum sponsae faciem caelestis sponsi aperiamus adventum“), aus: Morin: Deux petits discours, S. 4, Z. 39–41.

22 Siehe unten, Kap. 4.1.2.

23 Vgl. Wilhelm Ülhof: Weihegrade, in: Josef Höfer / Karl Rahner (Hg.): Lexikon für Theologie und Kirche, Freiburg 1965, Sp. 981, hier: Sp. 981.

24 Vgl. Kirsten Wallenwein: Corpus subscriptionum. Verzeichnis der Beglaubigungen von spätantiken und frühmittelalterlichen Textabschriften (saec. IV–VIII), Heidelberg 2017, S. 78–79; 265–266.

25 „Sic egregius Christi pontifex Zeno signorum virtutibus approbatur: quod in sacerdotio gessit, multiplicat in sepulchro“, aus: Morin: Deux petits discours, S. 4, Z. 27–29.

schen Ursprungs ist.[26] Zwar enstand die Handschrift in Regensburg, allerdings konnte Gamber zeigen, dass die Messe wohl aus Verona stammt, was angesichts der Herkunft des Kultes auch naheliegt.[27] Die frühe Verbreitung in Regensburg spricht darüber hinaus für eine gewisse Bekannt- und Beliebtheit des Kultes.

Unsicherheit besteht hinsichtlich der oben erwähnten Kirche am Grab des Heiligen.[28] Mehrere Quellen der Karolingerzeit – darunter Paulus Diaconus – legen nahe, dass bereits in langobardischer Zeit oder davor eine Kirche außerhalb der Stadt am Grab existierte.[29] Diese Berichte haben in der Forschung mitunter zu Vermutungen über eine vorkarolingische monastische Gemeinschaft an diesem Ort geführt, die dann als Verehrergemeinschaft des Heiligen zu gelten hätte.[30] Allerdings basiert diese These auf einer fehlerhaften Identifikation eines in einer langobardischen, durch eine Kopie von 806 überlieferten Urkunde, genannten „domus sancti Zenonis“[31] mit einer solchen Gemeinschaft. Mittlerweile wurde bewiesen, dass sich diese Bezeichnung nur mit dem in der Stadt gelegenen Dom in Verbindung bringen lässt.[32] Zwar ist die Existenz eines Sakralbaus am Grab

---

26 Vgl. Klaus Gamber: Die gallikanische Zeno-Messe. Ein Beitrag zum ältesten Ritus von Oberitalien und Bayern, in: Münchener Theologische Zeitschrift 10, 1959, S. 295–299, hier: S. 295.

27 Vgl. ebd., S. 298.

28 Lange hat die Forschung versucht, die Kirche zu verorten, in der das von Gregor berichtete Mirakel der Etschüberflutung stattgefunden haben soll. Es wurde verschiedentlich für den Dom, das Kloster San Zeno Maggiore sowie für die kleine Kirche San Zeno in Oratorio argumentiert. Diese Identifizierung gestaltete sich immer als problematisch, weil das Mirakel in einer neben der Etsch gelegenen Kirche stattgefunden haben soll, wo auch Zeno begraben sei. Dabei war es unmöglich, eine Kirche mit beiden Merkmalen zu finden: Entweder ereignete sich das Mirakel dort, wo Zeno begraben war, nämlich im Kloster San Zeno Maggiore. Dieses ist aber zu weit entfernt von der Etsch. Der Dom und San Zeno in Oratorio sind hingegen näher an der Etsch und konnten überflutet werden, allerdings gibt es keinerlei Hinweise, dass der Heilige jemals hier bestattet worden war. Elisa Anti löste das Problem überzeugend, indem sie vorschlug, in der Kirche des Mirakels und der Grabkirche Zenos zwei unterschiedliche Orte zu sehen, da Gregor nicht deutlich von einer Einheit beider ausginge. Sie legt dar, dass Gregor für sein Mirakel an den Dom dachte, während Zeno seit seinem Tod außerhalb der Stadtmauer lag. Vgl. Elisa Anti: Note sulla prima sepoltura di san Zeno e sulla sede del miracolo delle acque, in: Annuario storico zenoniano 17, 2000, S. 11–18.

29 Vgl. Paulus Diaconus: Historia Langobardorum, in: L. Bethmann / G. Waitz (Hg.): Scriptores rerum langobardicarum et italicarum saec. VI–IX (Monumenta Germaniae historica), Hannover 1878, S. 45–187, hier: Buch III, Kapitel 23, hier S. 104.

30 Vgl. Vittorio Fainelli: L'abbazia di S. Zeno nell'alto medioevo, in: Miscellanea Roberto Cessi (Storia e letteratura. Raccolta di studi e testi 71), Rom 1958, S. 51–62, hier: S. 51.

31 Fainelli: Codice diplomatico Veronese, Nr. 71, S. 88.

32 Vgl. Anti: Verona e il culto, S. 32. Dass der Terminus eindeutig den Dom bezeichnet, zeigen auch die Urkunden, dazu: Andrea Brugnoli: „Pares illorum famuli“. Una tipologia documentaria veronese per negozi tra persone di condizione servile, in: Andrea Brugnoli / Gian Maria Varanini (Hg.): Studi Pierpaolo Brugnoli. Magna Verona vale. Studi in onore di Pierpaolo Brugnoli, Verona 2008, S. 27–48, hier: S. 33. Außerdem: Pierpaolo Brugnoli (Hg.): La Cattedrale di Verona, S. 81. Auf ähnliche Weise wird das Episkopium Mailands als „domus Ambrosii“ bezeichnet, Giovanni B. Sannazzaro: L'architettura dal Medioevo al Rinascimento, in: Adele Buratti Mazzotta (Hg.): Domus Ambrosii. Il complesso monumentale dell'arcivescovado, Mailand 1994, S. 35–59, hier: S. 35.

des Heiligen durchaus anzunehmen; dass hier aber eine vom Dom getrennte und institutionalisierte Verehrung stattfand, ist eher unwahrscheinlich.

Bis zum Ende der Langobardenzeit hatte sich also in Verona um den heiligen Zeno ein Kult gebildet, der in erster Linie am Dom gefeiert und vom Bischof und seinen Klerikern getragen wurde. Zwar umfasste dieser Kult bereits eine liturgische Praxis, die sich im Rahmen der Messe nachweisen lässt, eine auf den Heiligen direkt zugeschnittene Liturgie ist allerdings nicht belegt. Dies änderte sich mit Beginn der fränkischen Herrschaft über Norditalien unter den Karolingern.

4.1.2 Die Etablierung Zenos als Heiliger: 8.–10. Jahrhundert

Mit der Ankunft der Karolinger, die Verona 774 nach einem Sieg gegen die Langobarden ins fränkische Reich eingliederten,[33] erfuhr die Verehrung Zenos tiefgreifende Veränderungen. Die Integration Oberitaliens in das fränkische Reich bedeutete, dass die wichtigsten politischen und organisatorischen Posten mit Vertretern der fränkischen Eliten besetzt wurden. Während die Comites die Verwaltung des Militär- und Wirtschaftswesens beaufsichtigen, pflegten die Bischöfe die Administration des politischen und gesellschaftlichen Lebens und waren für die Anbindung der ihnen anvertrauten Städte an das Zentrum des Reiches verantwortlich. De facto gewannen die Bischöfe zunehmend an Einfluss und wurden zu den wahren Herren der Städte.[34]

Auch auf den Veroneser Bischofsstuhl wurden sehr bald nach der Eingliederung fränkische Exponenten gesetzt. Zwischen dem Ende des 8. und der ersten Hälfte des 9. Jahrhunderts waren es die von der Reichenau stammenden Mönche Egino und Ratold, die Verona nicht nur mit dem Königshof, sondern auch mit wichtigen fränkischen Klöstern nördlich der Alpen verbanden. Besonders in zwei Bereichen ist das Wirken dieser Bischöfe für eine Untersuchung des Zenokultes zwischen dem 8. und 10. Jahrhundert relevant: in der Gründung und Förderung von religiösen Verehrergemeinschaften sowie in der Erweiterung und Reform der Liturgie.

Egino (gest. 27. Februar 802) war ein Alemanne – so berichten es die *Miracula sancti Marci*[35] – und wurde nach der fränkischen Eroberung Italiens wahrschein-

[33] Vgl. Carlo G. Mor: Dall'età carolingia alle prime lotte sociali, in: Vittorio Cavallari / Piero Gazzola (Hg.): Verona e il suo territorio, Verona 1960–1984, S. 5–142, hier: S. 67–142.

[34] Vgl. Michele Pellegrini: Vescovo e città. Una relazione nel Medioevo italiano (secoli II–XIV), Mailand 2009, S. 26–28. Außerdem: Andrea Castagnetti: Aspetti politici, economici e sociali di chiese e monasteri dall'epoca carolingia alle soglie dell'età moderna, in: Giorgio Borelli (Hg.): Chiese e monasteri a Verona, Verona 1980, S. 43–119, hier: S. 45. Zu den Bischöfen und ihren Handlungsspielräumen im Frühmittelalter siehe auch: Sean Gilsdorf: The Favor of Friends: Intercession and Aristocratic Politics in Carolingian and Ottonian Europe (Brill's Series on the Early Middle Ages 23), Leiden 2014.

[35] Vgl. Walter Berschin / Theodor Klüppel: Der Evangelist Markus auf der Reichenau, Sigmaringen 1994, S. 38.

lich gegen 780[36] zum Veroneser Bischof erhoben.[37] Über sein Leben ist vergleichsweise wenig bekannt, sein Tod hingegen interessierte die Geschichtsschreiber der Reichenau, da er sich nach seinem Rücktritt vom bischöflichen Amt, wahrscheinlich um die Mitte der 90er Jahre des 8. Jahrhunderts,[38] dorthin zurückgezogen hatte. Auf der Bodenseeinsel gründete Egino die Peterskirche in Niederzell, wo er wenige Jahre später (802) begraben wurde.[39] Auch wenn seine Amtszeit nicht allzu lang gewesen ist, spielte Egino als Initiator eines regen Transfers von Büchern zwischen Verona und der Reichenau sowohl bei der Reform der Liturgie am Veroneser Dom als auch im Bereich der Handschriftenproduktion im Veroneser Skriptorium eine entscheidende Rolle.[40]

Das beste Beispiel für Eginos Wirken am Veroneser Dom ist die Handschrift Berlin, Deutsche Staatsbibliothek, Phillipps 1676.[41] Paläographische und kodikologische Untersuchungen dieses Codex stellen das handwerkliche Niveau heraus, das das Skriptorium des Veroneser Doms unter Egino erreicht hatte.[42] Vor allem aus liturgiewissenschaftlicher Sicht ist der Codex interessant, weil er die Reform der Veroneser Liturgie und ihre Anbindung an fränkische Traditionen zeigt. Es handelt sich bei dem Codex um ein liturgisches Homiliar, also eine Sammlung

---

[36] Vgl. Walter Berschin / Alfons Zettler: Egino von Verona. Der Gründer von Reichenau-Niederzell (799) (Reichenauer Texte und Bilder), Stuttgart 1999, S. 48.

[37] Zu Egino siehe: Alfons Zettler: Die karolingischen Bischöfe von Verona I. Studien zu Bischof Egino (+ 802), in: Sebastian Brather (Hg.): Historia archaeologica: Festschrift für Heiko Steuer zum 70. Geburtstag, Berlin u. a. 2009, S. 363–388.

[38] Vgl. Berschin / Zettler: Egino von Verona, S. 52.

[39] Vgl. ebd.

[40] Eine ganze Reihe von Handschriften, die man als Egino-Gruppe bezeichnet, weist bezüglich der Schrift klare Veroneser Merkmale auf, viele davon befanden sich aber sehr bald nach ihrer Anfertigung auf der Reichenau, wie zeitgenössische Korrektureinträge oder Nachträge zeigen, vgl. Elias A. Lowe: Codices Latini Antiquiores: A Palaeographical Guide to Latin Manuscripts Prior to the 9th Century. Vol. 8: Germany: Altenburg-Leipzig, Oxford 1959, VIII. 1076, V. 601, VII. 907. Vgl. Martin Steinmann: Neue Fragmente von Hieronymus in psalmos und das Scriptorium Bischof Eginos von Verona, in: Deutsches Archiv für Erforschung des Mittelalters 48, 1992, S. 621–624.

[41] Vgl. Bernhard Bischoff: Katalog der festländischen Handschriften des neunten Jahrhunderts. Aachen-Lambach, Wiesbaden 1998, S. 86, Nr. 410.

[42] Veroneser Schreiber waren mit einer „firm, massive Caroline miniscule" (Lowe (wie Anm. 255), Nr. 1057) an der Anfertigung des Codex beteiligt und partizipierten somit bereits gegen Ende des 8. Jhdts. (die Handschrift wurde 796–799 datiert, vgl. Susanna Polloni: Manoscritti liturgici della Biblioteca Capitolare di Verona (secolo IX). Contributo per uno studio codicologico e paleografico, in: Medioevo. Studi e documenti 2, 2007, S. 151–228, hier: S. 158.) an der neusten fränkischen Schriftentwicklung. Vgl. Mirella Ferrari: Libri liturgici e diffusione della scrittura carolina nell'Italia settentrionale, in: Culto cristiano, politica imperiale carolingia (Convegni del Centro di Studi sulla Spiritualità Medievale 18), Todi 1979, S. 265–279, hier: 269–272; außerdem: Beniamino Pagnin: Formazione della scrittura carolina italiana, in: Guiscardo Moschetti (Hg.): Atti del Congresso internazionale di diritto romano, Verona 1951–1953, S. 243–266. Insbesondere zu liturgischen Handschriften siehe auch: Giacomo B. Baroffio: Manoscritti liturgici e musicali sull'arco alpino fra i secoli IX e XII, in: Carlo Magno e le Alpi: atti del XVIII Congresso Internazionale di Studio sull'Alto Medioevo, Susa, 19–20 ottobre 2006, Novalesa, 21 ottobre 2006, Spoleto 2007, S. 141–150.

von Homilien der Kirchenväter für die Lesung im Stundengebet,[43] die Egino in Anlehnung an die Sammlung des Alanus von Farfa zusammenstellte.[44] Der Bischof ließ den Codex explizit für den Gebrauch an dem der Jungfrau Maria gewidmeten Dom anfertigen, wie aus dem Widmungsbrief auf f. 23v hervorgeht: „Schiedsrichter des Himmels, Vater der künftigen Zeit, gebe dem Bischof Egino deine gute Belohnung, der dieses Buch in Auftrag gab und es der Kirche deiner heiligen Mutter Maria schenkte."[45] Eginos Homiliar stellt eines der frühesten Exemplare dieser Gattung von Handschriften dar. Das Werk wurde im Gebrauch zwar wenig später vom *Homiliarius* des Paulus Diaconus in der fränkischen Liturgie abgelöst,[46] die Handschrift bezeugt aber die Bemühungen des alemannischen Bischofs um die Reform der Liturgie am Dom von Verona entsprechend dem fränkischen Programm. In deren Rahmen wurden unter anderem auch neue Text- und Handschriftengattungen eingeführt, wie beispielsweise das gregorianische Sakramentar.[47]

Das Engagement Eginos für eine Reform der Veroneser Kirche endete nicht mit dessen Rückkehr auf die Reichenau. Vielmehr wurde es von seinem engen Vertrauten und Nachfolger auf dem Bischofsstuhl weitergeführt, dem ebenfalls von der Reichenau stammenden Ratold. Ratold, der um 770 wahrscheinlich in eine hochadlige alemannische Familie geboren wurde, war Hofkaplan König Pippins und enger Vertrauter Bischof Eginos.[48] Als wahrscheinliches Datum der Weihe Ratolds zum Bischof gibt Hlawitschka aufgrund eines Eintrages in einem Kalender des 9. Jahrhunderts, wo von einer „Consecratio domini episcopi Ratoldi" die Rede ist, den 26. September 801 an.[49] Über 30 Jahre später, wahrscheinlich ab 834, wurde Ratold als Unterstützer Ludwigs des Frommen die Rückkehr zu seinem Bischofssitz Verona verwehrt, das in Italien und damit im Machtbereich Lothars I. lag.[50] Ratold zeichnete sich durch seine Unterstützung für die religiösen Institutionen Veronas so sehr aus, dass er in den lokalen Geschichtsbüchern als großer Wohltäter erinnert wird.[51] Dies kam insbesondere den Verehrergemeinschaften um den heiligen Zeno zugute.

---

43 Vgl. Palazzo: A History of Liturgical Books, S. 154.

44 Vgl. Berschin / Zettler: Egino von Verona, S. 19–20.

45 „Arbiter excelsi poli, pater futuri seculi, Egino presuli, tuo famulo, redde mercedem optimam, qui hunc librum scribere iussit sanctaequae matris tui filii Mariae [...] tradidit aecclesiae [...]", aus: Valentin Rose: Verzeichniss der Lateinischen Handschriften der Königlichen Bibliothek zu Berlin, Erster Band: Die Meermann-Handschriften des Sir Thomas Phillipps (Die Handschriften-Verzeichnisse der Königlichen Bibliothek zu Berlin. 12), Berlin 1893, S. 81.

46 Vgl. Palazzo: A History of Liturgical Books, S. 155.

47 Vgl. ebd., S. 154–155.

48 Vgl. Eduard Hlawitschka: Ratold, Bischof von Verona und Begründer von Radolfzell, in: Hegau 54 / 55, 1997, S. 5–44, hier: S. 9.

49 Die Kalenderblätter befinden sich nun in einer Handschrift in Berlin, Berlin, Staatsbibliothek, lat. 128. Vgl. Meersseman u. a.: L'orazionale, S. 21–23.

50 Vgl. Hlawitschka: Ratold, S. 25.

51 Vgl. Vittorio Fainelli: Grandi benefattori: il Vescovo Ratoldo e l'arcidiacono Pacifico, in: Zenonis Cathedra. Miscellanea di studi in onore di S.E. l'arcivescovo mons. Giovanni

So beförderte Ratold die bauliche Umgestaltung des Areals um den Dom und die Erneuerung der Gebäude in diesem Bereich: Er renovierte die Kathedrale Santa Maria Matricolare, die angegliederte Taufkirche San Giovanni in Fonte und die bischöflichen Wohnungen. Auch neue Gebäude wurden dort errichtet, nämlich die Kirche San Giorgio e San Zeno, ein Krankenhaus für die Pflege von Kranken und Armen sowie weitere Gebäude für die Kleriker (Räume für den Unterricht und die Ausbildung sowie private Wohnungen).[52] Die räumliche Struktur des Komplexes um die Kathedrale von Verona im Frühmittelalter ist in einem Beitrag von Silvia Lusuardi Siena und Cinzia Fiorio Tedone abgebildet.[53]

Besonders bemühte sich Ratold um die Kleriker am Veroneser Dom. Diesen kam nicht nur seine Bautätigkeit zugute, sondern auch wirtschaftliche Zuwendungen. In einer Urkunde von 813 garantierte ihnen der Bischof Güter und Einkommen aus Kirchen und Klöstern in und außerhalb der Stadt. Auch stellte Ratold den Domklerikern Räume und Häuser sowie eine eigene Kirche zur Verfügung, in der sie den alltäglichen liturgischen Dienst verrichten konnten, nämlich die kleine Kirche San Giorgio e San Zeno, die durch eine überdachte Halle[54] mit der Hauptkirche des Doms verbunden war.[55] Mit diesen Maßnahmen garantierte Ratold die finanzielle und teilweise räumliche Unabhängigkeit der Kanoniker vom Bischofsstuhl. Seine Vorkehrungen, die vor allem wirtschaftlicher Natur waren, bedeuteten darüber hinaus die Gründung des Kapitels der Domkleriker, die bereits seit dem 6. Jahrhundert am Dom wirkten, als eine eigene Körperschaft. Bischof Ratold hatte daher mehr als bloß die wirtschaftliche Fundierung einer religiösen Institution bewirkt. Vielmehr ermöglichte er dieser die Entwicklung einer unabhängigen und erkennbaren Identität in einer eigenen Kirche, in

---

Urbani (Nova historia. Numero speciale 7/III–IV), Verona 1955, S. 23–27.

52 Vgl. Silvia Lusuardi Siena / Cinzia Fiorio Tedone: Il complesso episcopale nell'alto medioevo alla luce delle testimoninaze scritte, in: Pierpaolo Brugnoli (Hg.): La Cattedrale di Verona nelle sue vicende edilizie dal secolo IV al secolo XVI, Venedig 1987, S. 79–82.

53 Dies.: Ipotesi interpretativa sullo sviluppo del complesso episcopale veronese, in: Pierpaolo Brugnoli (Hg.): La Cattedrale di Verona nelle sue vicende edilizie dal secolo IV al secolo XVI, Venedig 1987, S. 83–87, hier: S. 87.

54 Zu dieser architektonischen Konstruktion, deren Anwesenheit und Funktion sich mit den Anforderungen der Liturgie der Kanoniker erklären lassen, da diese täglich von San Giorgio in die Hauptkirche gingen, siehe: Fabio Coden: Il portico detto „santa Maria Matricolare" presso il complesso episcopale di Verona, in: Arturo C. Quintavalle (Hg.): Medioevo: L'Europa delle cattedrali. Atti del convegno internazionale di studi, Mailand 2007, S. 339–349.

55 Vgl. Fainelli: Codice diplomatico Veronese, N. 97, N. 101–102. Vgl. Castagnetti: Aspetti politici, economici, S. 49–50: „La dotazione assegnata al capitolo fu massiccia e a buon diritto possiamo considerarla come la base degli sviluppi successivi. [...] Il capitolo della cattedrale veronese assume una propria autonomia giuridica, economica ed amministrativa all'inizio del secolo IX. Anticipando quella che di li a poco sarebbe stata realizzata dai Carolingi e conosciuta come la riforma di Aquisgrana, che introduceva la vita comune del clero nei capitoli delle cattedrali, il vescovo franco Ratoldo decise nell'813 di istituire una mensa canonicale affinché servisse, con i cospicui redditi che ne potevano provenire, di supporto economico ad un regolare svolgimento della vita canonicale presso la cattedrale."

der sie neben anderen Heiligen besonders Zeno verehrten, dem sie ihre Kirche widmeten.[56]

Ratolds Bemühung um eine Profilierung der Identität des Domkapitels wird auch in den Neuerungen deutlich, die er in die Liturgie der Kleriker einführte. Diese lassen sich besonders in einem liturgischen Codex nachvollziehen, der in der ersten Hälfte des 9. Jahrhunderts im Skriptorium des Domes angefertigt wurde, dem Kollektar Verona, BC, CVI(99). Diese Handschrift gibt außerdem Auskunft über die Lebensweise des Kapitels in der frühen Karolingerzeit. Das Kollektar enthält die Gebete, die ein Zelebrant während des Stundengebetes aussprach und erfüllte somit die gleiche Funktion wie ein Sakramentar, in dem ebenso die im Rahmen der Messe zu betenden Partien enthalten sind.[57] Der Bestand an Gebeten für das Stundengebet wird in dieser Handschrift durch ein Kalendar (in der Handschrift als Martyrologium gekennzeichnet)[58] und eine Reihe von Benediktionen vervollständigt. Auch weiteres liturgisches Material, wie das Athanasische Glaubensbekenntnis, einige Ordines und eine Litanei, sind Teil der Veroneser Handschrift.[59]

Das Kollektar wurde bereits von Meersseman und Venturini untersucht und datiert. Beide gingen davon aus, dass die Handschrift durchgängig von einer einzigen Hand geschrieben worden sei, und waren zuversichtlich, Pacificus, den Erzdiakon der Veroneser Kathedrale in der ersten Hälfte des 9. Jahrhunderts, als Schreiber identifizieren zu können.[60] Außerdem datierten sie die Handschrift aufgrund eines Eintrages im Kalender, in dem der Tod Pippins fixiert wurde, vor 810.[61] 2007 wurde der Codex erneut untersucht. Dabei wurde nicht nur festgestellt, dass er nicht von einer Hand geschrieben wurde, sondern auch, dass die Handschrift in zwei Teile zu unterteilen ist, die jeweils von sechs beziehungsweise vier unterschiedlichen Händen geschrieben worden sind.[62] Auch die Datierung musste somit neu bestimmt werden. Der erste Teil der Handschrift, in dem der Kalender, das Glaubensbekenntnis, das Kollektar und ein Ordo eingetragen worden sind, lässt sich wegen des kalendarischen Eintrages zum Tode Pippins weiterhin vor 810 datieren.[63] Aufgrund eines Nachtrages kann die zweite kodikologische Einheit datiert werden. Auf fol. 62v lässt sich trotz einer Rasur ein

[56] Vgl. Forchielli: Collegialità di chierici, S. 38–41. Außerdem: Miller: The Formation of a Medieval Church, S. 42–43.

[57] Vgl. Palazzo: A History of Liturgical Books, S. 145.

[58] Vgl. Meersseman u. a.: L'orazionale, S. 138–145.

[59] Vgl. ebd., S. 14–15.

[60] Vgl. ebd., S. 5. Außerdem: Maria Venturini: Ricerche paleografiche intorno all'Arcidiacono Pacifico di Verona, Verona 1929, S. 149. 1995 konnte von La Rocca herausgearbeitet werden, dass die Figur des Pacificus vor allem im Laufe des 12. Jhdts. besonders aufgeladen und zum Symbol und mythischen Ursprung für das Domkapitel gemacht wurde. Vgl. La Rocca: Pacifico di Verona.

[61] Vgl. Meersseman u. a.: L'orazionale, S. 17.

[62] Vgl. Polloni: Manoscritti liturgici della Capitolare, 161, Fußnote 21.

[63] Bei Meersseman fälschlicherweise als 8. August angegeben, vgl. Meersseman u. a.: L'orazionale, S. 17; vgl. auch: Venturini: Ricerche paleografiche, S. 92.

Eintrag nachvollziehen, in dem für die Bewahrung des Kaisers Karl gebetet wurde.[64] So wurde diese zweite Einheit, die die Benediktionen, die Litanei und einen weiteren Ordo enthält, sicher vor 814 angefertigt, als Karl der Große noch am Leben war.[65]

Meiner Ansicht nach lässt sich der Abfassungszeitpunkt des ersten Teils insofern näher bestimmen, als dass eine Hand des frühen 9. Jahrhunderts die später im Detail zu untersuchende Übertragung der Reliquien des Heiligen ins neu errichtete Kloster San Zeno Maggiore nachtrug. Das Kollektar dürfte daher vor dieser Translation entstanden sein. Da der genaue Zeitpunkt dieser Translation nach heutigem Wissensstand allerdings nicht gesichert ist, bleibt es bei einer Datierung in das erste Jahrzehnt des 9. Jahrhunderts. Die Handschrift überliefert somit das früheste vollständige Beispiel für ein Kollektar, da ansonsten aus dem 8. und 9. Jahrhundert nur Fragmente oder unvollständige Exemplare eines solchen Handschriftentypus überliefert sind.[66]

Auch die Lokalisierung der Handschrift in Verona ist unumstritten: Sowohl im Kalender als auch in der Litanei sind Feste und Heilige erwähnt, die typisch für das frühmittelalterliche Verona sind, darunter der Todestag Zenos am 12. April und das Zenofest am 8. Dezember.[67] Auf den Dom verweisen darüber hinaus die Verzeichnung der Domweihe im Kalender sowie verschiedene nekrologische Nachträge, die weiter unten noch genauer untersucht werden und explizit auf Kleriker des Kapitels verweisen.

Auch wenn sich das Kollektar durch die neuen paläographischen Befunde Pollonis nicht mehr als Produkt des mythischen Pacificus bestimmen lässt, kann es mit Bischof Ratold in Zusammenhang gebracht werden. Das zeigt die Tatsache, dass die Vorlage direkt von der Reichenau, dem Herkunftskloster der beiden frühen Veroneser Bischöfe, nach Verona kam. Bei dieser Vorlage handelte es sich nach Meersseman um ein nun verschollenes Kollektar der Abtei, das noch vor dem heute nur noch fragmentarisch überlieferten Kollektar der Abtei, Karlsruhe BLB Aug. perg. XXII,[68] auf der Reichenau angefertigt wurde.[69] Dies belege sowohl der Kalender der Veroneser Handschrift, in dem wichtige Feste für die Abtei (Maria und Petrus) verzeichnet wurden, als auch die Aufnahme von umfangreichem monastischem Material.[70] Es ist vor allem die Sammlung von Benediktionen und Gebeten, die Meersseman als Benedictionale bezeichnet, die ihren monastischen Ursprung verrät. Hier sind nämlich Segnungen und Gebete für die Räume eines Klosters enthalten.[71]

---

64 Vgl. ebd., S. 90–91.
65 Vgl. Polloni: Manoscritti liturgici della Capitolare, S. 163–164.
66 Vgl. Klaus Gamber: Codices liturgici latini antiquiores. Pars II (Spicilegium Friburgense. Subsidia 2), Freiburg 1968, S. 548–550.
67 Vgl. Meersseman u. a.: L'orazionale, S. 18.
68 Nr. 1503 in Gamber: Codices liturgici latini, S. 550.
69 Vgl. Meersseman u. a.: L'orazionale, S. 53–55.
70 Vgl. ebd., S. 54–55.
71 Vgl. ebd., S. 177–183.

Die Aufnahme dieser Texte wurde nicht nur mit der Treue des Veroneser Kopisten zu seiner Vorlage erklärt. Vielmehr hätte Ratold die Kleriker des Domkapitels bereits vor der Aachener Reform von 816 zur Vita communis verpflichtet.[72] Tatsächlich lässt sich diese These eines gemeinsamen Lebens des Kapitels auch durch das Urkundenmaterial stützen. So ist in der bereits erwähnten Gründungsurkunde des Kapitels vom 24. Juni 813 von einem gemeinschaftlichen Einkommen der Körperschaft die Rede, das unter den Kapitelmitgliedern zu teilen war.[73] Dass das Einhalten der Vita communis von den Klerikern des Kapitels erwartet wurde, zeigt auch der Tadel Bischof Rathers, der ebenfalls Mönch gewesen und etwa um 930 zum Bischof von Verona ernannt worden ist: Seiner Ansicht nach hätten die Kleriker den Weg des gemeinsamen Lebens verlassen.[74]

Dass Ratolds Maßnahmen zur Förderung der Identitätsbildung des Kapitels als erfolgreich beurteilt werden müssen, belegen die bereits erwähnten nekrologischen Einträge, die im Laufe des 9. Jahrhunderts in das Martyrolog eingetragen wurden. Neben den Festangaben wurden die Todesdaten vieler Mitglieder des Kapitels notiert, die dadurch erkennbar sind, dass diese Personen als „presbyter", „clericus", „archipresbyter" und so weiter bezeichnet wurden. Einige dieser Namen sind außerdem auch in Urkunden aus dem Domkapitel zu finden.[75] Die Tatsache, dass Kleriker des Kapitels das Bedürfnis verspürten, die Namen verstorbener Mitglieder zu notieren, drückt einen Sinn für Identität und Gruppenzugehörigkeit aus.

Es kann nicht verwundern, dass sich gerade in dieser Situation die ersten profilierenden liturgischen Texte um den Heiligen finden lassen, nämlich der sogenannte *Sermo de vita sancti Zenonis* eines sich selbst als *Coronatus notarius* bezeichnenden Autors. Als *Sermo* bezeichnet man die früheste Vita Zenos, die in unterschiedlichen Fassungen vorliegt, die mit den BHL-Nummern 9001–9008 unterschieden werden. Bis heute existiert keine historisch-kritische Edition dieser Fassungen, die auf die genaue Entstehung und Verbreitung dieser frühen hagiographischen Texte für Zeno Licht werfen könnte. Gedruckt wurde der Text auf Basis einer Handschrift durch die Gebrüder Ballerini 1739.[76]

Der *Sermo* ist in neun episodenhafte Kapitel gegliedert. Die Vita wird im ersten Kapitel mit einer dreifachen Metapher eröffnet, die die menschliche Neugier für das Leben der Heiligen thematisiert. Die brennende Neugier der Menschen

---

72 Vgl. ebd., S. 55–57. Siehe dazu auch: Borders: The Cathedral of Verona, S. 61.

73 Vgl. Fainelli: Codice diplomatico Veronese, Nr. 102, S. 127–132.

74 Vgl. Dario Cervato: Raterio di Verona e di Liegi. Il terzo periodo del suo episcopato veronese (961–968). Scritti e attività, Verona 1993, S. 270–271.

75 Vgl. Vittorio Lazzarini: Scuola calligrafica veronese del secolo IX, in: Vittorio Lazzarini (Hg.): Scritti di paleografia e diplomatica, Padua 1969, S. 10–27, hier: S. 15–17. Lazzarini ist der einzige, der explizit auf die Anwesenheit dieser Nachträge hinweist. Weder Meersseman, der den Kalender edierte (vgl. Meersseman u. a.: L'orazionale, S. 138–145, noch Venturini (vgl. Venturini: Vita ed attività, S. 94.) oder Polloni (vgl. Polloni: Manoscritti liturgici della Capitolare, S. 161–164) drucken diese Nachträge ab.

76 Vgl. Ballerini / Ballerini: Sancti Zenonis Episcopi, S. CXLVII–CL.

gegenüber den Erzählungen über Heilige wird zunächst mit dem Begehren eines Dürstenden nach Wasser verglichen, dann mit der Ungeduld eines Menschen, der auf eine Nachricht wartet und die Ankunft eines Boten wünscht, und zuletzt mit der Sehnsucht eines Reisenden, der von den Speisen und Köstlichkeiten seiner Heimat träumt. Der Autor erklärt auch, dass er erzählen wolle, was er über Zeno habe erfahren können, und dies verschriftlichen wolle, um die Heiligkeit von Zeno außer Zweifel zu stellen. Im Kapitel 2 werden die Persönlichkeit und asketischen Gewohnheiten des Heiligen beschrieben: Er ist friedlich („*mitis*") und angenehm im Gespräch („*in sermone affabilis erat*"),[77] er fastet und betet unaufhörlich („*Erat enim sedens in monasterio in secretiori parte in oppido Veronensi continuis ieiuniis et crebris orationibus*").[78] Sein erstes Wunder wird in Kapitel 3 erzählt: Zeno, der in der Etsch fischt, rettet einen Bauern vor dem Teufel, der ihn durch Einwirken auf die Rinder, die seinen Karren ziehen, ertrinken lassen wollte. Der Teufel ist daraufhin erbost und rächt sich, indem er die Tochter des Kaisers Gallienus quält. Er fordert Zeno heraus und Kaiser Gallienus lässt nach Zeno suchen. Die Gesandten des Kaisers treffen auf Zeno, der, wieder fischend, nach kurzer Unsicherheit – der Kaiser sei nämlich ein Feind der Christen – den Soldaten folgt. In Kapitel 5 besiegt Zeno nochmals den Teufel und kann das Mädchen ihrem Vater wohl und gesund zurückgeben. Gallienus ist von Zeno so beeindruckt, dass er ihm seine eigene Krone schenkt. Zeno nimmt die Krone entgegen, um sie unmittelbar den herbeigelaufenen und um die Taufe bittenden Armen zu schenken. In Kapitel 7 verwandelt der Heilige die Stadt in einen christlichen Ort voller Kirchen und frei von heidnischen Idolen. In Kapitel 8 stirbt der nun berühmt gewordene Heilige, und eine Kirche wird für ihn in der Nähe der Etsch gebaut, in der sein Leichnam auch bestattet wird. Kapitel 9 beschreibt, in Anlehnung an Gregor den Großen, Zenos postumes Wunder, in dem er die versammelten Gläubigen vor einer Überschwemmung durch die Etsch rettet.

Der *Sermo* kann nun recht sicher am Anfang des 9. Jahrhunderts und ins Umfeld der Kleriker am Dom verortet werden. Der *Sermo* wurde sicher vor circa 810 verfasst, da in diesem ersten Jahrzehnt des 9. Jahrhunderts die Überführung der Reliquien von Zeno ins Kloster San Zeno Maggiore stattfand, das weiter unten näher thematisiert wird. Dies kann wohl als ein einschneidendes Ereignis gesehen werden, das kein Hagiograph verschwiegen hätte, das vom Autor des *Sermo* aber nicht erwähnt wird.[79] Bezüglich des Terminus post quem kann mittlerweile gelten, dass er nach 774, also in der karolingischen Zeit verfasst worden ist. Elisa Anti beobachtet eine in diesem Zusammenhang bedeutsame Tatsache: während in Kapitel 9 des *Sermo* Gregors Schilderung der Etschüberflutung von Coronatus fast wortwörtlich übernommen wird, bleibt ein Detail der Vorlage unerwähnt, nämlich die Nennung des langobardischen Königs Autari sowie anderer lango-

[77] Ebd., CXLVII.
[78] Ebd.
[79] Er wird erst in der Mitte des 12. Jhdts., also mehr als dreihundert Jahre später, schriftlich fixiert, siehe dazu Kapitel 4.3.2.

bardischer Autoritäten als Garanten des Mirakels. Diese Zensur, infolge derer die langobardischen Persönlichkeiten aus der Erzählung getilgt werden,[80] spricht dafür, dass der Text bereits unter karolingischer Herrschaft verfasst worden ist.

Sowohl textliche Eigenschaften des *Sermo* als auch kodikologische Aspekte der frühesten Handschrift, die ihn überliefert, erlauben nun eine Lokalisierung im Milieu der Kleriker und legen nahe, dass der *Sermo* von einem Kleriker für seine Gemeinschaft verfasst wurde. Außerdem lässt sich zeigen, dass der Text dort im Rahmen der liturgischen Lesung rezipiert wurde. Zunächst ist die Autorenfrage näher zu erörtern. Die vielen zitierten biblischen Passagen sowie seine Kenntnis von Gregors von Tours Werk *Liber in gloria confessorum*, das in der Episode zur Heilung der Königstochter anklingt, weisen darauf hin, dass der Autor ein gut ausgebildeter Kirchenmann war.[81] Außerdem wird dem *monasterium* von Zeno eine prominente Rolle zugeschrieben: Dort bereitet sich der Heilige durch geistige und körperliche Übungen auf das Predigen vor, in dessen Nähe wird Zeno beim Fischen dargestellt. Allerdings bezeichnet der Terminus hier nicht eine Kloster-, sondern vielmehr eine Bischofskirche, und zwar den Veroneser Bischofsitz, eine Besonderheit, die – wie Golinelli zeigte – auch ein weiterer hagiographischer Text aus Verona aufweist, nämlich die *Passio Firmi et Rustici*.[82] Diese Hinweise lassen darauf schließen, dass der Autor Kleriker des Veroneser Domkapitels gewesen ist.[83] Auch der Beiname Coronatus wurde von Elisa Anti als ein Hinweis darauf gedeutet, dass der Autor ein Kleriker sei: der Beiname Coronatus drücke aus, dass er ein mit der Krone des Priesteramtes ausgezeichneter Notar sei.[84]

Ebenso ist der intendierte Rezipientenkreis des Textes in der Gemeinschaft der Kleriker am Dom zu suchen. Dies lässt sich aufgrund lexikologischer und thematischer Aspekte des *Sermo* vermuten: Für diese Gruppe wurde Zeno im *Sermo* vor allem als Sacerdos und nicht nur als Episcopus dargestellt, für sie wird auch im Prolog die besondere Würde eines Lebens als Sacerdos betont und auch die Mirakel, die Zeno bewirkt, stellen ein eindeutiges Signal dar, dass der Heilige einen besonderen Grad der Priesterweihe innehatte, nämlich den eines Exorzisten.[85]

Auch andere Hinweise legen diese Identifikation nahe: Es wird berichtet, wie Zeno vor seinen Reisen ein Gebet spricht und wie er dies auch vor dem Eintreten in den Palast des Kaisers Gallienus tut, der die Christen verfolgte. Auch die Handlungen Zenos bei den Exorzismen werden präzise beschrieben: Zunächst macht er das Kreuzzeichen, dann erhebt er seine Hand und spricht passende

80 Vgl. Elisa Anti: Verona e il culto di San Zeno tra IV e XII secolo, Verona 2009.

81 Bezüglich der Episode der Heilung des besessenen Mädchens und ihres literarischen Vorbildes siehe: Golinelli: Il Cristianesimo nella Venetia, S. 287.

82 Vgl. ebd., S. 283–284.

83 Die frühere Forschung vertrat die These, dass der *Sermo* von einem Mönch des Zenoklosters verfasst worden sei, wie zum Beispiel Mario Carrara: Gli scrittori latini, in: Vittorio Cavallari / Piero Gazzola (Hg.): Verona e il suo territorio, Verona 1960-1984, S. 349–420, hier: S. 367. Diese Hypothese erschien nach und nach weniger haltbar.

84 Vgl. Anti: Verona e il culto, S. 51.

85 Vgl. Golinelli: Il Cristianesimo nella Venetia, S. 284–285.

Gebete. Diese Passagen lassen sich nahezu als Handlungsanweisungen lesen, die das priesterliche Publikum in alltäglichen Bereichen anleiten sollten: „Sprich vor jeder Reise ein Gebet", „Sprich ein Gebet, wenn du einen profanen Ort betrittst", oder auch: „Verhalte dich bei einem Exorzismus auf diese oder jene Weise". Diese Aspekte veranschaulichen den pragmatischen Charakter des *Sermo* und erlauben es, die Gemeinschaft der Priester am Dom als primäre Rezipienten des Textes zu identifizieren.

In der Frage nach der Abfassungsmotivation des *Sermo* ist sich die Forschung weitgehend einig. Aufgrund der erwähnten historischen Verhältnisse, in denen die Vita verfasst wurde – der Machtwechsel, die Ankunft neuer, fremder Herrscher im geistlichen sowie säkularen Bereich – wird der *Sermo* oft als ein Mittel der bischöflichen Propaganda oder, neutraler, der Verbreitung und Verstärkung des Zenokultes gedeutet, und zwar sowohl innerhalb Veronas, wo er für den Vortrag im Rahmen einer Lectio publica vorgesehen gewesen wäre, als auch außerhalb der Stadt:[86]

> Die Kultur und Sensibilität der Veroneser Bischöfe, die in den ersten Jahrzehnten nach der fränkischen Eroberung auf den Bischofsstuhl kamen, machte sie für einen Text besonders empfänglich, der sich sehr für die Zelebrierung des Veroneser Bischofssitzes eignete.[87]

Auch wenn die Abfassung der Zenovita im Umfeld des Domkapitels verortet werden kann,[88] wurde sie bald vom Bischof genutzt, um damit episkopale Propaganda zu betreiben. Diese propagandistische Kampagne sei auch nördlich der Alpen betrieben worden, wofür die Vita exportiert worden sei, etwa zu Hinkmar von Reims.[89]

Bei näherer Betrachtung kann von einer propagandistischen Absicht aber keine Rede sein. Auch eine Nutzung im schulischen Kontext, wie Golinelli vermutet,[90] ist auszuschließen, wie eine Untersuchung der frühesten Handschrift eröffnet. Trotz seiner Zerstörung 1744 kann der älteste Codex für eine Untersuchung herangezogen werden, da wir über eine Beschreibung, Transkription sowie Abbildungen des Bandes, angefertigt durch den Veroneser Gelehrten Scipione Maffei verfügen. Dieser konnte die Handschrift anlässlich einer Gelehrtenreise nach

---

86 Vgl. Anti: Verona e il culto, S. 49–52.

87 „La cultura e la sensibilità dei vescovi di Verona che si avvicendarono nei primi decenni della dominazione franca, li rendevano particolarmente ricettivi nei confronti di un testo che si prestava docilmente all'operazione di celebrazione del seggio episcopale veronese", aus: Giorgia Vocino: Santi e luoghi santi al servizio della politica carolingia (774–877). Vitae e Passiones del regno italico nel contesto europeo, Venedig 2010, S. 221.

88 Vgl. Anti: Verona e il culto, S. 49. Vgl. Golinelli: Il Cristianesimo nella Venetia, S. 284–285. Dafür sprechen lexikologische Beobachtungen (die Häufigkeit der Benennung von Zeno als „sacerdos" gegenüber „episcopus") und die Typologie der von Zeno bewirkten Mirakel, die darauf schließen lassen, dass Zeno als Exorzist geweiht war, aber auch der Hinweis auf den Namen des Autors, der sich „coronatus notarius" nennt, der also möglicherweise ein ‚Geweihter', also ein Kleriker war. Siehe Anti: Verona e il culto, S. 50–51.

89 Vgl. Vocino: Santi e luoghi santi, S. 216–221.

90 Vgl. Golinelli: Il Cristianesimo nella Venetia, S. 287.

Frankreich 1720 in Paris inspizieren und die Ergebnisse seiner Untersuchung den Brüdern Ballerini, den ersten Editoren des *Sermo* und der *Tractatus* von Zeno, mitteilen.[91] Es handelte sich um eine Pergamenthandschrift von 140 Blatt im Kleinfolioformat, bei der zwei Schreiberhände am Werk waren. Aufgrund der Schrift wird sie zwischen dem Ende des 8. und dem Beginn des 9. Jahrhunderts datiert, also zeitlich sehr nah zur Entstehung des *Sermo* verortet.[92] Zu einem unbestimmten Zeitpunkt kam der Codex in den Besitz von Hinkmar von Reims, der ihn dann seiner Bischofskirche St. Denis schenkte. Dies wird von einer Notiz auf dem ersten und zweiten Blatt des Codex bezeugt: „Hinkmar der Erzbischof schenkte [dieses Buch] der [Kirche des] Heiligen Remigius."[93] Der Codex enthielt neben dem *Sermo* auch die Predigtsammlung von Zeno, die in zwei Bücher aufgeteilt wurde, denen jeweils ein Inhaltsverzeichnis vorangeht.

Interessanterweise deutet gerade diese an Hinkmar gesendete Handschrift darauf hin, dass sich die These einer Propagandaabsicht allein nicht halten lässt. Die Organisation der Handschrift, die aus zwei Teilen, nämlich der Vita sowie dem *Opus* des Heiligen besteht, weist auf ein Verständnis von Zeno als Autor hin. Mit der Zusammenstellung des Codex versuchte man ein Dossier um Zeno zu kompilieren, eine Art Autorenportrait, in dem die Abschrift der Homiliensammlung *Tractatus* zusammen mit der Lebensbeschreibung seines Autors zusammengebunden wurde. So betrachtet richteten sich der Codex sowie die darin überlieferten Texte tatsächlich nicht nur an die Verehrergemeinschaft der Veroneser Kleriker, sondern auch an ein weiteres Publikum. Dieses konstituierte sich allerdings hauptsächlich aus Gebildeten – wie Hinkmar –, die sich für Zeno nicht nur als Heiligen, sondern auch als Theologen und Autor interessierten.

Schwerer wiegen allerdings die Hinweise auf eine liturgische Nutzung der in der Handschrift enthaltenen Texte. Eine wichtige Besonderheit des Codex, die Maffei notierte, sind eine Reihe von Marginalia, die von einer alten aber zweiten Hand („antiqua sed secunda manu"[94]) eingetragen wurden und die darüber Auskunft geben, welche Predigt von Zeno bei welchem liturgischen Anlass vorzutragen sei. So findet man zu Beginn der dritten Predigt des zweiten Buches den Hinweis: An Weihnachten von den Brüdern in der Kammer nach dem Einzug der Diakone vor dem Bischof zu lesen („In Natali Domini fratribus legenda in cubiculo post Diaconorum ingressionem ante Pontificem"[95]). Oder bei der dreizehnten Homilie des ersten Buches: Bei der Weihnachtsoktav, die neunte Lesung des Bischofs („In octaba [sic] Domini, Pontificis nona lectio"[96]). Wichtig sind insbesondere zwei Hinweise, die erlauben, ohne Zweifel Verona als Nutzungskontext

---

91 Ballerini / Ballerini: Sancti Zenonis Episcopi, V.

92 Vgl. Lazzarini: Scuola calligrafica veronese, S. 14.

93 „Hincmarus Archiepiscopus dedit Sancto Remigio", Ballerini / Ballerini: Sancti Zenonis Episcopi, S. 6.

94 Ebd., VII.

95 Ebd.

96 Ebd.

dieser Handschrift zu identifizieren. In einer dieser Notizen wird eine Stephanskirche erwähnt: Zu lesen in der Stephanskirche am zweiten Ostertag vom Ambo, bevor der Bischof beginnt, die Gabe des Heiligen Geistes zu feiern („Ad S. Stephanum ad martyres secunda feria paschae legenda in ambone, antequam Pontifex consignationem sancti spiritus celebrare incipiat"[97]). Die Predigt 43 ist demnach bei Sankt Stephan ad martyres am zweiten Tag der Osterwoche, also am Ostermontag, auf der Kanzel zu lesen, bevor der Bischof mit der Feier der Consignatio, eines Weihritus für das Taufwasser, beginnt.[98] Die Stephanskirche war seit dem 5. Jahrhundert ein wichtiger und traditionsreicher Ort der sakralen Topographie Veronas.[99] Auch eine zweite Notiz lässt auf Verona als Nutzungskontext der Handschrift schließen: Die Predigt 70 soll am Festtag der Märtyrer Firmus und Rusticus für die Brüder gelesen werden: Beim Fest von Firmus und Rusticus vorzulesen („In festivitate sanctorum Firmi et Rustici fratribus recitanda"[100]), ein Fest, das nur für Verona charakteristisch ist.

Die Handschrift wurde also, zumindest für den Teil, der die Predigten von Zeno enthielt, in Verona *liturgisch* genutzt. Dafür, dass auch der *Sermo* des Coronatus im Rahmen des nächtlichen Stundengebets der Kanoniker Verwendung fand, spricht nicht nur die Tatsache, dass der Text im gleichen Codex enthalten war, sondern auch seine Einteilung in neun kurze Kapitel, deren Anzahl den benötigten neun Lektionen der Matutin in einer Kathedralkirche entspricht. Diese Einteilung lässt sich übrigens auch in den jüngeren Handschriften des *Sermo* nachweisen. Außerdem wird das neunte Kapitel, das eine Anleihe von Gregor dem Großen darstellt, als ein unabhängiges neuntes Kapitel der Vita gesehen und des Öfteren durch eine Rubrik ausdrücklich als eigene Lesung ausgewiesen.[101] Es

---

97 Ebd.

98 Ebd., VIII.

99 Vgl. Pierpaolo Brugnoli (Hg.): La Cattedrale di Verona, S. 8. Dass die Stephanskirche für die Liturgie des Domes wichtig war, zeigt auch das Lektionar für die Messe Verona BC LXXXII(77), um die Mitte des 9. Jahunderts. Hier werden die Messlesungen für den Samstag nach Pfingsten angegeben und der Rubrik ist zu entnehmen, dass die Messe in Sankt Stephan gefeiert wurde. Die römische Vorlage des Messlektionars hätte hingegen die Messe in Sankt Peter vorgesehen. Vgl. Sieghild Rehle: Lectionarium plenarium Veronense (Bibl. Cap., Cod. LXXXII), in: Sacris erudiri 22, 1974, S. 321–376, hier: S. 323. Auch in Verona wurde im 9. Jhdt. eine stationale Stadtliturgie gefeiert. Zu der Stationsliturgie nach dem Vorbild Roms im Frühmittelalter siehe: Johann Dorn: Stationsgottesdienste in frühmittelalterlichen Bischofsstädten, in: Andreas Bigelmair (Hg.): Festgabe Alois Knöpfler zur Vollendung des 60. Lebensjahres gewidmet, München 1907, S. 43–55. Außerdem: Ursmer Berlière: Les stations liturgiques dans les anciennes villes épiscopales, in: Revue liturgique et monastique 5, 1920, S. 213; Rolf Zerfass: Die Idee der römischen Stationsfeier und ihr Fortleben, in: Liturgisches Jahrbuch 8, 1958, S. 218–229; John F. Baldovin: The Urban Character of Christian Worship. The Origins, Development and Meaning of Stational Liturgy (Orientalia Christiana Analecta 228), Rom 1987

100 Ballerini / Ballerini: Sancti Zenonis Episcopi, VIII.

101 In der Handschrift Roma Biblioteca Casanatense 718, fol. 17v wird die Passage als „Lesung des Papstes Gregors über das Wunder von Sankt Zeno" („Lectio sancti Gregori pape de miraculo sancti Zenonis") markiert; in der Handschrift Trento Biblioteca Capitolare 173, fol. 22v macht die Passage Gregors die neunte Lesung aus.

ist wahrscheinlich, dass zu dieser Zeit neben den Lesungen aus dem *Sermo* für die Zenofeste am Dom Antiphonen und Responsorien gesungen wurden, die aus dem Commune entnommen wurden. Darauf deutet die erste für Zeno spezifische Historia hin, die, wie später ausführlich behandelt wird,[102] im 10. Jahrhundert entstand. Diese erste Historia für Zeno stellt meines Erachtens eine gänzlich neue Komposition dar. Ihre Analyse legt nahe, dass sie fast ausschließlich auf der Grundlage einer neuen Überarbeitung der Zenovita basierte und ansonsten keine weiteren Quellen für den Text der Antiphonen und Responsorien benutzt wurden. Wenn es eine ältere, spezifische Zenohistoria gegeben hätte, hätte der Offiziendichter sie wahrscheinlich überarbeitet und in die neue einfließen lassen. Daraus ergibt sich, dass die Kleriker bis zu dem Zeitpunkt der Entstehung einer spezifischen Historia für Zeno wohl Gesänge aus dem Commune verwendeten. Auch lässt sich vermuten, dass sie dafür die Antiphonen und Responsorien aus dem Commune eines Bekenners wählten. In den Lesungen aus dem *Sermo* trat Zeno als Priester hervor und so wären auch diese Gesänge für eine entsprechende Profilierung des Heiligen besonders gut geeignet gewesen.

Zusammenfassend ergibt sich aus diesen Beobachtungen, dass die älteste Vita Zenos im Rahmen der Liturgie des Domkapitels entstand und nicht als Propagandamittel. Sie war der inhaltliche Nukleus der Identität einer zunehmend auf den Heiligen bezogenen Verehrergemeinschaft, nämlich der Gruppe der Kanoniker an der bischöflichen Kathedrale von Verona. In deren Kirche erklang die Stimme des rhetorisch begabten Zeno auch vierhundert Jahre nach seinem Tod, indem seine Homilien in den jährlichen Zyklus der liturgischen Feiern eingebunden wurden. Auch wurde der Heilige durch das Lesen seiner Lebensbeschreibung im Rahmen des nächtlichen Gebets von den Klerikern memoriert. Hier wurde Zeno insbesondere als Sacerdos, Exorzist und zuletzt auch als erfolgreicher Bischof dargestellt und bot für die Kleriker ein nachzuahmendes Modell an.

Das Ziel Ratolds war weniger die Förderung des Heiligenkultes für Zeno an sich. Vielmehr ging es ihm darum, das religiöse Leben seiner Stadt zu fördern und im Zuge dessen auch die kirchlichen Institutionen Veronas zu stärken. Dies geschah zum einen, wie gerade beschrieben, durch die Reformierung des Domkapitels, ging aber auch mit der Etablierung weiterer kirchlicher Institutionen einher. So erhielt auch der Zenokult weiteren Aufschwung, nämlich durch die Gründung eines Benediktinerklosters am Grab des Heiligen: des Klosters San Zeno Maggiore. Auch wenn wohl bereits seit der Zeit des Petronius eine kleine Kirche das Grab des Heiligen bewachte, so stand dieser Ort bis ins frühe Mittelalter kaum im Zentrum der liturgischen Praxis. Vielmehr ist wahrscheinlich, dass die Kirche von Mitgliedern des Domes offiziert wurde und lediglich Schauplatz einer Verehrung in kleinem Umfang war.

Dies änderte sich schlagartig in der Zeit Ratolds, auch wenn die komplizierte Quellenlage keine einfachen Aussagen erlaubt. Eine Urkunde von 853 bezeugt,

102 Siehe unten, Kapitel 4.2.1.

dass der italische König Pippin und Bischof Ratold eine zerstörte Kirche für den heiligen Zeno wieder errichten ließen: „Aber wir entdeckten, auf welche Art und Weise zur Zeit von Karl dem Großen der berühmte König Pippin zusammen mit dem Veroneser Bischof Ratold die Kirche von Sankt Zeno wiederaufbaute, die schon durch Schulden so geschwächt war, dass sie fast vernichtet war."[103] Zwar berichtet eine angeblich frühere Urkunde, dass sich am Ort dieser von Ratold errichteten Kirche bereits ein Zenokloster „auf dem Land bei der eben erwähnten Stadt" („in suburbio praedictae civitatis"[104]) befand, allerdings konnte diese Urkunde als nachträgliche Fälschung identifiziert werden und ist daher nicht belastbar.[105] Es sollte vielmehr davon ausgegangen werden, dass am Grab des Heiligen lediglich eine Kirche bestand, die zur Zeit Ratolds zerstört gewesen ist. Davon berichtet auch Paulus Diaconus, der am Ende des 8. Jahrhunderts in seiner *Historia Langobardorum* von einer Kirche außerhalb der Stadtmauer von Verona gelegen („extra veronensis muros sita"[106]) redet. Dass die von Ratold erbaute Kirche des heiligen Zeno mit dem Kloster zu identifizieren ist, belegt die Nennung des Klosters Moratica in der Urkunde von 853, die bis in spätere Zeit mit dem Zenokloster verbunden war.[107]

Die Kirche am Grab des Heiligen wurde durch Ratold wohl zwischen 802 und 810 erneuert, wobei nicht bekannt ist, wann genau dies geschah. Das Veroneser Urkundenbuch spricht von einer Dedicatio im Dezember 806. Diese Nennung basiert aber nicht auf einer überlieferten Urkunde, sondern wurde wohl aus dem mutmaßlichen Datum der Translation im Frühling 807 abgeleitet.[108] Tatsächlich gibt es auch für dieses Datum keine belastbaren Hinweise, auch wenn es in der Forschung allgemein akzeptiert wird.[109] Wann genau das Kloster gegründet wor-

---

[103] „Sed in domni Karoli augusti invenimus, qualiter Pippinus gloriosus rex cum Rataldo ipsius sedis episcopo ecclesiam sancti Zenonis confessoris Christi renovassent cum iam rebus debitis privata adeo fuerat adtenuata ut ad nichilum esset redacta". Fainelli: Codice diplomatico Veronese, Nr. 190, S. 287–291. Außerdem: Die Urkunden Ludwigs II., hrsg. von Konrad Wanner (MGH DD L II), München 1994, Nr. 13, S. 88–91.

[104] Fainelli: Codice diplomatico Veronese, N. 117, S. 153.

[105] Vgl. Egidio Rossini: Giurisdizioni e proprietà fondiaria del monastero di s. Zeno dedotte da documenti pubblici anteriori all'anno mille. La nascita del „Burgus Sancti Zenonis", in: Studi Zenoniani. In occasione del XVI centenario della morte di S. Zeno, Verona 1974, S. 68–168, hier: S. 79.

[106] Vgl. Paulus Diaconus: Historia Langobardorum, hrsg. von Ludwig C. Bethmann / Georg Waitz (SS rer. Lang.), Hannover 1878, S. 104.

[107] Vgl. Wanner: Die Urkunden Ludwigs, S. 88. Außerdem: Gian Maria Varanini: Il monastero di San Zeno di Verona nell'età "romanica" (metà XI–metà XIII secolo). Aspetti economici, istituzionali e politici, in: Francesco Butturini / Flavio Pachera (Hg.): San Zeno Maggiore a Verona. Il campanile e la facciata. Restauri, analisi tecniche e nuove interpretazioni, Verona 2015, S. 29–42, hier: S. 30.

[108] Vgl. Fainelli: Codice diplomatico Veronese, Nr. 74, S. 92–94.

[109] So spricht Anti von einer „traditionellen Datierung", bezieht sich in den Fußnoten aber weitgehend (und zum Teil mit fehlerhaften Seitenangaben) auf Titel, in denen lediglich allgemein vom Anfang des 9. Jhdts. die Rede ist. Eine Ausnahme ist Giovanni B. C. Giuliari (Hg.): S. Zenonis episcopi Veronensis Sermones, Verona 1883, S. 21, der tatsächlich 807 als Datum ins Spiel bringt, sich dabei aber auf Literatur stützt, aus der dies nicht hervor-

den ist und die Gebeine des Heiligen feierlich dorthin überführt worden sind, ist somit fraglich. Da der Translationsbericht des 12. Jahrhunderts davon spricht, dass König Pippin an der Translation beteiligt gewesen sei, hat die Forschung daraus gefolgert, dass dies nicht nach 810 geschehen sein kann, da Pippin dann verstorben ist.[110] Inwiefern man dieser Quelle vertrauen kann, soll an dieser Stelle nicht entschieden werden, insgesamt erscheint das erste Jahrzehnt des 9. Jahrhunderts aber als wahrscheinlich.

Eindeutiger lässt sich belegen, dass das Kloster tatsächlich am Grab des Heiligen errichtet wurde. Nicht nur stellte das Areal im Nordwesten von Verona, auf dem das Kloster heute liegt, während der Spätantike eine Begräbnisstätte außerhalb der Stadtmauern dar.[111] Auch wurden andere Bischöfe von Verona nachweislich an diesem Ort begraben. Das belegt eine kleine Kirche, in der der Bischof Prokulus (260–304) bestattet ist.[112] Außerdem wurde zu Recht festgestellt, dass es sich für die Karolinger kaum gelohnt hätte, das Kloster an einem abgelegenen Ort zu gründen, um dann die Gebeine des Heiligen dorthin aufs Land vor den Mauern der Stadt zu bringen.[113] Unabhängig von der Frage, wann genau die Translation vollzogen wurde, kann mit Sicherheit gesagt werden, dass sich vor den Toren der Stadt im ersten Jahrzehnt des 9. Jahrhunderts ein Benediktinerkloster etablierte, das dezidiert dem heiligen Zeno gewidmet war und bald mit der Pflege seiner Gebeine betraut wurde. Diese Verpflichtung ging mit einer ausgiebigen Förderung durch Bischof und Kaiser einher, die das Kloster reich beschenkten.[114]

Auf der Ebene der Liturgie zeigt sich eine deutliche Intensivierung des Zenokults zu Beginn des 9. Jahrhunderts, die vor allem in der Erweiterung der Feierlichkeiten für den Heiligen zum Ausdruck kommt. Während bislang lediglich der 8. Dezember, das Datum der Bischofsweihe Zenos, welches sein Wirken am Dom markierte, liturgisch gefeiert wurde, wurde dieses Fest nun auch vom Kloster für sich in Anspruch genommen, das an diesem Tag seine Dedicatio feierte. Damit nicht genug: Ratold etablierte noch weitere Feste, die vor allem mit dem Kloster in Verbindung gebracht und dort gefeiert wurden. Zum einen das Fest zum Todestag des Heiligen am 12. April, zum anderen das Fest der Translatio

---

geht. Auch Franco Segala: Le reliquie del vescovo, in: Annuario storico zenoniano, 1983, S. 11–23, hier: S. 14 und Fußnote 12 auf S. 23, spricht von 807 als Datum der Translation, bezieht sich aber nur unspezifisch auf nicht näher genannte „documenti“, die dies belegten. Denkbar ist, dass er sich auf die Notizen im Urkundenbuch bezieht, die aber wie erwähnt lediglich Interpolationen darstellen.

110 Vgl. Anti: Verona e il culto, S. 55.

111 Vgl. Lanfranco Franzoni: Verona. Testimonianze archeologiche, Verona 1965, S. 55–58.

112 Vgl. Ederle / Cervato: I vescovi di Verona, S. 16. Außerdem Anti: Verona e il culto, S. 33. Vgl. außerdem: Valenzano: La basilica di San Zeno, S. 8.

113 Vgl. Anti: Note sulla prima, S. 14.

114 Dem Kloster standen unter anderem Erträge aus weiteren Klöstern in Verona, Mantova und Umgebung zu. Siehe dazu die Urkunden, ediert in Fainelli: Codice diplomatico Veronese, Nr. 77, 78, 80, 81, 83. Siehe auch: Hlawitschka: Ratold, Bischof von, S. 13–15.

am 21. Mai, dem Datum der Überführung der Reliquien ins Kloster San Zeno Maggiore.[115]

Diese neuen Feste wurden im Laufe des 10. und 11. Jahrhunderts in vielen Handschriften nachgetragen, in denen sie ursprünglich nicht vorgesehen waren, zum Beispiel Verona BC LXV(63).[116] Hier wurden am Rande des Haupttextes, nämlich des Martyrologiums von Beda, im Laufe des 10. und 11. Jahrhunderts und nicht von der Haupthand, wie Meersseman behauptet,[117] einige liturgische Notizen angebracht, die uns über die Verehrung von Heiligen in Verona informieren. Von einer Hand des 10. Jahrhunderts wurden zunächst die Feste für Prokulus, Syrus und am 8. Dezember die *Dedicatio eclesiae sancti Zenonis* hinzugefügt, eine Hand des 11. Jahrhunderts vervollständigte die Handschrift dann auch mit weiteren in Verona verehrten Heiligen, und zwar neben Eufemia besonders das Zenofest am 12. April und das Fest des Firmus und Rusticus am 9. August.[118] Im 11. Jahrhundert sind daher bereits zwei Feste für Zeno etabliert, neben dem bereits erwähnten Fest des 8. Dezembers, das für den Dom wichtig war, weil damit Zenos bischöfliche Weihe memoriert wurde, auch das Fest am 12. April, bei dem der angebliche Todestag des Heiligen zelebriert wurde. Liturgische Nachträge mit Veroneser Bezug sind auch im berühmten Sakramentar von Padova, Cod. D 47, ein Gregorianum des II. Typus, zu beobachten.[119] Die Handschrift wurde in Nordfrankreich, Belgien oder Oberitalien angefertigt, dann zunächst im 9. Jahrhundert in Lüttich verwendet und landete zuletzt, wahrscheinlich dank Bischof Hilduin oder Bischof Rather, im 10. Jahrhundert in Verona, wo sie durch Zusätze für die lokale Nutzung tauglich gemacht wurde: Neben Zusätzen, die eine Art Veroneser Supplement darstellen,[120] wurden auf ff. 149v–150v in der zweiten Hälfte des 10. Jahrhunderts eine Messe für das Zenofest am 12. April und auf f. 161v die Messe für die Translation von Zeno von einer Hand der ersten Hälfte des 11. Jahrhunderts nachgetragen. Diese Messen können also nicht als Quellen des 9. Jahrhunderts gelten, wie Segala referiert.[121] Die Formulare für zwei Zenomessen, am 12. April und 8. Dezember, sind auch in der Handschrift Verona, BC LXXXVII(82) zu finden. Das Sakramentar, eine Prachthandschrift, in der der Kalender in Gold- und Silberschrift eingetragen wurde, wurde gegen Ende des 10. Jahrhunderts in Regensburg geschrieben und ist als Wolfgangs-Sakramentar bekannt.[122] Im Kalender wurden die Feste des Veroneser Propriums ebenso wie der Haupttext in Gold- und Silberschrift hinzugefügt. Außerdem wurde vor dem Beginn des Sakramentars und vor dem Beginn des Kanons, auf der Rectoseite des Foliums 12, und somit in extrem prominenter Position, die Messe für

[115] Vgl. Meersseman u. a.: L'orazionale, S. 18.
[116] Vgl. ebd., S. 67–68.
[117] Vgl. ebd., S. 67–68.
[118] Vgl. Polloni: Manoscritti liturgici della Capitolare, S. 177.
[119] Vgl. Vogel: Medieval Liturgy, S. 94–95.
[120] Vgl. Meersseman u. a.: L'orazionale, S. 69–71.
[121] Vgl. Segala: Il culto di San Zeno, S. 27–28.
[122] Vgl. Gamber: Codices liturgici latini, Nr. 940, S. 418.

das Zenofest am 12. April ebenso wie der Rest der Handschrift von Regensburger Schreibern eingetragen. Der Text dieser Zenomesse ist wie der erste Teil des Kanons in goldener Schrift auf Purpurgrund eingetragen worden.[123] Da eine weitere Zeno-Messe, nämlich für das Fest am 8. Dezember, bereits auf fol. 153v, also im Corpus der Handschrift, von erster Hand eingetragen worden und somit im Programm der Handschrift bereits zum Zeitpunkt der Anfertigung vorgesehen war, deutet diese Hinzufügung der Messe für das Fest des 12. April zu Beginn der Handschrift und nicht nach dem liturgischen Kalender auf die zunehmende Wichtigkeit des Aprilfestes in Verona hin. Dies war allerdings den Regensburger Schreibern nicht bekannt und so musste das zweite Fest, wahrscheinlich entsprechend dem Wunsch des Veroneser Auftraggebers des Codex, ergänzt werden.

Bereits seit der Zeit Ratolds feierte man im Kloster den Heiligen an drei Tagen, von denen zwei direkt mit dem Standort des Klosters verbunden waren. Auch wenn der Todestag Zenos im April zugleich auch vom Kapitel übernommen und bis ins jüngere *Carpsum* beibehalten wurde,[124] führte dieser Umstand doch zu einer liturgischen Ungleichgewichtung der Institutionen, die dadurch verstärkt wurde, dass an einem dieser Feste, nämlich im Dezember, vor dem Kloster ein Markt veranstaltet wurde, durch den dem Kloster besonders viele Spenden und Zuwendungen zukamen.[125] Zwar versuchte Ratold, dieser Ungleichheit entgegenzuwirken, indem er die Teilung der Spenden an den heiligen Zeno zwischen den zwei Institutionen verfügte,[126] die sich beide mit gewissem Recht auf den Heiligen berufen konnten. Nichtdestotrotz drohte das Kloster, den Domklerikern ihr bisheriges Monopol auf die Verehrung des Heiligen streitig zu machen.[127] In der von Ratold bewirkten Multiplizierung der Verehrergemeinschaften des heiligen Zeno war so ein Konfliktpotential angelegt, das bis ins hohe Mittelalter das Verhältnis der beiden Institutionen zueinander belastete und auch ihre Liturgie nachhaltig beeinflusste. Diese Entwicklungen sollen im Folgenden nachgezeichnet werden.

Zusammenfassend lässt sich sagen, dass nach einer langen Phase der unbestimmten liturgischen Verehrung Zenos am Dom mit Beginn des 9. Jahrhunderts und der Integration der Stadt ins Karolingerreich der Kult des Heiligen erheblich verfestigt wurde. Dies geschah nicht nur durch die Förderung der Kleriker am Dom, die sich auf den Heiligen beriefen, sondern vor allem durch die Organisation und Institutionalisierung der bis dahin nicht belegbaren Verehrung am Grab des Heiligen durch die Gründung und Förderung des Benediktinerklosters San Zeno Maggiore. Gleichzeitig wurde der Kult durch die Einführung neuer Feste intensiviert: Nun feierte man den Heiligen nicht nur am 8. Dezember, sondern

---

123 Vgl. Meersseman u. a.: L'orazionale, S. 72–73.

124 Vgl. ebd., S. 244.

125 Vgl. Fainelli: Codice diplomatico Veronese, Nr. 231, S. 352.; außerdem: Golinelli: Il Cristianesimo nella Venetia, S. 290.

126 Vgl. Fainelli: Codice diplomatico Veronese, Nr. 122, S. 163.

127 Vgl. ebd., Nr. 102 S. 130–131, Nr. 117 S. 155.

auch seinen Todestag am 12. April sowie die Translation seiner Gebeine am 21. Mai. Was die Konstruktion des Heiligen angeht, lässt sich vor allem durch die Abfassung einer Vita, des sogenannten *Sermo*, eine vorsichtige Profilierung erkennen, gleichzeitig war mit dem Fehlen einer Historia der Bereich der Hagiopraxis auf das unspezifische Commune beschränkt und erlaubte damit noch keine individualisierte Verehrung. Dies änderte sich erst im Verlauf des 10. Jahrhunderts, mit dem Wirken Bischof Rathers in der Stadt.

4.2 Verehrergemeinschaften von Zeno in Verona im 10. und 11. Jahrhundert

4.2.1 Die erste eigene Historia für Zeno

Die Etablierung einer individualisierten liturgischen Verehrung für Zeno lässt sich erst ab dem 10. Jahrhundert nachweisen und ist mit Bischof Rather und der Gemeinschaft seiner Kleriker verbunden. Bis zu diesem Zeitpunkt wurde Zeno, wie oben gesagt, mit einer Commune-Historia, wahrscheinlich aus dem Commune eines Bekenners, gefeiert. Die darin enthaltenen Antiphonen und Responsorien bestanden aus umfunktionalisierten Psalmversen, die je nach Typus zur Verehrung einer ganzen Gruppe von Heiligen genutzt wurden. Die für Zeno verwendete Commune-Historia wurde daher auch für andere Heilige, die als Bekenner galten, gesungen. Zwar bewirkt die Auswahl einer bestimmten Commune-Historia eine gewisse Profilierung des Heiligen – am Beispiel Zenos eben als Bekenner –, dies aber ließ den Heiligen nicht als individualisierte Figur hervortreten. Erst wenn in den Antiphonen und Responsorien der Heilige namentlich erwähnt und für die spezifischen Verdienste seiner Biographie besungen wird, kann er als in der liturgischen Praxis vollständig konstituiert gelten. Dies geschah mit Bischof Rather. Er förderte die Entstehung der ersten Historia für Zeno, mit der der Heilige mit einem auf ihn zugeschnittenen Set an Antiphonen und Responsorien verehrt wurde. Erst dies bewirkte – nach dem Verständnis dieser Arbeit – die wahre Geburt des individuellen Heiligen.

Die hier zum Ausdruck kommende Rolle einer Historia für den Kult des Heiligen liegt in der Zentralität dieses Hauptbestandteils des Offiziums begründet, die sich auf zwei unterschiedlichen Ebenen beobachten lässt. Zum einen aus einer produktions-, zum anderen aus einer rezeptionsästhetischen Perspektive. Produktionsästhetisch bedeutet das Verfassen einer spezifisch auf den Heiligen abgestimmten Historia das Aufkommen des Bedürfnisses der Verehrergemeinschaft, den Heiligen besser zu ehren und zu besingen. Auch wenn Commune-Historiae durch die Performanz am Tag des Festes immer einen Bezug zum aktuell gefeierten Heiligen gewannen, konnte erst die auf ihn spezifizierte Historia den besonderen Stellenwert des Heiligen sowie die Bindung der Gemeinschaft an die Figur ausdrücken: Zunächst mit einer im Rahmen der liturgischen Feier vorgelesenen

Vita, dann mit dem Offizium wird der Heilige zum ausdrücklichen Protagonisten der Hagiopraxis, indem ihm neben einer eigenen heiligen Biographie auch ein eigenes liturgisches Gedenken zugeschrieben wird:

> Nebst allen diesen Formen und Manifestationen des Heiligenkultes erlaubt die Komposition eines eigenen Offiziums – komponiert besonders für den Heiligen auf der Grundlage einer Vita oder Passio – ihn von den Heiligen des Commune zu unterscheiden [und] ihn auf die gleiche Ebene zu stellen, wie die sogenannten ‚Universalheiligen' des römischen Kalenders. Die Historia setzt sich also als höchste Krönung des Heiligenkultes durch."[128]

Nicht nur wirken die auf der Vorlage der Vita basierenden Antiphonen und Responsorien wie ein Echo der im Laufe der selben Zeremonie erzählten Geschichte des Heiligen („Bestimmte Episoden der Biographie der Heiligen wurden somit durch die Antiphonen und Responsorien hervorgehoben, die sie wie ein Echo wiederholten."[129]), auch wird der performative Wert[130] der hagiographischen Erzählung gesteigert:

> Der transformierende Schritt von der biographischen auf die kultische Ebene bedeutet zugleich eine signifikante Steigerung des Dignitätsanspruchs, weil die liturgische memoria aufgrund ihres sakralen Charakters eine Überbietung des durch die Vita vorgegebenen erinnerungskulturellen Modells und eine gesteigerte, fast ‚realpräsentische' Form von Aktualisierung reklamiert.[131]

Der Heilige verwandelt sich von einem „erzählten" oder „erinnerten" zu einem „angebeteten" Heiligen.[132] Dies hat aus rezeptionsästhetischer Perspektive weitreichende Folgen: Die Rezitation der Vita im Chor und das Singen ihrer poetischen Überhöhung – der Historia – erweitert nicht nur das Publikum der Rezipienten des hagiographischen Stoffes;[133] auch die Geschichte und der Name des Heiligen werden zu einer auditiven und physischen Memoria.[134]

Aufgrund dieser besonderen Bedeutung des Offiziums im Rahmen des Verhältnisses zwischen dem Heiligen und der Verehrergemeinschaft soll im Folgenden die Historia für Zeno genauer untersucht werden. Diese Historia wird hier mit

---

128 „Ainsi toutes ces formes et expressions différenciées du culte de saints, la composition d'un office propre, spécialement composé pour le saint à partir de la rédaction d'une vita ou d'une passio, permet de le distinguer du commun, de le placer à niveau égal avec les saints dits universel du calendrier romain. L'Historia s'impose donc comme la consécration suprême de son culte." Goudesenne: Les Offices historiques, S. 29.

129 „Des épisodes de la vie des saints étaient ainsi mis en évidence par les antiennes et les répons qui les rérecutaient comme un écho", aus: de Gaiffier d'Hestroy: Hagiographie et historiographie, S. 148.

130 Vgl. Sedda zu den „leggende corali" francescane, Filippo Sedda: La *Legenda liturgica vaticana* per l'ottava di San Francesco. *Franciscus alter evangelista*, in: Frate Francesco. Rivista di cultura francescana 78, 2012, S. 83–126, hier: S. 84–85.

131 Felix Heinzer: Der besungene Heilige: Aspekte des liturgisch propagierten Franziskus-Bildes, in: Wissenschaft und Weisheit 74, 2011, S. 234–251, hier: S. 234.

132 Vgl. Sedda: La Legenda liturgica, S. 83.

133 Vgl. de Gaiffier d'Hestroy: Hagiographie et historiographie, S. 148.

134 Vgl. ebd., S. 154.

dem Incipit der Magnificat-Antiphon als *Dum Zeno pontificatus honore* bezeichnet (hier in Kapitel 3.3.1 auf S. 61–80 ediert).[135]

Die Historia *Dum Zeno pontificatus honore* ist sehr langlebig und wird von einer Gruppe von ungefähr 15 Handschriften überliefert, die zwischen dem 11. und dem 15. Jahrhundert entstanden sind. Es lassen sich zwei Fassungen dieser Historia identifizieren, eine kanonikale[136] und eine monastische Fassung.[137] Die Gruppe mit der höchsten Zahl von Zeugnissen ist, wie zu erwarten war, die aus Verona: die kanonikale Version des Offiziums wird von einem Liber ordinarius, auch als *Carpsum* des Stephanus cantor bekannt (Verona BC XCIV(89)) belegt, in dem das Offizium nur durch Incipits der Gesänge angegeben ist, und von drei Antiphonaren des 12. und 14. Jahrhunderts überliefert (Verona BC XCVIII(92), Verona BC MLII und Verona BC MLIII). Vereinzelte Gesänge, und zwar nur die Antiphonen für die Tageshoren, sind auch in einem Brevier des 13. Jahrhunderts (Verona BC CIII(96)) bezeugt. In einem Antiphonar der zweiten Hälfte des 15. Jahrhunderts (Verona BC MLXV), in dem die Gesänge für das Comune sanctorum enthalten sind, sind als Nachtrag Antiphonen für die erste und zweite Vesper, die Laudes und die Tageshoren für das Fest von Zeno zu finden.

Die monastische Version des Offiziums lässt sich ebenso in Veroneser Handschriften auffinden, und zwar in einem Brevier des 15. Jahrhunderts, heute in Kremsmünster (Kremsmünster SB CC60), und in einem Antiphonar des Veroneser Zenoklosters des späten 15. Jahrhunderts (Verona BCi 739 I). Vereinzelte Gesänge sind auch in einem monastischen Hymnar aus dem Zenokloster, das auf das Ende des 11. Jahrhunderts datiert worden ist, überliefert: Verona BC CIX(102). Außerhalb von Verona ist das Offizium in kanonikaler Version von einer Gruppe von Handschriften des 14. und 15. Jahrhunderts aus Cividale (Cividale MAN XLVII, Cividale MAN XXX und Cividale MAN XXXIV) sowie von zwei ähnlich datierten Handschiften aus Bad Reichenhall in der Diözese Salzburg überliefert (München BSB Clm 23143 und München BSB Clm 24882). Die monastische Version liefert auch ein Brevier des 15. Jahrhunderts, das in Augsburg für ein oberitalienisches Kloster (Verona oder Trento) angefertigt wurde (Augsburg StStadtB 2° 204).

Um die Frage nach der Entstehung dieser Historia zu klären, und somit herauszufinden, wann und von welcher Gemeinschaft die Initiative des Verfassens von spezifischen Gesängen für Zeno ausging, ist eine Analyse dieser abweichenden Fassungen notwendig.

Die Antiphonen und Responsorien der Historia in kanonikaler Form (cursus romanus) bedienen sich ausschließlich des Textes einer Zenovita als Vorlage, die

135 Eine weitere Historia, ein Reimoffizium mit dem Incipit *In lege sui Domini Zeno meditatur* ist in der Handschrift Padova BC A 20*, ff. 181r–187v überliefert. Sie scheint außerdem, abgesehen von der genannten Handschrift, wo sie auch nur fragmentarisch überliefert ist, keine Rezeption erfahren zu haben.

136 Hier ediert in Kapitel 3.3.1 auf S. 60–72.

137 Hier ediert in Kapitel 3.3.1 auf S. 73–80.

weiter unten noch zu identifizieren sein wird. Ausnahmen bilden die Magnificat-Antiphon der ersten und zweiten Vesper, das Invitatorium und das erste und letzte Responsorium der Matutin, welche entweder aus dem Commune entnommen oder keinem spezifischen hagiographischen Subtext zuzuordnen sind. Thematisch werden im kanonikalen Offizium folgende Aspekte der Zenogeschichte behandelt: Zenos angeborene Heiligkeit (A1 Ab utero, R2 Ab utero), die Ernennung zum Bischof aufgrund seiner Verdienste (A2 Probitatis, R2 Ab utero), seine asketische Lebensweise und die Bitte an Gott um Unterstützung bei der Bekehrung der heidnischen Stadtbevölkerung (A3 Continuis, R3 In secretiori), Zenos milde Art (A4 Affabilis, R4 Affabilis), das Fischen Zenos und ein erstes Mirakel, in welchem ein Mensch vor dem Ertrinken gerettet wird (A5 Dum exercitio, A6 Vir Dei, R5 Dum in fluvio, R6 Elevata), die Auseinandersetzung mit dem Teufel (A7 Beatus Zeno) und schließlich das Mirakel der Heilung der Tochter des Gallienus (A8 Miserabilis, A9 Sacerdos Dei, R7 Festinans, R8 Ingrediente). Die Antiphonen-Reihe der Laudes (L-A1 Dominus Iesus Chrstus bis L-A5 Christi namque sacerdos), die in einigen Handschriften auch als Antiphone der ersten und zweiten Vesper verwendet werden, behandeln erneut und ausschließlich den Exorzismus des Mädchens. Darauf folgend schließt auch die Benedictus-Antiphon (B-A Acceptam beatus Zeno) die Laudes mit dieser Episode ab und erzählt, wie Gallienus seine Krone dem Heiligen schenkt und wie der Heilige sie unmittelbar an die Armen weitergibt. Einige Aspekte der Geschichte von Zeno, darunter wichtige Episoden wie das auch von Gregor dem Großen erzählte Mirakel der Etschüberschwemmung, die Massenbekehrung der Bevölkerung oder Zeno als Kirchenbauer und Zerstörer von heidnischen Tempeln werden nicht erwähnt. Ebenso unerwähnt bleiben der Tod des Heiligen und der anschließende Bau einer Basilika in seinem Namen durch die kaiserliche Familie

Im monastischen Offizium, das etwas umfangreicher ausfällt, um den Bedürfnissen des monastischen Stundengebets gerecht zu werden, werden zwei zusätzliche Aspekte der Geschichte erwähnt: Zeno zerstört die heidnischen Idole und baut stattdessen christliche Kirchen in Verona (A11 Coepitque, R8 Beatissimus Christi). Außerdem befiehlt Zeno den Bau einer weiteren Kirche neben der Etsch und wird dort nach seinem Tod bestattet (R4 Iuxta Athesis, A12 Iuxta Athesis). Zwei der Antiphonen und Responsorien, die im monastischen Offizium zu den kanonikalen hinzugefügt wurden, A11 Coepitque und R8 Beatissimus, basieren auf weiteren Kapiteln der Zenovita. Die zwei weiteren zusätzlichen Antiphonen der monastischen Version (R4 und A12) sind auch lose von der Vita inspiriert, die Aussage der Vita wird allerdings an diesen Stellen der Historia geändert. Auf diese Eigentümlichkeiten des monastischen Offiziums wird später zurückzukommen sein.

Die Elemente aus der Vita werden vom Offiziendichter in der kanonikalen Version der Historia in chronologischer Reihenfolge aus der Vorlage übernommen: Zunächst wird in den Antiphonen der Matutin und der Laudes die Geschichte des

Heiligen von der Geburt bis zur Befreiung der Tochter Gallienus' erzählt, dann werden die gleichen Episoden durch die Responsorien der Matutin von Anfang an wiederholt. Somit ist es wahrscheinlich, dass der Offiziendichter zunächst alle Antiphonen, sowohl die der Matutin als auch der Laudes, in einem Zug auf der Grundlage der Zenovita verfasste und die Responsorien – gattungsgemäß musikalisch anspruchsvoller und textlich umfangreicher als Antiphonen – in einem zweiten Schritt komponierte.

Die chronologische Ordnung der Erzählung hingegen wird in der monastischen Historia teilweise unterbrochen. An einigen Stellen wurden mitten in der Erzählung auch nicht-narrative, gebetsartige Antiphonen und Responsorien hinzugefügt. So entsteht der Eindruck, dass die klerikale Version des Offiziums zuerst komponiert wurde und anschließend für den monastischen Cursus erweitert werden musste: Wie in der unten stehenden Tabelle zu erkennen ist, wurden alle vorhandenen Antiphone der ersten und zweiten Nokturn im klerikalen Cursus vollständig für die erste Nokturn im Cursus monasticus aufgebraucht und in gleicher Reihenfolge übernommen, während die drei übrigbleibenden Antiphonen des klerikalen Cursus zusammen mit drei neuen Antiphonen (A10, A11 und A12) für die zweite Nokturn im monastischen Offizium verwendet wurden. Die Laudes-Antiphonen wurden en bloc übernommen.[138]

Tabelle 1 Vergleich der Antiphonenreihen der Historia im CR und CM

Dum Zeno pontificatus honore – Cursus romanus	*Dum Zeno pontificatus honore – Cursus monasticus*
A1 Ab utero A2 Probitatis A3 Continuis	A1 Ab utero A2 Probitatis A3 Continuis A4 Affabilis ita A5 Cum[139] exercitio A6 Vir Dei
A4 Affabilis ita A5 Dum exercitio A6 Vir Dei	A7 Beatus Zeno A8 Miserabilis A9 Sacerdos *A10 Beate Zeno* *A11 Coepitque* *A12 Iuxta Athesis*
A7 Beatus Zeno A8 Miserabilis A9 Sacerdos	*A13 Iste est*

[138] Dabei handelt es sich um ein typisches, auch sonst zu beobachtendes Verfahren. Vgl. Eva Ferro: „Suavissime universorum Domine". Eine „konstanzische" Maria Magdalena-Historia in Hirsau?, in: Archiv für Liturgiewissenschaft, 2014, S. 49–74, hier: S. 60–67.

[139] Die monastische Antiphon verwendet die Konjunktion *cum*, nicht *dum*.

Dum Zeno pontificatus honore – Cursus romanus	*Dum Zeno pontificatus honore – Cursus monasticus*
L-A1 Dominus L-A2 Exsurgens L-A3 Ingrediente L-A4 Tenens L-A5 Christi B-A2 Acceptam	L-A1 Dominus L-A2 Exsurgens L-A3 Ingrediente L-A4 Tenens L-A5 Christi B-A2 Acceptam

Bei der Übernahme der Responsorien aus der klerikalen Version ging der Offiziendichter der monastischen Historia anders vor, doch auch hier wird deutlich, dass die klerikale Version die ursprüngliche war, die dann für den monastischen Cursus adaptiert worden ist: Die jeweils drei Responsorien einer Nokturn des kanonikalen Cursus werden im monastischen Offizium durch jeweils ein neues viertes Responsorium ergänzt (R4, R8, R11).

Tabelle 2 Vergleich der Responsorienreihen der historia in CR und CM

Cursus romanus	*Cursus monasticus*
R1 Hic est R2 Ab utero R3 In secretiori	R1 Hic est R2 Ab utero R3 In secretiori *R4 Iuxta Athesis*
R4 Affabilis R5 Dum in fluvio R6 Elevata	R5 Affabilis R6 Dum in fluvio R7 Elevata *R8 Beatissimus Christi*
R7 Festinans R8 Ingrediente R9 Sancte	R9 Festinans R10 Ingrediente *R11 Sacerdos Dei* R12 Sancte

Die Adaption und die Hinzufügungen im monastischen Offizium und die dadurch entstehenden chronologischen Unstimmigkeiten, wie zum Beispiel im Fall von R4 im Cursus monasticus, wo der Tod von Zeno bereits im ersten Teil des Nachtgebets behandelt wird, geben einen entscheidenden Hinweis auf den Entstehungsort des Offiziums. Sie belegen, dass das Offizium zunächst für den Cursus romanus komponiert worden ist, womit das Kloster San Zeno Maggiore als Initiator einer solchen liturgischen Aufwertung ausscheidet. Vielmehr rückt das Domkapitel als klerikale Institution ins Zentrum der Aufmerksamkeit. Tatsächlich legt auch die Überlieferung diesen Schluss nahe, da die frühesten Zeugnisse des Offiziums aus dem Dom stammen. Es handelt sich zum einen um ein Antiphonar des 11. Jahrhunderts, die Handschrift Verona BC XCVIII(92), und zum zweiten um das berühmte *Carpsum* des Stephanus cantor Verona BC

XCIV(89), einen Liber ordinarius, der für das Domkapitel von Verona gegen 1060 geschrieben wurde.[140] Das Antiphonar kann trotz einiger Unsicherheit in Verona lokalisiert[141] und entweder in das erste[142] oder zweite Viertel des 11. Jahrhunderts (nur wenige Jahre vor der Verschriftlichung des *Carpsums*[143]) datiert werden. Trotz dieser Unstimmigkeit in der Datierung stellt die Handschrift tatsächlich den ältesten Zeugen des Zeno-Offiziums dar, sie ist aber im Zusammenhang mit der Frage nach der Entstehung der Historia weniger entscheidend als das etwas jüngere *Carpsum*.

Diese Handschrift enthält die Incipits aller Gesänge für die Liturgie des Stundengebets und der Messe für das ganze liturgische Jahr, so wie diese vom Bischof und den Klerikern des Domkapitels im 11. Jahrhundert zu verrichten waren.[144] Zum Anlass des Fests der Depositio des Heiligen am 12. April befindet sich auf fol. 30v–32r die Historia *Dum Zeno pontificatus honore*, die wie alle anderen Gesangstexte durch ihre Incipits angegeben ist. Sie stammt von der Haupthand, die den größten Teil der Handschrift – die Quaternionen II bis XI, die den Liber ordinarius enthalten – kurz nach der Mitte des 11. Jahrhunderts niederschrieb.

Dieser früheste handschriftliche Beleg für die Historia fügt sich in das skizzierte Bild der Entstehung des Offiziums, das anhand der Strukturanalyse erzeugt wurde: Am Dom von Verona entstand – sicher vor Mitte des 11. Jahrhunderts, als ihre frühesten Quellen, das Antiphonar und das *Carpsum* angefertigt wurden –

---

140 Vgl. Venturini: Vita ed attività, S. 69–70.

141 Die Historia *Dum Zeno pontificatus honore* wurde auf einem unabhängigen Doppelblatt geschrieben, das an einer ungewöhnlichen Stelle in der Handschrift angebunden wurde, nämlich zwischen dem Fest Inventio sanctae crucis und Fronleichnam. Das Zenofest für die Depositio hätte allerdings früher angebunden werden sollen, und zwar im April, zwischen dem Ambrosius- (am 4. April) und dem Georgsfest (am 23. April). Da der Schreiber des Binios allerdings der gleiche ist wie der Veroneser Schreiber der restlichen Handschrift, und da hier alle weiteren Veronesischen Feste beinhaltet und an der richtigen Stelle im Kirchenjahr verzeichnet sind, gilt es als gesichert, dass die Handschrift in und für Verona angefertigt wurde. Vgl. Maria Venturini: Vita ed attività dello „scriptorium" veronese nel secolo XI, Verona 1930, S. 79; vgl. Ropa: Liturgia, cultura e tradizione, S. 23; vgl. Hesbert: Corpus Antiphonalium Officii, S. XXII; vgl. Borders: The Cathedral of Verona, S. 243–244. Das Problem mit der Positionierung des Binios in der Handschrift kann nicht, wie von Ropa vorgeschlagen, damit gelöst werden, dass das hier gemeinte Zenofest das der Translation sei. Zum einen wird das Fest „natale" genannt und zum zweiten war das Fest der Translation im 11. Jhdt. und vor allem für das Domkapitel nicht relevant. Das bestätigt die Tatsache, dass das Fest der Translation im *Carpsum* gar nicht erwähnt wird. Wahrscheinlicher ist, dass das Zenooffizium zunächst im Binio als unabhängige kodikologische Einheit kopiert und dann an einer günstigen Stelle, und zwar dort, wo das Ende eines Foliums mit dem Ende eines Offiziums und der Beginn eines Foliums oder einer Lage mit dem Beginn eines weiteren Offiziums übereinstimmte, platziert wurde. Die Frage, warum überhaupt der Schreiber der Handschrift das Zenooffizium nicht von vornherein in die Handschrift eingeplant hatte, sondern es getrennt niederschrieb, muss unbeantwortet bleiben. Vielleicht hatte er das wichtige Zenooffizium zuerst kopiert, noch bevor er das ganze Material für den Codex bekam.

142 Vgl. ebd., S. 243–250.

143 Vgl. Venturini: Vita ed attività, S. 80.

144 Ediert in: Meersseman u. a.: L'orazionale, S. 204–309.

die Historia für Zeno *Dum Zeno pontificatus honore* in ihrer ursprünglichen Form im Cursus romanus. Abgesehen von der Bestimmung eines Terminus ante quem bleibt die Frage nach einer genaueren Datierung der Historia aber noch offen. Es bleibt also weiterhin möglich, dass sie im 9. Jahrhundert entstand, als, wie oben erläutert, der Veroneser Dom im liturgischen Bereich sehr produktiv war und den Zenokult, unter anderem mit einer neuen Vita, intensivierte.

Die Hinweise des *Carpsums* sind für die Datierung der Historia besonders wichtig, leider aber nicht ganz eindeutig zu interpretieren. Obwohl der Codex, der das *Carpsum* überliefert, präzise datierbar ist, beziehen sich einige der darin überlieferten liturgischen Texte auf älteres Material. Dies geht aus dem Prolog hervor, in dem der Schreiber, ein gewisser *Stephanus cantor*, Kleriker am Dom,[145] sagt, er habe das *Carpsum* nicht selbst verfasst, sondern auf der Grundlage älterer liturgischer Bestände lediglich aktualisiert („divina renovavi inspiratione"). Dabei habe er lediglich Notwendiges ergänzt („que congruenter addenda erant, addidi"), beziehungsweise Überflüssiges beseitigt („que superflua, sollerter resecare studui").[146] Auch die Bezeichnung *Carpsum* habe er von seinen Vorgängern übernommen: „huius libelli opusculum, quod ex nostrorum antecessorum nuncupatione carpsum vocatur."[147]

Bereits 1974 konnte Merssemann zeigen, dass der Großteil des im *Carpsum* überlieferten Materials in der Zeit des Bischofs Rather, also etwa von 931 bis 968 entstand.[148] Er argumentierte zum einen mit der Struktur des Buches[149] und zum anderen mit der Erwähnung von fränkischen liturgischen Bräuchen im *Carpsum*. Diese wurden zunächst auch von Stephanus übernommen, mussten aber nachträglich von ihm angepasst werden.[150] Unter diesen fränkischen Bräuchen fällt besonders die Feier des Trinitätsfestes auf. Dieses Fest wurde in Verona nach der Überlieferung im *Carpsum* nicht nur mit einem eigenen Offizium gefeiert, was für das frühmittelalterliche Italien besonders bemerkenswert war, darüber hinaus wurde es mit dem Offizium des Stephanus von Lüttich begangen. Dies spräche deutlich für eine Entstehung des liturgischen Materials in der Zeit von Rather,

145 Er beschreibt sich selbst als „geprägt und ausgebildet im Pfarrhaus der in Verona gelegenen Kirche zur Heiligen Mutter Gottes Maria" („in canonica sancte matris domini Marie, Verone site, imbutus et educatus"), ebd., S. 218.

146 Zitate ebd.

147 Ebd.

148 Vgl. ebd., S. 88.

149 Vgl. ebd.

150 Vgl. ebd., S. 88–91. Der erste Hinweis betrifft die Quatembertage. Im Fall der Quatembertage wird im Verona des 9. und 10. Jhdts. dem fränkischen Brauch gefolgt, nach dem diese Fastentage im Frühling und Sommer während der ersten März- beziehungsweise der zweiten Juniwoche zu begehen waren. Somit wird in Verona ausdrücklich der Brauch der römischen Kirche außer Acht gelassen, nach dem die Quatembertage des Frühlings und Sommers in der ersten Woche der Quadragesima und während der Pfingstwoche begangen werden. Dieser Brauch blieb während des Episkopats von Rather gültig und wurde auch im *Carpsum* berücksichtigt (Kapitel 54–57), musste aber von Stephanus nachträglich korrigiert werden, als die Veroneser Liturgie den neuen Vorschriften des Konzils von Seligenstadt (1022) angepasst werden musste.

der das Trinitätsoffizium aus seiner Heimat (Lüttich) nach Verona importierte und am Dom feiern ließ.[151]

Diese Datierung des liturgischen Materials ist allerdings nicht notwendigerweise auch als Datierung des Zeno-Offiziums zu verstehen, denn das Offizium muss nicht zwangsläufig schon Teil der älteren Fassung des *Carpsums* gewesen sein. Stattdessen könnte es auch zu den wenigen Addenda gehören, die Stephanus in seine Fassung des *Carpsums* integrierte.

Gegen diese Möglichkeit spricht zunächst die Tatsache, dass das Zeno-Offizium, wie die meisten anderen Korrekturen des Stephanus,[152] nicht als Nachtrag auf hinzugefügten Zetteln in den Codex eingeschrieben wurde. Stattdessen findet man es nach der Ordnung des liturgischen Jahres im Hauptteil der Handschrift. Darüber hinaus gibt es weitere Hinweise dafür, dass die Zeno-Historia in der Version des *Carpsums* schon beinhaltet war, die im 10. Jahrhundert während der Zeit Rathers verfasst wurde. Für diese Annahme spricht insbesondere die hagiographische Vorlage, auf deren Grundlage das Offizium verfasst wurde, da sie auch im 10. Jahrhundert entstand. Da allerdings gleich mehrere Zeno-Viten als solche Vorlage in Frage kommen, muss zunächst die Frage der Abhängigkeiten zwischen dem Offizium und dem hagiographischen Material geklärt werden. Bislang hat sich die Forschung lediglich mit zwei der vielen Fassungen der Zenovita befasst, nämlich mit der bereits erwähnten karolingischen Fassung BHL 9001 (*Sermo*) und mit BHL 9010 sowie dem dazugehörigen Translationsbericht BHL 9011, die beide als Produkt des Zenoklosters gelten und ins 11. oder 12. Jahrhundert datiert werden.[153]

---

[151] Vgl. ebd., S. 93–95. Während in den meisten Diözesen Europas, und vor allem den italienischen Diözesen inklusive Rom, am ersten Sonntag nach Pfingsten bis ins Spätmittelalter kein spezifisches Fest für die Dreieinigkeit vorgesehen war, wird im *Carpsum* stattdessen explizit eine „dominica de S. Trinitate" gefeiert, für die außerdem ein eigenes Offizium vorgesehen war, das Trinitätsoffizium des Stephanus von Lüttich. Der Schluss liegt somit auf der Hand: Es waren die Lütticher Mönche und Bischöfe von Verona, Hilduin und Rather, die nicht nur den Lütticher Brauch des Feierns eines Trinitätsfestes, sondern auch das Trinitätsoffizium ihres Landsmannes Stephanus nach Verona importierten. Stephanus, der Schreiber des *Carpsum*, musste übrigens gerade an dieser Stelle das Ratherianische *Carpsum* nachträglich korrigieren: Nach der Versöhnung der Veroneser Bischöfe mit dem umstrittenen Papst Alexander II. wurde auch die Liturgie dem römischen und eben von diesem Papst propagierten Brauch angepasst, nach dem der Trinität kein spezifischer Feiertag zukam. Glücklicherweise ergänzte Stephanus das *Carpsum* mit bewahrendem Habitus, statt das Trinitasfest und das Lütticher Offizium zu tilgen: Er fügte auf einem Zettelchen für den ersten Sonntag nach Pfingsten ein Offizium ein, das den bisherigen Brauch ersetzen sollte.

[152] Die Korrektur der Quatembertage zum Beispiel wurde auf die leer gebliebenen Blätter nach dem Kalendar kopiert (fol. 7v–8v), die Korrektur bezüglich des ersten Sonntags nach Pfingsten und des Trinitätsfestes auf einem zusätzlichen Zettel (54A). Auf einem weiteren Zettel (30A) modifizierte Stephanus die Liturgie für die erste Vesper der Septuagesima und auch in diesem Fall ließ er die zu korrigierende Stelle im Corpus der Handschrift unangetastet. Vgl. ebd., S. 90; 95–96.

[153] Elisa Anti hat die Fassung mit der BHL-Nr. 9008f als Transkription einer Handschrift aus Bovino (Napoli) publiziert. Diese Fassung kommt aber als Vorlage für die Historia aus textlichen Gründen nicht in Frage und wird hier nicht weiter behandelt. Siehe: Elisa Anti:

Die weiter unten erfolgende Analyse dieser beiden Viten kann allerdings zeigen, dass keine der beiden Fassungen als Vorlage für das Offizium in Frage kommt. BHL 9010–11 scheidet aus chronologischen Gründen als Vorlage für die Historia von Anfang an aus. Sie wurde von Anti überzeugend als ein Produkt des 12. Jahrhunderts identifiziert und in die Zeit des Abtes Gerhard (1138–1178) datiert.[154] Der karolingische *Sermo de vita sancti Zenonis* (BHL 9001) hingegen könnte zwar wegen seines hohen Alters als Vorlage des Offiziums in Frage kommen, zumal er sich großer Beliebtheit erfreute. Eine nähere Untersuchung des Wortlauts des Offiziums (siehe Tabelle 7) zeigt aber entgegen den Erwartungen, dass auch die karolingische Vita nicht die Vorlage für die Historia gewesen sein kann. An vielen Stellen wurde die Formulierung des *Sermo* modifiziert – meistens erweitert und ausgeschmückt – wobei deutlich wird, dass sich der Offiziendichter einer anderen Vita-Fassung als Vorlage für die Historia bediente.

Aus der Analyse aller Fassungen der Vita, die als Vorlage für das Offizium in Frage kommen könnten, weil sie vor 1060 (dem Terminus ante quem der Entstehung des Offiziums aufgrund der Überlieferung im *Carpsum*) handschriftlich vorhanden waren, also BHL 9001, 9003, 9004, 9006 und 9007,[155] geht allerdings hervor, dass lediglich eine dieser Fassungen erhebliche Übereinstimmungen mit dem Offizium aufweist, nämlich die bislang in der Forschung nahezu unbeachtete BHL 9007. In der untenstehenden Tabelle (Tabelle 7) wird der Wortlaut der Historia (linke Spalte) mit dem Text von BHL 9001, 9003, 9004, 9006 und BHL 9007 verglichen.

Die Gegenüberstellung der Texte macht deutlich, dass die Zeno-Historia im Cursus romanus nicht von der ältesten Fassung der Zenovita abhängt, sondern vielmehr die als BHL 9007 gekennzeichnete Fassung als Vorlage hatte: Neben inhaltlichen Aspekten entnimmt die Historia aus BHL 9007 auch sprachliche Formulierungen, die sonst in keiner anderen Fassung der Vita vorkommen. Interessant sind zum einen die Übernahmen, in denen der Wortlaut von BHL 9007 gar nicht oder nur geringfügig verändert wird. So wird zum Beispiel aus *a matris utero*

Un'inedita redazione della *Vita I sancti Zenonis* nel ms. XV.AA.15 della Biblioteca Nazionale di Napoli, in: Annuario storico zenoniano, 1998, S. 27–32.

154 Die Gründe dafür sind vielfältig: zum einen ist kein handschriftliches Zeugnis der Vita älter als das Endes des 12. Jhdts. Zum zweiten legen auch inhaltliche Aspekte vor allem im Miracula-Teil den Schluss nahe, dass die Vita zwischen 1138 und 1178 verfasst wurde, und zwar in der Zeit, als ein neuer Kirchturm gebaut und die klösterlichen Bauten renoviert wurden. Besonders Abt Gerhard, der die Abtei von 1163 bis 1187 leitete, kommt nach Antis Auffassung als Auftraggeber der Vita in Frage. Die Initiative einer neuen, auf das Kloster zugeschnittenen Vita von Zeno passt sehr gut in Gerhards Programm einer Renovierung und Stärkung des Klosters, wie er sie auch durch bauliche, wirtschaftliche und politische Maßnahmen betrieben hat. Vgl. Anti: Verona e il culto, S. 104–105.

155 Da nicht alle diese Fassungen ediert sind, mussten teilweise die einzelnen Handschriften herangezogen werden. Für Hinweise über die handschriftlichen Zeugnisse der einzelnen Fassungen der Zenovita sowie ihrer Datierung habe ich mich auf die tabellarische Darstellung von Elisa Anti gestützt, in der alle der Forscherin bekannten Handschriften mit Zenoviten aufgelistet sind, vgl. ebd., S. 117–129.

(BHL 9007) *ab utero matris* (A1) anstatt *a ventre* in allen anderen Fassungen.[156] Außerdem werden kurze Elemente hinzugefügt, zum Beispiel A5 *per preceps in amnem demergi* und R4 *ad eum properantes.* Vor allem sind aber die Stellen interessant, an denen die Historia neue Ideen und Formulierungen von BHL 9007 übernimmt, die in keiner anderen Vita-Fassung vorkommen. Beispiele dafür sind der Zusatz *Probitatis et scientiae iugibus incrementis* (BHL9007/A2), welcher zu Beginn der zweiten Antiphon der Matutin übernommen wurde oder der Ausdruck *et artis apostolicae instrumenta baiulans* (BHL9007/A9), der in A9 zu *et artis apostolicae documenta sequens* wurde, oder auch der Satz *ab omni daemonicae incursionis ludificatione* (BHL9007/A5), welcher in der fünften Antiphon der Laudes identisch übernommen wurde. Auch in der Benedictus-Antiphon wird BHL 9007 gefolgt, indem die kurze Redepartie von Zeno von *Si Dominus operatur excelsa, ipsi referatur et gloria* zu *Si Dominus operatur excelsa, ipsi perpetue laudes referantur et gloria* geändert wurde. In dem kurzen Zusatz von BHL 9007 *domus regia in tristitiam versa cruciatu et maerore ingenti affligebantur*, der auch in der Historia übernommen wird, versteckt sich sogar ein kleines Cicero-Zitat,[157] in welchem Cicero die schmerzhafte Erfahrung von Eltern beschreibt, die ihre Kinder verlieren.[158] Auffällig ist auch, dass die in der Historia übernommenen Wörter sehr oft in der exakt gleichen Position wie in BHL 9007 zu finden sind. A2 beginnt zum Beispiel mit *Probitatis et scientiae*, L-A3 mit *Ingrediente Christi confessore*, genauso wie in BHL 9007, wo sie am Anfang eines neuen Satzgefüges platziert sind.

4.2.2 Bischof Rathers Überarbeitung der frühesten Zenovita als Vorlage der Historia: BHL 9007

BHL 9007, die bislang weder kritisch ediert noch beachtet wurde, erweist sich somit für die Frage nach der Entstehung der Historia als entscheidend. Daher soll sie hier hinsichtlich ihrer Überlieferung und möglichen Datierung eingehend

156 Andere Beispiele wären: *ut per sacerrimam vitam* (BHL 9007/A2) anstatt *ut per vitam sanctam* (Rest); *in Athesis fluvio piscationis excercitio fungeretur* (BHL 9007/R5) anstatt *in fluvio Athesi piscationem dum ageret* (BHL 9001); *acriter* (BHL 9007/A8) statt *crudeliter* (Rest); *luculenter emicuit* (BHL 9007/ R2) statt *emicuit* (Rest); *die noctuque* (BHL 9007/R3) statt *de die in diem* (Rest).

157 Cic. Verr. 2,5,123: „Utrum ego desipio et plus quam satis est doleo tanta calamitate miseriaque sociorum, an vos quoque hic acerbissimus innocentium *cruciatus et maeror* parentum pari sensu doloris adficit?“, Marcus T. Cicero: Il processo di Verre, hrsg. von Nino Marinone / Laura Fiocchi, Mailand [8]2013, S. 1180. Die Verrinen zirkulierten im 10. Jhdt. in Italien, wie ein Bifolium mit Teilen aus der zweiten Rede bezeugt, das einer Handschrift aus Montecassino hinzugefügt wurde. Das Doppelblatt wurde nach Bischoff von einer möglicherweise italienischen Hand der zweiten Hälfte des 10. Jhdts. geschrieben. Vgl. Leighton D. Reynolds / Peter K. Marshall: Texts and Transmission. A Survey of the Latin Classics, Oxford 1986, S. 71.

158 Die textliche Übernahme ist zwar sehr begrenzt, die Stelle aus Ciceros Rede allerdings ganz passend, da auch in der Vita ein Vater, nämlich Gallienus, der hier übrigens nur als *pater* und nicht als Kaiser, König oder mit seinem Namen identifiziert wird, und seine ganze Familie (*tota domus eius*) wegen der teuflischen Krankheit der Tochter trauern.

untersucht werden. Die Fassung wird von etwa achtzehn bisher bekannten Handschriften aus dem 10. bis 14. Jahrhundert überliefert.[159] Die frühesten Zeugnisse dieser Gruppe sind Novara BC II und Novara BC LXIII.[160] Die Handschriften enthalten Viten von Heiligen, wie zum Beispiel Gaudentius, Ambrosius und Sirus, die auf eine Verwendung in Novara oder Umgebung hinweisen.[161] Auch Zeno wurde in diesen Sammlungen berücksichtigt und BHL 9007 war für die Lesungen am Fest des 8. Dezembers vorgesehen.[162] Neben der Vita enthalten die Codices auch ein bisher unbekanntes Gedicht von zwanzig elegischen Distichen mit dem Incipit *Pontificum splendor*, das eine kondensierte Zenobiographie anbietet.[163]

Über die Datierung dieser frühesten Zeugnisse ist wenig bekannt: Elisa Anti datiert beide ins 11./12. Jahrhundert und identifiziert Novara BC LXIII als Kopie von Novara BC II. Sie liefert aber keine Begründung für ihre Datierung und ihre Einschätzungen.[164] In Giuseppe Mazzatintis mehrbändigem Werk *Inventari dei manoscritti delle biblioteche d'Italia* wird Novara BC. LXIII ins 10. Jahrhundert,[165] ms. II ins 11. Jahrhundert datiert.[166] Somit wird nicht nur Elisa Antis Datierung der Handschriften, sondern auch das von ihr postulierte Abhängigkeitsverhältnis zwischen den Codices in Frage gestellt: Wenn die Datierung in Mazzatintis *Inventari* stimmt, kann Handschrift LXIII keine Kopie der Handschrift II sein, da die erste Handschrift älter ist. Nach paläographischer Untersuchung der Codices scheint mir die frühere Datierung wahrscheinlicher als die Datierung Antis.[167]

---

159 Hier stütze ich mich auf die von Elisa Anti aufgelisteten Funde (vgl. Anti: Verona e il culto, S. 120–123), allerdings gehe ich davon aus, dass die Überlieferung von BHL 9007 bereits im 10. Jhdt., und nicht erst im 11. einsetzt. Anti hingegen geht von einer Überlieferung ab dem 11./12. bis ins 14. Jhdt. aus. Vgl. ebd., S. 123.

160 Elisa Anti erwähnt eine weitere Handschrift von BHL 9007, Firenze BN Conv. Soppr. A.I.1213, welche auf das erste Viertel des 11. Jhdts. zu datieren sei, ebd., S. 121. Bei näherer Betrachtung allerdings hat sich gezeigt, dass die Handschrift nicht BHL 9007, sondern eher eine geringfügige Überarbeitung von BHL 9001 überliefert, in der aber die markanten Überarbeitungen von BHL 9007 fehlen.

161 Siehe dazu: Mazzatinti: Inventari dei Manoscritti, 74; 78–79. Auch Elisa Anti glaubt, dass die Handschriften für das Domkapitel von Novara angefertigt wurden, vgl. Anti: Verona e il culto, S. 120.

162 In beiden Handschriften wird die Vita in *lectiones* unterteilt: vier Lesungen werden in der Hs. LXIII und neun in der Hs. II vorgesehen.

163 Das Gedicht wurde von der gleichen Hand wie die Vita, aber mit einer dünneren Feder eingetragen (charakteristische Buchstaben wie -a, -g, -r sind identisch). Für die Edition von BHL 9007 und des Gedichtes siehe Kapitel 3.3.3, S. 87–91.

164 Vgl. Anti: Verona e il culto, S. 120.

165 Mazzatinti: Inventari dei Manoscritti, S. 74.

166 Ebd., S. 78–79.

167 Die Schrift der Handschrift LXIII weist einige Merkmale auf, die von Armando Petrucci als typisch für die karolingische Minuskel in der Zeit 870–970/980 erkannt wurden: Die Linienführung der Buchstaben wirkt schwerer; Ober- und Unterlänge sind gleichmäßig oder weisen eine spachtelförmige Vergrößerung an der Spitze (-b, -d); die Buchstaben sind zusammengerückt, die Räume zwischen den Wörtern hingegen eher unregelmäßig gehalten. Der Buchstabe -y erscheint in zwei Formen (einmal ganz auf der Linie, einmal mit der rechten Unterlänge unter der Linie); die et-Ligatur ist im Modul etwas vergrößert im Vergleich zu den einzelnen Buchstaben und erscheint auch am Anfang und Ende sowie

Auch bezüglich der Abhängigkeit der Handschriften deuten kleine Hinweise, wie zum Beispiel einige Rubriken der Hs. II, die nahezu an eine Textualis erinnern,[168] sowie die Änderung einer Textstelle[169] entgegen Antis Vermutung eher auf eine Abhängigkeit der Handschrift Novara BC II von Novara BC. LXIII hin. Damit lässt sich ein Terminus ante quem für die Entstehung von BHL 9007 festlegen, nämlich das Jahr 1000, in welches Novara BC LXIII zu datieren ist. Eine genaue Datierung des in der Handschrift überlieferten Textes ergibt sich daraus aber noch nicht.

Eine eingehende Analyse der hagiographischen Überarbeitung erlaubt es, in dieser Frage weitere Schlüsse zu ziehen. Verschiedene inhaltliche und stilistische Eigenschaften der Vita deuten nämlich darauf hin, dass, wie der Text im *Carpsum*, auch die Vita in der Rather-Zeit entstanden sein muss, ja sogar auf Rather selbst zurückzuführen ist.

Rather, der dreimal auf dem Bischofsstuhl von Verona saß und dreimal aus der Stadt verjagt wurde,[170] zeigte mindestens in zwei Angelegenheiten sein Interesse für Hagiographie: zum einen hatte er in den zwei Jahren seines Exils in Como (937–939) eine Überarbeitung der alten Vita des Heiligen Ursmarus verfasst und an die Mönche von Lobbes geschickt,[171] zum zweiten hatte Rather während seiner dritten Amtszeit als Bischof von Verona zwischen 962 und 968 – neben einundvierzig weiteren Werken[172] – auch einen Bericht über den Kult des heiligen Metro und über den Diebstahl seiner Reliquien aus Verona verfasst, die *Invectiva de translatione sancti Metronis*. Wie der Titel des Werkes schon erahnen lässt, widmet sich der Autor hier weniger der hagiographischen Erzählung als der polemischen Invektive. Beide Werke sind allerdings für die Frage nach einer Zuschreibung von BHL 9007 relevant. Während die *Vita Ursmari* ein passendes

in der Mitte der Wörter. Das Unziale -f ist stark unter der Linie gezogen. Die Abkürzung *rum* wird ausschließlich für -orum verwendet und bildet die Form einer 2, deren horizontale Line gerade und auf der Linie verläuft. Es werden mehrere Abkürzungen für -que benutzt. Die Schrift der Handschrift II rückt sie hingegen eher ins 11. Jhdt.: Die Schrift ist nun gerade gerichtet (zum Beispiel wie der Rücken des Buchstaben -a, der nun nicht mehr schräg liegt), ein kurzer Strich verzeichnet am Ende der Zeile die Worttrennug, -st und -ct sind enger und höher; Abkürzungen werden häufiger. Vgl. Armando Petrucci: Censimento dei codici dei secoli XI–XII. Istruzioni per la datazione, in: Studi medievali 9, 1968, S. 1115–1126. Für eine baldige Verbreitung von BHL 9007 nach der Abfassung spricht auch eine Anmerkung am Rande eines Codex des 10. Jhdts., die von einer jüngeren Hand eingetragen wurde, die sich ins 11. Jhdt. datieren lässt.

168 Vgl. Bernhard Bischoff: Paläographie des römischen Altertums und des abendländischen Mittelalters (Grundlagen der Germanistik 24), Berlin [2]1986, S. 171–173.

169 *Raptatus* in Novara BC LXIII wird in *raptus* in Novara BC II korrigiert.

170 Zu Rather grundlegend: Cervato: Raterio di Verona.

171 Vgl. Rather von Verona: Die Briefe des Bischofs Rather von Verona, hrsg. von Fritz Weigle (MGH Epistolae 2), Weimar 1949, Brief Nr. 4, 27–29. Für die Edition der Vita Ursmari von Rather siehe: ders.: Opera omnia, hrsg. von Jacques P. Migne (Patrologia Latina 136), Paris 1881.

172 Vgl. Peter L. D. Reid: Tenth-Century Latinity. Rather of Verona (Humana Civilitas 6), Malibu 1981, S. 5.

Vergleichsbeispiel derselben hagiographischen Gattung bietet und Rathers Überarbeitungsverfahren nachvollziehbar macht,[173] tritt in der *Invectiva* Rathers charakteristischer Stil deutlich zu Tage und ermöglicht einen Vergleich der Werke unter sprachlich-stilistischen Gesichtspunkten.

Rather selbst berichtet in einem Brief an die Mönche von Lobbes, wie er im Fall der Überarbeitung der *Vita Ursmari* vorgegangen ist: Während seines Exils in Como habe er ein kleines Büchlein entdeckt, in dem sich einige wenige Informationen über die Taten des Heiligen Ursmarus befänden, der Patron von Rathers Mutterkloster war. Es handelte sich dabei um die gegen 765 verfasste *Vita Ursmari* des Anso von Lobbes.[174] Während die Inhalte der Vita nach Rathers Aussage sehr wertvoll seien, sei ihre Sprache so verdorben und voll von Fehlern im Wortgefüge und Satzbau – Stichwort: Soloecismus –, dass er sie nicht einfach abschreiben und den Brüdern zurückschicken könne, sondern sie zuerst korrigieren müsse:

> Wir fanden ein Büchlein [...], das ein wenig Stoff über den Heiligen und unseren besonderen Patron, nämlich Bischof Ursmarus, enthielt. Diese Inhalte sind zwar feinem Gold und Edelstein vorzuziehen, doch sie sind in ihrer sprachlichen Form dermaßen voll von Fehlern, dass sie schwer zu verstehen sind [und ich frage mich, ob dies] entweder aufgrund der Fahrlässigkeit des Schreibers oder der Ignoranz des Vorlesers geschah. Daher, da wir gerade viel Zeit haben, pflegten wir allein die Fehler aus diesem Werk zu korrigieren [...].[175]

Zwar bleibt Rather dem Text des Anso in seiner Überarbeitung größtenteils treu,[176] gleichwohl lassen sich einige deutliche Interventionen feststellen. Diese bestehen vor allem in der Hinzufügung eines Prologes und einer weiteren erklärenden Textpassage.[177] Daneben verwies bereits Golinelli in seiner Analyse der Bearbeitung Rathers auf eine gesteigerte Sprach-Ästhetik der Überarbeitung:

> Von Anfang an bemerkt man die Übereinstimmung der zwei Texte und gleichzeitig die Aufmerksamkeit Rathers für ein reineres Latein: aus vocata est wird vocatur; zwei Sätze des Originaltextes werden durch ein geschicktes syntaktisches Spiel in einem zusammengeführt, und zwar durch die Einführung der Hypotaxe anstelle der Parataxe.[178]

---

173 Golinelli hat dies in einem kurzen Aufsatz geschildert: Paolo Golinelli: Nota su Raterio agiografo, in: Mittellateinisches Jahrbuch 24–25, 1989–1990, S. 125–131.

174 Vgl. Walter Berschin: Biographie und Epochenstil im lateinischen Mittelalter. Ottonische Biographie: Das hohe Mittelalter: 920–1220 n. Chr., Halbbd. 1: 920–1070 n. Chr. (Quellen und Untersuchungen zur lateinischen Philologie des Mittelalters), Stuttgart 1999, S. 50–51.

175 „reperimus libellum [...] pauca de virtutibus continentem domni ac specialis patroni nostri sancti videlicet Ursmari episcopi, continentia rerum quidem auro obrizo topazioque praeferenda, locutionis vero soloecismis ita pro sui modulo refertissima, ut difficile fuerit deprehendere, utrum scriptoris negligentia an dictatoris hoc contigerit insipientia. Quod cum non parum pro tempore nos offendisset, curavimus ea eiusdem operis solummodo corrigere vitia [...].“ Rather von Verona: Briefe, S. 28.

176 Vgl. Golinelli: Nota su Raterio, S. 126.

177 Vgl. Berschin: Biographie und Epochenstil, S. 53.

178 „Fin dall'esordio si nota la corrispondenza dei due testi e insieme una attenzione verso un latino più puro in Raterio: vocata est diventa vocatur; le due proposizioni del testo originario sono unite in una sola con un sapiente gioco sintattico, consistente nell'introduzione dell'ipotassi in luogo della paratassi.“ Golinelli: Nota su Raterio, S. 127–128.

An dieser Stelle kann man noch eine weitere Überarbeitungstechnik Rathers nennen. Rather bemühte sich, gewöhnliche Vokabeln durch elegantere Synonyme zu ersetzten. In der zitierten Passage wird *laus* durch *praeconium*, *nasceretur* durch *saeculo daretur* ersetzt. Weiterhin wird deutlich, dass Rather einerseits dem Text des Anso zwar weitestgehend treu bleibt, ihn andererseits aber durch Präzisierungen und Neustrukturierung eleganter gestaltet:

> In dieser Passage erkennt man – trotz der Treue zum Ausgangstext – die Entwicklung des Textes des Anso durch Rather. Man bemerkt gewisse Präzisierungen (aus suis tribulationibus wird huiusmodi atque aliis tribulationibus) und die Neustrukturierung der Periode, die verdoppelt wird und in welcher das letzte direkte Zitat in ein indirektes Zitat verwandelt wird. Das Ganze wirkt ohne Zweifel viel eleganter.[179]

Auch hier könnte man den Beobachtungen Golinellis den Hinweis auf zwei weitere Besonderheiten des Stils Rathers hinzufügen, die in der kurzen Passage hervortreten: erstens seine ausgiebige Nutzung von Adverbien, die einen emphatischeren Ton erzeugen (*Tanta quoque eius*), zweitens die besondere Anwendung des Adverbs *econtra*, welches hier, wie an einigen anderen Stellen seiner Werke, von Rather mit der Bedeutung „auf der anderen Seite“ benutzt wird.[180] Zur besseren Veranschaulichung dieses Sachverhalts seien hier in aller Kürze die Passagen abgedruckt, die Golinelli für seine Analyse von Rathers Überarbeitung der *Vita Ursmari* unter die Lupe nimmt.

Passage Nr. 1:[181]

Anso, Vita Ursmari	Rather, Vita Ursmari
Beatus igitur Ursmarus Episcopus, dignus laude bonorum, in pago Haina vel Theoracense, in villa quae vocata est Fleon, oriundus fuit. Qui a domino est electus a caelo per praedestinationem, priusquam nasceretur in terra per originem.	Beatus igitur Ursmarus episcopus, bonorum omnium *praeconio* dignus, pago Teoracenis, et villa quae vocatur Fleon oriundus, a domino est electus per praedestinationem, priusquam *saeculo daretur* per originem.

[179] „In questo passo si può notare lo sviluppo del testo di Ansone operato da Raterio, pur nella sostanziale fedeltà. Si notino alcune puntualizzazioni (suis tribulationibus che diventa: huiusmodi atque aliis tribulationibus) e la ristrutturazione del periodo, che viene sdoppiato, e nel quale la citazione finale da diretta si trasforma in indiretta. Il tutto con un effetto di indubbia maggiore eleganza.“ Ebd., S. 128.

[180] Vgl. Reid: Tenth-Century Latinity, S. 87.

[181] Golinelli: Nota su Raterio, S. 127.

Passage Nr. 2:[182]

Anso, Vita Ursmari	Rather, Vita Ursmari
Tanta erat patientia illius in suis tribulationibus, ut cumparari queat beati Iob, quia non peccavit labiis murmurando contra Deum neque dolus inventus est in ore eius, sed laudes domini iugiter concinnebat, sicut propheta ait: Benedicam Dominum in omni tempore, semper laus eius in ore meo.	Tanta quoque eius erat patientia in humiusmodi atque aliis tribulationibus, ut posset comparari patientiae Job beatissimi, qui non peccavit labiis suis, nec stultum quid contra Deum locutus est. Laudem econtra domini iugiter concinebat, atque secundum Prophetam benedicebat Dominum in omni tempore, laus eius semper in ore ipsius resonabat.

Zusammenfassend kann die Analyse der erwähnten Passagen aus der alten *Vita Ursmari* und aus Rathers Überarbeitung dieser Vorlage den Modus operandi des Veroneser Bischofs in der Rolle eines Hagiographen und Redaktors sehr gut beleuchten. Rathers Treue zur Vorlage bei gleichzeitiger Weiterentwicklung des Textes, die Art der syntaktischen und sprachlichen Interventionen und seine Vorliebe für emphatische Adverbien sind im Zusammenhang mit der Frage einer Autorschaft von BHL 9007 entscheidend. Anhand dieser Ergebnisse soll nun die mögliche Autorschaft Rathers für die Redaktion BHL 9007 untersucht werden. Dafür werden die Texte von BHL 9007 und ihrer Vorlage BHL 9001 in einer Tabelle gegenübergestellt (Tabelle 8, S. 337). Die folgenden, kursiv markierten Zitate beziehen sich zur besseren Nachvollziehbarkeit jeweils auf diese Tabelle und nicht auf die Edition.

Der erste Hinweis auf eine Autorschaft Rathers besteht darin, dass in BHL 9007 wie im Fall der Vita Ursmari ein Prolog hinzugefügt wurde, der die äußerst knappe Einleitung der älteren Fassung ersetzte (Tabelle 8, S. 377, Nr. 2).[183] In diesem neuen Prolog wird über den Brauch von weisen Männern der Vergangenheit reflektiert, die das Leben der Heiligen erforschten und niederschrieben, um

182 Ebd., S. 128.

183 Auch Elisa Anti beobachtet dies: „Tatsächlich ist es vor allem der Prolog, der die unterschiedlichen Versionen des Textes unterscheidet. In ihrer ursprünglichen Version (wie wir gleich sehen werden, nämlich BHL 9002) hatte die Vita praktisch keinen, eine Lücke, die man in den folgenden Jahrhunderten unbedingt füllen wollte, wie die Verbreitung von Prologen zeigt, die, wenn verglichen, [...] unabhängige Überarbeitungen des ersten Kapitels zu sein scheinen, welches ursprünglich auch die Funktion einer Einleitung hatte. Man kann also aus gutem Grund vermuten, dass derjenige, der die Viten überarbeitete, den Prolog erweiterte und ihn mehr vom Rest des Textes trennte, eben BHL 9002 als Modell hatte." „In effetti, è proprio il prologo che differenzia maggiormente le varie versioni del testo. Nella sua forma originaria (come vedremo a breve identificabile in BHL 9002) la Vita ne era praticamente priva, lacuna che deve essere sembrato indispensabile colmare nei secoli successivi, come dimostra il proliferare di prologhi che, posti a confronto, [...] sembrano elaborazioni indipendenti del primo capitolo, che in origine assolveva anche alla funzione introduttiva. Si può dunque ragionevolmente ipotizzare che chi riscrisse la Vita ampliandone il prologo, distaccandolo più nettamente dal resto della narrazione di quanto non avvenisse in precedenza, avesse come modello di riferimento appunto la versione 9002." Anti: Verona e il culto, S. 122.

anderen die Nachahmung der Heiligen zu ermöglichen. Im Anschluss dazu kehrt der Redaktor zur Vorlage zurück, übernimmt größtenteils ihren Text, verändert ihn aber mit einigen Eingriffen, die die Passage flüssiger gestalten und ihr sprachliches Register erhöhen. Die drei Beispiele, die Coronatus in BHL 9001 für das Verlangen des Geistes nach Heiligengeschichten angeführt hatte, werden in BHL 9007 nicht mehr durch sehr kondensierte Ausdrücke eingeleitet: (*tamquam quis ille..., aut quis..., vel etiam quis*). Stattdessen werden sie durch *si aliquis..., vel etiam si quis..., aut certe si quislibet...* strukturiert und damit das Tempo der Passage etwas verlangsamt. Außerdem werden dabei folgende Syntagmen ergänzend hinzugefügt, mit denen die geschilderten Vergleiche verständlicher werden: *ex remota regione, esuriens, ad solitam sui ventris satietatem*. Dies gleicht dem bereits beschriebenen Vorgehen Rathers im Fall der ersten Passage seiner *Vita Ursmari*. In beiden Fällen erzielt der Redaktor eine Stilerhöhung. So werden einige Vokabeln der Vorlage, welche dem *sermo rusticus* entsprechend einem niederem Register entstammen, durch ein eleganteres Synonym ersetzt: *instat* für *est*, *ambiat* für *cupiat*, *dapibus* für *epulis*. Im Hinzufügen eines Prologes sowie in der Art der Eingriffe im ersten Teil von BHL 9007 (syntaktische Eingriffe, kleine Zusätze, Änderung des Vokabulars) werden also die Ähnlichkeiten im Modus operandi des Redaktors von BHL 9007 und der *Vita Ursmari* Rathers deutlich.

Auch an weiteren Stellen wurde die Vita des Coronatus in BHL 9007 modifiziert. Der vage Ausdruck der Vorlage *In diebus illis*, der aufgrund seiner Uneindeutigkeit an die Eröffnung einer Evangelienperikope erinnerte,[184] wird nun durch den folgenden Satz präzisiert: *In diebus imperatoris Gallieni, qui per successiones caesarum vigesimus septimus in eorum est catalogo subrogatus, quo etiam tempore, Dionisius vir reverentissimus a beato Petro apostolo vigesimus tertius Romanae praesidebat ecclesiae* (Tabelle 8, S. 337, Nr. 2). Dies dient der historischen Kontextualisierung des Lebens Zenos: Es wird erörtert, dass Zeno im 3. Jahrhundert lebte, da seine Vita erzählt, er habe mit Kaiser Gallienus zu tun gehabt. Außerdem fügt der Redaktor die historiographische Information hinzu, dass Gallienus der 27. Kaiser gewesen sei. Zur gleichen Zeit habe auch Dionysius als 23. Papst im Rom gewirkt. Mit diesen Zusätzen versuchte der Redaktor von BHL 9007, die Geschichte des Bischofs von Verona historisch zu kontextualisieren und zeigt gleichzeitig sein fundiertes Wissen über die politische und kirchliche Geschichte der Spätantike. Auch dieser Hinweis spricht für eine Autorschaft Rathers von BHL 9007, ist ihm doch eine solche historische Bildung und ein Interesse für das historische Geschehen außerhalb Veronas zuzutrauen.[185]

---

184 Vgl. Christoph Markschies: Liturgisches Lesen und die Hermeneutik der Schrift, in: Peter Gemeinhardt (Hg.): Patristica et Oecumenica. Festschrift für Wolfgang A. Bienert zum 65. Geburtstag (Marburger theologische Studien 85), Marburg 2004, S. 77–88, hier: S. 83.

185 Vgl. Albrecht Vogel: Ratherius von Verona und das zehnte Jahrhundert, Jena 1854, S. 25–26. Außerdem: Benny R. Reece: Classical Quotations in the Works of Ratherius, in: Classical Folia 22, 1968, S. 198–213.

Diese Identifizierung des Redaktors von BHL 9007 mit Rather wird auch durch eine Reihe weiterer kleinerer Hinzufügungen, Wortumstellungen und Umformulierungen im Vergleich zur älteren Vorlage gestützt. Davon seien hier nur einige als Beispiel erwähnt:[186] Zum einen vereinfachte der Redaktor von BHL 9007 die etwas verwirrende Stelle der Vita des Coronatus, in welcher Zenos angeborene Heiligkeit erwähnt wird. Coronatus hatte die Stelle wie folgt formuliert: *et quia ipse Dominus dixit bona operantibus: Priusquam te formarem in utero novi te, et antequam exires de ventre sanctificavi te. Ille enim a cunabulis benedictus et a ventre sanctificatus erat* (Tabelle 8, S. 337, Nr. 2). In BHL 9007 wird nun der Satz *Priusquam te formarem in utero novi te, et antequam exires de ventre sanctificavi te*, ein Zitat aus Jeremias,[187] sinnvoller platziert, nämlich nach dem Satz, in dem von Zenos angeborener Heiligkeit berichtet wird. Dazu wird auch eine kurze Parenthese eingeschoben (*ut assertione divina in eo repeti videretur*), die das Zitat und seinen Bezug zu Zeno auf folgende Weise erklärt: *Fuit quippe a matris utero sanctificatus, et a cunabulis benedictus, ut assertione divina in eo repeti videretur, quod Hieremiae dictum est: „Priusquam te formarem in utero, novi te et antequam exires de ventre sanctificavi te*“ (Tabelle 8, Nr. 2). Auch die darauffolgende Aussage des *Sermo*, dass Zeno aufgrund seines heiligen Lebens zum Bischof erhoben wurde (*ut per vitam sanctam pastor in populo esse mereretur*), wird in BHL 9007 ausführlicher begründet, nämlich durch den Zusatz *Denique probitatis atque scientiae iugibus incrementis.*

Außerdem wird an einer weiteren Stelle in BHL 9007 die syntaktische Struktur der Vorlage modifiziert. Aus folgendem Satz der Vorlage: *iuxta civitatem Veronam, quae in propinquo erat itinere, egrediente eodem viro a monasterio, in fluvio Athesi piscationem dum ageret, erectis sursum oculis vidit* (Tabelle 8, Nr. 4) macht der Redaktor von BHL 9007: *iuxta urbem Veronam, dum egrediens idem vir a monasterio in Atesi fluvio piscationis exercitio fungeretur, erectis sursum oculis.* Dabei ersetzt er den Ablativus absolutus *egrediente viro* durch ein Participium coniunctum im Präsens (*egrediens*) und bezieht es auf *idem vir.* Auch die Konjunktion *dum*, die den Temporal-Satz *piscationem ageret* einleitete, wird in BHL 9007 an den Anfang des Satzgefüges verlegt. Ebenso wird die einfache transitive Konstruktion *ageret* + Akkusativ (*piscationem ageret*) nun durch eine Konstruktion mit dem Deponens *fungor* + Ablativ ersetzt. Auch das Objekt *piscationem* wurde in BHL 9007 durch die Periphrase *piscationis exercitio* modifiziert. Auch Substitutionen im semantischen Bereich werden in dieser Passage in BHL 9007 vorgenommen. Dabei werden gewöhnliche Begriffe durch ihre eleganteren Synonyme ersetzt: *flumen* wird zu *amnis*, *omnibus demonstraretur* zu *cunctis cernentibus daretur intellegi*, *elevans oculos* zu *intentis luminibus*, *videret* zu *prospicieret*, *vidit* zu *aspexit*. Da sich sehr ähnliche Eingriffe auch im ersten Kapitel der *Vita Ursmari* Rathers beobachten

186 Weitere kleinere Hinzufügungen in BHL 9007 sind zum Beispiel: *melliferae praedicationis, quoniam sanctus ei spiritus purarum illuminator mentium doctor existebat, alacer et splendifico nitore facundiae vividus* (vgl. Tabelle 8, S. 335).

187 Vgl. Jer 1, 5.

lassen, kommt darin ein weiterer Hinweis auf eine Autorschaft Rathers für BHL 9007 zum Ausdruck.

Zusammenfassend kann festgehalten werden, dass der Redaktor von BHL 9007 und Rather in ihrer Überarbeitung der *Vita Ursmari* auf gleiche Art und Weise vorgegangen sind: Die Vorlagen wurden jeweils an mehreren Stellen übernommen, aber auch modifiziert, wobei die Überarbeitungen sowohl die syntaktische Struktur als auch die semantische Ebene betreffen. Außerdem wird in beiden Fällen die Vorlage durch Zusätze ausgedehnt und durch Präzisierungen verdeutlicht. In beiden Überarbeitungen wurde im Allgemeinen der Text der Vorlage verbessert und der Stil eleganter gestaltet. Die Ähnlichkeit dieses Vorgehens spricht für eine Identifikation Rathers als Redaktor von BHL 9007. Diese These soll im Folgenden anhand detaillierterer Analysen weiter geprüft werden.

Eine besonders aufschlussreiche Modifizierung der Vorlage befindet sich am Schluss von BHL 9007, unmittelbar vor einer Passage aus den *Dialogi* des Gregorius Magnus, in der Zenos Mirakel bei der Etschüberschwemmung erzählt wird. Diese Stelle ist wichtig, da sie das Ende des Textes markiert, der auf den Redaktor zurückgeht. Der darauffolgende Teil ist wortwörtlich aus den *Dialogi* Gregors des Großen übernommen (vgl. Tabelle 5, Nr. 8). Vor der Erzählung Gregors wird im *Sermo* sowie in BHL 9007 die Kirche erwähnt, die für Zeno gebaut wurde. Diese Kirche (*venerabilis locus*) sei, laut Coronatus, durch die Mirakel Zenos verherrlicht, die im Namen Christi geschehen seien: *qui etiam venerabilis locus in Christi nomine miraculis coruscat*. Der Redaktor von BHL 9007 behält den Hinweis auf die Kirche und auf die Mirakel Zenos, ändert aber den Bezug auf Christus und ersetzt ihn durch einen auf die Dreifaltigkeit: *Qui etiam venerabilis locus in recta ineffabilis ac beatae Trinitatis confessione signis et miraculis coruscat*. Es stellt sich die Frage, aus welchem Grund sich der Redaktor von BHL 9007 entschied, genau an dieser Stelle die Vorlage zu ändern und anstelle von Christus die Dreieinigkeit zu erwähnen. Gerade diese Nennung der *Trinitas* liefert meines Erachtens einen stichhaltigen Hinweis auf die Identität des Redaktors von BHL 9007, nämlich auf Rather.

Als Grund für die Nennung kann ein Trinitäts-Patrozinium der Kirche Zenos nicht in Betracht kommen. Der *venerabilis locus*, der im Text als Ort des Wirkens Zenos erwähnt wird, stand nie unter einem solchen Patrozinium, und zwar unabhängig davon, ob der Autor der Passage an die Grabkirche Zenos oder an eine andere Kirche in Verona dachte. Der Grundstein der ersten der Trinitas gewidmeten Kirche in Verona, der 1117 geweihten Kirche der Mönche von Vallombrosa, wurde erst im Jahr 1073 gelegt.[188] Sie kann hier also nicht gemeint sein, da BHL 9007 schon vor diesem Datum zirkulierte.[189] Der Redaktor muss daher andere Gründe gehabt haben, die ihn dazu veranlassten, sich genau an dieser Stelle von der Vorlage zu entfernen. Diese haben meiner Ansicht nach als persönlich zu gel-

188 Vgl. Miller: The Formation of a Medieval Church, S. 77–78.

189 Wie die handschriftliche Überlieferung zeigt, siehe S. 212.

ten. Eine besondere Verehrung der Trinitas war typisch für Lüttich und wurde, wie oben bereits erwähnt, erst im 10. Jahrhundert durch die Lütticher Mönchs-Bischöfe Hilduin und Rather nach Verona gebracht.[190] Auch die Feier eines speziell der Trinität gewidmeten Festes war durch diese Bischöfe in Verona etabliert worden. In Italien sowie im übrigen hochmittelalterlichen Europa außerhalb Lüttichs und Fuldas war dieser Brauch keineswegs üblich.[191]

Dabei legte besonders Rather eine lebhafte Trinitätsfrömmigkeit an den Tag: Nicht nur schloss er Predigten und Urkunden mit einem Hinweis auf die Dreieinigkeit,[192] auch Buch 5 seiner *Praeloquia* endet mit den Worten:

> So soll der Text unserer Rede mit dem Lob der Heiligen Dreifaltigkeit enden: Dir das Lob, Dir die Ehre, Dir die Danksagungen, o selige Dreifaltigkeit. Erbarme, erbarme, erbarme Dich meiner, der ich, obwohl ich dessen nicht würdig bin, ausgewählt wurde, über Dich ungeschickt zu reden und dessen Namen Du kennst.
>
> Huius itaque nostri scilicet textus sermonis in laudem desinat sanctae Trinitatis. *Tibi laus, tibi gloria, tibi gratiarum actio, o beata Trinitas.* Miserere, miserere, miserere, licet indignissimo, de te tamen indecenter loquenti crinito, cuius nomen non ignoras, mihi.[193]

Der kursivierte Satzteil stellt sogar ein vom Editor der *Praeloquia* nicht identifiziertes Zitat aus dem Trinitätsoffizium des Stephan von Lüttich (Responsorium der ersten Vesper und Vers von zwei Laudes-Antiphonen) dar.[194]

Vor allem aber hatte Rather auch seine Überarbeitung der *Vita Ursmari* unter das Patrozinium der *Trinitas* gestellt: „bei dessen Barmherzigkeit [scilicet von Jesus Christus, A. d. V.] wir sogleich gewürdigt wurden, einen sehr frommen Fürsprecher, den heiligsten Ursmarus zu finden, dessen Leben wir in diesem Werk zum Lob und zur Ehre der allmächtigen Dreifaltigkeit zu beleuchten pflegten."[195] Die-

---

190 Dies hatte bereits Meersseman dazu bewegt, die erste Fassung des Liber ordinarius des Domkapitels (die Handschrift Verona BC XCIV(89) in die Zeit Hilduins und Rathers zu datieren. Vgl. Meersseman u. a.: L'orazionale, S. 93–95.

191 Vgl. Peter Browe: Zur Geschichte des Dreifaltigkeitsfestes, in: Archiv für Liturgiewissenschaft 1, 1950, S. 65–81, hier: S. 79.

192 Wie zum Beispiel die Predigt Nr. 6, Rather von Verona: Sermones monacenses, in: Paul Tombeur (Hg.): Thesaurus Ratherii Veronensis necnon Leodiensis. Series AB, formae et lemmata; lemmata et formae, lemmata a tergo ordinata, tabulae frequentiarum, formae et lemmata, formae a tergo ordinatae, lemmata singulorum operum, concordantia lemmatum et formarum (Corpus Christianorum. Thesaurus Patrum Latinorum), Turnhout 2005, hier: S. XXXVIII. und das Diplom des Otto I. zu Gunsten der Veroneser Kirche und zum besonderen Schutz des Bischofs Rather, vgl. Theodor Sickel: Die Urkunden Konrad I., Heinrich I. und Otto I. (MGH DD O I), Hannover 1879, S. 474.).

193 Aus: Rather von Verona: Ratherii Veronensis Praeloqviorvm libri VI Phrenesis. Dialogus confessionalis, hrsg. von Peter L. D. Reid (Corpus Christianorum. Continuatio Mediaevalis 46A), Turnhout 1984, S. 168.

194 Vgl. Antoine Auda: L'École musicale liégeoise au Xe siècle. Etienne de Liège (Mémoire de la Classe des Lettres 2, 1), Brüssel 1923, S. 113. Siehe dazu außerdem: Jonsson: Historia, S. 164–176.

195 „apud cuius clementiam piissimum intercessorem iugiter invenire mereamur Ursmarum sanctissimum, cuius vitam in praesenti elucidare disposuimus *ad laudem et gloriam omnipotentissimae Trinitatis.*" Rather von Verona: Opera omnia, Sp. 346.

ser Hinweis auf die *Trinitas*, mit dem Rather den Prolog der *Vita Ursmari* schloss, wurde von ihm sehr bewusst gewählt. Sein Prolog stellt gleichzeitig auch den Widmungsbrief dar, den er zusammen mit seiner Überarbeitung der *Vita Ursmari* an seine Brüder in Lobbes schickte. Mit dem Hinweis auf die *Trinitas* teilte Rather seinen Adressaten eine deutliche Botschaft mit, nämlich, dass er, nun Bischof und Exilant in fernen Ländern, seiner Heimat und ihren Heiligen wie Ursmarus und der Verehrung der göttlichen Dreieinigkeit treu blieb.

Die Anwesenheit des Hinweises auf die *Trinitas* – quasi eine Signatur Rathers – in BHL 9007 spricht für dessen Urheberschaft dieser Vitafassung. Diese These kann und soll hier durch eine eingehende Analyse belegt werden, mit der der Text von BHL 9007 aus stilistischer, grammatikalischer und syntaktischer Perspektive näher erörtert und mit dem Stil Rathers verglichen wird.

4.2.2.1 Zur Identifizierung Rathers als Redaktor von BHL 9007

Rathers Stil wurde bereits von Peter L. D. Reid ausführlich untersucht, seine Ergebnisse können somit für die Prüfung einer Autorschaft Rathers von BHL 9007 herangezogen werden.[196] Die folgende Analyse konzentriert sich auf jene Textpartien, die nur in BHL 9007, aber nicht in ihrer Vorlage (*Sermo*) vorkommen, und deshalb als origineller Beitrag des Redaktors zu sehen sind. Vor allem in fünf Bereichen lassen sich die auffälligsten Analogien zwischen der Sprache von BHL 9007 und dem Stil Rathers beobachten:

1. Die erste Analogie betrifft die großzügige Nutzung von Adverbien. Rather zeige, so Reid, eine deutliche Präferenz für Adverbien mit dem Suffix -iter[197] sowie eine Vorliebe für nachdrückliche Adverbien, wie *immo*, *nempe*, *nimirum*, *sane*, *penitus*, *prorsus*, *utique*, *quippe*, *saltem*, [...] *absque dubio* [...], *videlicet*, *omnino*, *profecto*, *certe*, *precipue*, *ideo*, und *necessarie*.[198] Auch BHL 9007 zeichnet sich durch den intensiven Gebrauch entsprechender Adverbien aus, die sich sowohl eingebettet in umfangreichere Zusätze als auch als allein stehende kurze Hinzufügungen im Text finden. Allein in der Gruppe der Adverbien mit Rathers Lieblingsendung -iter wurden vom Redaktor von BHL 9007 zum ursprünglichen knappen Text der Vorlage fünf Adverbien hinzugefügt (*perniciter*, *acriter*, *lamentabiliter*, *unanimiter*, *rationabiliter*). Dazu kommen vier weitere Adverbien mit der Endung -nter: *incessanter*, *patenter*, *luculenter* und vor allem Rathers Favorit *indesinenter*,[199] sowie drei weitere auf -im (*paulatim*, *confestim*, *affatim*) und zwei auf -itus (*penitus*, *funditus*) endende. Aber auch andere Adverbien werden in BHL 9007 hinzugefügt, vor allem die von Rather bevorzugten nachdrücklichen und emphatischen Adver-

[196] Vgl. Reid: Tenth-Century Latinity.

[197] „Rather shows a marked preference for this type [scilicet Adverbien in -iter]“, ebd., S. 79.

[198] „Also apparent from the passage quoted is his fondness for assertive and aggressive adverbs“, ebd., S. 56; 81.

[199] Bei Reid wird das Adverb *indesinenter* als „freq.“, also häufig gekennzeichnet, vgl. ebd., S. 80.

bien, die teilweise sogar mehrmals vorkommen: *sane*, *nempe* (2x), *certe*, *quidem*, *nimirum*, *quippe* (2x), *videlicet*. Außerdem kommen weitere Adverbien sowie eine adverbiale Konstruktion vor, die beide auch bei Rather häufige Verwendung finden: *iure* (wird von Rather insgesamt über 70x verwendet), *dire* und *luce clarius* (insgesamt 3x bei Rather).[200]

2. Die Vorliebe für solche Adverbien spiegelt Rathers allgemeine Neigung zu einem hyperbolischen Stil wieder.[201] Diese drückt sich auch in der häufigen Anwendung von Superlativen sowie von Paaren oder Triaden von Adjektiven und Synonymen aus und stellt eine weitere Stileigenschaft dar, die auch in BHL 9007 zu finden ist.[202] Superlative kommen an vier Stellen vor. Zum einen im Prolog, wo von den weisesten Männern (*peritissimorum ... virorum*) die Rede ist (Tabelle 8, S. 337, Nr. 2). Zum zweiten als Attribut von Papst Dionysius, der als ehrwürdigst beschrieben wird: *Dionisius vir reverentissimus*. Gerade dieses Syntagma lässt einen weiteren Aspekt des Stils Rathers in BHL 9007 sichtbar werden, nämlich seine Vorliebe für Superlative, die aus dem Partizip Präsens gebildet werden. Reid nennt als Beispiel: *amantissimus* (in aktiver Bedeutung), *credentissimus*, *presentissimus* und so weiter.[203] Auch in BHL 9007 wird *reverentissimus* als Superlativ aus dem Partizip Präsens von *reverens* gebildet. Weitere Superlative finden sich, wie zum Beispiel im Ausdruck *veluti fulgidissimum sidus* oder *per sacerrimam vitam*. Hier wird die Botschaft der Vorlage (*per vitam sanctam*) durch den Superlativ besonders betont. Zum dritten zeigt auch die Hinzufügung von Adjektiven und Adverbien Rathers Tendenz zu einem hyperbolischen Stil. Diese werden entweder ganz neu hinzugefügt (*sollicite ac rationabiliter*, *ineffabilis ac beatae*) oder bereits in der Vorlage bestehenden Adjektiven angehängt, um deren Wirkung zu steigern (zu *cruciatu* wird *et maerore* hinzugefügt; zu *pura* auch *et rectissima fides*).

3. Eine dritte Auffälligkeit von BHL 9007, in der Rathers Stil ans Licht tritt, betrifft die extensive Nutzung des Hyperbatons. Dieser Aspekt, der unter anderem Rathers Prosa als komplex und schwierig berüchtigt gemacht hat,[204] betrifft auch BHL 9007 und zwar nicht nur in den originellen Zusätzen des Redaktors, sondern auch dort, wo der Redaktor die Reihenfolge von Worten geändert hat, um einen entsprechenden Effekt zu erzielen. Man gewinnt den Eindruck, Rather habe eine solche Umarbeitung des Textes als seine Aufgabe gesehen und sei daher konsequent durch die ganze Vorlage gegangen, um mittels der Reihung ihrer Wörter ein Hyperbaton zu erzeugen. Ein typisches Beispiel: Aus *Indicemus pro*

---

200 Diese Zahlen basieren auf meiner Recherche. Hierfür habe ich in der Datenbank Library of Latin Texts: LLT-A, https://katalog.ub.uni-freiburg.de/link?id=116897937 das Vorkommen bestimmter Wörter in den Werken Rathers gezählt. [1. Februar 2018]

201 Vgl. Reid: Tenth-Century Latinity, S. 95.

202 „Synonymous extensions in pairs is of course such a regular feature of Rather's style that it is hardly worth looking for examples", ebd., S. 52.

203 Vgl. ebd., S. 95.

204 „A second source of difficulty is the confusing word order Rather deliberately adopts. [...] The separation of a word from its phrase [...] is a routine feature of his style; [...]", ebd., S. 52–53.

qua re missi sumus ad virum istum wird in BHL 9007 die Formulierung *Indicemus pro qua re istum destinati sumus ad virum* (Tabelle 8, S. 339).[205]

4. Eine weitere stilistische Eigenschaft von BHL 9007 bestätigt Rathers Autorschaft. Auch sie betrifft, wie im Fall des Hyperbatons, den Komplexitätsgrad des Satzbaus. Rather selbst hat beobachtet, dass seine Werke schwierig zu lesen sind. Dabei nennt er seine Anwendung einer eigentümlichen Wortstellung – eben das gerade geschilderte Hyperbaton – sowie seine häufige Nutzung von Parenthesen als Gründe dafür.[206] Dieser Aspekt tritt besonders in Erscheinung, wenn Rather als Redaktor seiner eigenen Werke tätig wird. Durch den Vergleich der zwei existierenden Versionen von Rathers *Invectiva de translatione S. Metronis* konnte Peter Reid nicht nur zeigen, dass Rather seine Werke (und wie im Fall der *Vita Ursmari* auch die Werke anderer) umfassend zu überarbeiten pflegte, sondern eben auch, dass er dabei vor allem die Hinzufügung von Parenthesen einsetzte.[207]

Auch ein großer Teil der Änderungen, mit denen BHL 9001 zu BHL 9007 ‚verbessert' wurde, besteht aus der Hinzufügung von parenthetischen Sätzen. Einige davon kamen oben schon zur Sprache. Da gerade diese parenthetischen Zusätze auch in der Nutzung der Legende für das Offizium übernommen wurden, seien sie hier nochmal eigens erwähnt. Die erste Parenthese betrifft den erwähnten Zusatz zu Beginn der Vita, mit dem die Unbestimmtheit der historischen Daten der Vorlage durch genaue Angaben vervollständigt wird: *In diebus imperatoris Gallieni, qui per successiones caesarum vigesimus septimus in eorum est catalogo subrogatus, quo etiam tempore, Dionisius vir reverentissimus a beato Petro apostolo vigesimus tertius Romanae praesidebat ecclesiae* (Tabelle 8, S. 337). Darüber hinaus finden sich sowohl geringfügige[208] als auch umfangreichere Parenthesen, in denen auch biblische Zitate eingearbeitet werden (vgl. etwa: *ut assertione divina in eo repeti videretur, quod Hieremiae dictum est*; *ne diutius absconderetur civitas supre montem domus Domini posita; nempe talibus et his similibus incedebat opinatus virtutibus, ut compleretur in eo, quod Dominus apostolis ait* [...] *virtutem inimici* (Tabelle 8, S. 340). Anders als in anderen Überarbeitungen Rathers, beeinträchtigen die hinzugefügten parenthetischen Sätze in BHL 9007 nicht die Nachvollziehbarkeit des Textes.[209]

205 Vgl. auch: *At ille publica voce coepit clamare* der Vorlage BHL 9001, in BHL 9007: *At ille publica coepit et horribili voce clamare*. Es lassen sich viele weitere Beispiele für die Anwendung des Hyperbatons in BHL 9007 beobachten: *peritissimorum disciplinabilis mos extitit virorum; avide fontium concupiscat fluenta; desideratissimum ex remota regione audire ambiat nuntium; ad solitam sui cupiat ventris pervenire satietatem; ad tuum perniciter abire impedimentum; ubi sanctum potuisset invenire virum; milites velocibus ad virum Dei gressibus pergunt;talibus et his similibus incedebat opinatus virtutibus; sacrosanta agebat antistes pro populi intercessione salutaria* (Tabelle 8, S. 336).

206 Vgl. Peter L. D. Reid: Tenth-Century Latinity. Rather of Verona (Humana Civilitas 6), Malibu 1981, S. 42.

207 Vgl. ebd., S. 45.

208 So zum Beispiel: *et artis apostolicae documenta proficiens*; *mox ab omni daemonicae incursionis ludificatione*; *cuius in omni vitae transeuntis tempore nutui oboedierat*.

209 Das ist im Übrigen auch der Fall in der Invectiva: „The parentheses are often short enough to cause no difficulty – merely irritation. *Ut ita loquar* (Metr. 14), *ut conici utique valet* (18),

5. Der fünfte und letzte Bereich, in dem sich die analoge Vorgehensweise Rathers und des Redaktors von BHL 9007 manifestiert, besteht in den angedeuteten Substitutionen von gebräuchlichen Wörtern durch ein selteneres Synonym, etwa der schon erwähnte Begriff *dapibus* (BHL 9007) für *epulis* (BHL 9001).[210] Diese Substitutionen erhöhen zusammen mit weiteren kleinen Zusätzen[211] den Stil des Werkes. Auch in diesem Vorgehen zeigt sich eine Ähnlichkeit des Redaktors von BHL 9007 zur Überarbeitungstechnik Rathers, der „plumpe oder banale" durch „spannendere oder seltenere Wörter" ersetzte.[212] Insgesamt bemühte sich Rather in seinen Überarbeitungen um einen pathetischen und ausdrucksvollen Stil, der sich eben auch in BHL 9007 nachweisen lässt.

Zusätzlich zu diesen fünf Überarbeitungstechniken, die sich sowohl in der *Vita Ursmari* als auch in BHL 9007 feststellen lassen, lassen sich in beiden Texten eine Reihe von sprachlichen Eigentümlichkeiten feststellen, die Rathers Latinität auszeichnen. So ersetzt Rather gerne *sum* durch Synonyme wie *exsto*, *exto* und *existo*.[213] Auch in BHL 9007 wird *sum* vermieden und an drei Stellen durch Synonyme ersetzt.[214] Außerdem verwendet Rather öfters das Infinitiv Perfekt im Sinne eines Präsens und *nosse* anstatt des Infinitiv Präsens.[215] Auch in BHL 9007 findet man eine solche Verwendung des Infinitivs Perfekt von *noscere*: hier wird der Satz der Vorlage *audiant populi omnes, qui eius cupiunt miracula* zu *nempe audiant populi omnes, qui eius cupiunt nosse miracula* modifiziert (siehe Tabelle 8). Das letzte Beispiel dieser Art betrifft Rathers Nutzung von Verba deponentia in passiver Bedeutung.[216] Ein von Reid aus Rathers *opus* erwähntes Beispiel findet sich sogar fast identisch in BHL 9007: In seiner *Conclusio deliberativa* von 955 bezeichnet Rather Gregor den Großen als „opinatissimus [...] Gregorius" und Reid übersetzt entsprechend „renowned Gregory".[217] In BHL 9007 wird Zeno auf ähnliche

---

quam confundit Deus (25), *mystico nec sine sensu* (50), *ut conicere cogamur...* (81), *nisi Dei parcat eis contra meritorum pietas* (90), *hereo confessoris dicam an martyris* (104), *proh nefas* (115), *quod est tutius ac rationabilius (129), quod veracius* (134) – these are merely nuisances. But sometimes asides like these have confused his editors." Reid: Tenth-Century Latinity, S. 45–46.

210 Weitere Beispiele sind *amnis* für *flumen*, *cunctis cernentibus daretur intellegi* für *omnibus demonstraretur*, *intentis luminibus* für *elevans oculos*, *prospicieret* für *videret*, *aspexit* für *vidit*, *innotuit* für *audivit*, *coactus migrabo* für *per imperium ipsius egrediar* und *velut fumus vento raptatus* für *evanuit velut fumus*.

211 Z. B. *et splendifico nitore facundiae vividus*, *per praeceps*, *limphaticam ruinam*, *saeviens incessanter moliebatur*.

212 „Some of his changes in Metr. show him substituting a more exciting or rare word for a dull or hackneyed one: 61 *ornamenta* for *opes*, 145 *subdola* for *impia*, 163 *refutasse* for *fugisse* and 97 *mestiloquo* for *moesto*. [...] We can see him striving for a more expressive, more grandiloquent, style of writing." Reid: Tenth-Century Latinity, S. 53.

213 „*Exsto*, *exto*, *existo* frequently appear for *sum* [...]", ebd., S. 73.

214 Dies geschieht dreimal: 1. *Olim peritissimorum disciplinabilis mos extitit;* 2. *Revera quoniam sanctus ei spiritus purarum illuminator mentium doctor existebat;* 3. *Sic etenim instat sapientis mens ad investigandas sanctorum vitas* (siehe Tabelle 8, S. 336–337, Nr. 2 und 3).

215 Zum Beispiel in Metr. 15.159 *nosse volo*, vgl. Reid: Tenth-Century Latinity, S. 73.

216 Vgl. ebd., S. 69–70.

217 Ebd., S. 70.

Weise als „opinatus“ bezeichnet: *Nempe talibus et his similibus incedebat opinatus virtutibus* (Tabelle 8, S. 340). Auch in diesem Fall scheint es sinnvoll, wie von Reid vorgeschlagen, „opinatus“ als passiv zu übersetzen: „Zeno trat hervor durch solche und ähnliche Mirakel berühmt.“

Im Bereich der Substantive legt Rather eine Präferenz für Substantive der u-Deklination an den Tag, die er meist im Ablativ oder im Dativ einsetzt.[218] In den Zusätzen von BHL 9007 finden sich auch vermehrt Substantive der u-Deklination im Ablativ (*impetu*, *cruciatu*, *manu* und *noctuque*) und einmal auch im Dativ (*nutui*). Was die Adjektive angeht, merkt Reid an, dass Rather öfters ein Adjektiv statt des Genitivs eines Substantivs benutzt, zum Beispiel *regulari collirio* statt *Regulae collirio* (*die Salbe der Regel*).[219] Erneut sei hier ein Beispiel von Reid erwähnt, das fast identisch in der Zenovita vorkommt. In Rathers *Praeloquia* 4.9, 255C findet man den Ausdruck *lupina* [...] *incursione*, eine Formulierung, die stark an die Passage von BHL 9007 *mox ab omni daemonicae incursionis ludificatione* (Tabelle 8, S. 340) erinnert. Dieser Ausdruck ist auch in der Historia *Dum Zeno pontificatus honore*, Antiphon 5 (siehe Kapitel 3.3.1, S. 61) zu finden.

Auffallend bei Rather ist außerdem im Bereich der Pronomina seine wenig präzise Verwendung von *aliquis* / *quis*. Insbesondere fällt sein nach den Standards des klassischen Lateins inkorrekter Gebrauch des Pronomens *aliquis* nach der Subjunktion *si* beziehungsweise *ne* auf: In seiner zweiten Predigt für die Fastenzeit von 964 schreibt der Bischof: *et si aliquis ... aliquid fecerit boni*.[220] Auch im Prolog von BHL 9007 findet sich eine solche Anwendung von *aliquis* nach *si*: *Sic etenim instat sapientis mens ad investigandas sanctorum vitas, tamquam si aliquis sitiens ardore solis adustus, avide fontium concupiscat fluenta* (Tabelle 8, S. 337).

Zuletzt seien zwei Besonderheiten im Bereich der Syntax erwähnt. Rather verwendet ab und zu die Subjunktion *quatenus* + Konjunktiv statt *ut* + Konjunktiv, um einen Finalsatz einzuleiten, zum Beispiel *quatinus ... liberet Deus*.[221] Gleich zu Beginn von BHL 9007 findet man eine solche Anwendung von *quatenus* in einem Finalsatz: *quatenus ob suae studium doctrinae ipsorum in orbe imitatione potirentur et eorum quandoque consortio in perhennis vitae gloria fruerentur* (Tabelle 8, S. 337). Ähnlich bemerkenswert ist Rathers Nutzung von *siquidem* zur Einleitung eines Kausalsatzes. Teilweise erscheint die Subjunktion in Rather sogar gefolgt von einem Partizip.[222] In BHL 9007 kommt interessanterweise auch dieses Phänomen vor und zwar aufgrund eines Zitierfehlers Rathers: Als der Redaktor von BHL 9007 die Mirakelerzählung Gregors des Großen wortwörtlich wiedergibt, findet man nicht – wie in der kritischen Edition von Gregors *Dialogi* – *Sicque stans aqua*, sondern *Siquidem stans aqua* (Tabelle 8). Dieses letzte Beispiel zeigt auf besonders prägnante Art, dass Rathers persönlicher Stil auch dann durchdringen kann,

218 Vgl. ebd., S. 77.
219 Vgl. ebd.
220 Vgl. ebd., S. 85.
221 Vgl. ebd., S. 102.
222 Vgl. ebd., S. 101–102.

wenn er nicht als Autor, sondern als bloßer Redaktor tätig ist und sogar dann, wenn er aus dem Werk eines anderen Autors zitiert.

Die sprachlichen Eigenheiten von BHL 9007, die sich auf stilistischer, grammatikalischer und syntaktischer Ebene beobachten lassen, sind insgesamt ein starkes Argument für die These, dass der Redaktor des Textes mit Rather von Verona zu identifizieren ist.

Zwischenfazit

Insgesamt wird deutlich, dass BHL 9007 nicht das Werk eines einfachen, anonymen Redaktors ist, sondern Rather selbst am Werk war. Er sah es, wie im Fall der *Vita Ursmari*, als seine Aufgabe, die Vita eines so wichtigen Patrons wie Zeno aufzuwerten und sie seinen Maßstäben und seinem Stil entsprechend zu verbessern. Dafür spricht nicht nur die Tatsache, dass BHL 9007 auf die gleiche Weise wie die *Vita Ursmari* bearbeitet wurde. Die Art der Eingriffe, mit denen der *Sermo* des Coronatus modifiziert wurde, sind typisch für Rather: Auf der einen Seite wurde der bestehende Text respektiert, so dass „nichts verloren geht",[223] auf der anderen wurden Syntax und Sprache der Vorlage an mehreren Stellen geändert, um sie eleganter, emphatischer und ausdrucksvoller zu gestalten. Auch Zusätze wurden eingearbeitet, die Rathers Gelehrsamkeit demonstrieren sollen. Aber nicht nur Rathers Vorgehensweise als Redaktor lässt sich in BHL 9007 festhalten. In dieser Überarbeitung kommen auch ganz persönliche Aspekte ihres Urhebers ans Licht: Neben Rathers besonderer Verehrung der *Trinitas* sind es vor allem die sprachlichen und stilistischen Eigentümlichkeiten des Textes, zu denen besondere Favoriten und charakteristische Redewendungen Rathers zu zählen sind.

Mit der Identifizierung des Urhebers der hagiographischen Vorlage der Historia ergibt sich daher auch ein Terminus post quem für die Entstehung der Historia, die nicht vor der Ratherzeit entstanden sein kann. Tatsächlich lässt sich über die folgende Analyse der Historia belegen, dass auch diese ein Werk des Veroneser Bischofs ist.

4.2.2.2 Rather als Autor der neuen Historia

Diese Analyse wird allerdings dadurch erschwert, dass die Historia *Dum Zeno pontificatus honore* in der ursprünglichen Fassung im Cursus romanus äußerst nah am Text ihrer Vorlage BHL 9007 bleibt. In der Historia werden ganze Sätze des Vitatextes wortwörtlich übernommen, höchstens geringfügig modifiziert und als Antiphonen, Responsorien und Verse eingesetzt. Da für diese übernommenen Teile logischerweise auch die Beobachtungen der sprachlichen und stilistischen

223 „Gleich einem Paulus Diaconus hat er [Rather] als Revisor einer Vita so viel Entsagung aufgebracht, daß er stehen ließ, was immer grammatisch noch zu vertreten war. Nichts ist bei Rathers Korrektur verlorengegangen," Berschin: Biographie und Epochenstil, S. 52.

Analyse der Vita zutreffen, lässt sich aufgrund dieser Bestandteile keine Aussage über die Urheberschaft der Historia treffen. Glücklicherweise trifft dies nicht auf alle Bestandteile der Historia zu: so wurden die Magnificat-Antiphon der ersten und zweiten Vesper, das Invitatorium sowie das erste und letzte Responsorium der Matutin (und die dazu gehörenden Verse) nicht auf der Grundlage der Vita komponiert, denn sie verwerten Gesänge aus anderen Heiligenoffizien oder wurden in Gänze neu gedichtet. Daher wird sich die folgende Analyse auf diese Bestandteile der Historia im Cursus romanus beschränken, die im Editionsteil auf den Seiten 58–70 dargestellt sind. Die entsprechende Stelle wird jeweils durch das liturgische Element angegeben (z.B. R1).

Zunächst sollen hier Stil und Terminologie der Zusätze untersucht werden. Die neu gedichteten Antiphonen und Responsorien der Historia weisen einige bereits erwähnte Merkmale des Stils Rathers auf. So zeigt sich in der Magnificat-Antiphon der ersten Vesper die Verwendung des Hyperbatons wie auch des Verbs *exsistere*, das hier, wie in der Rather'schen BHL 9007, anstelle von *esse* eingesetzt wird: *meritis non paucis existentibus* (M-A1). Auch kommt in dieser Antiphon das Adjektiv *ruinosa* (*a ruinosa peste*) vor, welches nur in BHL 9007 (und nicht in der Vita von Coronatus) zu finden ist, hier allerdings als Substantiv (*limphaticam viri ruinam*) verwendet wird. Außerdem bietet das erste Responsorium der Matutin zwei Beispiele des Hyperbatons (R1 *cuius praeclara fulserunt in mundo miracula* und *gemina virtute Dominus sanctitatis et sapientiae decoravit*).

Auffälliger ist allerdings die Nutzung des eher ungeläufigen Substantivs *antistes* als Synonym für *episcopus* im ersten Responsorium der Matutin, das nicht auf der textlichen Grundlage der Historia oder anderen Heiligenoffizien verfasst wurde: R1 *Hic est sacer antistes Zeno quem gemina virtute Dominus sanctitatis et sapientiae decoravit, cuius praeclara fulserunt in mundum miracula et in caelis adeptus est angelorum commercia.* Insbesondere zeigt die Formulierung *sacer antistes* in Verbindung mit dem Verb *fulgere* einen Zusammenhang mit dem Gedicht in elegischen Distichen, das in den Handschriften von BHL 9007 aus Novara dem Text der Vita vorangestellt wurde. Auch dort hieß es in den Versen 5–6 *Sed tamen e multis perstringam pauca legenti, / In quibus antistes fulserit ille sacer* (vgl. Kap. 3.3.3 auf S. 87). Dies deutet sowohl im Fall der Historia als auch des Gedichts stark auf eine Autorschaft Rathers hin. Nicht nur hatte Rather an mehreren Stellen seiner Predigt über den heiligen Donatianus (*Pauca de vita sancti Donatiani*[224]) dem geläufigen *episcopus* die Bezeichnung *antistes* vorgezogen.[225] Auch hatte er sein philologisches Interesse ausgerechnet für das entsprechende Verb gezeigt: In seiner Kopie von *De nuptiis Philosophiae et Mercurii* des Martianus Cappella hatte Rather sich am Rande das Partizip Präsens *antistans* notiert. Diese Gewohnheit

224 Vgl. François Dolbeau: Pauca de vita sancti Donatiani, in: Peter L. D. Reid (Hg.): Ratherii Veronensis Praeloqviorvm libri VI Phrenesis. Dialogus confessionalis (Corpus Christianorum. Continuatio Mediaevalis 46A), Turnhout 1984, S. 275–283.

225 Vgl. ebd., S. 280, Z. 50–52 und S. 283, Z. 153.

Rathers, seltene und ausgefallene Wörter *in margine* seiner Bücher zu notieren, beschreibt Claudio Leonardi auf folgende Weise:

> Diese Leseanmerkungen [scilicet Rathers marginalia, A. d. V.] zielen nicht darauf ab, am Rande des Codex einen Index des Werkes zu bilden [...], vielmehr entsprechen sie Rathers lexikalischer Neugier: er sucht, markiert am Rande und kommentiert teilweise seltene Wörter oder technischen Wortschatz aus der quadrivialen Wissenschaft. Was ihm auffällt ist nicht – so scheint es – der Inhalt des De nuptiis in seiner Gesamtheit, sondern das einzelne Wort. Seine Sammlung ist eine der sprachlichen Raritäten.[226]

Das Verb *antistare* / *antistans* fiel Rather wegen seiner linguistischen Interessen auf, wie auch das davon abgeleitete Substantiv *antistes*, das er in seiner Predigt für den heiligen Donatianus, im Prolog-Gedicht und in der Historia für Zeno verwendete.

Nicht nur die sprachlichen Hinweise deuten auf eine Autorschaft Rathers hin. Vielmehr kann die folgende Analyse der liturgischen Bezugsmodelle der Historia zeigen, dass sie perfekt in Rathers Vorstellung seines Bischofsamtes passte. Der älteste handschriftliche Zeuge der Historia, das berühmte Antiphonar Verona BC XCVIII(92), liefert diesbezüglich eine Spur. Das letzte Responsorium der Matutin (R9) ist nicht auf der Grundlage der Vita komponiert, sondern bedient sich eines bereits existierenden Gesanges und wurde in diesem Codex mit folgender Rubrik angegeben: Es sei beim Martinsfest gesucht (*Requiratur in sancti Martini*). Das gleiche Responsorium war auch im zweitältesten Zeugen der Historia, nämlich im *Carpsum* (Verona BC XCVI(89)) vorgesehen und gehörte daher wahrscheinlich zum ursprünglichen Textbestand des Offiziums. Solche Anlehnungen an Offizien anderer Heiliger waren nicht selten. Des Öfteren wurden bestimmte Elemente aus anderen Offizien entlehnt, um einen Heiligen mit einem ganz bestimmten Profil zu versehen.[227] Mit dem Responsorium aus dem Martinsoffizium wird Zeno mit dem berühmten fränkischen Bischof und Modell eines Confessors Martin in Verbindung gebracht und als Martinellus dargestellt.[228] Diese Verbindung liefert aber einen weiteren Anknüpfungspunkt zu Rather: Eine direkte Linie zwischen Zeno und Martin hatte Rather nämlich schon in seinem frühesten Werk *Praeloquia* gezogen, das er nach der ersten Amtszeit in Verona aus dem Gefängnis in Pavia schrieb. Hier erwähnt er Martin und Zeno als Vorbilder seines eigenen

---

226 „Queste note di lettura non tendono a costruire, nel margine del manoscritto, un indice dell'opera [...], rispondono piuttosto alle curiosità lessicali di Raterio: egli cerca, annota in margine, qualche volta commenta, parole rare [...] o termini tecnici quadriviali. [...] Ciò che lo colpisce non è, si direbbe, il contenuto del De nuptiis nel suo insieme, ma il singolo termine. La sua è una raccolta di rarità linguistiche." Claudio Leonardi: Notae et glossae autographicae, in: Peter L. D. Reid (Hg.): Ratherii Veronensis Praeloqviorvm libri VI Phrenesis. Dialogus confessionalis (Corpus Christianorum. Continuatio Mediaevalis 46A), Turnhout 1984, S. 291–314, hier: S. 294.

227 Dazu auch bei: Heinzer: Der besungene Heilige.

228 Zu dieser Verbindung vgl. Jean-François Goudesenne: Historiae from Alta Italia and their Frankish Models: A Progressive „Romanisation" by the Carolingian Franks (750–950), in: Roman Hankeln (Hg.): Political Plainchant? Music, Text and Historical Context of Medieval Saints' Offices (Wissenschaftliche Abhandlungen 91), Ottawa 2009, S. 13–29, hier: S. 20.

Amtes: „Hic est, dicent, novellus propheta, recens apostolus, subito angelus effectus; iste sanctus Martinus, Zeno est iste sanctus [...].“[229] Alles in allem legen die neu gedichteten Partien der Historia sowie die aus anderen Offizien entliehenen Elemente den Schluss nahe, dass Rather auch als Urheber der Historia gelten muss: seine stilistischen Eigentümlichkeiten und terminologischen Vorlieben sowie die von ihm vertretenen Bezugsmodelle treten klar zum Vorschein.

Kehren wir zu der Frage zurück, die zu Beginn dieses Kapitels aufgeworfen wurde: Wo, wann und durch wen wurde die Zeno-Historia *Dum Zeno pontificatus honore* verfasst? Die Historia wurde in ihrer ursprünglichen Version für eine kanonikale Institution, den Dom von Verona, verfasst, welcher im 9. und 10. Jahrhundert den Zenokult noch primär verwaltete. Sie wurde sicher vor der Verschriftlichung im Antiphonar Verona BC XCVIII(92) im ersten Viertel des 11. Jahrhunderts verfasst und war im *Carpsum* enthalten, also der ersten Version des Liber ordinarius, das während der Episkopatszeit von Rather entstand. Doch die Hinweise der Vorlage, auf der die Historia basiert, erlauben den Kontext ihres Verfassens noch deutlicher einzugrenzen: die Historia enthält Formulierungen und Eigentümlichkeiten, die lediglich BHL 9007 enthält, die wiederum anhand sprachlicher, stilistischer und inhaltlicher Merkmale auf Rather zurückzuführen ist. Damit wurde sowohl die Vita als auch die Historia im Rahmen jener allgemeinen Aufwertung des liturgischen Lebens in Verona verfasst, die Rather während seiner Episkopatszeit initiierte.

Zwischenfazit

Der Kult von Zeno erfuhr im Laufe des 10. Jahrhunderts in Verona eine erneute Entfaltung. Dies wurde vor allem mit der Komposition einer Historia erreicht, mit der der Heilige im Rahmen des Stundengebets individuell profiliert und gefeiert werden konnte. Somit wurde der Heilige nun nicht mehr bloß in der Vita ‚erzählt‘, sondern liturgisch für seine besonderen Verdienste verehrt und seine spezifische Biographie memoriert. Der Hauptakteur dieser Aufwertung des Kultes von Zeno im 10. Jahrhundert ist die Verehrergemeinschaft des Veroneser Doms, und vor allem Bischof Rather, welcher für entscheidende Maßnahmen im liturgischen Bereich verantwortlich war: Neben der Historia wurde auch eine generelle Erneuerung und Systematisierung der Liturgie vorgenommen und in der frühesten Version des *Carpsums* verschriftlicht. Für Zeno verfasste Rather wohl persönlich nicht nur eine neue Vita, sondern auf deren Grundlage auch eine Historia. Im Folgenden soll die Frage untersucht werden, wie und mit welchen Inhalten die Figur Zenos im 10. Jahrhundert profiliert und mit Bedeutung

[229] Vgl. Peter L. D. Reid: Introduction, in: Peter L. D. Reid (Hg.): Ratherii Veronensis Praeloqviorvm libri VI Phrenesis. Dialogus confessionalis (Corpus Christianorum. Continuatio Mediaevalis 46A), Turnhout 1984, S. VII–XIV, hier: VII.

versehen wurde. Dies soll nun anhand einer Analyse der liturgischen Aufführung des Zenofestes im Dom beleuchtet werden.

4.2.3 Zeno: heiliger Bischof und Vorbild für Priester

Im Laufe des 10. Jahrhunderts wurde zum ersten Mal in der Geschichte des Zenokultes in Verona ein liturgisches Ensemble geschaffen, in dem Zeno für seine spezifischen Verdienste und mit Bezug auf seine biographischen Gegebenheiten gefeiert wurde. Wie dies zuvor geschah, bleibt unbekannt, möglich ist aber, dass die alte Vita des Coronatus zusammen mit einer Historia aus dem Commune im Stundengebet der Kleriker vorgetragen wurde. Nun ergeben sich zwei Fragen. Erstens: Wie sah das Offizium – hier nicht nur als Historia, sondern als Gesamtheit aller Elemente des Stundengebets, nämlich als liturgisches Ensemble verstanden – für die Feier des Zenofestes am Dom im 10. Jahrhundert aus? Und zweitens: Welches Bild von Zeno entstand in diesem Offizium? Diese Fragen sollen anhand einer Analyse der im Kapitel 3.4.1 erfolgten Rekonstruktion beantwortet werden.[230]

Zunächst zum Festanlass. Obwohl eigentlich der 8. Dezember das ursprüngliche Fest Zenos darstellte, wurde der Heilige an diesem Tag nur mit einer kleineren Feier gewürdigt. Vermutlich lag dies daran, dass dieses Fest durch die Weihe des Klosters San Zeno Maggiore bereits monastisch belegt war. Die Historia des Heiligen wurde nach Auskunft des *Carpsums* (Verona BC XCIV(89)) auf den 12. April verlegt und für die Feier der Depositio Zenos verwendet (vgl. Kapitel 3.4.1, Rekonstruktion 1). Auch im Antiphonar (Verona BC XCVIII(92)) wurde dieses Fest gefeiert, dabei wurde es als Natale bezeichnet. Das Fest am 8. Dezember ist im *Carpsum* auch angegeben, wobei es dort bereits zu „in dedicatione s. enonis" umbenannt worden ist und seiner geringen Relevanz für das Kapitel entsprechend lediglich mit Commune-Texten begangen wurde.[231]

Da sowohl im *Carpsum* eine Magnificat-Antiphon für die Feier am 12. April zu Beginn des Offiziums (M-A1) und eine am Ende der Historia (M-A2) als *ad vesperum antiphona* gekennzeichnet werden, und das Antiphonar die identischen Antiphonen an gleicher Stelle überliefert,[232] lässt sich die Bedeutung des Zeno-Festes erschließen: Die Feier von gleich zwei Vespern – am Vorabend sowie am Abend des Festtages – deutet auf ein, wie zu erwarten, wichtiges Fest für den Dom von Verona hin. Der liturgische Ablauf dieser Vespern kann leider nicht rekonstruiert werden, da weder das Antiphonar noch das *Carpsum* entsprechende Gesänge angeben, sondern direkt mit dem Invitatorium, also mit der Eröffnung der Matu-

230 Siehe Rekonstruktion 1: Das Zeno-Offizium am Veroneser Dom ab dem Ende des 10. Jhdts., S. 119.
231 Vgl. Meersseman u. a.: L'orazionale, S. 296.
232 Verona BC XCVIII(92), fol. 147r.

tin fortfahren.[233] Nach den Psalmen und ihren Antiphonen wird das Magnificat mit einer Antiphon gesungen, in der ein expliziter Bezug auf Zeno formuliert wird: Bischof Zeno, ruhmreich und verdienstvoll, heilte die Tochter des Gallienus von dem Angriff des Teufels (M-A1). Die Magnificat-Antiphon ist die einzige Stelle im Offizium, an der Zeno explizit als *episcopus*, genauer: als *pontifex* charakterisiert wird. Weitere Angaben bezüglich der restlichen Elemente der Vespern, zum Beispiel der Kurzlesung, des Responsoriums, des Hymnus und so weiter sind nicht überliefert.

Die Feier wurde während der Nacht fortgesetzt und zwar in der Matutin: Im Invitatorium wurde Zeno mit einem Gesang besungen (I), der als Erweiterung des Commune-Invitatoriums für Bekenner zu sehen ist. Hier wird zum Lob Gottes und nicht des Heiligen eingeladen. Zeno erscheint daher nicht als direktes Objekt der Verehrung, sondern als Objekt der Gnade Gottes, der ihm die Ehre des himmlischen Reiches gegeben hat. Dabei muss betont werden, dass das Invitatorium anders als andere Antiphonen nach jedem von einem Solisten vorgetragenen Psalmvers als eine Art Antwortgesang vom ganzen Chor gesungen wird.[234]

Nach einem Hymnus, zu dem sich in den Quellen keine Angaben finden,[235] ist die erste Nokturn explizit Zeno gewidmet. Hier ergeben sich durch die performanzbedingte Interaktion zwischen Antiphonen und Psalmen einige inhaltliche Analogien, die teilweise durch sprachliche Resonanzen hervorgerufen werden. Die Antiphonen der Nokturn werden zu der Psalmenreihe 1, 2, 3, 4, 5, 8, 14, 20 und 23 gesungen, die traditionsgemäß für das Fest eines Bekenners ausgewählt wurden.[236] In der ersten Nokturn wird Zeno vor dem Hintergrund der Psalmen 1, 2 und 3 dem *beatus vir* der Bibel gleich gestellt. Dabei werden vor allem zwei Aspekte hervorgehoben: zum einen Zenos asketisches Leben, zum zweiten seine Tätigkeit als Prediger. Der Heilige, welcher in Analogie mit dem *beatus vir* auch *beatus Zeno* genannt wird, widmet sich den spirituellen Exerzitien und der Askese – in A1 *probitatis et scientiae iugibus incrementis* und A2 *continuis ieiuniis et orationibus crebris*) ebenso wie der *beatus vir* von Psalm 1, welcher Tag und Nacht das Gesetzt Gottes reflektiert (Ps 1, 2: „et in lege eius meditabitur die ac nocte").

Zeno erfüllt die Aufgabe seines psalmischen Vorbildes aber auch dadurch, dass er seine Predigten an Menschenmengen richtet. Diese Idee wird in A3 *Continuis ieiuniis et orationibus crebris a Domino petebat ut sibi aditum praedicationis in populos aperiret* und A2 *ad hoc pertingere meruit ut per sacerrimam vitam pastor in populis efficeretur* ausgedrückt und damit eine Resonanz zu den heidnischen Völkern

233 Jüngere Antiphonare des 14. Jhdts. aus Verona, die Handschriften Verona BC MLII und Verona BC MLIII geben an, dass bei den beiden Vespern die gleichen Antiphone der Laudes zu singen waren, allerdings gekoppelt an die für die Vesper typische Psalmenreihe 109–112 (vgl. Pascher: Das Stundengebet, S. 171.). An fünfter Stelle geben sie Psalm 131 an, der üblicherweise für die Feier eines Bischofs vorgesehen war (vgl. ebd, S. 172). Ob diese Antiphone bereits im 10. Jhdt. genutzt wurden, ist nicht rekonstruierbar.

234 Vgl. Hiley: Western Plainchant, S. 99.

235 Möglicherweise wurde der Hymnus aus dem Commune eines Confessors vorgetragen.

236 Vgl. Pascher: Das Stundengebet, S. 200–201.

(*populi*) des Psalms 2 kreiert, zu denen David predigt: *Quare fremuerunt gentes, et populi meditati sunt inania?* [...] *Ego autem constitutus sum rex ab eo super Sion, montem sanctum eius, prædicans præceptum eius.* Außerdem wird die Analogie zu der biblischen Figur des *beatus vir / David* durch die Interaktion von Antiphon 3 und Psalm 3 vollständig. Zeno bittet in A3 um die Hilfe Gottes (*a Domino petebat*) wie es auch David tut, der in Psalm 3, 5 singt: „Voce mea ad Dominum clamavi et exaudivit me de monte sancto suo." Der Psalmvers erklang nochmal als Versikel zum Abschluss des psalmischen Teils der ersten Nokturn und verstärkt so die Analogie zwischen Zeno, der an diesem Tag gefeiert wird, und David, seinem biblischen Vorbild.

Nach Versikel, Vaterunser und kurzer Segnung als Ende des ersten, psalmischen Teils der ersten Nokturn wird mit den Lesungen begonnen. Dieser Teil der ersten Nokturn, der aus der Abwechslung von Lesungen und Responsorien besteht, ist vor allem erzähltechnisch und performativ interessant: Die Lesungen bilden einen erzählerischen Rahmen für die Aussagen der Responsorien, die entweder aktualisierend auf den Heiligen hinweisen oder ausgewählte Aspekte des Narrativs der Lesungen pointiert wiederholen und durch den musikalischen Vortrag hervorheben. Die erste Lesung, die aus dem Prolog der Rather'schen Vita besteht, behandelt zunächst im Allgemeinen den Wert der Erforschung von Heiligenviten (*indagatione diligenti sanctorum vitas exquirere*). Diese sind Gegenstand der Sehnsucht des Geistes und liefern auch ein Vorbild zur Besserung des eigenen Lebensstils.

Im ersten Responsorium wird aber deutlich gemacht, dass bei dem aktuellen Anlass nicht irgendein Heiliger gefeiert wird, sondern dass es um Zeno geht. An einer der performativ wichtigsten Stellen des Offiziums,[237] nämlich dem ersten Responsorium der Nokturn, wird Zeno ins Zentrum der Aufmerksamkeit gestellt. Das Responsorium beginnt mit einem Demonstrativpronomen, das direkt auf Zeno verweist, quasi als ob der Heilige sich im Raum befände: R1 *Hic est quem gemina virtute Dominus sanctitatis et sapiencia decoravit, cuius preclara fulserunt in mundum miracula et in celis adeptus est angelorum conmercia.* Auch im dazugehörigen Vers wird ein Demonstrativpronomen an die erste Stelle gesetzt und so die imaginierte Präsenz des Heiligen im Raum erzeugt: V *Iste est qui ante Deum magna virtutes operatus est et omnis terra doctrina eius repleta est. Et in celis adeptus est angelorum commercia.*

237 Der besondere Wert dieser Stelle, die mit einem anspruchsvollen Solo die Eröffnung des responsorialen Teils der Matutin markiert und oft auch für die Historia namensgebend ist, wird auch durch ihre künstlerische Aufwertung hervorgehoben: Hier befindet sich nämlich meistens eine größere oder illuminierte Initiale. Vgl. Hughes: Medieval Manuscripts, S. 161–162. Das ist auch der Fall im Antiphonar Verona BC XCVIII(92), wo eine vierzeilige Initiale (H) das Responsorium einleitet, sowie in jüngeren Handschriften aus dem Veroneser Dom, wo eine figurative Initiale mit einem Zenobild zu finden ist, siehe Verona BC MLII, fol. 153r und Verona BC MLIII, fol. 153r. Dazu siehe auch Felix Heinzer: Eucharist and Holy Spirit: Hidden Mass-Theology in an Early Thirteenth-Century Office Book Fragment, in: Harvard Library Bulletin 21, 2011, S. 5–17, hier: S. 6–9.

An dieser sowie an weiteren Stellen im Offizium, an denen der Heilige direkt angesprochen wird, wie zum Beispiel in gebetsartigen Gesängen, wird die Veränderung des medialen Status der hagiographischen Texte in der Liturgie deutlich: Beim Heiligenfest wird nicht nur *über* den Heiligen erzählt, wie in den in der Matutin vorgelesenen Abschnitten der Vita, sondern der Heilige selbst ist im Raum präsent und kann angesprochen und um Hilfe gebeten werden. Neben den Gesängen des Offiziums, die auf die Präsenz des Heiligen im Raum verweisen, sind auch diejenigen Responsorien relevant, die im Zusammenhang mit den begleitenden Lesungen gewisse Aspekte der Biographie des Heiligen auswählen, hervorheben und durch den musikalischen Vortrag intensivieren. Das ist zum Beispiel in der Einheit Lesung 2 – Responsorium 2 der Fall. Während die Lesung die Figur des Heiligen historisch kontextualisiert, besingt das Responsorium Zenos angeborene Heiligkeit sowie sein vorbildliches heiliges Leben, das ihn zum Bischofsamt (*pastor*) führte. Zenos angeborene Heiligkeit wird dann in Lectio 3 thematisiert, die antizipierend auf R2 beruht.

Mit dem Hinweis, dass Zeno bereits im Mutterschoß heilig und in der Wiege gesegnet ist, und vor allem durch den Wortlaut dieses Responsoriums, in dem die Begriffe *uterus*, *mater* und *sanctificatus* erwähnt werden, wird Zeno liturgisch mit einer anderen wichtigen Gestalt verbunden, der pränatale Heiligkeit zugesprochen wurde, nämlich mit Johannes dem Täufer. Dieser wird unter anderem mit folgenden Antiphonen und Responsorien besungen: CAO 2400 „Dominus ab utero vocavit me, de ventre matris meae recordatus est nomini mei",[238] oder CAO 2669 „Erit enim magnus coram Domino, et Spiritu Sancto replebitur adhuc ex utero matris suae"[239], und CAO 7435 „Priusquam te formarem in utero novi te, et antequam exires de ventre sanctificavi te, et prophetam in gentibus dedi te."[240] So wird Zeno unter dem Aspekt der angeborenen Heiligkeit assoziativ in die Nähe eines Propheten gerückt.

Allerdings wird nicht nur Zenos angeborene Heiligkeit, sondern auch sein Verdienst hervorgehoben: Er habe nicht allein wegen seiner pränatalen Auserwähltheit, sondern auch durch seine heilige Lebensweise zum Hirten unter den Völkern aufsteigen können. Diese Idee erklang gleich zu Beginn des Festes, in der Magnificat-Antiphon der ersten Vesper (*Dum Zeno pontificatus honore, meritis non paucis existentibus*) und nochmal in A2: *Probitatis et scientiae iugibus incrementis...*, in R2: *ad hoc pertingere meruit ut pastor in populis per sacerrimam vitam efficeretur*, in R3 sowie in seiner Repetenda, wo die Idee durch das Verb *dignaretur* wieder aufgenommen wird und im Vers von R4, in dem Zenos eifriges Leben als ent-

238 René-Jean Hesbert: Corpus Antiphonalium Officii. Bd. 3 Invitatoria et antiphonae (Rerum Ecclesiasticarum Documenta. Series Maior. Fontes 9), Rom 1968b, S. 71. Im Folgenden: CAO.

239 Ebd., S. 204.

240 René-Jean Hesbert: Corpus Antiphonalium Officii. Bd. 4 Responsoria, versus, hymni et varia (Rerum Ecclesiasticarum Documenta. Series Maior. Fontes 10), Rom 1970, S. 357.

scheidend für die Bekehrung der Stadt zum Christentum beschrieben wird: V *Ita existebat alacer ut mox ad eum properaret relictis idolis Domino crederent Ihesu Christo.*

Ein weiterer Aspekt, der in diesem Zusammenhang relevant zu sein scheint, ist die Tatsache, dass Zeno auch für seine Weisheit und sein Wissen gelobt wird. In der gerade erwähnten A1 wird nicht nur die Tüchtigkeit (*probitas*) des Heiligen, sondern auch seine Ausbildung (*scientia*) erwähnt, im ersten Responsorium der Matutin wurde Zeno die Zwillingstugend der Heiligkeit und Weisheit zugeschrieben: R1 *sacer antistes Zeno quem gemina virtute Dominus sanctitatis et sapientiae decoravit.* Diese Betonung der Bildung von Zeno scheint auf Rather zurückzuführen zu sein, denn im ersten Fall handelt es sich um einen Zusatz Rathers zum Vitatext, der im Offizium übernommen wird, während R1 möglicherweise komplett auf ihn zurückgeht.

L3 bietet eine konzise Zusammenfassung dieses Bildes: Hier wird sowohl die im R2 schon gesungene Stelle *Ab utero* wiederholt, als auch eine weitere Stelle erwähnt, die erst in R3 gesungen wird. Diese lautet: *Erat enim sedens in monasterio in secretiori parte oppidi Veronensis continuis ieiuniis et orationibus crebris a Domino petens ut sibi dignaretur aditum melliferae praedicationis in populos aperiret.* Zenos asketischer Lebensstil, sein intensives Fasten und Beten, seine Predigertätigkeit sowie seine Bitte an Gott werden somit wiederholt. Es wird aber auch hinzugefügt, dass der Heilige in der Verborgenheit eines Klosters außerhalb der Stadt verweilt. Während allerdings in der Vita von einem *monasterium* (*sedens in monasterio in secretiori parte in oppidi Veronensis*) die Rede ist, wird im Offizium ein Gebetshaus (*oratorium*) erwähnt. Zeno ist somit in einem verborgenen Teil eines Gebetshauses mit seinen Exerzitien beschäftigt: *in secretiori parte oratorii.*

Während die erste Nokturn mit dem Bild von Zeno abschließt, der in der Verborgenheit eines kleinen Gebetshauses der Askese nachgeht und sich dann an die Bekehrung der Stadt durch das unermüdliche Predigen macht, erscheint der Heilige in der zweiten Nokturn als aktiver Seelsorger und Exorzist. Die zweite Nokturn verläuft im Gegensatz zur ersten und, wie später zu zeigen sein wird, zur dritten, ohne bemerkenswerte textliche oder inhaltliche Resonanz zwischen den Psalmen und den Antiphonen sowie zwischen den Lesungen und Responsorien. Allerdings wird in der Historia auf bestimmte Aspekte der Figur und Biographie von Zeno insistiert. Zum einen wird Zeno in A4 und R4 für seine Wortgewandtheit und sein eifriges Leben besungen: Er ist leutselig und mild und kümmert sich um die Gläubigen, die zu ihm kommen. Zum zweiten wird er in A5 und R5 während des Fischens porträtiert. Diese auf den ersten Blick eher unscheinbare Stelle verweist allerdings auf einen wichtigen Aspekt der Modellierung des Heiligen im Offizium, denn Zeno wird nicht nur, wie oben angesprochen, in der Liturgie mit einem Propheten, sondern als Apostel dargestellt. Die Profilierung Zenos als Apostel zieht sich wie ein roter Faden durch das ganze Offizium und vollzieht sich gerade in der Darstellung von Zeno als Angler. Gleich mehrmals, und zwar in den A5 und A9, in L3 und L5 und nochmal im R5, erscheint Zeno mit dem Fischen beschäftigt. Es ist vor allem A9 mit dem dazugehörigen Psalm 23, der diese Idee bildlich entwickelt: Der Heilige erscheint hier erneut während des Angelns: A9 *Sacerdos Dei Zeno sedebat super lapidem*, nur wird diesmal die Parallele zu der apostolischen Tätigkeit explizit: *et artis apostolicae documenta sequens piscabatur in flumine*. Das Bild wird auch in dem der A9 folgenden Psalm 23 wiederaufgenommen, in dem eine ähnliche fluviale Bildlichkeit angewendet wird: Ps 23, 2–4: „ipse super maria fundavit eum et super flumina praeparavit eum. Quis ascendit in montem Domini aut qui stabit in loco sancto eius? Innocens manibus et mundo corde“. Die Figur von Zeno, welcher über den Fluss emporsteigt, auf einem Stein sitzt (*super lapidem*) und dort der apostolischen Tätigkeit nachgeht, bekommt in der performanzbedingten Interaktion mit Psalm 23 einen biblischen Hintergrund. Bereits in der ersten Nokturn war Zeno als Apostel profiliert worden, aber dort mehr durch seine Predigertätigkeit. Im Vers von R2 (*In omnem terram sonus exiit conversationis eius et sanctitas luculenter emicuit*) war die Predigertätigkeit Zenos mit einem Auszug aus dem Offizium für das Fest eines Apostels beschrieben worden. Auch wird deutlich, dass die Vita die Quelle für die Auswahl dieses Textes darstellt – der Vers bezieht sich auf eine Stelle der Vita, die in der folgenden L3 vorkommt. So ergibt sich erst im liturgischen Kontext eine Verbindung zu den Festen für die Apostel. Gerade im Antiphonar XCVIII(92) wird der Vers nicht nur im Zeno-Offizium, sondern auch in gleicher liturgischer Funktion im Offizium für das Commune apostolorum,[241] in den Offizien für Petrus und für Paulus[242] und als Responsorium auch in den Offizien für Johannes Evangelista und für Petrus[243] eingesetzt. Auch die weitere Überlieferung des liturgischen Gesanges zeigt, dass er sowohl als Vers als auch als Responsorium oder Antiphon einheitlich für die Apostel besetzt wurde, und zwar wahrscheinlich schon aufgrund des ursprünglichen Kontexts des Textes, der nämlich im Brief des Paulus an die Römer (Röm 10, 18) und dort als Zitat des Psalms 18, 5 vorkommt. Zeno wird also nicht nur wie in der zweiten und dritten Nokturn als Angler und Menschenfischer dargestellt, auch für seine Tätigkeit als Prediger, der das Wort Gottes auf Erden verbreitet, wird er, wie in R1, mit den Aposteln verbunden.

Der dritte Aspekt, der in der zweiten Nokturn eingeführt und in der dritten sowie in den Antiphonen der Laudes fortgeführt wird, ist Zenos Darstellung als Exorzist. Zenos Auseinandersetzung mit dem Teufel wird in A6 und R6 sowie in A7 und R8 geschildert: Der Heilige besiegt den Teufel mit einem Exorzismus und rettet die besessene Tochter des Gallienus. Der Sieg Zenos in der Auseinandersetzung mit dem Teufel wird bereits gegen Ende des antiphonalen Teils der zweiten Nokturn im Zusammenspiel zwischen A6, dem Psalm und dem Versikel erzählt. A6 bezieht sich mit dem Satz *hominem, quem Deus creavit* auf die Idee des darauf folgenden Psalmes, Psalm 8, in dem es auch um die Schöpfung des

[241] CAO 6289 „In omnem terram exivit sonus eorum, et in fines orbis terrae verba eorum“, ebd., S. 74.
[242] CAO 7014 ebd., S. 254.
[243] CAO 6918 ebd., S. 231.

Menschen durch Gott geht: Der Mensch wird nicht nur von Gott geschaffen, sondern nimmt auch eine privilegierte Position innerhalb der Schöpfung ein, er ist deren Krönung (Ps 8, 6–7: „minuisti eum paulo minus ab angelis, gloria et honore coronasti eum et constituisti eum super opera manuum tuarum"). Die Idee von Psalm 8, nach dem der Mensch die Krönung der Schöpfung darstellt, wird dann im Versikel wieder aufgenommen, diesmal aber in Bezug auf die besondere Position des Heiligen, welcher von Gott gekrönt wurde: V *Posuisti Domine super caput eius coronam de lapide pretioso.*

Als siegreicher Exorzist erscheint Zeno, wie erwähnt, auch in der dritten Nokturn. Der antiphonale Teil der letzten Partie der Matutin öffnet sich erneut während der Auseinandersetzung des Heiligen mit dem Teufel: Die Worte, mit denen Zeno den Teufel vertreibt (*Non te permittit Dominus aliquid agere adversus servum suum*), werden durch einen Vers des folgenden Psalms 14 wiederaufgenommen: „et obrobrium non accepit adversus proximos suos". Die Interaktion zwischen dem siegenden Exorzisten und dem durch die Psalmen vorgegebenen biblischen Rahmen wird auch im Versikel betont, das den psalmischen Teil der dritten Nokturn abschließt. Der letzte Teil des Psalms 23, 7–10

> 7 Attollite portas, principes, vestras, et elevamini, portae aeternales, et introibit rex gloriae. 8 Quis est iste rex gloriae? Dominus fortis et potens, Dominus potens in praelio. 9 Attollite portas, principes, vestras, et elevamini, portae aeternales, et introibit rex gloriae. 10 Quis est iste rex gloriae? Dominus virtutum ipse est rex gloriae.

> 7 Machet die Tore weit und die Türen in der Welt hoch, dass der König der Ehren einziehe! 8 Wer ist der König der Ehren? Es ist der Herr, stark und mächtig, der Herr, mächtig im Streit. 9 Machet die Tore weit und die Türen in der Welt hoch, dass der König der Ehren einziehe! 10 Wer ist der König der Ehren? Es ist der Herr Zebaoth; er ist der König der Ehren.

wird hier wieder aufgenommen: *Amavit eum Dominus et ornavit eum, stolam gloriae induit eum, et ad portas paradisi coronavit eum.* Der antiphonale Teil der dritten Nokturn schließt also mit dem Bild eines siegenden Heiligen, der bei den Toren des Paradieses von Gott gekrönt wird. So ergibt sich eine Verbindung mit den Bildern der Antiphonen der Laudes, in denen Zenos Sieg über den Teufel und seine erfolgreiche Bekehrung der Bevölkerung besungen werden.

Vielleicht passend zu der Idee der Laudes, die dem Lob Gottes gewidmet sind,[244] wird in der Benedictus-A ein doppeltes Lob Gottes und des Heiligen auf eindringliche Weise besungen: Der triumphierende Zeno, der gerade die Krone von Gallienus bekommen hat (*acceptam beatus Zeno coronam a rege*), welche als Symbol des Sieges des Heiligen über den Teufel und seine Herrschaft über die Stadt zu verstehen ist, ruft zum Lob Gottes: *Si Dominus operatur excelsa ipsi perpetuae laudes referantur et gloria.* Bereits vor den Laudes wurde die Zenogeschichte in den Responsorien und Lesungen der dritten Nokturn zu Ende erzählt. Während die Lesungen den ganzen Text der Vita unterbringen und somit die Geschichte

[244] Vgl. Pascher: Das Stundengebet, S. 225–226.

von Zeno im Ganzen erzählen, bricht die Narration der Responsorien in R8 ab, und zwar an dem Punkt, an dem Zeno den Teufel aus der Tochter von Gallienus vertreibt und dieser Verona verlässt. Weder die Schenkung der Krone durch Gallienus, noch die Bekehrung der Stadtbevölkerung durch Zeno werden in den Responsorien der Matutin erwähnt. Stattdessen endet die Matutin in R9 mit einer direkten Ansprache an Zeno: Er wird von seinem Diener (*servulos*) um Gehör und Erbarmen gebeten. R9 beendet somit die Matutin nicht einfach inmitten der Narration, sondern schließt viel mehr den Rahmen, der in R1 durch den Hinweis auf die Präsenz des Heiligen geöffnet worden war (R1 *Hic est...*). Auch an dieser Stelle wird deutlich, dass es im Offizium um mehr als um die Erzählung der *gesta* des Heiligen ging. Vielmehr wird der Aspekt der Präsenz des Heiligen im Rahmen der liturgischen Feier stark gemacht: Er kann von den feiernden Klerikern um Hilfe angerufen werden.

Darüber hinaus ist zu beobachten, dass Zeno durch das ganze Offizium hindurch nur unterschwellig als Bischof charakterisiert wird. Das Attribut *episcopus* wird vermieden und es werden lediglich an drei Stellen Formulierungen verwendet, die auf Zenos Rolle als Bischof anspielen; in der Magnificat-Antiphon: „Damals erblühte Zeno sehr durch die Ehre des Bischofsamtes" (*Dum Zeno pontificatus honore valde polleret*); in A2, wo er als Hirte (*pastor in populis*) erscheint – eine Formulierung die sich auch im Offizium für Gregor den Großen und im Commune eines Bischofs finden lässt,[245] und zuletzt in R1, wo Zeno als heiliger Vorsteher (*sacer antistes*) charakterisiert wird. Viel deutlicher tritt hingegen Zenos Charakterisierung als einfacher Priester hervor. Modelliert auf dem Vorbild des *beatus vir* der Psalmen und eines Apostels tritt Zeno dezidiert als Priester und Exorzist auf. Diese Profilierung des Heiligen wird zum einen in den Bezeichnungen deutlich, die im gesamten Offizium verwendet werden, um Zeno zu beschreiben. Oft wird er als *sacerdos Dei* (1×), *Christi sacerdos* (3×) und *sanctus Christi confessor* (3×) bezeichnet. Auch Formulierungen wie *vir Dei* (1×) und *beatus Zeno* (5×) werden im Vergleich zum Attribut *episcopus* deutlich bevorzugt.[246] Ebenso sind die Tätigkeiten, denen sich der heilige Priester in der Historia widmet, weni-

[245] CAO 4673 *Sacerdos et pontifex, et virtutum artifex, bonus pastor in populo, qui placuisti Domino* Hesbert: Corpus Antiphonalium Officii, S. 448.

[246] Zum Vergleich: Syrus von Pavia: CAO 6224 *Beatus pontifex Syrus, et Ticinensium civium mirabilis doctor, in coelis perenniter exsultat, qui primus Liguriae partes catholicae fidei praeclaris fulgoribus illustravit*; CAO 6724 *Felix namque es, almifice pontifex Syrus, et omm laude dignus, qui extremos ad occasus Italiae fines pretiosae fidei gemmis primus condecorasti.* V *Ora pro populo, interveni pro clero, et pro plebe postula*; CAO 6972 *Insignis pontifex Syrus dum Lodensium oppidum ingressus est, turba ad eum plurima convenit, in qua divino fultus auxilio a nativitate caecum illuminavit.* Eusebius von Vercelli: 6208 *Beatus Eusebius, pontifex et martyr, in fide Christi perseverans, hodie terrae corpus beatam coelo animam intulit*; CAO 7775 V *Vinctis manibus post tergum, beatus pontifex et martyr Eusebius verberibus caesus est ab Arianis.* Barbatus von Benevent: CAO 6818 *Hic est Barbatus, egregius pontifex, quem Omnipotens tanta gratia donare dignatus est, ut imperio ex obsessis corporibus daemones pelleret, et colla ardua Creatori subderet.* Martin: CAO 7076 *Laudabilis et praeclarus pontifex, sapiens negotiator Martinus, data partem chlamydis accepit regna coelorum, ideo gloriosus exsultat inter omnes sanctos.*

ger für einen Bischof, sondern eher für einen einfachen Priester typisch. Sie sind nicht nur alltäglich, sondern weisen möglicherweise auch auf den Weihegrad hin, den Zeno vor seiner Benennung als Bischof innehatte: Neben dem Angeln, das Zenos Modellierung als Apostel deutlich macht, erscheint Zeno am häufigsten mit der Vertreibung des Teufels beschäftigt und ist so deutlich als Exorzist zu erkennen. Darüber hinaus werden seine asketische Lebensweise (das Fasten und Beten im *oratorium*) und die Verdienste, die er durch eine solche Lebensweise erreicht, betont.

Mit dieser Charakterisierung von Zeno, der als einfacher Priester und nicht nur als Bischof profiliert wird, ist auch das Ausbleiben jeglicher Erwähnung der Stadt Verona verbunden. Weder die Stadt noch ihre Bürger noch die Idee einer Veroneser Kirche werden im Offizium des 10. Jahrhunderts thematisiert. Verglichen mit der spätmittelalterlichen Texttradition des Offiziums und anderen Offizien für oberitalienische Heilige ist dies besonders auffällig. In den Handschriften des Zeno-Offiziums aus Cividale zum Beispiel wird an mehreren Stellen ein direkter Bezug zu Verona hergestellt (vgl. Kapitel 3.3.1, Edition der Historia im *cursus romanus* S. 58–72). Dort wird die Veroneser Kirche dazu aufgefordert, sich zu freuen, da sie von einem solchen Helfer (Zeno) gestützt und von einer solchen Gnade gestärkt ist: *Exsultet magno gaudio Veronensis ecclesia tali freta subsidio et fulcita clementia.* Auch in den erwähnten Offizien für heilige Gründer von oberitalienischen Diözesen wird auf ähnliche Weise wie in Cividale ein direkter Bezug zur Stadt hergestellt, sei diese bloß namentlich erwähnt oder auch, genau wie in Cividale, zum Jubeln aufgerufen. Pavia und seine Bürger erlangen zum Beispiel durch ihren Vorsteher Syrus selbst Berühmtheit: „O quam gloriosi sunt Ticinicolae cives, quibus talis ac tantus praesul est datus; nam et beatum Syrum invitabant dicentes: „Ingredere, pater desiderabilis, ingredere, nobisque callem pande ad atria vitae ducentem aeternae."[247]

Außerdem finden sich in den Offizien, in denen der Heilige als *episcopus* oder *pontifex* beschrieben wird und die Beziehung zu Stadt in den Vordergrund gerückt wird, Hinweise auf die Berühmtheit des besungenen Heiligen. Darin wird er häufiger mit Adjektiven wie *insignis* und *praeclarus* und Verben wie *illustrare* (verherrlichen, berühmt machen) charakterisiert. Möglich ist, dies vor einem patriotischen Hintergrund zu interpretieren: Der berühmte Heilige macht mit seinem Wirken die Stadt nach innen und nach außen ruhmreich. Auch dieser Aspekt fehlt gänzlich in der frühesten Historia für Zeno. Die im Verona des 10. Jahrhunderts performierte Historia präsentiert Zeno nicht als patriotischen Heiligen oder als ruhmreichen Vorsteher für die Stadt und ihre Bürger, sondern profiliert ihn als einfachen Exorzisten, der sich intensiv der Askese an einem ver-

[247] CAO 4062. Siehe zum Beispiel auch: CAO 2145 *Delectare gaudiis, gloriosa urbs Papia, quia veniet tibi ab externis montibus exsultatio; non vocaberis minima sed copiosa in finitimis civitatibus.* CAO 3528 *Iussu consors beati Eusebii tribus annis, beatus Gaudentius post ipse Vercellensem corroboravit ecclesiam.* CAO 5365 *Vere cognoscent omnes quia sanctus Apollinaris est gloriosus martyr in civitate Ravenna, praestans beneficia in Christo credentibus, alleluia.*

borgenen Ort widmet und nach dem Vorbild der Apostel in Seelsorge und Predigt tätig ist. Aufgrund seines verdienstvollen und eifrigen Lebens stieg er zum Bischof auf.

Zusammenfassend lässt sich festhalten, dass Zeno in seinem frühesten Offizium ein deutlich erkennbares individuelles Profil erhielt und als asketisch lebender Priester mit niederen Weihegraden dargestellt wurde. Der so charakterisierte Heilige wurde durch die Performanz des Offiziums einer bestimmten Verehrungsgemeinschaft in der Liturgie vor Augen geführt, nämlich den Klerikern des Veroneser Domkapitels. So ergibt sich die Frage, warum diese Profilierung so und nicht anders vorgenommen wurde und ob diese Profilierung mit dem intendierten Publikum des Heiligen zusammenhing. Um diese Frage zu klären, ist es sinnvoll, diese Verehrergemeinschaft und die sie betreffenden historischen Vorgänge im 10. Jahrhundert zu untersuchen.

4.2.4 *Klerikerleben in der* Veronensis ecclesia *im 10. Jahrhundert unter Bischof Rather*

Die Verehrergemeinschaft am Dom bestand, wie bereits geschildert wurde (vgl. Kapitel 4.1.2) aus den Klerikern, Priestern, Diakonen und Subdiakonen, die zu der *schola sacerdotum Veronensis ecclesiae* gehörten. Sie waren also nichts anderes als die Mitglieder des Kapitels des Domes,[248] und damit eine unter vielen Klerikergemeinschaften, die im städtischen wie im außerstädtischen Raum von Verona angesiedelt waren.[249] Die hauptsächliche Aufgabe der Kleriker des Kapitels war das Verrichten des liturgischen Dienstes an der bischöflichen Kathedrale, Santa Maria Matricolare, bei der sie an Hochfesten offizierten, also wenn der Bischof die Liturgie leitete. Feste Einkommen aus Kirchen und Besitzungen in der Stadt und Provinz bildeten das finanzielle Vermögen des Kapitels, das vom bischöflichen Besitz getrennt war. Dies bedeutete nicht nur, dass die Kleriker ihr Vermögen in Eigenverantwortung verwalteten, sondern auch, dass sie – zumindest teilweise – räumlich und finanziell unabhängig vom Bischof waren. Dieser Drang zur Autonomie, der mit Ratold bereits im 9. Jahrhundert begann, kulminierte im 12. Jahrhundert mit der Unterstellung des Kapitels unter die direkte Aufsicht des Patriarchen von Aquileia.[250] Eine solche Autonomie des Kapitels bedeutete natürlich auch, dass den Bischöfen von Verona nur begrenzte Mittel zur Verfügung standen, um die Kleriker zu kontrollieren, da sie über keine finanziellen Druckmittel verfügten. Dies war nur ein Aspekt, wenn auch wahrscheinlich der wichtigste der Veroneser Kirchenstruktur, an dem sich Rather im 10. Jahrhundert störte.

---

248 Vgl. Forchielli: Collegialità di chierici, S. 67.

249 Die Kirchen der Provinz werden in den Urkunden als *plebes* (it. *pievi rurali*) identifiziert. Vgl. ebd., S. 103–104.

250 Vgl. Pio Paschini: Le vicende politiche e religiose del Friuli nei secoli nono e decimo, in: Nuovo Archivio veneto 21, 1911, S. 37–88; 399–432, hier: 426.

Über das Kapitel und die Situation der Veroneser Kleriker berichtet uns Rather in drei Werken, die er während seiner dritten Amtsperiode in Verona zwischen 962 und 968 verfasste: zum einen in einem Brief an Bischof Hubertus von Parma vom November 963; zum anderen in dem als *Synodica* bekannten Sendbrief, den Rather während der Fastenzeit 966 allen Klerikern der Diözese zusandte und schließlich im *Judicatum*, einem Dekret vom November 967. Diese Texte sind vor allem deswegen interessant, weil sie Auskunft über das Reformprogramm geben, dem Rather das Kapitel unterziehen wollte, und das den historischen Subtext für seine Historia für Zeno liefert.

Aus dem Brief, den Rather 963 an Bischof Hubertus von Parma schickte und der mit dem in der Handschrift Laon, Bibliothèque municipale, Ms. 274 überlieferten Titel *De contemptu canonum* bekannt geworden ist, wird deutlich, dass Rather mit den Zuständen am Domkapitel nicht zufrieden war und einige Missstände sah:

> Et ut ad nostra, id est, pro nefas, sęcularia redeam, cum rarissime videas gratis aliquos aut timore aut confoederari amore, unde te verebitur, cui nihil vales auferre, unde amabit, cui nihil potes conferre? Si ergo ad episcopum nihil de rebus pertinet, quibus clerici vivere debent, aut ipse eis non debet ut animalem ita et corporalem dare in tempore tritici mensuram, et si, ut actus continent apostolorum, non dividitur singulis ab episcopo vel quolibet alio ab eodem ad id officium instituto, prout cuique opus est, sed ipsi clerici dividunt inter se, prout quilibet eorum potentior est, et non iuxta consuetudinem aliarum ecclesiarum omnibus ecclesiae clericis, sed iuxta propriam voluntatem solis diaconibus et presbyteris, debent, quę Veronensi ecclesiae collata sunt, cedere, ut ditati videlicet habeant, unde contra episcopum suum valeant rebellare, et ut dominentur ceteris et ad sui auxilium per potestatem possint eos, cum volunt, compellere et iuramentum alteri, quem illi scilicet attraxerint, episcopo fidelitatis fecisse iubere et, si non oboedierint, de ecclesia eos eicere posse, ut habeant quoque, unde filiis uxores, filiabus adquirant maritos, vineas et campos, postremo unde mammonę iniquitatis sine intermissione valeant deservire, subdiaconi, acoliti et ceteri in ordine clerici quid debent agere, unde vivere, pro qua re militare ecclesię, excubias custodire, flagella pro discendis litteris saltem perferre [...].[251]

> Und um zu unserem Anliegen zurückzukommen, nämlich zum Weltlichen: da du nur sehr selten Menschen siehst, die ohne den Zwang der Furcht oder Liebe zusammenkommen, weswegen soll sich jemand vor dir fürchten, dem du nichts wegnehmen kannst, oder weswegen soll dich jemand lieben, dem du nichts schenken kannst? Wenn der Bischof nicht über die Mittel verfügen kann, mit denen die Kleriker leben müssen, oder wenn derselbe ihnen nicht einen spirituellen und körperlichen Lohn zur richtigen Zeit geben muss, und wenn es nicht, wie die Apostelgeschichten erzählen, vom Bischof oder irgendeinem anderen, den der Bischof beauftragt hat, zwischen den Einzelnen geteilt wird, soviel wie es jedem Einzelnen zusteht, sondern die Kleriker es selbst unter sich verteilen, und zwar je nachdem welcher stärker ist als der andere, und wenn sie das, was für die Veroneser Kirche zusammengetragen wurde nicht gemäß dem Brauch aller anderen Kirchen allen Klerikern der Kirche, sondern gemäß dem eigenen Willen nur den Diakonen und den Presbytern abgeben müssen, so dass sie so bereichert etwas besitzen, wodurch sie gegen ihren Bischof rebellieren können und die anderen beherrschen

[251] Rather von Verona: Briefe, S. 76–77.

können und sie diese durch ihre Macht zu ihrer Unterstützung zwingen können, und so dass sie diese nötigen, wie sie wollen und sie zwingen können, einem anderen Bischof, den sie nämlich gerufen haben, Treue zu schwören, und, wenn die Kleriker nicht gehorchen, sie auch aus der Kirche herausjagen können, und auch so dass sie die Mittel haben, um ihre Söhne mit Frauen zu verheiraten und um ihre Töchter zu verheiraten, so dass sie Weinberge und Felder, und zuletzt die Brust der Ungerechtigkeit ohne Unterbrechung saugen können, was sollen die Subdiakone, die Akolyten und die anderen tun, wovon sollen sie leben, für welchen Lohn sollen sie den kirchlichen Dienst verrichten, Liturgie feiern, bei der Ausbildung den Stab erleiden?

Zum einen kritisiert Rather darin das Verwaltungssystem des Vermögens des Kapitels. Er ärgert sich darüber, dass nicht ihm, dem Bischof, die Verteilung der Güter zustand, die er je nach Bedarf („prout cuique opus est“) aufgeteilt hätte, sondern dass diese von den Klerikern unter sich verteilt wurden. Ärgerlich fand er vor allem, dass die Kleriker in der Verteilung der Einkommen ungerecht vorgingen: nur die mächtigeren Diakone und Presbyter bekamen alles, für alle anderen blieb nichts übrig. Diejenigen, die die meiste Mühe im liturgischen Dienst (militare ecclesie, excubias custodire) und wegen der Ausbildung (pro discendis litteris) aufbringen mussten, bekamen keine Belohnung und kein Entgelt. So wurden Diakone und Presbyter reich, während die Kleriker mit den niederen Weihegraden in Armut leben mussten.

Zum Zweiten kritisiert Rather auch die Missstände, die diese ungerechte Vermögensverteilung mit sich brachte, und zwar vor allem, dass die Kleriker in keiner Weise das Zölibat respektierten. Reiche Kleriker konnten sich private Wohnungen leisten, heirateten, und hatten sogar Nachwuchs, dem sie ihren Besitz, also eigentlich Kirchengüter, vererbten. Aber auch die Kleriker der niederen Grade waren unkeusch. Sie seien, so schreibt er in einem anderen Brief, eben aufgrund ihrer Armut gezwungen, Frauen zu nehmen.[252] Außerdem beklagt Rather, dass die Kleriker sich in Lebensstil, Bekleidung und Erscheinung so sehr an das säkulare Leben angepasst hätten, dass sie kaum von einem Laien zu unterscheiden gewesen seien.[253]

Darüber hinaus war Rather auch mit der Ausbildung der Kleriker unzufrieden, die ihm besonders am Herzen lag.[254] Als er den Klerikern des Kapitels der Kathedrale befohlen hatte, eine Prüfung der Bildung der *titularii* – das heißt der Kleriker, die in den städtischen Kirchen von Verona offizierten – und der Kleriker der Provinz durchzuführen, hätte er festgestellt, dass die Kleriker des Kapitels selbst nicht gut ausgebildet waren. Auch wenn die für die Prüfung zuständigen Kleriker berichtet hatten, dass nichts Schlechtes zu finden gewesen sei, hatte Rather herausgefunden, dass die Priester nicht einmal das Apostolische Glaubensbekenntnis auswendig konnten:

[252] Vgl. Ep. 29, ebd., S. 165–166.
[253] Ebd., S. 101.
[254] Vgl. Sarah Hamilton: The Practice of Penance, 900–1050, London 2001, S. 66.

Ihr erinnert euch, ich weiß, dass ich befahl, dass die Erzpriester und die Erzdiakone zusammen mit den Kanonikern der Kathedrale – alle anwesend – zwei Tage lang ohne mich alle Pfarreien besuchen und Abfragungen machen sollten, und dass sie mir am dritten Tag berichten und erklären sollten, was zu korrigieren sei. Dies wurde getan. Als ich saß, fragte ich ab, was getan wurde. Der Befragte antwortete, dass ihr bezüglich der Psalmen und Ähnliches gefragt hattet und dass, Gott sei Dank, nichts Schlechtes gefunden worden war. [...] Wozu soll also eine Synode gehalten werden, wenn ihr nichts mehr gefunden hattet, das zu korrigieren war? Als ich sie aber über den Glauben befragte, fand ich heraus, dass viele nicht einmal das apostolische Glaubensbekenntnis rezitieren konnten.[255]

Es sei gerade dieser Umstand gewesen, der Rather dazu bewegt hätte, sich an alle Kleriker der Diözese zu wenden und ihnen eine schriftliche Mahnung zu schicken, eben die kurz nach dem Brief an Hubertus verfasste *Synodica*: „Bei dieser Gelegenheit wurde ich gezwungen, eine Mahnung an alle Priester zu verfassen."[256]

In dieser 966 verbreiteten Schrift entwarf Rather ein umfassendes Reformprogramm, das er in einer Linie mit den in der älteren *Admonitio synodalis*[257] ausgelegten Prinzipien entwickelte. In der *Synodica* wurden die Kleriker unterwiesen, so dass sie „das Volk durch gutes Beispiel unterrichten sollten."[258] Der Bischof versuchte somit nicht nur auf die Kleriker, sondern durch sie auch auf die Laienbevölkerung erbaulich einzuwirken.[259] Die primären Adressaten der Schrift sind allerdings seine Kleriker. Sie sollen nach dem kanonischen Gesetz leben: Sie sollen keine Frauen haben, sondern neben der Kathedrale wohnen, um ihre liturgische Pflicht pünktlich und ehrfürchtig verrichten zu können.[260] Ihre Gebärden sollen sauber und passend sein, ebenso die Kirchen- und Altarausstattung: auf jeden Fall soll jede Kirche ein „missalem plenarium", ein „lectionarium" sowie ein „antiphonarium" besitzen.[261] Das Singen sollen die Kleriker gut beherrschen, und auch Lesungen und Gebete sollten „singulariter distincteque" gesprochen werden.[262]

Drei weitere Punkte fügt Rather außerdem eigenständig zu der *Admonitio* hinzu, die ihm besonders wichtig zu sein scheinen. Zum einen besteht er darauf,

---

255 „Recolitis namque, cognosco, me praecepisse, ut duobus diebus archipresbyter et archidiaconus me absente advenientes cum ordinariis omnibus pariter residentibus discuterent, die tertia emendanda mihi omnia recitarent. Factum est. Residens interrogavi, quid actum fuisset. Respondit, cuius intererat, vos inquisisse de psalmis et huiusmodi et, Deo gratias, non malum adeo invenisse. [...] Unde igitur synodus ageretur, nil amplius, quod emendaretur, invento? Sciscitatur itaque de fide, illorum inveni plurimos neque ipsum sapere symbolum, qui fuisse creditur apostolorum [...]", Rather von Verona: Briefe, S. 144–145.

256 „Hac occasione synodicam scribere omnibus presbyteris sum compulsus [...]", ebd., S. 145.

257 Vgl. Hamilton: The Practice of Penance, S. 64.

258 „[...] bono exemplo Dei populum erudire [...] studeatis", Rather von Verona: Briefe, S. 129.

259 „Rather gave his sermon an educational aspect, seeking through his clergy to promote the proper observance of the Christian life by the laity [...]", Hamilton: The Practice of Penance, S. 65.

260 Vgl. Rather von Verona: Briefe, S. 130.

261 Ebd., S. 131.

262 Ebd., S. 134.

dass nur Männer, die ein Mindestmaß an Bildung genossen haben, als Priester geweiht werden dürfen:

> Über diejenigen, die geweiht werden sollten, solltet ihr wissen, dass ich sie auf keinen Fall befördern werde, es sei denn, sie wurden für eine gewisse Zeit entweder in unserer Stadt oder in irgendeinem Kloster oder bei einem Lehrer ausgebildet und es sei denn sie sind ein wenig gebildet, so dass sie des kirchlichen Dienstes für würdig gehalten werden können. [263]

Auf diesen Punkt besteht Rather später im gleichen Brief erneut: „Niemand von euch soll ohne meine Erlaubnis einen Priester weihen, weder einen, der stottert, noch einen, der zu schwer verletzt ist oder einen, der nicht ausgebildet werden kann."[264] Der Bischof plädiert außerdem für eine brüderliche Verteilung der Ressourcen unter den Klerikern nach dem Vorbild der Apostel.[265] Das Einkommen soll nun „nicht in Feldern und Weinbergen, sondern in Scheffeln und in Sechsteln",[266] also detailliert, aufgeteilt werden. So sollen die Einkommen aus den Besitzungen verteilt und nicht die einzelnen Eigentümer an die Kleriker abgegeben werden. Zum Dritten betont er nochmals die Wichtigkeit des Fastens und schildert ausführlich die Formen der sexuellen Enthaltsamkeit und der Enthaltung von Speise und Trank. Diesem Thema werden über 28 Zeilen des Briefes gewidmet.[267]

Auch wenn Rather sich in dieser Schrift an alle Kleriker der Diözese wandte und somit Reformbedarf auf allen Ebenen der Veroneser Kirche diagnostizierte, wird durch ein ein wenig später verbreitetes Dekret, das *Judicatum*, klar, welches das wahre Ziel der Reformbemühungen des Bischofs war, nämlich das Domkapitel von Verona und darin insbesondere die Kleriker mit den niederen Weihegraden. Mit diesem Dekret versuchte der Bischof in November 967 sein

---

263 „De ordinandis pro certo scitote, quia a nobis nullo modo promovebuntur, nisi aut in civitate nostra aut in aliquo monasterio vel apud quemlibet sapientem ad tempus conversati fuerint et litteris aliquantulum eruditi, ut idonei videantur ecclesiasticae dignitati", ebd. Dabei erwähnt er drei Formen der Ausbildung, die in Verona und in Oberitalien während des 10. Jhdts. offensichtlich offen standen. Eine Ausbildung konnte nach Rather entweder in einer Kathedral- oder Klosterschule erlangt werden, aber auch eine private Form des Unterrichts, nämlich bei einem „weisen Mann" („apud quemlibet sapientem") scheint möglich gewesen zu sein.

264 „Clericum nemo vestrum sine licentia faciat nostra, nullus balbum vel ultra mensuram blesum, nullus eum, qui de litteris durum habet sensum", ebd., S. 137.

265 „Bezüglich euren Eigentums, ihr solltet euch gegenseitig vertrauen und es gemeinschaftlich teilen, egal ob dies klein ist oder groß, und ihr solltet nicht vergessen, was der Apostel sagte, nämlich dass niemand seinen Bruder im Geschäft oder bezüglich etwas anderem betrügen soll, da Gott über all diese Dinge urteilt, sowie ich euch schon sagte und bezeugte" („De ipsa vero, que ad vos pertinet, fidem inter vos habetote et communiter eam dividite, sive sit magna sive sit modica, scientes apostolum dixisse: Nemo circumveniat in negotio, id est causa aliqua, fratrem suum, quoniam vindex est Dominus de omnibus his, sicut praediximus vobis et testificati sumus"), ebd., S. 136–137.

266 „non per campos tamen et vineas, sed per modios atque sextaria". Vgl. Cervato: Raterio di Verona, S. 264.

267 Vgl. Rather von Verona: Briefe, S. 136–137.

Reformprogramm in die Tat umzusetzen. Im *Judicatum* wird zunächst noch einmal auf die Situation der Kleriker mit den niederen Weihegraden (lat. *minores clerici*) aufmerksam gemacht:

> Ich habe festgestellt, dass diejenigen, die die größten Mühen in der Kirche auf sich nahmen, auch gleichzeitig so arm waren, dass sie ohne Pause sich beklagten und auch wegen der Armut zur widerrechtlichen Weihe eilten, um ein bisschen wirtschaftliche Erleichterung, aber mit größtem Schaden für ihre Seele, zu finden, weil ihr Alter sie fortschreiten ließ, und weder ihre Bildung ihnen half noch ihre Tüchtigkeit sie auszeichnete. [268]

Diese Kleriker mit den niederen Weihegraden waren regelrechte „liturgical functionaries",[269] diejenigen, die liturgische Pflichten erfüllten und somit auch die größte Mühe auf sich nahmen. Ungeachtet dieser Tatsache waren sie aber auch diejenigen, die wegen der Gier von Presbytern und Diakonen in Armut leben mussten. Aufgrund ihrer Armut wollten sie daher gegen die Regeln möglichst rasch zu der Priesterweihe kommen, und konnten sich nicht dem Erlangen einer angemessenen priesterlichen Ausbildung widmen. So waren sie gezwungen, sich die Priesterweihe nicht rechtens zu beschaffen und litten infolgedessen unter dem Mangel an Wissen (*scientia*) und Redlichkeit (*probitas*),[270] der damit einherging.

Rathers Lösung für diese Missstände war einfach aber einschneidend: die Kleriker mit den niederen Weihegraden mussten aus der Abhängigkeit von den anderen Klerikern (lat. *maiores*) gelöst werden. Rather intervenierte gerade an den Stellen, an denen diese Abhängigkeit perpetuiert wurde, und zwar zum einen durch eine korrektere Verteilung des Einkommens des Kapitels und zum zweiten durch eine Reform des Umgangs mit der Priesterweihe.[271] Presbyter und Diakone verwalteten nämlich, wie bereits erwähnt, nicht nur das Einkommen des Kapitels und verteilten dies ungerecht unter sich selbst, sondern sie entschieden auch, ob und wann ein Priester der niederen Weihegrade in die höheren Grade aufgenommen werden durfte. Auch konnten sie bewirken, dass ein minor clericus aus dem Kapitel ausgeschlossen und so zur vollständigen Armut verurteilt wurde. Um dies zu vermeiden, entschloss Rather, dass den Minores ein unabhängiges Einkommen[272] und eine eigene Kirche, die in der Nähe des Domes gelegene Santa

---

268 „Considerans itaque, qui maiorem in ecclesia laborem et fortiorem sustineret adeo paupertatem, ut sine intermissione murmurarent et ob inopiam ad sacros ordines inlegaliter etiam accedere festinarent, ut aliquid ex his cum detrimento quoque animae maximo invenirent subsidii, cum nec aetas utique eos admitteret nec scientia commendaret nec morum probitas illustraret [...]", aus: Fritz Weigle: Urkunden und Akten zur Geschichte Rathers in Verona, in: Quellen und Forschungen aus italienischen Archiven und Bibliotheken 29, 1938, S. 1–40, hier: S. 26–27.

269 Borders: The Cathedral of Verona, S. 62.

270 Siehe Fußnote 267.

271 Vgl. Cervato: Raterio di Verona, S. 177.

272 Dieses setzte sich aus den Einnahmen aus Santa Maria Consolatrice und anderen Kirchen und Besitzungen in Verona und der Provinz zusammen, zum Beispiel Santa Maria in Stelle, San Procolo, einem Bauernhof (*casale*) im Sala-Tal und so weiter. Siehe: Weigle: Urkunden und Akten, S. 28.

Maria Consolatrice, zustehen sollte. Die Minores – insgesamt zweiunddreißig[273] – sollten sich selbstständig um die Verwaltung und brüderliche Verteilung ihres Einkommens kümmern. Außerdem sollten sie einen unter den Minores und von ihnen selbst ausgewählten Praepositus wählen, der das Vermögen zu verwalten hatte und dafür mit einem kleinen Obulus belohnt wurde.[274] Außerdem verhinderte Rather, dass die Maiores den Ausschluss anderer Priester aus dem Kapitel bewirken konnten: Falls einer der Minores als Rache aus dem Kapitel ausgeschlossen werden sollte, konnte er sich nach Santa Maria Consolatrice zurückziehen und dort den liturgischen Dienst verrichten, für den er aus dem getrennten Vermögen der Minores entlohnt werden sollte.[275]

Rathers Maßnahmen erlaubten so den Minores, deren Lebensunterhalt nun gesichert wurde, sich auf die Feier der Liturgie[276] und auf die Ausbildung zum Priester zu konzentrieren:[277]

> Die Begründung betont nicht nur die Wichtigkeit des religiösen Dienstes, sondern auch die Wichtigkeit des Lernens. Von dieser Perspektive kann Rathers Maßnahme nicht nur als Gründung einer Bruderschaft der Priester mit niederen Weihen, sondern auch als eine Neuordnung der Schule und der Beginn der Schule der Akolyten interpretiert werden.[278]

Rathers institutionelle Erneuerung ist in der Geschichtsschreibung als Gründung einer Bruderschaft der Priester mit niederer Weihe („congregazione del clero inferiore")[279] bekannt und aus kirchenhistorischer Perspektive untersucht worden. Rather bewirkte allerdings mit seinen Maßnahmen, wie Cervato im erwähnten Zitat auch bemerkt, noch mehr als nur die Einführung einer neuen Form der kirchlichen Organisation. Vielmehr gab er den Klerikern der niederen Weihegrade neben einem sicheren Einkommen auch einen Lebensort (Santa Maria Consolatrice) sowie eine korporative Identität und das Bewusstsein für die eigene Funktion und Aufgabe. Das Verrichten der Liturgie, das Engagement für die priesterliche Ausbildung sowie ein Leben im Einklang mit Rathers Ideal eines auf

---

273 Vgl. Weigle: Urkunden und Akten, S. 27; Cervato: Raterio di Verona, S. 264.

274 Vgl. Weigle: Urkunden und Akten, S. 28.

275 Vgl. ebd., S. 30.

276 „Seine Neubewertung hätte das Ausgeben der kirchlichen Besitzungen vermieden und den Besuch der Liturgie seitens der Kleriker mit niederen Weihen befördert" („La sua rivalutazione avrebbe contribuito a evitare la dilapidazione dei beni ecclesiastici e avrebbe favorito l'assiduità al servizio liturgico da parte dei chierici inferiori"), Cervato: Raterio di Verona, S. 182.

277 Eine schola ist bei Santa Maria Consolatrice übrigens ab 1020 bezeugt, vgl. Miller: The Formation of a Medieval Church, S. 49–50.

278 „La motivazione sottolinea non solo l'importanza del servizio divino ma anche l'importanza del momento dello studio. Da questo punto di vista l'atto di Raterio è interpretabile, oltre che come costituzione di una congregazione del clero inferiore [...] anche come una riorganizzazione della schola e un inizio di quella che sarebbe stata nel futuro la scuola degli accoliti", aus: Cervato: Raterio di Verona, S. 267.

279 Ebd.

Askese und Seelsorge konzentrierten priesterlichen Alltags sind die Bestandteile dieser Identität.

Die thematischen Schwerpunkte und die Profilierung des Heiligen in seiner Historia für Zeno legen nun nahe, dass für Rather auch die Liturgie ein Mittel zur Implementierung seines Reformprogramms darstellte. Zeno war von Rather bereits als nachzuahmendes Vorbild in Anspruch genommen worden: er bezeichnete ihn als *specialis patronus noster* und bezog sich an mehreren Stellen auf Zenos Schriften als Rechtfertigung der eigenen Positionen.[280] Mit der oben geschilderten Profilierung des Heiligen in der Historia ging Rather aber noch einen Schritt weiter: er nahm den Heiligen in der Historia als Paradigma nicht nur für den Bischof selbst, sondern auch eines guten Klerikers in Anspruch, und bot ihn als nachahmbares Vorbild den Klerikern der Kathedrale von Verona an.

Zum einen wird Zeno zum Modell des perfekten Priesters gemacht. Er lebt ein asketisches Leben und widmet sich der Predigt und der Seelsorge: A3 *continuis ieiuniis et orationibus crebris* [...] *aditum praedicationis*; R2 *in omnem terram sonus exiit conversationis eius*. Das Aufsteigen zum bischöflichen Amt wird als Belohnung für seine Bemühungen und Verdienste charakterisiert: M-A1 *Dum Zeno pontificatus honore, meritis non paucis existentibus*; R2 *ad hoc pertingere meruit ut pastor in populis per sacerrimam vitam efficeretur*; Vers von R4 V *Ita existebat alacer ut mox ad eum properaret relictis idolis Domino crederent Ihesu Christo*.

Auch Zenos Gelehrsamkeit wird im Offizium betont: A2 *Probitatis et scientae iugibus incrementis* und R1 *Zeno quem gemina virtute Dominus sanctitatis et sapientiae decoravit*. Es soll auch nochmal daran erinnert werden, dass in beiden Fällen die textlichen Partien der Historia auf Rather selbst zurückgehen, der den Text der karolingischen Vita modifizierte und mit der Änderung im Offizium übernahm oder den liturgischen Gesang stets ex novo kreierte. Daher ist es nicht verwunderlich, dass auch in Rathers Dekret *Judicatum* auf die Wichtigkeit der priesterlichen Ausbildung mit den identischen Begriffen hingewiesen worden war: *nec scientia commendaret nec morum probitas illustrare*.

Die Historia präsentiert Zeno aber nicht nur als ideales Modell eines Priesters, das es zu imitieren gelte. Das Offizium hat auch eine starke identitätsbildende Funktion, denn die Kleriker konnten sich selbst in dem von Rather modellierten Heiligen erkennen. In der liturgischen Medialisierung erkennen die Minores, die als „liturgical functionaries"[281] tatsächlich diese Historia sangen, in Zeno nicht nur den berühmten ersten Bischof der Stadt Verona, sondern auch einen Priester, ja sogar einen Kleriker mit niederem Weihegrad, einen einfachen Exorzisten. So

---

[280] Es seien hier nur ein paar Beispiele genannt: „ut Zeno sanctus affirmat [...]", vgl. Rather von Verona: Briefe, S. 95; „et cum specialis noster doctor atque prouisor beatus utique zeno dicat in sermone utique quem de iuda filio iacob et thamar nuru ipsius elegantissime composuit quod [...]", ebd., S. 129; „sicut et in sermone de adventu domini beatus Zeno dixit [...]", vgl. François Dolbeau: Ratheriana III. Notes sur la culture patristique de Rathier, in: Sacris erudiri 29, 1986, S. 151–221.

[281] Borders, The Cathedral of Verona, S. 62.

wie sie, die für das Verrichten des liturgischen Dienstes zuständig waren, verbringt Zeno seine Zeit vertieft im Gebet. In der Historia wird auch an dieser Stelle der Wortlaut der Vita modifiziert. Während in der Vita von einem *monasterium* die Rede ist (L2 *sedens in monasterio in secretiori parte in oppidi Veronensis*), wird im Offizium ein Gebetshaus (*oratorium*) erwähnt. Zeno betet im verborgenen Teil dieses Gebetshauses: *in secretiori parte oratorii*.

Die Differenz mag klein sein, ist aber wichtig. Zum einen verschwindet im gesungenen Teil des Offiziums das Wort *monasterium*, was die Möglichkeit einer Assoziation mit dem Zenokloster in Verona ausschließt. Zum zweiten erscheint das Wort *oratorium*, das im Frühmittelalter eine kleine Kirche oder Kapelle bezeichnet, die einer weiteren Kirche oder einem Kloster unterstellt war. Ein *oratorium* war außerdem explizit dem alltäglichen liturgischen Dienst gewidmet und dem breiteren Publikum nicht zugänglich.[282] Hier wird deutlich, dass durch diese Modifizierung des Vitatextes in der Historia bewusst eine Anspielung auf die kleine Kirche Santa Maria Consolatrice gemacht wurde, die dank Rather den Minores zur privaten Nutzung zu Verfügung stand und deren Einkommen den Lebensunterhalt der Kleriker liefern soll.

Sogar der Zustand von relativer – im Vergleich zu dem Wohlstand der Presbyter und Diakone des Kapitels – Armut entspricht Zenos asketischem Leben und spiegelt die Lebenseinstellung eines echten Priesters wider, ganz im Gegensatz zu den Maiores, die wegen ihres säkularisierten Lebensstils kaum noch von einem Laien zu unterscheiden waren. Gekonnt verwandelt Rather so in seiner Zeno-Historia die einfacheren Lebensumstände der Minores in etwas Positives und Erstrebenswertes. Die entgegengesetzten Werte, die Rather in Verona vorfand – Kleriker, die sich wie Laien verhalten, heiraten, keine Liturgie singen, nach Reichtum und gesellschaftlichem Ansehen streben –, werden von Rather konterkariert und somit berichtigt.

Ähnlich geht Rather im Übrigen im Fall seiner eigenen Gesellschaftsgruppe, nämlich mit Bischöfen, vor. In der Schrift *Qualitatis coniectura* will Rather selbst Material für seine Kritiker liefern („Cavillatoribus igitur materiem [...] ipse uti ministrem“[283]). Er tadelt, kritisiert und erniedrigt sich selbst für all die Aspekte, unter denen er mit seinem Verhalten nicht tut, was von jemandem in seiner Position erwartet wird: Er ist arm, er pflegt die richtige Art des Liturgie-Singens, er liest zu viel, er züchtigt sich selbst ständig, er kümmert sich nicht um seine Bekleidung und im Allgemeinen um Reichtümer, er verachtet den *curulis pontificalis* (die Liege eines Bischofs), sondern schläft lieber auf dem Boden:

---

282 Vgl. Du Cange, Charles du Fresne: Glossarium mediae et infimae Latinitatis. 10 Bde., Niort 1883–1887, t. 6, Sp. 054b. Online unten: http://ducange.enc.sorbonne.fr/ORATORIUM1 [04. September 2018].

283 Rather von Verona: Qualitatis coniectura cuiusdam, Ratherii utique Veronensis, hrsg. von Peter L. D. Reid (Corpus Christianorum. Continuatio Mediaevalis 46), Turnhout 1976, S. 117.

Er kritisiert die Gewohnheiten, das Lesen und Singen der Kleriker. Er nennt eine widerrechtliche Ehe ‚Ehebruch'; er behauptet, dass das Gesetz eher als der Brauch zu achten ist. Er verbietet die Arbeit am Sonntag. Er befiehlt, dass diejenigen, die Gott dienen, ihm auf ungewohnte und nie dagewesene Art dienen. Er hört nicht auf, zu rufen: „Einer kann keine Belohnung ohne Mühe bekommen." Wohin also mit den Königen? Wohin mit all den Reichen? Wohin mit all denen, die hedonistisch leben? Weil laut ihm steht der Himmel nur für die Leidenden offen. Er hat immer die Nase in einem Buch, er hört nicht auf darüber zu reden. Er tadelt jeden: „Sei kein Freund von jemandem, dessen Gewohnheiten dem Teufel gefallen." Aber wen lobt er, dieser Mann, der sich die ganze Zeit tadelt? [...] Was soll ich noch sagen? Sein Leben unterscheidet sich von dem Leben derjenigen, die Ehre anstreben. Seine Kleider sind vernachlässigt, seine Schuhe dreckig, er sammelt keine Teppiche, ihm fehlt das Tischgeschirr; er ist zufrieden mit bescheidenen Möbeln und anderen Geräten, er möchte keine wertvollen Dinge. Nicht des Ruhmes oder Ehre ist in ihm zu finden. Er wäscht sich die Hände und den Mund vor und nach dem Essen, das Gesicht selten. Möglicherweise war er in seiner Heimat Zimmerman, daher interessiert er sich nicht für Ehre, obwohl uns anders gesagt worden ist, wir glauben, dass er der Sohn eines Tischlers ist; daher ist er so erfahren und willig, Kirchen zu bauen und zu renovieren, und daher dreht er jeden Stein um und trägt sie oft selber. Er schämt sich nicht, sich wie ein Sklave zu benehmen; er verachtet die Bräuche eines Herrn so sehr, dass er viel öfters auf dem Boden als im Gemach des Bischofs schläft [...].[284]

Die Selbstkritik ist natürlich ein literarischer Kunstgriff, mit dem Rather ein durchaus positives Porträt von sich selbst zeichnet. Er, Rather, steht trotz scheinbarer Kritik und Tadel überlegen da, eben weil er nicht das erwartete (aber verdorbene) Verhalten der Bischöfe seiner Zeit an den Tag legt, sondern in der Nachfolge der Apostel und letztendlich Jesu steht. Mit Jesus vergleicht sich Rather, wenn er sich vor seinen Klerikern als Sohn eines Zimmermannes bezeichnen lässt (*forsitan in patria sua fuerat bacularis, ideo illi honor omnis est uilis, longe aliter sepe licet dictum sit frequentius nobis filius carpentarii*), in klarer Anlehnung an Matthäus, 13, 55 und Markus 6, 3.

Bemerkenswerterweise tadelt Rather sich selbst für gerade jene ‚Verfehlungen', die er versucht, in den Minores anzuspornen, nämlich apostolische Armut, regel-

284 „Mores, lectionem et cantum carpere clericorum. Inlegale coniugium nominat adulterium; legem quam consuetudinem dogmatizat tenendam. Opus servile interdicit dominica die. Non modo inusitato sed et inaudito commissos deo iubet modo servire. ‚Ad magna premia perveniri non posse nisi per magnos labores' non quiescit clamare. Ubi ergo reges, ubi omnes divitiis affluentes, indeque voluptuose vadunt viventes? Calamitosis nam iste solum regnum Dei hoc dicto promittit. Nasum semper tenet in libro; inde garrire non cessat omnino. Redarguit omnes ‚contiguus nulli cuius mores placeant illi.' Quem vero laudat, qui seipsum semper vituperat? [...] Quid plura? Dissimilis omnibus honorem curantibus eius est vita. Vestibus non comitur, calceamentis turpatur, scamnalia non querit, mensalibus indiget; lectisterniis mediocribus ceteraque supellectile delectatur, pretiosa non ambit. Nil quod gloriae pertineat in eo videtur, nil quod honori. Manus tantum et labia cibum lavat sumpturus, necnon et sumpto, faciem raro. Forsitan in patria sua fuerat bacularis, ideo illi honor omnis est vilis, longe aliter sepe licet dictum sit frequentius nobis filius carpentarii; ideo tam gnarus tamque voluntarius est basilicas struendi uel restruendi, lapides semper versat et reversat, ipse eos sepe convectat. 3. Quae sunt servorum, agere non dedignatur; dominorum, adeo negligit usum, ut posthabito curule pontificali frequentius decubet humi [...]", aus: ebd., S. 117–118.

mäßiges Besuchen und korrektes Ausführen der Liturgie, Zölibat, Anstrengung und Ausbildung („Nasum semper tenet in libro“[285]). So wie die Feinde Rathers, die ein standesgemäßes, aber aus seiner Sicht verdorbenes Leben führten, standen auch die Maiores für das Verderben und die Umkehrung der apostolischen Werte und des priesterlichen Lebensstils. Die Minores hingegen, die wie er selbst nicht die verdorbenen Bräuche der Zeit beachten, sondern dem ursprünglichen apostolischen Modell folgten, waren die guten Kleriker und wahren Nachfolger Zenos.

Gerade dieses Bewusstsein sollte die Historia mit ihrer Profilierung von Zeno als eifrigen aber einfachen Sacerdos den Minores vermitteln. Neben dem Predigen und der Unterweisung durch Briefe und Schriften, die der Bischof den Klerikern zum aufschreiben und memorieren mitgab („Istud cum et mediante quadragesima illis atque memorie mandanda dedissem“[286]) tritt somit auch Liturgie als weitere Maßnahme Rathers für die Implementierung seiner Reform hervor. Wahrscheinlich war die Historia auch eines der wirkungsvolleren dieser Mittel, da sie im Gegensatz zu anderen Texten ein großes Identifikationspotential besaß. Dank der medialen Erhöhung in der liturgischen Performanz gewannen die aus dem hagiographischen Material ausgewählten und gezielt aufbereiteten Themen des Offiziums an Aussagekraft, weil sie im Alltag ihrer Akteure einen Platz fanden. Die Charakterisierung Johnsons der Situation der Franziskaner im 13. Jahrhundert beschreibt dies meines Erachtens auch gut:

> [...] the person who performs in liturgy participates, through the body, in the interpretation of meaning which is accepted by the individual, yet determined by another. Indeed, liturgical action goes beyond simply recognizing a particular meaning; it substantiates and enfleshes the predetermined understanding of communal identity. Words uttered in liturgical settings bring institutional realities such as identity into being with tangible force.[287]

Die Konstitution einer klar verortbaren und durch Aufgaben und Lebensstil definierten Verehrergemeinschaft war nicht nur für die Minores relevant. Auch nach außen, gegenüber den Maiores, wurde durch Rathers Reform die Verehrergemeinschaft der Minores abgegrenzt. Wenn die Minores das apostolische Lebensideal verkörperten, gerieten nun die Maiores in den Zwang, ihren – vom Bischof so häufig kritisierten – abweichenden Lebensstil zu rechtfertigen. Aber auch gegenüber den Laien und weiteren in Verona aktiven Verehrergemeinschaften war dies eine klare Botschaft: In den Klerikern des Domes, die im Einklang mit dem ursprünglichen apostolischen Modell lebten, sind die wahren Nachfolger des Sacerdos Zeno zu suchen. Der Heilige sollte somit nach innen als Vorbild für die Kleriker und nach außen als Abbild der Kleriker dienen.

---

[285] Ebd., S. 117.

[286] Rather von Verona: Briefe, S. 145.

[287] Timothy J. Johnson: Choir Prayer as the Place of Formation and Identity Definition: The Example of the Minorite Order, in: Miscellanea francescana 111, 2011, S. 123–135, hier: S. 134.

4.3 *Im Dienste des Klosters*

Bis zum Ende des 10. Jahrhunderts war der Prozess der Profilierung von Zeno und der damit verbundenen Identitätsbildung der Verehrergemeinschaft der Kleriker des Domes abgeschlossen. Bischof Rather hatte diesen Prozess mit der Einführung einer neuen Zenovita und der darauf basierenden Historia ermöglicht und gelenkt. Darin wurde Zeno als Modell eines guten Priesters stilisiert. Die Kleriker, die wie die Minores nach diesem Modell lebten, konnten sich in dem Heiligen wiederfinden und als seine Nachfolger verstanden werden. Hier aber, am Dom von Verona und bei den Kanonikern, endete Zenos Geschichte nicht. Seit dem Beginn des 9. Jahrhunderts gab es in Verona eine weitere Gemeinschaft, die sich auf Zeno beziehen konnte, nämlich die Mönche des Klosters San Zeno Maggiore.

Mitten in einem langobardischen Begräbnisareal außerhalb der Stadt hatten zu Beginn des 9. Jahrhunderts Bischof Ratold und Pippin, der König von Italien, ein benediktinisches Kloster an dem Ort gegründet, wo vermutlich eine Grabkirche für Zeno gestanden hatte.[288] Die wichtigsten Bezugspersonen für das Kloster waren also seit dessen Gründung der König beziehungsweise Kaiser und der Veroneser Bischof. Dies änderte sich auch im weiteren Verlauf der Klostergeschichte im 9. und 10. Jahrhundert nicht: Nachdem für die ersten fünfundzwanzig Jahre nach der Gründung des Klosters wahrscheinlich der Bischof selbst die Abtei geleitet hatte, findet sich erst 833[289] der Hinweis auf einen Abt. Die eigentliche Aufsicht über die Abtei scheint allerdings weiterhin beim Bischof geblieben zu sein, und auch Stiftungen und Zuwendungen seitens der Könige und Kaiser dem Kloster gegenüber gingen im Früh- und Hochmittelalter meistens auf eine Initiative des Bischofs zurück, wie die urkundliche Überlieferung zeigt. Die Veroneser Prälaten stilisierten sich dabei immer wieder als Unterstützer und Überwacher des Klosters.[290] So ermöglichte auch Bischof Rather 968 die Erneuerung des Klosters mit von ihm dafür eingeworbenem Geld.[291]

Gleichzeitig war dieses Verhältnis aber auch von einem Konflikt bestimmt, der sich immer wieder entzündete und an die Oberfläche gelangte. Zentraler Punkt dieser Problematik war der Anspruch, den sowohl der Bischof als Hausherr der „domus sancti Zenonis“, als auch das Kloster als Grabkirche von Zeno auf den selben Heiligen erheben konnten. Vor allem ging es hierbei um die Frage nach

[288] Vgl. Franco Segala: L'abazia benedittina di San Zeno. Breve profilo storico 2, 1984, S. 35–40, hier: S. 35. Anti merkt dazu an, dass diese Gründung perfekt in Linie mit der karolingischen Politik war: das Kloster konnte, auch dank seiner strategischen Position auf dem Weg nach Norden und Westen, einen sicheren Ort für die Könige auf Reisen anbieten. Vgl. Anti: Verona e il culto, S. 56–57. Entgegen der früheren Forschungsmeinung (zum Beispiel Fainelli: L'abbazia di und neulich auch Miller: The Formation of a Medieval Church, S. 123, Fußnote 27) gab es vor der Translation der Reliquien von Zeno kein Kloster, sondern eine Kirche.

[289] Vgl. Fainelli: Codice diplomatico Veronese, S. 193, Nr. 140.

[290] Vgl. Anti: Verona e il culto, S. 56–58.

[291] Vgl. Fainelli: L'abbazia di, S. 59.

den Spenden „ad sanctum Zenonem“.[292] Mit diesem Begriff wurden bereits in den frühmittelalterlichen Urkunden die Spenden bezeichnet, die von den Gläubigen an den heiligen Zeno entrichtet wurden. Dabei zeigt die urkundliche Überlieferung, dass die Institutionen, die diese Spenden erhielten, im Laufe der Zeit wechselten: Zu Beginn des 9. Jahrhunderts spendeten Laien zum Fest des Heiligen im Dezember. Diese Spenden kamen wiederum zu gleichen Teilen dem Bischof und den (Dom-)Klerikern zu.[293] Dies erklärt sich dadurch, dass das Fest im Dezember die bischöfliche Weihe von Zeno würdigte und daher vor allem den Bischof und seine Kleriker betraf. In einer Urkunde von 815 wurde hingegen geregelt, dass die „oblationes, quae fiunt ad sanctum Zenonem“[294] prinzipiell den Mönchen zustünden, abgesehen von einem Teil, den sie dem Bischof und den Kanonikern weitergeben sollten. Diese Unentschiedenheit spiegelt sich auch in den Quellen wieder, in denen die Spenden als ungenügend an den Heiligen gerichtet bezeichnet sind. Erst 820 erscheint in einer Urkunde des Bischofs Ratold eine deutlichere Bezeichnung dieser Spende: Es handelt sich um die Spenden „ad corpus“, also an die Reliquien des Heiligen, die im Kloster lagen. Bemerkenswerterweise scheint in dieser Urkunde Ratold allerdings den Klerikern die Spende zugesprochen zu haben.[295]

Es kann nicht verwundern, dass diese Situation aufgrund der Konkurrenz um finanzielle Ressourcen ein erhebliches Konfliktpotential beinhaltete. Dieses eskalierte offenbar im Laufe des 9. Jahrhunderts so sehr, dass sich Ludwig der Fromme 866 einschalten musste, um zwischen den Klerikern des Domes und dem Abt von San Zeno zu schlichten.[296] Es sei nämlich zu einem großen Streit („grandis altercatio“[297]) zwischen den Klerikern und dem Abt gekommen, und zwar gerade bezüglich „der Kirche des seligen Zenos, wo sein Körper begraben liegt“[298] und bezüglich „der Spende, die jedes Jahr das Volk dieser Kirche mit frommem Sinn anbietet.“[299] Die Kanoniker behaupteten, Anspruch auf die Hälfte dieser Spenden zu haben, die Mönche hätten aber dieses Abkommen nicht respektiert, indem sie die Spenden in größerem Umfang für sich behalten hätten. Ergebnis dieser Schlichtung war, dass sich die Parteien erneut auf die Teilung der Spenden einigten. Die Mönche wurden dabei auch gewarnt, die Spenden, die das ganze Jahr über an den Heiligen adressiert werden, ohne jegliche Entwendung („sine omni subtractione“[300]) aufzubewahren. Auch sollten sie bereit sein, auf ihre Weihe zu schwören, dass sie nichts entwendet hatten („ita ut si necessum fuerit iurati dicant per suum sacerdotium quod nichil exinde minuassent“[301]). Die Mönche waren offensichtlich bereits zu diesem Zeit-

[292] Fainelli: Codice diplomatico Veronese, Nr. 102, S. 130.
[293] Ebd.
[294] Vgl. ebd., Nr. 117, S. 154.
[295] Vgl. ebd., Nr. 122, S. 163.
[296] Hier und im Folgenden vgl. ebd., Nr. 233, S. 356–357.
[297] Ebd., S. 356.
[298] „de ecclesia beati Zenonis ubi corpus eius humatum quiescit“, ebd.
[299] „et de oblatione que ad eandem ecclesia devota mente populus offert annualiter“, ebd.
[300] Ebd., S. 357.
[301] Ebd.

punkt eigentlich nicht mehr einverstanden, die Spenden an den Körper des Heiligen, den sie schließlich bewahrten, mit dem Bischof und den Kanonikern zu teilen, und konnten nur durch die kaiserliche Autorität dazu verpflichtet werden.

Zusammenfassend lässt sich beobachten, dass das Zenokloster im 9. und 10. Jahrhundert in einem ambivalenten und konfliktträchtigen Verhältnis zu den Bischöfen und den Klerikern des Veroneser Domes stand: Auf der einen Seite war das Kloster auf Initiative des Bischofs hin gegründet worden und war lange auf dessen Unterstützung angewiesen gewesen; auf der anderen Seite konkurrierten beide Institutionen um die Einnahmen aus den Spenden an den Leib des Heiligen, der im Kloster begraben war. Es ist wenig verwunderlich, dass sich diese Ambivalenz auch in den liturgischen Quellen aus dem Kloster niederschlägt.

4.3.1 Die erste Phase: Das Zenokloster und seine liturgische Produktion im späten 10. und im 11. Jahrhundert

Für das frühe Mittelalter hat sich aus dem Zenokloster leider nur eine spärliche liturgische Überlieferung erhalten, nämlich eine Historia und Hymnen für das Zenofest (Depositio) am 12. April. Die Untersuchung des Materials ist außerdem durch die Tatsache erschwert, dass die handschriftliche Überlieferung nicht zeitgleich zur Entstehung der Texte, sondern erst wesentlich später einsetzt: im Fall der Historia sogar mit Codices des 15. Jahrhunderts. Um den Entstehungskontext dieser Quellen untersuchen zu können, ist daher zunächst eine sorgfältige Datierung und Beschreibung des Materials notwendig.

Eine Historia für Zeno entsprechend dem Cursus monasticus wird in einer Gruppe von spätmittelalterlichen Handschriften überliefert. Dazu zählen ein großformatiges Antiphonar (Verona BCi 739 I) und zwei kleinformatige Breviere (Augsburg StStadtB 2° 204 und Kremsmünster SB CC60). Zumindest zwei dieser Handschriften sind explizit mit der benediktinischen Abtei San Zeno Maggiore in Verona verbunden. Auf dem ersten Blatt des großformatigen Antiphonars der Biblioteca Civica findet man den Hinweis, dass das darin überlieferte Material die Gewohnheiten der benediktinischen Mönche von San Zeno widerspiegelt: „Incipit proprium sanctorum secundum consuetudines monachorum ordinis sancti Benedicti in venerabili cenobio sancti Zenonis maioris Verone."[302] Auch das Brevier der Bibliothek von Kremsmünster kann anhand seines Kalenders und der darin und im Corpus der Handschrift als wichtig markierten Heiligenfeste mit San Zeno Maggiore in Verbindung gebracht werden.[303] Hier finden sich nämlich die Angaben für drei liturgische Feste für Zeno: Neben dem Fest des 8. Dezembers, an dem Zenos Bischofsweihe und gleichzeitig die Weihe des Klosters gefeiert wurde, sind auch das Fest des Todestages (am 12. April) und die Translation (21. Mai) zu finden. Dies legt nahe, möglicherweise wenig überraschend, dass

302 Verona BCi 739 I, 1r. Dazu auch: Castiglioni: Note sui codici, S. 409.
303 Vgl. Fill: Katalog der Handschriften, S. 302.

die in diesen Codices überlieferte Historia im Veroneser Kloster für die Feier der Zenofeste – und zwar offensichtlich aller drei – gesungen wurde.

Ein Vergleich der Antiphonen und Responsorienreihe der Historia in der kanonikalen und monastischen Version wurde bereits im Kapitel 4.2.1, Tabelle 1, durchgeführt. Die Ergebnisse dieses Vergleichs seien hier aber der Übersichtlichkeit halber zusammengefasst. Die vergleichende Untersuchung der Struktur der zwei Fassungen der Zenohistoria verdeutlichte, dass die monastische Historia keine vollständig neue Kreation des Zenoklosters war. Viel mehr stellte sie eine Erweiterung der Rather'schen Historia im Cursus romanus dar, die mit gebetsartigen und narrativen Gesängen für den monastischen Gebrauch vervollständigt wurde. Es scheint also, dass der komplette Bestand an Antiphonen der Matutin, die in der kanonikalen Version vorzufinden waren, der Reihe nach übernommen wurde, während die fehlenden vier Antiphonen neu geschaffen oder aus dem Commune übernommen wurden.

Tabelle 3 Vergleich Antiphonenbestand der Historia CR-CM

	Historia *cursus romanus*		Historia *cursus monasticus*
A1	Ab utero	A1	Ab utero
A2	Probitatis	A2	Probitatis
A3	Continuis	A3	Continuis
A4	Affabilis	A4	Affabilis
A5	Dum exercitio	A5	Cum exercitio
A6	Vir Dei	A6	Vir Dei
A7	Beatus Zeno dixit	A7	Beatus Zeno dixit
A8	Miserabilis pater	A8	Miserabilis pater
A9	Sacerdos Dei Zeno sedebat	A9	Sacerdos Dei Zeno sedebat
		A10	*Beate Zeno praesul*
		A11	*Coepitque beatus pontifex*
		A12	*Iuxta Athesis fluvium*
		A13	*Iste est de sublimibus*

Das Gleiche gilt für die Responsorien der Matutin, mit dem einzigen Unterschied, dass hier jeweils das vierte Responsorium jeder Nokturn vervollständigt wurde. Dies scheint bei der Adaptierung von kanonikalen Offizien für den monastischen Cursus ein beliebtes Verfahren gewesen zu sein.[304]

Tabelle 4 Vergleich Responsorienbestand der Historia CR-CM

	Historia Cursus romanus		Historia Cursus monasticus
R1	Hic est	R1	Hic est
R2	Ab utero	R2	Ab utero
R3	In secretiori	R3	In secretiori

304 Vgl. Ferro: Suavissime universorum Domine, S. 63.

R4	Affabilis	R4	*Iuxta Athesis*
R5	Dum in fluvio	R5	Affabilis
R6	Elevata	R6	Dum in fluvio
R7	Festinans	R7	Elevata
R8	Ingrediente	R8	*Beatissimus*
R9	Sancte Zeno	R9	Festinans
		R10	Ingrediente
		R11	*Sacerdos*
		R12	Sancte Zeno

Weitere Gesänge, wie das Invitatorium und die Magnificat-Antiphonen der ersten und zweiten Vesper wurden in der Historia im Cursus monasticus auch modifiziert, die Änderungen sind aber eher ästhetischer Natur (das ursprüngliche Invitatorium zum Beispiel wird durch das hexametrische *Aeternum trinumque*[305] ersetzt) und hätten jederzeit vorgenommen werden können. Sie sind daher für eine Untersuchung der Entstehung der monastischen Historia wenig aufschlussreich.

Interessanter ist die Übernahme der Laudes, bei der nicht nur die Antiphonen-Reihe, sondern auch die Psalmenreihe und die säkulare (und kürzere) Struktur des Morgenlobes mitsamt der säkularen Historia übernommen wurden. Das wird bei einem Vergleich der Standardform der Laudes im monastischen und kanonikalen Cursus mit den Laudes der Historia für Zeno in den monastischen Handschriften deutlich:

Tabelle 5 Vergleich Struktur der Laudes in CR und CM

	Laudes in CM	Laudes in CR	Laudes der Zeno-historia in CM
1	Psalm 66 ohne A	Psalm 92 oder 50 mit A	Psalm 92 mit A *Dominus Iesus Christus*
2	Psalm 50 oder 92 mit A	Variabler Psalm mit A	Psalm 99 mit A *Exsurgens*
3	Variabler Psalm mit A	Psalm 62 und 66 als ein Psalm mit A	Psalm 62 [66 wird nicht expliziert] mit A *Ingrediente*
4	Variabler Psalm mit A	Alttestamentarisches Canticum mit A	Benedicite omnia [Canticum aus Daniel 3, 56–88] mit A *Tenens*
5	Alttestamentarisches Canticum mit A	Psalmen 148–150 als ein Psalm mit A	Psalmen 148 [149–150 nicht expliziert] mit A *Christi namque*
6	Psalmen 148–150 als ein Psalm mit A	/	/

(Tabelle basiert auf Harper, The Forms and Orders, S. 97–98 und Hughes, Medieval Manuscripts, S. 52)

305 Hesbert: Corpus Antiphonalium Officii, Nr. 1020.

Dies bedeutet, dass die Übernahme der kanonikalen Historia durch das Zenokloster auch mit der partialen Übernahme eines säkularen Cursus einherging.

Die Frage nach der Vorlage der monastischen Historia ist also damit rasch geklärt. Weniger offensichtlich ist der Zeitpunkt ihrer Entstehung. Die handschriftliche Überlieferung scheint auf den ersten Blick für die monastische Historia im 15. Jahrhundert zu sprechen, da alle drei liturgischen Codices der zweiten Hälfte des 15. Jahrhunderts angehören. Es gibt aber Hinweise, die darauf hindeuten, dass dieses Offizium bereits seit dem 11. Jahrhundert im Zenokloster in Gebrauch war – doch seit wann? Das von Rather im letzten Drittel des 10. Jahrhunderts geschaffene und am Dom etablierte Offizium (siehe Kapitel 4.2.2) kann bald danach auch im Kloster übernommen worden sein; eine Präzisierung wird jedoch durch die Tatsache erschwert, dass vom einstmals relativ üppigen Bücherbestand der Veroneser Abtei leider wenig übrig geblieben ist, und dass der verstreute Bestand bisher noch nicht gänzlich identifiziert werden konnte.[306] Der älteste Textzeuge der Historia, das Antiphonar des Zenoklosters, stammt aus dem späten 15. Jahrhundert.[307] Die weitere Überlieferung der monastischen Historia und vor allem die Überlieferung außerhalb des Zenoklosters bieten allerdings Indizien dafür, dass das Offizium in dieser monastischen Version schon früher zirkuliert haben musste.

Neben den zwei ebenso wie das Antiphonar aus San Zeno Maggiore aus dem 15. Jahrhundert stammenden Brevieren Augsburg StStadtB 2° 204, das sicher vor 1457 zu datieren ist, und Kremsmüster SB CC 60, das um 1467 angefertigt wurde, sind vor allem die Hinweise von Handschriften aus Aquileia-Cividale wichtig. Die zwei Antiphonare Cividale MAN XLVII und Cividale MAN XXXIV überliefern, da sie für den Gebrauch im Dom von Aquileia angefertigt wurden, eine Historia für Zeno im Cursus romanus. Teilweise wird aber das kanonikale Offizium von Rather mit Gesängen aus der monastischen Tradition der Historia interpoliert. Dies zeigt, dass in Cividale die monastische Version des Offiziums bekannt gewesen sein muss. Diese Codices wurden von ihrem Katalogisator Cesare Scalon ins 14. oder 15. Jahrhundert datiert, sie wurden sicher vor 1433 angefertigt.[308] Auch wenn dadurch der Terminus ante quem nicht wesentlich nach hinten gerückt werden kann, zeigt doch die Verbreitung der monastischen Version der Histo-

[306] Die älteste überlieferte Bücherliste von San Zeno stammt aus dem Jahr 1317 und schließt lediglich 29 Codices ein. Sie enthält allerdings nur die Bücher, die zusammen mit weiteren liturgischen Werkzeugen wie Paramenten, Kelchen, Altarbedeckungen und so weiter in der Sakristei aufbewahrt wurden. Der erste vollständige Bibliothekskatalog ist auf das Jahr 1400 datiert und listet 131 Codices auf. Vgl. Alessia Parolotto: La biblioteca del monastero di San Zeno in Verona, 1318–1770, Verona 2002, S. 7–9. Die älteste Bücherliste ist ediert in Luigi Montobbio: Il più antico elenco di codici del monastero di S. Zeno di Verona (1318), in: Rivista di storia della chiesa in Italia 14, 1960, S. 94–101. Der Bibliothekskatalog von 1400 in Antonio Avena: Guglielmo da Pastrengo e gli inizi dell'umanesimo a Verona, in: Atti dell'Accademia di agricoltura, scienze, lettere, arte e commercio di Verona 82, 1907, 65–73, hier: S. 65–73.

[307] Vgl. Castiglioni: Note sui codici, S. 411.

[308] Scalon / Pani: I codici di Cividale del Friuli, S. 185–187 und S. 158–159.

ria sogar außerhalb Veronas, dass sie vor ihrer Aufzeichnung in der Prachthandschrift des Zenoklosters im 15. Jahrhundert existiert haben muss.

Einen weiteren Hinweis liefert eine Handschrift aus Verona (Verona BC CIX(102)), ein Hymnar aus der zweiten Hälfte des 11. Jahrhunderts, das Spuren des monastischen Offiziums *Dum Zeno pontificatus honore* enthält. Die Handschrift enthält außerdem die ältesten Hymnen für Zeno. Auf Grund der Aufbewahrung in der Kapitelbibliothek der Kanoniker wurde die Handschrift als Produkt des Skriptoriums des Kapitels angesehen.[309] Dass es sich hingegen um ein monastisches Hymnar handelt, bezeugt die Tatsache, dass nach der Kurzlesung und dem Hymnus der Laudes das Singen eines Responsoriums mit seinem Vers vorgesehen war. Dies war eine Praxis, die dem kanonikalen Brauch fremd war, da dort kein Responsorium vor dem morgendlichen Laudes-Hymnus gesungen wurde.[310] Außerdem deutet die Tatsache, dass in der Handschrift die Hymnen am Tag des Todes des Heiligen, dem 12. April platziert wurden, auf eine Provenienz aus San Zeno Maggiore, da dieses Datum für das Kloster wichtig war.[311] Matthew Borders hat in seiner Untersuchung der musikalischen Handschriften des Kapitels von Verona ein plausibles Szenario für den Transfer der Handschrift aus dem Kloster ins Kapitel entworfen, indem er die Hand einiger Nachträge mit einem Mitglied des Kapitels identifizierte:[312]

> Copied in the scriptorium of the abbey of S. Zeno, Cod. CIX may have remained there for as long as a century. During the late twelfth century however, the canons borrowed it for consultation as they were preparing their own hymnal [...]. Upon completing this project, they neglected to return the older book to the monks. From that time onward, Cod. CIX was stored with the other liturgical books in the treasury of the chapter.[313]

Des Weiteren wird diese These von der Tatsache untermauert, dass gerade in der von ihm vermuteten Zeit des Besitzerwechsels der Handschrift (im späten 12. Jahrhundert) das Zenokloster erneut liturgisch produktiv geworden war und, wie später eingehend zu klären sein wird, neben einer neuen Vita, einem Translationsbericht und einem Mirakel-Bericht, auch sein altes Set an Zeno-Hymnen mit neuen ersetzt hatte.

Aber zurück zu der Historia von Zeno und ihrer Einführung ins Kloster. Dieses Hymnar liefert einen wichtigen Hinweis auf eine Verwendung der monastischen Historia im Zenokloster spätestens im 11. Jahrhundert. Auf ff. 89r–90r enthält dieser Codex nämlich den Hymnus für die Vesper des Zenofestes, wo ausweislich des gegebenen Incipits das Responsorium *Ab utero* mit seinem Vers *In omnem terram* vorgesehen war. Dieses Responsorium entstammt der Zeno-Historia, die Rather für die Nutzung am Dom komponiert hatte, die zu diesem Zeitpunkt aber offenbar auch im Kloster verwendet wurde.

---

309 Vgl. Venturini: Vita ed attività, S. 84–86.
310 Vgl. Harper: The Forms and Orders, S. 98.
311 Vgl. Anti: Verona e il culto, S. 94.
312 Vgl. Borders: The Cathedral of Verona, S. 254.
313 Ebd., S. 254–265.

Es kann also als gesichert gelten, dass man im Kloster San Zeno Maggiore bereits in der zweiten Hälfte des 11. Jahrhunderts die Historia aus dem Dom kannte. Auch wenn damit streng genommen nicht belegt ist, dass zu diesem Zeitpunkt die kanonikale Historia mit den Zusätzen erweitert wurde, die in den Quellen des 15. Jahrhunderts überliefert sind, sprechen zwei Gründe dafür. Die überlieferten monastischen Zusätze zeigen, dass sie nicht auf der Grundlage der neuen Vita kompiliert wurden, die, wie später zu zeigen sein wird, in der zweiten Hälfte des 12. Jahrhunderts verfasst wurde. Sie sind also älter als diese Vita und wurden bereits vor dem 12. Jahrhundert im Kloster gesungen. Auch der einfache, fast eucologische Stil und die Inhalte dieser Zusätze zeigen, dass sie von einer älteren hagiographischen Vorlage abhängig sind, die ohne große Änderungen für die Zusätze übernommen wurde. Dies deutet darauf hin, dass die Erweiterung für den monastischen Gebrauch eher eine schnelle Angelegenheit war, die durchaus zum gleichen Zeitpunkt der Übernahme der Historia aus dem Dom geschehen konnte.

Zusammenfassend legen all diese Hinweise nahe, dass die Historia sicher nicht erst kurz vor der Aufzeichnung in den spätmittelalterlichen Codices der Abtei eingeführt worden war. Sie wurde im Zenokloster wohl schon vor dem Verfassen der neuen monastischen Zenovita des 12. Jahrhunderts übernommen und dort bereits im 11. Jahrhundert gesungen, wie die Spuren im Hymnar vermuten lassen. Der handschriftliche Befund aus dem Spätmittelalter deutet also nicht auf ein junges Alter der Historia hin. Viel mehr spricht er für ihre extreme Langlebigkeit. Sie blieb im Gegensatz zu der Vita und den Hymnen, die, wie wir gleich sehen werden, im Laufe des 12. Jahrhunderts neu geschaffen wurden, von dem Moment ihrer Einführung am Kloster bis zu ihrer erneuten Fixierung in den Handschriften des 15. Jahrhunderts – möglicherweise aus Respekt für ihre lange Tradition – unangetastet.

Es ist sogar möglich, dass die Historia bereits im letzten Viertel des 10. Jahrhunderts, und zwar noch zur Zeit des Bischofs Rather, ins Kloster gelangte. Dies legt der historische Kontext nahe. Im letzten Viertel des 10. Jahrhunderts erlebte die monastische Gemeinschaft vor den Mauern der Stadt eine Wiedergeburt. Vermutlich wegen der verheerenden Einfälle der Ungarn war es in dieser Zeit notwendig geworden, Kloster und Basilika umfangreichen Renovierungsmaßnahmen zu unterziehen.[314] Wieder war es Bischof Rather, der die Erneuerung einer religiösen Institution seiner Diözese in die Wege leitete. So erbat er erfolgreich von Kaiser Otto I. eine Geldsumme für die Vollendung der „basilica sancti Zenonis".[315] Das

[314] Vgl. Valenzano: La basilica di San Zeno, S. 9; siehe dazu auch: Anti: Verona e il culto, S. 62–63; Andrea Castagnetti: Dalla caduta dell'Impero Romano d'Occidente all'Impero Romano-Germanico (476–1024), in: Andrea Castagnetti / Gian Maria Varanini (Hg.): Il Veneto nel medioevo. Dalla „Venetia" alla Marca Veronese, Verona 1989, S. 1–80, hier: S. 39. Vgl. auch Miller: The Formation of a Medieval Church, S. 69–70.

[315] Vgl. Rather von Verona: Briefe, Ep. 30, S. 169–170. Rather musste sich zwar kurz darauf gegen die Vorwürfe verteidigen, das ihm von Otto I. anvertraute Geld für den Umbau des Klosters zu anderen Zwecken genutzt zu haben, doch das Kloster war bereits 983 offen-

liturgische Material aus dem Zenokloster deutet nun darauf hin, dass sich diese Wiedergeburt nicht nur auf das bauliche Äußere des Klosters beschränkte, sondern, wie im Fall der Kleriker des Domes, auch mit einer liturgischen Erneuerung einherging. Es ist sehr wahrscheinlich, dass Rather die Zenoliturgie, die im Kloster bisher wahrscheinlich auf unspezifischen Commune-Gesängen basierte, bei dieser Gelegenheit mit dem auf Zeno zugeschnittenen Material aus dem Dom ersetzte. Dazu gehörte wohl neben der Historia auch Rathers Überarbeitung der Zenovita, auch wenn die Überlieferung dieses Textes für das Zenokloster in dieser Zeit nicht bezeugt ist. Darauf deutet die Tatsache, dass, wie wir sehen werden, im 12. Jahrhundert eine neue monastische Vita auf der Vorlage der Vita Rathers (BHL 9007) verfasst wurde. Auch wenn nur eine Handschrift von BHL 9007 aus Verona überliefert ist (das kanonikale Lektionar Paris BN Lat. 9739), muss dem Verfasser der neuen Vita im Zenokloster im 12. Jahrhundert eine Kopie zur Verfügung gestanden haben, die er teilweise abschrieb und veränderte.[316]

Mit diesem Material war also gegen Ende des 10. Jahrhunderts ein auf Zeno zugeschnittenes Set liturgischer Texte für die Nutzung im Kult gegeben. Die Wiedergeburt des Klosters bedeutete also nicht nur die Wiederinstandsetzung verfallener Gebäude, sondern auch die Restitution der monastischen Verehrergemeinschaft, die nun auch ihren eigenen Bezug zu Zeno und somit ihre eigene Identität in der Liturgie entwickeln und behaupten konnte. Hinweise über die Inhalte dieser neuen monastischen Identität sowie über das Profil, mit dem der Heilige nun versehen wurde, liefern die Inhalte des liturgischen Materials aus diesem Kloster.

Zunächst sollen in diesem Zusammenhang die frühesten Hymnen des Zenoklosters analysiert werden, die in Kapitel 3.3.2, ab S. 79, ediert sind (die hier angegebenen Zitate entstammen dieser Edition). Die ältesten überlieferten Hymnen für Zeno finden sich in jenem Hymnar vom Ende des 11. Jahrhunderts, das bezüglich der Verwendung der Historia von Zeno im Zenokloster zu Rate gezogen wurde, nämlich der Handschrift Verona BC CIX(102). Hier werden für das Zenofest am 12. April drei Hymnen vorgesehen, und zwar jeweils ein Hymnus für die Vesper, einer für die Matutin und einer für die Laudes. All diese Hymnen basierten auf unterschiedlichen Vorlagen. Der Hymnus für die Matutin *Iesu redemptor omnium* wird direkt aus dem Commune eines Bekenners übernommen: In der Handschrift findet sich nach dem Incipit *Iesu redemptor omnium* die Anweisung *requiratur in natale confessorum*. Auch der Laudes-Hymnus war zumindest von einem Commune-Hymnus inspiriert, den Hymnus für einen Märtyrer *Deus tuorum militum*. Es ist unklar, ob die Kontrafaktur dieses Hymnus der Profilierung Zenos als Märtyrer diente, da im Text die Vorlage nur vage wiederaufgenommen wird und

sichtlich so weit renoviert, dass Otto II. hier einen Reichstag versammeln konnte und sich sein Nachfolger Otto III. zwischen dem Jahr 996 und 1000 mehrmals in San Zeno Maggiore aufhielt. Vgl. Valenzano: La basilica di San Zeno, S. 9.

316 Dazu mehr in Kapitel 4.3.2.

Zeno viel mehr als Bischof (Strophe 2: *Qui Zenonem episcopum...*) angesprochen wird. Nur der Hymnus der Vesper *Zeno pontifex inclite* wird nicht aus dem Commune entnommen. Auch er wurde allerdings von einer Vorlage adaptiert, die sich nach Farfa lokalisieren lässt und dort für das Fest *Cathedra sancti Petri* verwendet wurde. Die Tatsache, dass auch für ein wichtiges Fest wie das Zenofest im Kloster kaum individualisierte Hymnen verwendet wurden, spricht dafür, dass sie älteren Datums waren und wahrscheinlich nicht erst am Ende des 11. Jahrhundert entstanden, als sie schließlich verschriftlicht wurden. Im Kloster wurden diese Hymnen also lange Zeit gesungen, bevor das sie überliefernde Hymnar in der zweiten Hälfte des 12. Jahrhunderts dem Kapitel geschenkt wurde.[317]

Vor allem im Hymnus der Vesper *Zeno pontifex inclite* wird die Profilierung des Heiligen sichtbar. Darin wird Zeno ausdrücklich für seine Rolle als Bischof zelebriert: Zum einen wird er ausdrücklich als *pontifex* und *pastor* angesprochen. Zum zweiten scheint auch die Tatsache signifikant, dass das Stück in Farfa für das Fest *Cathedra sancti Petri* verwendet worden war und also ursprünglich Peter als erster Inhaber des römischen Bischofsstuhls feierte.[318] Es ist möglich, dass in San Zeno Maggiore gerade dieser Hymnus ausgewählt wurde, weil er die bischöfliche Rolle von Petrus betonte, die nun auch für Zeno in den Vordergrund gestellt wurde. Zeno wird in diesem Hymnus aber darüber hinaus auch als Patron des Klosters (*patronus*) bezeichnet und die Mönche als seine *famuli* (*adesse tuis famulis*) charakterisiert. Die Profilierung von Zeno als Bischof und Patron, die in den Hymnen des Zenoklosters zum Thema wird, zeigt auf der einen Seite, dass zu dieser Zeit das Episkopium eine wichtige Instanz für die monastische Gemeinschaft darstellte und auf der anderen Seite, dass Zeno auch als spezieller Patron der Klostergemeinschaft fungierte. Zu diesem Zeitpunkt wurde daher zwischen diesen zwei Rollen kein Widerspruch empfunden. Allerdings kommt in den monastischen Zusätzen der Historia auch ein weiterer Aspekt des Heiligen ans Licht, der für die Mönche ebenso relevant war.

Die Übernahme der Historia von Rather ging mit der Übernahme eines bestimmten Profils des Heiligen seitens der monastischen Gemeinschaft einher.

---

317 Vgl. Clemens Blume (Hg.): Die Hymnen des Thesaurus Hymnologicus H. A. Daniels und anderer Hymnen-Ausgaben. Pars I Hymni antiquissimi saec. V–XI (Analecta Hymnica Medii Aevi 51), Leipzig 1908, S. 220–221. Auch zwei weitere Hymnaren des 11. Jhdts., Zürich ZB Rh. 82 und Zürich ZB Rh. 91 aus Farfa, die zu einem unbestimmten Zeitpunkt nach Rheinau kamen, überliefern diesen Hymnus. Vgl. Jakob Werner: Die ältesten Hymnensammlungen von Rheinau, in: Mitteilungen der antiquarischen Gesellschaft in Zürich 13, 1891, hier: 84 (x). Der Hymnus wurde auch für andere Heilige verwendet. In einer Handschrift aus Reims des 13. Jhdts. wurde er für Remigius verwendet, in einer Handschrift des 12. / 13. Jhdts. aus Cambrai für Autbertus und in mehreren Handschriften aus Verdun für Vitonus. Ein spätmittelalterliches Brevier, heute in Wien ÖNB 4089, zeugt von einer Nutzung des Hymnus für den Heiligen Benedikt (vgl. http://www.vhmml.us/research2014/catalog/detail.asp?MSID=17466) [25. Juni 2018]. Siehe dazu AH 51, Nr. 190; AH 19, Nr. 448; AH 12, Nr. 151 und 448; AH 4, Nr. 197.

318 Vgl. Michael Buchberger (Hg.): Lexikon für Theologie und Kirche. Bd. 1, Freiburg [2]1957, Sp. 743.

Dieses Profil war vom Bischof ausdrücklich für seine Kleriker entworfen worden und konnte somit für die Kanonikergemeinschaft als Modell verstanden werden. Die Benediktinermönche übernahmen Ende des 10. Jahrhunderts gezwungenermaßen auch dieses Profil von Zeno. Allerdings zeigen gerade die Zusätze, mit denen sie die klerikale Historia für die Nutzung im Kloster adaptierten, den Wunsch, den eigenen Bezug zum Heiligen auszudrücken. Darin wird auf zwei Punkte der Zenobiographie Bezug genommen, die bisher in der kanonikalen Historia keine Rolle gespielt hatten.

Zum einen wird Zeno als Stifter von Kirchen dargestellt. Es wird an mehreren Stellen in der monastischen Historia (siehe Kapitel 3.3.1, S. 73–80) erzählt, dass Zeno den Kaiser nach der Heilung dessen Tochter bittet, in Verona die heidnischen Idole zerstören zu dürfen, um an deren Stelle christliche Kirchen zu errichten. Dies erwähnen A11 und R8.[319] Im Rahmen dieses Kirchenbaus wird im Offizium vor allem eine Kirche hervorgehoben. In A12 wird berichtet, dass Zeno befohlen hätte, neben dem Fluss eine Kirche zu bauen und dass er darin starb.[320] R4 betont außerdem noch ausdrücklicher, dass Zenos Körper in dieser vom ihm erbauten Kirche begraben liegt.[321] An dieser Stelle wird klar, welche Kirche damit gemeint ist. Es geht um das Kloster selbst, denn dort, und dies war dem monastischen Urheber der Zusätze bewusst, lagen Zenos Reliquien immer noch begraben.

Mit der Nennung des Zenoklosters in der monastischen Historia für Zeno wurde zweierlei bewirkt. Zum einen wurde die Verbindung zum Bischof gekappt und das Kloster wurde, eingerahmt in die Bautätigkeit von Zeno, zur Gründung des Heiligen selbst. In diesem Punkt weicht die monastische Historia von der Vorlage der Vita sowie von der urkundlichen Überlieferung ab. Beide zu diesem Zeitpunkt zirkulierenden Zenoviten, und zwar sowohl die des Coronatus[322] als auch Rathers Überarbeitung,[323] hatten in Verwandten von Gallienus die Verantwortlichen für den Bau einer Kirche im Namen des heiligen Zeno identifiziert. Die urkundliche Überlieferung des Frühmittelalters sprach bezüglich der Gründung und Ausstattung eines Zenoklosters sogar von einer Petitio des Bischofs von Verona beim Kaiser.[324] In der Historia hingegen wird die Gründung des Klosters direkt auf Zeno zurückgeführt.

319 A11 *Coepitque beatus pontifex in Verona destruere omnia idola et fabricare Christi ecclesias*; R8 *Beatissimus Christi confessor Zeno petiit a rege ut in urbe Verona destruerentur omnia manufacta idola et conderetur cum omni honore Iesu Christi catholica ecclesia* V *Cumque sanasset filiam regis petiit a rege ut in urbe Verona.*

320 A12 *Iuxta Athesis fluvium iussit beatus Zeno construi oratorium in quo quievit in Domino.*

321 R4 *Iuxta Athesis fluvium iussit beatus confessor Zeno construi oratorium ubi post modum quievit in Domino* V *Ibique sepultus corpore et in caelo spiritus eius.*

322 „in honore Dei et in ipsius sancti sacerdotis, quidam ex genere Gallieni fecit sancto nomini ipsius basilicam haud procul a fluvio", vgl. Sala: Il culto di Zeno nei secoli VIII–IX, S. 31.

323 *in honore dei et ipsius sancti sacerdotis quidam ex genere Gallieni fecit reverendo eius nomini basilicam, haud procul a fluvio*, vgl. Edition, Kapitel 3.3.3, S. 91.

324 Vgl. Fainelli: Codice diplomatico Veronese, Nr. 117, S. 154.

Mit der Nennung der Grabkirche von Zeno wird, zum zweiten, ein für die monastische Gemeinschaft entscheidender Punkt erwähnt, nämlich die Tatsache, dass das benediktinische Kloster auf dem Grab des Heiligen entstanden war. Da der heilige Körper nur an einem Ort, nämlich im Kloster, liegen konnte, konnten nur seine Mitglieder, die Mönche, über die körperlichen Überreste des Heiligen rechtmäßig verfügen und sich als Hüter der Reliquien des Heiligen verstehen.

In diesem Zusammenhang ist es auch relevant, dass das Kloster in der urkundlichen Überlieferung ab 841 mit einem deutlichen Bezug zum Leib und zum Grab von Zeno beschrieben wird.[325] Das Kloster wurde stets als der Ort, „wo sein Körper begraben ruht" („ubi corpus eius humatum quiescit"[326]) bezeichnet. Die Formulierung des vierten Responsoriums der monastischen Historia R4 *ubi post modum quievit in Domino* V *Ibique sepultus corpore et in caelo spiritus eius* ähnelt dem Ausdruck der Urkunde und ist wahrscheinlich nicht zufällig gewählt. Vielmehr wurde sowohl im urkundlichen Bestand als auch in der Liturgie des Klosters die gleiche Idee ausgedrückt. Das Kloster sah in der Tatsache, dass es die Reliquien des Heiligen aufbewahrte, ein Alleinstellungsmerkmal und definierte seine Identität durch den Bezug dazu.

Diese Verbindung zwischen dem Kloster und den Reliquien war aber nicht nur klosterintern relevant, sondern auch nach außen von Bedeutung. Während sie nach innen eine Identifizierung der monastischen Mitglieder mit einer genauen Funktion als Bewahrer der Reliquien ermöglichte, diente sie nach außen der Legitimierung der klösterlichen Ansprüche im Konflikt mit dem Bischof und den Klerikern um die Spenden „ad corpus".

Zusammenfassend lässt sich sagen, dass das liturgische Material des monastischen Zenokultes einer weiteren Verehrergemeinschaft Zenos eine Stimme verlieh. Als das Kloster gegen Ende des 10. Jahrhunderts renoviert wurde, erlebte auch die dort angesiedelte monastische Gemeinschaft eine Wiedergeburt und fixierte ihren Anspruch auf Eigenständigkeit selbstbewusst in der Liturgie. Doch diese Identität war ambivalent und von dem gleichzeitigen Bezug auf zwei unterschiedliche Instanzen bestimmt. Auf der einen Seite bestand eine traditionelle Abhängigkeit vom Episkopium: Viel liturgisches Material kam aus dem Dom und das Kloster blieb dabei Empfänger der liturgischen Produkte des Bischofs. Außerdem wurde vor allem in den monastischen Hymnen für Zeno ein Bild des Heiligen entworfen, in dem er vornehmlich als Patron, aber auch ausdrücklich als Bischof (*pontifex*, *pastor* und *episcopus*) hervortrat und von seiner monastischen Gemeinschaft um Unterstützung gebeten werden konnte. Andererseits wird in den Zusätzen der monastischen Historia ein weiteres Element erwähnt, welches für die Herausbildung der Verehrergemeinschaft im Kloster entscheidend war, nämlich ihr Bezug zu den Reliquien von Zeno, dessen körperliche Überreste im

325 Elisa Anti beobachtet, dass dieser Bezug in den Urkunden ab 905 immer ausgedrückt wurde, vgl. Anti: Verona e il culto, S. 64.

326 Fainelli: Codice diplomatico Veronese, Nr. 233, S. 356.

Kloster lagen und dessen Mönche daher auch die an ihn gerichteten Spenden beanspruchten.

Durch diese Profilierung hatte sich die Identität Zenos allerdings verdoppelt: Während die Gemeinschaft der Kleriker am Dom Zeno als Bischof und Priester verehrte und in dem Heiligen ein Modell erkannte, verehrten ihn die Mönche des an seinem Grab entstandenen Klosters nicht nur für die ihm zugeschriebene Biographie, sondern mehr noch für das, was er für sie war: Ein toter, aber heiliger und daher wirkmächtiger Leib. Die Zusätze der monastischen Historia erscheinen in diesem Zusammenhang nicht nur als selbstbewusste Aussage über das eigene Verhältnis zum Heiligen, sondern auch als Instrument im Konflikt um die wirtschaftliche Nutzung seiner Reliquien.

4.3.2 Die zweite Phase: Weiterhin Konkurrenz und eine neue Profilierung von Zeno

Vorerst blieb es still um die Spenden „ad corpus", die bis zum 11. Jahrhundert in Urkunden nicht mehr erwähnt wurden. In einer Urkunde von 1014 bestätigte Heinrich II., dass die Mönche den Klerikern einen Anteil an den Spenden schuldeten, wobei nicht mehr von gleichen Teilen die Rede war. Dem Bischof und seinen Klerikern sollte nun eine feste Summe zukommen, egal wie viel dem Kloster gespendet wurde, nämlich zwanzig mancusi bzw. fünfzig solidi.[327] Dies wurde in weiteren Urkunden des 11. Jahrhunderts zunächst bestätigt. Gegen Ende des Jahrhunderts lässt sich die Pflicht der Mönche zur Abgabe eines Teils der Spenden an Bischof und Domkapitel nicht mehr fassen. 1084 regelte Heinrich IV.[328] dann, dass die „heilige Gemeinschaft der Mönche"[329] alle Spenden „zum heiligen Leib des sehr seligen und vornehmen Bischofs und Bekenners Christi Zeno"[330] sicher und ohne Störungen besitzen und behalten sollte.[331] Auch bestätigte er, so wie seine Vorfahren vor ihm (zum Beispiel Konrad II.[332]), dass niemand, auch nicht der Bischof, dem Kloster etwas wegnehmen dürfte. Bemerkenswerterweise wurde aber in dieser Urkunde das Recht zur freien Abtwahl des Klosters nicht mehr wie in früheren Urkunden erwähnt. Es scheint also 1084 weggefallen zu sein.

Das Kloster wurde so gegen Ende des 11. Jahrhunderts auf der einen Seite offiziell und vom deutschen Kaiser selbst als rechtmäßiger Besitzer der Reliquien und daher einzelner Empfänger der Spenden „ad corpus" erkannt. Auf der anderen Seite erlangte es dadurch aber noch keine vollständige Emanzipation vom

---

327 Vgl. Die Urkunden Heinrichs II. und Arduins, hrsg. von Harry Bresslau / Hermann Bloch / Robert Holtzmann (MGH DD H II), Hannover 1900–1903, Nr. 309, S. 387–388.

328 Vgl. Die Urkunden Heinrichs IV., hrsg. von Dietrich von Gladiss / Alfred Gawlick. 3 Bde. (MGH DD H IV), Weimar 1952, Nr. 363, S. 482–484.

329 Ebd., „sancta congregatio monachorum".

330 Ebd., „ad sacrum corpus beatissimi egregiique pontificis atque confessoris Christi Zenonis".

331 Ebd., „securiter teneat atque possideat sine ulla inquietudine alicuis persone".

332 Vgl. Die Urkunden Konrads II., hrsg. von Harry Bresslau / Hans Wibel / Alfred Hessel (MGH DD K II), Hannover 1909, Nr. 95, S. 1132–133.

Bischof. Vielleicht aufgrund dieser bleibenden Spannung wurde das Kloster im Laufe des 12. Jahrhunderts erneut aktiv. Es produzierte neue liturgische Texte, die einen deutlichen Schwerpunkt auf die Mirakel des Heiligen legten und somit als letztes Wort im Streit um seine Überreste fungieren sollten.

Der erste Text, mit dem das Zenokloster seine Liturgie erneuerte, ist ein hagiographischer Bericht, der als *Vita beatissimi Zenonis* bekannt ist. Dieser Bericht setzt sich aus zwei klar voneinander unterscheidbaren Teilen zusammen: Im ersten Teil (BHL 9010) wird das Leben von Zeno beschrieben, im anderen (BHL 9011) die Reliquienübertragung und die Wunderwirkung des Heiligen erzählt. Frühere Editoren des Textes, etwa Scipione Maffei und die Bollandisten, waren der Meinung, dass die Teile zwei unterschiedliche Werke darstellten, wenn auch möglicherweise beide auf den gleichen Autor zurückzuführen wären. Daher gaben letztere dem Text auch zwei unterschiedliche BHL-Nummern.[333] Mittlerweile hat sich aber die Ansicht etabliert,[334] dass BHL 9010 und 9011 die zwei Teile eines einzigen Werkes darstellen. Die Gründe dafür sind vielfältig: Nicht nur werden sie öfters als zusammenhängender Text in den handschriftlichen Zeugen überliefert,[335] auch strukturelle und sprachliche Hinweise sprechen für eine einheitliche Komposition der inhaltlich unterschiedlichen Teile.[336] Gerade aufgrund der inhaltlichen Strukturierung des Textes kann man eigentlich sogar von einem dreiteiligen Werk sprechen, das in einen Vita-, einen Translatio- und einen Miracula-Teil unterteilt ist. Auf diesen Aspekt wird später näher einzugehen sein.

BHL 9010–9011 ist, im Vergleich mit weiteren Versionen der Zenovita wie BHL 9001 (Coronatus) und BHL 9007 (Rather), weniger verbreitet. Elisa Anti konnte 2009 lediglich zwanzig Handschriften auflisten, die BHL 9010 und zum Teil auch BHL 9011 überliefern. Aus Antis Liste müssen allerdings mindestens zwei Handschriften[337] gestrichen werden, weil sie nicht diese Version der *Vita Zenonis* überliefern und zwei weitere[338] als nicht identifizierbar gelten, da sie mit inkorrekter Signatur angegeben wurden.[339] Zwei Handschriften liturgischer Natur, die in dieser Arbeit für die Edition herangezogen wurden, sollen zu dieser Liste hinzugefügt werden. Es handelt sich um die bereits erwähnten Breviere Augsburg StStadtB 2° 204 und Kremsmünster SB CC60, welche neben weiteren Elementen für das Stundengebet auch Lesungen enthalten, die aus BHL 9010–9011 stammen. Dazu kommt eine weitere Handschrift, Leipzig UB 1264, die unten noch weiter

---

333 Vgl. Anti: Verona e il culto, S. 98. Auch Golinelli geht von zwei Werken aus, vgl. Paolo Golinelli: Italia settentrionale (1130–1220), in: Guy Philippart (Hg.): Hagiographies. Histoire internationale de la littérature hagiographique latine et vernaculaire en Occident des origines à 1550 (Corpus Christianorum. Hagiographies), Turnhout 1994–2006, S. 125–153, hier: S. 132–133.

334 Vgl. Sala: Il culto di Zeno dal X al XII, S. 15. Vgl. Marchi: Le antiche storie, S. 34–35. Vgl. Anti: Verona e il culto, S. 98–99.

335 Vgl. ebd., S. 99.

336 Vgl. ebd.

337 München BSB Clm 1090 und Nürnberg SB Cent. VII 99.

338 Verona BCi 327 und Verona BCi 923.

339 Vgl. ebd., S. 126–127.

zur Sprache kommen wird. Einige Handschriften überliefern neben der Vita und der Translatio auch ein Gedicht in elegischen Distichen (Inc. *Qui praecepit aquam populo producere petram*), das vor dem Beginn des eigentlichen Vitatextes platziert wurde.[340]

Der erste Teil des monastischen Textes, nämlich die eigentliche Vita (BHL 9010) änderte den bereits bekannten Plot des Lebens Zenos nicht wesentlich.[341] Auch hier ist Zeno bereits im Mutterschoß heilig, er lebt auf asketische Weise, predigt und bekehrt nach und nach die noch heidnische Bevölkerung. Zu den bereits bekannten Mirakeln, nämlich der Rettung eines Bauern und der Befreiung der Königstochter von der Besessenheit des Teufels, wurden aber zwei teilweise unbekannte Episoden hinzugefügt.[342] Das erste neue Wunder ereignet sich, als Zeno von den Gesandten des Kaisers aufgesucht wird. Nachdem Zeno der Forderung des Kaisers, sich zum Palast zur Hilfe seiner Tochter zu begeben, zustimmt, lädt er die Soldaten des Kaisers dazu ein, sich aus seinem Fang drei Fische zu holen. Diese sind aber gierig und nehmen sich unerlaubt auch einen vierten Fisch dazu. Als die Soldaten den Fisch in heißes Wasser werfen, um ihn zu kochen, bleibt er unversehrt und schwimmt weiterhin friedlich im kochenden Wasser. Der Heilige verzeiht aber den Soldaten den Diebstahl und diese sind durch das Wunder so beeindruckt, dass sie nun uneingeschränkt an seine Heiligkeit glauben. Im Anschluss reist Zeno zum Palast von Gallienus und befreit dessen Tochter vom Teufel. Davon höchst beeindruckt, schenkt der König dem Heiligen seine eigene Krone und gibt ihm außerdem die Erlaubnis, christliche Kirchen in Verona zu bauen und die heidnischen Götzenbilder zu zerstören. Im Zusammenhang mit der Bekehrung Veronas wird nun das zweite bisher unbekannte Wunder erzählt. Eine Gruppe von Heiden fordert Zeno heraus, einen Ertrunkenen wieder zum Leben zu erwecken, und verspricht, dass sie sich, falls Zeno dies bewirken könne, zum Christentum bekehren würde. Zeno betet zu Gott und der Tote steht wieder auf, die Heiden sind überzeugt und rufen nun: *Wir glauben, wir glauben und so lasst uns die frevelhafte Idole abstoßen.*[343] Im Anschluss an diese Episode wurden vom monastischen Verfasser der Vita einige längere Exzerpte aus der Homiliensammlung von Zeno eingefügt, in der der Heilige die Taufe und die Tugend der Geduld erörtert. Nach diesen Passagen aus dem *Tractatus* wird noch einmal auf Zenos Kampf gegen den Teufel angespielt und kurz darauf sein Tod geschildert. Auch in dieser Version der Vita wird am Schluss das bisher einzig bekannte post-

---

340 Verona BC L, Verona BC CXII, Verona BC CCXXVII; Verona BCi 2007 und Firenze BML Ash. 135.

341 Der durch Maffei (Maffei, Istoria diplomatica, Mantova 1727) edierte Text von BHL 9010–9011 wurde in: Sala: Il culto di Zeno dal X al XII, S. 18–24 wieder abgedruckt. Aus praktischen Gründen wird aus Sala zitiert, wenn die Texte nicht in dieser Arbeit ediert wurden (z. B. der Prolog von BHL 9010).

342 Das zweite Mirakel wurde bereits im Gedicht *Versus de Verona* erwähnt, vgl. Marchi: Le antiche storie, S. 32.

343 *Credamus, credamus et idola fallacia dimittamus*, siehe Edition, S. 96.

mortale Wunder des Heiligen eingefügt, nämlich die bereits von Gregor dem Großen erzählte Rettung der Stadt vor einer Etschüberflutung.

Die Ereignisse nach dem körperlichen Tod des Heiligen werden im zweiten Teil des monastischen Dossiers zu Zeno ausführlich behandelt.[344] Zunächst wird im Translationsbericht die Übertragung der Reliquien in das durch König Pippin und Bischof Ratold renovierte Zenokloster erzählt. Der Leib von Zeno, der bislang in einer kleinen Kirche ruhte, wurde dank Pippin und Ratold *schöner und erhabener*[345] begraben. Dafür wurde das ursprüngliche Gebäude vergrößert und eine Krypta mit Säulen gebaut, in der auch ein Marmorsarkophag platziert wurde. Als aber der König, der Bischof und die ganzen Kleriker der Stadt sich beim alten Grab sammelten, um es zu öffnen, wurden sie vom Schrecken überwältigt und trauten sich nicht, solch ehrwürdige Gebeine zu berühren. Erst dank eines am Gardasee lebenden Asketen, Benignus, der die Gebeine mit der Hilfe von wenigen Auserwählten aus dem alten Grab herausholte, konnte die Translation erfolgen. Die Reliquien wurden zunächst in einer Prozession, bei der sich unzählige Wunder ereigneten, durch die Stadt geführt, und dabei von der jubelnden und singenden Bevölkerung empfangen. Anschließend wurden die unversehrten Überreste[346] des Heiligen im neuen Grab versiegelt. Weiterhin wird berichtet, wie sich nach der Reliquienübertragung, und dank zahlreicher Schenkungen, die im Translationsbericht aufgelistet werden, die monastische Gemeinschaft etablieren konnte. Dank der liebevollen Zuwendung der Kaiser, der uneingeschränkten Unterstützung Ratolds und auch dank Schenkungen durch Laien, wurde das Kloster, so berichtet uns der Autor, sehr reich: *illa ecclesia ditissima facta est*.[347] Aber auch spirituell war die monastische Gemeinschaft vorbildhaft: Die älteren Mönche zeichneten sich durch ihre Würde und ihr regelkonformes Leben aus und waren auch für die Jüngeren ein Vorbild:

> das Verhalten und die moralische Würde zeigten, dass die alten Mönche und der Abt selbst die monastische Regel wunderbar respektierten und dass sie Modell und Spiegel der Anhänger waren, so dass gute Väter gute Söhne hervorbrachten.[348]

Die Erzählung endet mit dem Hinweis auf die vom Grab aus bewirkten Mirakel des Heiligen. Diese seien so zahlreich und hätten Zeno so berühmt gemacht, dass der Erzähler nicht davon absehen könne, auch diese zu schildern. Er verfasste daher ein *opusculum*,[349] in dem über einige Heilungen und Besessenenbefreiungen berichtet wird:

---

[344] Siehe Edition, Kapitel 3.3.3, S. 100–106.

[345] *decentius et sublimius*, siehe Edition, S. 100.

[346] *integritate membrorum servata*, siehe Edition, S. 101.

[347] Siehe Edition, S. 102.

[348] *seniores illos cum abbate eadem institutio et moralis gravitas tales exhibuit, quibus gubernaculum coenobiale regule mirifice servaretur et formula atque speculum sequacibus essent et ut boni patres bonos heredes efficerent*, siehe Edition, S. 103.

[349] Siehe Edition, S. 103.

> Aber der selige Priester zog viele Menschen aus entfernten Orten zu sich, einige von dem Glauben bewegt, andere von der Krankheit gezwungen. Und um nicht alles zu verschweigen, lasst uns einige seiner Mirakel in diesem Büchlein erläutern.[350]

Sprachlich zeichnen sich die monastische Vita und die Translatio durch einen relativ eleganten Stil mit klassisch-antiken Anklängen aus, die später ausführlicher behandelt werden. Der Mirakelteil ist hingegen aufgrund des behandelten Materials und den Charakteristiken der Gattung entsprechend eher schlicht. Er besteht im Wesentlichen aus einer Liste von zusammenhanglosen Wundern.[351] Das einzig beobachtbare Ordnungsprinzip der Liste ist, dass die Wunder in chronologischer Reihenfolge präsentiert werden, und zwar vom älteren zum jüngeren.

Da in diesem Teil des Werkes einige Wunder mit verschiedenen historischen Ereignissen verknüpft werden, bietet sich die Möglichkeit einer Datierung der Texte. Allerdings wurden diese Hinweise in der Forschung unterschiedlich gedeutet und entsprechend verschiedene Datierungen vorgeschlagen, zum Beispiel ins 11.,[352] 12.[353] und auch ins 13.[354] Jahrhundert. 2009 konnte allerdings Elisa Anti eine Datierung in die zweite Hälfte des 12. Jahrhunderts belegen.[355] Hinweise im Text beziehen sich zum Beispiel auf einige Besitzungen des Klosters, so ein Waldstück bei Mantico.[356] Diese lassen erkennen, dass der Autor wahrscheinlich zur Zeit des Abts Gerhard lebte, der den Anspruch des Klosters auf einige dieser Besitzungen nach langwierigen rechtlichen Streitereien durchsetzen konnte.[357] Auch der Hinweis auf den Bau eines Glockenturmes, von einigen mit einer Erweiterung in den Jahren 1045–1049 identifiziert, geht Antis Ansicht nach auf eine zweite Renovierung des gleichen Turmes zurück.[358] Die Vita hebt nämlich die Höhe des Turmes besonders hervor. Eine solche Betonung ist aber eher im Fall des Glockenturmes passend, der dank des Abtes Gerhard fertig gestellt wurde. Der Turm wurde von den Zeitgenossen für seine Höhe bewundert und als erstaunlich gebaut („mirabiliter constructum“[359]) beschrieben. Dieser zweite Umbau des Turmes gehörte zu umfangreichen Renovierungsmaßnahmen, die Abt Gerhard

---

350 „*Sed beatissimus confessor vires a Domino datas quam sepe excitans, multa memoratu, digna perficiens ex longinquis regionibus plures vocaverat; alios religione motos, alios aegritudinis necessitate coactos. Sed pretereamus omnia suorum per hoc opusculum diseramus aliqua*“, siehe Edition, S. 103.

351 Vgl. Heinzelmann: Translationsberichte, S. 63, der von einem Schematismus der Wunderberichte spricht.

352 Vgl. Marchi: Le antiche storie, S. 35.

353 Vgl. Maffei: Istoria diplomatica, S. 316; Vgl. Giambattista Biancolini: Notizie storiche delle chiese di Verona. 8 Bde.), Verona 1771, S. 76.

354 Vgl. Carrara: Gli scrittori latini, S. 365.

355 Vgl. Anti: Verona e il culto, S. 104.

356 Vgl. Varanini: Il monastero di San Zeno, S. 36–37.

357 Vgl. Castagnetti: Aspetti politici, economici, S. 67.; vgl. Valenzano: La basilica di San Zeno, S. 217.

358 Auch Sala sieht das so, vgl. Sala: Il culto di Zeno dal X al XII, S. 16.

359 Der Text der Inschrift ist in: Valenzano: La basilica di San Zeno, S. 214, abgedruckt. Siehe dazu auch Anti: Verona e il culto, S. 104.

während seines Abbatiates zwischen 1163 und 1187 initiierte.[360] In Abt Gerhard, der sich stark um eine finanzielle und bauliche Erneuerung des Klosters bemüht hatte,[361] ist nach Anti daher auch der wahrscheinliche Auftraggeber der neuen Lebensbeschreibung des Heiligen zu sehen.[362]

Darüber hinaus deutet auch der Befund der handschriftlichen Überlieferung auf eine solche Datierung hin, denn es ist kein Textzeuge vor BHL 9010–9011 vor dem Ende des 12. Jahrhunderts überliefert.[363]

Insgesamt gilt also die Zeit des Abts Gerhard als eine besonders positive Phase für das Zeno-Kloster, das sich in der zweiten Hälfte des 12. Jahrhunderts auf dem Höhepunkt seiner Macht befand.[364] Neben den umfangreichen baulichen Renovierungen betraf diese Blüte des Klosters auch die literarischen und liturgischen Texte des Zenokultes. Zu dieser Zeit wurde zwar nicht die äußerst langlebige Historia, dafür aber die Lesungen der Zenofeste und die Hymnen für Zeno geändert. Diese sollen im Folgenden zunächst vorgestellt und in ihren historischen und liturgischen Entstehungskontext eingeordnet werden.

In den Handschriften des 11. Jahrhunderts waren drei Hymnen vorgesehen, nämlich eine für die Vesper (*Zeno pontifex inclite*, ediert in Kapitel 3.3.2 auf S. 81–82) sowie zwei weitere aus dem Commune entnommene Hymnen für Matutin und Laudes. In den spätmittelalterlichen Handschriften aus San Zeno sind diese Hymnen nicht mehr zu finden. Zur Vesper sang man den Hymnus *Effulget orbis speculum* (ediert auf S. 82–83), und auch die bislang dem Commune entnommenen Hymnen für Matutin und Laudes wurden nun mit auf Zeno zugeschnittenen Stücken ersetzt: *Post haec curavit* (ediert auf S. 83–84) und *Praesulis sancti redeunt colenda* (ediert auf S. 84–85).

Die ersten zwei neuen Hymnen von Vesper und Matutin stellen eine einheitliche Komposition dar: Im ersten Teil des Vesper-Hymnus wird nach einer Strophe, in der auf die Wichtigkeit des aktuellen Festanlasses hingewiesen wird, Zeno für seine Weltverachtung und die Vielfalt seiner Mirakel gelobt. Anschließend wird sein erstes Mirakel erzählt. Hier endet der für die Vesper vorgesehene Teil der Komposition. Zwei weitere Mirakel des Heiligen, der Exorzismus der Tochter des Gallienus und die Rettung der Bevölkerung vor der Etschüberflutung, werden im Hymnus der Matutin erzählt. Die hier positionierte und durch das Incipit *Praesta, pater piissime* vertretene Doxologie weist darauf hin, dass erst hier der Hymnus zu Ende ist, und die Gesänge für Vesper und Nokturn damit als eine einheitliche Komposition zu sehen sind.

---

360 Vgl. Valenzano: La basilica di San Zeno, S. 214–218.

361 Vgl. Castagnetti: Aspetti politici, economici, S. 66. Wie Varanini erinnert, vgl. Varanini: Il monastero di San Zeno, S. 36, war die Zeit des Abts Gerhard noch zur Zeit Dantes positiv in Erinnerung geblieben.

362 Vgl. Anti: Verona e il culto, S. 105.

363 Vgl. ebd., S. 104.

364 Vgl. Varanini: Il monastero di San Zeno, S. 35.

Auch formal bilden diese Hymnen eine Einheit. Sie bestehen aus insgesamt zwölf Strophen von jeweils vier Versen von acht Silben und weisen einen proparoxitonischen Rhythmus (8pp) auf, mit dem die Struktur eines jambischen Dimeters rhythmisch nachgeahmt wird. Der Hymnus der Laudes weist hingegen eine unterschiedliche formale Struktur auf. Es handelt sich um einen Hymnus in sapphischen Strophen. Auch inhaltlich zeigt sich, dass dieser Hymnus als eigene Komposition anzusehen ist. Wie der erste Hymnus beginnt er nämlich mit einem Hinweis auf die Wichtigkeit des Festes, der als Eröffnung einer neuen Komposition gut platziert ist. Danach werden die Predigttätigkeit des Heiligen und seine Mirakel behandelt. Nachdem der Heilige um Gehör gebeten wird, schließt auch dieser Hymnus mit einer Art Doxologie, in der Gott gepriesen wird.

Wie im Fall der Historia im Cursus monasticus des Heiligen sind die Hymnen erst in Handschriften des späten Mittelalters erhalten: Neben den zwei bereits erwähnten Handschriften Augsburg StStadtB 2° 204 und Kremsmünster SB CC60 überliefert auch ein weiteres Brevier die Hymnen, nämlich eine Handschrift aus dem 14. Jahrhundert München BSB Clm 23143. Bei den Hymnen allerdings, die in dieser Handschrift fragmentarisch überliefert sind, handelt es sich um den Nachtrag einer Hand des 15. Jahrhunderts. Auch zwei Psalterien-Hymnare aus dem Zenokloster überliefern die Hymnen, nämlich die Handschriften Yale BL 744 und Verona BCi 745. Weiterhin bezeugt auch das bereits in Zusammenhang mit der Historia erwähnte Antiphonar des späten 15. Jahrhunderts, die Handschrift Verona BCi 739 I, dass diese Hymnen zum traditionellen Bestand der liturgischen Gesänge für die Zenofeste gehörten. Hier werden nämlich zu den jeweiligen Momenten des Stundengebets die Incipits der Hymnen angegeben: Für die beiden Vesper der Hymnus *Effuget orbis speculum*, für die Nokturn *Post hec curavit* und für die Laudes der Hymnus *Praesulis sancti*.

Vor allem die zwei Psalterien-Hymnare aus dem Zenokloster können Hinweise bezüglich der Datierung dieser Hymnen geben. Obwohl sie von dem Kunsthistoriker Gino Castiglioni als „gemelli",[365] also Zwillingshandschriften, charakterisiert wurden, wurden sie unterschiedlich, wenngleich durchweg mindestens vor 1450 datiert.[366] Sie sind somit die ältesten Handschriften, die die Hymnen überliefern.

Es stellt sich also auch im Fall der neuen Hymnen für Zeno aus dem Zenokloster die Frage, wie ihre Entstehung zeitlich zu verorten sei: Soll man, wie der handschriftliche Befund nahe zu legen scheint, von einer spätmittelalterlichen Entstehung der neuen Hymnen ausgehen oder stellen sie ein Erzeugnis älteren

---

365 Castiglioni: Tre salteri, un officio, S. 213.

366 Robert G. Babcock und Walter Cahn datieren die Handschrift aus Yale aufgrund einiger Nachträge im Kalender vor 1425–1427. Im Kalender wurden nämlich nachträglich die Namen von deutschen Heiligen wie Ulrich, Kilian und Wolfgang hinzugefügt. Dies passiert, nachdem 1425–1427 deutsche Mönche zum Bewohnen der Abtei gerufen wurden. Vgl. Babcock / Cahn: A New Manuscript, S. 109–110. Castiglioni bezieht sich auf die gleichen Hinweise des Kalenders, datiert die Handschrift 745 der Biblioteca Civica aber vor 1450, als eine Verbrüderung mit St. Ulrich und Afra und mit Tegernsee geschlosssen wurde, vgl. Castiglioni: Tre salteri, un officio, S. 213.

Datums dar, das zum Zeitpunkt der Erneuerung der liturgischen Codices der Abtei im 15. Jahrhundert[367] beibehalten wurde? Auch wenn durch die Überlieferung in den zwei Hymnaren aus San Zeno der Terminus ante quem für die Entstehung der Hymnen im besten Fall ein wenig nach hinten (vor 1425) gerückt werden kann, verbleiben wir bei einer sehr späten Datierung des Materials. Wenn die Hymnen tatsächlich erst im zweiten Viertel des 15. Jahrhunderts in die Abtei eingeführt worden sind, würde dies bedeuten, dass zwischen dem 11. und dem 15. Jahrhundert die Mönche die Hymnen sangen, die in der Handschrift Verona BC CIX(102) überliefert sind. Das wäre durchaus erstaunlich, da diese Hymnen lediglich Entlehnungen aus dem Commune darstellten und wenig spezifische Informationen über den wichtigen Klosterpatron enthielten.

Tatsächlich gibt es einige Hinweise darauf, dass dies nicht der Fall war. Da sich das Hymnar bereits zu Beginn des 13. Jahrhunderts nachweislich im Dom befand, also nicht mehr in San Zeno Maggiore benutzt wurde, war sein Inhalt dort möglicherweise bereits obsolet geworden. Dies bedeutet, dass etwa zu dieser Zeit (Ende des 12. Jahrhunderts) neues Material im Kloster vorhanden war. Auch inhaltliche und formale Aspekte legen diesen Schluss nahe.

Vor allem die Hymnen der Vesper (*Effulget orbis speculum*, hier ediert auf S. 82–83) und Matutin (*Post haec curavit*, hier ediert auf S. 83–84) weisen thematische und semantische Berührungspunkte mit der Vita und dem Translationsbericht des 12. Jahrhunderts (BHL 9010–11) auf. In der zweiten Strophe des Hymnus der Vesper (S. 81) wird Zeno als Beispiel eines Lebens nach dem monastischen Ideal der Weltverachtung dargestellt.

Qui Christi fide fervidus
hoc praesens spernens saeculum,
flore virtutum praeditus,
caeli possedit praemium.

Zeno, der die irdische Welt verachtete, kann nun den Preis des himmlischen Lebens genießen.

Der Aspekt der Weltverachtung war in der Figur von Zeno immer schon präsent gewesen, so in der frühmittelalterlichen Vita des Coronatus, wo Zeno fast als Asket dargestellt wurde, aber auch in Rathers BHL 9007. Allerdings ist es die Vita des 12. Jahrhunderts, BHL 9010, in der diese Idee am meisten Raum einnimmt. Hier wird nicht nur Zeno, sondern auch, expressis verbis, die Mönche des Klosters für eine monastische Lebensweise gepriesen. Besonders die Mönche des Zenoklosters wurden nicht nur für ihr regelkonformes und vorbildhaftes Leben als Modell und Spiegel für die Anhänger, sondern auch dafür gelobt, dass sie Laien inspirieren, das Saeculum zu verlassen und den Habit anzuziehen:

---

367 Castiglioni redet von einem „rinnovo“ derjenigen Codices, die in dem Katalog der Abtei von 1400 als „antiquus“, „valde antiquum“, „vetus“ und „antiquissimum“ bezeichnet worden waren und bemerkt, dass gerade aufgrund dieser Erneuerung nur große Choralhandschriften aus dem Zenokloster auf uns gekommen sind, vgl. Castiglioni: Note sui codici, S. 391.

Auch die Stadt und das Umland freuten sich gemeinsam; so dass viele Menschen die schattenreiche Welt des irdischen Lebens flohen und ähnlich zu solchen vornehmen Menschen [scilicet der Mönche von San Zeno, A. d. V.] werden wollten, und dies hatten sie vor, nicht wegen Armut, sondern wegen des Hungers und Durstes nach der heiligen Bekehrung. So zogen sie das monastische Habit an und brachten der Abtei nicht wenige Reichtümer.[368]

Der Hymnus, in dem Zenos monastische Attitüde der Weltverachtung gepriesen wird, lässt sich daher gut in dem gleichen Entstehungskontext verorten, in dem auch die monastische Vita BHL 9010–9011 verfasst wurde.

Darüber hinaus werden in den neuen monastischen Hymnen zwei weitere Themenkomplexe angesprochen, die ausschließlich in BHL 9010–11 zur Sprache kommen. Dies sind zum einen die Metapher von Zeno als hellem Licht, das die Finsternis des Heidentums verjagt. Zum zweiten die Darstellung der angeblichen Bekehrung der Bevölkerung Veronas durch den Heiligen als *triumphus* über die Feinde. In der dritten Strophe des Hymnus der Vesper (hier ediert auf S. 83) sangen die Mönche:

Hic onus carnis baiulans
plura fecit miracula,
ut floret lux clarissima
caecas fugavit tenebras.

Die erste Zeile schließt wieder an das Thema der Last des irdischen Lebens an, während in der zweiten Zeile die Mirakel von Zeno angesprochen werden. In der dritten und vierten Zeile wird Zeno mit einem hellen Licht gleichgestellt, das die blinde Finsternis vertrieb. Dieses Bild findet man in Ansätzen bereits in der Rather-Vita (BHL 9007), in der der Autor einen Satz von Coronatus mit dem Zusatz *a tenebris infidelitatis et errore conversa gentili* (hier ediert auf S. 90) ergänzt. Diese Idee wurde aber besonders in BHL 9010–9011 erweitert: Hier kommt sie nämlich gleich mehrere Male zum Ausdruck. Zunächst im Prolog, in dem die Heiligen mit den Fackeln und Leuchtern eines Hauses gleichgestellt werden, die den Glanz Gottes verbreiten. Unter den Heiligen ist Zeno wegen der Vielfalt seiner Wunder der hellste Stern: er schimmert wie Lucifer, der Morgenstern.

Solche tugendhaften und nützlichen Gaben schenkt Gott seinen Heiligen, so dass das Licht der Heiligkeit leuchten kann und wie eine Kerze, nicht unter dem Scheffel, sondern auf dem Leuchter, allen denen, die im Haus sind, Licht schenken kann. Viele Heilige können heilen, aber unter diesen glänzte Zeno aufgrund der großen Zahl seiner Wunder wie der Morgenstern.[369]

---

368 *Urbs et suburbana communiter huiusmodi contubernio gaudebant. Unde plures fallacis saeculi umbratilem auram vitantes ut couterini tantorum virorum fierent satagebant, quos non penuria id facere cogebat sed esuries et sitis sanctae conversationis inhiantes non minimas opes Zenoni ferentes monasticum habitum induerunt*, siehe Edition, S. 102.

369 „Haec honesta et utilia munera Iesus sanctis suis est pollicitus, ut iubar sanctitatis sic claresceret, et lucerna non sub modio, sed super candelabrum posita omnibus, qui in domo sunt, eluceret. Sed gratiam curationis plurimi sanctorum sunt adepti; inter quos multitudine miraculorum beatissimus Zeno, velut Lucifer matutinus rutilat", Sala: Il culto di Zeno dal X al XII, S. 19.

In dieser Passage verbirgt sich die Anspielung auf eine Bibelstelle. Es handelt sich um das Evangelium von Lukas, Kapitel 11, Zeile 33: „Nemo lucernam accendit et in abscondito ponit, neque sub modio sed super candelabrum, ut qui ingrediuntur, lumen videant". Dank der Rekonstruktion (Kapitel 3.4.2) wird deutlich, warum gerade diese Bibelstelle in die monastische Vita einfloss. Diese Passage aus dem Evangelium wurde nämlich traditionell während der dritten Nokturn am Fest eines Bekenners und Bischofs gelesen. Im monastischen Stundengebet war es üblich, die Lesungen der dritten Nokturn nicht aus der Vita des Heiligen, sondern aus einer Homilie der Kirchenväter zu entnehmen. Die Auslegung behandelte die Passage des Evangeliums, die an jenem Tag in der Messe gelesen wurde und die zu Beginn der dritten Nokturn nochmal durch Nennung ihres Incipits erklang.[370] Die handschriftliche Überlieferung zeigt, dass auch im Zenokloster diese Evangeliumsstelle und ihre Auslegung durch Beda gelesen wurden. An dieser Stelle wird deutlich, dass die Vita nicht nur ein literarischer Text war, sondern Teil des liturgischen Arrangements, auf das ihr Autor Bezug nimmt.

Das Bild des Lichtes wird noch einmal in BHL 9010–9011 verwendet, diesmal auf Zenos Bekehrung Veronas bezogen:

> Aber jener Lehrer des richtigen Glaubens kräftigte die Wurzel des Glaubens in Verona und vertrieb alle Lügen der Heiden, wie das helle Licht die Dunkelheit.

> Sed Veronensis fidei radicem hic orthodoxae fidei doctor firmavit et omnia deliramenta paganorum, velut clara luce tenebras, ab urbe sua fugavit.[371]

Auffällig ist hier auch der Wortlaut der Vita, der teilweise mit dem Wortlaut des Hymnus *Effulget orbis speculum* (hier ediert auf S. 82–83) übereinstimmt: *velut clara luce tenebras* (BHL 9010) – *ut floret lux clarissima* (Hymnus, Str. 3); *tenebras ab urbe sua fugavit* (BHL 9010) – *caecas fugavit tenebras* (Hymnus, Str. 3). Da dieser Themenkomplex um das Licht in der Vita mehrmals auftritt[372] und auch aufgrund der ähnlichen Formulierung in der Vita und im neuen Hymnus der Vesper, könnte man sogar die Vermutung äußern, im Autor der Vita und des Hymnus die selbe Person zu sehen. Diese war wohl ein Mönch von San Zeno, der in dem heiligen Zeno das hellste Beispiel für das regelkonforme monastische Leben sah, das auch er und die Mönche seines Klosters, San Zeno Maggiore, führten.

Eine gewisse Ähnlichkeit zwischen BHL 9010–11 und den Hymnen lässt sich auch auf einer allgemeineren, semantisch-terminologischen Ebene beobachten. Das Vokabular von BHL 9010–9011 ist relativ gehoben und weist einige klassisch-antike Reminiszenzen auf. Im Prolog der Vita[373] stößt man zum Beispiel auf das Wort *gaza*, *gazae* (die Reichtümer des persischen Königs), das vornehmlich

---

[370] Vgl. Harper: The Forms and Orders, S. 87.

[371] Siehe Edition, S. 92.

[372] Zum Beispiel: *et sanctitas luculenter emicuit*, siehe Edition, S. 93.

[373] „Hic diligens patronus imminentium periculorum impetum dissipat, et inimicorum visibilium, et invisibilium molimina eliminat, cui servire si sapis, opulenta eris satis, tam divinis armis, quam terrenis gazis", Sala: Il culto di Zeno dal X al XII, S. 19.

bei den Dichtern der klassischen Zeit (Vergil, Lukrez und Horaz) zu finden ist.[374] Antik anmutend ist auch die Diskussion über die Siege (*triumphos*) der paganen Helden, die in ihrer erbaulichen Funktion mit den Kämpfen und Siegen der Heiligen verglichen werden:

> Es ist lobenswert, diese Siege hervorzuheben und sie den Nachfahren anzuvertrauen, sodass der siegende Heilige würdiges Lob bekommt und gleichsam der fromme Glaube des Volkes Zeugnisse der Heiligkeit bekommt und verstärkt wird. Die Heiden sahen sich die Bilder der siegenden Helden an und priesen ihre Kriege und, so verführt von einem solchen Beispiel, gaben sie sich Mühe, sie nachzuahmen. Werden etwa unsere Rechtgläubigen, nun über die Siege des sehr berühmten Mannes durch das Zeugnis der geschriebenen Sprache besser belehrt als die Ungebildeten, die die schweigenden Statuen anschauten, nicht die Tugenden mit weiteren Tugenden vermehren?
>
> Dignum est hos triumphos [scilicet von Zeno, A. d. V.] attollere, et nostris posteris relinquere, ut dignas laudes victoriosus sanctus suscipiat, et devota religio populi documenta sanctitatis, et incrementa debitae servitutis accipiat. Gentiles videntes imagines triumphantium, eorum bella extollebant, et tali exemplo illecti, ut illis similes fierent, satagebant. Orthodoxi nostri, dum triumphos praeclarissimi viri melius per monimenta loquentis literae editos, quam per silentis, et mutae statuae formam vulgatos viderint, nonne virtutes virtutibus auxerint?[375]

Gerade dieses Bild eines triumphierenden Heiligen wird auch im Hymnus der Laudes *Praesulis sancti* eingesetzt, in dem die Rede von einem *pastor aeterno radians triumpho*[376] ist. Außerdem zeichnen sich die Hymnen wie BHL 9010–9011 im Allgemeinen durch ein ausgesuchtes Vokabular und eine gewisse Vorliebe für bestimmte Ausdrücke aus. Darunter ist zum Beispiel die Bezeichnung des Heiligen als *praesul* zu erwähnen, die kein einziges Mal in BHL 9001 und 9007, in BHL 9010–9011 aber gleich dreimal und in den neuen Hymnen *Effulget orbis speculum*, *Post haec curavit* und *Praesulis sancti* ebenso dreimal verwendet wird; auch die Adjektive *mirificus*, das kein Mal in BHL 9001 und 9007, zweimal in BHL 9010–9011 und einmal im Hymnus der Vesper (*Effulget orbis speculum*) eingesetzt wurde, und *excelsus*, das sowohl im Hymnus der Laudes *Praesulis sancti* (*Magnus excelsus fuerat sacerdos*) als auch im einleitenden Gedicht in BHL 9010–9011[377] (*In quibus excelsus crescis*) sind in diesem Kontext zu erwähnen. Zusammenfassend sprechen diese inhaltlichen und semantischen Berührungspunkte zwischen Vita und Hymnen dafür, dass beide im selben Umfeld entstanden sind, nämlich in der zweiten Hälfte des 12. Jahrhunderts, während des Abbatiats Gerhards.

Allerdings wurde unlängst aus formaler Sicht angemerkt, dass der dritte Hymnus für die Laudes eine humanistische Schöpfung aus dem 15. Jahrhundert sei.[378] Hierfür spräche die metrische Struktur dieses Hymnus, bei dem es sich um sechs

---

374 Vgl. Georges: Ausführliches lateinisch-deutsches Handwörterbuch, Bd. 1, Sp. 2907.
375 Sala: Il culto di Zeno dal X al XII, S. 18–19.
376 Siehe Edition, S. 85.
377 Sala: Il culto di Zeno dal X al XII, S. 18.
378 Vgl. Tommaso Migliorini: Girolamo Avanzi e l'inno *O diem gemma* a santa Toscana, S. 1–41, hier: S. 17.

sapphische Strophen von drei sapphischen Hendekasyllaben und einem Adoneus handelt, die Migliorini daher als humanistische Komposition sehen möchte. Gegen diese Einschätzung sollen zwei Punkte erwähnt werden. Zum einen die Tatsache, dass die sapphische Strophe durch das ganze Mittelalter hindurch eine durchaus beliebte metrische Form für Hymnen gewesen ist, welche auch aufgrund des prominenten und extrem erfolgreichen Vorbildes des Hymnus *Ut queant laxis* immer wieder aufgenommen wurde.[379] Auch das Vokabular ist, wie gerade gezeigt, auch wenn es humanistisch klingen mag, eher der antik anmutenden Vita BHL 9010–9011 entlehnt.

Das Beispiel eines genuin humanistischen Hymnus *Summe rex regno* (hier ediert in Kapitel 3.3.2 auf S. 85–87) liefert hingegen das liturgische Material für Zeno, das aus dem Stift Bad Reichenhall stammt. Die Handschrift München BSB Clm 16402, eine Pergamenthandschrift des 15. Jahrhunderts in Folio-Format mit Exzerpten aus Pseudo-Augustinus,[380] sowie ein Brevier des 14. Jahrhunderts (München BSB Clm 23147) in einer hinzugefügten Lage aus Papier (16. Jahrhundert) überliefern einen ins Jahr 1498 datierten und als *carmen* bezeichneten Hymnus für Zeno. Im Brevier ist er dezidiert als *carmen sapphicum* überschrieben und sein Autor, Andreas aus Schwaben, in der Überschrift erwähnt: *Carmen saphicum* [sic] *in divi Zenonis laudem editum ab Andrea svevulo canonico huius cenobii Sancti Zenonis*. Die neue Komposition benötigte das Placet des Bischofs, da sie eben nicht zum traditionellen Bestand an liturgischen Gesängen des Zenofestes gehörte. Auch dies fixierte der Schreiber in die Handschrift München BSB Clm 16402 f. 91v: „Hoc carmen reverendissimus in Christo pater dominus Ludovicus Ebmer episcopus Chiemensis concessit atque autorizavit ut in ecclesia nostra in festis divi Zenonis pro hymno cantetur anno Domini 1498." Nicht nur die Charakterisierung als Gedicht und die Zuschreibung zu einem gelehrten Autor, sondern auch seine Sprache weisen den Hymnus dezidiert als eine humanistische Kreation aus. Darin finden auch genuin antike Begriffe und Konzeptionen ihren Platz: Gott ist zum weisen Lenker des Olymps geworden (*Summe rex regno dominans superno, / rector et celsi sapiens Olympi*) und er wird so wie Petrus Kephas (Felsen) genannt (*Tu Chephe, navi pelago natanti / provides nautas maris alta doctos*), wobei die Bezeichnung im Gedicht weniger wegen der Stelle in der Vulgata, sondern wahrscheinlich eher wegen ihres altgriechischen Klanges ausgewählt wurde. Der von Gott gewährte Schutz ist hier in Analogie zu dem Schild eines römischen Soldaten als *clypeus*[381] (*At tuo tutus clipeo beatus / ne sacros daemon laniaret artus*) dargestellt, das himmlische Leben ist zum erhabenen Hafen des Äthers (*ut ipsi / eius ad portum meritis vehamur aetheris altum*) geworden.

Im Gegensatz zu dieser genuin humanistischen Kreation fällt also der Hymnus für Zeno *Praesulis sancti* inhaltlich und semantisch nicht besonders als humanis-

[379] Vgl. Hiley: Western Plainchant, S. 141–142.
[380] Vgl. Halm u. a.: Catalogus codicum latinorum, S. 64. Lang: Das Erzbistum Salzburg, S. 89.
[381] Vgl. Georges: Ausführliches lateinisch-deutsches Handwörterbuch, Sp. 1210.

tisch auf. Auch die Wahl der sapphischen Strophen deutet, wie erwähnt, nicht unbedingt auf eine spätmittelalterliche Entstehung hin,[382] sondern der Hymnus konnte wohl in der zweiten Hälfte des 12. Jahrhunderts entstanden sein. Während der Blütezeit des Klosters gab es dort nämlich eine Gruppe von gebildeten Mönchen, die die Fähigkeit besaßen, eine neue, stilistisch elegante und antik anmutende Biographie des Klosterpatrons zu verfassen. Auch in der Metrik waren sie geschickt. Neben dem bereits erwähnten Prolog-Gedicht zu BHL 9010–9011 in elegischen Distichen ist auch eine beachtliche Gruppe von metrischen Inschriften zu erwähnen, welche die Renovierungsarbeiten am Klostergebäude sowie seine Ausschmückung mit Skulpturen und Reliefgruppen begleiteten und in Stein fixierten.[383] Zu diesem Aspekt des Klosterlebens im 12. Jahrhundert wurde angemerkt, dass als Autor der vielen Inschriften – von denen die meisten in leoninischen Hexametern verfasst wurden – ein gelehrter Mönch der Abtei zu sehen sei,[384] welcher nicht nur mit dem Metrum vertraut war, sondern auch über Kenntnisse zu den Kirchenvätern, aber auch den antiken (Vergil), spätantiken (Prudentius) und frühmittelalterlichen (Wahlafrid Strabo und Hrabanus Maurus) Dichtern verfügte.[385] Unter diesen Umständen waren also auch für das Verfassen des neuen Zeno-Hymnus mit seinen sapphischen Strophen im 12. Jahrhundert die Bedingungen im Kloster gegeben.

Ein letzter Hinweis sei hier gegen eine humanistische Entstehung von *Praesulis sancti* erwähnt. Seine ersten Editoren, die Veroneser Priester Raffaele Bagatta und Battista Peretti, die in der zweiten Hälfte des 16. Jahrhunderts in Verona tätig waren, kannten diesen Zenohymnus und veröffentlichten ihn in ihrer Sammlung von Dokumenten über Veroneser Heilige. Sie leiteten den Text mit diesen Worten ein: „Sehr alter monastischer Hymnus für die Laudes.“[386] Eine Entstehung des Hymnus im 15. Jahrhundert, also kurz vor der Anfertigung der einzigen heute noch überlieferten Codices aus San Zeno Maggiore, würde seine Charakterisierung durch Autoren des 16. Jahrhunderts als „sehr alt“ kaum rechtfertigen.

---

382 Für Eusebius, den Patron von Vercelli, ist ein ähnlich gestalteter Hymnenkomplex aus ähnlicher Zeit überliefert. Die älteste Quelle, ein Brevier aus dem 13. Jhdt. (vgl. Giacomo B. Baroffio: Iter liturgicum italicum, online: http://www.hymnos.sardegna.it/iter/iterliturgicum.htm [03. März 2021]), überliefert nämlich neben zwei Hymnen für die Matutin und die Laudes auch einen Hymnus von neun sapphischen Strophen mit dem Incipit *Praesul insignis, martyr Eusebi* für die zweite Vesper, siehe Guido M. Dreves (Hg.): Hymni inediti. Liturgische Hymnen des Mittelalters (Analecta Hymnica Medii Aevi 22), Leipzig 1895, Nr. 155, 156 und 157.

383 Siehe dazu: Valenzano: La basilica di San Zeno, 211–236.

384 Vgl. Saverio Lomartire: Testo e immagine nella Porta dello Zodiaco, in: Dal Piemonte all'Europa: esperienze monastiche nella società medievale. Relezioni e comunicazioni presentate al XXXIV Congresso storico subalpino nel millenario di S. Michele della Chiusa (Torino, 27–29 maggio 1985), Turin 1988, S. 431–474, hier: S. 445.

385 Vgl. Valenzano: La basilica di San Zeno, S. 225.

386 „Hymnus antiquus ad laudes in officio ordinis S. Benedicti [...]“, Raffaele Bagatta / Battista Peretti (Hg.): Sanctorum episcoporum Veronensium, c. 15r.

Zusammenfassend lässt sich festhalten, dass sowohl die Vita (inklusive des Translations- und Mirakelberichtes) als auch die neuen Hymnen sehr wahrscheinlich ein gleichzeitiges Produkt aus der Zeit des Abts Gerhard darstellen und eventuell sogar vom gleichen Autor verfasst worden sind. Damit fällt diese liturgische Erneuerung in eine Phase des wirtschaftlichen Aufschwungs und der baulichen Erweiterung des Klosters in der zweiten Hälfte des 12. Jahrhunderts.

Als Nächstes sollen nun die Inhalte dieses Materials untersucht werden. Es wird sich zeigen, dass sich in der Betonung von gewissen Aspekten Zenos der Versuch ausdrückte, dem Kloster und der monastischen Gemeinschaft eine prominente Rolle in der Verwaltung seines Kultes zuzuschreiben. Dabei wurde der Anspruch des Klosters auf eine solche prominente Rolle im Zenokult vor allem mit der Anwesenheit der Reliquien des Heiligen im Kloster legitimiert. Die Produktion dieser Texte war daher ein weiterer Schachzug im langanhaltenden Streit um den Leib des Heiligen und um die Emanzipation des Klosters vom Bischof.

Zunächst ist hierbei wichtig, die Abhängigkeitsverhältnisse der neuen Vita zu ihren Vorlagen zu klären. Während der Translations- und Mirakelbericht eine Neuschöpfung des 12. Jahrhunderts darstellte, bezog sich die Lebensbeschreibung Zenos (BHL 9010) auf die Vita Rathers (BHL 9007) und nicht, wie oft behauptet,[387] auf die karolingische Vita des Coronatus (BHL 9001).[388] Dies zeigt die wörtliche Übernahme von Ausdrücken aus der Ratherschen Vita in BHL 9010. Die Übernahme (hier kursiv markiert) ist so deutlich, dass der Vergleich von nur zwei Passagen ausreicht, um dies zu demonstrieren:

Tabelle 6 Vergleich von BHL 9001, BHL 9007 und BHL 9010

BHL 9001[389]	BHL 9007[390]	BHL 9010[391]
Ille enim a cunabulis benedictus et a ventre sanctificatus erat, et ad hoc	Fuit quippe a matris utero sanctificatus, et a cunabulis benedictus, ut	*Fuit quippe a matris utero sanctificatus, et a cunabulis benedictus, ut*

[387] Vgl. Sala: Il culto di Zeno dal X al XII, S. 17; vgl. Golinelli: Italia settentrionale, S. 132. Auch Anti argumentiert mit der Abhängigkeit von BHL 9010 von dem *Sermo* (von Coronatus notarius), obwohl sie sehr wohl merkt, dass der Autor von BHL 9010 BHL 9007 als Modell vor sich liegen hatte, vgl. Anti: Verona e il culto, S. 95 und S. 123.

[388] Für Elisa Anti stellt BHL 9007 eine Brücke zwischen der Vita des Coronatus und der monastischen BHL 9010 dar. Sie stellt auch fest, dass der monastische Autor für das Verfassen seiner BHL 9010 BHL 9007 als Modell nahm: „Questa versione [scilicet BHL 9007, A. d. V.] appare particolarmente interessante perché si presenta come una sorta di ‚ponte' tra il *Sermo* e la *Vita beatissimi Zenonis*, dato che in essa compaiono alcune espressioni che ritroveremo letteralmente riprese nella *Vita II* [BHL 9010]. Viene pertanto da chiedersi se sia l'autore di BHL 9010 ad avere lavorato avendo come modello BHL 9007 oppure l'autore di BHL 9007 ad avere scritto, o meglio riscritto, avendo sottomano tutte e due le *Vitae*, e attingendo ad entrambe. Considerando la datazione dei manoscritti, l'ipotesi più attendibile sembrerebbe la prima." Ebd., S. 123.

[389] Aus: Sala: Il culto di Zeno nei secoli VIII-IX, S. 29–32.

[390] Hier ediert in Kapitel 3.3.3 auf S. 87–91.

[391] Hier ediert in Kapitel 3.3.3 auf S. 91–105.

pertingere meruit, ut per vitam sanctam pastor in populo esse mereretur; et ideo quia in omnem terram exiit sonus conversationis eius et sanctitas emicuit audiant populi omnes, qui eius cupiunt miracula.	assertione divina in eo repeti videretur, quod Hieremiae dictum est: „Priusquam te formarem in utero, novi te et antequam exires de ventre sanctificavi te." Denique probitatis atque scientiae iugibus incrementis ad hoc pertingere meruit, ut per sacerrimam vitam fieri pastor in populo mereretur. Nempe audiant populi omnes, qui eius cupiunt nosse miracula, quia in omnem terram sonus exiit conversationis eius et sanctitas luculenter emicuit.	*assertione divina in eo repeti videretur, quod Hieremiae dictum est: „Priusquam te formarem in utero novi te, et antequam exires de ventre sanctificavi te." Denique probitatis atque scientiae*[392] *iugibus incrementis ad hoc pertingere meruit, ut per sacerrimam vitam fieri pastor in populo mereretur. Nempe audiant populi omnes qui eius cupiunt nosse miracula. Quia in omnem terram sonus exiit conversationis eius, et sanctitas luculenter emicuit.*
Ille enim sedebat super lapidem, qui in proximo monasterii erat, et piscabatur in flumine.	Ille vero sedebat super lapidem, qui in proximo erat monasterii, et artis apostolicae documenta proficiens, ex more piscabatur in flumine.	Ille vero sedebat super lapidem qui in proximo erat monasterii, *et artis apostolicae baiulans instrumenta ex more piscabatur in flumine.*

Diese Vorlage wird bezüglich des Plots der Vita des Heiligen weitgehend respektiert, sie wurde aber auch an einigen entscheidenden Punkten geändert, die hier nun ausführlich zu behandeln sind.

Eine Abweichung von der Vorlage stellt die Hinzufügung von Exzerpten aus der Homiliensammlung (*Tractatus*) des Heiligen dar. Es werden mehrere Passagen zitiert, in denen Zeno die Tugend der Geduld behandelt.[393] Die Auswahl des Themas der Geduld (*patientia*) passt zum monastischen Autor der Vita und zu seinem Publikum von Mönchen, da die Geduld traditionell als monastische Tugend galt.[394] Abgesehen von den zwei neuen Mirakeln, die hinzugefügt wurden und bereits zusammengefasst worden sind, wird die Vorlage an zwei weiteren Stellen modifiziert. Diese stehen in deutlichem Zusammenhang mit dem Konflikt zwischen Kloster und Dom. Zum einen wird der Prolog von Rather eliminiert. Statt diesem wird nun BHL 9010 von einem umfangreicheren Vorwort eröffnet. Schon die erste Zeile dieses neuen Prologes verrät, worum es dem Autor dieser Vita vor allem ging, nämlich um die Wunderwirkung Zenos:

> Euch, liebste Brüder, will ich einige Taten des heiligen Zeno kurz und klar erzählen: entweder solche, die er während seines Lebens vollbrachte, oder solche, die nach sei-

392 Maffei ediert an dieser Stelle fälschlicherweise „sanctitatis", Maffei: Istoria diplomatica, S. 322. Die Überprüfung einer Auswahl von Handschriften, hat ergeben, dass alle „scientiae" überliefern.

393 Sala: Il culto di Zeno dal X al XII, S. 22.

394 Vgl. Barbara H. Rosenwein: Anger's Past. The Social Uses of an Emotion in the Middle Ages, Ithaca 1998, S. 99.

nem Tod zu Stande kamen oder sich später, nach einiger Zeit zeigten. Und ich darf auch nicht diejenigen Wunder verschweigen, die die religiösen Männer, mit denen ich wohnte, selbst mit ihren glaubwürdigen Augen gesehen haben.[395]

Der Prolog Rathers hatte den Taten des Heiligen offensichtlich zu wenig Platz eingeräumt, ein Terminus („gesta“) der hier deutlich als Synonym für Mirakel verwendet wurde. Auch wenige Zeilen später, nachdem der Autor sich als eifriges Bienchen („operosa apicula“[396]) definiert hat – mit einer im monastischen Bereich sehr beliebten und aus der Antike (Seneca) kommenden Metapher[397] –, wurde erneut auf diesem Thema insistiert: Wie soll er denn schweigen, fragt er sich, wenn gleichzeitig der Heilige so viele Wunder bewirkt? „Quae lingua sileat, dum sepultus viventem aegrotum aut extendit, aut illuminat, aut mundat, aut aliquo modo curat, vel iam mortuum suscitat?“[398] In diesen wenigen Eröffnungszeilen ist schon ein wesentlicher Teil des Programms der hochmittelalterlichen monastischen Ré-écriture der Hagiographie Zenos im Kloster zu lesen: Vor allem die Wunderwirkung des Heiligen und somit der *locus* der Mirakel, San Zeno Maggiore, und seine Bewohner („religiosi viri, quibus cum stetimus“[399]) sollen hier erzählt, memoriert und gepriesen werden.

Auch an einer zweiten Stelle wird von der Vorlage, BHL 9007, abgewichen. Das Gedicht von Rather wurde durch ein neues, im gleichen Metrum gehaltenes Gedicht ersetzt und zwar durch das Gedicht *Qui praecepit*:

Qui praecepit aquam populo producere petram
Hic valet ingenium mollificare meum.
Unde tuam vitam, Zeno sanctissime, scribam:
Arbitror esse pium signa referre stylum
In quibus excelsus crescis velut alta cupressus.
Talia dum nitor, gaudeo si superor
Si quis praeteritos sancti numeravit actus,
Computet arva soli, computet astra poli.
Paucula de multis iactemus semina sulcis,
Incrementa dabis ditia, Christe, satis.[400]

---

395 Der Prolog wurde im Rahmen der liturgischen Feier im Zenokloster nicht vorgelesen und wurde deshalb in den hier edierten liturgischen Handschriften nicht überliefert. Der Text hier stammt daher aus der Edition von BHL 9010 in: Sala: Il culto di Zeno dal X al XII, S. 18–30. „Vobis fratres carissimi, breviter et aperte S. Zenonis quaedam gesta narramus; vel quae olim dum viveret fecerat, vel quae post obitum mature futura reliquerat seu quae per intervalla temporum deinde enituerunt nec praetereunda sunt quae religiosi viri, quibuscum stetimus fidelibus oculis viderunt“, ebd., S. 18.

396 Ebd.

397 Vgl. Fiona J. Griffiths: The Garden of Delights. Reform and Renaissance for Women in the Twelfth Century, Philadelphia 2011, S. 82–108.

398 Sala: Il culto di Zeno dal X al XII, S. 18.

399 Ebd.

400 Maffei und Sala edieren in V. 4 *stylo* für *stylum*. Ich habe hier den Wortlaut der Handschriften Verona BibCiv 2007 und Firenze BML Ash. 135 wiedergegeben.

Hier wird im Gegensatz zu dem früheren *Pontificum splendor* komplett auf eine Schilderung der Biographie des Heiligen verzichtet. Stattdessen wird das Augenmerk zum einen auf die Wunderwirkung von Zeno und zum zweiten auf die Tätigkeit des Dichters gelegt.

Prolog und einleitende Gedichte waren traditionell auch in hagiographischen Texten für die Darstellung der Causae scribendi und der Ziele des Textes reserviert. [401] An diesen Stellen traten daher auch die Autoren der Werke prominent auf. Die Tatsache, dass die monastische Vita sich ausgerechnet an diesen Stellen von der Vorlage entfernt, drückt den Wunsch des neuen monastischen Autors aus, sich an die Stelle des alten Autors (Rather) zu setzen. So erfolgte die Verschiebung des Fokus in BHL 9010 gleich auf zwei Ebenen. Zum einen inhaltlich, durch die Konzentration auf die Mirakel des Heiligen statt auf seine Biographie, und zum zweiten durch den Wechsel der Urheber der Texte: Bischof Rather wird nun von einem Mönch ersetzt, der wiederum für die ganze hinter ihm stehende monastische Gemeinschaft des Zenoklosters steht.

Gegen Ende des Vita-Teils fällt aber eine weitere Erneuerung gegenüber der Vorlage auf: In der monastischen Vita wird dem Tod des Heiligen viel Platz eingeräumt. Vor allem im Vergleich mit der äußerst kurzen Formulierung in BHL 9007 *non multo post in pace receptus est*, fällt die detaillierte Schilderung des Heiligen auf dem Sterbebett, seiner Abschiedsrede und der Reaktion des trauernden Volkes besonders auf. Der Grund für diese umfangreiche Schilderung des Todes des Heiligen ergibt sich aus dem weiteren Verlauf der Vita, in der nach wenigen Zeilen das Kloster als Ort des Grabes des Heiligen und Hotspot der Wunder hervorgehoben wird:

> *Solche Gelübde äußerten Menschen jeden Alters und weinten vor Liebe zu dem Bischof. Sie veranstalteten ihm eine würdige Begräbnisfeier und begruben ihn nicht weit von der Stadt, dort wo er pflegte, glücklich zu Gott zu beten. Viele und vielfältige Wunder ereigneten sich bald drauf bei seinem Grab.* [402]

Der Moment des Todes stellt natürlich für das Zenokloster einen entscheidenden Moment dar, und zwar aus zwei Gründen: Zum einen wurde der tote Heilige unweit von der Stadt im Zenokloster begraben. Auch geht der Autor hier wie in den bereits analysierten Zusätzen der monastischen Historia davon aus, dass Zeno selbst in diesem Kloster lebte: *ubi Deo feliciter sacrificare consueverat*. Die Lebensgeschichte des Heiligen wird so zum Gründungsmythos des Klosters; die Orte, an denen Zeno wirkte und starb, werden mit den für den Schreibenden reellen Gegebenheiten verschmolzen. In diesem Sinne wundert es nicht, dass die Erzählung der Reliquienübertragung in der Translatio und den postmortalen Mirakeln des Heiligen in dem Miracula-Teil fast so lang ausfallen wie die seines Lebens. Es

---

401 Vgl. Monique Goullet: Écriture et réécriture hagiographiques, Turnhout 2005, S. 31.

402 *Haec vota animi omnis aetas fundebat, et pro amore pastoris eiulabat, cui dignas exequias persolverunt, sepelientes non longe ab urbe, ubi Deo feliciter sacrificare consueverat. Multiplices et variae mirabilium species repente circa tumulum eius apparuerunt, siehe Edition*, S. 99.

entsteht der Eindruck, dass nicht mehr Zeno als der eigentliche Protagonist der Erzählung zu sehen ist, sondern dass eher das Kloster diese Rolle einnimmt.

Diese Botschaft sollen auch die zwei weiteren Texte vermitteln, die zusätzlich zur Erzählung des Lebens von Zeno im Kloster neu verfasst wurden, nämlich der Bericht über die Übertragung der Reliquien des Heiligen und die Liste von Mirakeln, die Zeno post mortem bewirkte. Beide Texte enthalten reichlich Lob der eigenen Institution und ihrer Bewohner sowie eine klare Fokussierung auf die Wunderwirkung des Heiligen. Auch Ereignisse von „staatspolitische[r] und ‚publizitäre[r]' Bedeutung",[403] wie Schenkungen und Stiftungen durch Bischöfe oder Könige und im Allgemeinen die Betonung der Unterstützung des Klosters vonseiten der Laien und der politischen Institutionen spielen im Translations- und Mirakelbericht eine große Rolle.

Neben diesen inhaltlichen Aspekten ist aber vor allem die Tatsache entscheidend, dass das Kloster überhaupt neue Texte produzierte sowie dass es sich dabei gerade um eine Reliquienüberführung und um einen Mirakelbericht handelte. Qua Gattung zeichnen sich solche Texte nämlich durch große Zeit- und Ortsbezogenheit aus:

> Zu den inhaltlichen Charakteristiken der Translationsberichte gehört aber vor allem, daß sie sich – anders als die hagiographische Biographie und deren exemplarischer, überzeitlicher Heiliger – auf konkrete Ereignisse in einem genau beschriebenen Raum zu einem festgehaltenen Zeitpunkt beziehen.[404]

Martin Heinzelmann betont in diesem Zusammenhang, dass die Orts- und Zeitbezogenheit dieser Texte im Sinne einer urkundlichen Beglaubigung der erzählten historischen Ereignisse zu verstehen sei.[405] Zwar ist die Beglaubigung sicherlich eine wichtige Funktion der Texte, entscheidender ist meiner Ansicht nach aber eine andere, mehr auf das Diesseits bezogene Funktion, nämlich die der Identitätsstiftung. Die in der zweiten Hälfte des 12. Jahrhunderts verfassten schriftlichen Berichte zur Überführung der Gebeine sowie der am Grab gewirkten Wunder von Zeno sollten den Anspruch des Klosters legitimieren, aufgrund von vergangenen Ereignissen die wichtigere Rolle im Zenokult zu spielen. Die Ereignisse der karolingischen Zeit werden zur Kulisse für das hochmittelalterliche Geschehen und das Kloster des 12. Jahrhunderts ist nicht nur faktisch, sondern auch spirituell identisch mit dem Kloster, in dem der Heilige lebte und das er als sein Grab auswählte. Die Erzählung der Überführung der Reliquien von Zeno entwickelt sich somit von einer Beglaubigung hin zum Gründungsmythos des Klosters: Sie erzählt weniger die Geschichte des Heiligen, als vielmehr die Geschichte der monastischen Gemeinschaft selbst.

---

403 Heinzelmann: Translationsberichte, S. 59.
404 Ebd., S. 57.
405 Vgl. ebd., S. 57–58.

Eine solche Zeit- und Ortsbezogenheit ist im Fall der Mirakelliste (das *opusculum*[406]) noch stärker. Hier geht es weniger um die Memorierung und Re-Aktualisierung der an den Anfängen der Klostergeschichte stehenden und fast mythisch gewordenen Überführung der Reliquien, sondern stärker noch um Ereignisse, die chronologisch näher am Verfasser stehen. Darauf weist auch die Erwähnung von Augenzeugen der Mirakel im Prolog der Vita: „Nec praetereunda sunt quae religiosi viri, quibuscum stetimus fidelibus oculis viderunt."[407]

Auch Heinzelmann beobachtet, dass Wunderberichte sich bezüglich ihres Realismus und ihrer Aktualität von der Lebensbeschreibung eines Heiligen unterscheiden:

> Im Gegensatz zu den exemplarischen, weitgehend typisierenden Wundern der hagiographischen Biographie zeichnen sich die Wunderberichte der Translation häufig durch größeren Realismus und durch größere Gegenwartsbezogenheit aus [...].[408]

Der Mirakelbericht besaß also größere Aktualität, weil er zeigen sollte, dass die Kraft des Heiligen nicht nur zur Zeit seines Lebens und der Überführung der Reliquien wirkte, sondern auch nach seinem Tod bis heute unversehrt geblieben war.[409]

Den Translations- und Mirakelberichten kommt daher in komplementärer Weise eine doppelte Funktion zu: Während der Bericht über die Überführung der Gebeine des Heiligen an den Ort des Zenoklosters die räumliche Verbindung des Klosters mit dem Heiligen betont, bezeugen die Mirakel dessen fortwährende Wundertätigkeit bis in die Gegenwart. Diese Tätigkeit diente zum einen der Identitätsstiftung für die Gemeinschaft am Grab des Heiligen, gleichzeitig aber auch der Werbung des Klosters um Zuwendungen und Unterstützung bei den Zeitgenossen. Hierin liegt eben die von Heinzelmann betonte „publizitäre [...] Bedeutung"[410] solcher Berichte. Das Wissen darüber, dass sich die Wunderkraft des Heiligen immer noch am Kloster manifestierte, konnte ein Publikum von Laien anziehen, die zu einem Besuch des Klosters (mit anschließender Spende) bewegt werden konnten.

---

[406] Siehe Edition, S. 103.

[407] Sala: Il culto di Zeno dal X al XII, S. 18.

[408] Heinzelmann: Translationsberichte, S. 65.

[409] „[...] celui qui veut composer un recueil de miracles n'est absolument pas lié par des contraintes chronologiques puisqu'après sa mort, le saint vit éternellement en Dieu. Ses miracles peuvent donc se manifester à n'importe quel moment. Quelle est alors l'attitude de l'hagiographe? Il écrit, nous le savons, pour susciter, maintenir ou réactiver le culte d'un saint. Il doit donc montrer que la puissance posthume du saint, qui se manifeste par des miracles, est toujours aussi forte que de son vivant [...]", Pierre-André Sigal: Histoire et hagiographie. Les Miracula aux XIe et XIIe siècles, in: L'historiographie en Occident du Ve au XVe siècle: actes du congrès de la societé des historiens médiévistes de l'enseignement supérieur; Tours, 10–12 juin 1977/1980 (Annales de Bretagne et des pays de l'Ouest), Tours 1980, S. 237–257, hier: S. 242–243.

[410] Vgl. Heinzelmann: Translationsberichte, S. 59.

Dass es sich dabei nicht nur um Laien niederen Standes handelte, legen auch die Nutzungsszenarien dieser Texte abseits der Liturgie nahe.[411] Unter anderem sei es denkbar, so Heinzelmann, dass sich Translations- und Mirakelberichte aufgrund ihrer historiographischen und gleichzeitig enkomiastischen Aspekte besonders für das Vorlesen beim Besuch des Klosters von prominenten Gästen eigneten:

> [...] bedeutenden Besuchern eines Klosters [wurden] die Taten des eigenen Klosterheiligen beim Mahle vorgelesen: Bei solchen Gelegenheiten mußten solche Texte besonders gefallen, die durch ihren aktuellen Bezug praktischen Geschichtsunterricht mit entsprechender Verherrlichung des jeweiligen Klosters (oder Kirche) und durch die durchaus konkret geschilderten Wundergeschichten Staunen, Ermahnung [...] und Erbauung gleichzeitig boten.[412]

Anlass für ein solches Szenario gab es in San Zeno Maggiore in der zweiten Hälfte des 12. Jahrhunderts zuhauf. So waren regelmäßig Kaiser im Zenokloster zu Gast, wie zum Beispiel Friedrich I., der sich 1163 dort aufhielt und den Treueschwur des Abtes Gerhard entgegennahm.[413] Da Verona ein wichtiger Verkehrsknotenpunkt zwischen Alpen und Rom darstellte, ist es sehr wahrscheinlich, dass auch andere prominente Gäste, etwa Bischöfe, Äbte oder Adlige, auf ihrer Reise im Kloster einkehrten und dort von der Wundertätigkeit des Heiligen überzeugt werden konnten. Dies würde die frühe Verbreitung der Vita nördlich der Alpen erklären, die sich bereits zum Ende des 12 Jahrhunderts im Sächsischen Kloster Pegau nachweisen lässt.[414] Diesen Besuchern wollte die monastische Gemeinschaft der zweiten Hälfte des 12. Jahrhunderts vor Augen führen, dass die Fackel des Zenokultes nicht mehr am Dom brannte, sondern weitergegeben wurde und nun *non longe ab urbe*,[415] in San Zeno Maggiore leuchtete.

Zeno als Märtyrer und Kreuzfahrer

Die Untersuchung des hagiographischen Dossiers für Zeno, das in der zweiten Hälfte des 12. Jahrhunderts im Zenokloster angefertigt wurde, hat ergeben, dass die Fokussierung auf den Körper des Heiligen und auf die durch die Reliquien bewirkten Mirakel mit der Verherrlichung der Abtei und seiner Bewohner einher-

---

411 Vgl. ebd., S. 116–118.

412 Ebd., S. 118.

413 Die Urkunden Friedrichs I. 1158–1167, hrsg. von Heinrich Appelt (MGH DD F I), Hannover 1979, Nr. 422, S. 309–311. Siehe auch dazu: Varanini: Il monastero di San Zeno, S. 36. und Anti: Verona e il culto, S. 106.

414 Die Handschrift Leipzig, UB, 1264 überliefert auf fol. 180r–202r und zwar im Teil der Handschrift, der auf das Ende des 12. Jhdts. datiert worden ist, die Vita und Translation von Zeno (BHL 9010–9011). Die Überschrift „Liber de vita sancti Zenonis confessoris ecclesiae pigaviensis" auf fol. 180r deutet daraufhin, dass dieser Teil der Handschrift vor der Bindung als unabhängiger *libellus* zirkuliert hatte. Vgl. http://www.manuscripta-mediaevalia.de/dokumente/html/obj31570169 [26. August 2018]. Mir sind zurzeit weitere Verbindungen zwischen Verona und Pegau nicht bekannt.

415 Siehe Edition, S. 99.

ging. Eine nähere Untersuchung des liturgischen Materials sowie der liturgischen Performanz des Klosters an den Tagen der Zenofeste bringt aber auch einen weiteren, bisher unbeachteten Aspekt ans Licht.

Zum einen fallen das von Bildern des Kampfes durchdrungene Imaginarium und die martialischen Begrifflichkeiten der monastischen Vita auf. Die Passage des Prologes, in der die christlichen Heiligen mit den siegenden Herrschern der Heiden verglichen werden, wurde bereits oben erwähnt. Sie sei hier der Nachvollziehbarkeit halber nochmal abgedruckt:

> Es ist lobenswert, diese Siege hervorzuheben und sie den Nachfahren anzuvertrauen, sodass der siegende Heilige würdiges Lob bekommt und gleichsam der fromme Glaube des Volkes Zeugnisse der Heiligkeit bekommt und verstärkt wird. Die Heiden sahen sich die Bilder der siegenden Helden an und priesen ihre Kriege und, so verführt von einem solchen Beispiel, gaben sie sich Mühe, sie nachzuahmen. Werden etwa unsere Rechtgläubigen, nun über die Siege des sehr berühmten Mannes durch das Zeugnis der geschriebenen Sprache besser belehrt, als die Ungebildeten, die die schweigenden Statuen anschauten, nicht die Tugenden mit weiteren Tugenden vermehren? [416]

Der Autor möchte, dass auch die christlichen Heiligen wie die paganen Herrscher von früher imitiert werden. Dabei seien die guten Christen, so der Autor weiter, dank der schriftlichen Berichte der Hagiographen besser informiert als die Heiden, die nur durch Bilder beziehungsweise durch Statuen zu einem tugendhaften Verhalten bewegt wurden. Diese Stelle fiel einigen Forschern bereits auf und wurde für eine Datierung der Vita herangezogen. Sie merkten an, dass der Autor an dieser Stelle die Überlegenheit seines schriftlichen Berichtes über Leben und Wirken von Zeno den Bildern der Maler und den Statuen der Steinmetze entgegenstellen möchte. Die Polemik des monastischen Autors gegen die bildende Kunst soll als Reaktion auf einige Objekte derselben entstanden sein, die im Zenokloster auch von Zeno erzählten. Diese wurden entweder mit der Bronzetür des Portals der Basilika, auf der einige Szenen aus der Vita von Zeno abgebildet sind, oder mit der polychromen Lunette desselben Portals identifiziert, wo ebenso ein auf den Teufel tretender Zeno bewundert werden kann. Da diese Kunstobjekte aber gegen 1140–1160 entstanden, sei die Vita auch in dieser Zeit entstanden und ihr Autor sogar Augenzeuge der Anfertigung der Objekte.[417]

Neben der Polemik gegen die bildende Kunst fällt aber auch auf, dass der Autor sich nicht einfach auf irgendwelche Statuen der Antike bezieht, sondern gerade an die Statuen von kämpfenden und siegenden Kriegern („Gentiles viden-

---

416 Dignum est hos triumphos attollere, et nostris posteris relinquere, ut dignas laudes victoriosus sanctus suscipiat, et devota religio populi documenta sanctitatis, et incrementa debitae servitutis accipiat. Gentiles videntes imagines triumphantium eorum bella extollebant, et tali exemplo illecti, ut illis similes fierent, satagebant. Orthodoxi nostri, dum triumphos praeclarissimi viri melius per monimenta loquentis literae editos quam per silentis, et mutae statuae formam vulgatos viderint, nonne virtutes virtutibus auxerint?, aus: Sala: Il culto di Zeno dal X al XII, S. 18.

417 Vgl. ebd., S. 15–16 und Anti: Verona e il culto, S. 103.

tes imagines triumphantium eorum bella extollebant“[418]) denkt. Meiner Ansicht nach bezieht sich der Autor gerade auf diese Bilder, um durch diesen Vergleich die Wunder von Zeno als „triumphos“ („dum triumphos praeclarissimi viri [...]“ [419]) bezeichnen zu können und aus Zeno, dem friedlichen Confessor, nun einen „siegreichen Heiligen“ („victoriosus sanctus“[420]) zu machen.

In diesem Zusammenhang ist auch eine weitere Passage von BHL 9010 relevant. Nach dem Prolog wird der historische Kontext der Lebenszeit Zenos geschildert.[421] Diese Schilderung wird im monastischen Text viel ausführlicher gestaltet als in der Vorlage BHL 9007. Der Autor behandelt hier aber, etwas verwirrend, nicht Gallienus, den Kaiser, mit dem Zeno im weiteren Verlauf des Textes zu tun haben wird, sondern seinen Vorfahren, Valerianus. Warum eigentlich? Sowohl mit der gerade erwähnten Diskussion über die Siege der Heiligen als auch mit der Schilderung der Regierung des Kaisers Valerianus wird, meines Erachtens, die Bühne für Zenos Auftreten als Märtyrer vorbereitet. Valerianus ist zunächst gegenüber den Christen wohlwollend, er verwandelte sich als alter Mann aber in einen Christenverfolger. Er befahl, so die Vita, die gerechten und heiligen Männer zu töten (*ut iustos et sanctos viros interimi iuberet*) und so wurde im ganzen Reich das Blut der Christen vergossen (*fuso per omnem Romani regni latitudinem sanctorum sanguine*). Vor diesem Hintergrund kann Zeno wenige Zeilen später dezidiert als Sieger über den Wahn der Heiden (*deliramenta paganorum*) erscheinen und das bis dahin heidnische Volk durch das Christentum neu geprägt (*et populum adhuc informem sigillo formae Dei imaginavit*). Als Sieger über die Heiden tritt Zeno übrigens auch in einem der zwei hinzugefügten Wunder von BHL 9010 auf. Die heidnische Masse (*multitudo prophana*[422]), die Zeno herausgefordert hatte, ist durch sein Wunder geschlagen und bezeugt laut ihre Bekehrung: *Illi duplici capti animo, tum faedere promissionis, tum spectaculo visionis clamarunt: ‚Credamus credamus, et idola fallacia dimittamus!‘*[423]

Auch in einer weiteren Passage von BHL 9010 wird erneut auf die Idee eines Kampfes des Heiligen gegen die Heiden und den sie anstiftenden Teufel Bezug genommen. In dieser Szene erscheint Zeno sogar in Begleitung einer Truppe von *tyrones*, ein Begriff mit starker militärischer Konnotation und ein Synonym von *miles*.[424] Der Teufel, neidisch auf die Reichtümer der Kirche, stört die Rekruten des Heiligen und wirft seine besten Anhänger gegen sie: *Hic artifex fraudolentus idololatriae magistros eorumque discipulos multis argumentis contra sancti Zenonis tyrones adhuc rudes infestabat.*[425] Gott aber lässt Zenos Jünger einen glorreichen Sieg über die geschlagenen Feinde erlangen: *At Deus, qui dedit illis se nosse, auxit et*

418 Sala: Il culto di Zeno dal X al XII, S. 18.
419 Ebd.
420 Ebd.
421 Siehe Edition, S. 91–92.
422 Edition, S. 96.
423 Edition, S. 96.
424 Georges: Ausführliches lateinisch-deutsches Handwörterbuch, Sp. 3131–3133.
425 Siehe Edition, S. 98.

posse, ut per signum miraculorum Zenonem sequentes, gloriosam victoriam triumphatis hostibus reportare.[426] Auch Zeno selbst unterstützt die Seinen und hört selbst nach dem Sieg nicht auf zu kämpfen, sondern befiehlt ausdrücklich, die Waffen nicht niederzulegen. Mit seinem Beispiel verleiht er ihnen Kraft, damit sie im verbleibenden Kampf stärker sein können:

> *Ipse vero sanctus, accepta palma, non proiecit*[427] *arma, neque suos proicere permisit, nec nudis verbis, sed factorum exemplis illos exagitabat. Nam vigilando, orando, ieiunando, elemosinando, miraculis coruscando, magnum robur constantiae illis inculcavit et, ut certatim fortiores essent in residua pugna, indulcavit. Iustus Zeno ut palma in Dei domo florebat et sua plantatio in eadem aula, et in atriis domus Dei vehementer crescebat.*
>
> *Der Heilige aber, auch nachdem er den Sieg errungen hatte, legte die Waffen nicht ab und er erlaubte es auch seinen Anhängern nicht, hingegen feuerte er sie nicht nur mit bloßen Worten, sondern mit Taten an. Und so ließ er durch das Wachen, durch das Fasten, mit dem Spenden und mit Wundern die große Kraft der Standhaftigkeit in sie einfließen. Und um sie für den weiteren Kampf zu stärken, redete er mit Lieblichkeit. Der gerechte Zeno blühte wie eine Palme im Haus Gottes und seine feste Verwurzelung im Haus Gottes wuchs kräftig.*[428]

Somit ist Zeno in BHL 9010 in einen Märtyrer verwandelt worden: Aus dem friedlichen und asketisch lebenden Sacerdos ist ein bewaffneter Kämpfer geworden.

Diese neue Profilierung wurde aber nicht nur durch die literarische Stilisierung der Vita generiert. Auch in der liturgischen Performanz außerhalb der Lesungen wurde Zeno nun als Märtyrer gefeiert. Wie aus der Rekonstruktion ersichtlich wird, wurde die Matutin der drei Zenofeste im Kloster anders als im Dom mit einer Psalmenreihe gefeiert, die traditionell für das Fest eines Märtyrers reserviert war.[429]

Da sich in der Vita ein Zitat aus dem letzten Psalm dieser Reihe findet – nämlich aus Psalm 91, 13–14: „Iustus ut palma florebit; sicut cedrus Libani multiplicabitur. Plantati in domo Domini, in atriis domus Dei nostri florebunt" – ist es naheliegend, dass diese Reihe ebenfalls im Kontext der Überarbeitung der Liturgie im Kloster in der zweiten Hälfte des 12. Jahrhunderts eingeführt wurde. Obwohl man dort die traditionellen Antiphone und Responsorien bewahrte, konnte so dennoch auch auf der Ebene der Historia, oder genauer gesagt des Wechselgesangs zwischen Historia und Psalmen, der Heilige neu profiliert werden. Tatsächlich führt gerade diese performative Adaption der Psalmen zu einem fast stärkeren Effekt als die literarische Stilisierung in der Vita: Die Verknüpfung dieser Psalmenreihe mit dem Profil eines Heiligen als Märtyrer war jedem liturgisch geschulten Hörer sofort erkennbar.

In diesem Zusammenhang kommt dem Moment des Todes eine entscheidende Bedeutung zu. Der Autor der monastischen Vita wich, wie bereits erwähnt, gerade an dieser Stelle von der Vorlage ab und erweiterte die dort extrem knapp

---

426 Siehe Edition, S. 98.

427 Sala ediert hier „proiecint".

428 Siehe Edition, S. 98.

429 Vgl. Pascher: Das Stundengebet, S. 200–201.

behandelte Szene des Todes des Heiligen. Die Herausforderung war dabei, aus dem friedlich gestorbenen Bischof einen durch Folter, Kampf oder unrechte Verurteilung getöteten Märtyrer zu machen. Ob dies dem Autor gelang, soll nach der Lektüre dieser unterhaltsamen Passage überprüft werden:

> *Sed tempus instabat ut legitimi certaminis coronam acciperet et animam ex corruptione exutam incorruptioni redderet. Quod virum Dei plenum non latuit. Mox gregem multo labore et sudore quaesitum quo iacebat vocari praecepit quibus inspectis ait: „Filii carissimi diutius vobiscum esse mallem sed Dominus ergastulum animae pulsat et quam dedit ad se vocat. Nunc vestrae fidei, spei et caritati ecclesiam Dei commendo, quam ille quovis pretio sed proprio sanguine quaesivit ut eam doctrinae lumine illustretis et exemplorum fultu roboretis. Vigilate in fide, viriliter agite, confortamini in Domino et omnia vestra in caritate fiant. Scitis, qui legitime certaverit, coronabitur. Hic certate, hic pugnate, hic contra vitiorum aciem dimicate ut coronam non tabentibus floribus aut lauro fluitura textam capiatis. Sed gemmis perenniter fulgentibus et auro numquam perituro Dei digito fabricatam possideatis." Post multiplices et elegantes sermones mysterium tali aptum negotio sumpsit et osculum singulis – velut iturus Ierusalem – dedit. Post haec signavitt eos et benedixit. Mox sanctam animam creatori suo reddidit.*[430]

> *Aber die Zeit nahte, in der er die Krone des richtigen Kampfes bekommen sollte und er die Seele, befreit vom Verderben, der Ewigkeit zurückgeben sollte, und dies blieb dem heiligen Mann nicht verborgen. Bald befahl er, dass seine Herde, die er mit Mühe und Anstrengung geleitet hatte, zu seinem Sterbebett komme. Den Anwesenden sagte er: „Liebste Kinder, ich würde lieber länger bei euch bleiben, aber der Herrgott klopft bereits an der Tür der Seele und verlangt das zurück, was er schenkte. Ich vertraue eurem Glauben, Hoffnung und Liebe die Kirche Gottes, die er nicht zu irgendeinem Preis, sondern mit seinem Blut gründete, an, so dass ihr sie mit dem Licht der Doktrin beleuchtet und mit der Stütze des Beispiels stärkt. Seiet wach im Glauben, handelt tapfer, habet Trost in Gott, alle eure Handlungen sollen mit Gott geschehen. Ihr solltet wissen, dass der, der richtig kämpfte, gekrönt wird: kämpfet ihr so, strebet ihr so, führet ihr Krieg gegen die Heere der Sünde, so dass ihr keine Krone aus welkenden Blumen oder aus Lorbeer bekommt, sondern eine aus immerglänzenden Edelsteinen und immerwährendem Gold, von der Hand Gottes geschmiedet." Nach vielen und überzeugenden Predigten feierte er die Messe und küsste jeden, als ob er im Begriff gewesen wäre, nach Jerusalem zu fahren. Danach zeichnete und segnete er sie und bald darauf starb er.*

Die Szene findet eigentlich, wohl ganz anders als bei einem Märtyrer, am Sterbebett des Heiligen statt. Trotzdem wird der Moment des Todes durch eine Kampfmetapher eröffnet (*tempus instabat ut legitimi certaminis coronam acciperet*). Diese Metapher wird auf der einen Seite häufig benutzt, um das christliche Leben als Kampf zu charakterisieren.[431] Doch im Zusammenhang mit der Rede, die der Heilige direkt vor seinem Tod hält, wird deutlich, dass sie hier die Funktion erfüllt, die ganze Szene auf ein imaginäres Schlachtfeld zu verlegen. Zenos Rede besteht aus einer Collage von Bibelzitaten, die von Gian Paolo Marchi bereits identifiziert

---

[430] Siehe Edition, S. 98.

[431] Vgl. Felix Heinzer: *Hos multo elegantius, si ecclesiastica loquendi consuetudo pateretur, nostros heroas uocaremus.* Sprachbilder im frühchristlichen Märtyrerdiskurs, in: Ralf v. d. Hoff u. a. (Hg.): Imitatio heroica. Heldenangleichung im Bildnis (Helden – Heroisierungen – Heroismen 1), Würzburg 2015, S. 119–136, hier: S. 123–124.

worden sind.[432] Bemerkenswert ist aber vor allem der allgemeine Ton und der Inhalt der Rede, in der die Gläubigen um den sterbenden Heiligen dazu aufgefordert werden, mit ihrem Blut für die Kirche zu kämpfen (*ecclesiam Dei commendo, quam ille non quovis pretio, sed proprio sanguine quaesivit*), sie mit der Verbreitung der christlichen Lehre berühmt zu machen und mit ihrem Beispiel zu stärken (*ut eam doctrinae lumine illustretis et exemplorum fultu roboretis*) und für sie tapfer zu handeln (*viriliter agite*). Auch, so Zeno weiter, sollten sie kämpfen, Krieg führen und gegen das Heer der Sünde fechten (*Scitis quia qui legitime certaverit, coronatur: hic certate, hic pugnate, hic contra vitiorum aciem dimicate, ut coronam* [...]), um den Preis des himmlischen Lebens zu erlangen. Der Autor funktionalisierte an dieser Stelle die Sprache und Bilder des Kampfes nicht, um lediglich eine allgemein verbreitete Metapher für das christliche Leben zu verwenden. Er hatte vielmehr ein wirkliches Schlachtfeld und einen genauen Ort im Sinn, wie ein kurzer aber doch auffallender Zusatz verrät: *und er gab jedem einen Kuss, als ob er auf dem Weg nach Jerusalem wäre* (*et osculum singulis, velut iturus Ierusalem, dedit*).

In diesem Sinne ist wohl auch der im monastischen Hymnus für die Laudes *Praesulis sancti* erwähnte Ausdruck: *praedicans gentes bene transmarinas*[433] zu verstehen. Es wird hier nämlich auf eine Missionierung von Zeno im Heiligen Land hingedeutet.

Diese Profilierung von Zeno als Märtyrer mag vor dem Hintergrund der realen und den Zeitgenossen bekannten Biographie des Heiligen verwundern. Besonders die hier zuletzt genannten Anspielungen auf den Kampf für die Kirche und der deutliche Bezug zur Stadt Jerusalem können aber dabei helfen, diese neue Profilierung zu erklären. Den Subtext dieser agonalen Sprache liefern die das hohe Mittelalter bestimmenden Kreuzzüge ins Heilige Land. Zeno wird in dieser Vita nicht nur im Allgemeinen als Märtyrer dargestellt, sondern ganz konkret mit den Kreuzzügen und vor allem den Kreuzfahrern in Verbindung gebracht: Er habe, so die monastische Vita, viele Menschen zu *religionis milites*,[434] Soldaten des Glaubens, gemacht.

Es scheint, als habe das Kloster versucht, nicht nur aus dem Wunder wirkenden Körper Zenos politisches und wirtschaftliches Kapital zu schlagen, sondern auch von der sich ausbreitenden Kreuzzugsbegeisterung des 12. Jahrhunderts zu profitieren. Da sich die Erneuerung des monastischen Dossiers Zenos grob in die Zeit Gerhards datieren lässt, sind hierfür zwei Szenarien denkbar: Zum einen, dass sich das so gewonnene Profil Zenos an Personen, die aus dem zweiten erfolglosen Kreuzzug zurückgekehrt waren, oder an deren Angehörige richtete. Für diese war der im Profil des Klosters zum Märtyrer stilisierte Heilige, der auch einen Bezug zum Kampf und zu Jerusalem aufwies, wohl ansprechender als der Sacerdos und Bischof des kanonikalen Offiziums. Dies mag insbesondere auf Kaiser Friedrich

432 Vgl. Marchi: I Manoscritti della Capitolare, S. 57.
433 Siehe oben, S. 84.
434 Siehe Edition, S. 99.

selbst zugetroffen haben, der im Gefolge Konrads III. am zweiten erfolglosen Zug ins Heilige Land teilgenommen hatte.[435]

Zum anderen ist denkbar, dass sich das Kloster mit diesem Profil von Zeno an diejenigen richten wollte, die im Zuge des dritten Kreuzzuges in den 80er Jahren des 12. Jahrhunderts aufbrachen, und vor ihrem Aufbruch oder als Ersatzleistung geeigneten Heiligen eine Zuwendung geben wollten.[436]

Tatsächlich lässt sich feststellen, dass gerade Verona zu dieser Zeit von einem regelrechten Kreuzzugsfieber befallen war, das durch die Anwesenheit prominenter Personen im Jahre 1184 in der Stadt weiter befeuert wurde: Zu diesem Zeitpunkt traf sich hier Kaiser Friedrich I. mit Papst Lucius III., um die Notwendigkeit eines weiteren Kreuzzuges zu diskutieren. Zu diesem Anlass weilten auch der Patriarch von Jerusalem Heraklius und die Großmeister der Templer und des Hospitals von Jerusalem in Verona.[437]

Dieses Kreuzzugsfieber hatte nicht nur solche prominenten Gäste Veronas erfasst: In den Kirchen der ganzen Stadt wurde für den Kreuzzug gepredigt. Am 4. November 1184 wurde die Dekretale *Ad abolendam*, das Ergebnis der Gespräche zwischen Kaiser, Papst und den Großmeistern der Ritterorden, veröffentlicht. Am gleichen Tag hielt der Bischof von Ravenna im Dom von Verona eine flammende Kreuzzugpredigt.[438] Gegen 1188–1189 predigte auch der kurz zuvor berufene Bischof von Verona, Adelard, für den Kreuzzug und führte selbst eine Gruppe Veroneser Kämpfer in das Heilige Land.[439]

Welches dieser Szenarien zutrifft, lässt sich schwer entscheiden. Sie verdeutlichen aber beide den von der Auseinandersetzung um das Heilige Land geprägten Zeitgeist des 12. Jahrhunderts, dem sich die Mönche des Zenoklosters und ihr Heiliger durch die Umprofilierung in den liturgischen Quellen anzupassen versuchten.

---

435 Vgl. Ekkehard Eickhoff: Friedrich Barbarossa im Orient. Kreuzzug und Tod Friedrichs I., Tübingen 1977, S. 28–30. Vgl. außerdem: Rudolph Hiestand: „precipua tocius christianismi columpna“. Barbarossa und der Kreuzzug, in: Alfred Haverkamp (Hg.): Friedrich Barbarossa. Handlungsspielräume und Wirkungsweisen (Vorträge und Forschungen 40), Sigmaringen 1992, S. 51–108 und ders.: Kingship and Crusade in Twelfth-Century Germany, in: Alfred Haverkamp / Hanna Vollrath (Hg.): England and Germany in the High Middle Ages, London 1996, S. 236–265.

436 Vgl. Anne L. Bysted: The Crusade Indulgence. Spiritual Rewards and the Theology of the Crusades, c. 1095–1216 (History of Warfare 103), Leiden 2015, 160–163. Außerdem: Jonathan S. C. Riley-Smith: The Crusades, Christianity, and Islam, New York 2008, S. 29–44.

437 Vgl. Gian Maria Varanini: Lucio III, la curia romana e una Chiesa locale. Verona 1184–1185, in: Amedeo de Vincentiis (Hg.): Studi Massimo Miglio Roma e il papato nel Medioevo: studi in onore di Massimo Miglio, Rom 2012, S. 185–200, hier: S. 185–186, und auch: Dario Cervato: Iacet ad monasterium Sancti Zenonis: Adelardo II cardinale e vescovo di Verona, in: Annuario storico zenoniano, 1991, S. 41–54, hier: S. 52. Außerdem: Annamaria Ambrosioni: Federico I e il papato dal Congresso di Verona alla partenza per la I crociata (1184–1189), Mailand 1986.

438 Vgl. Cervato: Iacet ad monasterium, S. 52.

439 Vgl. ders.: Adelardo cardinale vescovo di Verona (1188–1214) e legato pontificio in Terra Santa (1189–1191), Verona 1991, S. 18.

Zwischenfazit

Nachdem im vorherigen Kapitel die liturgischen Quellen aus dem Dom von Verona analysiert wurden, wurde in diesem Kapitel das liturgische Material für die Zenofeste einer weiteren Institution untersucht, die sich in Verona durch den Bezug zum heiligen Zeno profilierte, nämlich das Kloster San Zeno Maggiore. Die liturgische Überlieferung lässt sich grob in zwei Phasen gruppieren. In einer ersten Phase, ungefähr zwischen dem Ende des 10. und der Mitte des 12. Jahrhunderts, entstand im Kloster eine Gruppe von liturgischem Material. Dieses schloss eine Historia, die wahrscheinlich gegen Ende des 10. Jahrhunderts durch die Kontakte mit Bischof Rather das Kloster erreichte, und Hymnen ein. Die Untersuchung dieser Materialien zeigte, dass in dieser ersten Phase das Kloster über eine distinkte Identität verfügte, aber noch sehr stark von dem Episkopium abhing: die Historia wurde aus dem Dom übernommen, gleichzeitig aber auch so adaptiert, dass der Bezug des Klosters zum Heiligen, nämlich die Anwesenheit seines Körpers in San Zeno Maggiore, betont werden konnte. Gleichzeitig zeigt die Profilierung von Zeno als Bischof in den ältesten Hymnen der Abtei, dass der bischöfliche Einfluss noch eine lebenswichtige Rolle für das Kloster spielte.

Eine zweite Phase des Klosters lässt sich anhand der liturgischen Überlieferung identifizieren, die in der zweiten Hälfte des 12. Jahrhunderts dort entstand. Für den Vortrag an den Zenofesten und als Begleitung der etablierten Historia wurden nun eine neue Vita, ein Translations- und Mirakelbericht sowie neue Hymnen verfasst. Darin tritt ein viel deutlicheres Bild der Verehrergemeinschaft des Klosters zu Tage: Die Fokussierung auf den Leib sowie auf die von diesem bewirkten Mirakel verdeutlicht die klare Inanspruchnahme des Heiligen für das Kloster, das sich nun explizit als Hüter der Reliquien profilierte und dadurch seine Emanzipation vom Bischof und gegen seine prominente Rolle in der Verwaltung des Zenokultes behauptete. Gleichzeitig kommt auch der Versuch des Klosters ans Licht, weitere Publika für sich und den eigenen Heiligen zu gewinnen. Zeno wurde als Märtyrer und Kreuzfahrer profiliert und dadurch auch für die zahlreichen Kreuzzugsbegeisterten attraktiv gemacht.

Aus der Auseinandersetzung mit dem Bischof und dem Dom um den Kult von Zeno, die bereits in der Mitte des 9. Jahrhunderts entflammte und noch im 10. und 11. Jahrhundert die Geschichte der Abtei prägte, ging das Kloster letztendlich als Sieger hervor. Dass das Episkopium sich nach außen nicht mehr allein durch den Bezug zu Zeno präsentieren konnte, verdeutlichen einige liturgische Quellen aus der zweiten Hälfte des 14. Jahrhunderts. Gegen 1368 gibt das Kapitel neue Handschriften für den Chor in Auftrag und unterzieht in diesem Rahmen auch das liturgische Repertoire einer Erneuerung.[440]

440 Es geht um neun Codices, teilweise Zwillingshandschriften, die für die Nutzung im Chor der Domherren angefertigt wurden und als „corali di Turone“ bekannt sind, vgl. Castiglioni: I corali tardotrecenteschi.

Zwar wurde Zeno hier auch zu dieser Zeit weiterhin mit der bekannten Historia *Dum Zeno pontificatus honore* gefeiert, allerdings finden sich nun weitere Historiae für andere Veroneser Bischöfe, nämlich Theodorus und Anno.[441] Dabei handelt es sich um Kulte, die bereits in der Kathedrale vorhanden waren, die aber bis zu diesem Punkt kaum gefeiert wurden.[442] Die Kreation neuer Gesänge für diese Bischöfe hatte einen doppelten Effekt: Auf der einen Seite wurde damit ein ‚Pantheon' von heiligen Veroneser Bischöfen kreiert und somit die Rolle dieser Heiligen als Prälaten der Veroneser Kirche in den Vordergrund gestellt. Auf der anderen Seite verlor Zeno unter diesen Umständen seine herausgehobene Stellung und wurde zu Einem unter Mehreren. Dieser Umstand deutet daraufhin, dass nun das Amt des Bischofs ins Zentrum der Außendarstellung des Domes rückte. Auf Zeno alleine konnte man sich am Dom nicht mehr berufen. Der Heilige gehörte nun allein dem Kloster.

---

441 Das Offizium für Theodorus zum Beispiel wurde als Paraphrase der Psalmen aufgebaut, die es begleiten. Für diese Art der Offiziendichtung siehe Benjamin Brandt, „Psalm paraphrase and biblical exegesis. An early office for St. Stephen" (nicht veröffentlichter Vortrag bei der Konferenz Historiae, Venezia, Fondazione Ugo e Olga Levi, 26.–29.01.2017).

442 Im *Carpsum* Verona BC XCIV(89) war ein Fest für Anno vorgesehen, bei dem sich in der Handschrift nur der Hinweis „De conf." befindet (vgl. Meersseman u. a.: L'orazionale, S. 276; für Theodorus sind dort zwei Feste vorgesehen (*natale* und *translatio*), beide wurde lediglich mit Commune-Gesängen gefeiert (vgl. ebd., S. 290 und S. 296).

5 Schluss

In dieser Studie wurde untersucht, wie Heilige im Mittelalter durch die liturgische Performanz von religiösen Verehrergemeinschaften konstruiert wurden. Dabei wurde die Untersuchung am Beispiel des heiligen Zeno von Verona und der ihm dort gewidmeten Verehrergemeinschaften durchgeführt, nämlich dem Veroneser Domkapitel und dem Kloster San Zeno Maggiore.

Grundlage der Arbeit stellte die Annahme dar, dass die Figur des Heiligen nicht bloß durch das Verfassen von Texten über ihn konstruiert wurde, sondern vielmehr Resultat eines vielfältigen kommunikativen und sozialen Prozesses war, der in Praktiken der Verehrung vollzogen wurde. Da diese Praktiken nur selten durch die Forschung in den Blick genommen werden, bestand eines der Ziele dieser Arbeit in der Verschiebung der Aufmerksamkeit von der Hagiographie hin zur Hagiopraxis, also von der Vita als Quelle der Heiligenverehrung auf die von Verehrergemeinschaften veranstaltete liturgische Feier. Daher rückten in dieser Arbeit vor allem die liturgischen Quellen des Kultes des heiligen Zeno in den Fokus. Sie erlaubten, die jeweils unterschiedlichen historischen Verehrergemeinschaften des Heiligen zu identifizieren sowie deren räumliche und zeitliche Kontexte zu bestimmen. Aus rezeptionsästhetischer Perspektive ermöglichten sie außerdem, die Bedeutung des jeweiligen Festes des Heiligen für seine historische Verehrergemeinschaft herauszustellen.

Für eine so geartete Untersuchung war es notwendig, die überlieferten Quellen der Hagiopraxis nicht nur wie üblich durch eine Edition, sondern auch im Rahmen einer Rekonstruktion zu erschließen. Hierfür wurden in einem ersten Schritt (Kapitel 3.3) die liturgischen Quellen jeweils nach Gattung separat ediert. Dabei wurde nicht ein ursprünglicher Text rekonstruiert, sondern durch eine synoptische Darstellungsweise die gegebenenfalls vorhandene Varianz wiedergegeben und betont. Da liturgische Quellen immer eine rituelle Praxis widerspiegeln, stellt jede überlieferte Version eine valide Version eines liturgischen Textes dar, die entsprechend gewürdigt werden muss. Diese Edition ermöglicht es, abweichende Texttraditionen zu identifizieren und somit die Inhalte der Feste der Hagiopraxis für die jeweiligen Kultkontexte genau zu bestimmen. Darüber hinaus wurde durch die Edition das Material zugänglich und unabhängig von der in dieser Arbeit durchgeführten Analyse konsultierbar gemacht.

Anschließend (Kapitel 3.4) wurden die in der Edition getrennt erstellten Texte je nach Kultkontext in einer Rekonstruktion zusammengeführt. Dafür wurden die handschriftlichen Träger historischen Kultkontexten zugeordnet und anschließend in einer Tabelle zusammengeführt. Das in den Handschriften und der Edition separat überlieferte liturgische Material wurde somit in den performativen und historischen Kontexten der jeweiligen liturgischen Feier wiedergegeben. Dabei sollte die Eigenheit liturgischer Quellen deutlich werden, die nur als Teil und im Rahmen der liturgischen Praxis zu verstehen sind.

Diese Rekonstruktion wurde für zwei konkrete Verehrungskontexte erstellt: Zum einen für das Zenofest des Domes in 10. Jahrhundert, zum anderen für die Feste, die das Kloster San Zeno Maggiore ab der zweiten Hälfte des 12. Jahrhunderts feierte. Die Quellen dieser Kontexte wurden nach ihrem Vorkommen in der Choreographie des Stundengebets nahezu in Gänze wiedergegeben. Hiervon profitiert die anschließende Analyse der Quellen, da textliche Resonanzen, Synergien zwischen den unterschiedlichen Elementen der Feier und das gegebenenfalls wiederholte Vorkommen einzelner Ideen und Bilder nachvollzogen werden können. Nur dadurch wird die Gesamtheit der liturgischen Feier als sinnvolles Ganzes wahrnehmbar.

Nach der methodischen Fundierung der Arbeit und der Aufbereitung der Quellen durch Edition und Rekonstruktion wurden Zenos historische Verehrergemeinschaften im Spiegel ihrer Hagiopraxis in den drei darauffolgenden Kapiteln analysiert. Ein besonderes Augenmerk lag dabei auf der Frage, wie der Heilige jeweils von einer Verehrergemeinschaft in der Liturgie konstruiert und mit welchem Profil er versehen wurde. Daraufhin wurde versucht, die Motive herauszuarbeiten, die die Gemeinschaft zu einer solchen Konstruktion führten und auch die Folgen zu identifizieren, die eine solche Konstruktion des Heiligen für die Verehrergemeinschaft selbst und ihr Verhältnis zu anderen sozialen Gruppen in der Stadt hatte. Für die Beantwortung dieser Fragen wurden zwei Verehrergemeinschaften Veronas ausgewählt, die einen besonderen Bezug zum heiligen Zeno aufwiesen: das Kapitel des Veroneser Doms und das Kloster San Zeno Maggiore.

Zunächst wurde in Kapitel 4.1 die Entstehung des Kultes und der beiden Verehrergemeinschaften untersucht. Hierfür wurde ein Überblick über Zenos historische Person und den Anfang des Zenokultes von dem Erscheinen der ersten Spuren seiner Verehrung hin zur zaghaften Entwicklung einer Hagiopraxis in der Karolingerzeit gegeben. Die Untersuchung ergab dabei eine fundamentale Rolle dieser Zeit für die Entwicklung des Zenokults, da hier die Grundsteine der zwei Institutionen gelegt wurden, die mit dem Heiligen wesentlich verbunden waren und dessen Verehrergemeinschaften in der Stadt darstellten: das Kapitel der Kleriker am Veroneser Dom und die Mönche von San Zeno Maggiore.

Obwohl die Karolingerzeit für die Entwicklung der Institutionen des Zenokultes sehr wichtig war, konnte diese Arbeit zeigen, dass gerade das 10. Jahrhundert für die vollständige Konstruktion des Heiligen entscheidend war, insbesondere die Veroneser Zeit des Bischofs Rather. Erst dank ihm wurde in Verona, genauer: am Dom, die erste Hagiopraxis für Zeno entwickelt, in der Zeno nun zum ersten Mal als vollständig profilierte Figur hervortreten konnte. Im Rahmen einer Untersuchung der ersten Historia für Zeno, der kanonikalen Historia *Dum Zeno pontificatus honore*, konnte eine bisher unbeachtete Fassung der Vita Zenos (BHL 9007) als ihre Vorlage identifiziert werden. Überdies entpuppte sich BHL 9007 nach eingehender inhaltlicher, sprachlicher und stilistischer Analyse als Werk Rathers, der hier, wie in der *Vita Ursmari*, als Redaktor einer älteren hagiographischen Vorlage tätig wurde. Die Untersuchung der auf BHL 9007 basierenden frühesten Zeno-Historia ergab außerdem, dass auch diese als Produkt des aus Lüttich stammenden Bischofs anzusehen ist: Darin vorkommende sprachliche und stilistische Eigentümlichkeiten sowie der Bezug auf den heiligen Martin, auf den Rather sich bereits berufen hatte, weisen den Lütticher Bischof als Urheber der Historia aus. Das so herausgearbeitete liturgische Ensemble des Zenofestes am Dom ab dem Ende des 10. Jahrhunderts wurde anschließend anhand der Rekonstruktion analysiert. Es wurde deutlich, dass in diesem liturgischen Kontext Zeno vor allem als einfacher und nach dem Modell der Apostel lebender Priester und Bischof profiliert wurde. Als patriotischer Heiliger wurde er hingegen kaum definiert.

Dieses in der Hagiopraxis konstruierte Profil von Zeno wurde daraufhin im Zusammenhang mit der Reform untersucht, die Rather am Domkapitel implementierte. Der inhaltliche Vergleich des von Rather propagierten Reformprogrammes mit dem Profil des Heiligen, wie dieser in der Hagiopraxis konstituiert wurde, konnte erhebliche Analogien offenbaren. In beiden Kontexten wurden auf die Wichtigkeit eines asketischen priesterlichen Lebens sowie die Ausbildung der angehenden Priester insistiert, die durch wirtschaftliche und räumliche Unabhängigkeit der eifrigen Minores von den Maiores gewährleistet wurden, die hingegen einen verdorbenen Lebensstil an den Tag legten. In diesem Kontext wurde die Liturgie zu einem Vehikel der Reform Rathers und der heilige Zeno in den Dienst der Reform genommen. Er wurde als asketisch lebender Priester zum Modell, das von den Klerikern des Domkapitels nachgeahmt werden sollte.

Eine solche Profilierung Zenos bedeutet seine Inanspruchnahme für die Kleriker des Kapitels, die sich als seine Nachfolger auszeichnen konnten. Sie waren aber nicht die einzigen, die einen speziellen Bezug zum Heiligen aufweisen konnten, denn auch das Kloster San Zeno Maggiore konnte diesen für sich vereinnahmen, da es immerhin auf Zenos Grab errichtet worden war. In der Tatsache, dass es zwei Gemeinschaften gab, die sich durch den Bezug zum gleichen Heiligen definierten, verbarg sich ein Konfliktpotential. Diese Spannung bestimmte langfristig das Verhältnis der Verehrergemeinschaften zu dem Heiligen und untereinander. Sie kam im Zusammenhang mit den Spenden für den Kult des Heiligen und der Frage, wem sie rechtmäßig zustanden, an die Oberfläche, lag aber eigentlich tiefer. Sie entstand nämlich dadurch, dass die jeweilige Rolle der mit Zeno unterschiedlich verbundenen Institutionen in der Verwaltung des Zenokultes nicht eindeutig geklärt war.

Im Kapitel 4.3 wird die zweite Verehrergemeinschaft Zenos in Verona, das außerhalb der Stadtmauer gelegene Benediktinerkloster San Zeno Maggiore, genauer in den Blick genommen und die dort entwickelte Profilierung des Heiligen untersucht. Auch wenn das Kloster bereits seit dem 9. Jahrhundert, als es auf dem ursprünglichen Grab Zenos errichtet wurde, mit der Aufgabe der Pflege der Reliquien des Heiligen betraut war, setzte die Überlieferung seiner liturgischen

Produktion erst im 11. Jahrhundert ein. Gleichwohl zeigte die Untersuchung, dass die monastische Fassung der Zenohistoria *Dum Zeno pontificatus honore* sowie die Vita BHL 9007 bereits ab dem Ende des 10. Jahrhunderts im Kloster Verwendung fand. In dieser ersten Phase bis zur Mitte des 12. Jahrhunderts war das Kloster in seiner Inanspruchnahme Zenos noch zögerlich. Auch wenn die zusätzlichen Gesänge, mit denen die Historia im Cursus romanus für die Nutzung im Kloster adaptiert wurde, zeigen, dass der monastischen Gemeinschaft ihre privilegierte Rolle als Bewahrer der Zenoreliquien bewusst war, wird Zeno immer noch auch als Bischof profiliert. Dieses mehrdeutige Profil des Heiligen, der auf der einen Seite als Gründer des Klosters und dort begrabene Reliquie, auf der anderen aber immer noch primär als Bischof präsentiert wurde, drückt das ambivalente Verhältnis der Abtei zu den Veroneser Bischöfen in dieser Phase ihrer Geschichte aus, das sowohl in einer politischen Abhängigkeit als auch dem selbstbewussten Wunsch nach Unabhängigkeit bestand.

Erst in der zweiten Hälfte des 12. Jahrhunderts, als das Kloster dank Abt Gerhard zu einer wirtschaftlichen und kulturellen Blüte gelangte, wurde die monastische Gemeinschaft auch liturgisch aktiver. Die monastische Hagiopraxis des Zenofestes wurde in dieser Zeit mit Lesungen aus einem neuen hagiographischen Dossier und neuen Hymnen angereichert. Darin nimmt das Kloster nunmehr deutlich eine prominente Rolle im Zenokult für sich in Anspruch. Auch lässt sich in der monastischen Hagiopraxis der zweiten Hälfte des 12. Jahrhunderts eine Profilierung Zenos erkennen, in der der individuelle Bezug der monastischen Gemeinschaft zum Heiligen deutlich zum Ausdruck kam. Zeno wird nun vor allem als toter, aber wirkmächtiger Körper für das Kloster relevant, dessen Mönche sich als Bewahrer seiner Reliquien und Verwalter seiner wundersamen Kraft definieren konnten. Damit nahm das Kloster eine eindeutige Position im Konflikt mit dem Dom ein und präsentierte sich als rechtmäßiger Verwalter des Kultes des gemeinsamen Heiligen.

Etwas überraschen mag die Tatsache, dass Zeno in der monastischen Hagiopraxis ab der zweiten Hälfte des 12. Jahrhunderts außerdem auch als Märtyrer profiliert und dadurch für Kreuzfahrer attraktiv gemacht wurde. Diese Umprofilierung des Heiligen ließ sich als Symptom des in der zweiten Hälfte des 12. Jahrhunderts Verona beherrschenden Kreuzzugsfiebers deuten. So behauptete sich das Kloster nicht nur innerhalb des städtischen Mikrokosmos gegenüber dem Bischof und dem Domkapitel als rechtmäßige Verwalter des Zenokultes, sondern machte sich damit auch für von außen kommende Verehrer erkennbar und attraktiv. Diese letzte Umprofilierung Zenos, mit der er als Märtyrer für mehrere Gruppen auch außerhalb der Stadt als verehrungswürdig präsentiert wurde, war der abschließende Schachzug im Wettbewerb um den Heiligen. In der spätmittelalterlichen Liturgie des Domes, wie sie in Codices des 14. Jahrhunderts fixiert ist, ist Zeno hauptsächlich durch sein bischöfliches Amt definiert, und damit tendenziell nur noch einer, wenn auch der erste, unter Veronas vielen Bischöfen.

6 Anhang

Tabelle 7 Vergleich Historia im CR mit verschiedenen Versionen der Zenovita

Historia *Dum Zeno pontificatus honore* (CR)	BHL 9001[1]	BHL 9003[2]	BHL 9004[3]	BHL 9006[4]	BHL 9007 [5]
A1 Ab utero matris fuit sanctificatus beatus Zeno et a cunabulis benedictus.	Ille enim a cunabulis benedictus et a ventre sanctificatus erat.	Igitur ille a cunabulis benedictus et a ventre sanctificatus erat.	Ille enim a cunabulis benedictus et a ventre sanctificatus erat.	fehlt	Fuit quippe a matris utero sanctificatus et a cunabulis benedictus.
A2 Probitatis et scientiae iugibus incrementis ad hoc pertingere meruit ut per sacerrimam vitam pastor in populis efficeretur.	fehlt et ad hoc pertingere meruit, ut per vitam sanctam pastor in populo esse mereretur.	fehlt et ad hoc pertingere meruit ut et vita sancta et pastor in populo esse mereretur.	fehlt et ad hoc pertingere meruit ut et vita sancta et pastor in populo esse mereretur.	fehlt	Probitatis atque scientiae iugibus incrementis ad hoc pertingere meruit ut per sacerrimam vitam fieri pastor in populo mereretur.

[1] Aus: Sala: Il culto di Zeno nei secoli VIII–IX, S. 29–32.
[2] Aus: Angelo Grazioli: San Zenone di Verona, in: La scuola cattolica 68, 1940, S. 174–199, hier: S. 193–195.
[3] Wortlaut der Handschrift Firenze BN Conv. Soppr. 182, ff. 216r–218r (10. Jhdt.).
[4] Wortlaut der Handschrift Firenze BML Plut 30.I sin., ff. 24v–25v (12. Jhdt.).
[5] Aus meiner Edition von BHL 9007 (siehe Kapitel 3.3.3, S. 87–91).

A5 Dum exercitio piscationis fungeretur in fluvio vidit quendam hominem in plaustro sedentem per praeceps in amnem demergi.	in fluvio Athesi piscationem dum ageret, vidit de contra quemdam hominem in plaustro sedentem, bubus subiunctis, mergi in flumine.	in fluvio Adese piscationem dum ageret erectis sursum oculis vidit e contra quendam hominem in plaustrum bovibus subiunctum mergi in flumine.	in fluvio Atise piscationem dum ageret vidit de contra quendam hominem in plaustro bovibus mergi in flumine.	Cum quadam die a monasterio egressus in flumine Attice piscationem ageret vidit de contra quendam hominem in plaustro bovibus mergi in flumine.	Dum egrediens idem vir a monasterio in Athesis fluvio piscationis exercitio fungeretur erectis sursum oculis vidit ex adverso quendam hominem in plaustro sedentem bubus subiunctis per preceps in amnem dimergi.
A6 Vir Dei, elevata sursum manu, fecit signum crucis dicens: „Revertere retro Sathanas, ne perimas hominem quem Deus creavit."	Et quidem sanctus vir [...] Elevata sursum manu fecit sanctae crucis signum frequenti vice dicens: „Revertere retro Satanas, ne perimas hominem, quem Deus creavit."	Et quidem sanctus vir [...] Elevata sursum manu fecit sanctae crucis signum frequenti vice dicens: „Revertere retro Satanas, ne perimas hominem, quem Deus creavit."	Et quidem sanctus vir [...] Elevata sursum manu fecit sanctae crucis signum frequenti vice dicens: „Revertere retro Satanas, ne perimas hominem, quem Deus creavit."	Et quidem sanctus vir [...] Elevata sursum manu fecit sanctae crucis signum frequenti vice dicens: „Revertere retro Satanas, ne perimas hominem, quem Deus creavit."	Sanctus itaque vir Dei [...] elevata sursum manu fecit sanctae crucis signum frequenti vice et dixit: „Revertere retro Satana ne perimas hominem quem Deus creavit."
A7 Beatus Zeno dixit: „Non te permittit Dominus aliquid agere adversus servum suum."	Tunc sanctus Dei Zeno ait: „Non te permittat Dominus agere adversus servum suum."	Tunc sanctus Dei Zeno ait: „Non te permittat Dominus agere adversus servum suum."	Tunc sanctus Dei Zeno ait: „Non te permittat Dominus agere adversus servum suum."	Tunc sanctus Dei Zeno ait: „Non te permittat Dominus agere adversus servum suum."	Sanctus autem Dei Zeno dixit: „Non te permittit Dominus aliquid agere adversus servum suum."

A8 Miserabilis pater totaque domus regia maerore affligebatur eo quod acriter puella suffocaretur.	Tunc miserabilis pater simulque tota domus regia in tristitiam versa cruciatu affligebantur, eo quod sic crudeliter suffocaretur	Tunc miserabilis pater simulque et tota domus regia in tristitiam versa cruciatu affligebatur eo quod sic crudeliter soffocaretur.	Tunc miserabilis pater simulque et tota domus regia in tristitiam versa cruciatu affligebatur eo quod sic crudeliter suffocaretur.	Tunc miserabilis pater simulque tota domus regia in tristitiam versa cruciatu affligebantur, eo quod sic crudeliter suffocaretur.	Miserabilis ergo pater simulque tota domus regia in tristitiam versa cruciatu et maerore ingenti affligebantur eo quod tam acriter puella suffocaretur.
A9 Sacerdos Dei Zeno sedebat super lapidem et artis apostolicae documenta sequens piscabatur in flumine.	Ille enim sedebat super lapidem, qui in proximo monasterii erat, et piscabatur in flumine.	Ille einm sedebat super lapidem quod in proximo monasteri erat et piscabat in flumine.	Ille enim sedebat super lapidem qui in proximo monasterio erat et piscabat in flumine.	Ille enim sedebat super lapidem, qui in proximo monasterii erat, et piscabatur in flumine.	Ille vero sedebat super lapidem qui in proximo erat monasterii et artis apostolicae instrumenta baiulans ex more piscabatur in flumine.
R2 Ab utero sanctificatus beatus Zeno et a cunabulis benedictus, ad hoc pertingere meruit ut pastor in populis per sacerrimam vitam efficeretur. V In omnem terram sonus exiit	Ille enim a cunabulis benedictus et a ventre sanctificatus erat, et ad hoc pertingere meruit, ut per vitam sanctam pastor in populo esse mereretur; et ideo quia in omnem terram exiit sonus	Igitur ille a cunabulis benedictus et a ventre sanctificatus erat et ad hoc pertingere meruit ut et vita sancta et pastor in populo esse mereretur; et ideo quia in omni terra exiit sonus	Ille enim a cunabulis benedictus et a ventre sanctificatus erat et adhoc pertingere meruit ut et vita sancta et pastor in populo esse mereretur. Ideo quia in omnem terram exivit sonus	Ille enim a cunabulis benedictus et a ventre sanctificatus erat et adhoc pertingere meruit ut et vita sancta et pastor in populo esse mereretur. Ideo quia in omnem terram exivit sonus	Fuit quippe a matris utero sanctificatus et a cunabulis benedictus [...]. Denique probitatis atque scientie iugibus incrementis ad hoc pertingere meruit ut per sacerrimam vitam fieri pastor in

conversationis eius et sanctitas luculenter emicuit.	conversationis eius et sanctitas emicuit.	conversationis eius et sanctitas emicuit.	conversationis eius et sanctitas emicuit.	conversationis eius et sanctitas emicuit.	populo mereretur. […] in omnem terram sonus exiit conversationis eius et sanctitas luculenter emicuit.
R3 In secretiori parte oratorii continuis ieiuniis et crebris orationibus a Domino petebat ut sibi dignaretur aditum praedicationis in populos aperire. V Ad convertendas in amore Christi animas hominum die noctuque deditus erat.	Erat enim sedens in monasterio in secretiori parte in oppido Veronensi, continuis ieiuniis et crebris orationibus a Domino petens, ut sibi dignaretur aditum praedicationis in populos aperire. Denique ad convertendos in Christi amorem animos hominum de die in diem deditus erat.	Erat enim sedens in monasterio in secretiori parte in oppido veronense Continuis ieiuniis et crebris orationibus a Domino petens ut sibi dignaretur aditum praedicationis in populo adaperire. Denique ad convertendas in Christi amore animas hominum de die in diem deditus erat.	Erat enim sedens in monasterio in secretiore parte in oppido Veronense ad convertendas in Christi amore animas hominum petitus erat.	Erat enim sedens in monasterio in secretiore parte in oppido Veronense ad convertendas in Christi amore animas hominum petitus erat.	Erat enim sedens in monasterio in secretiori parte oppidi veronensis continuis ieiuniis et orationibus crebris a Domino petens ut sibi dignaretur aditum mellifluae praedicationis in populos aperire. […] ad convertendas in amore Christi animas hominum die noctuque deditus erat.
R4 Affabilis ita erat in sermonibus et mansuetudine atque habitu mitis ut Deus	Ita ergo in sermone affabilis erat, et in mansuetudine et in habitu mitis, ut Deus	Ita ergo in sermone adfabiilis erat et in habitu mitis ut Deus in ipso a quibus	Ita ergo in sermone ac fabulis erat et in mansuetudine mitis ut Deus in ipso	Ita ergo in sermone ac fabulis erat et in mansuetudine mitis ut Deus in ipso	Ita sane affabilis erat in sermone et in mansuetudine seu in habitu mitis ut iure

in ipso conlaudaretur ab omnibus ad se venientibus. V Ita existebat alacer ut mox ad eum properantes relictis idolis Domino crederent Iesu Christo	in ipso conlaudaretur ab omnibus venientibus ad se; et ita alacer, ut mox relictis idolis Domino Iesu Christo crederent.	poterat videri conlaudaretur ad omnibus apparentibus et venientibus ad se ita alcer erat ut mox relictis idolis Domino Ihesu Christo crederatur.	conlaudaretur ab omnibus apparentibus et veniendo ad se. Ita alacris ut ex ipsius sancto eloquio mentes vel corda hominum accenderentur.	conlaudaretur ab omnibus apparentibus et veniendo ad se. Ita alacris ut ex ipsius sancto eloquio mentes vel corda hominum accenderentur sicut scriptum est.	Deus in ipso collaudaretur ab omnibus venientibus ad se. Ita alacer et splendifico nitore facundiae vividus ut mox ad eum properantes relictis idolis et pravitate gentilitatis exempti Domino crederent Iesu Christo.
R5 Dum in fluvio Athesis piscationis exercitio fungeretur, erectis sursum oculis, vidit quendam hominem in plaustro sedentem, bubus subiunctis, in amnem dimergi.	in fluvio Athesi piscationem dum ageret, erectis sursum oculis vidit de contra quemdam hominem in plaustro sedentem, bubus subiunctis, mergi in flumine.	in fluvio Adese piscationem dum ageret.	in fluvio Atise piscationem dum ageret erectis sursum oculis vidit de contra quendam hominem in plaustro bovibus mergi in flumine.	per idem tempus iuxta eam civitatem Veronam haec in propinquo itinere egrediente eodem viro a monasterio in fluvio Atise piscationem dum ageret erectis sursum oculis vidit de contra quendam hominem in plaustro bovibus mergi in flumine.	dum egrediens idem vir a monasterio in Athesis fluvio piscationis exercitio fungeretur erectis sursum oculis vidit ex adverso quendam hominem in plaustro sedentem bubus subiunctis per preceps in amnem dimergi.

V Tanta enim velocitate ferebatur ut cunctis ostenderetur antiqui hostis arte peractum.	Tanta enim velocitate ferebatur, ut omnibus demonstraretur diaboli arte fuisse gestum.		Tanta enim velocitate ferebatur ut omnibus demonstraretur diaboli arte fuisse gestum.	Tanta enim velocitate ferebatur ut omnibus demonstraretur diaboli arte fuisse gestum.	Tanta quippe miserabilis velocitate ferebatur ut palam cunctis cernentibus daretur intellegi hoc diaboli arte fuisse peractum.
R7 Festinans itaque daemon ingressus est palatium caesaris Gallieni et comprehensam eius unicam filiam coepit eam crudeliter vexare. V Miserabilis pater simulque tota domus eius cruciatu et maerore affligebatur.	Festinans daemon ingressus est domum palatii Gallieni; comprehensam filiam eius, quae eo tempore parentibus unica erat, coepit crudeliter vexare. Tunc miserabilis pater simulque tota domus regia in tristitiam versa cruciatu affligebantur.		Festinans daemon ingressus palatium Gallieni comprehensa filia quae tunc in tempore parva erat et a parentibus unica coepit crudeliter vexari. Tunc miserabilis pater simulque et tota domus regia in tristitiam versa cruciatu affligebatur eo quod sic crudeliter suffocaretur.	et festinans daemon ingressus palatium Gallieni comprehensa filia quae tunc in tempore parva erat et aparentibus unica coepit crudeliter vexari. Tunc miserabilis pater simulque et tota domus regia in tristitiam versa cruciatu affligebatur eo quod sic crudeliter suffocaretur.	Festinans itaque daemon ingressus est concite palatium caesaris Gallieni arreptamque filiam eius quae tunc temporis unica parentibus erat, coepit crudeliter vexare. Miserabilis ergo pater simulque tota domus regia in tristitiam versa cruciatu et maerore ingenti affligebantur.
L-A1 Dominus Iesus Christus omnipotens est, oportet enim ut mirabilia Dei	„Dominus Iesus Christus omnipotens est. Ite“ – inquit – „ecce ego subsequor		quia Dei mirabilia oportet ut omnibus	Ille vero dixit eis: Ite, inquid, ecce ego subsequor vos quia Dei mirabilia oportet	Dominus Iesus Christus omnipotens est. Ite“, inquid, „ecce ego paulatim

omnibus manifestentur.	vos, quia Dei mirabilia oportet ut omnibus manifestantur.“		manifestentur.	ut omnibus manifestentur.	subsequor vos. Oportet enim ut mirabilia Dei luce clarius manifestentur.“
L-A2 Exurgens beatus sacerdos fecit orationem perrexitque ad palatium ubi affligebatur pro sua filia rex.	Exsurgens vero sanctus fecit orationem, et perrexit ad palatium ubi cruciabatur et affligebatur pro sua filia imperator.		Exurgens autem sanctus sacerdos fecit orationem perexitque ad palatium ubi cruciatus rex affligebatur per sua filia.	Exurgens autem sanctus sacerdos fecit orationem perexitque ad palatium ubi cruciatus rex affligebatur per sua filia.	Exsurgens vero beatus sacerdos vero ne diucius absconderetur civitas super montem domus Domini posita fecit orationem perrexitque ad palatium ubi affligebatur pro sua filia rex.
L-A3 Ingrediente Christi confessore palatium facto crucis signo per os puellae daemon clamavit dicens: „Tu, Zeno, venisti ad expellendum me et propter tuam sanctitatem stare non possum.“	Facto vero crucis signo, ingrediente Christi sacerdote palatium, coepit mox per os infantulae daemon clamare dicens: „Ecce tu, Zeno, venisti ad expellendum me, et ego propter tuam		Facto vero crucis signo ingrediente sacerdote palatium coepit mox per os infantile daemon adclamare dicens: „Ecce, Zenon, tu venisti ad expellendum me et ego stare propter tuam sanctitatem	Facto vero crucis signo ingrediente sacerdote palatium coepit mox per os infantile daemon adclamare dicens: „Ecce, Zenon, tu venisti ad expellendum me et ego stare propter tuam sanctitatem	Ingrediente siquidem Christi confessore sacerdote palatium et facto crucis signo coepit confestim per hos infantulae daemon clamare dicens: „Ecce, tu Zeno, venisti ad expellendum me et ego propter tue

	sanctitatem stare non possum.“		non possum.“	non possum.“	pavorem sanctitatis hic stare non possum.“
L-A4 Tenens beatus Zeno manum puellae dicens: „In nomine Domini mei Iesu Christi praecipio tibi exi ab ea daemon.“	tenens sacerdos manum puellae dixit: „In nomine Domini Iesu Christi praecipio tibi, exi ab ea daemon.“		tenens sacerdos manum puellae continuo exit daemon.	tenens sacerdos manum puellae continuo exit daemon et adclamare publica iam voce coepit dicens.	tenens sacerdos manum puellae dixit: „In nomine Domini nostri Iesu Christi praecipio tibi exi ab ea daemon.“
L-A5 Christi namque sacerdos ab omni daemonicae incursionis ludificatione sanam restituit filiam regis.	Christi itaque sacerdos sanam restituit imperatoris filiam.	Sanam vero reddens restituit regi filiam.	Sanam vero reddens restituit regi filiam.[6]	sanam vero reddens restituet regi filiam.	Christi namque sacerdos sanam mox ab omni daemonicae incursionis ludificatione restituit filiam regis.

[6] Sanam...filiam] Der Text von BHL 9004 wird in Firenze BN Conv. Soppr. 182 durchgestrichen und mit dem Wortlaut von BHL 9007 ersetzt: *Christi namque sacerdos sanam mox ab omni demonice incursionis ludificatione resitutit filiam regis.* Sowohl die Handschrift als auch die Hand, die den Nachtrag hinzufügte, können ins 10. Jhdt. datiert werden. Sie liefern somit einen weitereren Beleg dafür, dass BHL 9007 im 10. Jhdt. im Umlauf war.

Tabelle 8 Vergleich BHL 9001 – BHL 9007

	BHL 9001[7]	BHL 9007[8]
1		*Pontificum splendor, iustorum norma virorum,* *Aequilibra Zeno trames et ordo boni.* *Acta viri, cuius totum respersa per orbem,* *Quanta nequit dextra scribere lingua loqui.* *Sed tamen e multis perstringam pauca legenti,* *In quibus antistes fulserit ille sacer.* *Pro dolor!, antiquo quidam correptus ab hoste* *In fluvium sese precipitando ruit.* *Tunc crucis efficiens sacratae signa subinde* *Mortis ab articulo sustulit ipse pater.* *Ipse domum petit Gallieni caesaris in qua* *Nata iacet gravibus exagitata malis.* *Illam namque taeter vexabat spiritus unde* *In luctum mater vertitur atque pater.* *Sed Domini veniens ad regis iussa sacerdos.* *Cum iubet obsessam deserit alta gemens.* *Hoc etiam minitans quod non post multa Veronae,* *Impedimenta sui sint subeunda sibi;* *Cuius amore stilo depinximus ista redemptor* *Illius munda crimina nostra prece.*

7 Aus: Sala, Il culto di San Zeno nei secoli VIII e IX, in: Annuario storico Zenoniano 7 (1990), S. 19–36, hier: S. 29–32.
8 Eigene Edition aus den zwei ältesten Textzeugen, Novara BC II und Novara BC LXIII (siehe Kapitel 3.3.3., S. 87–91). Rathers Zusätze kursiv.

2	In diebus illis in provincia Italia, in civitate Verona, in qua beati Zenonis acta claruerunt, evolvimus tanti viri virtutes. Sic enim est humana mens ad investigandas sanctorum vitas, tamquam quis ille sitiens, ardore solis adustus concupiscat fontium fluenta, aut quis desideratissimum nuntium audire cupiat, vel etiam quis deliciarum epulis enutritus, in quodam longinquo itinere positus, ad rem pervenire suae mentis satietatem cupiat. Ita et ego tanti viri, quamvis ad omnia quaeque egit vel in conversatione vel etiam in miraculis explere non valeo, attamen quantum adtingere pro parte possum, enarrare non desisto, ne quis ille lector deroget, aut audiens legentem desidioso animo detrahat, cum scriptum sit: Qui retribuunt mihi mala pro bonis, detrahunt mihi; et quia ipse Dominus dixit bona operantibus: Priusquam te formarem in utero novi te, et antequam exires de ventre sanctificavi te. Ille enim a cunabulis benedictus et a ventre sanctificatus erat, et ad hoc pertingere meruit, ut per vitam sanctam pastor in	*Olim peritissimorum disciplinabilis mos extitit virorum indagatione diligenti sanctorum vitas exquirere earumque seriem stili officio sollicite ac rationabiliter memoriae posteritati assignare, quatenus ob suae studium doctrinae ipsorum in orbe imitatione potirentur et eorum quandoque consortio in perhennis vitae gloria fruerentur.* Sic *etenim instat sapientis* mens ad investigandas sanctorum vitas, tamquam *si aliquis* sitiens ardore solis adustus, *avide* fontium concupiscat fluenta, *vel etiam si quis* desideratissimum *ex remota regione* audire *ambiat* nuntium, *aut certe si quislibet* deliciarum *dapibus* enutritus, in quodam longinquo itinere positus *esuriens*, ad *solitam* sui cupiat *ventris* pervenire satietatem. *Nos itaque licet eis, qui talia conscripsere, simus scientia impares, et penitus ad exprimenda, quae gestimus inefficaces, quoniam rei materiam verborum composito non aequiperat, ea tamen, quae de beati Zenonis virtutibus vel scriptis vel faminibus ediscere valuimus disserãmus.* *In diebus imperatoris Gallieni, qui per successiones caesarum vigesimus septimus in eorum est catalogo subrogatus, quo etiam tempore, Dionisius vir reverentissimus a beato Petro apostolo vigesimus tertius Romanae praesidebat ecclesiae,* in provincia Italia in civitate Verona beati Zenonis acta claruentur. *Cuius* viri virtutes *ad liquidum, quas in conversatione vel in miraculis peregit, explicare non sufficientes, aliquas tamen iuxta, quod attingere possumus, ennarrare veridica ratione conamur. Fuit quippe a matris utero* sanctificatus, et a cunabulis benedictus, *ut assertione divina in eo repeti videretur, quod Hieremiae dictum est:* „Priusquam te formarem in utero, novi te et antequam exires de ventre sanctificavi te.“ *Denique probitatis atque scientiae iugibus*

	populo esse mereretur; et ideo quia in omnem terram exiit sonus conversationis eius et sanctitas emicuit audiant populi omnes, qui eius cupiunt miracula.	*incrementis* ad hoc pertingere meruit, ut per *sacerrimam* vitam *fieri* pastor in populo mereretur. *Nempe* audiant populi omnes, qui eius cupiunt *nosse* miracula, quia in omnem terram sonus exiit conversationis eius et sanctitas *luculenter* emicuit.
3	Erat enim sedens in monasterio in secretiori parte in oppido Veronensi, continuis ieiuniis et crebris orationibus a Domino petens, ut sibi dignaretur aditum praedicationis in populos aperire. Denique ad convertendos in Christi amorem animos hominum de die in diem deditus erat. Revera quia in ipso spiritus sanctus doctor erat, sicut ipsa veritas per se loquitur dicens: „Non enim vos estis qui loquimini, sed spiritus patris vestri, qui loquitur in vobis" et illud: „Ego sum pastor bonus, et animam meam pono pro ovibus meis". Ita ergo in sermone affabilis erat, et in mansuetudine et in habitu mitis, ut Deus in ipso conlaudaretur ab omnibus venientibus ad se; et ita alacer, ut mox relictis idolis Domino Iesu Christo crederent.	Erat enim sedens in monasterio in secretiori parte oppidi Veronensis, continuis ieiuniis et orationibus crebris a Domino petens, ut sibi dignaretur aditum *melliferae* praedicationis in populos aperire. Igitur ad convertendas in amorem Christi animas hominum *die noctuque* deditus erat. Revera quoniam sanctus ei spiritus *purarum illuminator mentium* doctor existebat, sicut ipsa veritas loquitur dicens: „Non enim vos estis, qui loquimini, sed spiritus patris vestri, qui loquitur in vobis." Ita *sane* affabilis erat in sermone et in mansuetudine, seu in habitu mitis, ut *iure* Deus in ipso collaudaretur ab omnibus venientibus ad se, ita alacer et *splendifico nitore facundiae vividus*, ut mox *ad eum properantes* relictis idolis et *pravitate gentilitatis exempti* Domino crederent Iesu Christo.
4	Per idem vero tempus cum iuxta civitatem Veronam, quae in propinquo erat itinere, egrediente eodem viro a monasterio, in fluvio Athesi piscationem dum ageret, erectis sursum oculis vidit de contra quemdam hominem in plaustro sedentem, bubus subiunctis, mergi in flumine. Tanta enim velocitate ferebatur, ut omnibus demonstraretur diaboli arte fuisse gestum. Et quidem sanctus vir, elevans oculos dum vidisset, cognovit hoc factum diaboli esse. Elevata sursum manu fecit sanctae crucis signum frequenti vice dicens: „Revertere retro Satanas, ne perimas hominem, quem	Per idem tempus iuxta urbem Veronam, *dum egrediens idem vir a monasterio in Atesi* fluvio *piscationis exercitio fungeretur*, erectis sursum oculis vidit *ex adverso* quendam hominem in plaustro sedentem bobus subiunctis *per praeceps in amnem dimergi*. Tanta *quippe miserabilis* velocitate ferebatur, ut *palam cunctis cernentibus daretur intellegi*, hoc diaboli arte fuisse *peractum*. Sanctus itaque vir, *dum intentis luminibus* hoc *a longe prospiceret*, cognovit *limphaticam viri ruinam* factum diaboli esse. *Interea* vir Dei elevata sursum manu fecit sanctae crucis signum frequenti vice et dixit: „Revertere retro Sathana, ne perimas hominem

	Deus creavit“. Quod signum diabolus ut vidit, evanuit velut fumus, ita ut clamoribus ac stridore nefando quasi de alta rupe inruperit, dicens: „Etsi quidem nunc me non permittis animas hominum lucrari, tamen paratus sum in patrias ignotas, quae circumquaque sunt, ire ad impedimentum tuum“. Tunc sanctus Dei Zeno ait: „Non te permittat Dominus agere adversus servum suum“. His ita actis, cum ululatu et clamore discessit.	quem Deus creavit“. Quod *videlicet* signum ut diabolus *aspexit*, velut fumus vento *raptatus* evanuit et clamoribus *nimiis* ac stridore nefando, quasi de alta rupe *cum impetu decideret* ait: „Etsi non hic me permittis animas hominum *mea obsessione* lucrari, tamen paratus sum in patrias notas circumquaque *sitas*, ad tuum *perniciter abire* impedimentum.“ Sanctus autem Dei Zeno dixit: „Non te permittit Dominus *dire* aliquid agere adversus servum suum“. His ita *peractis*, cum *detestabili* ululatu et clamore discessit.
5	Festinans daemon ingressus est domum palatii Gallieni; comprehensam filiam eius, quae eo tempore parentibus unica erat, coepit crudeliter vexare. Tunc miserabilis pater simulque tota domus regia in tristitiam versa cruciatu affligebantur, eo quod sic crudeliter suffocaretur. Quae dum crudeli vexatione correpta esset, coepit per os infantulae imperatoris filiae daemon clamare dicens: „Non egrediar a corpore isto, nisi Zeno episcopus venerit, ac per ipsius imperium egrediar.“ Mox vero ut hoc imperator Gallienus audivit, missis apparitoribus ad perquirendum sanctum virum, coepit sollicite investigare. Tunc ex iussu imperatoris milites pergunt ad virum Dei. Ille enim sedebat super lapidem, qui in proximo monasterii erat, et piscabatur in flumine. Venientes vero milites, quia inscius illis erat, coeperunt sollicite interrogare sanctum Dei sacerdotem dicentes: „Quis es tu, homo Dei? Indica nobis, si vidisti Zenonem episcopum, quem nos ex iussu imperatoris perquirimus.“ At ille respondit dicens: „Quamvis plura sint nomina in monasterio nostro de nomine	Festinans *itaque* daemon ingressus est *concite* palatium caesaris Gallieni *arreptamque* filiam eius, quae *tunc* temporis unica parentibus erat, coepit crudeliter vexare. Miserabilis ergo pater, simulque tota domus regia in tristiam versa, *cruciatu et maerore ingenti* affligebantur, eo quod *tam acriter* puella suffocaretur. Quae dum crudeli vexatione corriperetur, coepit per os infantulae regis filiae daemon clamare dicens: „Non egrediar a corpore isto, nisi Zeno venerit episcopus, ac per ipsius imperium *coactus migrabo*.“ Mox itaque ut hoc regi Gallieno *innotuit*, missis aparitoribus *sollicita intentione* coepit investigare, *sic ubi sanctum potuisset invenire virum*. Ex iussu autem regis milites *velocibus* ad virum Dei *gressibus* pergunt. Ille vero sedebat super lapidem, qui in proximo erat monasterii *et artis apostolicae documenta proficiens, ex more* piscabatur in flumine. Venientes ergo milites, quoniam *ignotus* eis erat, coeperunt sollicite sanctum Dei sacerdotem interrogare dicentes: „Quis es tu, homo Dei? Indica nobis, si vidisti Zenonem episcopum, quem nos ex iussu regis perquirimus.“ At ille repondit: *„Ad quod missi estis edicite*. Ego enim quamvis tantillus servus Christi, tamen Zeno

<table>
<tr><td></td><td>isto, quem vos dicitis, tamen quod missi estis dicite. Ego enim, quamvis tantillus, servus tamen Christi sum, Zeno vocor". Tunc vero conferentes milites ad invicem dicebant inter se: „Quid multa conloquimur? Indicemus pro qua re missi sumus ad virum istum". Respondentes vero dixerunt: „Rogat te imperator, et te vult videre". Respondit Zeno: „Quid meam vult humilitatem videre imperator, qui omnium Christianorum inimicus esse non desistit?". At illi dixerunt: „Ita enim rogat te imperator, ut filiam ipsius, quae a daemonio vexatur, sanam reddas, quae unica illi est". Ille vero dixit eis: „Dominus Iesus Christus omnipotens est. Ite – inquit – ecce ego subsequor vos, quia Dei mirabilia oportet ut omnibus manifestantur". Quo dicto abierunt milites.</td><td>vocor." Igitur conferentes ad invicem milites dicebant inter se: „Quid multa colloquimur? Indicemus pro qua re istum destinati sumus ad virum." Tunc patenter intimantes beato sacerdoti dixerunt: „Rogat te rex venire ad se, quia vult faciem tuam videre." Zeno respondit: „Quid meam rex vult humilitatem cernere, qui omnium Christianorum manifestis indiciis inimicus esse non desinit?" At illi respondentes dixerunt: „Obsecrat enim te rex, ut filiam ipsius, quae immani atrocitate a daemonio vexatur, sanitati restituas, quia unica illi est." Ille vero dixit eis: „Dominus Iesus Christus omnipotens est. Ite", inquit, „ecce ego paulatim subsequor vos. Oportet enim ut mirabilia Dei luce clarius omnibus manifestentur." Quo dicto milites viam, qua venerant, repedarunt.</td></tr>
<tr><td>6</td><td>Exsurgens vero sanctus fecit orationem, et perrexit ad palatium ubi cruciabatur et affligebatur pro sua filia imperator: quo sanctus Dei episcopus, dum iter ageret, ante pervenit, quam hi, qui missi fuerant milites.

Facto vero Crucis signo, ingrediente Christi sacerdote palatium, coepit mox per os infantulae daemon clamare dicens: „Ecce tu, Zeno, venisti ad expellendum me, et ego propter tuam sanctitatem stare non possum".
Quo dicto tenens sacerdos manum puellae dixit: „In nomine Domini Iesu Christi praecipio tibi, exi ab ea, daemon". At ille publica voce coepit clamare dicens: „Etsi hinc a te expulsus fuero eo Veronam: invenies me et eos, in quibus habitem, stantes in platea exspectantes te". Christi itaque sacerdos sanam</td><td>Exurgens vero beatus sacerdos, ne diutius absconderetur civitas supra montem domus Domini posita, fecit orationem perrexitque ad palatium, ubi cruciabatur et lamentabiliter affligebatur pro sua filia rex. Sanctus quoque Dei episcopus Zeno, dum celeri peragratione iter ageret, ante eo pervenit, quam hi qui missi fuerant milites. Ingrediente siquidem Christi sacerdote palatium et facto crucis signo coepit confestim per os infantulae daemon clamare dicens: „Ecce tu, Zeno, venisti ad expellendum me et ego propter tuae pavorem sanctitatis hic stare non possum." His quidem auditis tenens sacerdos manum puellae dixit: „In nomine Domini nostri Iesu Christi praecipio tibi: „Exi ab ea, daemon!" At ille publica coepit et horribili voce clamare dicens: „Etsi hinc a te expulsus fuero, eo Veronam ibique invenies me et eos in quibus habitem stantes in platea expectantes te." Christi namque sacerdos sanam mox ab omni daemonicae incursionis</td></tr>
</table>

	restituit imperatoris filiam.	*ludificatione* restituit filiam regis.
7	Quod vero factum ut vidit imperator Gallienus, admiratione comprehensus, coronam regalem, quam capite suo gestabat, sancto sacerdoti obtulit dicens: „Tali medico, qui sanam unicam filiam meam restituit, nullis aliis muneribus placere possum, nisi ei ipsam quam habeo coronam meam offeram". Quod factum, dum gereretur, videns multitudo populi qui ad palatium convenerat, ab errore conversa gentili crediderunt in Christum Iesum Dominum nostrum, petentes sacerdotem Christi, ut docerentur viam salutis et baptismum in remissionem perciperent peccatorum. At ubi sacerdos accepit coronam imperatoris, statim distribuit pauperibus dicens: „Si Dominus operatur excelsa, ipsi referatur et gloria".	*Protinus autem* ut rex Gallienus vidit hoc factum, *attonitus* admiratione coronam regalem, quam capite gestabat sancto sacerdoti obtulit dicens: „*Tam salutifero* medico qui sanam unicam filiam meam restituit, nullis *muneribus aliis* placere possum, nisi *ipsam ei* quam habeo *meam* offeram *coronam*." *Cumque*, hoc gestum, multitudo *vidisset* populi, quae ad palatium convenerat, *a tenebris infidelitatis* et errore conversa gentili, crediderunt *unanimiter* in Iesum Christum Dominum nostrum, *obsecrantes* sacerdotem Christi, ut docerentur viam salutis et baptismum *mererentur* in remissionem *percipere delictorum*. At ubi sacerdos coronam accepit a rege, statim *in partes divisam* distribuit pauperibus dicens: „Si Dominus operatur excelsa, ipsi *perpetuae laudes* refer*antur* et gloria."
8	His ita gestis petiit beatissimus Zeno ut ei licentia tribueretur omnia idola destruendi et in Christi nomine ecclesias fabricandi. Cuius precibus adquievit imperator omnibus quae ille poposcerat. Post haec ingressus sacerdos Veronam civitatem intrepidus praedicabat in Christi nomine verbum, ut diaboli idola destruerentur et in Christi famulus pateretur.	His ita gestis, petiit beatissimus Zeno, ut ei licentia tribueretur omnia idola destruendi *et basilicas* in Christi nomine fabricandi. Cuius *almificis* precibus adquievit rex *affatim* in omnibus, quae ille poposcerat. *Nempe talibus et his similibus incedebat opinatus virtutibus, ut compleretur in eo, quod Dominus apostolis ait: „Ecce dedi vobis potestatem calcandi supra serpentes et scorpiones et omnem virtutem inimici"*. Post haec *igitur* ingressus sacerdos civitatem Veronam, intrepidus praedicabat in Christi nomine verbum et hoc *instanter* agebat, ut *funditus* idola destruerentur et in honorem Domini aedificarentur ecclesiae. *Denique, dum haec agerentur, multitudo populi paganorum saeviens incessanter moliebatur, ut impedimentum Christi famulus pateretur.* Sed

	Sed vigilans in suis servis Christus vincebat mendacium, quod purafides tenebat in corde.	vigilante in servis suis Christo vincebatur mendacium, quod pura *et rectissima fides ab infidelium cordibus abigebat.*
9	Perfectis igitur his agebat salutaria pro populi intercessione, quod ab ineunte aetate in Christi amore solitus erat. Qui dum hoc instanter ageret, Dei voluntate non multo post receptus in pace est. Et quia in miraculis omni populo claruit, in honore Dei et in ipsius sancti sacerdotis, quidam ex genere Gallieni fecit Sancto nomini ipsius basilicam haud procul a fluvio, ubi nunc sanctum ipsius corpus requiescit, qui etiam venerabilis locus in Christi nomine miraculis coruscat.	*His equidem ita patratis sacrosancta* agebat *antistes* pro populi intercessione salutaria, seu ab ineunte aetate in Christi amore solitus erat. Qui *nimirum* dum haec *indesinenter* ageret *operante manu* voluntatis Dei, *cuius in omni vitae transeuntis tempore nutui oboedierat*, non multo post in pace receptus est. *Porro* quia *in virtutibus exhibitae sanctitatis veluti fulgidissimum sidus* omni populo claruit, in honore Dei et ipsius sancti sacerdotis quidam ex genere Gallieni fecit *reverendo eius nomini* basilicam, haud procul a fluvio, *ubi longo tempore corpus ipsius requievit. Qui etiam venerabilis locus in recta ineffabilis ac beatae Trinitatis confessione signis et miraculis coruscat.*
10	Post vero aliquod tempus, apud eamdem Veronensem urbem, cum die sancti natalii ipsius devote populus una cum clero vel sacerdotibus ad missarum solennia convenissent, fluvius Athesis, ubi super ripam eius reconditum esse dignoscitur corpus, subito tanta inundatione excrevit ut aqua fluminis usque ad fenestras vel tectum ascenderet. Cuius ecclesiae dum essent ianuae apertae, aqua in eam minime intravit, sicque stans aqua ecclesiae ianuam clausit, ac si illud elementum liquidum in soliditatem parietis fuisset immutatum. Quod etiam factum videns populus admiratione comprehensus, qui illic ad	LECTIO SANCTI GREGORII DE MIRABILIBUS BEATI ZENONIS EPISCOPI Quando apud Romanam urbem alveum suum Tiberis egressus est, tantumque crescens, ut unda eius super muros urbis influeret atque in ea maximas regiones occuparet apud Veronensem urbem fluvius Athesis excrescens ad beati Zenonis martyris atque pontificis ecclesiam venit. Cuius ecclesiae, dum essent ianuae apertae, aqua in eam minime intravit. Quae paulisper crescens usque ad fenestras ecclesiae, quae erant tectis proximae, pervenit. *Siquidem* stans aqua ecclesiae ianuam clausit ac si illud elementum liquidum in soliditatem parietis fuisset immutatum cumque essent multi interius inventi, sed aquarum

	honorem Dei et sancti sacerdotis convenerat, fame sitique se perire acclamabat. Cum ergo essent multi interius inventi et aquarum multitudine ecclesia omnis circumdata, et ipsi in quam possint partem egredi non haberent ibique se siti et fame deficere formidarent, ad ecclesiae ianuam veniebant ad bibendum, hauriebant aquam quae, ut praedixit, usque ad fenestras excreverat et tamen intra ecclesiam nullo modo diffluebat. Hauriri itaque ut aqua poterat, sed diffluere ut aqua non poterat. Stans autem ante ianuam ad ostendendum cunctis meritum Confessoris, et aqua erat ad adiutorium, et quasi aqua non erat ad invadendum locum. Et dum tanta esset inundatio aquae, velut murus cicumquaque ecclesiae eractus erat, et intus aqua minime ingrediebatur. Quanta enim putamus virtus orationis ipsius apud Deum obtinere poterat, cum et aqua in specie muri erecta erat, et ingredi locum venerabilem non audebat. Unde adcrevit veneratio et timor circa Christi sacerdotem, ut etiam, si fide exigat, infirmi curentur, daemoniaci veniant et liberentur. Et si quis ex vera fide sanctum eius nomen invocaverit, sine dubio eius petitioni annuitur. Multi etenim de longinquis regionibus venientes obsessa infirmitate corpora ad eius sepulcrum iacentes per ipsius intercessionem ad propria cum sanitate et gaudio revertuntur. Ecce multis miraculis ego inutilis Coronatus notarius, quod compertum tenui, in parvo conclusi, ne legentibus vel audientibus fastidium generarem. Praestante Domino nostro Iesu Christo, cui est honor et gloria in saecula saeculorum. Amen.	multitudine ecclesia omni circumdata, qua possent egredi non haberent ibique siti ac fame deficere formidarent, ad ecclesiae ianuam veniebant. Ad bibendum hauriebant aquam, quae – ut praedixi – usque ad fenestras excreverat et tamen intra ecclesiam nullo modo defluebat. Hauriri itaque ut aqua poterat, sed defluere ut aqua non poterat. Stans autem ante ianuam ad ostendendum cunctis meritum martyris et aqua erat ad adiutorium et quasi aqua non erat ad invadendum locum.

Literaturverzeichnis

Quellen

Ambrosius von Mailand: Sancti Ambrosii Opera. Epistularum liber decimus, Epistulae extra collectionem, Gesta Concilii Aquileiensis, hrsg. von Michael Petschenig / Michaela Zelzer (Corpus Scriptorum Ecclesiasticorum Latinorum 82,3), Wien 1982.

–: Sancti Ambrosii Opera. Epistularvm libri VII–VIIII, hrsg. von Otto Faller (Corpus Scriptorum Ecclesiasticorum Latinorum 82,2), Wien 1990.

Augustinus: Contra Faustum, hrsg. von Ioseph Zycha (Corpus Scriptorum Ecclesiasticorum Latinorum 25,1), Wien 1891.

–: In Iohannis evangelium tractatus CXXIV, hrsg. von Radbodus Willems (Corpus Christianorum. Series Latina 36), Turnhout 1954.

Beda Venerabilis: In Lucae evangelium expositio. In Marci evangelium expositio, hrsg. von David Hurst (Corpus Christianorum. Series Latina 120), Turnhout 1960.

Benedikt von Nursia: La Règle de Saint Benoît Bd. 2 Ch. VIII–LXXIII, hrsg. von Adalbert d. Vogüé / Jean Neufville, Paris 1972.

Cicero, Marcus Tullius: Il processo di Verre, hrsg. von Nino Marinone / Laura Fiocchi, Mailand [8]2013.

Davril, Anselme u. a. (Hg.): Guillelmi Duranti Rationale divinorum officiorum (Gvillelmi Dvranti Rationale divinorvm officiorvm / ed. A. Davril), Turnhout 2000.

Die Urkunden Friedrichs I. 1158–1167, hrsg. von Heinrich Appelt (MGH DD F I), Hannover 1979.

Die Urkunden Heinrichs II. und Arduins, hrsg. von Harry Bresslau / Hermann Bloch / Robert Holtzmann (MGH DD H II), Hannover 1900–1903.

Die Urkunden Heinrichs IV., hrsg. von Dietrich von Gladiss / Alfred Gawlick (MGH DD H IV), Weimar 1952.

Die Urkunden Konrads II., hrsg. von Harry Bresslau / Hans Wibel / Alfred Hessel (MGH DD K II), Hannover 1909.

Die Urkunden Ludwigs II., hrsg. von Konrad Wanner (MGH DD L II), München 1994.

Gregor der Große: Dialogues – Livres I–III. Bd. 2, hrsg. von Adalbert d. Vogüé / Paul Antin, Paris 1979.

Paulus Diaconus: Historia Langobardorum, in: L. Bethmann / G. Waitz (Hg.): Scriptores rerum langobardicarum et italicarum saec. VI–IX, Hannover 1878, S. 45–187.

–: Homiliarius, hrsg. von Jacques P. Migne (Patrologia Latina 95), Paris 1851.

Rather von Verona: Opera omnia, hrsg. von Jacques P. Migne (Patrologia Latina 136), Paris 1881.
Rather von Verona: Die Briefe des Bischofs Rather von Verona, hrsg. von Fritz Weigle (MGH Epistolae 2), Weimar 1949.
–: Qualitatis coniectura cuiusdam, Ratherii utique Veronensis, hrsg. von Peter L. D. Reid (Corpus Christianorum. Continuatio Mediaevalis 46), Turnhout 1976.
–: Ratherii Veronensis Praeloqviorvm libri VI Phrenesis. Dialogus confessionalis, hrsg. von Peter L. D. Reid (Corpus Christianorum. Continuatio Mediaevalis 46A), Turnhout 1984.
–: Sermones monacenses, in: Paul Tombeur (Hg.): Thesaurus Ratherii Veronensis necnon Leodiensis. Series A– B, formae et lemmata; lemmata et formae, lemmata a tergo ordinata, tabulae frequentiarum, formae et lemmata, formae a tergo ordinatae, lemmata singulorum operum, concordantia lemmatum et formarum, Turnhout 2005.
Zeno von Verona: Zenonis Veronensis tractatus, hrsg. von Bengt Löfstedt (Corpus Christianorum. Series Latina 22), Turnhout 1971.

Sekundärliteratur

Ambrosioni, Annamaria: Federico I e il papato dal Congresso di Verona alla partenza per la I crociata (1184–1189), Mailand 1986.
Andrieu, Michel: Les Ordines Romani du haut moyen âge. 5 Bde. (Spicilegium Sacrum Lovaniense: Etudes et documents), Löwen 1931–1961.
–: Les Ordines Romani du haut moyen âge. Bd. 2 Les textes (Ordines I– XIII) (Spicilegium Sacrum Lovaniense: Etudes et documents), Löwen 1960.
–: Les Ordines Romani du haut moyen âge. Bd. 1 Les manuscrits (Spicilegium Sacrum Lovaniense: Etudes et documents), Löwen 1965.
Angenendt, Arnold: Heilige und Reliquien. Die Geschichte ihres Kultes vom frühen Christentum bis zur Gegenwart, München 1994.
–: Liturgie im Mittelalter, in: Patrizia Carmassi (Hg.): Präsenz und Verwendung der Heiligen Schrift im christlichen Frühmittelalter, Wiesbaden 2008, S. 211–238.
Anti, Elisa: Animali e ambiente nell'agiografia zenoniana, in: Annuario storico zenoniano, 1993, S. 25–34.
–: Un'inedita redazione della *Vita I sancti Zenonis* nel ms. XV.AA.15 della Biblioteca Nazionale di Napoli, in: Annuario storico zenoniano, 1998, S. 27–32.
–: Note sulla prima sepoltura di san Zeno e sulla sede del miracolo delle acque, in: Annuario storico zenoniano 17, 2000, S. 11–18.
–: Verona e il culto di San Zeno tra IV e XII secolo, Verona 2009.
Antony, Franz J. A.: Archäologisch-liturgisches Lehrbuch des gregorianischen Kirchengesanges. Mit vorzüglicher Rücksicht auf die Römischen, Münsterschen und Erzstift Kölnischen Gesangsweisen, Münster 1829.

Arlt, Wulf: Neue Formen des liturgischen Gesangs: Sequenz und Tropus, in: Christoph Stiegemann / Matthias Wemhoff (Hg.): 799 – Kunst und Kultur der Karolingerzeit. Karl der Große und Papst Leo III. in Paderborn. Bd. 3 Beiträge zum Katalog der Ausstellung Paderborn 1999. Handbuch zur Geschichte der Karolingerzeit, Mainz 1999, S. 732–740.

Auda, Antoine: L'École musicale liégeoise au Xe siècle. Etienne de Liège (Mémoire de la Classe des Lettres 2, 1), Brüssel 1923.

Avena, Antonio: Guglielmo da Pastrengo e gli inizi dell'umanesimo a Verona, in: Atti dell'Accademia di agricoltura, scienze, lettere, arte e commercio di Verona 82, 1907, 65–73.

Babcock, Robert G. / Cahn, Walter: A New Manuscript from the Abbey of San Zeno at Verona, in: The Yale University Library gazette 66, 1992, S. 105–116.

Bagatta, Raffaele / Battista Peretti (Hg.): Sanctorum episcoporum Veronensium antiqua monumenta et aliorum sanctorum quorum corpora, et aliquot, quorum ecclesiae habentur Veronae, Venedig 1576.

Baldovin, John F.: The Urban Character of Christian Worship. The Origins, Development and Meaning of Stational Liturgy (Orientalia Christiana analecta 228), Rom 1987.

Ballerini, Pietro / Ballerini, Girolamo: Sancti Zenonis Episcopi Veronensis Sermones nunc primum, qui par erat, diligentia editi, Verona 1739.

Balogh, József: „Voces Paginarum". Beiträge zur Geschichte des lauten Lesens und Schreibens, in: Philologus 82, 1927, S. 84.

Baroffio, Giacomo B.: Manoscritti liturgici e musicali sull'arco alpino fra i secoli IX e XII, in: Carlo Magno e le Alpi: atti del XVIII Congresso Internazionale di Studio sull'Alto Medioevo, Susa, 19–20 ottobre 2006, Novalesa, 21 ottobre 2006, Spoleto 2007, S. 141–150.

–: Lo spazio concettuale e reale della filologia liturgica, in: Rivista Internazionale di Musica Sacra 31, 2010, S. 169–192.

Baroffio, Giacomo B. / Kim, Anastasia E. J.: Cantemus domino gloriose. Introduzione al canto gregoriano, Cremona 2003.

Bauer, Dieter u. a. (Hg.): Heilige – Liturgie – Raum (Beiträge zur Hagiographie 8), Stuttgart 2010.

Berlière, Ursmer: Les stations liturgiques dans les anciennes villes épiscopales, in: Revue liturgique et monastique 5, 1920, S. 213.

Berschin, Walter: Biographie und Epochenstil im lateinischen Mittelalter Bd. 4,1: Ottonische Biographie. Das hohe Mittelalter, 920–1220 n. Chr., Halbbd. 1: 920–1070 n. Chr. , Stuttgart 1999.

Berschin, Walter / Klüppel, Theodor: Der Evangelist Markus auf der Reichenau, Sigmaringen 1994.

Berschin, Walter / Zettler, Alfons: Egino von Verona. Der Gründer von Reichenau-Niederzell (799) (Reichenauer Texte und Bilder 8), Stuttgart 1999.

Biadego, Giuseppe: Catalogo descrittivo dei manoscritti della Biblioteca comunale di Verona, Verona 1892.
Biancolini, Giambattista: Notizie storiche delle chiese di Verona. 8 Bde.), Verona 1771.
Bischoff, Bernhard: Paläographie des römischen Altertums und des abendländischen Mittelalters (Grundlagen der Germanistik 24), Berlin [2]1986.
–: Katalog der festländischen Handschriften des neunten Jahrhunderts. Aachen – Lambach, Wiesbaden 1998.
Bjur, Hans / Santillo B. Frizell (Hg.): Via Tiburtina. Space, Movement and Artefacts in the Urban Landscape, Rom 2005.
Blume, Clemens (Hg.): Die Hymnen des Thesaurus Hymnologicus H. A. Daniels und anderer Hymnen-Ausgaben. Pars I Hymni antiquissimi saec. V–XI (Analecta Hymnica Medii Aevi 51), Leipzig 1908.
–: Vorwort und Einleitung, in: Clemens Blume u. a. (Hg.): Thesauri hymnologici hymnarium. Die Hymnen des 5.–11. Jahrhunderts und die irisch-keltische Hymnodie, Leipzig 1908, S. V–XLVII.
Borders, James M.: The Cathedral of Verona as a Musical Center in the Middle Ages. Its History, Manuscripts, and Liturgical Practice. 2 Bde., Chicago 1983.
Browe, Peter: Zur Geschichte des Dreifaltigkeitsfestes, in: Archiv für Liturgiewissenschaft 1, 1950, S. 65–81.
Brown, Peter: Society and the Holy in Late Antiquity 1989.
Brugnoli, Andrea: „Pares illorum famuli". Una tipologia documentaria veronese per negozi tra persone di condizione servile, in: Andrea Brugnoli / Gian Maria Varanini (Hg.): Studi Pierpaolo Brugnoli. Magna Verona vale. Studi in onore di Pierpaolo Brugnoli, Verona 2008, S. 27–48.
Brugnoli, Pierpaolo: Le case del capitolo canonicale presso il duomo di Verona, Verona 1979.
– (Hg.): La Cattedrale di Verona nelle sue vicende edilizie dal secolo IV al secolo XVI, Venedig 1987.
Buchberger, Michael (Hg.): Lexikon für Theologie und Kirche. Bd. 1, Freiburg [2]1957.
Bullough, Donald A.: Texts, Chant, and the Chapel of Louis the Pious, in: Peter Godman / Roger Collins (Hg.): Charlemagne's Heir. New Perspectives on the Reign of Louis the Pious (814–840), Oxford 1990, S. 489–508.
Bysted, Anne L.: The Crusade Indulgence. Spiritual Rewards and the Theology of the Crusades, c. 1095–1216 (History of Warfare 103), Leiden 2015.
Camilot-Oswald, Raffaella: Die liturgischen Musikhandschriften aus dem mittelalterlichen Patriarchat Aquileia (Monumenta Monodica Medii Aevi. Subsidia 2), Kassel 1997.
Carrara, Mario: Gli scrittori latini, in: Vittorio Cavallari / Piero Gazzola (Hg.): Verona e il suo territorio, Verona 1960–1984, S. 349–420.

Castagnetti, Andrea: Aspetti politici, economici e sociali di chiese e monasteri dall'epoca carolingia alle soglie dell'età moderna, in: Giorgio Borelli (Hg.): Chiese e monasteri a Verona, Verona 1980, S. 43–119.
–: Dalla caduta dell'Impero Romano d'Occidente all'Impero Romano-Germanico (476–1024), in: Andrea Castagnetti / Gian Maria Varanini (Hg.): Il Veneto nel medioevo. Dalla „Venetia" alla Marca Veronese, Verona 1989, S. 1–80.
Castiglioni, Gino: Note sui codici quattrocenteschi del Monastero di San Zenone Maggiore nella Biblioteca Civica di Verona, in: Emanuela Sesti (Hg.): La miniatura italiana tra Gotico e Rinascimento: atti del II Congresso di Storia della Miniatura Italiana 1985, S. 389–413.
–: I corali tardotrecenteschi del capitolo veronese, in: Gian Maria Varanini (Hg.): Gli scaligeri 1277–1387. Saggi e schede pubblicati in occasione della mostra storico-documentaria allestita dal Museo di Castelvecchio di Verona (giugno–novembre 1988), Verona 1988, S. 421–426.
–: Tre salteri, un officio e qualche riflessione sulla miniatura veronese in età tardogotica, in: Rivista di storia della miniatura, 2007, S. 213–228.
Cervato, Dario: Adelardo cardinale vescovo di Verona (1188–1214) e legato pontificio in Terra Santa (1189–1191), Verona 1991.
–: Iacet ad monasterium Sancti Zenonis: Adelardo II cardinale e vescovo di Verona, in: Annuario storico zenoniano, 1991, S. 41–54.
–: Raterio di Verona e di Liegi. Il terzo periodo del suo episcopato veronese (961–968). Scritti e attività, Verona 1993.
Cipolla, Carlo: Il velo di Classe, Verona 1972.
Coden, Fabio: Il portico detto „santa Maria Matricolare" presso il complesso episcopale di Verona, in: Arturo C. Quintavalle (Hg.): Medioevo: L'Europa delle cattedrali. Atti del convegno internazionale di studi, Mailand 2007, S. 339–349.
Corbin, Solange: La cantillation des rituels chrétiens, in: Revue de musicologie 47, 1961, S. 3–36.
Da Lisca, Alessandro: La basilica di S. Stefano in Verona, in: Atti e memorie dell'Accademia di Agricoltura, Scienze e Lettere di Verona 14, 1936, S. 45–119.
–: La basilica di San Zenone in Verona, Verona 1941.
Dalmais, Irénée H. u. a. (Hg.): Volume IV: The Liturgy and Time. The Church at Prayer. An Introduction to the Liturgy, Collegeville 1985.
De Gaiffier d'Hestroy, Baudouin: La lecture des Actes des martyrs dans la prière liturgique en Occident. A propos du passionaire hispanique, in: Analecta Bollandiana 72, 1954, S. 134–166.
–: Etudes critiques d'hagiographie et d'iconologie (Subsidia Hagiographica 43), Brüssel 1967.
–: Hagiographie et historiographie, in: La storiografia altomedievale, Spoleto 1970, S. 139–166.

Dolbeau, François: Pauca de vita sancti Donatiani, in: Peter L. D. Reid (Hg.): Ratherii Veronensis Praeloqviorvm libri VI Phrenesis. Dialogus confessionalis, Turnhout 1984, S. 275–283.
–: Zenoniana. Recherches sur le texte et sur la tradition de Zénon de Vérone, in: Recherches Augustiniennes et Patristiques 20, 1985, S. 3–34.
–: Ratheriana III. Notes sur la culture patristique de Rathier, in: Sacris erudiri 29, 1986, S. 151–221.
–: Les hagiographes au travail: collecte et traitement des documents écrits (IX–XII siècles), in: Martin Heinzelmann (Hg.): Manuscrits hagiographiques et travail des hagiographes, Sigmaringen 1992, S. 49–76.
Dorn, Johann: Stationsgottesdienste in frühmittelalterlichen Bischofsstädten, in: Andreas Bigelmair (Hg.): Festgabe Alois Knöpfler zur Vollendung des 60. Lebensjahres gewidmet, München 1907, S. 43–55.
Dreves, Guido M.: Einleitung, in: Guido M. Dreves (Hg.): Historiae rhythmicae. Liturgische Reimofficien des Mittelalters. Erste Folge. Aus Handschriften und Wiegendrucken, Leipzig 1889, S. 5–16.
– (Hg.): Historiae rhythmicae. Liturgische Reimofficien des Mittelalters. Erste Folge. Aus Handschriften und Wiegendrucken (Analecta Hymnica Medii Aevi 5), Leipzig 1889.
–: Vorwort, in: Guido M. Dreves (Hg.): Sequentiae ineditae. Aus Handschriften und Frühdrucken, Leipzig 1890, S. 5–8.
– (Hg.): Hymni inediti. Liturgische Hymnen des Mittelalters (Analecta Hymnica Medii Aevi 22), Leipzig 1895.
Du Cange, Charles du Fresne: Glossarium mediae et infimae Latinitatis. 10 Bde., Niort 1883–1887.
Dunstan, Alan: Hymnody in Christian Worship, in: Cheslyn Jones (Hg.): The Study of Liturgy, London 1992, S. 507–519.
Dyer, Joseph H.: Monastic Psalmody in the Middle Ages, in: Revue bénédictine 99, 1989, S. 41–74.
–: The Singing of Psalms in the Early Medieval Office, in: Speculum 64, 1989, S. 535–578.
Ederle, Guglielmo / Cervato, Dario: I vescovi di Verona: dizionario storico e cenni sulla Chiesa veronese, Verona 2002.
Eickhoff, Ekkehard: Friedrich Barbarossa im Orient. Kreuzzug und Tod Friedrichs I., Tübingen 1977.
Eisenberg, Ronald: Dictionary of Jewish Terms. A Guide to the Language of Judaism, Lanham 2011.
Fainelli, Vittorio: Codice diplomatico Veronese. Bd. 1 Dalla caduta dell'impero romano alla fine del periodo carolingio. 2 Bde. (Monumenti storici. Nuova serie 1), Venedig 1940.

–: Grandi benefattori: il Vescovo Ratoldo e l'arcidiacono Pacifico, in: Zenonis Cathedra. Miscellanea di studi in onore di S.E. l'arcivescovo mons. Giovanni Urbani, Verona 1955, S. 23–27.
–: L'abbazia di S. Zeno nell'alto medioevo, in: Miscellanea Roberto Cessi, Rom 1958, S. 51–62.
Farmer, Sharon: Communities of Saint Martin. Legend and Ritual in Medieval Tours, Ithaca 1991.
Ferrari, Mirella: Libri liturgici e diffusione della scrittura carolina nell'Italia settentrionale, in: Culto cristiano, politica imperiale carolingia, Todi 1979, S. 265–279.
Ferro, Eva: „Suavissime universorum Domine". Eine „konstanzische" Maria Magdalena-Historia in Hirsau?, in: Archiv für Liturgiewissenschaft, 2014, S. 49–74.
Fill, Hauke: Katalog der Handschriften des Benediktinerstiftes Kremsmünster. Teil 2 Zimeliencodices und spätmittelalterliche Handschriften nach 1325 bis einschliesslich CC 100. 2 Bde. (Denkschriften der philosophisch-historischen Klasse 270), Wien 2000.
Fischer-Lichte, Erika: Semiotik des Theaters. Die Aufführung als Text, Tübingen ^{5}2009.
Flanigan, Clifford C. u. a.: Liturgy as Social Performance: Expanding the Definitions, in: Thomas J. Heffernan / Ann E. Matter (Hg.): The Liturgy of the Medieval Church, Kalamazoo 2001, S. 635–652.
Forchielli, Giuseppe: Collegialità di chierici nel veronese dall'VIII secolo all'etá comunale, in: Archivio veneto 58, 1928, S. 1–117.
Franzoni, Lanfranco: Verona. Testimonianze archeologiche, Verona 1965.
–: La campana di Cansignorino per la torre del Gadello (1370), in: Gian Maria Varanini (Hg.): Gli scaligeri 1277–1387. Saggi e schede pubblicati in occasione della mostra storico-documentaria allestita dal Museo di Castelvecchio di Verona (giugno–novembre 1988), Verona 1988, S. 322.
Galli, André: Zénon de Vérone dans l'antiphonaire de Bangor, in: Revue bénédictine 93, 1983, S. 293–301.
Gamber, Klaus: Die gallikanische Zeno-Messe. Ein Beitrag zum ältesten Ritus von Oberitalien und Bayern, in: Münchener Theologische Zeitschrift 10, 1959, S. 295–299.
–: Codices liturgici latini antiquiores. Pars II (Spicilegium Friburgense. Subsidia 2), Freiburg 1968.
Georges, Karl E.: Ausführliches lateinisch-deutsches Handwörterbuch, Hannover ^{8}1913.
Gilsdorf, Sean: The Favor of Friends: Intercession and Aristocratic Politics in Carolingian and Ottonian Europe (Brill's series on the early Middle Ages 23), Leiden 2014.
Giuliari, Giovanni B. C. (Hg.): S. Zenonis episcopi Veronensis Sermones, Verona 1883.

Gneuss, Helmut: Zur Geschichte des Hymnars, in: Andreas Haug u. a. (Hg.): Der lateinische Hymnus im Mittelalter. Überlieferung, Ästhetik, Ausstrahlung, Kassel 2004, S. 63–86.

Golinelli, Paolo: Il Cristianesimo nella „Venetia“ altomedievale. Diffusione, istituzionalizzazione e forme di religiosità dalle origini al sec. X, in: Andrea Castagnetti / Gian Maria Varanini (Hg.): Il Veneto nel medioevo. Dalla „Venetia“ alla Marca Veronese, Verona 1989, S. 237–331.

–: Nota su Raterio agiografo, in: Mittellateinisches Jahrbuch 24–25, 1989–1990, S. 125–131.

–: Italia settentrionale (1130–1220), in: Guy Philippart (Hg.): Hagiographies. Histoire internationale de la littérature hagiographique latine et vernaculaire en Occident des origines à 1550, Turnhout 1994–2006, S. 125–153.

Goudesenne, Jean-François: Les Offices historiques ou Historiae composés pour les fêtes des saints dans la province ecclésiastique de Reims (775–1030), Turnhout 2002.

–: Historiae from Alta Italia and their Frankish Models: A Progressive „Romanisation“ by the Carolingian Franks (750–950), in: Roman Hankeln (Hg.): Political Plainchant? Music, Text and Historical Context of Medieval Saints’ Offices, Ottawa 2009, S. 13–29.

Goullet, Monique: Écriture et réécriture hagiographiques, Turnhout 2005.

Grazioli, Angelo: San Zenone di Verona, in: La scuola cattolica 68, 1940, S. 174–199.

Griffiths, Fiona J.: The Garden of Delights. Reform and Renaissance for Women in the Twelfth Century, Philadelphia 2011.

Gy, Pierre-Marie: Le culte des saints dans la liturgie d’Occident entre le IXe et le XIIIe siècle, in: Robert Favreau (Hg.): Le culte des saints aux IXe-XIIIe siècles. Actes du Colloque tenu à Poitiers les 15–16–17 septembre 1993, Poitiers 1995, S. 85–89.

Halm, Karl u. a.: Catalogus codicum latinorum Bibliothecae Regiae Monacensis. Codices num. 15121–21313 (Catalogus Codicum Manu Scriptorum Bibliothecae Regiae Monacensis 2,3), München 1878.

Hamilton, Sarah: The Practice of Penance, 900–1050, London 2001.

Harper, John: The Forms and Orders of Western Liturgy from the Tenth to the Eighteenth Century. A Historical Introduction and Guide for Students and Musicians, Oxford 1991.

Andreas Haug u. a. (Hg.): Der lateinische Hymnus im Mittelalter. Überlieferung, Ästhetik, Ausstrahlung, Kassel 2004.

Heinzelmann, Martin: Translationsberichte und andere Quellen des Reliquienkultes (Typologie des sources du Moyen Âge occidental), Turnhout 1979.

Heinzer, Felix: Die „heilige Königstochter“ in der Liturgie: Zur Inszenierung Elisabeths im Festoffizium „Laetare Germania“, in: Dieter Blume / Matthias Werner (Hg.): Elisabeth von Thüringen – eine europäische Heilige: Aufsätze, Petersberg 2007, S. 215–225.

–: Der besungene Heilige: Aspekte des liturgisch propagierten Franziskus-Bildes, in: Wissenschaft und Weisheit 74, 2011, S. 234–251.

–: Eucharist and Holy Spirit: Hidden Mass-Theology in an Early Thirteenth-Century Office Book Fragment, in: Harvard Library Bulletin 21, 2011, S. 5–17.

–: *Figura* zwischen Präsenz und Diskurs. Das Verhältnis des „gregorianischen" Messgesangs zu seiner dichterischen Erweiterung, in: Christian Kiening / Katharina Mertens Fleury (Hg.): Figura. Dynamiken der Zeiten und Zeichen im Mittelalter, Würzburg 2013, S. 71–90.

–: Hos multo elegantius, si ecclesiastica loquendi consuetudo pateretur, nostros heroas uocaremus. Sprachbilder im frühchristlichen Märtyrerdiskurs, in: Ralf von den Hoff u. a. (Hg.): Imitatio heroica. Heldenangleichung im Bildnis (Helden – Heroisierungen – Heroismen 1), Würzburg 2015, S. 119–136.

–: Poesie als politische Theologie. Texte und Kontexte der liturgischen Verehrung König Ludwigs des Heiligen, in: Francia 42, 2015, S. 73–92.

Heinzer, Felix u. a.: Einleitung: Relationen zwischen Sakralisierungen und Heroisierungen, in: Felix Heinzer u. a. (Hg.): Sakralität und Heldentum (Helden – Heroisierungen – Heroismen 6), Würzburg 2017, S. 9–18.

Herbers, Klaus: Hagiographie im Kontext – Konzeption und Zielvorstellung, in: Dieter Bauer / Klaus Herbers (Hg.): Hagiographie im Kontext. Wirkungsweisen und Möglichkeiten historischer Auswertung, Stuttgart 2000, S. IX–XXVIII.

Hesbert, René-Jean: Corpus Antiphonalium Officii. Bd. 1 Manuscripti „cursus Romanus" (Rerum Ecclesiasticarum Documenta. Series Maior. Fontes 7), Rom 1963a.

–: Corpus Antiphonalium Officii. Bd. 3 Invitatoria et antiphonae (Rerum Ecclesiasticarum Documenta. Series Maior. Fontes 9), Rom 1968b.

–: Corpus Antiphonalium Officii. Bd. 4 Responsoria, versus, hymni et varia (Rerum Ecclesiasticarum Documenta. Series Maior. Fontes 10), Rom 1970.

Hiestand, Rudolph: „precipua tocius christianismi columpna". Barbarossa und der Kreuzzug, in: Alfred Haverkamp (Hg.): Friedrich Barbarossa. Handlungsspielräume und Wirkungsweisen, Sigmaringen 1992, S. 51–108.

–: Kingship and Crusade in Twelfth-Century Germany, in: Alfred Haverkamp / Hanna Vollrath (Hg.): England and Germany in the High Middle Ages, London 1996, S. 236–265.

Hiley, David: Western Plainchant. A Handbook, Oxford 1993.

–: Gregorian Chant, Cambridge 2009.

Hlawitschka, Eduard: Ratold, Bischof von Verona und Begründer von Radolfzell, in: Hegau 54 / 55, 1997, S. 5–44.

Hoffman, Lawrence A.: Beyond the Text. A Holistic Approach to Liturgy (Jewish literature and culture), Bloomington 1987.

Hughes, Andrew: Medieval Manuscripts for Mass and Office. A Guide to their Organization and Terminology, Toronto 1982.

Huglo, Michel: Les manuscrits du processionnal. Bd. 1 Autriche à Espagne. 2 Bde. (Répertoire international des sources musicales 14,1), München 1999.
Huglo, Michel u. a.: Gallican Chant, in: Stanley Sadie (Hg.): The New Grove Dictionary of Music and Musicians, London 2001, S. 458–472.
Hülsen-Esch, Andrea v.: Romanische Skulptur in Oberitalien als Reflex der kommunalen Entwicklung im 12. Jahrhundert. Untersuchungen zu Mailand und Verona (Artefact 8), Berlin 1994.
Iversen, Gunilla: Problems in the Editing of Tropes, in: Text. An interdisciplinary annual of textual studies 1, 1981, S. 95–132.
–: Tropes and Prosulas Added to the Chant Gloria in Excelsis in the Medieval Mass: Editorial Problems and Proposed Solutions, http://hdl.handle.net/1807/32257.
Jensen, Brian M.: Lectionarium Placentinum as a Challenge to the Editor, http://hdl.handle.net/1807/32260.
Johnson, Timothy J.: Choir Prayer as the Place of Formation and Identity Definition: The Example of the Minorite Order, in: Miscellanea francescana 111, 2011, S. 123–135.
Jonsson, Ritva: Historia. Études sur la genèse des offices versifiés, Stockholm 1968.
– (Hg.): Tropes du propre de la messe (Corpus Troporum 1), Stockholm 1975.
Jungmann, Josef A.: Missarum sollemnia. Bd. 1 Messe im Wandel der Jahrhunderte. Messe und kirchliche Gemeinschaft. Vormesse, Wien 1962.
Kihlman, Erika: Expositiones sequentiarum. Medieval Sequence Commentaries and Prologues. Editions with Introductions (Acta Universitatis Stockholmiensis. Studia latina Stockholmiensia 53), Stockholm 2006.
–: Editing Fluid Texts: The Case of the Sequence Commentaries, http://hdl.handle.net/1807/32263.
Klauser, Theodor: Die liturgischen Austauschbeziehungen zwischen der römischen und fränkisch-deutschen Kirche vom achten bis zum elften Jahrhundert, in: Historisches Jahrbuch 53, 1933, S. 169–189.
Knape, Joachim: Zur Benennung der Offizien im Mittelalter. Das Wort „historia" als liturgischer Begriff, in: Archiv für Liturgiewissenschaft 26, 1984, S. 305–320.
Knibbs, Eric (Hg.): On the Liturgy, Amalar of Metz, Volume II, Books 3–4 (On the Liturgy / Amalar of Metz. Ed. and Transl. by Eric Knibbs), Cambridge / Mass 2014.
Kritzinger, Peter: The Cult of Saints and Religious Processions in Late Antiquity and the Early Middle Ages, in: Peter A. V. Sarris u. a. (Hg.): An Age of Saints? Power, Conflict and Dissent in Early Medieval Christianity, Leiden 2011, S. 36–48.
La Rocca, Cristina: Pacifico di Verona. Il passato carolingio nella costruzione della memoria urbana, Rom 1995.
Lang, Johannes: Das Erzbistum Salzburg. Teilband 2 Das Augustinerchorherrenstift St. Zeno in Reichenhall (Germania Sacra. Folge 3 9, 2), Berlin 2015.

Lazzarini, Vittorio: Scuola calligrafica veronese del secolo IX, in: Vittorio Lazzarini (Hg.): Scritti di paleografia e diplomatica, Padua 1969, S. 10–27.

Leonardi, Claudio: Notae et glossae autographicae, in: Peter L. D. Reid (Hg.): Ratherii Veronensis Praeloqviorvm libri VI Phrenesis. Dialogus confessionalis, Turnhout 1984, S. 291–314.

Lester, Anne E. u. a. (Hg.): Cities, Texts and Social Networks, 400–1500. Experiences and Perceptions of Medieval Urban Space, Florenz 2010.

Library of Latin Texts: LLT-A, https://katalog.ub.uni-freiburg.de/link?id=116897937.

Lipphardt, Walther: Solesmes, in: Friedrich Blume (Hg.): Die Musik in Geschichte und Gegenwart, Berlin 2001, S. 835–839.

Lodi, Enzo: Le due omelie di San Petronio vescovo di Bologna. Saggio critico-storico, in: Miscellanea liturgica in onore di Sua Eminenza il Cardinale Giacomo Lercaro, Rom 1967, S. 263–302.

Lomartire, Saverio: Testo e immagine nella Porta dello Zodiaco, in: Dal Piemonte all'Europa: esperienze monastiche nella società medievale. Relezioni e comunicazioni presentate al XXXIV Congresso storico subalpino nel millenario di S. Michele della Chiusa (Torino, 27–29 maggio 1985), Turin 1988, S. 431–474.

Lowe, Elias A.: Codices Latini Antiquiores: A Palaeographical Guide to Latin Manuscripts Prior to the 9th Century. Bd. 8: Germany: Altenburg-Leipzig, Oxford 1959.

Lusuardi Siena, Silvia: Puntualizzazioni archeologiche sulle due chiese paleocristiane, in: Pierpaolo Brugnoli (Hg.): La Cattedrale di Verona nelle sue vicende edilizie dal secolo IV al secolo XVI, Venedig 1987, S. 26–78.

Lusuardi Siena, Silvia / Fiorio Tedone, Cinzia: Il complesso episcopale nell'alto medioevo alla luce delle testimoninaze scritte, in: Pierpaolo Brugnoli (Hg.): La Cattedrale di Verona nelle sue vicende edilizie dal secolo IV al secolo XVI, Venedig 1987, S. 79–82.

–: Ipotesi interpretativa sullo sviluppo del complesso episcopale veronese, in: Pierpaolo Brugnoli (Hg.): La Cattedrale di Verona nelle sue vicende edilizie dal secolo IV al secolo XVI, Venedig 1987, S. 83–87.

Maffei, Scipione: Istoria diplomatica, Mantua 1727.

Marchi, Gian P.: Le antiche storie di San Zeno, in: Gian P. Marchi u. a. (Hg.): Il culto di San Zeno nel Veronese, Verona 1972, S. 13–61.

Marchi, Silvia: I Manoscritti della Biblioteca Capitolare di Verona. Catalogo descrittivo redatto da don Antonio Spagnolo, Verona 1996.

Markschies, Christoph: Liturgisches Lesen und die Hermeneutik der Schrift, in: Peter Gemeinhardt (Hg.): Patristica et Oecumenica. Festschrift für Wolfgang A. Bienert zum 65. Geburtstag, Marburg 2004, S. 77–88.

Markus, Robert A.: The End of Ancient Christianity, Cambridge 1990.

Martimort, Aimé G.: The Liturgy of the Hours, in: Irénée H. Dalmais u. a. (Hg.): Volume IV: The Liturgy and Time. The Church at Prayer. An Introduction to the Liturgy, Collegeville 1985, S. 151–256.

Mazzatinti, Giuseppe: Inventari dei Manoscritti delle Biblioteche d'Italia Bd. 6, Forlì 1896.
Meersseman, Gilles G. u.a.: L'orazionale dell'arcidiacono Pacifico e il Carpsum del cantore Stefano. Studi e testi sulla liturgia del duomo di Verona dal IX all'XI sec. (Spicilegium Friburgense 21), Freiburg 1974.
Migliorini, Tommaso: Girolamo Avanzi e l'inno *O diem gemma* a santa Toscana, S. 1–41.
Miller, Maureen C.: The Formation of a Medieval Church. Ecclesiastical Change in Verona, 950–1150, Ithaca 1993.
Montobbio, Luigi: Il più antico elenco di codici del monastero di S. Zeno di Verona (1318), in: Rivista di storia della chiesa in Italia 14, 1960, S. 94–101.
Mor, Carlo G.: Dall'età carolingia alle prime lotte sociali, in: Vittorio Cavallari / Piero Gazzola (Hg.): Verona e il suo territorio, Verona 1960–1984, S. 5–142.
Morin, Germain: Deux petits discours d'un évêque Pétronius, du Ve siècle, in: Revue bénédictine 14, 1897, S. 3–8.
Müller, Gerhard L.: Gemeinschaft und Verehrung der Heiligen. Geschichtlich-systematische Grundlegung der Hagiologie, Freiburg 1986.
Neuheuser, Hanns P.: Liturgische Bücher als Gegenstände der kulturhistorischen Betrachtung. Tendenzen neuerer Publikationsformen, in: BIBLIOTHEK Forschung und Praxis 34, 2010, S. 238–258.
Nowack, Petrus: Die Strukturelemente des Stundengebets der Regula Benedicti, in: Archiv für Liturgiewissenschaft 26, 1984, S. 253–304.
O'Loughlin, Thomas: The Monastic Liturgy of the Hours in the Nauigatio Sancti Brendani. A Preliminary Investigation, in: Irish Theological Quarterly 71, 2006, S. 113–126.
Orlandi, Angelo: Il culto dei vescovi veronesi: origine, sviluppo, testimonianze, in: Bollettino della diocesi di Verona 66, 1979, S. 199–213.
Ottosen, Knud: La problématique de l'édition des textes liturgiques latins, in: Otto S. Due u. a. (Hg.): Classica et mediaevalia. Francisco Blatt septuagenario dedicata, Kopenhagen 1973, S. 541–556.
Pagnin, Beniamino: Formazione della scrittura carolina italiana, in: Guiscardo Moschetti (Hg.): Atti del Congresso internazionale di diritto romano, Verona 1951–1953, S. 243–266.
Palazzo, Éric: A History of Liturgical Books from the Beginning to the Thirteenth Century, Collegeville 1998.
Paredi, Angelo: I prefazi ambrosiani: contributo alla storia della liturgia latina, Mailand 1937.
Parolotto, Alessia: La biblioteca del monastero di San Zeno in Verona, 1318–1770, Verona 2002.
Pascher, Joseph: Das Stundengebet der römischen Kirche, München 1954.
–: Die Methode der Psalmenauswahl im römischen Stundengebet (Sitzungsberichte / Bayerische Akademie der Wissenschaften), München 1967.

Paschini, Pio: Le vicende politiche e religiose del Friuli nei secoli nono e decimo, in: Nuovo Archivio veneto 21, 1911, 37–88; 399–432.

Patuzzo, Mario: Verona: romana, medievale, scaligera, Verona [4]2013.

Pellegrini, Michele: Vescovo e città. Una relazione nel Medioevo italiano (secoli II–XIV), Mailand 2009.

Petersen, Nils H.: Theological Construction in the Offices in Honour of St Knud Lavard, in: Plainsong and Medieval Music 23, 2014, S. 71–96.

Petrucci, Armando: Censimento dei codici dei secoli XI–XII. Istruzioni per la datazione, in: Studi medievali 9, 1968, S. 1115–1126.

Philippart, Guy: Introduction, in: Guy Philippart (Hg.): Hagiographies. Histoire internationale de la littérature hagiographique latine et vernaculaire en Occident des origines à 1550, Turnhout 1994–2006, S. 9–24.

Picard, Jean-Charles: Le souvenir des évêques. Sépultures, listes épiscopales et cultes des évêques en Italie du nord des origines au xe siècle (Bibliothèque des Ecoles Françaises d'Athènes et de Rome 268), Rom 1988.

Pighi, Giovanni B. (Hg.): Versvs de Verona, Bologna 1960.

Polidori, Valerio: L'edizione delle fonti liturgiche greche: una questione di metodo, in: Bollettino della Badia Greca di Grottaferrata 10, 2013, S. 173–198.

Polloni, Susanna: Manoscritti liturgici della Biblioteca Capitolare di Verona (secolo IX). Contributo per uno studio codicologico e paleografico, in: Medioevo. Studi e documenti 2, 2007, S. 151–228.

Reece, Benny R.: Classical Quotations in the Works of Ratherius, in: Classical Folia 22, 1968, S. 198–213.

Rehle, Sieghild: Lectionarium plenarium Veronense (Bibl. Cap., Cod. LXXXII), in: Sacris erudiri 22, 1974, S. 321–376.

Reid, Peter L. D.: Tenth-Century Latinity. Rather of Verona (Humana Civilitas 6), Malibu 1981.

–: Introduction, in: Peter L. D. Reid (Hg.): Ratherii Veronensis Praeloqviorvm libri VI Phrenesis. Dialogus confessionalis, Turnhout 1984, S. VII–XIV.

Reynolds, Leighton D. / Marshall, Peter K.: Texts and Transmission. A Survey of the Latin Classics, Oxford 1986.

Riché, Pierre: Les bibliothèques de trois aristocrates laics carolingiens, in: Le Moyen Âge 69, 1963, S. 87–104.

Riley-Smith, Jonathan S. C.: The Crusades, Christianity, and Islam, New York 2008.

Röckelein, Hedwig: Zur Pragmatik hagiographischer Schriften im Frühmittelalter, in: Thomas Scharff (Hg.): Bene vivere in communitate. Beiträge zum italienischen und deutschen Mittelalter. Hagen Keller zum 60. Geburtstag überreicht von seinen Schülerinnen und Schülern, Münster 1997, S. 225–238.

Rognini, Luciano: Notizie storico-artistiche sulla chiesa di S. Zeno in Oratorio, in: Annuario storico zenoniano 6, 1989, S. 59–72.

Ropa, Giampaolo: Liturgia, cultura e tradizione in Padania nei sec. XI–XII, in: Quadrivium 13, 1972, S. 17–156.
Rose, Els: Ritual Memory. The Apocryphal Acts and Liturgical Commemoration in the Early Medieval West (c. 500–1215) (Mittellateinische Studien und Texte), Leiden 2009.
Rose, Valentin: Verzeichniss der Lateinischen Handschriften der Königlichen Bibliothek zu Berlin, Erster Band: Die Meermann-Handschriften des Sir Thomas Phillipps (Die Handschriften-Verzeichnisse der Königlichen Bibliothek zu Berlin 12), Berlin 1893.
Rosenwein, Barbara H.: Anger's Past. The Social Uses of an Emotion in the Middle Ages, Ithaca 1998.
Rossini, Egidio: Giurisdizioni e proprietà fondiaria del monastero di s. Zeno dedotte da documenti pubblici anteriori all'anno mille. La nascita del „Burgus Sancti Zenonis", in: Studi Zenoniani. In occasione del XVI centenario della morte di S. Zeno, Verona 1974, S. 68–168.
Sala, Giuliano: Il culto di S. Zeno nei secoli VIII e IX, in: Annuario storico zenoniano 7, 1990, S. 19–36.
–: Il culto di S. Zeno dal X al XII secolo, in: Annuario storico zenoniano 8, 1991, S. 15–32.
Sandri, Gino: Gli Statuti Veronesi del 1276, Venedig 1940.
Sannazzaro, Giovanni B.: L'architettura dal Medioevo al Rinascimento, in: Adele Buratti Mazzotta (Hg.): Domus Ambrosii. Il complesso monumentale dell'arcivescovado, Mailand 1994, S. 35–59.
Scalon, Cesare / Pani, Laura: I codici della Biblioteca Capitolare di Cividale del Friuli (Biblioteche e archivi 1), Florenz 1998.
Sedda, Filippo: La *Legenda liturgica vaticana* per l'ottava di San Francesco. *Franciscus alter evangelista*, in: Frate Francesco. Rivista di cultura francescana 78, 2012, S. 83–126.
Segala, Franco: Il culto di San Zeno nella liturgia medioevale, Verona 1982.
–: Le reliquie del vescovo, in: Annuario storico zenoniano, 1983, S. 11–23.
–: L'abazia benedittina di San Zeno. Breve profilo storico 2, 1984, S. 35–40.
SFB 948 (Hg.): Antrag auf Einrichtung und Förderung des Sonderforschungsbereichs 948 Helden – Heroisierungen – Heroismen. Transformationen und Konjunkturen von der Antike bis zur Moderne, Freiburg 2011.
Sheerin, Daniel: The Liturgy, in: Frank Anthony Carl Mantello / A. G. Rigg (Hg.): Medieval Latin: An Introduction and Bibliographical Guide 1996, S. 157–182.
Sickel, Theodor: Die Urkunden Konrad I., Heinrich I. und Otto I. (MGH DD O I), Hannover 1879.
Sigal, Pierre-André: Histoire et hagiographie. Les Miracula aux XIe et XIIe siècles, in: L'historiographie en Occident du Ve au XVe siècle: actes du congrès de la societé des historiens médiévistes de l'enseignement supérieur; Tours, 10–12 juin 1977 / 1980, Tours 1980, S. 237–257.

Snijders, Tjamke: Celebrating with Dignity: The Purpose of Benedictine Matins Reading, in: Steven Vanderputten (Hg.): Understanding Monastic Practices of Oral Communication (Western Europe Tenth–Thirteenth Centuries), Turnhout 2011, S. 115–136.

Spilling, Herrad: Die Handschriften der Staats- und Stadtbibliothek Augsburg. Bd. 2 2° COD 101–250. Beschrieben von Herrad Spilling (Die Handschriften der Staats- und Stadtbibliothek Augsburg 2), Wiesbaden 1984.

Stäblein, Bruno: Hymnen. Die mittelalterlichen Hymnenmelodien des Abendlandes (Monumenta Monodica Medii Aevi 1), Kassel 1956.

Steinmann, Martin: Neue Fragmente von Hieronymus in psalmos und das Scriptorium Bischof Eginos von Verona, in: Deutsches Archiv für Erforschung des Mittelalters 48, 1992, S. 621–624.

Thacker, Alan T.: „Loca sanctorum“: The Significance of Place in the Study of the Saints, in: Alan T. Thacker (Hg.): Local Saints and Local Churches in the Early Medieval West, Oxford 2002, S. 1–44.

Ülhof, Wilhelm: Weihegrade, in: Josef Höfer / Karl Rahner (Hg.): Lexikon für Theologie und Kirche, Freiburg 1965, Sp. 981.

Valenzano, Giovanna: La basilica di San Zeno in Verona: problemi architettonici, Vicenza 1993.

van Uytfanghe, Marc: Le culte des saints et l’hagiographie face à l’écriture: les avatars d’une relation ambiguë, in: Santi e demoni nell’alto medioevo occidentale. (Secoli V–XI), Spoleto 1989, S. 155–202.

Varanini, Gian Maria: Lucio III, la curia romana e una Chiesa locale. Verona 1184–1185, in: Amedeo de Vincentiis (Hg.): Studi Massimo Miglio Roma e il papato nel Medioevo: studi in onore di Massimo Miglio, Rom 2012, S. 185–200.

–: Il monastero di San Zeno di Verona nell’età „romanica“ (metà XI–metà XIII secolo). Aspetti economici, istituzionali e politici, in: Francesco Butturini / Flavio Pachera (Hg.): San Zeno Maggiore a Verona. Il campanile e la facciata. Restauri, analisi tecniche e nuove interpretazioni, Verona 2015, S. 29–42.

Venturi, Giuseppe: Compendio della storia sacra e profana di Verona 1825.

Venturini, Maria: Ricerche paleografiche intorno all’Arcidiacono Pacifico di Verona, Verona 1929.

–: Vita ed attività dello „scriptorium“ veronese nel secolo XI, Verona 1930.

Vitacchio, Guido: I vescovi pre-zenoniani, in: Zenonis Cathedra. Miscellanea di studi in onore di S.E. l’arcivescovo mons. Giovanni Urbani, Verona 1955, S. 15–21.

Vocino, Giorgia: Santi e luoghi santi al servizio della politica carolingia (774–877). Vitae e Passiones del regno italico nel contesto europeo, Venedig 2010.

Vogel, Albrecht: Ratherius von Verona und das zehnte Jahrhundert, Jena 1854.

Vogel, Bernhard: Das hagiographische Werk Lantberts von Deutz über Heribert von Köln, in: Dieter Bauer / Klaus Herbers (Hg.): Hagiographie im Kontext.

Wirkungsweisen und Möglichkeiten historischer Auswertung, Stuttgart 2000, S. 117–129.

Vogel, Cyrille: Medieval Liturgy. An Introduction to the Sources, Washington, DC 1986.

Wagner, Peter: Ursprung und Entwicklung der liturgischen Gesangsformen bis zum Ausgange des Mittelalters, Leipzig [3]1911.

Wallenwein, Kirsten: Corpus Subscriptionum. Verzeichnis der Beglaubigungen von spätantiken und frühmittelalterlichen Textabschriften (saec. IV–VIII), Heidelberg 2017.

Weigle, Fritz: Urkunden und Akten zur Geschichte Rathers in Verona, in: Quellen und Forschungen aus italienischen Archiven und Bibliotheken 29, 1938, S. 1–40.

Werner, Jakob: Die ältesten Hymnensammlungen von Rheinau, in: Mitteilungen der antiquarischen Gesellschaft in Zürich 13, 1891.

Wollasch, Joachim: „Benedictus abbas Romensis": das römische Element in der frühen benediktinischen Tradition, in: Norbert Kamp / Joachim Wollasch (Hg.): Tradition als historische Kraft. Interdisziplinäre Forschungen zur Geschichte des früheren Mittelalters, Berlin 1982, S. 119–137.

Zerfass, Rolf: Die Idee der römischen Stationsfeier und ihr Fortleben, in: Liturgisches Jahrbuch 8, 1958, S. 218–229.

Zettler, Alfons: Die karolingischen Bischöfe von Verona I. Studien zu Bischof Egino (+ 802), in: Sebastian Brather (Hg.): Historia archaeologica: Festschrift für Heiko Steuer zum 70. Geburtstag, Berlin u. a. 2009, S. 363–388.

Zimpel, Detlev (Hg.): Hrabanus Maurus, De institutione clericorum – Über die Unterweisung der Geistlichen (Fontes Christiani 61), Turnhout 2006.

Register